# Cloud & Ashes

## Three Winter's Tales

# Cloud & Ashes

. . .

## Three
## Winter's
## Tales

. . .

## Greer Gilman

Small Beer Press
Easthampton, MA

Small Beer Press
150 Pleasant Street #306
Easthampton, MA 01027
www.smallbeerpress.com
info@smallbeerpress.com

Distributed to the trade by Consortium.

Library of Congress Cataloging-in-Publication Data

Gilman, Greer Ilene
  Cloud & ashes : three winter's tales / by Greer Gilman. -- 1st ed.
     p. cm.
  ISBN 978-1-931520-55-3 (hardcover : alk. paper)
  I. Title. II. Title: Cloud and ashes.
  PS3557.I453C56 2009
  813'.54--dc22
                        2009000450

First edition 1 2 3 4 5 6 7 8 9

Printed on 50# Natures Book Natural (30% PCR) by Thomson-Shore, Dexter, MI.
Text set in Centaur MT 11 PT. Titles set in Aquiline.
Cover art © 2009 by Kathleen Jennings (www.tanaudel.wordpress.com).

# Contents

*For Deb and Sonya, two of the Nine;*
*and for my mother, my North star*

# ONE: JACK DAW'S PACK

## The Crow

He is met at a crossroads on a windy night, the moon in tatters and the mist unclothing stars, the way from Ask to Owlerdale: a man in black, white-headed, with a three-string fiddle in his pack. Or in a corner of an ale house, querulous among the cups, untallied; somehow never there for the reckoning; though you, or Hodge, or any traveller has drunk the night with him. A marish man: he speaks with a reedy lowland wauling, through his beak, as they say. He calls Cloud crowland. How you squall, he says, you moorland ravens; how you peck and pilfer. He speaks like a hoodie crow himself, all hoarse with rain, with bawling ballads in the street. Jack Daw, they call him. A witty angry man, a bitter melancholy man. He will barter; he will gull. In his pack are bacca pipes, new ones, white as bones, and snuff and coney-skins and cards. He plays for nothing, or for gold; packs, shuffles. In a game, triumphant, he plucks out the Crowd of Bone, or Brock with her leathern cap and anvil, hammering at a fiery heart, a fallen star. (It brock, but I mended it.) Death's doxy, he calls her, thief and tinker, for she walks the moon's road with her bag, between the hedges white with souls; she takes. Here's a lap, he says, in his shawm's voice, sharp with yelling out for ale. Here's a blaze needs no bellows. Here's a bush catches birds. He mocks at fortune. The traveller in the inn forgets what cards he held, face down, discarded in the rings of ale; he forgets what gold he lost. He'd none in his pockets, yet he played it away, laid it round and shining on the sanded board, a bright array. On each is stamped a sun.

And elsewhere on that very night, late travelling the road between Cold Law and Soulsgrave Hag, no road at all but white stones glimmering, the sold sheep heavy in his purse, another Tib or Tom or Bartlemy will meet Jack Daw. He will stand at the crossroads, bawling in his windy voice, a broadside in his hand. There'll be a woodcut at the head: a hanged man on the gallantry, crows rising from the corn. Or this: a pretty drummer boy, sword drawn against the wood, and flaunting in her plumy cap. Two lovers' graves, entwined. A shipwreck, and no grave at all. You must take what he gives. Yet he will barter for his wares, and leave the heavy purse still crammed with coppers, for his fee is light. He takes only silver, the clipped coin of the moon: an hour of the night, a dream of owls. Afterwards, the traveller remembers that the three-string fiddle had a carven head, the face his own. With a cold touch at his heart, he knows that Jack Daw's fiddle wakes the dead; he sees their bones, unclad and rising, clothing with the tune. They dance. He sees his girl, left sleeping as he thought; Joan's Jack, gone for a soldier; his youngest child. Himself. They call him to the dance. He sees the sinews of the music string them, the old tunes, "Cross the Water to Babylon," "The Crowd of Bone." Longways, for as many as will, as must, they dance: clad in music, in the flowers and the flesh.

## What The Crowd Of Bone Sang

She is silent, Ashes, and she dances, odd one out. In the guisers' play, she bears a bag of ashes of the old year's crown to sain the hearths of the living, the hallows of the earth. The children hide from her, behind the door and in the shadow of the kist; not laughing, as they fear the Sun. Click! Clack! He knocks the old man dead, that headed him before. And tumbled by the knot of swords, he rises, flaunting in their gaze. The girl who put on Ashes with her coat of skins, who stalks them, bites her cheek and grimaces so not to laugh; she feels her power. She looks sidelong at the Sun.

They say that Ashes' mother got her gazing in her glass. *Undo*, the raven said, and so she did, undid, and saw her likeness in the stony mirror, naked as a branch of thorn. The old witch took it for herself; she cracked the glass, she broke the tree. They bled. Devouring, she bore her daughter, as the old moon bears the new, itself again; yet left hand to its right. And they do say the old one, Annis, locks her daughter in the dark of moon, winterlong and waning, and that Ashes' birth, rebirth, is spring. They say the sun is Ashes' lightborn brat. She is the shadow of the candle, the old moon's daughter and her mirror; she is tarnished with our breath and death. She's winter's runaway.

They are old who tell this.

But the girl who put on Ashes with her tattered coat walks silent, flown with night and firelight and masking. She is giddy with the wheel of stars. She sees the brands whirled upward, sees the flash of teeth, of eyes. The guisers shout and jostle. They are sharp as foxes in her nostrils: smoke and ale and eager sweat. She moves among them, nameless; she wears her silence like a cloak of night. Ah, but she can feel the power in her marrow, like a vein of stars. Her feet are nightfall. She could tuck a sleeping hare within her jacket, take a hawk's eggs from its breast. Her hand could beckon like the moon and bid a crone come dancing from the chimneynook to sweep about her and about; could call the sun to hawk at shadows, or a young man to her lap, and what he will.

And in the morning, she will lay by Ashes with her rags, and wash her face, and comb the witchknots from her hair; but Ashes in the tale goes on.

In spring, she rises from her mother Annis' dark; they call the snowdrops Ashes' Steps. The rainbow is her scarf. She dances, whirling in the April storm; she fills her hands with hailstones, green as souls. And there are some have met her, walking backward on the Lyke Road, that they call the white hare's trod, away from death; she leaps within the cold spring, falling, filling up the traveller's hands. She is drunken and she eats.

At May, the riddlecake, as round as the wheeling sun, is broken into shards, one marked with ashes; he that draws her share is Sun. But he was sown long since, and he's forgotten harrowing. He rises and he lies. Light work. He breaks the hallows knot of thorn; he eats the old year's bones for bread. Sun calls the stalk from the seeded earth, draws forth the green blade and the beard to swell his train. He gives the meadows green gowns. And flowers falling to his scythe lie tossed and tumbled, ah, they wither at his fiery kiss. They fall in swathes, in sweet confusion, to his company of rakes, his rade of scythesmen all in green. The hay's his dance. Vaunting, he calls the witchstone, Annis, to the dance, for mastery of the year, and wagers all his reckless gold. But he has spent his glory and must die. The barley is himself.

Ashes reaps him. By harvesting, she's sunburnt, big with light. She wears a wreath of poppyheads; her palms are gashed, they're red with garnering. They open like a cry. Her sickle fells the standing corn, the hare's last hallows, and he's gathered in her sheaf. She's three then, each and all the moon, his end: her sickle shearing and her millstone trundling round, her old black cauldron gaping for his bones.

## The Harper's Lad

His hair was yellow as the broom, as ragged as the sun. A ranting lad, a spark for kindling of the year. His name was Ash. It was Unhallows, in the grey between May Eve and morning. On the hills, the fires died. He'd leapt the nine hills in a turning wheel, from dusk to dusk, and rode rantipole with witches. Ah, they'd raged, howking at the earth with long blue nails. When they shook their tangled hair, the soulstones clattered, red as blood, and eyestones, milky white and black; and birdskulls, braided through the orbits, in their nightlong hair. He was drunk with dancing. He'd another girl to meet; had lingered, waking with his blue-eyed witch. *The owl flew out, the raven in,* sang mocking in his head, like Ashes in the old play. As he slouched along the moor, he heard a hoarse voice, in windy snatches, singing. Some belantered rantsman, he thought.

"*Oh, my name it is Jack Hall, chimney sweep, chimney sweep . . .*" A crow's voice, chanting, hoarded iron in a hinge.

There were some had sung all night, thought Ash; he'd gone to other games. It was lightward, neither sun nor moon, but the grey cock's hour. He was late. He hastened toward the beck.

"*And I've candles lily white, oh, I stole them in the night, for to light me to the place where I must lie.*"

They met by the trey stone, back of Law. A fiddler from a dance, it seemed, in a broad hat and battered jacket, with his face like the back of a spade. His hair was white as barley. "Out," he cries. "D'ye call this a road?"

"Flap ower it then, awd corbie. D'ye call that a voice?"

"Called thee."

A glance at the three-string fiddle. "Canst play us a dance on thy crowdy, catgut? Light our heels, then."

"What, is thy candle out?"

"I've a lantern to light it at."

"Of horn?"

But Ash was thinking of the blue-eyed witch, as rough as juniper, as fierce. She'd scratched him. Ash thought of the fire, how it whirled and crackled when they burned the bush; the sparks flew up like birds. The fire was embers: for a coal of juniper will burn a winter's night. Would burn a nine month at the heather's roots. Closing his eyes, he saw late-risen stars whirl round, the Flaycraw all one side afire, and rising, naked to his bones. The hanged lad in the sky. He played for the dancers in the starry hey. He played the sun to rise. But that was Hallows; they were winter stars, another turning of the wheel, and other witches. Vixens in a cage of straw. Hey up, he must be giddy drunk. Were all yon ale and randy turned his wits. But he'd a spark in him yet. And Ash thought of the dark-eyed lass who waited, like a sloethorn and a clear gold sky. A traveller. Whin. He'd best be going on. He tossed a coin to the fiddler. "Here's to thy bitch."

"And for thy pains."

They found the broadside in his jacket, after. Some said the woodcut was a high green gallows, and the harper's boy hanged dead. And others, it were nothing like: the white hare running and the hag behind. The black hare's bonny, but the white is death, they say: the moon's prey and her shadow.

Ash thrust the broadside in his pocket and went on down the road. His tousled head was bare, as yellow as the weeds called chimneysweepers, that are gold and come to dust.

### Scythes and Cup

Poor Tom o Cloud, and so he died?

*His husk*, an old wife says, and drinks. *Scarce bearded when he's threshed and sown.* Another, brown as autumn, broad-lapped, takes the cup; she kneads the cake. *Wha's dead? He's for thy belly, when he's risen, girl. He's drunken and he sleeps; his dreams are hallows, all a maze of light, of leaves. When's time, he'll wake wood.* And says the third, as thrawn as frost, the youngest of the three: *At dusk, at Hallows Eve, he rises, starry wi' a ceint o light: t'Sheaf, Awd Flaycraw, clapping shadows frae th' fields of night. Yon hanged lad i' th' sky.*

And Ashes?

*Ah, she mourns and she searches. And rounding wi' his child, she spins. D'ye see yon arain webs ont moor? Tom's shrouds, they call 'em. Bastards' clouts. And she may rive at Mally's thorn for shelter; owl's flown, there's none within. No hallows. So she walks barefoot and bloodfoot, and she lives on haws and rain. And moon's her coverlid, her ragged sheet.*

### Sheath and Knife

The girl lies waiting in the high laithe, knife in hand. Hail rattles on the slates. She cannot hear—what? Hunters. Closer still, she holds the knife, the same which cut the cord. Her breasts seep milk, unsuckled. Ah, they ache. Her blood wells, she is rust and burning; blood will draw *them*. Talons. Wings. Her mind is black and bright with fever. She would slip them, fight them, but her body clags her. It is sodden; it is burning. Sticks and carrion. The wind wauls, the rooftrees creak; below is muck and sleet and stone. She's drawn the ruined ladder up. Holed up. She stares at dark until the earth cants, until the knife's edge calls her back. Sharp across her palm: a heartline. White, then red. Her blood and milk spilled on the musty straw. That will call them, that will draw them from the dark, the tree, the bairn. But the earth starves for what she will not give it. Their voices tell her she is famine, she is hailseed, withering, the cold share in the dust.

She was Ashes. Ah, she'd flyted with them, wives and lasses, as they'd stripped her of her guising, scrubbed her, tugged the witchknots from her hair. *Cross all and keep nowt*, they'd told her, turning out the sooty pockets, folding up the tattered coat; and late and morning, privily, desperately, she'd drenched and drenched, but could not rid her belly of the seed. She's Ashes still. Still guising, in a tinker's jacket, oh, a brave lad, with her bloody hole. Caught in Ashes. Holed up. Crouching, clenching, in her darklong pain, she'd heard the shadows of the women mocking, turning out the pockets of the coat. Knife. Haws. Pebbles. Eggshells. There, the whirligig she'd cried for, that she'd broken, long years since. They hold up a skint and bloody hare. *Here's one been poaching*. Shivering, she shuts her eyes, but still she sees the brat like bruised fruit trodden in the grass, the cry between her legs. Windfall for the old ones. Ashes to ashes. His furled hand, like bracken. His blind mouth at her tit. If they'd found him there, they'd slain him, for the earth to drink. *Keep nowt*. She'd hung no rags to the hallows tree, when she'd left him. She'd not beg awd ones. And she'd nowt to give. Her hair was cut long since and burned. Her tongue was dry. But she'd wrapped him in a stolen jacket, nowt of Ashes. Twined a stranger's tawdry ring about his neck. Why? For the daws to pyke at? She's seen the crows make carrion of halfborn lambs, their stripped skulls staring from their mothers' forks. On the slates, the dry rain dances, shards of Annis, shards of souls. Heel of hands against her aching eyes, until it's red, all red as foxes, and their green stench in the rain.

### Coffer and Keys

At Hallows Eve, Ashes' mother hunts, unthralled from her stone. She is the wintersoul, the goddess of the high wild places, fells and springs and standing stones, the mistress of the deer. Her child's her prey.

Her mother Annis hates her, that her child (her child) is not herself. She wears her daughter at her throat in chains of ice, her blood as rings; she tears the new Sun, red with birthblood, from her daughter's side.

In winter, Ashes dies, is graved within her mother's dark.

*And her bairn's shut up in Annis' kist,* says an old wife, jangling her bunch of keys. *Down where she sits i' dark, and tells her hoard of souls. And he's Sun for her crown. So all t'world's cold as Law and blind as herself.* She leans and whispers. *D'ye hear her at window with her nails?* The dark-eyed children huddle by the hearth and stare at her, the old wife crouching with her cards of wool. Her shadows cross her shadows, like a creel unweaving. *Ah, but he's for Mally's lap, she haps him all in snow. It's winter and her loom is bare. Wood's her cupboard, and her walls are thorn; her bower's all unswept. Thou can't get in but she lets thee. And she's Tom Cloud's nurse. But Brock—ah, well now, Brock's death's gossip and she's keys to all locks. Will I tell ye how Brock stole him?*

*Why?* says the boldest.

*For a bagpipe that plays of itself,* says the eldest, as she rocks the babby. *Hush, ba. For a bellows til her blaze.*

*Not for Annis.*

But there are some say Ashes journeys on the river of her milk, that she's the lost star from the knot of stars they call Black Annie's Necklace, or Nine Weaving, or the Clew, that rises with the fall of leaves, a web like gossamer and rain. The Nine are sisters, and they weave the green world and the other with a mingled skein of light and dark, weave soul and shroud and sail; but Ashes winds the Sun within her, that the old Moon shears.

And some say no, that Ashes is a waif on earth, and scattered with the leaves. She rocks the cradle in the midnight kitchen, where no coal nor candle is, in houses where a child has died. And some have heard her lulling in the dying embers; seen her shadow in the moonspill, in the leaf's hand at the pane.

## Poppyheads

The woman in the stubble field moves slowly, searching. Her palms are creased with blood. Her tangled hair is grey. There is something that she's lost: a knife among the weeds, a stone from off her ring. Her child, she says. If you suckle at her dry breast, drink her darkness, she must speak your fortune, love and death. She once told other fates, with other lips. And still

she squats among the furrows, lifting up her ragged skirts for anyone or
none. She holds herself open, like an old sack in a barn. No seed within, all
threshed to chaff and silence. She was Ashes. She is no one. By the sticks
of the scarecrow, she crouches, scrabbling at the clodded earth and crying,
"Mam. Mam, let me in!"

### Sieve and Shears

There must be one called Ashes at the wren's wake, when they bring the sun.
At Hallows, she is chosen. All the girls and women go with candles, lating
on the hills. And if a man by chance (unchance) should see one, she will say
she's catching hares, she's after birds' nests, though it rattle down with sleet
and wind. They both know that she lies. Her covey are not seeking with their
candles, but are sought. And one by one, the tapers dwindle, or are daunted
by the wind; the last left burning is the chosen. Or they scry her in an O of
water from the Ashes spring, at midnight, when the Nine are highest. They
will see her tangled in their sleave of light, as naked as a branch of sloethorn,
naked as the moon. And though the moon in water's shaken by their riddling hands, its shards come round and round. Then swiftly as the newfound
Ashes runs, longlegged as a hare, she'll find the old coat waiting at her bed's
head, stiff with soot and sweat and blood. She walks in it at Lightfast, on the
longest night, the sun's birth and the dark of moon. She smutches children's
faces with her blacknailed hands. And their mothers say, *Be good, or she will steal
thee. Here's a penny for her bag.* Her mother's tree is hung (thou knows) with skins
of children, ah, they rattle like the winter leaves, they clap their hands.

### The Scarecrow

The starved lad in the cornfield shivers, crying hoarsely as the crows he
flights. He claps them from the piercing green, away like cinders into Annis' ground. Clodded feet, cracked clapper, and his hair like what's o'clock,
white dazzle. *Piss-a-bed,* the sheep-lads cry him. What he fears is that the
Ashes child will dance among the furrows, rising to his cry. What he fears
is that the crows will eat him. They will pick his pretty eyes. And he dreads
his master's belt. Yet he sings at his charing. At nights, he makes the maids
laugh, strutting valiant with the kern-stick, up and down. *Hunting hares?* calls
Gill. *Aye, under thine apron,* he pipes, as the Sun does, guising. And they laugh

and give him barley-sugar, curds and ale. *Thou's a bold chuck,* cries Nanny. *Will I show thee a bush for thy bird?* And he, flown and shining, with the foam of lambswool on his lip, *I's not catched one. But I will, come Lightfast. I'll bring stones, I'll knock it stark.* How they crow! And Mall with the jug cries, *My cage is too great for thy cock robin, 'twill fly out at door.*

Now he shakes with cold and clacks his rattle, and the cold mist eats his cry. The Ashes child will rise, unsowing from the corn: a whorl of blood, a waif. Craws Annis will crouch in the hedgerow, waiting; she will pounce and tear him with her iron nails, and hang his tatters from the thorn. Jack Daw will make a fiddle of his bones. He knuckles at his stinging eyes. He wants to cry. He sings. Back and forth, he strides the headland, as the guisers do, and quavers. *My mother was burned for a witch, My father was hanged from a tree ...* When he sees the hare start from the furrow, he yells, and hurls a stone.

### The Hare, The Moon

The moon's love's the hare, his death is dark of moon. He is her last prey, light's body, as the midnight soul, night's Ashes, is her first: All Hallows Eve, May Eve, her A and O. In spring, the waning of her year, she hunts in green: not vivid, but a cold grey green, as pale as lichened stone; afoot, for her hunt is scattered. And she hunts by night. Where her feet have passed is white with dew. Swift and mad, the hare runs, towards hallows, to the thicket's lap, unhallowing in white. He sees the white moon tangled in her thorn. Her lap is sanctuary. He would lie there panting, with his old rough jacket torn, his blood on the branches, red as haws. But at dawn, the hey is down. The white girl rises from the tree; she dances on the hill, unknowing ruth. Yet he runs to her rising, eastward to the sky. Behind him runs his deerlegged death, his pale death. There are some now blind have seen her, all in grey as stone, greygreen in moving. No, another says, as red as a roe deer or the moon in slow eclipse. At dawn, she will be stone.

They are sisters, stone and thorn tree, dark and light of one moon. Annis, Malykorne. And they are rivals for the hare, his love, his death: each bears him in her lap, as child, as lover and as lyke. They wake his body and he leaps within them, quick and starkening; they bear him light. Turning, they are each the other, childing and devouring: the cauldron and the sickle and the cold bright bow. Each holds, beholds, the other in her glass. And for a space between the night and morning, they are one, the old moon in the new moon's arms, the paling of her breast. The scragged hare slips them as they clasp. He's for Brock's bag, caught kicking.

## Masks

*Wouldst know thy fortune?* her lover says. And laughing, as his bright hair ruffles at her breath, *Ah. What's o'clock?*

*Not yet*, she says, low-voiced. (The stone in his ear, like the blood of its piercing. The bruised root stirring on his thigh.) *Not dawning yet. Nor moon nor sun.*

*Will not it rise?* he says, rounding.

*And go to seed.* She smiles, remembering. *Not yet. I've plucked it green.*

## The Rattlebag

The boy kneels, drunken, in the barn. They hold her down for him, the moon's bitch, twisting, cursing in the filthy straw. A vixen in a trap. He holds the felly of the cartwheel, sick and shaken, in the reeling stench. Cold muck and angry flesh. Their seed in snail tracks on her body, snotted in her sootblack hair. Their blood—his own blood—in her nails. She is Ashes and holy. He fumbles, tries to turn his face. He's not thirteen. "Get it into her, mawkin!" calls the bagman, wilting. Ashes and fear. "Thinks it's to piss with." "Hey, crow-lad! Turn it up a peg." "Spit in t'hole." And the man with the daggled ribbons, his fiddle safe in straw, cries, "Flayed it's thy mam?"

## The Hare, The Moon (Turned Down)

The black hare's bonny, as they sing: she lies under aprons, she's love under hedges. And she's harried to the huntsman's death, the swift undoing of his gun. But the white hare's death, they say: a maid forsaken or a child unmourned, returning from her narrow grave. A love betrayed. Her false lad will meet her on the moor at dusk, a pale thing fleeting; he will think he gives chase. But she flees him and she follows, haunting like the ghost of love. She draws him to his death. And after he will run, a shadow on the hills, a hare: the moon's prey and her shadow. Love's the black hare, but the white is death. And one's the other one, now white, now black, and he and she, uncanny as the changing moon. They say the hare lays eggs; it bears the sun within a moon. A riddle. Break it and there's nought within.

## Riddles

He holds her ring up, glancing through it with his quick blue eye; and laughs, and pockets it. A riddle. *What's all the world and nothing?*

O, says she, *thine heart. 'Tis for any hand. Thyself would fill it.*

And he, *Nay, it is th' owl in thine ivy bush. It sulks by day.*

*Aye,* says she, *and hares by night.*

*Thy wit, all vanity and teeth.*

*Thy grave.*

*At midnight, then? I'll bring a spade and we'll dig for it.* His white teeth glimmer, ah, he knows how prettily; and daring her, himself (for the thorn's unchancy, and this May night most of all), he says, *At the ragtree?*

*At moonrise.*

## Waking Wood

Between the blackthorn and the white is called the moon's weft, as the warp is autumn, Hallows, when her chosen sleeps. He dreams of lying in her lap, within the circle of her flowering thorn; his dreams wake wood. Between the scythe and frost he's earthfast, and his visions light as leaves. He keeps the hallows of the earth. And winterlong he hangs in heaven, naked, in a chain of stars. He rises to her rimes. When Ashes hangs the blackthorn with her hail of flowers, white as sleet, as white as souls, then in that moon the barley's seeded, and the new green pricks the earth. He's scattered and reborn. As in the earth, so in the furrows of the clouds, his Sheaf is scattered, whited from the sky until he rises dawnward, dancing in his coat of sparks. He overcrows the sun; he calls the heavens to the earth to dance. And in their keep, the Nine weave for their sister's bridal, and their threads are quick, their shuttles green and airy, black and white and red as blood. They clothe her in her spring and fall. In the dark before May morn, the Flaycraw dances, harping for the Nine to rise, the thorn to flower and the fires to burn, the wakers on the hills to dance. *The hey is down,* they cry. *Craw's hanged!* They leap the fires, lightfoot; crown their revelry with green. Not sloe. The blackthorn's death and life-in-death; the white is love. The bride alone is silent, rounding with the sun.

### Riddles, Turned

She looks at him though all her rings. There's mischief in her face, a glittering on teeth and under lids. *An you will, I may.*

### Quickening

At quickening, the white girl rises, lighter of herself; she undoes her mother's knots. Alone of all who travel Brock's road backward, out of Annis' country, out of death, she walks it in her bones, and waking. Neither waif nor wraith nor nimbling hare, but Ashes and alone. The coin she's paid for crossing is of gold, and of her make: her winter's son. Yet she is born unknowing, out of cloud. Brock, who is Death's midwife, sains her, touches eyes, mouth, heart with rain. She haps the naked soul in earth.

All the dark months of her prisoning, in frost, in stone, her shadow's walked the earth, worn Ashes outward, souling in her tattered coat. She's kept the year alive. But on the eve of Ashes' rising, the winter changeling is undone. From hedge to hall, the women and the girls give chase, laughing, pelting at the guisers' Ashes, crying, *Thief!* Bright with mockery and thaw, they take her, torn and splattered, in the street. *What's she filched? Craw's stockings. Cat's pattens. Hey, thy awd man's pipe! And mine. And mine.* Gibing, they strip her, scrub her, tweak the tangles from her hair, the rougher for her knowing. All she's got by it—small silver or the gramarye of stars—is forfeit. All her secrets common as the rain. And they scry her, and they whisper—*Is it this year? From her Ashes? Is't Sun for Mally's lap?* They take her coat, her crown, her silence. Naked and nameless then, she's cauled and comforted, with round cakes and a caudle of the new milk. She is named. Then with candles they wake Ashes, and with carols, waiting for the silent children and the first wet bunch of snowdrops at the door.

They say that Ashes wears the black fell of an unborn lamb; her feet are bare. She watches over birthing ewes and flights the crows that quarrel, greedy for the young lambs' eyes. Her green is wordless, though it dances in the wind; it speaks. Her cradle tongue is leaves. And where she walks grow flowers. They are white, and rooted in the darkness; they are frail and flower in the snow. It is death to bring them under a roof; but on the morn of Ashes' waking, only then, her buds are seely and they must be brought within, to sain the corners of the hearth. The country people call them Drops of Ashes' Milk. She is the coming out of darkness: light from the tallow, snowdrops from the earth, Bride from the winter hillside; and from Hell, the child returned.

She is silent, Ashes; but she sings her tale. The guisers strung the fiddle with her hair, the crowd of bone. It sings its one plaint, and the unwed, unchilded, dance:

> *My mother bare me in her lap,*
> *Turn round, the reel doth spin;*
> *As white the cloth she wove for me,*
> *As red my blood within.*
> *As black the heart she bore to me,*
> *As white the snow did fall;*
> *As brief the thread she cut for me:*
> *A swaddling-band, a pall.*

## The Ragthorn

It was lightward and no lover. Whin sat by the ragtree, casting bones. There were rings on her every finger, silver, like a frost. They caught and cast, unheeding, caught and cast. A thief, a journey by water. Sticks and crosses. All false.

The thorn was on a neb of moorland, at the meeting of two becks: a ragthorn, knotted with desires, spells for binding soul with soul and child in belly. Charms for twisting heartstrings, hemp. They were bright once and had faded, pale as winter skies. Bare twigs as yet. The sloe had flowered leafless, late; the spring was cold. In the moon-blanched heath a magpie hopped and flapped and eyed the hutchbones greedily. He scolded in his squally voice. "Good morrow, your lordship, and how is her ladyship?" called Whin. She knew him by his strut and cock: his Lady's idle huntsman, getting gauds in his beak. The bird took wing. The bare bones fell. "Here's a quarrel," she said, and swept them up, and cast again. When Ash came, she would rend him, with his yellow hair. Or bind him to her, leave him. Let him dangle, damn his tongue. She'd dance a twelvemonth on his grave. Ah, but she would be his grave, his green was rooted in her earth. And she thought of his white teeth in the greeny darkness and his long and clever hands. His hair like a lapful of flowers.

Whin was long-eyed, dark and somber, with a broad disdainful mournful mouth and haughty chin. But there was mischief in her face, as there was silver glinting in her hair: nine threads, a spiderwork of frost. Her clothes were patchwork of a hundred shades of black: burnt moorland, moleskin, crows and thunder; but her scarf was gold, torn silk and floating like a rag of sunrise. Looking up, she started—even now—and then she sighed and whistled softly, through her teeth. "Yer early abroad," she said. "Or late. T'fires are out."

Down the moor came a woman, slowly, feeling with a stick, and a child before her on a leash, its harness sewn with bells. Its hair was hawkweed. When it stumbled, it rang; she jerked it upright. Whin watched in silence as the two came onward: the beggar groping with her blackshod stick, the white child glittering and jangling. They were barefoot. She was all in whitish tatters, like the hook moon, scarved about her crowblack head, and starveling, with a pipe and tabor at her side. When she felt the rags on the branches brush her face, she called, "Wha's there?"

"A traveller," said Whin. "Will you break fast wi' us?"

"Oh aye," said the beggar, with her long hands in the ribbons, harping, harping. "Gi's it here." The blind woman slung down her heavy creel and sat, her stick across her knees, and held out her palm. Whin put bread on it. "Hallows with ye," she said. The long hand twitched like a singed spider; it snatched.

"Since ye'd be casting it at daws afore t'night," said the beggar.

"Wha said I's enough for twa?" said Whin.

The beggar crammed. She wolfed with her white eyes elsewhere, as if it were something else she wanted, that she tore. Her brat hid, grimed and wary, in her skirts, and mumped a crust. "And why else wouldst thou be laiking out ont moor, like a bush wi' no bird in it?" said the beggar. "Happen he's at meat elsewhere." She listened for Whin's stiffening. And grinning fiercely through her mouthful, "D'ye think I meant craw's pudding? Lap ale?" The bluenailed hand went out again, for sausage and dried apple, which she chewed and swallowed, chewed and spat into her fledgling's mouth. "Ye'd best be packing."

Whin drank. Too late to whistle up her dog, off elsewhere. The beggar took a long swig of Whin's aleskin. As she raised her arm to wipe her mouth, her sleeve fell back; the arm was scarry, roped and crossed with long dry welts. "Will you drink of mine?" she said, mocking; and undid her jacket for the clambering child, for anyone. Her breast was white as sloethorn.

Whin was cutting sausage with her streak of knife, and whistling softly through her teeth, as if her heart were thistledown, this way and that. *"... if I was black, as I am white as the snaw that falls on yon fell dyke . . ."*

The child suckled warily; it burrowed. The beggar pirled its hair; she nipped and fondled, scornfully. "It fats on me. D'ye see how I am waning?" She was slender as the moon, and white; and yet no girl, thought Whin: the moon's last crescent, not her first. Her hair was crowblack in a coif of twisted rags, the green of mistletoe, and hoary lichen blues. At her waist hung a pipe of a heron's legbone and a tabor of a white hare's skin. She had been beautiful; had crazed and marred. Her eyes were clouded, white as stones. There was a blue burn on her cheek, like gunpowder, and her wolfish teeth were gapped. Yet her breast was bell heather; her hands moved like moorbirds on her small wrists. They were voices, eyes. Looking elsewhere, she called to Whin, "You there. See all and say nowt. Can ye fiddle? Prig petticoats? I c'd do wi' a mort."

Whin said, "I's suited."

"And what's thou here about?"

"Gettin birds' nests," said Whin, all innocence.

"What for, to hatch gowks?"

"Crack eggs to make crowds of."

"And what for?"

"Why, to play at craw's wake."

The beggar wried her mouth. "Thou's a fool."

"And what's thou after?" said Whin. "Has thy smock blown away?"

"Hares," said the beggar.

"Black or white?"

"All grey to me." The beggar set the child down, naked in its cutty shirt. "Gang off, I's empty as a beggar's budget."

"Wha's brat is thou?" said Whin to the babby.

"No one's. Cloud's," said the beggar.

"Ah," said Whin.

The beggar did up her jacket. The child sat by her petticoats with a rattle: a wren tumbled round within a clumsy cage. "Will we do now?"

"How's that?" said Whin.

"Ah," said the beggar. "I give and take. My ware is not for town." She looked sidelong. Like a snake among heather roots, her hand was in her petticoats. She found something small and breathed on it, spat and rubbed and breathed. "Here," she said to Whin, holding out a round small mirror. "Is't glass?"

"It's that." It was clouded, cold; she held it gingerly. There was earth on it, and in the carving. It was bone. She looked in it and saw another face, not hers: a witch, a woman all in green, grey green. A harewitch. A green girl, gaunt and big with child. The beggar was listening with her crooked face. "No," said Whin. "My face is me own."

"A pretty toy," the beggar said. "An ape had worn it in his cap."

Whin turned it; she ran her thumb round the edge. Earth bleared it. There was gravedust on her hands; she dared not wipe them. She kept her voice light. There are witches on the walk, between times. If you meet them, you must parry. "Here's thieving. Does they wake when yer come and go?"

"They keep no dogs," said the beggar. "And they sleep. This?" Between her hands was a scarf like an April sky, warped with silver. It was cloud and iris, changing. It was earthstained, like the sky in water in a road, a rut. She drew it through and through her hands. A soul.

"Here's a fairing," said Whin, and shivered.

"Aye, then," said the beggar. "There's a many lads and lasses gangs to't hiring at that fair, cross river, and they bring twa pennies til their fee." Her voice grew deeper. "'Here's fasten penny,' they says. And mistress til them, 'Can tha reap? And can tha shear?'" Her fingers found the wafted scarf; they snatched it from the air. "And then they's shorn."

Whin watched it fluttering. The scarf had changed, like brown leaves caught in ice. "That's not on every bush. Was never a hue and cry when you—?"

"Cut strings? Wha said I did?" Her fingers brushed, ah, lightly, at Whin's neck, where the gold scarf flaunted, like a rag of dawn.

Whin flinched, but flung her chin up. "I's a fancy to't drum."

"I's keeping that," said the beggar. "For't guising."

"Did yer gang wi' them? Guisers?"

"I were Ashes."

"Ah," said Whin.

The child in the heather clapped its hands, it crowed. At its jangling, the small birds rose and called. Whin looked sidelong at it, smiling through her rings. "And you getten yer apron full. Here's catching of hares."

The beggar twitched its string. "I'd liefer gang lighter."

"Cold courting at Lightfast. Find a barn?"

"Back of Law, it were, and none to hear us. It were midnight and past, and still, but for t'vixens crying out on t'fell. On clicketing, they were, and shrieked as if their blood ran green. But for t'guisers ramping. See, they'd waked at

every door, they'd drank wren's death. And went to piss its health at wall. 'Up flies cock robin,' says one, 'and down wren'; and another, 'Bones to't bitches.' 'And what'll we give to't blind?' says third, and scrawns at fiddle. 'Here's straw,' they said. 'And threshed enough,' said I. But they'd a mind to dance, they'd swords. D'ye think brat's like its father sake? Is't Sun? Or has it Owler's face, all ashes? Hurchin's neb? Think it one of Jack Daw's get?"

"Nine on one?" said Whin, furious.

The stone-eyed beggar shrugged.

"Dogs."

"Boy and all," said the beggar. "They set him on." Thrub thrub went the fingers on the little drum and stopped the windless pipe. They pattered. "Happen not his brat. Nor old man's nowther. Cockfallen, he were." She leaned toward Whin's silence, secret, smiling with her wry gapped mouth. Her eyes were changeless. "But I marked 'em, aye, I marked 'em all." She drew a braid of hair from underneath her cap, undid the knot with swift sure fingers. Moving on the wind, the tress was silver, black and silver. It was wind, as full of blackness as the northwind is of snow. "There," she said. In her fingers was an earring, gold, with a dangling stone, a bloodred stone. "D'ye know its make?"

Whin sat. Her hands were knotted, rimed with rings. *False*, said her heart's blood. *False*. The black hair stirred and stirred, so much of it, like shadow. The beggar leaned toward her silence, with her scarred white throat. "Is't torn, his ear?" She flipped the earring, nimbly as a juggler, tumbling it and sliding it on and off each finger, up and down. "What will you give for't?"

The child's white hair was dazzling in her eyes, like snow, like whirling snow. Whin turned her face. "It's common enough." But the needles of the light had pierced her; she was caught and wound in hinting threads.

The beggar palmed it, pulled it from the air. "And which of nine?" she said, her white face small amid her hair. "There was one never slept that night, nor waked after. Drowned," she said. "Wast thine? They found him in Ash Beck. They knowed him by his yellow hair, rayed out i't ice. Craws picked him, clean as stars. Or will. Or what tha will. Wouldst barley for a death?"

Her fingers pattered on the drum. "That's one. And which is thine? There's one he s'll take ship and burn. He s'll blaze i't rigging, d'ye see him fall? And ever after falling, so tha'lt see him when tha close thine eyes. That's one.

"And one s'll dance ont gallows, rant on air. Is't thine? His eyes to feed ravens, his rags to flay crows. D'ye see them rising? Brats clod stones. And sitha, there's a hedgebird wi' a bellyful of him. And not his eyes. She stands by t'gallows. D'ye see her railing? That's one.

"And one s'll be turned a hare and hunted, dogs will crack his bones. There's a pipe of his thighbone and a drum of his fell. And tha s'll play it for his ghost to dance. And there's a candle of his tallow, for to light thee to bed. With such a one, or none, or what tha will. That's one. And which is thine?" She leaned closer. "D'ye take it? Is it done?"

Whin said nothing, caught in rime.

"Is't done?" said the beggar, chanting.

"And if it's done?"

Whin's fingers found the knot of the child's leash; undid it stealthily.

"Is't done?"

"Undone and all to do," cried Whin, springing up.

The whitehaired child had slipped his lead; he whirled and jangled as he ran. His hair was flakes of light. He whirled unheeding on the moor. And childlike fell away from him, like clouds before the moon, the moon a hare, the hare a child. He lowped and whirled and ranted. Whin caught him; he was light, and turning in her blood to sun. She bore it. By its light, she saw the beggar's shadow, like a raven on the rimy earth, that hopped and jerked a shining in its neb, a glass. A thief! the raven cried. Whin stood, as if the cry had caught her, in the whirring of the light like wings, a storm of wings; held fast. The child was burning in her hands, becoming and becoming fire. And she herself was changing. She was stone; within her, seed on seed of crystal rimed, refracted. She was nightfall, with a keel of moon, and branching into stars. She was wood and rooted; from her branches sprang the light, the misselchild. In that shining she was eyes of leaves, and saw her old love's blood, like holly, on the snow.

The child in the embers crowed, A thief!

And at his cry, Whin turned and ran, but still she held him fast. Behind her, the white-eyed woman shrank and whirred; the raven in her quillied out and rose, black-nebbed and bearded, with a woman's breasts. The waters of the beck leapt white. Amid the raven's storm of hair, its face, a congeries of faces, gaped for blood. Whitebrowed and ironbeaked; but its body was a woman's, cold and perfect to the fork: that too was beaked and gaping. It was shadow, casting none. Its very breath unhallowed.

Sun. The raven cried to its rising, "She's stolen my milk!" as Whin leapt the blackrocked foaming river. Cried and withered, like a flake of ash, and all its eyes went out.

The moor was sticks and ashes; frost and fire.

Whin held a heap of embers in her hands. They sang with dying, fell and faded into ashes. They were cold. She dared not spill them. With a shrug of her sleeve, she wiped her eyes, glittering with soot and tears.

The sun had risen. Whin turned from it and turned. White. A mist, a hag wreathed round and round her, cloud cold as Law. Beyond her, by the tree, she saw a white moor and a standing stone, unshaped. An iron crown was on it, driven deep with iron tangs, and rusting. There were nailholes where the eyes should be. The tree was silver, bowed beneath a shining weight of ice, in rattling shackles of glass. They cracked and glittered, falling. As she turned away, Whin saw a girl unbending from the tree, a knee as rough as bark; or nothing, wind among the rags.

And as she looked, the frost was flowering, the tree was white with bloom.

## The Thief

At the moorsend guisers came, in rags, in ashes, garlanded with green. They wore their coats clapped hindside fore; and a man in petticoats swept round them with a broom. *A thief! A thief!* they called, and clodded earth at the ravenstone. *Craw's hanged*, they cried. They paid no heed of Whin. A boy set garlands, rakish, on its crown. A girl in green tatters stooped for the beggar's blackshod stick, flung down; she strode it and she cantered, flourishing her whip. Moonbent and moledark, Hurchin tried his bagpipe, with a melancholy wheeze and yowl and buzzing, like a cat among wasps. Ragtag and bagpipe, they ranted and crowed.

There was one among them, in and out, unseen: a smutchfaced little figure, dark and watchful, with a heavy jangling pack. A traveller by kindred: breeched and beardless, swart and badgerly of shoulders. By its small harsh voice, a woman, so Whin guessed. And dressed as Ashes in the guisers' play. She wore grey breeches and a leathern cap, a coat of black sheepskins, singed and stained about the cuffs with ashes and with blood. Her hair was shorn across the brows and braided narrowly with iron charms. The hag had grizzled it; a hand undid the years.

"Hallows wi' thee," said Brock, nodding.

"And with ye," said Whin. What river had she leapt?

"Crawes Brig," the traveller said, and crossed to meet Whin at the beckside,

stone to stone. Sifting through the flinders in Whin's hands, she found a
something, round and tarnished; thumbed it to a gleam. A coin. She spun it
round. The one side was obliterate—an outworn face, a bird?—on the other
was a rayed thing, like a little star or sun. "That'll pay for't dance," said Brock,
and smiled, small and sharp as the new moon. She took a bag of craneskin
from her sleeve, and held it open for the ashes. There were coins in it and
bones; she drew it tight. "Undone," she said. "And all to do."

Whin bared her throat, undid her scarf and jacket to the heart; she bowed
her head beneath the cord. She saw at heart a shadow of the deepless water
and the pale boat riding, shrouded with her soul. Brock hung the soulbag at
her throat; she marked Whin's face with ash.

Whin gazed at her. "It's your coat Ashes wears."

"Aye," said Brock. "It's lent for travelling. Way's cold in but thy bones."

Whin said, "It's bonny on this earth, this morn; I'd linger."

And Brock said, "D'ye think it's dead alone as dance?"

Whin said, "I saw yon lady's scarf, her soul; she will not dance."

"Will she not?" A wind in the quickthorn shook the silver on the trees.
Whin saw a grove of girls, of sisters, woven in their dancing, scarved in light.
A hey as white as hag. Nine Weaving. "She dances now," said Brock. "She's
rising into dawn, and rooted; she is walking from her mother's dark, toward
winter, ripening until t'moon reaps her and she lies i' dark. Plum and stone.
And she'll gang heavy til she's light."

"What's she?" But Whin had seen her in the glass, and barefoot in the
shards of glass.

"Left hand til her mother's right, white's black. Not waning but t'childing
moon. Unwitch, unmaiden and unwise. Her mother's sister and her make.
Thysel."

"Her mother?" Whin did not name Annis.

"Aye, t'awd witch got her in her glass. And keeps her." Brock looked sidelong at the stone, the hill. Whin saw it, through and through, as black as sky.
It was a woman sleeping, with the hooked moon at her heart, and stars and
gatherings of stars within her side. She was the fell they stood upon, her hair
unwreathing in a coil of cloud.

"How—?"

"She quickens wi' herself," said Brock. "She's moon, and mews her daughter in her dark. But I's keys to all locks, and I come and go. When's time, I s'll
call on witch and steal her daughter to't dance. Will yer gang wi' me?"

Whin said, "I were Ashes."

"Ah," said Brock.

The scarf was in Whin's ashy hands; she ran it through and through a ring. "It were guising at Lightfast, and he'd bright long hair. Outlandish. I were fifteen, so I went down moor with him. I never see'd his face."

"So yer gotten a bairn?"

"Me mam and her gran—they'd've ta'en him and slain him. For an Ashes child. And sown his blood wi' t'corn. And they'd bind me til them, sleep and waking, while I's light of him. And whored me after. I left him under ragthorn." The scarf was knotted. "And I prayed no craws'd come, nor foxes. But I never stayed. I never turned til home. I's walking since."

Brock's eyes were shadowed in her hair. "And what d'ye think? Here's a woman weeping and she laps her child i't shroud; she lulls her fondling on her knee. Her nails are brocken, for she's graved it with her hands. Her milk is sore. And here's an old crone wailing, that she cannot comfort them. It's winter, and her loom is bare. And here's a fondbegotten brat, and nowther clout nor cladding til his arse. Tom Cloud. And thorn's his lap. And here's a vixen and her seven cubs; she dances like a flake of fire, crying, *Blood!* There's a many tales. And which is his?"

Whin said, "I'd want him well and growed."

"And thysel?"

"Away," said Whin. "I'd not be ended in a tale."

Brock tilted her face; the small cold iron clinked and jangled. "And here's a lad roved out wi' guisers—"

"No," said Whin, struck cold.

"And which?" said Brock. "And when? It's done, and long since done, and all to do."

Whin rubbed her hands against her breeches, crumpling the stormy scarf; the ash was pale against her clothes. Her blood was branching ice. *And which is thine?* the beggar said, herself met barefoot on the road. What child was sacrifice? And who had laid her down? "He's not—He's—"

"What moon makes of him."

Whin looked where the white tree shone. "And yet she dances."

"In her turn, and with him, in her turn. She bears him in her lap."

"I'd set her free."

"It's guisers turn all tales, and wake her to't dance. There's never endings. Will tha play for us?"

"A while," said Whin.

The rout came onward, fluttering with strips of rags. They shook a knot of bloody ribbons in her face. She knew them all by part. That broad-faced shepherd with the crown of horn. The old man with the bundled swords, the stripling with his pipe and drum. Those ranting lads. The Fool. The Awd Moon, with his petticoats and broom. Herself, with the box of coins, the bag of ashes. And the lad with bright unravelled hair. He bore a pole, with a cage of thorns, ungarlanded; the crow within it swung, down-dangled by a leg, its wings clapped open, and its beak agape and stark. Whin took her scarf and tore it, waif by waif, and hung the cage with rags of sun.

Aside and smiling, then she saw the white-haired fiddler raise his bow. Brock held the silver to him, beckoning Jack Daw; she called the tune.

And there began the wheedling of a little pipe, a small drum's thud.

## The Guisers

They come like hoarfrost and are gone. In their packs are dreams, lies, memories: the old moon's spectacles; a bunch of rusty keys; a baby's rattle like a wooden wren; spindles and whorls; blunt shears; a half burnt doll; a tangle of bright silks, bent nails; a tallow candle and a knife; a crowd of bone. It sings its old plaint in an outland tongue. They strung it with her hair. Or there are gold rings, chaffered at the door, for nothing, for a gnarl of ginger and a rime; cast shoes of leather. The lady left them, walking into song. 'Twas they who put the grey hawk's feather in her bed. And there's a shirt, a little slashed, once fine, but stained with hanging. They had it from his back. His eyes went to the crows; his bones dance.

If they come as guisers, you must let them in: the slouched one with her bag of ashes; the patched one with his broom of thorn. They bring the sun.

# TWO: A CROWD OF BONE

Margaret, do you see the leaves? They flutter, falling. See, they light about you, red and yellow. I am spelling this in leaves. When I had eyes and hands, and hair as red as leaves, I was Thea. My mother fed me to her crows, she burned my bones and scattered them; my braided hair she keeps. I am wind and memory who spells this; Thea who is spelled is stone. My mother got me gazing in her glass. Her raven held it up and told her: what I tell you, you must do. *Undo,* the sly moon said. And so she did, undid. Annis was herself her glass, and I her shadow, A and O. She saw me in the stony mirror, naked as a branch of thorn. Devouring, she bore me, as the old moon bears the new, itself again. But I am left hand to her right: not waning, but the childing moon. The dark has eaten me; I bear it light. I cloak myself in leaves, I fly. The wind unspells this.

I will spell this in the sliding water on a web. At my birth, the Necklace had its rising, Annis' chain of stones. But they do give it other names above, that Elsewhere it had set. The Skein, they call it in the Cloudish tongue; in Lune, the Misselbough; that cloud of stars we name the Clasp, they call Nine Weaving, or the Clew. So I did write when I had hands and learned to cipher and to spell. When I had eyes, I saw another heavens through her glass, another world. I walk there now and gather lightwebs, plucking them from thorns of night; I spin them in a skein, a clew. The dark is labyrinth, but not the maze I thought I knew. I wander like a moon. See, Margaret, how the heavens dance, they dance between my hands. When I had eyes, I thought my seeing bound the stars; I knew the Cup, the Hallows Tree, the Ship, as if my naming them were law. There is another law. The stars are messengers; their shining comes from far and farther still, from hearths long cold. Walking, I have seen the hearths beyond the stars, like ashes on a dark hill. But the stars that travel, they are dark and bright, like travellers with scarves of light, like beings newly blown of crystal, each a single note, nightblack, and rayed with burning silver. Their moving is their voice; they do not speak, but dance. Ah, now the drops of water slide away. The web is shaken bare.

I tell this in the frost, the rime. I am not for my mother's necklace. Margaret, have you seen it? It is strung with stones, all flawed: some round as waveworn pebbles, others long and sharpedged. They are souls, the souls of witches, cold long since: the eldest of them ash these nine thousand years. Witches turn themselves to stone. Their gaze is glass. But they are isolate, unknotted souls: they dance by one and one. The necklace is an eidolon, a ring that never was. The souls are gathered on one string, as shadows of the starry Chain. That cord is time; the knot is Law. It is a place. I lay there once, a white ground where the blood is spilled, a place of bones and coins. All witches came there, bent on darkness; none had met. They spelled in blood, cast bones; they spoke in tongues of fire. There are witches still in Lune, on Law. Yet none is living that could read the word my ashes spelled; nor find the nine bones that I left.


Beyond the circle of Whin's light, the sea moves, sleepless in its heavy gown. She walks beside it slowly, toward, away. And to her, from her, endlessly it shifts the longways of its slow pavane. Within her candle's burr, sparse flakes of snow blink, vanish. There is nothing there to see. Salt rime and shingle. Sea wrack. Stones, a curve of jetty, tumbled in a storm. Sticks and weed. They stir. A wave? They draw breath, harshly. The lantern swings and halts.

In the dark, a white face, staring: a man, all bone and shivering, three-quarters drowned. "Who's there?" he tries to call. Whin sets the lantern down. "A journeyman," she says. "A traveller." He sprawls against the stonework, tangled in an iron ring; the next wave frets at him, the next. His coat is gone, his head and feet are bare. A stranger out of Lune, thinks Whin. Uncloudish. Yet he bids her by her calling. "Ashes?" At his throat he wears a skin bag, smaller than a purse. His hands are white past bleeding, bruised; he signs to her, take this. She fumbles with the knots, she bites at them and tumbles out his hoard: cold rings.

"Will you tell a death?"

They are silver and endless on her hard brown palm. White stones like frost. A knot of blood. "Could yer not sell them?"

"None would take. No ship. They—"

"Throwed yer over? I see yer to hang."

He shudders. "It is not my passage that I seek."

"A fire," says Whin. "And drink ye. I'd not shift stones for yer grave."

She squats beside him, lugs him further up the strand. Stripping off his icy rags, she laps him in the old coat, black as nightfall, stiff as death. He'd not starve yet. She leaves him hallowed in the lantern's fleet.

There's wood enough, but sodden. Whin flings the heavy, takes the dry stuff, salt with frost. She stacks it, leeward of a quain of rock; strikes, kindles, drives her iron for the can. Waiting for the blaze, she chafes the stranger, lays him naked to her breast: blue hands, bruised feet, his starved and wrinkled cock and balls, his belly, slack against his spine, until the blood runs shining, sheeting on his dazed white face. The fire leaps. A boy, for all his haggard look. His eyes are sunken, shut; his beard is soft. Not twenty. Younger than herself. She lays him, not ungently, on the stones.

"Not sleep," he whispers. "Tell."

"Drink." The ale in the can's hot; she stirs a slurry of meal in, a scrape off her knuckled ginger. Strong. She holds it to his lips.

"Tell."

Whin drinks. "I will then." She turns the cold rings on her hand. They are silver and endless; they are night, moon, mourning. They would weigh her down. Whin sees the pale boat waiting and the soul that bellies in the dark wind, quick with death; the telling is the shroud that stays it, that the soul can journey. Let her go.

*It's what I is. Death's midwife.*

And she sets the first ring on.

*O death.* She sees the wheel hurled downward, burning, and the scattered crows. She sees a white wrist circled with a braid of burning hair, a bluenailed hand; it casts, it casts a blackness on the stony ground. Shards of witchglass, ashes of bone.

And she herself is scattered and restrung. She is the crowd of bone, the dead soul's stringing, and her voice.

Whin's hand is beating, beating on the earth. She sings.

It's in an outland tongue at first, a dancing driving lilt, a skirl and keening; then the tongue's her own. *There are pools in the river, and the river calls him.* All white in whiteness where it rises; swift in running, deepest where the red leaf eddies in the pool. Whorl and headlong, she sings the river's journey: glint

and shadow, dint of rain, the running to the downfall and the shivered bow
of light.

No more.

Even as she wakes from trance, the ring is ice, is water. Gone.

She sees the fire, sunken into embers; sees the drawn face staring. Far beyond, the sea shifts, turning its sleepless bed. Far gone.

"The child," he whispers.

Ah. The child. Whin presses at her eyes until the red's green as leaves, new
leaves. *Ashes. Ashes.* See, the crows at the furrows wheel and fall, they tear at—
*No. Leave off. That were back and elsewhere.* A long draught of the caudle, slab with
standing. Raking back her hair, salt-fretted with the roke and sweat, Whin
slips the small ring on her hand.

And there is nothing. Whiteness. Round she turns, and round; she stumbles, groping for a gossamer, a clew. No thread, there is no thread. A creak
of wood. A ship? And then a lalling nowhere, like a woman at her wheel; but
small. Arms crossed before her face, Whin blunders at the mist. It reddens
and dissolves; it dances. And she's in an empty room. She sees a cradle overset;
she sees a tangle of bright silks. In the roar and crackling of thorns, she sees a
burning doll, its blind face like a poppyhead, the petals like a cry.

"The child?" His voice is sharp with fear.

"Not dead."

He shuts his eyes. "Ah."

Whin slips the small ring up her finger, rocks it with her thumb. Not dead,
she'd swear it. How? Not born?

But where is here? The world is white now, greying like a ghost. Are they
now lost in what she'd sung? Whin stares a moment, mutely; then she turns
her palm and raises it. It fills with snow. She tastes the water in the hollow of
her hand, the salt and sweet.

Bending to the man, she brushes him; she touches eyes, mouth, heart.
"Thou sleep."


A girl is reading in a garden where no flowers grow. It is formal and math-
ematical, a maze, an abstract of the heavens done in yew and stone. A garden
made for moonlight and for winter, changeless but for sky and snow and
drifting leaves: a box of drowned green light. It is autumn now. The fountain's
dry; the stone girl weeps no more. Her lap is full of leaves. The lawn is grey

as gossamers with rime. The living girl's dishevelled, in a cloud of breath; she's hunched against the cold in woven velvet, wadded silk: old finery, too thin. Leaves light on her. She holds her book aslant to catch the light, and peers through cracked spectacles: "... one king's daughter said to another ..." Her breakfast's in a napkin: cake, an orange. Costly, alien, aglow. Round she turns it in her cold lap, cradles, sniffs. Straying from her hood, her tangled hair is pale red, light through leaves; her tumbled gown is stormcloud blue. Her slipshod feet are wet. Softly as she's come, she cannot hide her track: her feet, her draggling skirts have torn the hoarfrost, tarnishing. You cannot read her face: an egg, a riddle. What is it lives within a maze, within a wall, within a hedge of thorn? And on an island, not a winter's day in riding round. Yet she's never seen the sea.

A bird cries. *Margaret?* Startled, she looks up and round. The orange rolls unheeded from her lap. There, back of her, a black bird flutters to the earth, as ragged as an ash. Its cry fades like a cinder, glows and fades. Bearded, it regards her with its black eye; hops and drags a mirror in the wounded frost.


Ah, Margaret, it was cold in Cloud, the wandering. I mind a night of frost, a white hag on the hillsides; it was all ways white, whatever way we turned. Kit bore a lantern that he dared not light; my mother's crows have eyes. Round we turned like children in a game; like tops, still giddy, lest we fall.

Here's not yet dark, he said. And none to light our heels. I hear that Will the piper's to the hedgehogs' shearing.

A cup, I said, to drink their health.

A game, said he. Wilt thou have *Aprons all untied?* I'll show thee. Or *Cross my river to Babylon.*

Light words. But doubtful mind, I thought: elated, ill at ease. What should he with this bird of paradise? I was no hedgeling to be coaxed and whistled; yet had lighted on him, haggard to his hand. Brave plumes. And trailing jesses of another's leash.

Thy candle's quenched, said I. Will I light thee another?

And willing, said he. Wouldst bear it then?

And go the lighter for't.

Then soberly he said: the bridge is drowned. I know not the way.

We stood. And all the trees beyond us like a crowd of bones. No stars. I'd never gone by night, without to see the stars. And in my mind I saw what

I'd undone: my mother's chain of stones, the clasp of winter from my throat. Her chain of witches' souls. I saw them in the mist, the others in the game, caught out, cast out. They stood like stones, but clearer than the coldest night: in each, a dark witch rayed with blood; in each, the wintry stars. In the last, like an altar stone, there lay the image of a woman sleeping, with the hooked moon at her heart. She was the fell they stood upon, her hair unwreathing in a coil of cloud. This cloud. *I am braided in her hair,* I said, as if my mother lessoned me; and then recalling me, I touched my throat, all bare but for a scarf.

That chain was my knowledge. I put it off with my undoing and I walked unstarry in that mazing whiteness: unwitch, unmaiden and unwise. They say the moon does so. But I was never maid—ah, Margaret, thou'rt full young to see, but thou must see. Thou know'st my mother got me in her glass. And so I was as left hand to her right. I was her make in all things hidden, and I knew as I was known. Ah, but never with an other, I had never been unknown; nor seen, as through a cloud, the hearth and shadow of another's soul. My love, we got thee all unknowing, out of cloud.

But now your breath clouds the glass: too near, you gaze too near. And so see no one in the mist: a whiteness, waning with your breath. Oh, I am all undone. My mother loosed the knot long since; she laid the chain of me aside. The soul slipped by her. White in whiteness: what I am is white.

"So yer run off wi' a witch's daughter?" said Whin. "Were yer mad or what?"

"Dazzled," said the man at last, and softly.

"And t'lass?" A silence, long enough so that Whin thought he slept.

"Ah. No witch. In the end."

Kit stood. Whatever way he turned was white, as white as nowhere.

"Thea?"

"Soft," she said. "Catch hold."

Among the standing shapes of stones, a stone put back its hood and turned. He saw her, Thea, looking back at him, her curled hand at her throat. Stumbling in the mist, he caught her and he took her cold true hand. The lantern of her hair was grey. With hag, he saw: it ghosted them. Brocaded both alike: his russet and her raiment stiff and fine with it. Her face was muffled in a scarf, the whitest at her lips. His hair, when he put it from his eyes, was hackled with frost. "Where's this?"

"Cloud," said Thea. "Is there earth?"

"I know not," he said. He looked about, bewildered, at the mist. "How came we here?"

"By ship."

He remembered; or had dreamed the like. They were in her mother's garden, in among the stones like hooded watchers and the labyrinth of yews. 'Twas dusk and shadowless, the maze, the stones configured as the starry sky. They were playing at a game with lanterns? *Hide fox, and all after.* How the errant star of her shone out, now there, now elsewhere in the dark. Their lamps conjoined. He saw her, still, but as a light is still, still dancing in his eyes. He kissed her—ah, it drowned him deep, that kiss. In her, his soul translated, like a tree of fire, burning in her bluegreen dusk. *Come away with me,* he said, now ardent, now amazed, the words like Perseids. *To Cloud. And let thy mother—*

Nothing. He remembered nothing, like a sleeper waked. Cold moonlight, musty straw. A jangling, as of keys. The dream had troubled him with joy; he wore the stone of it, both bright and heavy, at his heart.

He said, bemused, "My lady sent for you. 'Twas in her closet."

"I had found a door," she said. "The sky has doors."

"And locks?"

"'Tis done. Undone."

He saw a little image, clear as in a dream: a string of stones cast by, like blood spilled on the hoary earth.

"But how—?"

"Thy fiddle was the ship."

Dismayed, he halted. "What?"

"'Twas wood of Cloud. It played the wind behind us."

"Ah," said Kit, and rubbed his eyes. Salt wind: it stung. "I gave it thee. And would again, were't all the sinews of my heart." And yet remembered nothing of the gift, the journey. *Ship?* As in a waking dream, he saw the sail of sky, bluegreen against a darker sky, all riddled with the stars. He saw the lantern at the mast. Their hands together at his lips were salt. "What tune?"

*"Light leaves on water."*

"Ah, it played that when its leaves were green. Waked wood." Still unsteady, his voice. That shock of severing still white, which at a thought would bleed. And so he laid light words to it, like cobwebs to a wound. He knelt to mend his lantern. "Here's a fret. 'Tis out. And I've left my flint and steel." He grimaced ruefully. "And come to that, thy book, and all. Hadst thou nothing thou wouldst take?"

"There was not time. The door stood open."

Suddenly he stood and said, "We've done it, then?"

"We do," said Thea. "Grammar."

"Ah," said Kit. "How the old crows' beaks will clack. Canst see them at their feast? Here's bones." And hopping on the ground, he cocked an eye at her, with such a glance of balked fury that she laughed aloud.

"*The crow and her marrow, they quarrel for the glass.*" Then gathering up her skirts, "Let's on," she cried.

"What way?"

"Any way. Away."

"All Cloud's to choose."

"I know. To where the fiddles grow."

"And shake the tree? I'll play no windfall, for the green are sharp."

"But we must cross a river by the dawn."

Round they turned like children in a game, and in and out among the stones. They called and bantered, dizzy with unlawful joy. Kit fell. His lantern slid away, it skated from his grasp; then he was up again, bruised and laughing. "Hey!" Then seeing her a-shake with cold, he sobered. "Canst thou make us fire?"

"No," said Thea.

"Nor can I," he said. "I doubt we'll starve then, but we find some cotter's hearth." He cast his coat round her, crazy with the ice. "Or a tinker's camp. And chaffer for his russet coat." *A mantle of the starry sky.* Her gown was thin, the color of the bloom on sloes, embroidered as the Milky Way: light shaken out, lace dandled. Not for travelling, he thought. A gown for walking in her mother's hall, from glass to glass. And it would snow.

"So this is Cloud," he said. "'Tis like a tale of witches, well enough by the fire. *Once afore the moon was round, and on a night in Cloud ...* Hast kindred here?"

"None," said Thea, "in this world. But hast not thou?"

"In Lune I had." He bent for the lantern. "We'd best on."

The night was uncompassed. Far off, they heard an endless rampage, not a shuttle but a reel of sound, cloud spinning into ice.

"What's that?" she said. "'Tis like the sea unmeasured."

"A river," he said. "Houses?"

So they set out for it, stumbling into brakes of thorn and bogs and pit-falls, snagged and mired. They went blindly, now toward and now astray. The roar grew louder in the dark. The hills re-echoed with the rush of it, behind, before, and everywhere. Above, a nightcrow cawed, once, in its coaly voice. An omen. Thea stilled.

"What is't?" said Kit.

"The clouds have eyes."

"An I had my fiddle, I would play them to sleep."

On the hills, the foxes yowled and yelped, as if their blood ran green. An eerie sound, that keening. Thea shivered.

"The hills have tongues. They wake."

"They wed. I'd light them with a dance." And wheeling backward, sliding—"Oh!" cried Kit. She caught his jacket as he stepped on nothing, on the brink of tumbling in a foss.

"Now what?" said Kit. "I'm for a glass castle and a bout with goblins. Or a ghost, or what you will. As we've tumbled in a winter's tale." He sat among the lashy thorns and rubbed his shins. "Ah," he said, and fumbled in his pockets. "Here." She felt a handful of nuts. "From thy mother's table, as I passed. We may sit and crack them while the crows take counsel."

"Or match them with a goblin, shell for soul."

"Unless he'd like a gingernut?"

"To cross his river?"

"Aye." Kit rose. "'Twill narrow upstream, far enough."

In the dark beyond the river, there and gone, they saw a fire.

Kit caught at Thea's arm. "A light. A house?"

"A torch," she said. "It moves."

"Thy mother's horsemen?"

"No. They bear no light."

He said, "Belike some lantered shepherd. Or a fiddler from a dance." Stumbling toward the light, he called out, "Hallows!"

An answer, lost in tumult.

"Hey! Where's this?"

"Crawes Brig," called the voice. "Wait on." They saw the wavering fire and the world made round it, swayed and ruddy. On the farther bank, a roughclad knarry shape held up a torch. It shuddered in the little wind. They saw the wolf-black water, snarling white; they saw the way, from stone to stepping-stone to span, the lighter as they leapt. A clapper bridge, a cromlech. They met on the span. "Here. Gi's that." The stranger took the lantern, thrust the torch in it alight, and latched the door; then hurled the brief end, whirling fire, in the beck.

They stood within a burr of light that brindled in the rushy dark. There was no other where. The stranger stared at them with long dark eyes, quirked mouth. Kit saw the hunch of shoulders bearing up the jangling pack. A traveller, he thought, a tinker or a tain by kindred: breeched and beardless, swart and badgerly of arms. And grey as any brock: with winters or the hag, he knew not. By the small harsh voice, a woman, so he guessed.

"Yer late abroad," said Brock. "Come on."

The candle wavers. Ah, thou frown'st, as if my shadow fell across thine elsewhere. I will spell this in the margins of thy book. Mine, once. See, Margaret, here the leaf's turned down where Perseis gave up. Her grave is Law. But I see thou read'st her spring, her journeying. The lady speaks:

> But thou art mazed, sweet fool. The wood is dark,
> And I th' moon's daughter in these rags of cloud
> Shall bear thee light.

Another world. I dreamed not of greenwood nor of crowns of May; nor thought on bread, sweat, childbed. Only I would not be Thea, and my lady's cipher. So I saw my chance: a bird in hand, a passager; an occultation of the Nine. I took.

Poor Kit. Wood with love of me. He mourned his fiddle; I do rue it now. His soul and livelihood and all. And yet he had of me a greater thing, unwitting. Not my maidenhead. Whatever ballads tell, 'tis nothing, anyone's. An O. That which annihilates all else. No, Margaret: the game is toyish, but the stakes are souls. My love, we ate each other back and belly, and the heartstrings: which are music, which are gut.

Ah, now the candle gutters. I am leaping; I am shroud and smoke. I snuff.

"Here," said the traveller. She stooped and they followed through a thicket of ice. The candle woke in it a flittering of lights; it chimed and rattled as they passed beneath it. "Rimes," said Thea, half aloud to Kit. "Glass castle," he whispered. "Did I not say?" Before them was a tumble of stones: hall fallen into hovel; a sill and dark within. At the door, the traveller stamped the clods from her boots. She set the lantern down; the fire made room. She turned in the doorway and said, "Walk in, awd Moon."

Kit caught her rime, though not her meaning. "Wi' broom afore, to sweep the ashes from the door," he said, as if they came a-souling at the empty house. He plucked at Thea's sleeve. "Go on, love, 'tis thy piece."

She turned her small moon's face on him. "Will there be oranges?"

"Thy lapful."

"I know not the words."

So Kit chanted, "Cold by the door and my candle burns low, so please let us in, for it's shrewd in the snow." He bent and bustled all around her with his broom of air; so they went in.

"Here's guising," said the traveller. "A sword and a bush." ·

Kit answered lightly. "So it ever was."

"Then let's to yer bout and have done wi' it. Smick smack, and up flies wren."

Thea lifted her face, bright with mischief. "Ah, but you must hear us out; you've bid us in. You must hear Moon's verses, since she's crossed your door."

The traveller looked them up and down: the tousled lad, all beak and bones; the girl in outlandish clothing, with her hair like braided fire. "Out o thy turning. If thou's Moon."

"Out of thy sphere, if thou'rt fire."

"Out of my depth," said Kit. "As I am drowned."

They clapped themselves and shivered. Dry within. No straw nor muck; but hay and heather, cut and heaped. Kit turned to and helped the stranger drag some branches to the hearth. It was bare enough, that ruin: a hovel for the lambing shepherds or the lasses binding broom. Kit whispered to Thea, "As for cakes and silver, we may bite old moon."

The traveller lit a fire with a stump of juniper. It burned with a sharp smoke, curling; then was firestruck, its every needle cast in gold, consuming. By its light, they studied her, a little smutchfaced woman, dark and watchful, in a coat of black sheepskins, singed and stained about the hem with ashes and blood. She wore grey breeches and a leathern cap. Her hair was unbound about her shoulders, roughly shorn across her brows; a few strands plaited narrowly with iron charms. She crouched by the fire and stirred it with her knife. "My forge is drowned," she said. The bough had fallen all to flinders, and the berries glowered in the ashes. "Get yer warm," she said, and quirked her chin at them. Then she stood and rummaged in her jangling pack, and went out.

They looked at one another, huddling by the fire. All the spanglings of the ice, their winter finery, had faded. There they sat in draggled clothes, ungarlanded, unwed. Bare strangers. By the wall where the bed had stood, a timeworn carving showed: a woman with a pair of shears, but what she sheared was gone. "I feel like a ghost," said Kit.

"How? Shadowy? Thou'rt blood and breath."

"Uncanny on this ground. And you?"

"No dwelling spirit. They do haunt; they have a bloodknot to this earth. A tale. And mine is all before me, all unmoored."

"An elfin, then."

"A waif. A soul unborn, and calling on the wind. Their tale is nothing: only, they are cold without, and would come in."

"I'd let them in," said Kit, "And warm them." White and shivering, her wisp of spirit. And a glass between their souls. He longed to take her in his arms: so small and cold and straight, so quick of mind. A candle and its light, he thought. And then: the fire was his. To have the daughter of so great a lady run away with him—'twas beyond all marvels. And a flawless maid. A dazzlement. A goblin in him danced, exulting; knocked at his breeches. Ranted on his grave. He knelt. "Thea. If thou wouldst—"

"Hush," said Thea, as they heard the traveller's goatshod step. They sprang apart, a little awkwardly. The fire had flushed them, that was all; the wind had tousled them. The traveller walked softly toward them, and turned to Thea with a cup.

"Here's to thy turning."

"With my heart," said Thea, with answering gravity. She took it in her hands and drank. "Oh," she said, and turned to Kit. "Do they not say in Cloud, hallows wi' thee?"

"And wi' thee," he said, and drank. It was milk, still warm. "Ah," said Kit, bemused. "Your lambs drop early, shepherd."

"Twa and twa," the traveller said. "T'ane black and t'other white." She drank. "And all me ewes give cheeses turn themsels."

"Cup and all?" said Thea.

The traveller smiled at her, small and sharp. "At tree, it were. They'll have left it for Ashes."

"Oh," said Kit. "I see." Though he did not.

But Thea, pinning up a braid, said, "Ashes?"

"Shepherds. They do wake her from her mother dark."

"Ah, Perseis. I know that tale."

"It's what I do," said the traveller. "Walk out and see."

Kit caught at straws. "You're late abroad."

"Been hunting craws. To mek a soulcake on."

"But where your dogs?" said Thea.

"Whistled home." She unhooked an aleskin from her pack, and teemed it out in a stoup. She pulled her knife from the fire, glowing, and she plunged it in the ale. "Ye'll be starved," she said. "Walking."

"Wanting bread," said Kit. "If you can spare."

"As for that." The traveller undid a rag and a knot and a clump of heather, and held out her scarred brown hand.

Kit saw a handful of stones, black scrawled with white, white scribbled over with a sort of wintry runes, like stars and their ascendants, prophecies of light. "I know this tale," said Kit. "You'll be wanting a bit of salt next. For the soup."

"What thou will," the traveller said. She chose a stone and thirled it with a pin and blew: a whorl of sun, widening, muddled with the ale.

"Eggs," he said, bewildered.

"Aye," said she, and tossed the shell away and broke another and another still, and stirred the pot. She teemed the ewe's milk in.

Kit raked through the embers for the few flawed shales of night. White, like the moon in flinders. Black, with a sleave of stars. Were they owl eggs, then? Or nightingales? "It's eating music," he said ruefully.

"O breve," said Thea. "Do they so in Cloud?"

"With bacon. Do we not in Lune?"

The traveller stirred the caudle round, with a race of ginger, knuckled like a witch's hand, a slurry of coarse sugar and a scrape of nutmeg. A pinch to the fire; it sparkled. "Wha said they'd hatch birds? Wha said they'd sing?"

"In Law," said Thea, "they do not."

So grave? Kit glanced at her, and pulled a fool's face, innocent. "They say the Lunish witches eat owl pies."

"Crack bones and craunch marrow, aye," said Thea. Fire and shadow on her face. "But of late they've grown dainty and will nothing coarse: venture on a junket of maidenheads—"

"Ah, that slips down," said Kit.

"—with a boy for a bergamot."

The traveller dipped her finger, tasted. "Aye, but seek as they will, their cupboard's bare. They may beg for't."

"They've sails," said Thea. In the silence, they heard the wind rise from the north and west, from Law.

"I's keeled for them," the traveller said. They looked at her, and at the eggshells, all shivered on the ground but one that whorled about the ale, and sank. "There's all their shallops."

"Will they follow so?" said Thea softly.

"But if their sails are souls, and all their riggins of thy hair."

"'Twas never cut," said Thea.

"Ah," the traveller said. "Reach to." They passed the caudle round and drank in silence. From her pack, the traveller shared out a bannock, spread with curds and new sweet cream. As round as the moon it was, and a little charred beneath. Ah, thought Kit, here's some hob goes supperless, and all the kitchen in a cludder with his sulking on't. He gazed at Thea, silent by the hearth. Her eyes were elsewhere.

Slowly, she unwound her scarf, unclouding heaven. Ah, but she was crescent, she was moonrise, even at the verge of dawn—O hallows—even to the rose.

But not for him, this glory. Bending toward the traveller, she held the scarf: a light silk woven of the sky, it seemed. He'd thought of it as grey, but it was shining, warped with silver like an April morning. Rain and bow. She laid it in the outstretched hands. Kit watching saw it fall on them, and thought their earthgrained furrows would spring green.

"For thy spell," she said. "A sail."

The traveller looked slantwise through her rough dark hair, her long black eyes unglittering. "A soul." It shifted in her hands, turned silver and a flowing dark, like cloud before the moon. And cleared then to a moonless dark. The stars ran through it still like rain. "Well, I's a rag on every bush, they say." She wafted it and caught it crumpled, bunched it in her pack all anyhow. "It's cawd without, thou knaws."

Thea said, "It would not keep me warm."

"It's thy petticoats are musty. Do them off."

"For thy breeches," Thea said. Kit looked at her, her bare throat white as thorn, her face alight. Her breasts—buds in January, whiter than its snow. No lad. She stood and paced, as he had seen her by the whiteskied windows of her mother's tower. Of darkest blue, her eyes, the night in which her fires burned. She turned on the traveller, fierce and cold. "Or thy cap or anything, thy hammer and thy sooty brat, so my mother would not see me in her glass."

"Break t'glass."

"It will not break, the moon. It goes with child unflawed, and of itself. And being full, itself devours, lighter of the dark. It gazes and it gnaws. I want to get back of it."

Kit looked at Thea, like the heavens' cold bright bow; and saw the dark that bent, that held her. There were walls he could not see.

The traveller held her gaze. "There is a door, they say."

"Then I would out of it."

He saw her fury; though her hair was braided close, she blazed as whitely as a falling star. He felt his spirit rise to her. Arrow to her bow. "Love, let me in."

She turned to him. "Crack the glass and I will."

It was his heart that cracked; but like an acorn, that the oak might spring. He slipped the ring from his finger. "Thea. Love," he said. "With my heart, 'tis what I have." His mother's ring of tawdry silver, black with years. A riddling posy.

Thea turned it round and read. *"Lief wode I fall, an light wode spring.* Or this way, look: *I fall and light: would spring leafwood."* Round again: *"Anne Lightwode: spring leaf. Would I fall?"* She looked to him and smiled; she slipped it on her finger.

O the falling star. 'Twas in his hands.

The traveller, watching as she would a play, took out her bacca and her bit of black pipe. "Key's under bush," she said. "Look well to yer locks."

And still Kit stood amazed.

"As for yer guising." The traveller undid her pack, and pulled from it a heap of leaves; she shook it out and there were sleeves to it, and dangling buttons made of horn. It was a coat in tatters. "Craws weren't having it," she said. "What's ta'en is anyone's."

"Is there a hat to it?" said Kit, recovering.

"And feather," said the traveller. She swung the coat round Thea's shoulders. It hung to her heels.

Kit grinned. "Ah. Wilt thou go for a ranting girl?"

"Aye, and bid them stand," the traveller said.

"Here's purses full," said Kit.

"I'll nothing but thy ring," said Thea, whirling round on him. "Or will it come to swordplay?"

"Wouldst kill me naked?"

"And would die beside thee."

He reeled her in. "And then I rise."

"Oh," said Thea. "'Tis my part. And I am of out it."

"So I am in," said Kit, and caught her by the coattail, laughing. "Turns," he said; so she let him try it on. He flaunted in it, up and down. He looked all mischief, with his leafish face. And in the flaycraw's voice, the fool's, he said, "I'll riddle thee. What leaves and still it stands?"

"A tree," said Thea. "Turns?"

The traveller shrugged. "For either, as it likes you. And if she's a lad, I's shears."

Thea rounded on her. "Where?"

"No," cried Kit, dismayed. "I beg thee. Not thy hair." He'd not yet seen it down, not played with it undone. It would unravel like a fugue. He thought of all the braided strands of it, the bright and somber and the burning strands, the viol and clarion. "And yet ..." His token glinting on her hand: he dared. "I'd have a lock of it, sweet witch, for journey's sake."

"In knots, as witches sell the wind?"

"Aye, knotted: for undone 'twould quicken stone."

A parry and no promise: "Thou wouldst thaw my lady's glass?"

"Like April snow. And all thy combs would flower, leafless, from the wood, and make of thy undoing, crowns of May." A tendril, like a wisp of fire, twining by her cheek: he traced it, marvelling. So cold, so bright and cold.

Not fencing now: the blade itself: "Wouldst braid thy gallows? Wear it?"

"Nearer than my breath. I'll knot my soul in it." It burned in him already, bright in every vein: a tree. He took her in his arms. "And being strung upon my bones, 'twill play the same tune still, for sun and moon, and all the starry hey to dance."

Her lips were colder than the moon's, and soft. He felt him falling in a drift of snow, bedazzled, over ears. Her lap, he thought, she lulls them in her lap. Moon and stars. He saw the burning bush. He saw the bird of her, flown up amid her branches—that he could not take. He shook himself, remembering the traveller's eyes, and shrugged the greatcoat off. "I'll go no more a-guising. 'Tis the fiddler's turn to dance."

"To pipe and drum," the traveller said.

Thea and the traveller took the coat between them, lofting it and laying it upon the springing heather, so it made a bed. They stood at head and foot of it, as in the figure of a dance; the traveller spoke.

"What thou gets here, thou mun leave betimes."

"I must bear it," Thea said.

"And will."

"Undone and done."

The traveller crouched and tweaked a corner of the coat aside, tucked something in, and rose. "What is ta'en here, cracks t'glass. What is tinder s'll be ash. Go lighter of it, intil dark." She flung a pair of shears on the makeshift bed. They lay there open, like a striding stork. She turned and gathered up her pack. "I's off."

They saw her go. They lay together on the coat, of leaves as deep as hallows. After a time, unspeaking, they undid her hair, and went into another night.

O the dark. Thou hear'st not, Margaret. I will tell this to the darkness.

I would not be Thea: so I did, undid. The thing of naught. Ablaze and all unhallowed in that night, I cracked the glass. Blasphemed my lady, that was Annis. That was all myself. Of my own will, I overset her holiest of laws; I broke her will of me, her mirror and her chain. Set Cloud for Law, and darkness for her glass. Blood in the stone's place, the place of secrets. Rose for thorn.

The traveller came to the stones. They stood looking out on darkness, on the bare white shoulder of the fell. That knowe is Law. The sky was starless; yet they mirrored in their O that constellation called Nine Weaving or the Clasp. The wintry mantle they had pinned was gone. Softly, she went in and out among them with her dying torch. All doors are hers; but these stood open. There was no one where the girl had been. The torch went out. The traveller turned among the empty stones, toward morning, sunwise.

*Ah!* cried Brock. She saw the falling star, now, nowhere, in the wintry sky. Her seeing sained it. Wheeling round, she dropped the black end of the besom to the earth, ashes on the frost. She snuffed the wind. It was rising, high above the earth. The sky had flawed with stars, with scarves and spanglings of light. Her eyes were good; she told the eight stars in the Nine, and one beside. It danced with them. The ashes told its name.

Beyond her lay the long bare fells, rimewhite, unwhitening. Through patches of the fading snow there pierced a greener white of snowdrops, that do spring in Ashes' wake. Her flowers. Drops of Milk, the country folk do call them, Ashes' Buds. They bring the light with them returning, rising from her mother's dark: all seely innocence. Yet they are death to pluck; and yet they must be gathered, woven for her crown by earthly hands. By Ashes. Not herself, but in her stead: a lass each winter who must wear the burden of her name, her silence, walking in her sleep. That godhead lights on whom she chooses: Ashes for her sake, her shadow, souling in a coat of skin. Her winter's lyke.

As Brock walked on, she passed a windbare thicket leaning all one way, and saw the curled green shoots of bracken, green amid the scrawl of last year's leaves; she saw the tassels of the oak unbraiding. Saw the selving wood. A hare loped by her, giddy with the moon; she slung no stone at it. It danced in a dizzy spiral. At last she came to where the Clew was caught, like sheep's wool, in the branches of a leafless thorn. Nearer to the earth there hung a garland and a tattered coat, cast by. And at its roots, asleep in winter's lap, there lay a greenwhite girl. Brock bent and sained her, touching eyes, mouth, heart with ashes. Until the dawn she watched by the sleeping girl.

Thea slept and she was kindled: all within her side the star became a knot of stars, a congeries, a cloud, a soul. It waked within her turning sky. Her hair unwreathing was the red of dawn.


Kit woke to see his new-made lover squatting naked in the ashy coat, her shorn hair flickering about her skull. So white, her goblin face. So young. *What have I done?* he thought. *O dark, what is she doing?* On the hearth lay the long sheaf of her sundered hair, not fading like shorn grass, but fiery. Bright as bracken in the rain, as bright as copper molten in a forge, a riverspill of fire on the muddy stones. She was burning it, strand by strand. Crouching, she stirred the embers with the shears.

"No," he said. "Thea."

The child witch turned to him. White as frost, as frail. Blood and ashes

on her thighs; the tuft of small fire that a breath would blaze. All naked but
the coat of skin. She rose and held a ring to him, white-gemmed, as if she
gave away her tears. She spoke in a child's imperious voice. "Go your ways.
You have well served me."

Coldstruck, he stared at her. The eyes saw no one. Mad?

She crouched again, to riddle through the ashes with a rusty sieve.
He caught her. Sharp and soft, a thornbush deep in snow. Like branches
she recoiled, and all her witchcraft fell away, like snow, like scattered snow.
She crouched amid the shards. "Not done," she said. "I was not done."

Kit knelt beside.

"Thea. Love. Wake up." He stroked the hackles of her hair, so cold, so
cold. "Thou'rt dreaming."

In his arms, she changed, thawed, cleft. His goblin rose.

And afterward, she slept at last. Lying watching her, the slight moon,
turning always from his gaze, he saw a fireglint beyond her: a long strand of
her hair, caught shining on a splint of wood. The last. He ran it through and
through his hands. He saw the girl in the wintry garden, turning back to call
him on; he saw the lantern of her hair. Again and yet again, he played the
fugue of its undoing. Heartstrings. Not for burning. With his fiddler's hands
he wound it round and round, and tucked it safe beside his heart.


"Gone," said Kit.

Whin said nothing; she could see it still, or the ghost of it: a bracelet of
bright hair about the bone. Like stolen fire. He'd wear it to his grave. *Beyond*,
she thought. *Would string his stars.* She shelled another mussel for the broth,
another; tossed the leavings on the heap. Clack. Click. Clack. At last: "And
wha'd take that and leave rings?"

"Crows. Her mother—I betrayed her. In the end."

Whin cracked and thumbed another mussel. Knife-edge and morsel.
Weed. "Ah. Craws wi' beards."

Kit turned his face. Not yet, thought Whin. And yet he'd tell.


Wet underfoot. Burnt moorland or bare stone; bracken, bent or tussock: all
were underlaid with squelch. "A world warped with water," Thea said, and
wrung her coat skirts. Water curling from the cloud, like raw wool from a

carder's combs. White water at a ford, frayed out, like torn lace at a roaring lad's throat. Fine icy water in the air. "At least," said Kit, "it's not raining." He did not say: we cannot lie in this. "There'll be a barn," he said. But now he could not tell if they were climbing, if they'd come this way before. Bright and brighter blazed the rust of bracken in its mockery of fire. The color of her hair, the color of desire, flickering on nothing, on the barren moor. Could water burn?

Her face turning back at him was like the moon from cloud; he leapt to it, it hooked him through the heart, the bone-caged heart.

"Look," said Thea, beckoning. "A walker on the hill." She called out, "Stay, thou shepherd!" And she ran. Kit ran after, calling, "Wait." And there was no one there: a waystone, squatting in the bracken like a hussif at her hearth. Thea touched the stone, her face between dismay and laughter. "See, she looms. 'Tis her weather."

"Hush," said Kit. "I doubt another day she brews." And fumbling beneath his pocket flap, he found a bit of bread, their last, and left it in a hollow of the stone. "There, awd lass. For a skein of sun."

And to Thea, "There'll be houses, wait on. We can barter and lie snug as hobs. Curds and barley straw."

"What way?" said Thea.

When they turned from her, the stone was fogbound, roofed and walled with cloud; they saw no way. "Away," said Kit. "'Tis all one." They heard the clank and rattle of a sheep on stones, a bird's disconsolate cry. And then a tap, a tapping, gathering like rain: a hammer on a forge.

"A fire," said Kit.

And stumbling, sliding down a track, they found a trod, stones driven edgewise for laden hooves; a wall, a fire in the mist. They tumbled from the old girl's lap, as if they'd been shaken from her apron, out of cloud and into rain.

And out of rain and by his fire sat a tinker at his work, his anvil driven in the ground, his lean bitch skulking by his side. A sere man, spare and shaggy, like a twist of tobacco. His dog, the mingled grey of ashes, smoke. He'd a tussy of coney skins hung to his tentflap; a jangle of saucepans and riddles and shears.

"How d'ye do?" said Kit, doffing his drowned hat. "Well, I hope, sir."

"What d'ye lack?" said the tinker.

"A knife," said Kit. "A cookpot. And a flint and steel. That blanket."

Clink! went the hammer on the rounding can. "A good cloak, is that. Awd bitch whelped on yon cloak. What d'ye give?"

Kit unfolded Thea's starry mantle.

The tinker eyed the velvet shrewdly; pinched a fold with black nails. "Molecatcher, ista? Owt else?"

"A glass."

An eyebrow. Then a shrug. "Gi's here." He ran his thumb round the frame of it, tilting his eye at them; considered; spat. "Done."

Kit knelt to bundle the stuff. A good knife indeed, well-hefted, sharp. "Yon road?"

"Goes longways." The velvet cloth had vanished in his pack. "And there's folk and not. Dogs."

"What honest work for strangers?"

A shrewd glance at Thea: draggled silk and drab russet, and a started vixen's brush of hair. "Whoring. Thieving."

Kit flushed. "Not while I've breath."

"Brave words to starve on. There's begging o course. Any trade in yer hands?"

"I could fiddle—" Kit began. And turned his palms up ruefully.

"And I could ride pillion, if I'd a horse and a whip."

Thea slipped the rings from her fingers. "Would these not bring us silver? For a crowd and a bow?"

"Aye, and a dance on the gallantry. Wha's to say they's not been thieved?" The bright eyes slid sideways at Kit. "I can see yer not to drown."

"They're not—" said Kit, and stopped. They were.

But Thea held a ring up, flicked it shining at the heather's roots. "If thou'd not stoop for it, then let it branch and bear silver."

There it lay. He looked at her, and spurned it with his toe. A swift unwreathing, a flicker in the grass and gone. A silver snake. "I'd keep dark yon bits o tawdry," he said. "There's folk'd cut throats for less. Thy stockings. Or a game or nowt." Thea nodded. "And if thou's a lad, thou doff thy hat, see. More to't than pissing upright." Then he bent to his camp and ferreted, set out a horn cup and a handful of coarse grey salt, a charred bird bound in herbs. "Hovel top o't trod."

"Thanks," said Kit. "My thanks. Hallows with ye."

"Sneck up," said the tinker.

Thea bowed.

As they started off up the trod in the closing rain, he called after. "If it's a fiddle thou's after, thou ask at Jack Daw."

"The fiddle. Ah." Kit gazed at the fire, pale in the wintry sun. No more than shaken air. "'Twas my father's. So my mother said. Of Cloud, as he was." He bit his lip. "I tell this badly."

"So yer no one's brat?" said Whin.

"Hers. Lightborn, we do say in Lune. We grow, like missel, in the air." His face was bright; then dark. "She died."

Whin drank, and passed the cup. A white bird tilted on the wind.

"Mine uncle—I was prenticed clerk. And fiddled at the wakes, and chafed."

"So yer went a-begging of a witch?"

"I was ta'en. By her servant."

"Ah."

"Coming from a dance," said Kit. "On Hare Law."

"And yer went with my lady's huntsman? Mad as a March hare, thou is."

"Drunk," said the fiddler, ruefully. "And thought I was in love."

Cold, toward moonrise, and the stars like rosin. Whirling. Not so drunk, he'd thought, but flown with fiddling. Ah, he'd never played so well as with Ned Hill, his serpent coiling in and out, and with Tib Lang's rowdy pipes and reed flute. They'd all the earth and heavens dancing to their tune, and half of Kempy Mag's great barn. Like hedgers laying thorn, they'd worked; and by some passing spell, their hey was quickset, green even as they wove, and flowering. A garland for a queen of May. That lass—ah, well he minded her, that straightbacked girl in green, triumphal, with a comet's tail of hair. In and out the mazes of the dance, he glimpsed her, arming with this shepherd and that scythesman, but fencing always with his tune, his air her make. As the music ended, she bowed to it: no partner but the air. His air. He lowered his bow and watched her as she coiled her tumbled braid, the bone pins in her soft stern mouth. The swift stabs. His heart. "Wed," said Tib drily. "Next month, to yon lame blacksmith. Get thee drunk."

And he had.

Five sets and six pints later, there was that other lass, at his elbow as he tuned. A brown girl, filching pears and russets; a green chit, all unripe. She'd a brow like a bird's egg, flecked and flawed, and mocking, shrewd grey eyes. "Why d'ye pull those faces, playing?" she'd said. "Toothache?" So he'd had to eat his hunch of Wake-bread, to show her he cared not, and had won a tiny leaden pair of shears, amid the crumbs. A mayfly toy. "They'll serve you for the wars," she'd said. "With a needle for spear." Afterward, he'd found a lady apple in his pocket, flawless, with a leaf.

He'd idled when they'd paid him, talking random, looking sidelong at the door until the girl in green went by. She'd turned at the threshhold, going, with a glance, half mockery and half challenge. Then he'd packed his fiddle up and walked on alone.

Not drunk. Unbounded, that was it: with darkness after fire, sky for rafters, silence for the stamp of boots, the clatter, and the clack of tongues. Light with love. As light as the Hanged Lad, Jack Orion, setting sidelong in his belt of sparks. Toward dawn, it was. As late as that? Well he defied his master's clock. Kit bowed to the skyclad fiddler, and doffed his hat, calling out, "Measure for measure, lad. Will I outplay thee?"

He walked on over Hare Law, his head a muddle of tunes, bright lasses, bowls of lambswool. *Cross my river to Babylon.* His nose sunk in froth. A bright and a dark head glancing up at him, then ducking low to laugh. His russet coat, Tom's old one turned, scarce worn. New buttons to it. ("Here's a flaycrow in a field goes bare," the brown girl said.) Ginger and marchpane. A leaden shears. The green girl whirling at his bow's end. Out of sight. Ah, still he played her over in his head.

Had passed the branching in the road long since. By Crowcrag, then, the gainest way. That striding bass. *Mall's Maggot.* Syllabub and damson cheese. Dull wool bales in the morning—ah, his head. Sand. Goosequills. Figures on a page, untallied. In and out the hey, and couples for another dance. Nine eight and longways. Silver in his pocket, ninepence, that made seven and a bit, near enough for Askwith's *Atomie of Starres.* For ribands—No, a carven glass. With verses round. A comb. New strings, though, call it six and coppers. All the broken cakes. And at the end of *Nine Weaving*, how the green girl raised her candle to him, like a sword, and blew it out. An apple with a leaf. And again, the tumbled braid, the coiling hands. But they undid; the long skein fell for him alone, unbraiding like a fugue about her moonwhite body.

He was on the high ground now, a puzzle of white stones.

"Lightwood?"

Whirling round in a blaze of stars, Kit saw no one. His coat-skirts settled; he felt the soft bump of his pocket, crammed with cakes, against his thigh. Stars still dancing.

He'd heard no rider; saw no horse. Yet on the road stood a horseman, spurred and booted: a stranger. Soberclad but richly, like a servant in a great house; yet outlandish. "Master Lightwood. Of Askrigg?"

"Sir?" When he stood the room spun, candlelight and dancers, whin and stars.

"I heard you fiddle at yon hobnailed rout."

"Ah." Had he seen that back amid the dancers? With the brown girl? With the lightfoot grizzled farmwife? Or with the lass in green?

"Small recompense among such folk."

Broken cakes. Lead trinkets. "They've ears."

"And so my lady has. And jewels to hang in them. She sends to bid you play for her. A wedding."

"Have you no fiddlers in far Cloud?" This was not going well.

"None of note."

Kit stood. Some wind, toward the morning, twangled in his fiddle strings.

"Nor time to further send. 'Tis by this next moon. I will bring you." A glint of silver. "Come, a handfast. To wet the child's head."

"Thought you said it was a wedding?"

"All the same."

"Ah," said Kit wisely. "'Twas ever thus. Brought to bed, either way." The stars were fading, paling to the east; he could see the long rise of Hawker Fell. "Little enough dancing for the bride," he said. "And the bairn his own piper."

"Brave company," the stranger said. "Here's one will look for you." He held a bone hairpin in his dark-gloved hand. "By this token, you are bid."

Kit took it in his hand, bemused. "Did she give—?"

"Is't yes?"

"Aye, but—"

Then the horseman sealed his bidding with a cold kiss, full on his mouth. Tongue, teeth, and all. Kit knew no more.


The wind is braided in my lady's hair.

Margaret. As thou sleep'st, a storm is rising. Ah, thou hear'st it, even in thy dream of Cloud. But thou art fathomless, thy sleep is ocean. Cowrie'd by thy cheek, thy hand curls inward, closing on the dream that spills away like starry sand. A shutter claps. The hangings of thy bed conceive; the clawed rings inch and jangle. Nearer. On thy coverlid, thy book, left open, stirs. The leaves lift, turning backward in the tale. Unwintering. Again, the dead girl turns and speaks; she plays in greenwood, in the spring of hope.

How cam'st thou by thy book? Dost know? I tell thee, there are rare things in thy bower, which is all thy world. See, that orange by thy pillow. Pith and bittersweet and curving. And when broke, a puzzlebox of sweets. Thy bedgown, of an antick fashion, rich but sadly tarnished with the salt. That rod of shrewd whalebone, that also I felt. Thy comb. And not least, the drowsy wine they gave thee. Aye, the physick and the cup.

All tangled in her seine.

But seldom now.

I have seen my lady with her braid undone, all naked in her glass.

*Here's a knot,* says Morag with the comb.

*Thou do. Undo.*

*Another.*

*Seven. And no more.*

And with each knot, the wind rose, howling, and now and now the lightning slashed, it winced and slashed, and then the clouts of thunder jarred. By the sixth, it was beyond all noise: one lightning, and a judder in the bones. And when the waves broke—It was Annis falling. It was burying alive in shards of sky.

I have seen ships cracked like jackstraws.

I have found things, walking by the sea. A coffer, cracked and spilling cinnamon and mace. A virginals. A bacca pipe, unbroke. The Nine of Bones. And sailors: drowned and shattered, drowned and frozen, trodden into sand. And some that Morag finished. I have found an orange lying by a tarry hand.


Thea blew her nails and huddled, pinch-faced. Kit rubbed his legs and sighed. So much for begging. Stones for breakfast and a long draught of Cloud ale; stones in shoes; dog's music at the last three farms; and brats at the pack-bridge with a hail of clods. And now they'd tumbled down a scree. He'd go home if he knew where home was. They were nowhere, halfway down a fell, and sliding from its bony knees. The tops were hid in dour cloud. "Here's

kites," said Thea. Higher up, they saw a shepherd, stooping with his burden
of a creel of hay. His crouching, prying, flying dogs made bow-knots of
a bedlam of sheep. Querulous and unrepentant Maudlins all, a-burst with
bastard lambs, and fellowed with their doting Toms, the crazed and kempy
wethers and the horn-mad tup. All trundled to fold. "On dirty toes," said
Thea. "Same as us."

To the north, they saw the bruised sky blacken, and the bentgrass flinch
and shiver in the rising wind. "Coming on bad," said Kit, standing. "We'll lay
up." Even as he spoke, the snow came, like a fury of ghosts.

Nowhere.

"Hey!" cried Kit. Stifled. Gloved hands of snow laid hold of him, clapped
eyes, mouth, ears. Seen out by February's footmen, to a ditch and crows.

"Hush," said unseen Thea. They could hear the sheep rattle and the shepherd call.

"Way here! Way here, Maddy. Come by, Gyp."

Kit caught hold of Thea's wrist, and scrabbled up the hillside toward the
voice. Not far, they'd not get far in this. "How far—?" bawled Kit.

A lean ghost, swathed in sacking. "Get by, thou bloody fool! Down dale."
"Where—?"

"Dog'll tek thee." Something like a hollybush leapt the wall, already chid-
ing at their heels. The shepherd called after, "Thou ask at Imp Jinny."

Down along an outcrop, rising into drystone wall; crook left, and down a
stony track between two walls, out of wind; past the shepherd's pony, like a
dejected chimney brush, beside his sledge of hay. The black bitch saw them
through the gate.

Trees, low and windbent, lapped and laden with the ghosts of leaves; a
lantern at the door, that turned their branching to bright webs.

"Hallows," called Kit, and beat muffled hands against the door.

"Will Shanklin?" called a woman's voice. "Owt wrong?" The door opened.
A small-faced strapping woman, knitting furiously. Sharp and brown as a
beechnut, with a beech's frazzled foliage, an old tree's knotted hands. Blue as
speedwell, her eyes. She looked them up and down. "If it's guising, yer a bit
few. And late."

"Have you a barn?" said Kit.

"I's a fire," said Imp Jinny. "Come in and keep wind out. I can see lass is
dowly."

They stamped and dripped and stared. A low room, bronzy with peat smoke, heaped with apples. Sweet and poignant with their scent. And not low after all, but racked and raftered, hung with anything to hand. Bunches of potherbs, besoms and birdsnares, shears and riddles and a swift of yarn. Swags of old washing—smocks and aprons—kippered in the air, as stiff as stockfish. Lanterns and pruning-hooks, ladles and rushlights. Strings of eggshells. Legs of mutton. Riddlecakes hung out to dry. A ball of thorn twigs, trailing ribands and old holly. Jinny ducked beneath. "Mind urchin," she called. A tiggy drank snuffling at a dish of milk. "Been at wort and gets to singing. Now then, thou rantipole. Mend tongue. Or I'll peg thee out i't apple trees, as a souling for t'birds." She nipped down a sallowed petticoat from under the thack, took a jacket from a kist, and bundled them at Thea. "Get thee doffed." She measured Kit with a glance. "Crouch up to't fire. Y'd look a right mawkin in my petticoats."

"Thanks," said Kit.

"Not at all. Thowt it were foxes at my ewes in lamb. Dropped a stitch, I doubt. Tea. Y've tea i' Lune?" Jinny swung the kettle over the fire; she scrabbled out leaves from a bright tin, painted gaudily with wrens and garlands. "Stockings and all, that's right. Peg 'em up. Lad can tek blanket. Now then, there's cock broth. And a tansy after."

Deep bowls of it, fork-thick with leeks and barley, fowl and carrots; Jinny broke them shards of oatcake for to sop the rich broth.

They ate. The snow pummeled at the windows; their clothes dripped and reeked. Imp Jinny walked to and fro, knitting and muttering and squinting at her heel, in a fury of pins: as thrawn as if her yarn were nettles and all her kindred swans. Born half a sleeve behind and not caught up. You'd think she knit them at the stake. "Purl and plain. Meks three. And—craws eat it!" She knit badly, Kit saw; the yarn snagged on her roughened hands, the stocking bunched and spiralled.

"Mistress Imp?"

Jinny turned, twanging with laughter. "And thy name's Kit Catgut. Imp's what I do. Graff apples to crabs. Hast etten Nonesuch? That were mine. And Sheepsnose, out o Seek-No-Further. And I's no Mistress, neither. Langthorn Joan's Jinny. Jane Owlet. Awd keeping pear's what I is. Warden. I'd eat dryly." The old hands crooked and looped and darted. "So yer out Lune? How came yer by Cloud?"

Kit, muffled in her patchwork quilt and downheeled slippers, tried for manly. "Seeking work."

"Can you do owt?"

"Undo," said Thea.

"What I can," said Kit.

Jinny pursed her lips. "Work. Well, there's threshing to Swang Farm. A rough gang for lasses; but there's straw and stirabout, and happen a few coppers. Got a knife?" She hefted it and tried the edge. "Aye, that's good." She gave it back to him. "Ye could try yer hand at binding besoms. Up moor." She was setting the heel now, storklegged with aggravation. "Come March, ye could clap eggs for Ashes. Do ye not i' Lune? No? Well, I'll set yer i't road on it. Craws!" Her ball bounded away; Kit caught it. "Thou keep petticoat."

"Ashes?" said Kit.

"Eh well, there's always Ashes. Or there's never spring. Gangs out wi' guisers." The Horn was rounded of her stocking; she sighed. "And byways, there's a barn up Owlriggs, void and dry. Ye could lig there for a piece. While lambing, anyroad."

"Many thanks," said Kit. "How—?"

"Shake snow from me apple trees, I doubt they'll crack. Lilt me yer fiddle tunes. I like a tune. Can't make, but I graff words til 'em."

"Ah. D'ye know this?" Softly, Kit sang through *Nine Weaving*; then clapped into *Jenny Pluck Pears* and *The Magpie's Bagpipe*. No great voice, but a true.

At his knee, by the fire, Thea crouched and set the cradle rocking to the rhythm of the dance. Full of skeins, it was.

"Soft," said Jinny sharply. "Do ye so i' Lune?"

"Do what?" said Thea. "Here's an ark for the urchin."

An odd blue glance; the needles stopped. "Rock empty cradles."

"No," said Kit, dismayed. "Moon turn from it."

Thea said, "I know not what it is. For bread or what?"

"I see," said Jinny. "Out Lune of Lune." She stilled the cradle with her hand. There was a wooden rattle laid in it, a tumbling, turning wren; a doll like a darning egg, a poppyhead unfaced with years; an acorn whirlywhorl. Undone, it spilled a marble in her palm. "That were Het's."

"Your lass?" said Kit softly.

"Imped out," said Jinny. "She were left by ragwell. Anyone's." She whorled the marble; smiled. "I'd've never such a lass. Wick as thistledown."

"Ah," said Thea. "She would braid of her mother then, the moon. I see thine orchard bears the Misselbough."

Jinny turned to Thea, puzzling. Something rueful; something awed. "So

thou'rt Ashes still. Poor lass." Almost, she touched the girl's thin cheek; but
went to feel her clothes instead, turned smock and stockings by the hearth.
"When I were Ashes—"

"Not a lad?" said Whin.
  "What?"
  "Her bairn that died."
  "Drowned," said Kit. "A lass. She said."
  "I see. Go on."

Jinny peeled a bowl of russets, broadlapped by the dozing fire. They watched
the long curls falling from the bright knife, the brown hands; they smelled
the sharp juice spring. "When I were Ashes—forty year ago, and more—I
kept back what I got. Oh, aye, come Kindle Night, they'd rived at me and
mocked me, for I'd not had maid nor man. Unploughed. Waste o darkness,
they'd said. Said nowt would spring of it. But what I'd hid weren't brat, nor
siller, nor a gallop on another's hobby. Sitha, when I'd put on Ashes coat, I'd
turned and wondered at glory o't world. All turning and endless. Stars and
seed. They caught me up i't dance, threadneedle. See, it's endless, yet there's
first and last. Same as like a spindle falling, thread and whorl. Same as peel."
And one long rose-moled spiralling fell flawless from the knife. "And I see'd
how things go on by dying. How they're born o fallow. That I kept."

They crossed a watersplash at dawn. The sky had put away its stars, undone
the clasp of winter from its throat. It stood, white and shivering, all bare
before the sun. No rose: a sudden glittering of frost, a lash of shadows, long
and sharp against the fell; and there, where the water sprang, the reddening
scratches of the alders. "Withies," said Kit. "I'll cut, an thou bind them."
  Clumsy with cold, they set to work with knife and twine. The day clouded up. The water brawled. A field away, a boy went huddling in his outworn
jacket, toward the lambs. Kit called to him, "Where's this?" but he ran away.
The sheep ran too, all which ways down the moor, their rumpling fleeces
heavy with the frost. They slowed from a trotting to a trundling, with their
stilted lambs beside them, slowed and stilled and cropped. Kit saw the boy

again, up lawside in a scud of stones, his hair as white as hawkweed. He
peered from behind a sheepfold. Kit swept him a bow, and he ducked.

"Do you steal children?" Thea said.

"Some run away with me," said Kit.

They sat among the bare wood by the waterside, and ate what they had
begged. It was scant enough, cold scrag-end and a lump of pease. A sup
of bratted milk. There was twopence in his pocket and his trade in Lune,
his fiddle for a ship and wracked, a witch's stolen daughter by his side. My
lady's malison on both. He looked at Thea, silvered by the cold fine mist.
He'd waked sometimes to see her watching, silent as the moon. He knew her
changing face, her dark and bright; he saw and he desired her as he would
the reachless moon. Her soul was elsewhere, even as he lay with her, amid
the bright leaves burning.

Jumping up, Kit looked about the lashy wood. "It's almost spring," he
said. "Here's blackthorn out." It flowered from its bare sticks, white as souls.
He gathered twigs of it, the bonniest of all. It twisted, green and sinewy;
he'd use no knife. He made a garland of it for her leaf-bright head: a crown
too sharp to wear.


Cross and cross between the ash pegs driven in her crucks, old great-armed
Imp Jinny told out her threads. Nine skeins unwinding, drawn as one, and
dancing in their creels; then down and down, from hand to peg and to and
fro, until their measured ending. Eight of wool; the ninth of moonlight,
turning on its reel of dark. She was making a warp.

The fire was of thorn. It caught the sway and draw and crooking of her
arms, and glinted in the scissors at her waist; it cast a creel of her in shadows,
cross and cross the room. Our cage is shadows and ourselves.

As Jinny told her warp, she sang, no louder than the rasp of wool, the
crackling of the little flame.

"O the broom blooms bonny, the broom blooms fair . . ."

Cross and cross, nine threads. That's one.

"I have lost a sheath and knife that I'll never see again . . ."

And loop and nine. That's two.

"And we'll never go down to the broom no more."

Kit remembered the kitchen in her mother's hall, stoneflagged and cavernous; the table, scoured saltwhite as a strand to windward, heaped with
wrack of bloody game. Ah, piteous, their eyes, and taunting now, with
acorns rattling in his gut. Blackcock and moorhen, ruffled and agape. Wet
heather on a red hind's flank. The lean and louring hounds rose hackling
at him, girning with their grizzled lips. They suffered him to pass; but
watched him, crouching on their bones or pacing, silent but for rattling
chains. Scoured as it was, the kitchen stank of them, of hair and blood and
ashes, dust of pepper and old damp. On the great gaunt dresser, fishwhite
pewter dully stared. The fire whirred and reeked. And Morag squatted with
a hare to gut, limp and lolling in her bloody apron. *Madam? I am sent to bid
you to my lady. In her closet, she did say.* The log fell in; the shadows jumped. And
perhaps Morag twitched at her high shoulder, like a preening crow; or it
was shadows, or his smoke-stung eyes. She rose to meet him, knife folded
in her apron, capped and barbed. *I come.* Formal and contemptuous, as always. Sheathed. Ah, but where were all the servants in so great a hall? Who
scoured and who swept? And he bethought him, late and suddenly: roe
deer? On that stony island? What had come of his wits, not to marvel? Yet
venison they had at table. No fish but eel pie, not a herring. Nothing salt.
Nor sodden, come to that. He saw again the haunch of meat, the charred
and shining spit withdrawn, the rusty cauldron tilted by the hearth. The
fur and flesh.

"Love? Who provisioned in thine hall?"

"Morag."

"Strange fish she caught."

"Gulls," said Thea. "Thou and I."

"But venison?"

"Ah. She hunts."


The witch rose twirling, turning in the air to raven. Or to ravenwise—a
something quilled and barbelled, clawfoot, but a woman to the fork. Thrice
round the broch she flew, in widening gyres, over scar and thornwood, sea
and skerry, tethered by my lady's will. At farthest of her swing was landfall,
rust and desolate. The bracken stirred. She stooped.

Margaret. Do you sleep now?

I will tell this in the moonlight sliding.

In my closet, Morag clasped the necklace round my throat. Cold souls, all witches, dead long since; cold hands, that late had plucked and foraged in the hare's blue meagre flesh. Untwisting it about my breast, she pinched me with her bloody nails. *Is't ripe?* And then the long robe on my shoulders—ah, but it was soft as snow, as sleeping in a drift of death. My mother keeps it still. 'Twas woven with the stars at Annis' wake: night sky and moonless, shading through the blue, bluegreen of twilight, seen as through the branches of the thorn. And naked else.

No sun, but at my fork.

The old crow held the glass. *My lady waits.*

*I come.*

And in her high unarrased room, from glass to moondark glass, my lady turned and paced. Her iron casket on the table was unlatched. At her throat, she wore the stone it held: no soul, but Annis' self, the true and only shard of night. The seed of Law.

I stood, as I was taught.

She turned and gazed at me. Bare as April.

I had not yet bled.

*My lady,* said I, to the stone. I knew its touch, ah, cold against the skin, and colder deeper still. Within. I knew her famished eyes.

*Her time comes,* said my lady to her woman. *By this moon. The souls?*

*Two are kept,* said Morag. *I have seeled them for the hunt. A mort in milk, a maid in blood.*

*And the third?*

*Is come. Seed full. A pretty piece, the huntsman says.*

*Shall have his fee.*

My mother touched my chin. *Come, Madam.* So she loosed the knot, undid the bright coil of my hair; she bid me to her table.


Whin slept. Lying silent by her, Kit woke long and heard the clash of the sea. He saw its pale thrums shine and ravel. Moonset. Darkness then, the wavebeat of his heart. He counted. Nine for a secret. There was something he'd not told.

That first night in the mist there was a third in bed with them. Half waking in the dark, he'd pulled her down on him, had murmured, fledged, had entered—ah, not Thea's air and fire, but the lap of earth. His grave. The spade bit deep. He saw the wriggling in the new-turned earth; breathed in the scent of earth and ashes, and of heather wet with rain. Still deeper. There, he touched a stirring, soft as moleskin, soft and dusk, and there, the quick and glistening neb. And at the very deep, a something, thrawn and wet: the root of dark, its flowering.

The cards. I had forgot them, slid between rough stone and worm-gnawn pan-elling, behind the kist. You puzzle at them, at this book of scattered leaves. Know thou, they are Cloudish magic. Not my lady's art, but tawdry: a sort of cantrips that their wiling beggars use. Hedge sortilege. I had them of a witch—a windwife or a sailor's whore, I know not. Cast up. Still living, when I'd hauled her on the sand, a-twitch and broken, like a windwracked gull. She'd signed: *Take. Keep.* A box, a book of spells? Skin bag and oiled silk. I slipped it warily within my skirts: forbidden hoard. And then came Morag with her stone.

I hid them. From her avid and contemptuous, her pebble eyes, her pry-ing hands: myself I could not hide. And all that winter of my threshold year, I looked not thrice at them. My lady basilisk had work. In the waning of the ashen moon, she called me down, in cold stiff cloth of silver and an iron busk, to look upon the last of three set dishes for my maiden feast. A banket of souls. There were two laid up in store, like picked meats from the cracking of a gilded nutshell bark: a child scarce old enough to call a virgin, the betrothed of an outland king; her nurse. Like cage birds fattening, like haggards, leashed and belled. I'd fed them with my hand. Had toyed: which I repent. A poor mad glowering girl; a woman, silent, spilling milk. I'd tasted of their souls, their essences: green quince and bletted medlar, quiddany and musk. And now the third, but lately come: a hare, caught kicking, from the huntsman's bag. A handful of brambles, green and flowering and all. Leaf and prick. I saw a beardless boy, astonished, ill at ease in country boots. He bowed to me. I took him up.

Thou turn'st the Hanged Lad on the gallantry; the Hare reversed.

I see.

*Is't riddles, then? A sort of stars?*

Go on. But soft now, I am at thy shoulder.

Ah, now thou hast them spread, in knots and gatherings and changeful congeries, across the nighted boards. Just so. They bear the names of earthly tales turned starry, as the Tower, and the Crowd of Bone, and all the figures of the moon and sky. What Imp Jinny called the wood above. And thou art lost in it. Thou hast no clew to wind thee through the mazes of that dance, unfellied and unfretted night. No windrose nor no wheeling Ship. O Margaret, I have read their painted book, an abstract of the airy world. But thou, thou know'st no tale of them, amazed as if thou mansionless looked up at heaven, saw its stars unstrung and scattering like a box of beads.

I will tell this in the cards.

Here's a black wench with a cap and anvil; see, she hammers at a fiery heart. That card doth signify that errant star which some call Mercury. But they do call her Brock. She's a cutpurse of great bellies, and does lighten them; a picklock of maidenheads; a thief of souls. On Whinnymoor she lurks, and bids the silent traveller stand; takes nothing of him naked, but a coin, a clip. Those waifs that shiver, dance and shiver on the moss, in nothing but their own brief souls, she laps in her rough jacket, earth and bone; she slaps them squalling into breath. She is death's midwife and her go-between, the third in marriage beds. Her clip is kindling. Twice did she sain me, doing and undoing: at the door where thou didst enter, love, and at the jagg'd rift of my going hence.

Here's Burnt Eldins. Burd Alone. She tosses up her golden ball outwith a hedge of bones. Its leaves are hands of children flayed, imploring. She is youngest of the Nine, those stars whose rising into dawn doth mark the stone of winter's death. I had the tale of Imp Jinny, how she winds the clew and finds her sisters locked up in Annis' kist. How she sets them free. That card I never drew.

Nor this: Nine Weaving. Eight are painted, bending to their wintry task. Ah, they blaze in their imprisoning. From their tower spills their endless web, the green world and that other, woven with a mingled skein.

And here's the Rattlebag, turned tail. It shows a lad, whiteheaded as a weed; he claps the crows that flacker from his field of corn, all rooted in a sleeping man, a sheaf whose binding is a belt of stars.

And turn, and he's the Hanged Lad, brave in winter, mid a winnowing of stars.

The Crowd of Bone. That fiddle that the old year plays of Ashes, of her bones. 'Tis strung with shorn red hair. Ah, it burns thy fingers, thou dost let it fall.

And Ashes. Not her smutched and tangled guise, as black as holly-blotch, that waif in tattercoats that walks behind a wren's cold corse: that is not Ashes but her mute. This Ashes dances lightfoot, and at every step a green blade springs. Her hair's like fires that the May lads leap, a-whirl in wind. Far far behind her is an O, a crow's eye or a cracked bright glass. Her end. But for now, she's walked away from Annis' glass, her eye of winter, out of that tale into this.

It was windy, with a clouted sky. The farm stood foursquare to the heavens, stonebuilt, with a line of trees to northward bending all one way. They danced. There were catkins on the hazels, taws of light, like whips to set the sun a-spin. Kit sneezed. There was pollen dusted in his hair and on his jacket, nebulas of bloom; he sleeved his face with Pleiades. "No geese," he said. "There's a comfort."

"I'll go this time," said Thea, peering through the hedge with him. They saw a drying yard, windriffled, up against the plainfaced farmhouse. There were two girls playing in the yard. They'd tied a rope to an iron ring in the housewall. One turned, the other skipped and sang. "My mother went to feed her crows, turn round and call them in . . ." The rope made rainbows in the plashy air; it slapped, slapped, slapped the stones. An unbreeched boy ran shouting with a whirligig. It flackered like a rising bird; it caught the sudden light. He tumbled in the mud. A woman in a cap and clanging pattens came out, a creaking wicker basket at her hip.

Kit and Thea slipped through the hedge. "Hallows with ye," he said, and bowed. His back was urchined out with brooms.

The woman nipped the small clothes up. She was rosy with the wind, and round-armed, with wisps of grey-brown hair straggling from her cap. "Here's a rade o scoundrels," she said to the peg box. "A-ligging and a-laiking, while us poor folk go to work. Well, I's counted shirts."

". . . one for t'rider and one for t'horse and one for t'boatman, for to row me across . . ."

The boy was crouching by a puddle, frothing his toy in it.

Fiercely, the woman pegged the washing out: smock, petticoat, shirt, breeches, smock. All dancing in the wind. Kit tweaked the breeches by the strings. "Here's thy chance," he said to them. "Do as I would."

"Huh," said the woman, but her shoulders quirked. "Would yer go to be hanged?

"Not I. And yet die bravely in a dance," he said.

Another woman looked out through the door. "Eh, Bet, what's to do?"

"A tain and his tally come a-begging. Lunish folk. Got besoms."

"Has they pins? We's short." She came out on the doorstep, flapping her apron. She was small and crumpled, with a smear of soap on her brow. Looking at the travellers, up and down, she said, "If it's guising, yer a bit few."

"A sword and a bush," said Kit.

"And late."

"The ways are very muddy," said Kit.

"And our shoes are very thin," said Thea.

"When's Lightfast i' Lune, then? Come May?" The woman with the basket looked at Thea. "Where's crown? Is t'wren in yer pocket, then?"

"Under her apron," said the woman at the door.

"Whisht," said the other. "Ista lad then? Or Ashes?"

"Turns," said Thea. "Whichever comes in next. Burnt Eldins."

"Aye well, if it's Eldins, yer first foot," said the woman at the door, relenting. "Not see'd Arrish lads as yet." Quirking at Kit: "What's he?"

Kit turned and shrank and darkened. The witch looked out through him, and cocked her shrewd black eye. Muck, said her mincing, and grubs, said her peck. Watching, Thea felt a thrill of uneasy laughter. He had Morag to the very nails. "The blood I brew, the bones I crack, I bear the childer on my back." The little girls watched, the rope slack, their faces uncertain. He clawed his hands at them and waggled.

The brown girl's thumb went in her mouth; she clung to her sister's apron. But the little dark one said, "Yer not a witch."

"Who said?" He swung the little dark thing in the air, and clapped her in the empty basket, shrieking delight.

Thea rounded on him, ranting in high style. It was her turn for Burnt Eldins; she had the coat. "Wha comes on stones?"

"Awd Crowdybones."

"What's that ye've got?"

"I's getting eldins for to boil me pot." Lantern and thornbush, like Mall-i'-th'-Moon.

"Wha's give thee leave to cut my wood?"

"Me glass and me riddle, they told me I could."

"All but nine, they may not go:

*The alder, the elder, the ash and the sloe,*
*The witchtree, the whitethorn, the hazel and oak:*
*Break one of their branches, and down with a stroke."*

"That's eight."

Thump, went the basket. Thump. And the girl peeked out, with her hair all tumbled, rough as juniper, her eyes as blue.

Thea whirled on her heel. "Burnt Eldins is youngest of all of the nine, I see by her stockins you've hung on the line."

"I's not been etten yet," said the girl. "It's all right, Tilda. Thou can look."

Kit crouched malefically. "Blood and bones, I'll crack, I'll crack, and fell and hair will patch me back. Eyes to me ravens, and breath to me bread, and fat for a candle to light me to bed."

Thea drew her sword of air.

"Take a broom," said Kit softly. "Plays better."

"Ah. Right then." Thea cleared her throat and struck a penny-plain bold stance. "Wha brings thee down but Hallycrown?" Turn and turn, they rimed.

"My tower's where thou'lt never find."

"They's left me a thread, and I walk and I wind." Round in merrills in the mud, she trod.

"I's ower t'riddles and back o Cawd Law."

"They's spinned me a clew and I's under thy wall." Thea ducked the clothesline.

"I's snecked t'door, thou shan't come in." All a-twitter.

"Brock turns locks and lifts thy pin."

"What's within but mirk and mist?"

"But I's a sun frae Mally's kist." She upraised a withered apple-john.

"Here comes my ravens to peck out thine eyes."

"And here comes my chopper, for to make 'em mince pies."

Once, twice, thrice they clashed and down fell Morag in the mud. Kit clutched his heart, turned tipple, kicked his heels and croaked. Tilda giggled uncertainly. Thea snatched the child from the basket, and Kit spun it round with his foot. Down went the child in it. Thea spoke.

*Now it's a ship and we all sail away,*
*So give us your hands for to finish our play.*

*The sail's o th' siller, the mast's o th' tree,*
*The moon's for a keel and the morrow's the sea.*

Kit whispered to the child, "Hang on." He jumped up beside Thea and
they took the handles of the creel. They hoisted it between them and they
swung it, one two three, and whirled it round.

*Up let her rise, and t'sisters take hands,*
*So gi' us some siller to bring them to land.*
*A sadcake, an apple, some eggs and old ale,*
*To help us poor guisers and weave us a sail.*

"Now Tilda's turn," said the child when she'd got her breath.

"Thou gut yon fish," said Whin. "It's that and slawk."

Kit turned from the bitter bright morning. Salt in candle flame: it sparkled. "Ah?" Carefully, from rock to driftwood, rock to rock, he hobbled back
to the fire, took the knife in stiff hands. "What's this, a dolphin?"

"Herring," said Whin. "Filched it. They'll blame cat." She prodded at the
pot of seaweed, doubtful. "So, where got yer that guising? Not i' Lune."

"Imp Jinny. Said it might get an egg or two."

"Thin wind for thieving, March. All green and mockery." Whin clapped
the lid to. "Wants a whet to it, does slawk. Verjuice or owt." She swiped the
ladle with her finger, licked it. "So yer kept them rings."

"And who'd buy them?" Kit's hands were glittering with blood and scales.
"Who'd make change? As good sell orchards in the moon."

"Spatchcocked, I think," said Whin. She took the fish. "Salt enough."

"There were two left. For the—for the child, she said. Her portion.
Those you took." He rubbed his fingers dry in sand. "One spent, one tossed
away in scorn. Three ta'en by—ruffians. And one she gave away."

"Did she, then?"

"To a boy. A whitehaired starveling boy. A scarecrow."

"Oh," said Whin, so poignantly that Kit knelt up by her.
"What is't then? At thy heart?"

⤳

They came by a ploughed field, pricked with the new green corn. A crow lad with his clapper cried, he clacked his sticks and cried, "Ban craws!" The cold wind shook his rags. The crows took up into the air. It was a brash day, bare and windy, with a sky of curds and whey. Thea stood in the furrows, watching; Kit stood by her. A stone's throw away, the birds swirled and settled, like a fall of ashes, calling out. Their voices glowed and faded like the sparks from the anvils of war.

Kit said, "He cries them barley."

"They defy him," said Thea. She was gazing at the sky. The clouds went swiftly. "Crows, that's all."

Cracked pepper, and a salt of smaller birds.

Hoarsely, hauntingly, the boy took up his chant.

> *Shoo all o't craws away,*
> *Shoo all o't craws:*
> *Out thrae John Barley's ground*
> *Into Tom Tally's ground;*
> *Out o Tom Tally's ground*
> *Intil Awd Mally's ground;*
> *Out frae Awd Mally's ground*
> *Into Black Annie's ground . . .*

Kit took up a stone and flung it in the birds' midst. They shrugged derisively; they hopped a little sidelong, pecked. He ran at them, flackering his coat and crying, "Craws! Ban craws!" He clodded them with earth. Huffed as dowagers, they ruffled in their black; they snapped their well-I-never beaks. "Sod off!" yelled Kit. They rose and scattered in the wide grey sky; went silver and were gone.

Turning back, triumphant, he saw Thea, pinched and shivering among the furrows. He clouded over. They'd had nothing all that day; she could eat nothing when they had, but picked and spewed. Coarse provender, he thought: no stomach for't. And it was cold and muddy in the lanes, her shoes were worn— ah, not her slippers, cast away in ruin. These were new old shoes, clodhopping country boots, ill-sorted with her rags of Lunish finery. And dearly they had cost her purse: her silver comb. Now he saw how odd her clothing looked, how tattery. Half tinsel and half drab. He'd thought of it as hers. Herself. How strange that started brush of hair, that boys cried *Vixen!* at. Cried whore.

Seeing him forlorn, she clapped and called to him, "Oh, bravely done."
He grinned and wiped a sword of air and sheathed it. "My turn for the
boy," he said. The coat flapped windily.

"I'll be Ashes, then; I'm tired of Eldins."

Kit came and held her. "Ah," he said. "Did I tell thee? I dreamed it hailed
moonseed. 'Twas full and it split."

"What sprang of it? Witches?"

"Children," he said. "All naked as the moon, and shining, as they were
made of sky. They danced."

Thea looked toward the barley-white boy, still crying. Further on, the
ashes fell. "What then?"

"A woman caught them in her apron."

"And then?"

"I woke," said Kit. "And seeing thee, forgot." There was straw still in her
hair: a garland. They were wed each day. Remembering, he plucked it out
and gave it, lightly, to the wind. Then turning with her gaze, he saw the boy.
"Poor lad, it's weary work, alone wi' crows."

Thea said, "Shall we play, and let him play?"

"I'll not hang ranting from a pole, even to please thee." He grimaced
fiercely, knotting up his brows. "But I'll play thee a tyrant rarely, or a crone
or what thou wilt."

"'Tis a strange play: we clap and they go."

"But an ancient play," said Kit. "The first true gallant of the part was
Tom o Cloud, who claps the shadows from the sky." He'd taught her all of
that: the names which country folk did give—Awd Flaycraw, Jack Orion—
to the sprawl of stars she'd called the Gallows Tree. A bookish name. "Wilt
play it naked, then?" said Thea.

"With a sword," said Kit. He sang the old tune from the masque, the
woodwo's brag:

> Orion wears a coat of sparks
> And starry galligaskins
> But men may see what man I be
> Without my first dismasking . . .

They were walking toward the crow lad's coign. The earth by the headland was scratched with mazes, glittering with shards of hoarded glass. The

crow lad blew his hands and stared. His coat was rags of sacking and his shoes were mud. His hempwhite head was bare, in a ravel of rope-ends.

"Hey, lad, would thy master hear a play?"

"Has dogs. And sets 'em on."

And a stick, thought Kit. And lays it on. He saw the wary face and wincing shoulders. The bruises. The boy stared back unblinking. He had eyes as green as hail. Kit found the last of what they'd begged, a sadcake and a scrape of fat. "Here's for thy piece," he said. The crow lad snatched it fiercely and he bit, he crammed. Kit waited. "What's thy name?"

"Called Ashlin."

"And thy kin? Who keeps thee?"

"No one," said the boy. "I's lightborn."

"So am I," said Kit. "We two are Mally's bairns." He saw a bright child made of azure falling, rolling naked in the dust. They come to dust. The woman in his dream turned elsewhere, as her lap was full. And still the lightborn fell: so many for the world to waste. Not all of them, he thought to say. Not ours to come.

But Thea said, "And I am darkborn."

"See'd," the crow lad said.

"But he and I go longways, out of Law." She looked about. "Her eyes?"

"Stoneblind. Off elsewhere, anyway."

"But if they follow—"

"I's a sling o stones. What I do."

Thea looked long at him. "Wouldst do it?"

"Owt I can."

Kit caught his breath, leapt in with, "Who's thy master, lad? I'd have a word with him. Wouldst come with us? Art fast?" He turned to Thea, bright with indignation, mischief, pleading. "He could play the boy."

"Got work. Hers," the crow lad said, and becked at Thea. He glanced at Kit's coat. "I see yer ta'en already. Go yer ways."

Thea said to the boy. "Is it fast, then?"

"Clap and done." He spat his hand; they shook.

Kit stood bewildered, like the child in the basket, whirled round in their play. Thea touched his arm. "Soft, love, 'tis a game we play." To the boy, she said, "What then?"

"Seek hallows."

"What way?"

"Gang wi' t'sun."

"How far?"

"While it's hallows."

Thea stretched her hand out, with its tawny ring. A turn and flick, and it was bare: she held a scrawny orange. "For thy noon."

The crow lad caught it and he tossed it in the air. He laughed, looking up at it, his bright hair scattering day. "What's ta'en is anyone's." Kit saw it fall.

"I'd an Ashes bairn," said Whin. Her turn, gazing through the fire, chin on close-hugged knee. "And left him. Naked as he came, for owt as found him. Craws or kin." And in a raw voice, small and wretchedly, she cried, "They would've cut his throat." Still raw. As if a horny hand, a sailor's or a drystone waller's, cracked and bled. "Me mam and her gran would. For t'harvest. Starving earth, I is."

Kit said softly, "Was he yours, the crow lad? D'ye think?"

"I knaw not. Like enough, I doubt." Whin rocked the small ring on her fingertip. "I cannot tell my blood."

"Ah," said Kit. The fire shifted, sighed.

"Thowt it were guising, being Ashes. When I ta'en her coat. And I laughed that I were chosen out of all, that I could take owt I willed. Whatever lad. So long as I did play her part, walk earth until she waked. So long as I kept nowt."

Kit looked for the child in her, as black as he was white. Broad cheekbones and a mournful lip, her long Ægyptian eyes. "And you would still be Ashes. If you'd kept the boy. Still hunted." Coverless as hares.

"What I is, is Ashes. Same as earth is earth. Her coat that she put on. And when I's doffed, I's done with, breath and bone. No giving back." Whin leaned from shadow into shying light. "I could ha' kept him, see."

The rain fell, water into water. After a time, Whin stirred the embers. "Blood or no. For his sake, for thy kindness, thanks."

"All mine, a hundredfold," said Kit. "He saved us. For a time."

Margaret, see. Bright Hesperus, the moon's epitome, hangs at thy window. Perseis her lamp. When I was Thea, I did love that star, her winding journey through the maze, the quickset stars. 'Tis lucent, there: a brilliant toy, a plaything from a mage's baby house. Burnt Eldin's bauble. Canst thou catch? Let my lady set her hedge as thick as gramarye, as high as ravens cry, the light will in at it.

In April of that wandering year, I spied a comet. In the Crowd of Bone it hung, toward Ninerise, in a thaw of fleeting snow. I waked and saw it, like a pearl dissolving in black wine; I drank that cup, light full of thee. And thou didst leap to it.

I knew then that I went with child.


Thea turned at the waystone, calling. What she said was blown away. And still she turned on the hillside, at the twelve winds' nave; the fellies of the wheel were hills. "What's that?" said Kit, coming breathless behind.

"Those folk. Here's all their petticoats away."

It rained, a hill beyond them and a hill behind: a cold fine windy rain. From the ragwell, where they stood in light, they saw the stormdark clouds onsailing. They were tall and tattery, their skirts of ragged silver draggling heedless through the hills. Then the thorn tree shivered in its rags; the spring winced light, it puckered with a sudden doubt. The sky darkened and a hail came on: small hail, but sharp and green. Kit cowered from it. Thea ran to it and whirled about, catching hailstones in her hands. They filled them, greener as they massed, bluegreen.

"Come back," called Kit. "Hey, Thea?" And he came a few steps, blindly, in the shattering of the hail. How it danced and it daunted, how it hissed and rattled on the ground. It beat him blind, it stung. "Hey!"

"Catching souls," she called.

As sudden, it was past. The hill was white: a spring made glass, the sky made soul and shattered. Slateblue to the eastward, slashed with rain, the heels of storm rolled onward. All above, the lift was blue. He shook himself. Thea's head was haily crowned; it glittered when she turned. Her neck was bare. She flung her hoard of stones away. They scattered on the earth like seed. Cold seed, he thought. No crows would take. A cloud away, a rainbow sprang. It spanned the storm. She clapped her wizened hands and laughed. "Do you turn and I'll dance to it."

Somewhere up Owlerdale they sheltered from a passing rain with tinkers in a hedge. Two women, old and young, with baskets of fairings: cowslip tossy-balls and bunches of bright ribands; toys and tawdry. Kit spread them his coat. The blackthorn was tarnishing, the white in bud. The younger of their chance-met company was breaking buds of it, to whet her bacon; the elder thumbed her cards and smoked. Rain and blackthorn fell.

"That comet," said Kit to Thea. "Ah, but it grows bright and bonny. Like a dandelion gone to seed and drifting."

"Whose clock?" said Thea. "And whose breath?"

Still wandering. It preyed on him, that wan and random look.

"Craws!" said the younger, counting wares. "Dropped whirlywhorl i't road."

The elder pointed with her pipestem. "Pick it up, then." There it lay in a puddle, gaudy and forlorn.

"I'll get it," said Kit, leaping up. Gallantry, perhaps; or smoke of shag. It mingled with the tinker's hair, smoke and spiralling like old man's beard.

The younger bit her bread, then turned and offered it to Thea, all but her thumbpiece. Cold fat bacon and wild garlic.

Pinched mouth and shake of head.

"I cry you mercy," Thea said. "A toothache."

A shrewd eye, like a stormcock's. "What did yer bite, then?"

But her aunt held out her pipe. "Here. Have a pull at me bacca. 'Twill dill thy pugging tooth."

Thea twisted, spewed and spat. Lay weeping.

"Ah," said Baccapipe. "Can read thy fortune wi' out cards."

And Bread-and-Bacon kicked her heels and sang, "... *when me apron were low, Ye'd follow me after through frost and through snow* ..."

"Whisht." The old one wiped Thea's mouth, felt her brow and wrist and belly with rough concern. "Not far gone, I'd say." She quirked her chin at Kit coming. "Does he—?"

No.

"And do yer—?"

No again.

"Knowst mouse-ear?"

"Where?" said Thea.

"Ninewood. Up Ask ways, a two three mile." She pointed over the hills. "Grows in among thorn."

And the younger sang again, blithe as a cuckoo that calls, *Not I!* at the nesting wren: *"... but now that my apron is up to my knee ..."*

"Sneck," said the elder.

Too late. Kit had tumbled. On his face, like wind in whitebeam, danced and paled his feelings: joy, awe, terror, tenderness, despair. "Thea?" He knelt and wreathed her in his arms. "Canst walk? Can I get thee aught?" he said foolishly. "From anywhere, the moon." He could not see her face. He thought he could feel the child; he saw it in his mind's eye, like a little comet, still travelling and trailing light: a seed-moon tumbling over and over through the air.

Now, Margaret, thou begin'st to wind. Slipping from thy bower, soft and warily, thou try'st the latch: my lady and her crow keep watch. Not always, thou hast found. The gore-crow hunts; my lady sleeps, but as the sun in Thule, riding on the rim of darkness. She but wets her lip in Lethe cup. Yet she sleeps. Locks and spells she's set on thee, and cage on cage: thou walk'st within a tower, in a maze, within a wall hedged round with thorn, encompassed in a bitter sea. Her lean hounds prowl the courts and coverts, and her huntsman wards the gates.

And further, they do keep thee innocent, they blanch thee, as a gardener doth a white root under stones. Thou art bedazed and physicked, purged, pinched, bled, stayed, examined, spied on. Whipped.

Yet they do not lock thy door, within so many locks. Nor mew thy seeking thoughts.

They slight thee, for thou canst not be dead Thea, thou unwanted wast her death; disdain thee for thy meddled blood. In their contempt is all thy hope. Thou art a dish that likes them not; they have no stomach for thy soul. Unconsidered, thou art half unseen, a sparrow in a wintry hedge. Whatever thou art let to find is all inconsequent, is haws.

Thou turn'st the key and slip'st.

Doors and doors. An arras and a winding stair.

Ah, these rooms I never saw. Thy journey, Margaret. Not mine.

Only to the next room, and the next.

Locked.

Nothing but a box of nutmegs.

Spectacles, in this, that make thy candle swerve and loom. Old iron. Rats.

A lock made like a witch, that bares her secrets to the key. That watches, mute and venomous. Not there.

In this, a heap of books, sea-ruined. Mooncalf'd bindings, white and swollen as a drowned face. Warp and white-rot, skin on skin. Down thou sit'st and try'st to pry the boards, to turn the bleared and cockled pages. Here, a drawing of a hand, anatomized. A riddle in geometry. A fugue of spiders. And behind a faded arras—ghost of roses, greensick blue—a bright dark closet full of wonders and of dust. A mute virginals. Thy fingers press the slack and clatter of its keys, unclose its fretty soundboard, gnawed and rustling with mice. The lid within is painted with brief garlands—violets and wood anemones—as if the music dreamed them in the dark. Spring flowers thou hast never seen: thy fingers, wond'ring, trace. They pleach the silk of scarves, as sheer as iris; trace the windings of a table carpet, blood of nightingales and cry-at-midnight blue. Thou strok'st a jar, round-bellied—blear with dust, yet lucent underneath—of china, blue and white as clouded May.

"So y'd not've been at leap fires, then," said Whin. "Being heavy."

"And light." Kit had seen them, other years, in Lune. Had begged the wood for them, from door to door:

> Sticks to burn vixens,
> Stones for the crow,
> Clips for us green lads
> And girls, as we go.

He'd danced with the highest: brave lads and bold heroes, and the lang tangly girls. Whirled higher, still higher, for the claps and cries, the eyes admiring or awed or scornful. Afterward, for clips and kisses. For the darker thing. By one and one, they'd pinched the embers—ah, another in thine hair. Thy shirt. By twos, had slipped away. He had lain on the dark hills; had made of charred petticoats, green gowns.

"No," he said. "No, we went to the greenwood. To get leaves."

"O," said Kit. "I drown." He stood in heaven, in the place where all doors lead. That wood was deep in flowers of the inmost curve of blue, the blue of iris her embrace. Her eye within her rainbow, as the moon within the old moon's clasp. And Thea walked in that unearthly floating haze of flowers, amid the leafing trees, knee-deep in Paradise. It was the heart; and yet at every further step, 'twas this. And this beyond. Each blue, the inwardest embrace, the bluest eye. An O annihilating all that's made.

The blue became his element, his air: he dove.

He saw a falling star beyond him. Thea.

Then 'twas past. He scuffled through old beech leaves, brushed by nettles. Stung himself and swore. Close by, he whiffed the green stench of a fox. He turned. A bluebell wood, the bonniest he'd ever seen. Young slender beeches. Holly, celandines, and wood anemones. And Thea gathering leaves, green branches.

Where she walked was heaven still.

He lay in sky, and watched her, errant in the sky below. She'd slipped from her tumbled smock, stood clad in sky. He saw the crescent of her, white and glimmering: in the dark of moon, the moon. That other sky she walked was on the verge of green, bluegreen, and turning deeper into blue. Beyond the new leaves, it was dusk. The trees were pointlace yet, or bare or budding out: an airy seine. A star hung trembling in the air, like water on a leaf, about to fall, unfallen. And the moon within his orbit, gilding as she set.

By a thorn tree, at his side, she sat and wove a garland in her lap. A knot of May.

Drowsily, he said, "We munnot sleep."

"Why not?"

"The morn will be the Nine. Wouldst see them rising?"

"Ah," said Thea, "but I am no maid."

He touched her small round belly. "Yet thou bringest may. A branch." The rank sweet scent of thorn hung faintly on the air; the petals fell, as if the moon unleaved. "Shall we set a hedge of them, a hey of girls?"

"And call it Lightwood?" Thea said.

Kit said,

> *Let no man break*
> *A branch of it, for leavy Tom doth wake.*
> *And keep his lash of girls ungarlanded.*
> *That wood is hallows.*

In another, rustic voice, he answered, "'Aye, 'tis where the bushes harry birds. I dare not for the owls go in."
Thea said:

> But thou art mazed, sweet fool. The wood is dark,
> And I—

"Go on," said Kit.

> And I th'moon's daughter in these rags of cloud
> Shall bear thee light.

"Oh," said Thea, "but I've left the book in Lune."
"Thou hast the way of it."
"By heart."
"And by thy heart." He wreathed his hands about their child, and spoke the woman's part:

> The lady goes with me.
> For that her star is wandering, I name
> Her Perseis . . .

And darting kisses in her neck, he said, "What think'st thou, for our lass, of Perseis?"

"Not Eldins?"
"Ah." Kit laughed softly for delight. "Will there be nine?"
"Less one," said Thea, bending to her wreath.

Whin said, "Did yer not guess what she twined?"
"No," said Kit. "I was a fool."
*Why d'ye pull that bitter little herb, that herb that grows so grey . . . ?* Ah, she'd pulled those leaves alone. "A man."

A silence. Somewhere in the wood, a bird poured silver from a narrow neck.

Thea stirred. "Kit?"

"Hmm?"

"Does it end so?"

"Which?"

"The tale. With Annis turned to stone."

"At sunrise? Aye, and it begins."

"There was another tale," she said. "About the moon in a thorn bush."

"Malykorne."

"What's she?"

"The Cloud witch. Annis' sister, some do say. Her bed's where the sun is waked. He sleeps the winter there."

"And now?"

"Wakes wood."

"Ah."

Darkness and the moonspill of the may. Green is nowhere, it unselves the wood. As lovers are unselved: not tree embracing tree, but one. But wood. A riddle, he thought drowsily. *Within a wood, another wood, a grove where grows no green; within a moon, another moon, and nowhere to be seen.* A bird in the dark leaves answered, but he never heard. *Two, two eyes,* the owl cried out. *Of tree, of tree, of tree.* Kit slept.

I will tell this in the dark. That crown I wove for thee. And on May Eve, of all unseely nights: that nadir of the wake of Souls, and darkness' dark of moon. Unhallows.

Ah, love, I had despaired of thee.

I was unwitched. Thou knitting reeled up all my powers, left us naked to my lady's malice. Soul and body, I went heavy with thy death. My great kite belly would undo us all. And so I did, undid. I would not have thee blood-fast, earthbound, for my dam to take. Nor turn thee Annis, stone within my stone.

Toward midnight, turning, Kit awoke and saw a fireflash amid the low woods, heard a brash of leaves: and there in the glade he saw a kitlin fox, a vixen dancing like a flake of fire in the wind.

He turned to Thea, shook her softly. "Hush, love. Look."

She woke and saw. He felt her at his side turned cold as hailstones. "Kill it," Thea said.

A stillness. "What?"

"I am heavy, I can do no spell. Now. Quick."

And still he watched. The patter of the paws was quick, like rain on leaves. A clickety vixen. April in its veins. It danced like a burning leaf, the aftercolor of the greenblue sky.

"What harm in it?" he said. "The pretty kitlin."

"Eyes," she said.

They turned and flashed, a deepsunk dazzling green. The fire was green.

She said, "It wears the fox's fell."

He'd heard no bark. No fox was ever so still, so fiery. None scented of green thorn. He rose, unsure. A stone?

But it was gone.

He turned back and saw Thea, huddled naked on the ground. He bent and wrapped her in her scattered clothes, for fear of eyes, of lairing eyes. Cold in his arms, she cried, "No witch. I am no witch. I cannot meet her in the air."

Kit said, "Who'd harm thee? I would keep thee. I would try." A hopeless tenderness consumed him, like a candle swaling in his bones. "It's what I'm for."

She twisted from him. To the child in her, she cried, "My blood is thy undoing."

"'Tis my blood as well," said Kit. "I do not use thee."

Thea said, "But I use thee. Poor fool, have you not seen? Thou wert my cock-horse, that I rid away."

No ship, no ship beneath him, and the cold wave's shock. Salt-blind, he flailed at her. "Then find thyself a jade to bear thee, and another when he's flagged. Any stick will do to ride on."

Silence. Her cheek went paler still. His hands unclenched. At last, softly, she said, "And to burn, at need. The slower, being green. I would not watch thee burn." She turned her face from him; he saw the white neck, the tumbled quenchless hair. "I am thy death."

And rising, naked in her smock, she ran. He followed blindly, pushing on at hazard through bushes and briars. Heedless of their lash, he scrambled onward, deeper in the wood. The wood was endless. Thea? Further on, he saw her glimmering; then white in whiteness, she was gone. His heart turned snow.

When I got thee, I had not yet bled. Nor will now, being air. That bower and that bed of state, my lady dressed for Annis, all in hangings of deep crimson velvet, rich as for the progress of a queen, though in her exile. Not that blue and meagre hag, that bugbear Annis, that doth stalk the fells of Cloud; not she, that winter's tale, that dwindled bloodfast crone: but Annis, air and dark made crystalline, before her fall.

I was born thirteen, as thou art now; I saw the Nine rise and the Gallows wheel and set an hundred enneads of times; and at thirteen, I lived a year, and died.

My lady did conceive, create me green and virgin for her sorcery; but kept me for herself. Her study and her moving jewel, her toy, her book. The pupil of her eye, that she did dote upon, so year by year put off the consummation of her art, for lessoning.

For play.

In her conjurations—often in her storms—my lady witch would gaze in me, the glass that Morag held: bare April, but for winter's chain. Herself was January, all in black and branching velvet, flakes of frost at neck and wrist. *Come, Madam,* she would say. *Undo.* And then undo my coil of hair, unbraid it through and through her hands. *Lie there, my art.* And still would gaze, devouring my stillness, as the eye drinks light. I shivered in her admiration. Then, only then, her wintry hand would touch, her cold mouth kiss; and quickening, the witch would toy and pinch and fondle, aye, and tongue her silent glass, till she, not I, cried out and shuddered. Cracked.

Cried out: her jewel, her epiphany, her nonpareil; her book of gramarye, her limbeck and her light. Her A and O.

And yet not hers.

Know you that the stone my lady wears is Annis, shattered in her fall and vanished, all but that cold shard of night. Her self that was.

That moment of her breaking, time began. Light wakened from its grave in her. Unbound, the moon did bind her to that sickled and disdained hag thou see'st, that ashes of herself: the witch. Time chained her to this rock. And for a thousand thousand changes of the moon did Annis brood on her disparagement, the lightwrack of her Law. She sought to gather up her flaws of night, anneal them in her glass: that glass from which she drew me, naked and unsouled. Her self.

With me, my lady did enact her fall: the cry and shattering. And with each reiterated crack, her glass would round itself, quicksilver to its wound. But not her soul. My brooch of nakedness did pierce her, bind her bloodfast to her baser self: that hag who eats children.

That was not what she designed.

She had made me for the stone. The seed of Law. And on the morrow of the night I fled her would have wound the stair, unlocked the bloodred chamber, set the stone within my womb. Bred crystal of my blood. That stone would turn me stone from inward, Gorgon to itself, until—

And then he saw her. Moonlight. 'Twas the moon had dazzled him. No more. Light fell, leaves shifted. Thea stood agaze. Stone still and breathing silence. *Hush. Look, there.*

He turned. A clearing, silver as a coin with dew, and tarnished as the moon's broad face. And in that O of light, like Mally-in-the-moon, a-bristle with her bush of thorn, he saw an elfish figure, to and fro. A child? (A tree afoot?) Not ancient, though as small and sickle as the old moon's bones: a barelegged child. A branching girl. They do get flowers of a hallows eve. Alone?

A lash of thorn whipped back and welted him. He sleeved the salt blood from his eyes. He blinked and saw her, not in leaves but rags: the ruins of a stolen coat, perhaps, a soldier's or a scarecrow's, or a lover's run a-wood. Mad Maudlin's, that was Tom's old coat. It fell from her in shards, as stiff as any bark with years. There were twigs of thorn in wilting flower in her hair, down, eggshells, feathers. Cross and cross the O she went, not getting branches: walking patterns to herself, as furious fantastic as a poet in her bower, her labyrinth her language. Then a start, and back she skitted, ticklish as a spider on her web, to tweak some nebulous chiasmus. A hussif of trees.

Daft as a besom, he thought. Poor lass.

But Thea said to her, "Is't hallows?"

"While it is. Thy time's to come." The green girl scrabbled in her rags, howked out a pair of crooked spectacles and rubbed them in the tatters of a leaf-red cap. She perched them on her nose. A grubby girl, with greenstained knees, scabbed knees and elbows. As she turned, Kit saw her crescent body shining through the rags. A downy girl. He stirred and her seeing mocked him: a fierce howlet's face. All beak and eyes. "Shift," she said. "I's thrang."

But Thea said, "I am what you do."

"Ah," said the girl. "What's that?"

"Undo."

The girl glanced at Kit. "I see thou's done already what thou can't undo." He felt her elfshot eyes. Her breasts were April, but the eyes were January, haily, and the tongue a cold and clashy March. Scathed, he felt himself, dishevelled in his raffish coat, with moss and toadstools in his hair. Leaves everywhere. And ramping after Thea, like a woodwose in a mumming. Mad for love.

There was nothing for it but to play the part. Her glazy eyes decreed. "Poor leavy Tom," he said. "Remember Tom his cup. He sees the craws at bones; they rouse the kittle wren, cock robin, and the tumbling owl."

Then he cared not for the hoyden; Thea touched his lips. "Softly. 'Tis her wood."

Kit looked about. There was no moon. The light was may. He saw the whiteness, heaped and hung about the branches, like all the petticoats of some untidy dreaming girl, a tangly lass who kept her bower. What she knew and drew had thorns.

"Come in," said the green girl, loftily. "Mind souls, I's flitting."

In was out. He saw the whitethorn petals fall and flitter as he passed: no wall or window else. Within was dark and waste. Thea, bending, took up a clumsy garland lying half-made on the ground. Kit saw the ashes of a fire, cold out; a crackpot, tipsy on its one leg, canted over. It was full of dry leaves.

Beyond her hedge—scant sticks, blown papers—lay the cold bare hills. The wind was smoke-edged.

"Fires on the hills," said Thea, shivering.

*Sticks to burn vixens.* Kit saw the whirling bodies, higher, leaping higher. Heard the cries. They would dance on every hill by dawning, round from Law to Law again, to close round Annis in her stone. The kindling was the hey.

The girl snecked air behind them. "Aye, they wake, and then I wake."

Thea said, "Are you their mistress, then?"

"They's no one's minions," said the girl. "Here's spring." It welled up through the leaves, a little constant twirl of silver, spilling secretly away. She cleared it with her heel, and crouched and filled her gnarly hands. "Thou's dry," she said to Kit. He drank of them, her hands within his hands. He tasted earth. "Cloud ale," she said. "Dost like of it?" He nodded, mute. She took him by the shoulders, light, as if she shook him out, her cloak of leaves. "Lie there. Wake wood."

And he was leaves. Brown leaves of oak, the lightfall of a thousand hallows. He was galls and tassels, traceries of veining; he was shards of acorns, shales of light. His lady's cups. He was turning earth, and through him sprang the starry flowers of the Nine. His earth had made them green. *No tongue, all eyes!* the witch commanded, and the eyes were myriad, were stars of earth.

As giddy as a god, he laughed.

"S'all we do?" said the witch to Thea.

"As you will."

They worked together, plaiting thorn and blackthorn in a garland. Round they turned and bound it, plashing branches in and inwards, as an O, a lightlashed eye. It made a crown too sharp to wear. For which? There was a glory in their laps, of quince and almonds, nettles, violets and goat-haunched catkins, all a-didder and a-dance.

"It turns," said the witch. "Turns O."

"O's naught," said Thea, with the garland in her lap.

"Or ay and anywhere, as swift as moon; or what thou will. O's tenfold."

Thea bent to her braiding. "If it were?"

"It quickens," said the witch. "Comes round. What's past is nowt til it, and all's to come."

Odd and even went the witch's fingers, in and out. Wood anemone and rue. She wove them in the nodding garland: eyebright and nightshade, cranesbill, crowsbane, and the honeyed primrose, ladysmocks, long purples. Turning, it was turning autumn: now the leaves they wove were red and yellow, fruited: haws and hazelnuts and trailing brambles, rowans, hips, and hazy sloes.

"That untwines," said Thea, of a mouse-eared herb. "I plucked it."

"Aye," said the witch, weaving in. "Wilta taste of it?"

"And wane?"

"And bear thysel, burd alone. Walk or wake, as thou wist."

Thea bent. "I am bound to them. My lady and this child. If I do bear it, I am hers; if I do not, I am herself."

"Allt same. Thou's moonfast."

Thea said, "I am uncastled. Will you keep me?"

"Where? I's nowhere."

"Here."

"Is nowhere. Hey is down, and there's no hallows i't green world. I't morning, I mun walk and Annis wake."

"Then I am lost," said Thea. "For my art is lost."

"Thou's bound as she is, rounding winter in thy lap. It will be born, I tell thee, and i't sickle o't moon." The witch tossed the tussymussy in her lap. "So mowt it be."

Kit watched them whispering secrets, close as moon and dark of moon, in one another's arms. They wove one burr of light. He saw the clew of stars in Thea's lap. He saw the witch's spectacles were frost; they faded as he looked, they trickled down and down her cheeks. He heard an owl's cry echoing, her windy laugh. He saw the green hills leap with vixens, blown like flames from hill to hill. *When the wheel comes round, 'tis sun,* he thought. He saw the blackened moon, the cavey moon, as slender as a share of bannock. Riddle cake. He thought the green witch bade him eat. It tasted sweet and bitter, of his dreams. His share was burnt. He saw a stone and a thorn tree, deep in green embrace. The moon was tangled in the leavy thorn, its roots its rimy crown. The stone was straked with lichens, of a bloodrust red; a crazy garland at its crown, aslant.

*Split the stick, and I am in it,* sang the wren. *I rise.*

*I crack the stone,* said the starry flower. *I will crack where I take root.*

He slept.


And so I waked that night, and whispered secrets with my sister moon. With Malykorne, that is my lady Annis' other face and elder: light and dark of one moon. Her cradling and my crescent self, still turning from my mother into light. And thou within me, braiding blood. A clasp of witches.

I had no heart for thy undoing.

*I am stone,* said I. *My lady's eidolon. How came I by this flaw?*

*Thy soul?* The green witch laughed. *Her glass were clouded.*

*Did you—?*

*Stir fire up? Not I.*

I thought on thy begetting. *Brock? Did she meddle?*

*Bloodroot i' thy lady's cauldron. Ashes i' thy cup.* The green witch drank. *What's done is done. Yet being kindled, thou might leave thy spill.*

Kit slept beside us. Why did I not leave him sleeping, let him grieve and live?

I tell thee, I could not, remembering how coldly I had culled him, out of all the bloodborn kenneled in my lady's dark. All in silver, I'd come down to view my prey, I'd held the candle to his dazzled face. Yes. He would do, I'd thought; yet stilled the triumph in my glance. My lady and her crow did watch. They'd uses for his soul and seed, designs of thrift and sorcery for bone, blood, fell and eyes. Ah, make no paragon of me—myself had marked him for my own false ends. His fiddle for a ship to bear me from that nighted isle; his cock to crow away her spell. 'Twould do, I judged. So one might heft a stick, a sling of stones, at need: to use, to cast away. He bowed; and as my lady bade, I offered drowsy wine to him, a draught amazing to the mortal sense. We'd toy with him before we slew.

*Is this the moon?* said he, and gazed about the hall. Awe and mischief in his face. *I've seen her owl and her ivy bush, but never tasted of her cup.*

I bit my lip, so not to laugh. All solemn then, alight with love, he drank to me. I saw him: tousled, sleepless, downy. He had brushed his twice-turned coat, as if he went not to his death but to a dance. *Poor fool,* thought I. And all unknowing, I was changed by him. His innocence his spell.

And so that green Unhallows eve, I waked by Malykorne and chose: to stay with Kit, to bear thee, for what end might come.

O Margaret, I was stark afraid. Of travailing, of birth. Of dying—ah, most bitterly; but more than death, I dreaded Annis in myself. Her stone I had averted; but the dark witch was in grain. I'd seen her in my lady's glass: bloodnailed and insatiate, the blind hag on the road. I was afraid of being her, of slaying what was not myself. Of whoring. Not the act—for I was schooled to that—but the devouring. Cold fire, turning sticks to Ashes, Ashes into Annis, endlessly: herself herself engendering.

Yet where thou wast, there Annis could not be. That secret did the green witch tell me, softly in mine ear: thou wouldst keep hallows in that place of blood, that O thine everywhere, thy keep; though I went naked to my lady's sky. And so I brooded thee, as doth a child its candle, lighting her the way to bed. Yet all about there lay the shadows of thine inward fire, the fears that winced and flickered in my brain. Of need and frailty and lumpishness. Of losing Kit, the fear of losing him. Of love.

"Craw's hanged!" cried the grey cock.

Kit woke. *Gone?* A something slipped from him, a ghost returning at the pale of night. It will not stay, that tide. The pale boat rides the mirk and shiver of that burning flood; it slips the moorings. Gone. Yet curled against him, Thea slept. Cap and acorn. They were lying by a scanty thicket, on the open hills. Not day yet, neither moon nor sun.

He heard a thump and twitter in the wood, a wild free scuffling and calling. Out from the greenwood burst a rout of guisers, clad in tattercoats and leaves.

"Hey is down!" they cried.

Children.

Thea hid her face, but she was laughing; Kit caught up their scattered clothes to lap her.

They'd a girl to play small music—hop and twitter, like a small bird on a briar—all but lost amid their charm. She'd a wheedling pipe and dowly drum. Another, a long lad, bore a garland of whitethorn with a dead crow swung from it, wryneck and agape. It dangled, claws upward, wings clapped wide and stark. Round it, in and out, there ran a thrang of boys and girls. One, crowned in oakleaves, clashed horns with another clad in holly. Lagman and tangling, walking in his sleep, a small boy gaped and swayed and staggered under all their jackets.

"Brant!" they cried. "Come in, here's game."

Not last but alone went a dark and clustering girl in torn russet and green crown; she bore a staff, and wore a fox tail jauncing behind.

"Craw's hanged!" she cried. "Get up!"

A stripling in petticoats swept round the lovers, whirling light and away. His skirts were singed with leaping fires. His broom was budded out, as if he'd swept stars with it. "Here's nest on 'em," he said. He poked at them and kittled them, left smears of pollen and of ashes.

"Hey!" cried Kit, sneezing, laughing all at once.

The others thronged. "We's late. They's been and done."

Undone.

The girl with the music played *Cuckoo!* on her little pipe

"My bout at broom? Yer said I could."

"Sneck up, thou mardy, or I's leave thee here for bears."

"Clartarse."

"Neshcock. Tell our dad of thee."

"Gi's a box," said another. "And we'll gang away."

Kit fumbled in his pockets, found a halfpenny. "Here's to your fires."

Brant bit, she pursed it. "And to yers. Where's riddle?"

"Here," said another. "In my apron."

They'd a round loaf of barley bread, with a face baked into it: a leafy glazy green man, scored and bossed on it, with clove-nailed eyes. Brant broke and shared it out with all. Kit took, and Thea. All tore it from within, the soft warm crumb; they left the crust of the green man, his face, for the last. At his end, a small boy took the heel, he pinched the raisins from the eyes. Round he went, guising in his mask of crust. Now crouching, now on tiptoe, peering round. A solemn mischief.

"I see you," he said to Kit. "You don't see me."

Then that, too, was devoured.


Whin tugged at Kit's long cotted hair; she eyed his salt-rimed straggling beard. "Time you was clipped."


"Day," said the woman. The sheep leapt, yellow-eyed and glaring, from between her knees. The fleece fell, the light sheep staggered giddily away. "Where yer bound?"

Kit said, "Thwaite. Is this the road?"

"We's all up here," said the woman with the shears, broad-backed, rosy, swathed in sacking. In the fold, the penned sheep blared and jostled.

"Oh," said Kit, looking round at the row of clippers kneeling or bending to their work, at the lappers and catchers, and the boy at the gate. Beyond them, it was cloudy, the hills hooded in morning.

"Way!" Behind him, a gangling lad brought on another ewe to clip, half-riding her. He threw her in the woman's lap. Her shears bit deep in the heathery wool; they scrunched and sang. "Walking on?"

Kit said, "Anywhere."

"If's a bite and a sup yer after, there's work. Can yer catch 'em? Can yer whet?"

"I'd think so. But ..."

The woman peered at Thea. A dishevelled girl, and silent. Like a tinker out sleepwalking. Hair like flakes of fire. The gown had been good, was tattered as lichen. It was undone at the waist. "Not so lish as yer were, is't? Can yer lap?"

"She's lapped," said a clipper.

Another sheep sprang away, a vengeful crone. Kit shielded Thea. "'S all right, she's been down afore," called a man. "Rigged ower."

"Pay 'em no mind," said the woman. "Fourpence and all found?"

"Done." Kit laid by his pack and jacket, and plunged into the throng of clamorous sheep.

"Hey up! Gi's a slipped 'un."

"Hey! Mind awd Sukey. She's gone on yer, like."

"Lovesick."

"Hod on, lad."

An old ewe cannoned into Kit. Down he went, embracing her for dear life, slathered, laughing. He got her somehow to a shepherd's lap. The man knelt on her head, grinning.

Kit felt his bones. "By, she's a brave 'un." He grinned at Thea, but she stood, looking out at the hills.

"Come on, then," said a lapper.

Thea gathered wool. There were loose locks everywhere. Two women stood at a board and hurdles, lapping fleeces. They plucked away the clarty bits—odds, bobs, and daggles by the tail—and threw them in a sack. They spread each fleece out, dark side up. Then they folded in the legs and rolled it up, dark outward inward, with a twist of the neck-wool drawn out and wrapped round. As they worked, they gossiped; but at every fleece, they said, "A soul, a sark. Out light, in dark."

Thea packed the fleeces in creels. Kit wrestled with the crones. The shears crunched on, inexorable; the light sheep skipped away. The lappers set riddles. "What rive at one another allt day, and lie in one another's arms all night?"

"I give up," said Thea. "Moon and her dark?"

"Wool combs."

From below, a long way off, came a girl, knitting beside a laden pony. A shepherd and a brisk black dog brought new sheep, down from the summer moors. They shone, brightdark and heavy as the thunderbreeding clouds.

The girl tied her pony, unlading hoggins, frails, and creels. She brought round a tray of cheesecakes, round and golden. "Noon."

Gooseberries and news. "Grey mare's foaled. A lad, and he's piebald.

Mistress? Yer Bet's been and thrawn one o yer good siller spoons i't beck, and me and Doll has fished it up. Young termagant." She sleeved her rosy face. "Oh, and a stranger come, asking at one Lightwood. Said he were an Outlune fellow, brown and beggarly, and ganging with a whey-faced breeding wench. A vixen." She stared at Thea. "There now! And that clotpoll of a crow lad sent him on up Houlsyke way. Will I fetch him back?"

"No," said Kit. "I thank you."

A blue-eyed shepherd looked to westward. Thunder. "Doubt he'll have tumbled i't hag by now."

Thea bit her seedcake. "Well done, my little page."

Whin's duckstone skipped and slapped across the waves. "Eight." She turned grinning. "That caps."

"You've nimmed all the smooth stones whilst I lay and slept." Kit's flicked once and sank. Still clumsy.

Whin turned out her pockets with a clattering flourish. "Halves." Stoop and flick. Three. "Yer still won't beat. I's worked at it." Still with her back to him, looking out at the bare green sea, she said, "Bairn's father."

"Ah?" Kit sorted through the stones.

"It were guising. I never see'd his face." Five. "So I see'd him a'where."

"A stranger." One with a leaf in it, too fair to cast away. And this ill-shapen. Ah, this would do. Four. "Yellow hair?"

"As chimneysweepers." A lad at leap fires. A thief at the gallows. Had he smiled, remembering her cries? A false love. A fiddler. A stranger with a scythe.

Sweetness of green hay. Midsummer. Endless dusk. And still the mowers, mothpale in their shirts, strode on. Kit watched the coil, recoiling of their backs, the long sweep of their scythes, in unison, and so enlaced that not a blade of grass between them stood. They struck and strode, advancing like the white edge of a wave: whish and tumble and the intricating arcs of edge. A long wave, standing with the sun. It stood; the flowers fell and withered with the grass. No sea, but slow green fire, kindled by the sun his kiss.

And after came the bending girls, to strow the grass. They'd not take rake to it, still green in bride-bed, bleeding from the scythe. Rakes to the lapcocks;

but straw girls to the swath, to shake and strew the hay in handfuls, east and west. Lay lighter that way.

The hay's the dance.

In Kit's long row, they raked and turned the fading flowers: matrons of a day, and sunburnt. Tossed and tumbled, all their brightness turned to breath of summer. Sweets compacted. He'd made hay since he could walk. He knew the dance. Scythe it and strow it, then to rakes. And turn and turn. Lapcocks to the hobs to windrows; windrows to the sledges. Crisp and blue.

And in among the cocks of hay, the lovers courted, striplings and hoydens, clip and cuff, like hares. Boys battled, whirling hay. And one to another, the straw girls sang: the grey-eyed girl behind him, tall and soldierly and brown; the elfin brat before.

Kit turned and gazed at Thea, in among the girls. Ah, lovelier than ever, fading. Inward turned, to sweet. His lass was growing thin and heavy. Bending to the grass, she strowed it, sun and moon. Skirts dovetailed, and her bare legs scratched. Her bright hair tumbled on her neck. Still white as thorn, her throat, her brow; no sun could burn them. Thea tossed her wraiths of flowers in the air, looked up and round within their falling. Whorl within whirlwind, slow and fast. *Move still, still so.* O my heart. Let it be *now* ever, at the solstice of my love. The blade but newly struck; my heart still standing. Yet will fall. Her blade's herself.

The long wave slowed, against the steepening shingle of the dark. And now the grass was ocean; slow and slower lagged their wading steps, their oars, against that tide. The lads cried challenges, lashed on their fellows, flagging, flagging with the sun; the lasses raked and sang:

> *You must kiss her and embrace her,*
> *Till she causes your heart to yield—*

One voice above the rest rang out, triumphant, hoarse:

> *For there's never a faint-hearted soldier*
> *Can win on a battlefield.*

The scythes struck on, against that tide of dark. Against the quenchless lap of earth, the grass that stood and shivered. Stood.

Up from Imber Beck came Kit, not spilling what he held. Deep pools and dappling, the rush and plunge of bright quick water on the stones. He'd washed him clean as dawn, walked naked in his old clean shirt. Grass at his ankles, wind stirring in his wet-combed hair, already lifting from its douse. A sparkling dancing day, a drying day. A day for playing hob. Wild thyme and trout, he thought: he'd lie and tickle.

He came to Thea, sitting in a circle of great stones, on one had fallen, at the green hub of the wheel of Cloud. Its nave, whence it breathed. Old stones, they were, and worn fantastical: wind-gnawed and water-cavey, flawed and rippled with the frosts. White stones, whorled with mosses. They'd not mown here. Would not: had left them whitelands to the wandering sheep.

Thea swung her heel and sang, like any shepherd's lass.

"A lovegift," said Kit, and held it out.

A cup of rushes, lined with cool green leaves of hazel, wet with dew. And brimmed with raspberries, most perfect ripe: as soft as foxes' paws, and with their prick. Their flowers wreathing round. A dowry for a queen of Elfin.

"Ah," said Thea. All her face alight with joy, as he'd not seen her. Taking them, she kissed him lightly on the wrist, just where his pulse beat blue. Where it was scratched with gathering, had beaded with bright blood. Love's bracelet. "Bravely won."

For that he'd pick them naked, from the inward of the thicket out. By Cockridden and by Childerditch, he would, were the brambles backside of the moon.

"Does it like thee, love?" he said. "That cup of imbers?"

"I shall give them to my eldest daughter," said Thea. And she ate.


Ah, Margaret, that was firstborn of my spells, my new-created magic. I will tell it in thy blood, in time. Nine drops. No more.


The field was called Crawcrooks. High and aslant the fell it lay, a stony piece, the last to harvest. They had reaped them all: Burnt Ridding, where the oats were lodged, the Light End and the Long Dark, and round by Mawkins Hey, by Brockholes, Beggary and Witchy Slang, the Whirl Ing and the Wren Graves, and out by Owler Hag. A nine day's stint.

Kit bent to the sheaving. The barley stood white. When he closed his eyes, he saw it glittering still, but awned with violet black. It scarred his eyes with light. Another sheaf, a knot of straw. He swam in it. Straw bristled up his shirt-tail, down his neck. His arms and legs were torn and welted, scarified with straw. Weeds nettled; stubble pierced. Sweat sidled and stung. He ached with stooping, beaten down, astounded by the clangor of the sun. He thought it screamed at him, defiant; looking up, he knew it for a hawk. A stunning and a brazen noon.

Before him went brown Madlin, Ailie Whinlaw, Kat and Bartlemy and Noll Ned Hewlin, with laggard Ciss to trail the rake. They moved breasthigh against the barley, all arrayed in its armor of light. Crouching, they cut it, striking off with their sickles: moon against sun. In their wake lay the barley, shorn and withering. Kit gathered it in armfuls, tying them with bands of straw that Thea twisted of the greenest corn. Beside him and behind worked Gib and Nick Scarrow, sheaving and stooking. No one spoke. The sun quelled them. Still he heard the rasp and rustle of the knives in corn.

The barley was one element, of sun, earth, wind, and rain. A hoary world. Time stilled. Before him rose a whirring and a clack of wings: a covey clattering away. He saw a scutter and a lop of coneys, and at his feet the fumblings of a dawstruck mole. A-sway on the nodding corn, the gressops leapt and chirred. He saw the plash of poppies falling, and the blue-eyed blink of cornflowers, clean petticoats of bindweed. He saw the scurry of the denizens laid bare to light: whitespinners, jinny-long-legs, harvestmen. He felt the sooty velvet of the smutched ears of slain corn, black as my lady's mask. In the sundered corn, he found a mouse's nest, two short ears bound together in a daddle of straw, as deftly plaited as any kirn witch on a stack. There were ratlins within, rosebald, but willowing out with a fuzz. They blindly wormed and squeaked. No dam. No help for it. He stuck it like a bauble in his sunburnt hat, and bent to work.

Then Ailie cried, "Whet!"

The bottle went round, hand to hand. Kit stood and eased his back. Looked first to Thea. He stared out beyond the barley at the whiteleached sky, the moorland bruised with sun. He turned. All below him and behind lay fields, a piecework stitched with drystone walls. He saw the hardwon ploughlands, pale and stooked, all glittering as a card of pins. Beyond lay fold and fallow, and the tilting meadows, green with aftermath, called fog. Above, stood only sheepwalk, cropped and stony, and tumbling becks. He thought of throwing down his glove and lying naked in the rush of water.

"Noon," said Ailie.

They'd an hour's halt. By ones and twos, they turned down the field, past the morning's thraves, sheaf leaning on sheaf, with another as henge. The men went flapping their shirts, their breeches with the knee strings undone. The women swung their sickles, in their broad hats and kerchiefs, their kilted petticoats, all urchined out with straw. Kit waited. Last of all came Thea, roundbellied in a borrowed apron, walking slow. Her hat was wreathed with poppyheads, how quickly bare: a few bright curving petals clung. He saw with a pang how sore her hands were, torn with spinning bands; how white her face. He said, "Thou wert to rest."

"Where's the penny, then?" she said.

He bent and stuck the mouse nest in a stook, carefully. It would not stand, being toppling heavy. "There's time. Shall we lie by the water?"

She looked up at the fellside. "I'd need wings."

"Rest then. Will I fetch thee water?"

"Kat's gone."

There was ale in the hedge. The reapers passed it round and drank; they sprawled and panted in the grass. Beneath an apron thrown over a hazelbush lay Madlin's baby, naked in a little shirt, beside his sleeping childish nurse. The cloth had been dabbled, for the cool; had long since dried taut, tented out on sticks. The shadows of the leaves moved lightly, dappled on the bairns. The baby waked and watched them, purse-mouthed, puzzling at air. "Ah," said Kit, crouching, all alight. The pretty poppet. Madlin wiped her mouth, undid her freckled breast. The little quaily brat set to with jugging. Ciss's Jacky played at the field edge, making pisspies in the dust.

They ate their baggin: curds and onions and the odd green bite; oatcake, cheese and ale. Kit had got brambles from a hedge for Thea. They were green and seedy, like eating broideries of beads; a few, as red as beaded blood: the needle's prick. Nothing else yet ripe. But there were crowcrooks on the moor; the sleeping girl had picked her apronful. Her mouth was stained with them. They had them for their afters: mistblue and midnight berries, tart, and bursting winy on the tongue.

Off by the beck, Kat and Bartlemy were wading, splashing. They leapt and clashed like kids. He snatched at what she flaunted, held high out of reach; Kat lashed him with a bunch of whins. Whoop! cried the boy, and under he went. They saw her ranting on the stone, as gleeful as a goblin. Up he came behind her, and he caught her by the petticoats. A splash like young dolphins.

"By dark," said Ailie, squinting at the glinty stubble and the dwindling standing corn. "Later n'r last year, by a farthing moon."

"It's coming on storm, I doubt," said Gib.

"We's have it done by then. Kirn and all."

Ciss said, "Is't witch or wench this year?"

Ailie looked crows at her, but thumbed her sickle. "As it falls."

The sickles lay about the grass, a halfyear's moons. A reiving wasp came on, and darted at the fruit. Ciss shrieked and cowered in her apron. Sibb in the hedgerow woke, saying, "Is't won yet? Mam?" Kit fanned Thea with his rushy hat. She was whitefaced, and her burning hair was flat with sweat. The red hair rode her like a demon.

Ailie said, "Yer want to be lying down."

Madlin put her baby to the other breast. "Are yer lighter by Gossamer? When is't?"

At Hallows. They would never speak so in the harvest field; Kit knew that much. "Toward Lightfall," he said.

"When's that i' Cloud?"

"The Nine stars' setting, that we call the Clew," said Kit. "Nine Weaving?"

"Cob's Web," said Ailie, nodding.

Nick Scarrow said, "I' Slaith, we call 'em Jack Daw's Seed." His teeth showed whitely in his sunburnt face. He was a hireling stranger; he walked the harvest north. A marish man. He'd said they reaped with scythes there: not creeping women, but a sweep of men.

"Aye, they's a queer lot, out Law," said Gib.

"Cunning wi' tools." Nick fleered at Thea's belly, with a sly and sidelong glance at Kit. "Will I thresh her for thee? Got a flail."

Hewlin sniggered.

"Aye, brock i't middle," said Ailie. "It hangs."

Kit said nothing, twisting straws. Nick shrugged. "Then hang her from a pole for t'crows. I seen yer crowland mawkins, out i't rain. A waste o seed." He sauntered off upfield, to sleep under the hedge. Kit threw away the knot of straw. Toward Whinside, the sky had turned; it shook like foil in the heat. The corn was yellower: not glinting now, but glowering. The sun was in it, brighter as it shrank.

Thea slept, and Madlin. Gib snored and Hewlin whistled; Ailie span hemp. The bluemouthed child made towns of pebbles. Ciss held Jacky in her lap and sighed. "At kirn feast, at Lowerstell, last year, they'd a fiddler til't dance."

Kit felt a whitecold sickle at his heart. The fear had grown in him that all the cunning of his hands was lost with Thea's art. He never spoke of it; he dreamed of ships. "Will he be coming?"

"Not up here, he won't. Up Annis' arse."

Ailie said, "Not for thy sake, Mistress Lightheels."

"Never mind," Kit said. "Do you rant, and I'll keep measure."

"Wi' yer tongue?" said Ailie. "Or have yer browt a pipe?"

"Packed away," he said soberly. "And the drum is broken."

Ciss went on, "A new tune? I do love a new tune."

"One I've made," he said. "The oldest in the world."

Ailie let her spindle fall, the coarse grey thread spin out. "There's Daw's awd crowd wants nobbut catgut. If y'd turn a penny. Hanged on a nail these ten years since."

Kit's heart leapt up.

Ciss poked at the stubble. "There's not," she said. "There was a beggar come, asking would I cross his palm. He telled my cards."

"No art i' that," said Ailie. "Thy fortune's i' thy fork." Down fell the spindle. "Wha tellt thee it were thine to give?"

"Caggy awd thing, wha'd want it?" Ciss pouted. "And I never turned me back, but when pot boiled ower. Asides, there's nowt else missed, I counted spoons and all. And I's to journey til a far country, and wed a stranger on a dapple horse." She turned to Kit. "Happen if yer see him ont road, yer could ask for it back. A tinker fellow like a white craw."

Before he'd framed an answer, Kat came running down the fellside, with her long legs twinkling, bare and scratched. There was gorse in her hair. She'd forgotten the water jugs; but grinned, holding out a great bunch of white heather, haws, crawcrooks. "For t'kirn."

Ailie took and laid it by her sickle, in its curve. "'Twill a' to do."

"So it better. Pains I taken wi't. Is there owt i' yon poke?" Kat rifled for her share of bread and bit it, grinning. "Bat's sulking. He's soused."

Kit watching thought he guessed the riddle. In Lune, in Askrigg, he had seen the images of bristling corn in kitchens down the dale, tied up with rags, with flowers dried to dust. The last sheaf was the Witch, they said; they gave her to the wrens to peck, at Lightfast: so the old year ate of her, to make it new. He said, "In my country, they do bind the Witch with rowans."

"Does they?" Ailie said.

Kat wrung her skirts. "I'd not wonder. For it's red and all."

The Witch was eaten, and in turn she ate. Long since, the old wives said, they'd slain a child for her, an Ashes child: each spring a fall. They said the Old Witch lulled him in her lap. Kit knew her cradle songs. And still in Lune the countryfolk kept law: they stoned the wren and burned his crown, sowed blood and ashes with their hoarded seed, to slake the Witch. Kit saw her, squatting in the corn, with her tangled shock of hair, her scrawny shanks and long toes; her cheeks were of the reddest grain.

"O' course," said Ailie. "Them outland folk is strange. I's heard they shear owls."

Kit looked at Thea sleeping. He said, "There is a tale in Lune. They say the barley is the black earth's daughter, shut all winter in her dark. She rises. So they say."

Ciss said, "They's witches all i' Lune, Gib says."

The spindle fell.

Kit closed his eyes. He saw the Maiden rising, running from her mother's ancient dark. A green girl, dancing in the wind; but long strings tethered her, white-wiry, to her mother's womb. They held her, ripening to stillness, caught and cut. Three servingmen with knives of stone, her mother's minions, struck her down; they beat her with their flails. Her lover looked for her among the sheaves. He took each Perseis in his arms, and she was Annis, hoar and silent. On her face, the shrouding spiders scurried at their work. They told her death in inches. So he laid her out amid the lykes of straw. His eyes were dry. But she was lighter of the sun, their child. He saw it, in its swaddling bands of straw, unslain. Kit saw it, even through his lidded eyes: a glory and a dazzlement. He slept.

Ailie glanced at him, scraw-boned as a rabbit, in his hempen shirt. "'Twill a' to do," she said.

To Luneward did they reap the Witch. Here in Cloud, his elsewhere, they did say the corn was lying in the Witch's lap; she combed his silver hair and he did sleep. And then her cronies crept on him, they cut him off at knee. Not one before another: all at once, they slashed. *Not I*, said each crone to her other. *Nor not I. 'Twas she, my sister slew him.* They were each and all the moon, his end: her sickle shearing and her millstone trundling round, her old black cauldron gaping for his bones.

They shared him out as riddlecake, as round as the wheeling sun. They drank him and he made them giddy: for the turning of the sun is in his cup.

As they drank, they played old bone games on their knuckles: moon reaps sun; sun mazes moon; and moon again wakes sun. They waked him through the winter and they scattered him: the earth his grave, his lap. His last sheaf was the Flaycraw. They hanged him on the Gallantry, to blacken in the wind and rain, to cry the crows. And so his green seed sprang.

Crows called in the harvest field. The bluemouthed child looked up. White crows. They dazzled in the sun; then fell like cinders, black. She watched. She looked around her, squinting. They were all asleep, her mam and all. She bent to her play again, moved pebble in their maze. The black crows quarrelled in the corn.

Kit woke hard. He saw crows rising in the field. His cheek was creased with straws; his arm, asleep where Thea lay on it. Drowsy and heavy, drenched with sleep, he rubbed his eyes and roused her. Ailie called them to the field. It shivered in the little wind; the dazed corn shook, it dazzled. To the east, the sky was sultry dark. They drank and hastened.

As Kit went to field, he met Nick Scarrow loitering by a stook: a burnt man, blue-eyed. He held a reaping-hook and smiled. "Word's out ont road," he said. "Thy Lunish piece. Wilt keep her when she's dropped yon brat? I's a mind to chaffer."

"Crows eat thee," said Kit.

"Crows gat me," said Nick, and slouched off.

Kit slashed with a fury at the rankest corn. A neck, he thought. A neck. "Come up," called Ailie, so he fell to binding, furthest out. He saw that Thea went among the women, safe enough. The work unknotted him, it combed. The women called and answered at their reaping, keeping measure.

*Wha knocks at stone?*
*Poor Peg alone.*
*What's poor Peg lack?*
*A rag t'her back.*
*For salt and bread to lay her dead.*
*And candlelight to gan by night.*
*And what's she beg?*
*A shroud to lap poor Tom.*
*Poor Peg.*

They were cutting in a long slow spiral now, coiled inward on the standing corn. They went sunwise.

*Here,* said the green witch. *I am here.*

And gone. She ran with a rustling, greenfoot. Slower now. She was heavy with the sun, he'd catch her. Then he took her in his arms. She turned, and she was hoary, spidery with years. A blue-eyed, bearded hag, ca'd Crawcrooks.

*Now you can lay me down and love me,* said the Witch. *If you will.*

So he did and he was rooted in her. He was Cloud. His name was Nightless and Bare Bones, Dearbought, Come by Chance. To the east, they called him Babylon, he bowed before the wind as Wiselack, Slobeard, Urchins Hey. To the south, his names were Long Nap, Little Knowe, Leap Hedges; to the west, Sheer Ash, Jack Nackerty, and Nine Tree Crowd; to the north, they reaped Cold Hallows, Hanging Crows, Hobs Graves. The cold wind played on him, the old tune always.

Then the slight moon and the dark of moon, the whitefaced breeding moon, came round him, bound him with their wreaths of straw. Their sickles ringed him like a running wheel. Then all at once, they slashed.

*A clip!* they cried. *A kiss, a clip!* He toppled in their arms.

"And so they ate thee," said Whin. "All but bit t'wren had, and there's an end."

"No," said Kit, smiling. "They did but taste." Kisses and a crown of poppies. Hurts and cream. A sweet mouth, blue with berrying; a shrewd mouth, taking sweets. And Ailie's warmest of them all and fierce, the brooding of a merlin's breast. Then he clouded. "No, 'twas Thea that the moon ate."

Autumn. Moving on. No work. The purple of the moors had gone from froth of jam to fleasblood, then from bruise to black; the trees, from blaze to ruin. Rimefrost on the swiddened heath took place of gossamers. The bracken and the bents were smithwork, smoldering in mist, and glinting, brazen in the strike of sun. And barren. While Kit could, he'd gathered haws, hips, brambles, sloes and rowans. Bags of nuts, his pockets full and Thea's apron. And one October afternoon, he'd found a milky way of mushrumps, penny buns, spilled out amid the leaves. They'd had a bit of mutton fat, just then. A feast. Their meal was long since giving out, their poke thin-flanked and dusty. It was poaching now. Hares, moorhens. Snared and spatchcocked. Aye, he'd looked at sheep, dared not. Not yet. He dared not hang and leave her.

Then it came to thieving. Which he did repent; yet cared not. Scant

enough scourings up here on Ask Moor. Back of beyond. A wary and a sken-
eyed folk, who cracked doors on long noses, clapped shut. High barred windows, hurtling dogs on chains. He'd eyed geese, but got none. Filched trifles.
Neeps and kindling and blue milk. Odd stockings. A smock for Thea, that
he'd had to crack, left cat-iced in a drying yard. Handfuls of oatmeal. Eggs
left for hobs.

Thin beggary and thinner shoes. More eyes, more spies, more calling
crows. More canting fellows on the road who turned and stared and mocked.
Their bold-eyed trulls, who called at Thea, crying out, *Brave rags with us. And
hiring for thy hobby-horse.* And then a broadside flapping at a crossroads: *Lunish
runagates,* it said. A kitfox and her cull. So they'd left the high road for the hags
and thickets, laying up on the moors, in folds rough-thatched with heather,
ruined barns. And moving on.

Thea had changed: all bones and belly, swollen fingers. Swollen buds,
yet flagging, fretted and embrowned. A side tooth lost with knitting bones.
Younger and older both, she seemed: a crone who danced her poppet on her
knee and lulled it, and a wizened imp. Great belly and her scabby knees, her
cracked and bluenailed hands. Nor mortal, neither, but a changeling, with
that pinched white face, that goblin's shock of hair. Yet her bonefast beauty
stayed.

She was—not happy, no. Ecstatic. Danced like chestnuts on a shovel. Slept
scarce at all. Since harvest, so he'd thought her sunstruck. Moonsick then.
Now still, now restless as a cat in pattens, to and fro. Thrang as Throp's wife,
and at nothing, all hours of the sun and moon. Waking and working. So she
called it, her work. Poor lass. As good brew ale in eggshells.

"Is't witchcraft?" he had asked.

"Riddles," Thea said.

He saw her, crouching in her ragged smock, intent on patterning. Ah, hallows on us, but she'd made some wondrous things. All fleeting, left behind to
wind, rain, earth, as soon as made. Unharvested, unheld. She scattered.

Sticks, stalks, leaves and stones. A living hazel branch, lapped all in poppy
petals, blood and branching. Leaves picked and shaded in a long streak on the
earth: from green through fire to dead black; from ashes to greenwhite. Twigs
in a round rattle. Labyrinths of leaves, bark, foxfire punk; or drawn in rime.
Spirals of cracked pebbles, scratched white with another. Cubbies of sticks.
Snailings and green horns of leaves, or burnished brown as copper: stitched
with thorns and plaited in one endless coil and spiral, nestled in the earth.

Leaves laid round nothing, bright and brighter toward the O. The same, with pebbles, white and whiter round abyss or origin.

One day he'd found her wading in a beck for more smooth stones, her apron full. In frost. Wet through and blue and shivering. And would not come with him until he'd waded in.

A night and day spent weaving stalks, an airy web of them, infilling all the crook and curving of a great low bough.

And in brief snow, a ball of it, built round and pierced by sharp small living wood. A ball that rolled its own maze, green laid bare; that rounded on its journeying.

O ever and alas, my Thea. O my dearest girl, my love.

Stark mad.


Ah, Margaret, I did make new heavens of the earth. Cast out of that cold sky in which my lucid soul was stringed, I did undo myself, redo: not Thea of the braided hair, but tangly Thea, tattery Thea, Thea of the grubby knees who crouched and plaited in a tinker's petticoats. I was inventing a new magic, for the old was lost with my virginity, with my immortal maidenhead. Oh, I was changing, changing fearfully; yet rounding with thy whiteheart self was Thea: we were sisters, twinned like cherries on a stalk.

O that was ragged bliss, that autumn. What I put my hand to, twisted of itself. Beyond astonishment, I did and did. Would lie but barely in the white of dawn. Wake new-inspired. Rise and work, outdoing what outdid the last, and of that latest making least again, transcending old with new. O Margaret, had I but lived, I would have lived so still: that whirling joy, that weaving steady hand.

Carriwitchets, Kit would say.

He'd come and go and bring his hard-won sticks of firing, his stock of provender, prigged rags; would sit and watch. Would coax me, bid me eat or sleep. I felt him sometimes at my shoulder: awed, exasperated, fearful. Dawning with delight. He kept the horn of leaves until it crumbled into dust.

I worked in what I had to hand, could gather. Sticks, stalks, leaves and stones. All found, unbound and scattering after. I was profligate as frost, as fern. As autumn, lavish, that does set a tree, a wood of trees, ablaze: a thousand thousand tongues to speak one word. As curious as nature's self, whose rarest work is secretest, embow'ring stars within bright clouds of stars, and seed in seed.

It was the raspberries began it.

In that cup of imbers did I spell thy blood: nine drops that would unbind my lady's will of thee. Set time going in her very stronghold. Yet I made no breach for thee in her shrewd hedge, but set a riddle for thyself alone. I would not have thee ride another's soul away. Walk barefoot, bloodfoot, if needs must: not use another creature, no, not Morag's dog, as I did Kit.

For the rest, 'twas winding spells, thyself thy clew. End and journeying and end, all rounded in a ball. Thine A and O.

Yet was I naked to the sky. I had no studied craft, no witchery, against my mother's furies, that would fall and rend. No roof.

In weaving of the garland, I had whispered secrets with that seely witch, that green unhallowed Malykorne. *No hallows until hallows,* she had said. As she, so I would be unhoused until her sister waked and hunted. Annis. If I could but win to Hallows—

So it came to stones. I strove, as Kit did, only to go on, to live and keep us until then. I had a garnet ring to stand for thee, that was a child's. I wish thou couldst have had it. Eight stones clustering about a ninth, a knot of seeds of blood. Much like the pomegranate I once found, that split and spilt within my hand. The riddle ring for Kit. And for myself, a ring like rain on gossamer, like cobwebs bright with dew. Nine Weaving. With my absence in't, the stone of Perseis I'd lost. Not wandering, but a falling star: astonishing and gone.


Her rings were woven in her fantasies. Her trash. One slid along a blade of grass, a small ring for her fingertip, a knot of drops of blood; another dangled from a scarlet thread, like rain in gossamer.

"Thea. Are there others?"

"Three. I have them safe." And showed her hand.

She would not give them over, though he begged and ranted, reasoned and cajoled, ah, coaxed her as he would a moonsick child to leave her toys. Her babywork. Alas, her wits waned even as she rounded. A greensick girl, and breeding. "Thou'rt worn, dear heart, beyond thy strength. Shouldst have a featherbed, a woman by thee. Physick."

"Wilt take them of me sleeping?"

"No," he said. "Not ever." And he came and knelt by her, he stroked her urchin head, he rubbed her nape. Inside his shirt, thrice-knotted round his wrist, the serpent of his cunning sleeked and shone. What's done is done, he thought. I rue me of that cheat. "Ah, that undoes."

He wanted her assent.

"For thine own sake, Thea."

Silence. And the twist and glittering of toys.

"Aye, scatter stones at scarecrow brats, leave none for thine own child."

Thea sat back on her heels, smudged her brow with her muddy wrist. "Ah, it comes."

Or softly, with his hands clasped round her belly. "Plum and stone." A rippling, as the round girl dived, down-dolphined in her eggshell ocean. "Sweet my love, thy lass wants nurture. Curds and cream. And swaddling. Thou hast not a clout for her."

At last, beyond all patience, starved and crazed with fear for them, he cracked her fist, uncurled her fingers from her hoard. Stone inward, she had worn them. Wore their imprint still, like Annis' kiss.

She had not cried out. He stood appalled; yet could not stay at that: put down the rings, caress the stone-bruised hand, so rudely forced. Could not undo.

"Thea?"

"As it must be."

He went out.

The door was warped with rain, white-molded. Margaret pushed until it gave upon an empty room, a tower that a storm had wracked. Bare muted walls, smashed glass; and in the naked window, for the first time, sea-blink. O. For a time she gazed at it and wondered; then she turned. Naught else but a daw's nest down the chimney, scattered sticks and trash. She bent and stirred it; she unwove. Smashed eggshells. Sticks and mutes. A key. A pebble. And a bent black ring. She thumbed it, rubbed it in her apron, peering at the outworn letters. This way and that in the wintry light. All gone but a word. *Lightwode.*

A voice in the air said, "Margaret."

That voice she knew; had heard it, ravelled with the wind, the sea. Not always. Since her doll was burnt, her dark-browed lulling nurse—O Norni—taken to her death. 'Twas now and nowhere, like a gossamer, at first: a glint and gone. Was now her galaxy. Her ground. As tangled in her thought as roots in earth, that flower seldom, yet inhere. But never until this aloud. *Is't you?*

"Thy daemon. Thou hast found the last, the lost star of the Nine, and overlooked. The one too quick for the eye."

Dusk. Late autumn, toward Hallows. Headlong on the road between Cold Law and Soulsgrave Hag, Kit hurtled. Three rings clenched in his right hand, thrust deep within his pocket; shame and fury at his heels. He knew not where he went. To Annis. Or to town. What town? Blind desperate, and pinched with argument and care, intent as a cat at kindling, he knew not where he was. The same place, always, the faster he ran. Round went the millstone, and over turned the wheel. *No bread, she has no bread. I had to. Anything they'd get. Bread, firing. One now, the others one by one. Bread, firing, a baby's coats. Ah, fool, a flock of sheep, a sheepwalk.* Fell and mutton, fleece and milk. He saw their lass run barefoot on the sward. Red hair, like fires on the hills. And round again: *no bread.*

He was at the crossroads before he saw the gang. A cronying of crows. Too late, he was among them. A slouching spade-faced man, whiteheaded, all in black, greenblack and broken swagger, like a swung cock at a fair. A gallows poll, that head, like hemp unravelling. Three trulls a-dangle at his heels. They fleered at Kit; they jostled. Cawed. A black mort, with a blue and scornful eye, her breasts at her kerchief bare and bruised. "Here's game," she said. "A goslin," said a pale and sluttish drab. Pissed petticoats and trodden shoes. And Maudlin-drunk, or mad. He swung. A ranting, taunting, roaring girl, a striding and a ride-moon doxy in a soldier's cap and feather, with his long sword buckled at her side. Red shoes.

Tighter still, he clenched his hand. His knife. He'd left his knife.

He made to pass by.

"Lightwood?"

Kit walked on.

"Heard tell thou was asking at Jack Daw." Almost, he turned. "For a fiddle."

Daw had it out for him; he drew the bow. And at that wauling sound, Kit's soul was snared. He turned and looked. Old and curious, far older than his own had been; rubbed shining as a fallen chestnut, newly split from its green burr. It had a carven woman's head. He yearned for it. *A trade,* he told himself: *not bread but years of bread.* A livelihood. He slipped two rings from off his fingers, deep within his coat; held out a third. White-gemmed. Like fleeces heavy with the dew. "Fair trade."

"What's this? Cuckoo-spit?" said Daw. "That, thy long knife, and a knock at thy vixen. I's a fancy to red hair."

"White-faced bitch is breeding," said Cap-and-Feather. "Maggot spied."

"She's a tongue," said Black Mort. "Can use it."

Jack Daw fleered. "I like a brave bellyful. Stir pot wi' my flesh hook and mek brat dance."

Kit spat. "Crows eat thee. Cock and eyes."

"They do," said Jack Daw, smiling.

Kit tried to shoulder past, but the doxies mobbed him, like crows at an owl by daylight. Jack Daw plucked at the fiddle. "Thou has strings for it, and all." His fingers at its neck and belly. "Owt else in yon placket?" Kit's face gave him away. He knew it. Daw twanged a string. "Done, is it? Say, two rings." He watched hope flicker. "Two rings. And thou serve yon nest o crows—ah, they gape for it. Now. Here. I like a play."

"No," said Kit. "No more."

The drabs were all about him, taunting, lifting up their petticoats. White belly and black joke. Craws wi' beards. Against all his will, Kit felt a stirring. And a sickening. Hobthrust rose and danced. He stared. A black scut, and a shitten fleece. Old ling. Rustbrown, and the red blood trickling down by her knee.

A cruel hand caught his wrist, bent backward. Wried his arm round his back until the socket started and the cold sweat sprang. No breaking Jack Daw's hold. Sinewy as yew, he was, inexorable. The voice was wasp honey. "Come, then. A bargain. For t'sake o that night's game thy dam once gave me. Salt and sweet, insatiable. A blue-eyed witch." Doubt and horror. Daw touched his cheek, mock gently; bent and whispered in his ear. "How cam'st thou by my face?" Kit swayed. In that brief slackening, the old man knocked him backward, winded, to the ground. Cap-and-Feather pinned his arms and Daw knelt on his shoulder, set a knife across his throat. "Where's thy vixen earthed?"

Clack! goes the old year and the new year tumbles down.

Kit turned his face. Shut his lips.

"By my lady's name, it will go ill with thee."

Skirts about her waist, the Black Mort straddled him; she squatted and undid his breeches flap. "Here's a knocking i't cellar. Here's a bird flies up."

Pissabed danced wildly, she whirled and wobbled in the road, like a slowing, sleeping top.

Cap-and-Feather chanted. *"The wren, the wren, the king of all birds ..."*

"Caught i't furze," said Black Mort. She spat between thumb and fingers. Laid on.

Kit gasped.

*"Although he is little, his family is great ..."*

"Wring it neck," said Pissabed.

"Darkmans and glimmer," said Jack Daw. "My lady bids. Then do."

A voice from somewhere cried, "Hang craws!"

"Craws!" answered from the hills. And all the dogs of Soulsgrave took it up.

"Cut," said Jack Daw. "Prig and run."

Crack! Blind lightning blast, a whirl and burring through his skull.

No more.


Kit woke, rolled naked in a ditch. *Fiddle's wracked,* he thought. *Where's here?* Himself was lash and scratch and throbbing, ice and fever, and a dizzy thud behind his eye. Dragged through whins, he thought. And tumbled down a bank. *That green girl at my bow's end. At the dance. That horseman?* His hand moved gingerly. No, his good hand—one was lame. Cracked bagpipes in his side. A broken crown. Wet blood on his mouth. Not his. From Cap-and-Feather. From her other mouth. Remembering, he retched and strangled. Nothing in his gut to puke.

Nothing left.

No clothes.

No rings.

And at his wrist, no braid of Thea's. Sharper still than all his hurts, he felt that ring of absent fire.

Gone.


Whin said in the dark, "Went naked back?"

"I robbed a scarecrow of his coat." A clear night mocking him. The Hanged Lad ranting on Cold Law. As naked as himself. They'd left him with one broken shoe, in haste. Derision.

"So yer done that. Ta'en rings."

"I did."

"Lost braid."

"I did." That desperate searching in the dark. He'd had a crazed hope it was somehow lost, not stolen for an end. That he would find it, tossed aside as naught. In a small voice, he said, "I didn't tell her. That I had it. That it was gone."

"Round thy wrist? Had she not see'd it?"

"No. I thought. We'd not—we hadn't lain together. Not since harvest." He would not force her crazy innocence, not take his will of her. And yet he had.

Long silence.

"At the stones," said Kit. "At Imber Beck. That kiss she gave me was the first time. Of her will." He drew one ragged breath. "That other, freely. Not her love." He was crying. "One other time. The last. I never knew it was. I never knew."

Waking in the night. Hard ground. And Thea with her back to him, within his curve, and cradling his hand against her breast. Like a child her doll. He felt his ring there, on a thread; he felt her quick heart tap and tap, like a branch at a windowpane; he felt the round drum of her belly thud and kick. She smelled of smoke and Thea. Not asleep.

She spoke, not drowsily, but low. "Kit. I do love thee. Know that."

Blood in my lady's place. Blood on her smock. It would not come out.

Margaret hurried through the dark and winding hallways, down toward her room. No sanctuary there, no more than in a hare's slight form, the impress of her crouch; but licit. Blood, suddenly. A spattering of drops, no more. Herself she'd washed and washed, no trace or tinge of it was left. Flung the water from her sill. But her smock. Would find her out. Bury it? The dogs would out. Burn it? No fire but in my lady's study. Up the chimney? Blood will out. Ah. Cut herself and mingle. Knife. She had a knife.

Softly now. She lifted the latch.

Morag and my lady waited with a rod of juniper. "Straying, and thy book undone. Come, Madam."

Margaret curtsied, rose. "My lady."

"Closer, girl. I am no basilisk."

The hand with its great ring held the face: a sere unshaking hand; a white face, like a scrap of paper to be written over, like a mirror to be filled. "There is something of my daughter in you."

"Aye, the whore," said Morag.

"Alike in straying," said my lady. Still she held her gaze. "Chastise her."

"Thy vixen, Madam." And when Margaret made no move, the servant took her bedgown, pushed her smock to her armpits. Held her wrists and bent her back across the kist, her new breasts and her belly all disclosed, a gibbous moon. Thrust her legs apart.

Slow blood.

My lady spoke, a cold still fury in her voice. "And who undid that knot?"

Morag said, "Not art, I'll warrant, but the worm in her. Your glass is carrion."

"Is of my adamant. A blank, but that I grave her with my icon and my law. And offscum else: yet will transmute."

"Or spoil, as did her dam. Your poppet. Waiting on the stars."

Whiter still, my lady's face. "It will be done, and presently. By this moon's dark."

A catechism then.

"What was thy mother?"

"Your daughter," Margaret said.

"A whore. Which is?"

She knew not. "One who strays?"

"'Twill do. Puts carrion in Annis' place. Which is?"

"We name it not."

"That errant part, wherein thy mother did betray me."

"Crow's fee," said Morag, pinching. "And the vixen's earth."

Margaret endured. The crow's contemptuous, efficient hands; my lady's avid eyes. And even in her dread and terror, sick with shame, she thought, *Like Thea?*

Then the rod, and no more thought.

They left her on the floor, amid the fallen needles, the scattering of twigs.

My lady turned at the door. "It is time thou learned thy glass."

A key snicked in the lock.

For a long time she lay weeping in her dabbled smock. Blood with hidden blood.

No voice. She heard no voice.


Kit hurried, huddled in his flapping coat. It would snow by dark. Black moor, white sky; but knit, the whiteness tangled in the ground as rime, the blackness branching up as trees. A scant wood, leafless now. Sloes, rowans, all gone by. Firing. He bent to get sticks. It still was light; but stiffening towards dusk. Ravenwards. And Thea waiting, pacing in their roofless shieling, by the ashes of a hearth. She made cairns of stones. She did and she undid. He dared not leave her; they would starve without. No sticks to burn; no bread. A handful of dampish meal, half acorns, bitter as the wind.

The braid was gone. He saw it glinting everywhere.

There. In that bush. He stumbled toward it.

Gone.

He stood. He would have wept, if he'd remembered how. It was all too much, too much. He stood. Dazed, cold, defeated, sleepless, starved, light-headed, lousy. Fizzing with lice. His feet recalled him, white cold, wet; he'd blundered. Cat ice.

Looking down, he saw a tump in the marshy ground: a spring, turfed over, housed with three great stones. Kneeling, he touched the lintel of the low door, lichened; found the blind runes graven in the rock. *Help us,* he said to darkness, spinning out a thread of silver. *Lighten her, my love.* He touched the water. No one. In the wood beyond, a stormcock sang. No solace here. He rose. On a tree hung knots of rags, frayed, faded to the blue of a winter sky. Another sky, some other now or then, caught here. And in among the ravellings of sky, a rag of iris. Thea's scarf.


Kit. Margaret. Ah, you do not hear me. She is gone until her time comes round; she cannot let you in. No hallows anywhere. Not yet.


At the corners of their shieling, raised on cairns, Kit saw her barricade: spiked crowns and spirallings of ice, frail caltrops. Morning stars. He dropped his sticks and ran. From wall to ashes, wall to wall, he found her, pacing and clenching. Blood on her lip. Then something wrenched her, as a laundress would a rag.

"Thea. How long—?"

She caught his sleeve, his coat, as on a breaking ship. Another wrench and shudder. "Kit." Like burning wax, her face: it warped and ran. Almost Thea leapt from it, as flame from a candle, blowing out. "Undo it."

"Love?"

"Undo the knot," said Thea. "That braid you took of me. Undo it."

Still he stood.

"To let the child be born. I cannot lighten else. I cannot meet them."

*O sweet hallows on us.* "Gone," he said.

"What?"

"Taken. Gone."

"Ah no." A great cry, twisting.

"Thea—"

She whirled on him, white-fiery. "Run. Now."

"I'll not leave thee. I will not."

"For a woman's help. I die else." Wrench and leap. "Now. Get thee hence."

He turned at the threshold. "O my heart's love."

"Go."

No time, no time.

He ran.


Whin dreamed of ravens. An ill-chancy dream, an omen. Then a telling. A trance. She saw a girl still barely living, filthy, naked on the icy ground. Her childbed. Saw the stubble of red hair, the new milk seeping from her breasts. The glazing eyes. A witch stood watching her, a corbie perched upon her hand. She stroked its beard, she ruffled it; it preened the bracelet at her wrist, of braided fire. *Ah, the sweetest morsels for my chuck, my Morag,* said the witch. *The crow's fee and the eyes.* Down it flapped, it picked the tidbits. Still the girl breathed, the blood ran, the death cry rattled in her throat. Then the witch called down her crows. They clustered at the bloody womb. They tore.

Whin woke yelling.

Still Kit slept on. He twitched and whimpered. Whin sat up and shook with rage. She cursed the raven and the witch; she cursed the knife that loosed the child, the braid, the shears that cut it. Cursed her master mistress Brock who had entangled her in this atrocity, to see and see and see. Change nothing.

Then up she got, and ran down to the shingle, to the water's edge. She'd drown the soulbag, wash the ashes from her face. Walk inland. She would be no more death's journeyman. Running, she tore her rings off, death by death, to hurl them in the sea.

Brock stood between salt water and the strand. "I'd not do that," she said.

"Could yer not have let her live?" cried Whin. "Not see'd to it that she went wi' child, smick smack, afore she'd much as bled? Thou meddlesome. And all for nowt. A tale of Ashes."

"It's done, and long since done," said Brock.

"And nowt to do wi' me."

"And all to do." The sea swashed, swashed. "There's bairn."

*O thank hallows.* There, a woman with a lantern. Hale and canny, she looked: brisk, in pattens and a hood. Kit caught her apron. "My lass. Please. Needs a woman by her." And she raised her candle, looking through him with a smile would scoop apples, a shankbone smile—I know two of that—and turned away. Up the fell.

He ran after. "Pity on us. For the love—"

Another crossed the trod. A sonsy girl, a goosedown girl and slatternly, who bore a flat candlestick, as if she tumbled up to bed. "Miss—? Can lead me to a midwife? My lass—" She blinked and giggled, turned away.

Another and another still. All with candles, all the girls and women of the dale end, lating on the hills. Now there, now elsewhere in the cloudy dark, as if they danced *Nine Weaving*. Round they turned like children in a game, a-bob and wheeling, in and out, through bushes and through briars. They were seeking with their candles—*lambs at Hallows? Birds' nests?* They were sought.

Hide fox, and all after.

As in a dream, Kit ran from one to the next, imploring, and they turned from him. None would speak. They shook their heads: some smiling, some pitying or shocked or scornful; some averting their eyes.

A weeping man, half naked, in a Bedlam coat.

One tossed a coin.

A knot of them, their backs turned. Gossips. Blindly, hopelessly, he touched a sleeve. "I beg of you—" A stone. A ring of them, like crones in cloaks. But one stone turned, the hood fell back. It was a woman with a darkened lantern, waiting, gazing out: like a sailor for landfall, like a scryer at eclipse. He was a gull at her masthead, a dog at her skirts: no more.

Down the fell, a light went dark. Another, upwind, and a girl knelt, doing up her shoe latch, looking round. And yet another, pinning up her hair. All waiting.

One by one, the candles all went out.

But one.

A child this woman, sheltering a dying candle in a tin. She brooded fiercely on it, willed it. In its doubtful glow, her face was rapt and shining. Awed. Her first time on the fells? Her flame lurched sideways, righted, leapt again. The last?

From up the fell, a voice called, *Ashes! We's Ashes!*

O the last. As her candle flickered out, she whirled for joy.

Another and another voice took up the cry, like vixens, greenfire in their blood. Hallooing to the dark of moon. *Ashes!* They were running now, a rout of women, whirling torches in the kindled dark. And still the child wheeled, giddy, in among the stones, the only silence. *Ashes!*

And alone, but for the ragman. She took to her heels.


I tell this to the air; yet I must speak.

My mother fed me to her crows, she burned my bones and scattered them; my braided hair she keeps. By that bright O of fire did she call me back from life to Law; by those shrewd knots torment me. She would not undo. Seven weeks she watched me naked, travailing from Hallows until Lightfast eve; then Morag's knife did let thee crying from my side, and I was light.


Margaret knelt and pried a stone up in the hearth; she dug. From under it, she took a ring, a clew of thread. A key.


Turning back from the stones, Kit saw the fire at their fold and ran, calling, stumbling on his whiteblind feet. He saw the ravens falling from the sky. One, another, turning women as they fell. They were clear as night, and starless;

where their wings beat back the thronging air was cloud and fire. As they touched the earth, it whitened, widening from their talons of the frost. They shrank as small as stones.

Kit fell. A thrawn hand caught him, and another, and a throng. Horned feet kicked through him like a pile of leaves; they scattered him like sparks. "Out!" he cried and struggled, held and haled. A torch was thrust at his face. There were witches all round him: men and crones, in black and rags of black, and goat fells, stiff with blood. They bore a cage of thorns and withies, hung with bloody rags and hair, with flakes of skin: the palms of children's hands, like yellow leaves, a-flutter.

Empty.

"Here's a fool," said one, a warlock.

"A soul," another said. A hag, all pelt and bones. The soulstones clattered in her hank of hair, with knops of birdskulls, braided through the orbits.

"A soul, a soul," the guisers cried.

Kit fought against their hands. "You let me go."

"You let us in," they chanted. "Let us in your house of bone."

And a man like a staghead oak, a blasted tree, cried, "Room!"

A tall witch with a great black fleece of hair flung back came striding through. It was a man, pale and sneering in a woman's robe, his strong arms naked to the shoulders, dark with blood. Death's midwife. Or a blasphemous Ashes?

"Annis!" they cried. "Annis wakes."

He prodded Kit with his staff. "What's this? A blindworm?"

"For your breakfast, my lady."

"For your bed."

"'Tis Ashes' bawd."

The stick against his throat had silenced him, half strangled him. He saw a black wood rising; it was leaved with faces. Thronged with crows.

"Bags I," said a voice.

The crowd parted. Kit saw a figure in a leathern cap, a coat of matted fleece. Ashes of juniper, a cloud of ashes at his eyes and lips. It whispered in his ear. "Thou's not to die for her," said Brock. "Thy lass did say."

"No," he tried to say. His mouth was full of ashes, he was blind with snow.

"Now," said Brock. "An thou will." And kissed his mouth.

He felt a tremor, a wind in his bones. She covered him like snow. Beneath

the sway of stars, he felt the green blades pierce his side, the awned heads
bow and brindle in the reaping wind. A sickle gathered him, a sheaf. Time
threshed. His chaff was stars, his bones were blackness, strung and shining. A
sword, a belt of stars. A crow called.

Then he knew no more.

Hallows morning.

Kit awoke on the hillside in the falling snow, all white and shades of white,
but for the black unkindly stones. After a time, he could stand, could hobble.
Halt and dazzled with the snow, and inch by crippled inch, he made his way
back to their shieling. Knowing what he'd find. Dread knowing.

Gone.

And more than gone. Pulled stone from stone, and torched and trampled
in a great wide circle, salt with snow. Cold out. All her toys.

"Go," she'd said. And so he'd gone.

He would have died for her.

He fell to his knees where their hearth had been, the ashes at the heart
of ashes. Nothing left: all taken, lost, betrayed. But there, a something like a
wren's dulled eye, its dead claw, in the snow. A ring. Not hoarded, so not lost.
He scratched for it, and found the other; turned them in his fingers. Blood
and tears.

Margaret knelt amid cold ashes, drawing mazes on the hearth. They'd left no
book to her, no ink, no candle: whips of juniper to gaze on, and the drowsy
wine. My lady's glass, which was black adamant: she could not break.

And so she did what she had left to her: undid. Ate nothing they had given
her, but dwindled out an orange she had kept, a heel of bread; drank snow
from her window sill. She worked by scant starlight at the puzzle of her cage.
Scrawled figures with a stick of charcoal; rubbed them out, redrew them, all in
black upon the hearthstone, what was white with snow without: the labyrinth
of yew and stone. If she did journey, she could not rub out.

So then: for her door, she had the jackdaw's key; then came the maze she
would unriddle and the hedge of thorn, the wintry sea. The world. Beyond
that, she could see no way. A ship? But only to have touched the sea, washed
Morag from her skin; to glimpse a world unbounded by my lady's walls. She

set herself to reach the sea. The garden was configured as the starry sky; that much she knew, had read her book beside the white girl crowned with leaves, with leaves and flowers in her stony lap. And water running down and down her face: it wept for her, who could not weep. Bound Ashes, in a box of yew.

She knew now what she was; what she was for. *A hole to fill,* said Morag truffling. *Naught else.* Yet had my lady smiled and pinched. *A limbeck. See, how sweetly she distills.* Had kissed: how scornfully, and yet had lingered. It was almost a caress. The bracelet burned against her skin. *I have sent to fetch thee a rare dowry. Dishes for thy maiden banket; jewels for thy chain. Thy first shall be thy father's soul.*

For a long time afterward, Margaret had sat, and turned and turned the hidden cards.

O the Nine, ah yes, the Nine would come and carry her away. She heard the clatter of their wings; she saw them, children of the rising light, like swans. Her heart rose up. Being mute, she could not cry to them; they lighted, children as they touched the earth, but a glory of their wings about them, like a snow. *Sister, come with us,* they said. *I will,* said Margaret's heart, *but have no wings. No ship.* And turned it up: that Ship whose mast is green and rooted, flowering as stars. And then bright Journeyman, the thief.

A rattle in the keyhole. A black stick on the floor. She'd risen to it, curtsied, with the cards behind her: all in haste. But three had fallen from her lap like leaves; their tales had withered at my lady's glance. *See, thou hast overlooked the Tower. That takes all.* The witch had stooped for it, mock-courteous, and held it to her branching candle; dropped it burning to the floor. *And which next shall I take? Thy cockboat? Or thy nest of geese?* Her gaze schooled Margaret's; they would bind her if she flinched. *Thy choosing, Madam. It will make a game.*

*The Hare.* My lady's wrist was bare, no braid.

*Aha, the Master Lightcock. Thou'rt seed of his, didst know? Shall watch him burn. And my sweet crow shall have his stones, to bait her dogs withal.* Then she had signed to Morag with the box. *Undo.*

And after they had gone.

It seemed that someone else took over, swift and secret, while the old lost Margaret sat, dreaming in a drift of cards. *Thou timorous, thou creeping hodmandod,* she thought: *thou snail that tangles in her trail of dreams. Draw in thy tender horns? Thou liest between the thrush and stone.* That other self, herself, had thought of riding, light a horseman as the moon; her mantle of the flying silver, fleeting on the wind. But now her new shrewd voice said, *Shoes and stockings, stout ones. In that room with the sea-chests. Thou needs must walk. Will need the way.*

And so she sat, and drew what she remembered of the labyrinth, the doors.

"No ship," said Kit. "When thou didst come on me, and take me up from drowning, there had been no ship. No storm. I'd gone in after her."

"I know," said Whin. "But thou was not to follow her. Thy lass did spell for thee."

"Not drown," said Kit. "I know. I am for hanging in yon braid. That I did twist myself."

"What for?" said Whin. "Thou's never telled."

"To hold fast." Kit clasped his hands, unclasped. "Ah, not to Thea—what I loved in her I held like moonlight in a sieve, I riddled rainbow. 'Twas a falling star, that nowhere is and yet is light. No, what I braided was a face she turned to me, a mask: that lady who did run away with me, did overturn her fortune for my sake. Mine own. The moon that turned and turned from me, yet bent within mine orb. Thought I. So kept that vanity, that she did shear. At first." A silence. "And after, I would keep myself, as I had thought I was. Would be. That Kit who called down witches with his airs. Not Thea's bow-stick, but a one who played." He bit his lip; looked up. "And she owed me a fiddle, I did tell myself. No matter; yet it rubbed. And at the last—moon blind me—I could not endure to tell her of my folly."

Whin passed the cup. "What now?"

"If not for Thea's sake, yet I will die, as all must die. And I would live ere then." A something lightened in his face. "And see our lass."

Asleep. Thy cards lie scattered on the floor, in knots and wheels, and painted gatherings. I cannot turn them. There, the Ship and the Rattlebag, the Hanged Lad and the Nine. Burnt Eldins. Ashes. And the Crowd of Bone: that fiddle that the old year plays of Ashes, of her bones. They strung it with her long bright hair. Itself and all alone, it sings, its one plaint always: of her death. Sings truth in riddles.

In a tale, thou Margaret wouldst brave my lady, even in her glass. Wouldst find my nine bones that were left; unbraid my hair and string the fiddle for thy father's hand to play. And thou wouldst dance to it, his daughter and my death. And down the witch would tumble, burning, in her iron shoes.

But I have sung my tale. Unstrung myself. Have told out all my thread but this, the endknot: they were always one, the braid that bound us and the strings that spoke.

Thou canst not hear the ghost now, Margaret: thou art child no more.

But thou art Margaret, thyself: no witch's blade can rive that knot intrinsicate we knit for thee, of love and pain. Thou art the daughter of my heart's blood and my soul. Bone of my bone, and heartstrings of my heart. To Kit I would restore thee: not his fiddle but my heart, translated. Not for him to play, but thou to dance for him, to sing thine own tale always, light and dark.

"So," said Whin. "Yer off."

They stood by her coble, sunk in snow to the black rim, as a mussel shell in sand. A white morning, toward Kindle Wake.

"I'll set thee on," said Kit.

Together, they dug out her boat and laded it; they pushed it down the blackweed shingle, salt and frost, to the water's edge. A wave crisped his boot. But only one. The tide was turning outward.

They clipped hard, clapped back and shoulder.

Kit said, "Thou ask at my daughter."

"And thou at my son," said Whin.

"I will that. Farewell."

Then they pushed her black coble into the sea. As it slipped, Whin leapt the gunwales; locked oars. It rode the swell, it hove. The next wave took her out. Kit watched from the shore. Whin rowed easily, strongly, turning only just to check her heading. Luneward. And to Law.

So they parted.

Kit took up his scant gear, new and raw. A knife, a cloak, a cookpot, and a flint and steel. Grey worsted stockings and a harden shirt. A stone in his pocket, with a leaf on it. He set out on his journeying; turned inland, in the snow.

I am walking, to the knees in earth: long-toed, reaching, rough of knees; gnarled wrists knotted, flowering at fingers' ends. They see, though I am blind. White, wet, my petals fall and fleck—like moons, like childing moons—my cold black bark. My lap is full of snow. In winter do I bear the misselbough, the Nine, entangled in my crown.

I was Ashes.

I am rising from the dark, and rooted; I am walking from my mother's dark.

My green leaves speak in season, in their turn, unfolding word by word till all is green and silent, lost in green, unselved. The green is wordless, though it spells the earth, it sings the wind. Rooted, I dance, unbraided to the wind. And then by leaf and leaf, I turn, take fire and prophesy. They spill, a tale of leaves, of endless leaves. My green is no one, everywhere, as wood as love; my age is selving. In my nakedness, I crouch and listen.

See, where I am split, my belly seamed. A curved blade caught me; I was reft. Yet I do bear, I ripen, plum and stone. They hang, my sloes, world-dark as winter nights, abloom with souls. They fall and sunder, worm and root.

I stand among a grove of girls. A garland, woven all of Ashes.

Touch my bark and I am elsewhere, though my lyke is earthfast, here and now. Break wood and I will burn. Do you see me? Now and nowhere, turning nowhere, telling light. But I am not my tongues. I rise with my sisters, woven in our dancing, scarved in light. We are pleached in an endless knot, an alley, in a cloud of stars: a hey as white as hag.

All ways led upward: not a door would let her to the wicket gate, the garden, to the maze that she would solve. She'd brought the clew to measure it; had sopped her manchet in the drowsy wine to brave the dogs withal. A hard frost glittering on snow: she'd hoped to leave small trace. Thin shoes, no mantle. She had only what was hidden left to take: the key, the clew, the ring. Her ravaged cards. Nine burnt.

No door. And higher still. A window? Could she get a wren's-eye view of it? Could draw it then. *Thou mole*, she thought. *'Tis black of night.* Moondark, so my lady and her raven hunted souls, and thought she slept. How long until they came to wake her? Found her gone? Dread struck her like an ice-axe to the shattered heart. *Go on*, she said, in darkness. All among her shards. *Old mole. 'Tis nowhere here. Get on.* Lightless, breathless with enormity, Margaret wound the stair.

She pushed through a last door, out onto the leads in snow. *O heavens.* Round she wheeled, within the greater wheel of stars.

The wood above.

That she had forfeited. Pasteboard and precious tawdry, turned celestial. All burning, unconsumed.

She'd never seen the stars at once; had learned them from her slit of window, from my lady's iron hoops, her brazen spheres. Her stones that hopped from perch to wire, dish to wire, like a cage of singing birds. But these were glorious: they flamed amazement in her eyes.

Giddy with the sky, she turned, until her breath had blinded her. Then she wiped her glazy spectacles, and stood and stargazed.

Knot by shining knot, she made them out—the Nine, the Hallows Tree, the Ship—yet wondered even in her wonderment. *But why a Ship? Why not a ladle or a swan? Why not bare stars, themselves? And why Nine Weaving? There are stars in clouds of stars, as if I breathed on frost. And which is the lost star of the Nine, amid so many?* She looked for the sisters, jumping edgewise in her slanted sight. Ah, she wished for those spectacles she'd found and left, that made the candle huge. They tangled in and out of focus, in a country dance, a hey. Five, a cloud of silver, three, four. Gone again.

And one bright planet threading through the maze. Like a knife round an apple, all askance. Or like a lantern through a labyrinth. *O yes.* Clasped hands flying to her lips: she bit them, so as not to cry out loud for joy. And ever after, when the Nine were named, she tasted rime on rough wool, and the oil of orange in her nails. *Yes.* The garden was the quickset stars. The key was errant: Perseis, and in her night house, at the wake of Souls. The Crowd of Bone. Those stars ascendant at her mother's birth.

She saw the way.

Down and round she ran, still downward with the falling spindle of the stairs, that twirled the heavens to a clew of light. That other chain, the necklace that she wore, broke loose in running, whirled and scattered on the steps. She left it as it fell. As later, in the time to come, she would outrun the world of her begetting, scatter it behind like leaves: her glass would crack my lady's heavens, would unstring the stars.

Margaret ran on.

# THREE: UNLEAVING

## Nine Weaving

When a star falls, we do say: *the Nine are weaving. Look!* The Road's their skein, that endlong from the old moon's spindle is unreeled. Their swift's the sky. *O look!* says Margaret. The children of the house gaze up or glance. The namesakes. *Look thou, Will. Look, Whin. They stitch your daddy's coat.* The twins, still whirling in the meadow, seem as heedless as the light, as leaves. Now one and now the other one, they tumble down and down the slope, lie breathless in the summer grass. *His mantle's of the burning gold,* says Whin; and Will, *His steed is January. I'm to have his spurs.*

Bright-lipped in her bower of meadow, imber-stained, small Annot gazes. She is like bright Annot fled; is like herself. *I've counted seven for the Ship. Like cherrystones. I've wished.*

*What Nine?* says Tom.

*Why, sisters in a tower—see yon smutch of silver, where it rises? Back of Mally's Thorn?*

He studies. *Aye. And stars in it. Like kitlins in a basket.*

*Their house. It is a nursery of worlds.*

*Is't far?* says Annot. *Can I walk there?*

*Not by candlelight,* says Margaret. *'Tis outwith all the heavens, sun and moon. I'll show thee in my glass.* But she is elsewhere now, remembering the Road beneath her, and the heavens that her glass undid. Remembering the Nine, the sisters at their loom of night.

And now, as once they ever did, they cast the shuttles, swift as memory, to and fro; they weave the green world and the other with a mingled skein. Leafgreen, light and dark, the lifeblood, and that other thread too quick for seeing. All that's fleeting is their weft: the wind in grass, the wavespell where it meets the rippling sand. Cloud shadow on the corn. They weave the spindrift and the wreathing snow, the whorl uprising in the fallen leaves, the spiring of the flame. Whatever's here and gone. Breath, body, and that *I* that wakes to dream—sleaved out, as light in rainbow ravels into air. What they do undoes.

But Ashes tells the warp. My lady's daughter—aye, herself that walked the longways out of winter—she, and all that wear her coat. Free maids, that weave their thread with bones.

We are storied in their web. Not held: our shadows, not our selves inwarped. We dance above it, like the light on water, like fireflies aslant the summer grass.

## May Margaret

Grey-cloaked, the skein of sisters wind the stair. Nine lanterns halo them, now mingling, now distinct; and in and out, like dancers in a dance. Wicksilver. At the sill, the eldest turns and lifts her candle, beckoning. Light spills through her fingers, stills her face. She draws her hood to shadow it. Without a word she turns from earth and swings the sightless door. No stair. And yet they mount on a spiral of sky, as if the faultless air were crystalline, were cracked. One by one, still climbing into air, they—

*Sisters?*

Rose and faded.

Air.

Earthbound, Margaret stood amid a silent throng, cloaked grey as ashes, emberless. The dancers banished from the dance, the earthfast stars. They look still toward morning and can find no stair.

*O sisters.*

Cold as stone, as silent.


Margaret woke amid a circle of grey stones and saw the spring stars fading into morning. Last and fairest, rising at the hem of day, she saw bright Perseis amid the Nine, with sleighting Brock, all tangled with a wraith of moon. One glyph: a riddle beyond rede, a rune of light. The stars at her nativity, her second birth. It dazed and dangled, like a cobweb set with dew; like a snarl of stuff from a celestial workbox. Her clew.

She gazed until it drowned in light.

A bird spoke, sleepily. And only then, she saw the wide world tilted at her feet. She was standing at the twelve winds' nave: the fellies of the wheel were hills. All round her, shade beyond shadow, dusk and blue, lay Cloud.

Too great to compass: she had never been unwalled. She laid a hand, a cheek, against rough stone to steady herself. *O,* she thought giddily, *it is the sky below.* She knew the charted heavens as she did her A and O; she had no map for this bewildering earth, but turned about her for a bearing. All unskied. She saw—not one Road but an interlace, an eddering of light. A maze. She saw a wood unrooted, floating in a lake of sky, of blue beyond the rainbow's edge. She saw a spark of fire like a falling star: a harbinger, a brand. *The Sun is in the Thorn at Ninerise.* Sun? In turning, she had lost her north. No stars. But counter to her whorling sprang a pale of fires on the hills, a wheel of suns. Even as she swung about, their light was swallowed in a nothingness, a chill white mist. At once she was lank with it, spangled and amazed.

Behind she heard a clank and rattle, and a horned thing sprang away. Startled, she cried out and reeled from it. And now a stone had shifted, dwindling. Standing in her way, it crooked a knee to her, it spoke.

"My lady?"

Stone still. All about them, fires dying on the hills.

Before her stood a small crookshouldered person in a coat and breeches, all in deadleaf brown. He bowed to her as to the new moon, louting low; then raised his shining, streaming face, his hair in ratstails. He spoke again in the old tongue, haltingly.

"My lady?"

"No," said Margaret, appalled. "No."

He flinched. He had a waning look, this apparition. "Lady, by this hand, if I offend you ..."

Still as a candle, gathering her will to run; then startling. "That?"

A grey ghost blaring in the mist.

"Ah. That. A sheep: no fellow." Still his bended knee to her. "Have you no company beside, no rade? No others of your folk?"

All about them, fires dying on the hills. A huddle of grey stones behind.

"They leave us," he said softly. Then, "How came you from this hillside?"

*Waking?* All behind her and before was cloud. They stood within a burr of morning, now and here. A bubble. "Oh ..." Now she saw his broad hat wreathed in flowers, violets and wood anemones, as fair as any painted book. But real, as blood is real, or feathers.

Gently, warily, he took the garland and held it out to her. She made no move. He crowned her unbent head, so carefully she felt no touch but green.

Stepped back and swept another bow. "I bid you good morrow, lady. Hallows with ye."

*Caught with flowers,* she thought. Spellbound.

Turning to the quick of day, he spoke as to himself: "... his fury's in the fall of leaf. Then scatt'ring of his wits, poor Tom lies naked in the slough, and shakes against the frost and February of his desolation. Being wood, the spring's his ecstasy, o'erspilling dark. His dreams do prick him and he flowers."

A hill aside of them—O marvellous—a blade of sunlight glinted like a sword unsheathing, raised in accolade. It slashed the silver to a sleave of rainbow. Mantle and scarf. It struck a flowering tree to mist and dazzle. A wonder: a cloud full of thorn. The birds woke shouting with joy.

And it was all too much, too much. The air was full of voices clamoring, hail-sharp; the light, white-fiery, furious: a glare as of unbroken lightning or the blinding of unbodied snow. A dazzlement, a tempest—

*Thea? Did you know all this?*

And still he touched her not, and still she felt his garland like a crown of hail.

She stirred and shivered.

He did off his coat and held out it to her. "It strikes cold at first," he said, in Cloudish now. *I thank you, no,* she said, with palm out-turned and bended knee; yet glanced at him, her hand against the doubtful sun, the water running down her face. They were of a kind, she saw—*like sister and like brother*—but his squirrel-red hair was faded. There were tufts of grey in it and squinches round his hazel eyes. "No place for a lass here alone." He gestured at the circling smudge of fires, at the revels. "They do make green gowns."

*They?*

"That bring the summer in."

In memory, she turned a card, now lost: the Rainers. Grave but joyful came a band of nymphs, the deer-legged votaries of Annis, who leapt and clashed with long braids flying, dark and fiery and fair. Still children. Cold as April: moon-cold crescent girls. On a pole wound Maywise with ribands, they bore the loveliest of garlands: hoops fixed crosswise in an orb, wound with ivy, crowned with flowers, trailing tendrils like a thyrsus. In it hung a Lady made of grass, a rake of grass blades in her hand. Reaper to herself, the mower mown.

Just then the grass bowed and darkened in a flaw of wind; white petals

fell. A cold bright rain drenched down and drifted on. Stunned and shivering,
Margaret raised her eyes to watch its ragged skirts retreating, grey and gleam.
As if the squall had rubbed away the tarnish of the night, the hills were green.
They ran with silver: tumbling becks and falls.

A voice on the hill cried, like an ember falling. "Craw's hanged!"

And voices echoed, hallooing. "Craw's hanged!" The rout was coming now,
by twos and threes, running down from the fellsides: toused and tangled, car-
rying great boughs of green. No silvery maids. Rough lads and rantipoles, a
sort of vixens and a sloth of bears. "Hey's down!"

No cover.

"Back way," said the stranger. Downward, sheer. The path was no more
than a sheen on grass, a flaw like bruised velvet. She wondered he could tread
so nimbly in this hail of light. Skidding and stumbling, she could manage her
water-heavy skirts, no more. Fell, slathered to the knee and scraped, yet shying from his proffered hand; went on. The flaw became a runnel, the runnel a
trod, deep-sunken in the hillside, set thwartwise with stones. On either side, a
foam of flowers, wild and delicate and rank. Deep hedgerows. Thrawn trees,
shock-headed, throwing roots across her path. At a stile, she looked back. *Oh.*
It pierced her heart with green, this world. This spring. The stones were out
of view, as vanished as the morning stars, the rainbow ravelled into cloud.
That door, that bridge were gone.

Sheer morning. Now the drystone walls turned hedges, the trod to churned
mud. They came through intakes to an onstead, barn and byres and a cross-
winged hall. In the courtyard, at the studded door, she balked. Locks and keys
again, another cell? In from all this ruthless beauty, into easeful dark?

As she wavered, the revellers came down on them like rooks that mob a
daystruck owl. Clawed creatures, raucous and hilarious, flown with ale. They
clustered and they cawed. Margaret shrank against the wall, hands crossed
before her face. Her fellow set hand to his hilts; yet spoke them fair enough,
if sharp.

"Here's silver for your sport. Away and dance." He cast a handful, scattering and shining.

But they cried, "In, summer! Let us in."

Like daws: and she a thing of glass. *Here's pretty.* If she fled them, they would
hunt. Eyes fixed upon the stranger's back, she fought her panic down. *Here's patterning. A covert in his coat.* Green leaves brocaded in the deadleaf silk, half seen,
and peering broideries of flowers, white and violet. A spring upwelling.

Some at back were elbowing and gawping; whispering behind their hands. *Thou ask. Nay, thou.*

A man doffed his broad hat, civil enough. "Morn t'ye, Master. Catched a hare?"

Wary; yet his fence was words. "I hunt not by the dark of moon."

"Then ye mun bring a candle," said a woman. "And t'moths will fly to it."

And another wench called out to Margaret, "Singed thy petticoats?"

From the back of the rout, a taunting voice said: "Singed *his* petticoats, more like."

White hand on the sword hilt. "Go your ways. Here's naught of your concerning."

"Nay, by yer leave, sir," said a woman, "our discerning's May. We bear it; ye mun bid us in."

"And if she bear it, then 'tis luck," said another with a rainwet garland on a staff, and shook it so the poppet danced. The water on the leaves rained down on Margaret. "Here's green to halse ye and this hall."

And half the revellers began confusedly to sing, a clash of carols.

But a high voice, hoarse with chanting, sang, "Me petticoat is lost, I left it at me granny's ..."

A marrow-deep bass took it up, "But I'll fetch it back i't morning ..."

"Peace, all on yer." In the doorway stood a woman in a cap and pattens, tall, ungarlanded, a box of bonefire in her hands. Down the long dark hall behind her stood another door, wide open to the silvery green. Bobbing, they swung to her, silenced. Keys at her belt. Was her courtier and captor huntsman to this lady? Margaret sank into a deep obeisance. A girl tittered. "That'll do," said Cap and Pattens, and quirked her chin upward. Margaret rose. Pattens turned to the men and maids. "Cold by t'door; come, speak thy piece." And at her beckoning, the garlander stood forth, rosepink with audience, wind-wantoned, petal-patched. They spoke their verses, turn and turn.

"How far have ye wandered?"

"By moonwise til morn."

"What got ye by moonlight?"

"What's yet to be born."

"Out o frost, fire; and ashes to thorn."

"Halse ye and this hall!" the May girl said, and shook her garland, so the lady danced within its orb.

"In, summer!" cried the throng.

And the doorkeeper swung it wide. "Hey's down." Another quick upward nod, and two or three blown girls went lingering to the byre and kitchen. "Nowt here nobbut rain to sup. Good ale within, and banketting. Come yer ways." Giggling and straggling, turning to stare, they obeyed, the hoarse voice and her tipsy swain last of all.

> *Yon duck has swallowed a snail*
> *Now isn't that a wonder?*
> *And it all came out it tail, it tail,*
> *It tail, it tail,*
> *It tail, it tail!*
> *And split it arse asunder, Gossip John.*

When they'd all gone in, the woman with the keys turned to Margaret and the stranger. "Cold by th' door, Master Grevil." Still he stood, with a face like the morning, doubt and glory. "Clapping craws? Here's fire within. Sack posset." He roused and they followed through the long cross-passage open to the kitchen garth, and into a high dim hall, arch-timbered. Rather gloomy, with a dank and doggish air. The fire was out, the hearth swept bare.

"Mistress Barbary," said the man, and set his prize forward.

Unheeding both, the woman knelt at the hearth. From her pierced earthen pot, she took a heap of embers, and rekindled the fire. "Tind ashes, take light." She sat back on her heels and watched it blaze, then rose, brushing her apron. A woman neither young nor old, close-grained and workworn as the haft of a rake. More tarnish than silver.

"Stockins," she said to the man. He shifted, dripping. There were puddles at his feet. "Gan up and doff yersel, Master. Lass'll not melt."

"Mistress Barbary," said master to maid. His voice shook with awe, with triumphant terror. "See." He looked at Margaret as if he'd picked her like a flowering branch. As if she were made of snow. Of lightning. "Is she not? What think you?"

The woman looked her up and down: tawdry finery. Smutched face and draggled petticoats, clagged feet.

"I'd get her dry."

So many faces, and all strange.

Garlands askew and singed petticoats. Faces glowing and heavy-eyed, giddy with waking or sullen with ale. Twigs of heather caught in frazzled plaits; a flecked breast starting from a pair of stays, tucked in with absent hands. New-bladed beards. A pair of startling blue eyes gazing from a mask of ashes. A wreath turned round and round in work-rough hands, between great gawking knees. Her kind.

O brave new world.

She was dizzy with the scent of it. Ale and woodsmoke and wet sheep, sharp sweat and wilting flowers.

Windows open to the green and rain.

No Master Grevil in his deadleaf jacket, when she turned to look; no passage to the door. Past all the thronging bodies, thick as bees, there lay a hearth and fire.

Down one long wall stood a dresser, crowded with plate: pewter and blue china, a few fair days amid the grey and gleam. It was dressed with green boughs, flowering and sleeting down, from bud to bare twig.

Laid out on a board were ranks of round dishes, white and gold, pranked out with knots of violets. A year of moons laid out in bowls of curds and cream, a moon of suns in frumenties and tarts. Gallipots of sweet spicery, a dish of sorrel and salmon. Hare pasties. Honeycomb. Margaret swallowed, lightboned suddenly with want. A quiddany of quinces, apricock marmalade. Green cheeses. Cakes and ale.

All untouched. They were waiting; all but a child in a feathery flat bonnet, half under the table with a black dog, licking a bowl. His elders had a rarer dish to sup.

Two breathless maids bore in a kit of syllabub, afoam; they set it on the dresser, slopping over in their haste, swiping up. They kicked off their mucky pattens with a scuffle and clang, unkilted their skirts, all agog. "Is't ower?"

"Not until thou's come, Doll Kickpail," called a man.

Mistress Barbary whist them with a glance. "Craw's hanged and world's ended," she said dryly. "Would yer finish wi' a jig?" She turned to Margaret. "Hey's down, this morning o't year. Come yer ways in."

That dance she knew: not these words, but their tune, the cadence of ritual. My lady had schooled her well. Margaret dropped a deep slow curtsey to the room.

When she rose, they were gaping. One or two horned their hands.

Barbary took a loaf with a green man's face baked into it, within a plaited wreath of bread. Clove eyes and sunburnt cheeks. Not a wood god, but the Sun in grain. She broke a piece, and held it out to Margaret. "Hallows with ye."

Margaret, hesitant, broke bread, and murmured, "And with you."

And at that, at last the household stirred. The Sun was torn to pieces, hand to hand, and devoured by a rabble of rantsmen. A gabble rose. Barbary stalked to the fire and set the kettle on.

The nine-day's wonder began.

Margaret sat dripping by the fire in a crowd of maids and men, her cup filled, her ruined finery appraised with rue and wonderment.

"Silk tiffany and cloth o silver. She mun be a princess o Lune."

"Prigged petticoats," said a sharp-faced man. "I doubt she's nobbut a tinker's lig-by, feigning daft. She'll wait while we's abed, and slip t'latch til him."

"Take silver and gold."

"Burn hall about our ears."

A maid scoffed. "That 'un? Couldn't catch moths wi' a candle."

A hind in a garland of wilted ivy, a great tawny man, drank deep. "What I think, is she's some great lord's lightborn. She were put to nurse ..."

"Wi' a bear?" said the piper, bag and chanter by his knee.

"Wi' a vixen," said the taborer. "And braids of her nurse."

"... wrapped i' yon petticoats. There'll be a mole on her."

A hind nudged his neighbor. "Eh, Jack, will we look for't?"

By the hearth sat a fair girl, untousled, brooding on a bowl of dainties like an ogress on a fondling child. She shook her head. "Sad ruin o velvet."

"Like a tinker out sleepwalking."

"Ashes?" said a wispy child, and blushed in confusion. "Not *Ashes*, but ..."

"Ashes i' May? Thou noddy. Imbers i' January." The scoffer drained her mug and held it out.

The ale went round again. The rain beat. The parliament of birds went on, owl and raven, wren and grouse.

"I knaw," cried a sonsy lass, "'Tis that lady left her lord and featherbed to gang wi' Ægyptians. In and out of a song."

"And wha'd tumble yon mawkin?" said a blackavised young man.

"Blind beggars," said a dark girl dancing. Cat face and clustering curls. "See at me. I's getten red shoon."

"Should have yon silver mantle." The young man glanced at Margaret, half mockery and half appraisal. All intent. A trig, dry, thirsty fellow, like a wasp on a damson. "As good hang it on a flaycraw as yon whey-face and ginger."

"Nay, a lady'd thee and thou us. See'd her bobbing at Wick Billy, same as a lord."

"Well, she didn't fall i' last rain."

"She did. Out o't moon."

"D'ye not see her bare toes? Mad Maudlin, lating after Tom o Cloud."

"Clarty feet, aye, but not travelled. Soft as my hand."

"Soft as thine head."

A hale old blue-eyed shepherd quavered: "His naunt"—he quirked his chin at his master's hall—"were stolen at her handfast. Away wi' t'fairies. They's gey fond o green fruit."

Barbary brought Margaret a dish of curds and cream and set it in her lap. Margaret tasted. Sharp-sweet and dowset, bronzed with nutmeg. And syllabub, ladled from the frothing bowl, and spangling on the tongue. O my. And buttered toasts. A banquet of rarities, and no enjoying it. As well eat honey in a hive.

All about her, they buzzed and pinched and pried and gazed.

"Happen she could be," said the shepherd. "I's heared folk gan there and back, and no more changed than delf in a dunghill."

"Cracked delf," another said.

"And painted."

"I thowt t'fair folk was *fair*."

"Thowt they was green. And lived on cresses."

Behind her, surreptitiously, a wench pinched salt on her.

"See'd her flicker," said a gangling lad. "Try toasting-fork, it's iron."

"Hey, Crook Tom, thou minds t'awd Mistress Grevil?"

"Dead. Aye, dead and tellt." The shepherd drank. "She'd not be walking."

"Nay, but her sister that were lost, young Mistress Annot. Were she russety?"

The shepherd pondered, deep in his mug. "Aye, she were an Outlune vixen, same as this. Airs and graces."

"What, this hedgebird?" sneered the sharp-faced man. "Beggar's velvet."

"A mooncalf."

"It's a changeling, I tell 'ee."

"A by-blow."

"A drab."

"Set her on shovel, and awa' up t'chimney."

Margaret cowered on her cutty stool. But Barbary was speaking, not over or behind, but to her. "How came you by Law?"

Darkness. She remembered nothing but abyss and roaring. Salt sting on her lips. Closing her eyes, she saw a storm-changed beach, a coffer, cracked and spilling cinnamon and mace. A shivered virginals. She saw an orange lying by a tarry hand. Bewildered, she said, "I was shipwrecked."

They howled.

"Drowned, by Dawcock!" cried the fiddler. "Here's a mermaid or a swan."

"Mind thy fingers, wench, he'll have 'em for fiddlepegs."

"What I say, she's a selkie. So what yer do, see, is yer fold her fell up in a kist. So's she can't swim away."

"If she was a selkie, she'd be bare as a needle."

"If she's seawrack," said a fattish fellow in drabbet, "then she's waif and stray. So finder keeps her, and he cracks her open."

The kitchen boy looked up. "My gammer see'd a ship once," he said. He licked his thumb dreamily, a shine of honey on his sooted cheek.

Mistress Barbary spoke. "Aye, but what ship? And what sea?"

Margaret saw the Lantern at her mast, the milkwhite shining of the Skein, the river and the road of death. The room swung. She fixed on the grey eyes as on a horizon. "I know not."

"What do they call you?"

By no name. *Crows' meat. Hole to fill.* "Thou."

Someone giggled. "Not sharpest knife i't drawer."

"Hold thy clap!" said Barbary. Turning back, "Are you honest?"

"Please you?"

"Do you lie with men?"

"Madam, I know none." If Barbary saw else, she said nought. Held Margaret's gaze and nodded. Then turned. "Dolly Jack, Jack Handsaw, Nick—if any on yer game wi' her, I s'll turn thee out ont road, bare arse and beggarstaff."

The sharp-faced man looked innocent. "By kit's catgut, her vixen is as safe wi' me as wi' t'master." Two or three laughed maliciously. One whistled a snatch of song.

But now the maids were clinging and wittering and twisting their aprons. "She's not staying here, is she? In our bower?"

"She'll elf us locks by night."

"Pinch us in our beds. Black and blue."

"Thou can pinch thysel i' bed well enough, Hob Ellender," said Barbary. "And thou, Cat Malison, if thou'd comb thy hair, she might tangle it." She turned to the company. "And hasn't she broke bread wi' us? And eaten salt?" Back she turned to Margaret, shivering by the fire. She held out her bunch of keys. "Will you break nowt nor take nowt, nor call craws down upon this hearth? Swear it." The old tune.

Margaret touched cold iron to her brow. "I swear."

"Then have thy keeping o this household, fire and fleet, until next hallows and a day."

Margaret curtsied again, rather shakily. The room roared and dizzied. The last of her command was crumbling, clods from pale roots.

"Come up, then." Barbary took up a jug and aired linen, and led her away.

Behind them, a girl called out to the company, "Well, I's for a jig. Clap us intil it."

Margaret followed her new mistress across the stone-flagged passage: back though the hall, where dogs and embers drowsed and mumbled on the bones of winter; through a low, dark room, half workroom and half parlor, full of snips and snaps of leather, bales of fleeces, glints of brass. Up a winding stair of oak. They came to a high room open to the rafters, panelled, with a stripped and shrouded bed. Swept bare. A bower once; a garret. There were planks in the roofbeams, thick-starred with apples drying, hung with bunches of greyed herbs, sweet and bitter. "T'awd mistress were an Outlune woman. Kept her stillroom." Turning cattycorner, Mistress Barbary undid a low door, like a cupboard in the chimneystack.

"There."

A low bed with a faded patchwork; a joint stool; a candlestick. Another blurred and faded patchwork at the window, made of glass and green and rain.

Barbary set the jug of water on the sill.

"Will I undo thee?"

*Here too.* Margaret shivered, waiting to endure. She dreaded what the sharp-eyed servant must see: the welts and bruises of her flawed virginity, the blood-dabbled smock. The cards. O hallows, would she find the cards?

"Here's a knot," said Barbary, softly. She let fall her hands. "Get on," she said. "And wash thysel. Thou's mucky. Bed's clean." She turned and rummaged in a kist.

A sleeve fell, stiff and heavy as a scab. Another. Spoils of dead queens drowned. Broideries rebroidered, trailing snarled and ravaged threads. Past mending. Rags of lace like last year's February. Waist and stomacher; petticoat and stays. Her sullied shift. *A strange world, Cloud,* she thought: *all changing.* Cloud and water, moving in the air; the sky unstayed. As if she laid aside the bands of heaven. Naked, Margaret dove into the coarse clean smock wrapped round the stone bottle. Warm. Tears started at the touch of it. So strange and light. So strange. She blinked them back; poured out the water for her hands and feet.

"Take these." Margaret turned. Barbary shook out an jacket and petticoat, ink-blue, the blue of midnight. Wool. "Her waiting-maid as were. Mek three o thee. Thou pin it up." She bent to the welter of tumbled clothes and gathered them. "That's as fine linen as ever I see'd, yon smock. Moon'll blanch it."

Gone.

No lock on the door.

Margaret stood at the window, looking out at the green. *Thea? Cold here.* Not the changeless cold of Law, but sudden. Kind unkind. No answer. They would hunt her. In a storm of ravens, in a shadow at the door. She must keep watch. Keep silence on her birth. She shivered. Colder here than in my lady's tower. Bone-cold. And she ached. How long had she been travelling? Turning back the quilt, she wrapped herself and huddled on the bed. A long road out of Law. For all her will to wake, she nodded.

*Hush, ba,* sang the wind.

*Norni?*

Here and nowhere. A remembrance. In their tower, Norni rocked an empty cradle by a fire of bone. At her knee, small Margaret held a tangle of bright silks; she saw a pale boat, rocking on a river of bright milk. Imbry's ship. Her sister's. Milk-twin and mother, child and nurse, they wove her journey between them, skein and song; made cradles in the air, of air. Then came a wind in the door, a rattling. The fire crouched and leapt.

Margaret started awake—keys jangling? No. She drew breath. No. Wind in the ivy. Wind. Her heart slowed, steadied. Soft featherbed. Small rain.

Unmooring, she remembered leaves blown backward in a vanished book, untelling winter. At the story's spring, she slept. But in the ease of driftedness, her mind still crouched at ward, a cloud full of thorns.

### Perseis, At Rise

*"The* morning Starre *doth lie this daybreak in the* Thorn," a later Margaret, turning from her glass, will write, *"wherein she joyeth most, her Pleasaunce and her Powre; Slae now falleth back and* Hulver *upriseth . . ."*

In the green dark of another morning, Annot rose. She laid aside her mantle and her gown of black for petticoats of green, May mourning; mirrorless, she combed her leaf-red hair, and as she braided it all down her back, she sang beneath her breath. *". . . and a thought come in her head to run in the wood . . ."* She left my lord's ring and my lady's baubles—though she traced the earrings with a finger, half-regretfully: her chains became her well. She left her needle in her work, too nearly done: the one unfinished sleeve. *". . . to pull flowers to flower her hat . . ."* A smock to be bedded in, a shroud. Too fine for the greenwood, to sully and snag. But she wore her old ring that had been her grandam's, her namesake: that she kept.

*An Lightwode.* And she turned it round on her finger. *Wode I fall?*

She'd cast cavels for this chance; bid Ashes for a tale. And happen she'd return a maid among her maidens all, green-garlanded, enchained; or happen she'd be lost forever. Lost like Perseis, to wander barefoot in the wood above, the sky; and bloodfoot on the Road. She had the tale of it by heart; had played it, most pathetically, before her bedpost and a velvet bolster and a brace of crooked chairs. *But thou art mazed, sweet fool. The wood is dark. And I th' moon's daughter in these rags of cloud Shall bear thee light . . .*

But now, this morrow, was no play, but Ashes' telling. She must gang to the greenwood, to keep tryst with a—What? A witch? A ghost? A daemon lover? All in silver and sable, fair-faced like the earl of Law. And at the thought, she laughed. *Thou greensick girl, thou gowk. To put thyself into a song.* And yet imagining his hand on her, imperious—*he asked of her no leave*—she blushed, as if half naked in a flaw of snow she'd drunk burnt wine. And shivered, hackled down her hause-bane with the thrill of it, ablaze with swallowed sun. Aglow with it and giddy. Drunk: and yet athirst.

*Tell me a ship. I would away.*

And Ashes turning in a clack of runes: *Thy ship's i't forest. Unleaving.*

*Unfelled?*

*T'keel's of thy laying. O' th' new moon, that will round wi' travelling. Thy mast's o't tree.* *What moon?*

*As thou may. Thou must til t'greenwood, til t'thorn; and break thou ae branch of it, but ane, and call on—*

*Ashes?* Air.

The birds had wakened, giddying. The night bled pale. She blew her candle out; and with it, all unknowing, she was past. Away like fire into air: but for a waft of honey and a wisp of soul. And in her bed, foreshadowed, unforeseen, another Annot slept, and dreamed her journeying. Long since. And yet to come: the O implicit in the origin, the new moon in the old, infurled; the rounding of the endless ring. *Lief wode I fall*—forever and again, the seed, root, flowering—*an light would spring.*

Far far in the greenwood, in the dark leaves of the wood, the owl cried out for her. *Two, two eyes.* And echoing, the small birds' plaint: *Of tree, of tree, of tree.* Forever: yet they bid her haste. No time. She had a tryst with story.

## Starglass

The child dreams. She is cradled in the moon's lap, who with gnarled hands combs her sleep, undoes the ravels of the hag-rid night. Her sleep is long as wind.

A small voice, like a fire of leaves: *She braids o her mother.*

And another, like the crackling of frost: *Aye, as left hand to this right. And Lightwood?*

*Of his root.*

As wind is braided with the flying leaves, so her sleep with falling stars. They speak through her in tongues of leaf. *A braid of birds,* she thinks. She's falling upward now, slow-wheeling through a hail of stars. They sain her, touching eyes, heart, mouth.

"Thou wake."

She's lying on the black earth in a drift of light. Looking upward, she sees bare wood and moonless night. No stars. Two cummers huddle on the ground beside her: a dark one, hulked in sooty sheepskins; and another, hung with tatters, like a tree that keeps her wintry leaves. That one bends to her with glinting spectacles; the other raises her with tarnished hands. Moving, this one jangles, like a tree hung with ice. "Time thou was waked."

So light. So strange and light. Her head is starless.

"How——?"

"Thou made thee a trance," says the leaf-witch.

She does not ask, *Where?*

"Wood above. Thou's come by unleaving."

She's lost her shoes along the way.

The dark one holds a wooden bowl to her. "Thou drink." A caudle of new milk. The child drinks deep of it, of dreams. It goes round.

From her lap, the leaf-brown other takes a barleycake, round as the honeyed moon. "Thou eat," she says, and shares it out. The child takes. It is warm. "Is't bread?"

"A riddle," says the leaf-witch.

And the dark one: "Barley. Thou break."

And so she does. The bread is hallowing. But in her share is something small and stony-sharp: a ring. A knot of seeds of blood. She turns it over in her hand; she holds it out to them. "I don't ..."

"That were thine," says Brock, the dark witch. "And will be."

"Will you keep it for me?"

"Till I won't," says leaf-brown Malykorne.

And Brock says, "As I will."

The child looks from one to the other. Malykorne holds out her long hand for the ring. "Mind thee, thou mun come for it."

"Will I know the way?"

"Thou knaws by th' moon," says Malykorne. She's pulled a long thread from her ravelled sleeve. Round her finger and her thumb, and in and out, she's wound it in a clew of light; she's done and done. "There's thy journey." A knot and a sleave, unbraiding starlight. Light as thistledown: she huffs it from her palm.

"Time is," says Brock. "I'll set thee on." Jangling, she doffs her coat of skins, and laps the child in it. "Cold in but thy bare soul." Ah, but colder still in Ashes' fell, in bone and blood. Stone cold. Then stirring, like a hive in winter; warm and fusty, with a tang of iron like a dying forge. Her blood rings like a new-struck nail. Brock touches the child's brow with her ashy hand. "What do they call thee, lass?"

By no name. "Thou." *Crows' meat. Hole to fill.*

"Thou's left that," says Malykorne. "Behind thee."

She looks back. Far far behind her is an O, a crow's eye or a cracked bright glass. A world, no bigger than a stone in someone's ring: she scries it in her hand. A child sits reading in a wintry garden, in a whorl of leaves, unfallen, walled about in glassy innocence. No flaw. A bird cries. *Margaret?* The child looks up; the leaves fall, scattering. Time runs. Unspelled, she spells in them her spring and fall, her journey.


Margaret lay amid a brangle of stars: their argument. Unselved: at once the riddle and unraveller, herself the key. But even as she knew the tale of it—so

nearly understood—she woke to birdsong, lay bewildered by the light. The
east looked down on her, dispassionate, the moon a white jug in its hand.

"Thou's o'erslept thysel," said Mistress Barbary. "Happen thou's weary, travelling." She set the jug down by the bedside. "Get thee washed afore it keels."

Rising barefoot and tousled, Margaret made her courtesy.

"Be still wi' yon bobbery. Thou's not a-guisering." A shrewd look. "Brought
up til it? Well, it won't do here. Folk think it mockery."

A careful nod.

Barbary went on. "Happen as thou's a stranger, thou won't know ways o't
hall. Master's Master Grevil. Bartolemy Grevil. He studies—Thy neck—And
I keep house for him. Joan Heron's Barbary." Her arms were full of clothes.
She ducked her chin at them. "Thou's gentry, so he'd have it. So thou lies
abed i' feathers. Gets thy water carried up." She laid down her bundle on the
joint stool, unfolded a smock. "And goes t'finer for't. But for a' that, thou's a
chit: so under governance. Thou does what thou's tellt."

Comb in hand. "Madam, at your will and his."

A look, an upward nod.

Bodies and petticoat. The servant shook them out. "His naunt's, these'd
be. Sisters out o Lune, they were—oh, 'twould be forty year agone. Damaris,
his mother were, t'awd master's Mistress Grevil, and young Annot." Stockings. Gown. "'Tis all else mourning." Fine falling bands, but out of starch;
a bitter tang to them, of wormwood. Mistress Barbary pinched the folds.
"Outlunish stuff. Still plainer than thy frippery. But I's set thee to furbish it.
See thy skill at thy needle."

"Madam, I know not the art of it."

Almost startled. "No? And they says t'fair folk's witches at their needles.
Fine as frost." She took the empty jug. "Dosta want doin up, or owt? No?
Quick then. Glass in t'awd mistress's chamber"—the apple room—"if thou
mun prink. Breakfast i't kitchen."

At the door, she turned back.

"And what shall we call thee?"

A deep breath. "An't please you, Margaret."

Grave approbation. "A good workday name. Wears well."


The maids were all at breakfast, sitting round the table with bowls of porridge and shares of oatcake, mugs of ale. Margaret stood at the sill, combed

and braided, very soberly clad. Forlorn. She heard a whisper: "Noll's fey." A nudge and a titter, a spurt of mirth silenced, like a kettle lid clapped to. At Barbary's nod, they all rose. They turned and bobbed to her, prim as pats of butter. And the little kitchen boy stood up and bowed solemnly, his hand to the hilts of his ladle.

"Good morn t'ye, lady," he piped.

Margaret curtsied: measure for measure.

"And the dog said bow-wow," called the dark girl. A smirk round the table, cut off by Mistress Barbary's glance: butter and knife.

Herself rose and beckoned Margaret to her side. "Here's Master Grevil's ward. She's called Margaret; and by bread and salt, she's o this household."

"Halse ye," they muttered, round the board.

"Hallows," said Barbary. "Table's laid for thee." Horn spoon and wooden bowl. Shyly, Margaret came and sat among them, folding herself small. Scrape and clatter, they took up their knives, and set to with a will. Eyes like shoe-nails. A stithy of tongues. She did as they did: sipped the strange bitter stuff, spooned up the salty mess of porridge. Glanced covertly. Five maids: the sly dark girl and the pale demure one, cheek to chin and whispering; a pair of sonsy country lasses, frankly curious and tucking in, with elbows well squared; and down at the foot of the table, a wispy, bewildered girl, spoon in the air and gazing. Only five. And the kitchen boy. Round as a hedgepig and as rough and dawdling. The swags of green had withered.

Barbary looked round the table. "Cat got yer tongues? Ye clatter quick enough when there's work toward."

Dark deftly licked her spoon. "An we'd cream til our porridge, then cats would have our tongues."

"And welcome," said Barbary. She becked her chin at the dark girl. "Now then. Yon malapert is Alys Kyteler ..."

"Cat Malison to thee. "

"And her gossip's Nell Blanchett."

"Hob Ellender."

"Cat's Paw," said one of the sonsy girls, scornfully. "Always i't cream."

"And here's Will Shanklin's daughters from up Owlriggs." The country girls. "Nan and Doll."

"Doll Kickpail and Nan Slutswool."

Barbary pointed her knife at Spoon-in-the-Air. "And yon mislaying clash-pot is Susannah Hawtrey."

"Morn t'ye," said the girl, and blushed.

"Sukey Bet Suckathumb."

"Sleeps wi' a babby."

"Who won't dust i't master's study?"

Awe and trembling assertion. "In his babbyhouse ..."

"Thou goslin. 'Tis a cupboard."

"... there's ghosts."

"Dead things," said Doll.

"So there's not, nobbut kickshaws," said Nan. "Won't eat thee."

But, "Mammysuck," jeered Cat.

"Enough o that, Mistress Lick-Luff-and-Wash-Whiskers." Barbary turned to the smutchy kitchen boy, round-eyed and agape. "And yon's Will Constant o Seventrees. Wick Billy."

"Cause he's slow."

He bobbed again.

"Shepherd's outwith, and t'men afield. They's nowt o thy concerning. Nor neither thine, Doll Draggletail." Barbary looked round the table. Bowls scraped and mugs empty. Crumbs.

Nan said, "Is she Mistress, then? Being one o't Grevilry."

"Just Margaret." But Barbary looked doubtful.

A poor shorn sort of name, said their faces.

Margaret set down her bowl. "... of Nine Law."

Uneasy respect for that, a shadow of awe.

Barbary rose. "Time we was to work. Thou, Margaret. T'master waits on thee. In his closet, he did say. Cat, Ellender, bedmaking. See they's aired. Nan, Doll, cheeses. Hens, Sukey."

Dark and fair caught Margaret by the dresser.

"Here's t'King's daughter o Elfland." Cat made a pretty leg and Nell a courtesy. They blocked the doors at either end. "My lady Nine Law. Your servants." All sincerity, caress: but with a sting in it, a spider in the cream. "What's come o yer siller gown? Tousled?"

"Turned arainwebs. Dead leaves."

"And my lady turned Margery Daw."

No getting by.

"Here's a dance. My lord Grevil's Maggot."

"For as many as will."

"Thinkst thou the dance can dance?"

"Wi' a fiddler afore. Will play on her."

"Thou, Magpie!" A pinch. "Mind thee, I's counted spoons."

"And what if she's prigged them? If she would she may. She's Noll Nut-tycrack's toy." Nell smiled. "Will keep her in's babbyhouse."

"His grasshop that he leashes wi' a silken hair."

"His bait. For t'pike to snap at."

No rise.

"Dost knaw Noll Grevil, what he is?" said Nell to Margaret.

Silence.

"He's a man-witch. Will learn thee to talk."

"Will slit thy tongue."

Margaret was sent up as garnish to a dish of marrowbones and a leathern jug of ale. Barbary led her through the hall and a wainscot parlor, beeswaxed and a little wormy, up a doglegged stair. She knocked with her elbow. "Here's breakfast and t'lass."

A little panelled room, low-ceilinged, looking out on ghostly trees. All white: she could not tell what was flower, and what fog. Master Grevil sat writing in a jackdaw's nest of ink and papers, book on open book. He wore a sober suit of mole-gray and nutgall brown, with many buttons; his linen very plain and fine. There was a little creature like a plume of fire on his shoulder, tuft-eared and pinchfaced; absently he fed it bits of crumb with inky fingers. His daemon? As he rose and bowed to her curtsey, it rode him, chittering and scolding. He glanced at Margaret's quenched and braided sobriety, and sighed. From a green child to a greensick girl.

"Hempen hampen! Is the imp not vanished with her suit of clothes?"

"We do stay her with cream," said Barbary. "Would you set her at brewing? At spinning?"

"Neither as yet. You may leave us."

"You'll be wanting more candles?"

"Anon."

He beckoned Margaret forward. Wary of the scolding imp, she came a step or two, and stood with downcast eyes that missed nothing. Books. Hundreds at least. What titles? Crusts and bones. An ape-headed cittern. A flute. Nutshells. Lees of wine. His table was covered with long folios and odd scraps of paper, written over in a thorny hand: scrawls, blotches, crossings-out. A drawing. *Stars?*

He saw, in her still face, her sidelong gaze. "The Nine."

"Please you, sir?"

"The stones. Where I found you, on Law. We do call them Nine Weaving, or Fiddler and Hey."

*The sky below.* "Are they always there?"

She'd puzzled him. "Before this hall. Before this world, I doubt. Do stones walk?"

*Are the stars made earthfast?* But she spoke no answer.

He began again, as dancers in a set dishevelled, on the proper foot. "You slept well? And have broken your fast? I would have you comfortably bestowed."

"Well. I thank you, sir."

"You may call me Grevil. I am master here. Low Askwith Hall." A hesitation. "Cloud."

Again she made her courtesy. "Master Grevil."

"Have you a name?"

"Margaret, sir."

"No other? Of what birth?"

"None."

"What? Did you grow like missel, in the air?"

"Like stone, I think, sir. In the earth."

"A cold lap for a nurse," he said. Took up a stone from a heap of writings; set it down. "Yet flowers spring of it." And again, that rueful measure in his voice: "*That legion of the grass that withers, all untold.*" He looked at Margaret. "So, Mistress Mouldwarp. I would hear your traveller's tale, your history of dark. Are there manors then beneath our wandering sheep? And courtiers of chrysoprase? Are all their midwives miners? For my nurse did say 'twas all a maze of gallantry, of music and of light."

She thought of the cracked virginals, the scuttling dark; but answered gravely. "None that I have heard."

"Are you not of that quality? Those folk that we call Unleaving?"

Her turn to startle. "Unleaving? Is that not a country of the air? The Wood Above?"

"Aye, those northern stars about the Ship that never set." He turned the outward of his hand to her, to show his ring. "Of old, my family took it as device: the Ship and Tree, whose ever-autumn is the sky. That fair folk live about its roots, 'tis written in philosophy. They fleet as do its leaves the stars."

"But I am none of theirs."

"I see," he said regretfully. "By daylight, you are someways earthier than first I saw, of none such subtle stuff. You breathe." A sideways smile. "Mistress Barbary will have it that you sneeze."

He shuffled through his papers, held one out. More drawings. "Grey Wethers at Askrigg." Another. "Long Meg and her Daughters at Imber Lap." She studied them.

"What think you?"

"As images? Most curious."

"But of the stones?"

"I know not."

"Some say they dance at Ninerise, when they hear the fiddler. And others, that when stones hear, they may dance. 'Tis said they are foxcastles, strongholds of a greener world. I think—I think they are knots between this world and another. Here. There. And one long seam, the Lyke Road, that we all must walk." He traced it with a finger; looked sidelong at Margaret. "But few of us backward."

She bent still closer to the leaves of drawings. "Sir. Here, where 'tis written *Scar Fell*, what place is that?"

"You can read?"

As if he'd asked, *Can you breathe?* "And cipher."

"Can you write?" He pulled up a lionheaded chair, set a half-scrawled leaf in front of her, found and mended a pen. "Copy that."

She bent to her task. *Qu'y: Whether ÿ Earthfasts at Tinding bee of lunish Stone or no?*

"An antick character," he said, bemused. "Where ... ?" He caught himself.

"Sir?"

Turning to the window, he looked out. "'Tis a history," he said, "of Cloud its ancientry, high Cloud. There are remnants of it, that in custom and in vulgar memory, the common tongue, yet live." Still his back to her, his arm raised to the windowframe, his brow to the glass. "A kind of monument."

"A book?" He turned round at her voice. Her face now one astonishment. "You've made a book?" As if he'd said, *I wrote this tree.*

Pink to the ears now. "Pieces of one. That is, 'tis matter for a book ..." He gestured at the table, helplessly. "... but in a sort dispersed."

Leaves scattered through the study. "Is there aught I can do?"

"I would not burden you."

She remembered kitchen talk. "My keep would burden you. Like ... a grasshopper." (She imagined a dwarfish fiddler all in silken green.) "Is there no work I could do?"

"Would you grovel in the ashes? Scrape trenchers? I'd not have you prey to these kitchen cullions and their hobbyhorses," he said fiercely.

"I am not schooled in kitchenry. But I can write. Would you have me copy for you?"

He relented. "Would it not weary you, to read this crabbed philosophy?"

"It is tales to me. New worlds."

He picked up her copy, studied it aslant. "'Tis an Outlune hand, and somewhat straggling in the character. But fair enough. 'Twill serve." He bent and scrabbled in the litter on his table for a silver coin; held it out to her. "So then: fair copy of foul papers. And thy wage is ..."

"I ask none."

"Come, you are a Cloudishwoman now. When I say *five*, your word is *seven*."

"Then ... might I read of your library?"

"And welcome. But that is—no, not fire and fleet, but air. What other?"

They had locked her in the dark, too often. "Candles?"

"Nine a week. Of wax. Brock's penny and a bargain. Clap?"

When she took his cool, dry, inky hand, it shook a little—doubting on her flesh?—then clasped.

"Here, as you write, we may talk at whiles, we grasshoppers. If we are burdens on the harvest, we at least may sing." He sat down caterwise to her, spread open one stout folio, as if to work; but walked and twirled his compasses, up and down the page, and up and down. Stalk and pirouette and stalk. He looked up at last at Margaret. "Tell me. How came you, thread-needle, out of Law?"


Beyond the wood lies nowhere. For a time, the witches walk through wreathed and drifted light; but that grows scanter, fading into rime. Is gone. They're on black moorland, climbing.

"A shrewd wind," says Malykorne.

"Aye," Brock says. "Colder, by and by,"

*No moon,* thinks Margaret, stumbling on. She sees unmeaning stars above her, scattered, like a broken chain of stones. And at her feet, stark nowhere. Mist and hag. They travel out of Law, unmazed, unislanded. *No walls,* she thinks, and shivers, awestruck. Yet a road: they walk the set stones of a trod, meet standing stones like hooded travellers, far seen and seldom come upon.

"No lantern," she says. "How is it we travel?"

"Dark o't moon," says Malykorne.

At a waystone, they part. There are coins on it, worn silver, lying in a shallow like a stoup. Brock chinks them, pockets. "I's off."

"Ah," says the leaf-witch.

"I's a tryst," says the dark witch. "Wi' a traveller."

"Your coat ... ?" says Margaret, and makes to doff it.

But the dark witch shrugs. "Best keep that whiles. Thou's colder than I s'll be." And jangling, she lopes away.

"Coming?" says the leaf-witch. "Farther back than onward." Margaret twists up her skirts and follows. The witch walks no straight path, from stone to stone, but wanders all askant the bushes, plucking lightwebs from the thorns. Margaret strays after. Apronless, she stuffs the pockets of the coat. Light stuff as thistledown; drifting as dreams. As wiry. She keeps close at the witch's heels: so vast a dark.

They go on.

"Oh," says Margaret, halting. "Oh, it's lost." On the fellside is a naked child, a waif that shivers, dancing on the moss. All naked as the moon.

The leaf-witch turns, glances. "Not yet."

Margaret stands. "Is it ... dead?"

"Unborn."

"Can you not comfort it?"

"Would have it so? His mam will die of him."

Still Margaret lingering, gazes, and still the waif-child whirls and shivers. Now she sees his bare feet bend no stem, nor break the blind ice of the hags. He dances open-eyed, unseeing. Naked: turning in a flare of silver, he's unclouded of his flesh. And for a moment, like a falling star, she sees him burning and unburnt with cold: as clear as adamant, aethereal, skyblack. Like crystal fiery from the blast, new-blown. It is the living that consume; this spirit holds: a glass that gathers in its bent the scattered stars, new-spells them in a soul. A child with child of its ascendants, great with light.

A trembling naked child.

"Far to go," calls Malykorne beyond her. Dark. She hurries after.

There are children back of Law. She scries them, cold as star-shot and as clear against the coalsack hills. That whirling, solitary wraith. A crouching child that scrabbles at the earth with bloodless hands, and weeps. A ranting ghost. And cowered in a thornbush by a silent beck, two sisters, wreathed in one another's arms. Like cherries twinned and rounding on a single stalk; like moonstones budded of a seed, ingeminate. One sky between them, and a single dream: a hooked moon at their hearts, re-echoed stars. As Margaret makes to pass, she sees one sister tinge with dawning, and her lifting hair, as if by wind; the other still lies dark.

The leaf-witch touches her cheek. "Come, lass. Farther still."

She lets herself be drawn. Stumbling in a waking dream, she thinks the lightwebs weigh her down; she thinks the leaf-witch draws her by a heart-string, ah, it tugs her by the ribs. Thorns pluck at her and thrawn roots trip. *No coin.* She tries to turn her pockets out, to pay her fare in light; but they are empty. She has gathered nothing.

"Here."

*Where?* she thinks, half-waking. Wading to the knee in drifted leaves. *No wood.* She sees a thorn tree by a tumbled wall, unleaving. All but leafless; yet there spills from it an endless tale of leaves. In her half-sleep, she could spell them, all the stories of a world. The wood above.

"In hallows," says the witch.

Beside the hawtree stands a hulk of tumbled stone. A fold once, or a shieling. Roofless huddle and a sill. The leaf-witch draws her in and laps her in a ragged patchwork. Of the leaves, and patched with sky? Of cloud and heaven, clouted with the leaves? In tatters now, however made: outworn undone. There's a needle rusting in the ravelled stuff. It pricks. She sees faint traceries of silver, patterns of a half-remembered sky: an earth unquilting of the stars.

"Light down wi' thee," the leaf-witch says. "Wake wood."

Margaret sleeps.


In his study, Grevil waked and read. He turned the pages over, written in that childish careful hand. "Of Leapfire, and the like Observances ..." Fair copy: she had set herself to make pleached alleys of his plash and thicket. He could see her as she bent to work: the inky fingers and ill-fortuned hair, pale sorrel,

wisping from its plaits. A child. A runaway. But of what kindred? By her carriage, gently born, and kitted like an antick queen (dragged backward through
a hedge); yet knew—or feigned to know—no more of courtship than a tinker's
brat. An innocent. No witch, he'd swear it. Nor an elfin, by her inky hands. A
changeling that the folk had blinded of her memory? Yet spoke the elder language, offhand, like a poet or a Lunish mage. The language of the dead.

"Of Leapfire ..."

But beyond the page he saw a daylit fire, pale, a troubling of the air; he saw
the dreadful gardener with his rake. *He sweeps the way for Ashes,* said the voices
at his back. His hand was in a colder hand; his new coat that was leafgreen
yesterday crowblack, as if the fire had burned it. Black amid black skirts behind
him. Through the tangled smoke, he saw the swirl and fall of birds, of leaves
like birds. Of ashes on the wind.

*All souls.*

The air was full of stories, silent voices that would speak.

A something cold and gentle brushed him, and another, cheek and chin. A
flurry. Eyes, mouth, heart: all ice. His mother snowed.

In his free hand, the flowers wilted in the bud. He cast them to the ground,
as he was told.

*Lyke to the earth's lap, lightly on the Road.*

Long after, he had asked the women, spinsters in the sun and gleaners,
Ashes all: *What unleafs in the Unleaving?* And the blue-eyed witch woolgathering
had said, *All souls that's not been tellt.* Her apron full, she'd plucked the tendrils
from the thorn. *If thou didst know their tongue, they'd tell thee allt stories o't world.*

He'd writ it down.

*Aye, prick it out,* the witch had said. *An thou were cloven, thou might hear. But thou's
an inch too many for yon sprights. At cockcrow, they's away.*

Alone of all the living, Ashes—any woman in her turn—could hear, trans-
late the spirits, wind their stories into shrouds. And being told, the stories of
the dead unbound them. Ropes of snow.

And still untold they thronged him, struck him whiteblind with their wings
of snow. They beat against the portals of his soul. The dead. Their silence was
their song, was time.

He looked again at Margaret's page.

A revenant?

An earthly nourice sits and sings, and ay she rocks an empty cradle by the hearth. She's spelling to her sea-drowned daughter, Imbry that she bore, to bring her to her landfall, to the shore of Cloud; as she has spelled these seven years. In Law is timeless, neither sun nor moon will ever be: and every breath is drawn a new bereavement and a hope. Her milk child, listening, lulls to sleep.

But at a sound elsewhere, the sleeper woke, was Margaret, remembering that her nurse was gone. Was taken: for those Scarrish arts she practiced. That she taught.

Cloud now.

Unbounded; yet bereft. The consolations of her cell—her nurse's touch, her mother's ghostly voice—were gone. No comb nor candlelight, no cradling play of string. No lap. No leaves—*Ah, Margaret, do you see them fall?* No tale.

Herself alone: then she would voyage.


Clouded from the view, bright Journeyman plies onward, slyest of the wandering stars. She's rising. She is never risen, ever at the brim of Law: dusk-diving, whelming in the wave of light. Her dance is with the sun; she dares it. Thief, they call her, and the Ferrier, whose River is the starry Road: her lading is of souls.

Coatless, Brock crouches by a fire of weed. Beyond it, there is nothing but the drub and hishing of the waves, the glint and fading of the shingle; and her boat, drawn up and laden. She awaits the tide.


In Grevil's study by the guttered candle lay a map of all the heavens; on it, like the unknown constellations of a dream—*of course*—there stood an empty wineglass and a pair of compasses, a flute, a quill, a congeries of nutshells and a knife, the twire of lemon peel it cut. A Vanitas. There lay the pages of a manuscript, emended in the writer's hand. The moonlight fell aslant, moved on. Across the heavens retrograde, towards dawn, there ran a scuttling scrying mouse. Unlike a falling star, it paused a moment, scenting marrow; and was gone. The still-life and the text remained.

"... two roads to a Life, as figur'd in the starry Sky, recross'd: the Lyke Road and the Zodiack, the river and the Mill it drives, the hallow'd and Profane.

"That one we call the Sun's road, that we tread with him, the slow wheel of the Year. So that company of Players that we call Brock's Journeymen doth lie a night at this Sign or at that in turn, as doth the Sun in his Houses: at the Keys, the Coffer, at the Harvester, the Hind, so many Inns. Then rising, they pack on.

"There is an Other road that is our dreams, their Play. It is what Ashes tells. From what Green room we know not, the Soul is call'd; and enters at that Crossroads where the Fiddler and the Witches meet. Their Scene is at the soul Spring in the roots of Thorn: as Countryfolk do say, in Mally's yard. So in a myriade of myriades of Lives one Comoedie is play'd: we play, disfiguring in turn the Fool, the knott of Swords, the Lanthorn-Bearer; brave the Ravens and the Scythe. How long's the Lyke Road? says the riddle: just as long as thou draw'st breath; however long, too brief. We die in Ashes' lap, wherein the Sun is born."

By the third of her allotted candles—they were dwindling—Margaret read. *I bid thee goodnight,* Mistress Barbary had said withdrawing: so she studied, waking nightlong with the dark, to bathe in it, renew herself. The day astounded her. It was—a clamoring of light, a forge, a chariot with fiery wheels, with horses fire-shod. A sea. And she an inland creature, of the underworld, bred up in darkness like a pot-blanched plant. Unbalanced with the light, she marvelled how these Cloudish creatures swam in it; stood, walked the dizzy earth. She staggered through their working hours, timesick, daunted by the bright and battering sun.

But now the failing day was quenched, the channer of the birds died down. Oblivious, she read until the candle crouched and flared. She startled. No one there. A wind had risen, that was all. The rain had stopped.

She knelt up on the bed, her finger in her place; twitched back the curtain.

Fire pooled and eddied in the quarrels of glass, that tilted it, now this way and now that, as on a choppy sea. Night wavered. Not the moon but her own face, pale amid the trees, looked in.

She bent and blew the candle out; then pushed the casement wide.

O heavens.

Stars. Thick as sparks from a fire of juniper. At first, a dazzlement, a shock of ecstasy: but even as she stood, her mind, swift-sorting, strung the patterns. Arm in arm, knee deep in apple trees, she saw the Witches on the Road. They looked as Norni drew them in the ashes of the hearth, in secret; like her card, but glorious. The fire-folk. One had a wisp of cloud for scarf, the tatters of a cloak of rain; the other swung the new moon at her hip, a budget with a star for coin.

And looking, Margaret laughed for wonderment: but silently. She'd learned that first of all, to make no sound, betray no vestige of her mortal blood. She sat back on her heels and rocked herself for joy and terror. And the household slept. No crowd of them ran out, half-dressed, to marvel at the city in the air. *Look, look up at the skies! O look.* So this was ... commonplace? What gods were they in Cloud, to leave such jewels scattered in a farmyard? Were they careless of their wealth? Or cunning? Did they mean to trap her, catch her gazing at forbidden stars? A thief of light. She shook with it. But even as she waited, shivering, for the sound of keys, the cold wind in the door, she thought: *So little of it.* But a strip of sky above the trees, a hem of petticoat. She would see more. And if they punished her, she would have seen.

No coal nor candlelight betrayed her. Soft as shadow now, she slipped into the greater room, the loft. She listened at the stairhead. Nothing but the wind in branches and the settling of the boards. No keys, no clattering of feet, no stench of butchery and fear. But she could smell the pears and apples on their slatted boards, like wine but sweeter far; could feel the buzz in them of prisoned summer, like the ferment in her blood. Could almost feel the tree in every timber, singing in its nailed captivity. Could feel the stones.

Barefoot on the wide bare boards, she stole to the farther window, clambered on a kist to reach the sill. Drew breath; and then undid the shutter, swung the glass.

Unleaving.

Norni's stars, that came not under Law, true North; and Thea's, painted in her cards: the Ship, the Ladle, and the bright Swan, barely risen, skimming low aslant the trees; the Lantern and the Knot of Swords. The Crowd of Bone that sang her mother's death. Ablaze. But not as painted: wheeling in a deepless sky, the Ladle spilling, and the great Ship overturned. *I spoke them truly; I am shipwrecked.* And again she laughed, astonished, through her tears. *O I am drowned.*

"Here," said Grevil, turning from his inlaid cabinet. "Here's elfshot. This—" He held a leafshaped blade of flint, no bigger than his thumbnail, white as salt. "—from Imberthwaite. It struck a tailor as he sat a-fishing. He was never at home in this world again. They say. His widow afterward did say he heard the bridles in his dream and followed."

He laid it on the page beside his drawing: like, but as the light to shadow.

"And this—" he said. Another, sharp as fire, gold as honey, wave-knapped. "This lay buried in a barrow mound. A thousand years, may be; or ten, a myriad. Perchance it lay in dark when first my lady's Ashes rose; slept still when she did wake."

*In dark.* She turned it over in her hand: so light. Small substance; all intent. He answered what she did not ask.

"An ashing. A tale of one who bore it. A map for journey after death. Like this—" He slid another and another drawer to show his curiosities. A coin, a shard of pottery, slip-glazed; a bear of ivory; a bone. "Like this—" He touched the gold ring at his ear. "—that will be mine." He looked at her. "We go not into dark untold." No emphasis, perhaps, on *we*.

Another drawer. He turned a jewel that was in it, of an owl-eyed deity. Of gold: the earth could mar it not. He bent his face from her, as if the telling were a secret, inmost of his heart. His hands that held a pen, a blade with skill, shook ever when he spoke.

"It is mine argument that men do write the map of heaven on this earth, in stone, in history, in myth; but that the heavens write it in ourselves, in earth." Again the sliding in and out of drawers. A leaf in stone; a pebble, water-thirled; a thumbling skull; a shell; a dragonfly. "That earth itself is ashing for the great world's soul."

*The Nine their book,* she thought. *'Tis writ in wind, in snow; and that he cannot keep.*

Now Grevil smiled. "A star appearing in the Anvil, they do say, was Tharrin's soul. A comet: for the which he ever wore his hair unbraided, so was caught by it. He hanged in riding out to hail his star, so he did fall with its return." He bent. "Now these—" This drawer was full of hailstones, rattling.

Witches' souls. Faint malice in them still. She looked away.

"'Tis said that witches do instone themselves—and others, aye. They draw their enemies by name, to braid them in their hair. To hoard." A click of pebbles as he raked through them. "They say my lady's crown is souls."

He could not know.

Shut and open. And this other drawer of ships, and each no bigger than a shell: as if a fleet were wracked in it. "Ah, these are pretty toys."

But Margaret stood elsewhere, in a storm of memory. As if a key had turned, a cabinet stood open, now she saw a white bed in a tower, and a book, its leaves blown backward in a wind. Her keep. *But I ran,* she said. *I am not locked in it.* And reason answered: *it is locked in you.* Box in box. Another storm: and Norni crouching, combing, by the bead of fire in a lamp, to bring the boat ashore, bring Imbry's boat ...

"... in Scarristack. They call them soulboats there. They brim them full of oil, and set them burning on the sea, 'tis said, to bring the dead to the Unleaving. As we walk the Road." He was all alight with it, imagining. "But see now." And he held to her a pebble scrawled and flecked. She took it; it weighed nothing in her hand. Not stone but eggshell.

Now she looked to him. "'Tis light."

"An owl's. And this a wren's—" He looked at her aslant. "So small a thing to hatch the summer. This now is a raven's; this—ah now, this beauty is a gyrfalcon's. It was taken of a nest atop a scar, ten fathoms fall on rock." At that, she looked at him, his scholar's bent, his hands. Catching at her disbelief, he said, "There is one climbs for me. He giddies not." And smiling now, "And this a nightingale's." To her astonishment, he whistled softly, like a bottle, narrow-necked, of crystal, filling up up up. *Jug jug wit wit.* "Thou gravity. There's asking in thine eyes. What wouldst thou know?"

"Wherein the music lies."

"Ah," said Master Grevil. "'Tis not in breaking it. That way is only slip and shivering. Here's glair in one hand; in the other, but a shell, as silent as thyself." She bent her head. "Aye, Mistress Mumchance, thou." He set the egg down in its nest of wool. "But verily, her music's in the stars. They say the nightingale sings nightlong in the wood above. In the Unleaving."

"I have read no little of the stars; but I know not this constellation."

"Ah, it stands not in the heavens, but the heart. Did I not say the sky is written in our souls? In our cosmography?" He traced the inlay of the cabinet, the flowers and the fruit of wood. "I have heard a nightingale in Lune, but long ago. In Gallwood, in the fellows' grove." He looked far inward, reminiscent. "*Quis quis quis,* it sings; and, *Cuius? Cuius?* cries the owl."

Then shaking off his melancholy, smiling, he unlocked the inmost door.

"But here ..."

Bright faces: portraits set in frames of ebony and gold and ivory, as small as coins. More precious still. Hand hovering, he chose.

Not this, the sad-eyed man: like Grevil in his look but greyer, all in black, a branch of almond in his hand. He sat in shadow in this very study. At his back, beyond the open window, lay his garden, greener than the sea, as fathomless. But he would dive no more.

Nor this, the young man standing in a field of barley, holding in his open shirt a chain, a something on it—what? a ring, a soul? another picture?—curled within his hand, unseen; nor yet his other self, his sister-twin by moonlight, at her music: sickle to his scythe. A glass unlooked-in at her back gave back the viewer's gaze in little, like the moon; it pupilled.

None of these, but two girls, side by side, a little elder than herself. He held them at his heart a moment; turned them. "This"—the fair one—"was my dearest mother, she who died when I was young." He did not look at Margaret. "I think my heart died with her." *I am sorry,* she would say; but knew not how. "And this—" As fair a maid but russety. Unsweet. The limner's brush had caught the mischief in her face: a stirring like a little wind that whirls the leaves in autumn, sets them all a-dance. "Her sister Annot, that was lost." A silence, but for wind in leaves, the birds. "She heard the bridles ring."


Barbary herself brought up the master's cup, leaving Margaret to poke and puzzle at her square of linen. At her heels, the clack of tongues began. Deft Ellender shook out her master's shirt, laid stitches in the band. "Not silk," she said. "Like some folk traipse about in." Margaret bent to her work. "He's nobbut backend gentry. Madam, now, his naunt—well, his mother come o high great folk."

"Up north," said Nan, and rummaged in the basket. "Here's tearing o sheets."

"Broad lands," said Ellender.

"And empty," said Nan.

"Her towers stand high," said Cat.

"Allt better to look down on thee," said Nan.

Cat flounced: no quashing her. "She's a ring til every finger, and a hawk til her hand. I see'd."

"Me and Bess Imberthwaite, we did her chamber," said Nan. "Orris til her water jug and sugar til her sack. Her fires laid wi' bark o cynament."

"I brock her stillery," said Doll, and sighed. "All glass it were. She had her waiting-women beat me."

"Two on 'em," said Nan. "And but to dress her. We was not to wash her stockings even."

"Cloyed wi' gold they were," saidCat.

And Ellender: "We was not to meddle wi' her coffers."

Sukey looked worried. "Was I there?"

"In thy cradle, thou goslin."

"Or she'd have made soap o thee. Suke-fat and violets."

Nan bit her thread. "Happen three year since she come a progress here." She glanced up at the door; spoke lower. "She given our master a rare good fretting: would he wed? And would he wed?"

"Were it a brave young lady?" said Doll. "I would we'd a mistress."

"Here's a fray," said Ellender. Folding back the master's shirt, her darns adorning it like snow on snow, she took a needleful. "I'd rather serve his aunt."

"Put gold til her hair," said Cat.

Nan snorted. "Swill her piss-pots, more like."

Ellender bent closely to her needlework. "I'd study."


The wind in leaves troubled her. *So many,* thought Margaret. *So many on the Road, still travelling. Untold.* She lit her candle, took her cards; but they—her Wood Above—had withered. Tale on tale, they fell from her. Unleaving. Even spelling out the cards, she stopped; she squared them. *Like and like.* But she would have the naked sky.

Up she knelt, undid the shutter: but the light seemed bitter as a frost, a wind of snow of stars, sharp-sided at her eyes. Inimical as Imbry's sea. Against the storm, she crooked her arm before her face. This sky now was too great for her: it stopped her breath. She fumbled with the latch to shut it out.

But Margaret had yet another sky, within her, not without: her toy, her consolation in the dayless dusk of Law. Hands curved about an emptiness, a space of air, she held the sky in thought: a crystalline of air, aethereal. A glass of smoke, in which the embers of imagination swirled and rose, un-burned and burning still. Upfalling to the wood above, they leafed, inlaid it with their fire. They flew, swift scattering, as dancers to their set. All there, the bright remembered stars. Did not her mother's mother set them in the sky? A beat of silence; then as one, they turned. Scarce breathing with the poise of light, she held them turning still. She set the errant stars a-dance.

*Within and out, in and out, round as a ball,*
*With hither and thither, as straight as a line . . .*

Whorl within wheel, she turned with them in mind, kept measure. Swift now, with their joyous tumbling; slow and slower, with the cradle of the summer stars. She swung in them. She spun sun and moon like jackstones, all a-jangle; swept and caught the five stars in her hand. Again she tossed her golden ball; and in its falling, all was changed.

Within was outward. She dove dolphin-backed amid the river of light, her sinews braided with light; and down and downward, into shadow. There was something that she dove for, glimmering: a bright ring blind with darkness, buried at the sill of dark.

She slept.

Margaret wakes to a rattle of rain on thack-stones, in a reek of down-driven smoke. Night still? A rushlight dips and dances. No sky. Black thatch above her and a taws of hazel in the rooftree, all a-bloom, that powders her with dust, a sift of sunlight. By the hearth, the witch sits wide-lapped, combing wool; a loom of her in shadows mocks and mows. Margaret hears the soft scritch of her wool combs and the embers hissing. Cards? There, pillowed at her cheek. And tangled in her braid, the ring. All there. She lies, lapped in nothing but a ragged patchwork, rough as a nettlebed, and all holes.

*Rooftree . . . ?*

Before she can speak, the leaf-witch answers. "Unleaving. We's out o't Road."

"Here?"

"Now."

Margaret sits up in the rough blanket and looks round. *No moor.* The witch's fire leaps and cowers in a hovel; or a hedge. The roof is plashed and eddered of the living thorn; the walls are tumbled stones. She lies in leaves on leaves, and lightwebs, downy as a cuckoo's nest, and vexed with twigs. O wonderful, most strange! A branch has flowered in the smoke. Of blackthorn, though she has no name for it: wood flowering in stars, whitenaked as the Nine.

And yet the starry sky is thack, the hedge a hovel, hung and flung about with crazy oddments. A tipsy cauldron, canted over in the leaves. A riddle and a rusty shears. A crook. A rattlebag. A garland, withered on a nail. But why? A ladle. Broken eggshells. Keys. What locks? A cratch full of wizened apples. A cage with no bird. A sheaf, unthreshed and sprouting, and a wormy wooden cup. On a shelf at her bedhead sits a green cheese by a whorl and spindle, wound with flax; a sickle, bound in straw. A cracked and unstrung fiddle, with a blindfold head. And up in the rafters hangs her own draggled petticoat, flimsy as frost, with a spider measuring the rents.

"Her coat," says Margaret, remembering the dark witch. Had she lost it?

"Off ranting," says the leaf-witch. "She'll have doffed her, breeks and all." She bends to her rovings.

And the witch. Not ancient as she'd seemed on moorland: ageless, fierce. A green girl in the husks of autumn. Gnarled hands and moon brow, shining cheek and chin; owl nose and peaked red cap. Straggles of her hair hang loose about her shoulders, mingling with the webs, now grey, now dark; her spectacles cast imps of light about the ceiling, glint and flitter.

"Nine," says the witch. "And one." She lays down her combs. "Not risen yet?"

Margaret makes her dishevelled courtesy. "Could I help?"

"Thou?" The witch is dishing up a cold green mass from the cauldron; she raps the ladle on the bowl. "Thou'rt as much use as a cat i' pattens. Here. Get it etten."

No small task. Struggling with her bowl of nettles and a broad horn spoon, Margaret chokes and swallows. "My thanks."

"Muggarts," says the witch. "For thy blood." She draws herself a horn of ale. Sleet falls hissing on the hearth. The witch drinks. "Dost knaw where thou's bound, lass?"

"Away."

"And wha's thou, when thou comes to it?"

*No one.* "A daughter?"

The witch looks shrewdly at her. Not my lady's gaze, avid and contemptuous; yet Margaret flinches, tallying her self: a coffer cracked on vanity, a windegg. A mole. Bruised privities and rifled heart. Green ignorance. "I can learn."

"Aye," says the witch, and passes the horn. "Thou's yet undone."

The drink is bitter, heartening. "Could I not stay here?"

"What's here? Now and nowhere. Thou's for t'Sun's road."

"The world?" O the dread of it, the great unknowing. "An I must."

"And how will thou keep thee, goslin? Knit nettles? Shear owls?"

"I know not."

"What canst thou?"

"Cipher. Read and spell," says Margaret. "Cast figures of the stars."

"Aye, canst thou? Riddle me: what's i' this house?"

Round she looks, and up and down. And round: she's giddy suddenly with ale. No sky in here. And come to that, no in nor out, no window nor a door. There's nothing but a clutter here of ... *Oh!* "Houses." And she laughs for sheer wonder. *Oh, I see.* The houses of the Sun: the Keys, the Coffer, the Riddle and the Shears. And yes, the stations of the soul's long Road: the Lantern and the Scythe. And there, the place of her begetting, in her mother's secrets, in the Crowd of Bone. Unleaving. "Stars. All the heavens."

"At thy birth," says the witch. "When thou comes to it. I s'll have stood thee as gossip." Dizzy with Cloud ale, her godchild only gawks. "We's kindred, sitha. Thou's daughter to my sister's daughter that's herself, that's one wi' me. So thou's me." She beckons back the horn, and drinks to Margaret's puzzlement. "A souling!"

A courtesy.

Down with the horn. The witch bustles. "There's an ashing for thee that I's kept."

"I thank you, but—"

"That's to be seen. T'ashing's what thou will; and what it wills, thou is to be." She huffs the dust from a great kist; opens it on mice and fragments. "There was books." She turns a smirched face on Margaret. "And which is thine?

Is it the ale? For there's a mischief in her now, an imp of curiosity. "If I were you, I'd have your spectacles," she says; and waits her death by owls.

The witch laughs until the leaves upwhirl around her and the spiders fold and fall. She turns her owlglass eyes on Margaret; tsks and rubs them in her cap. "Here's joy o them," she says; and sets them on her sister's daughter's nose.

And there is nowhere. Round the scryer turns and round: but there is nothing anywhere. No ground, no sky, no feel nor footing. Not a sound. All white in whiteness: a Cloud of unknowing.

"See? Thou can't see but I has my spectacles." The leaf-witch takes and folds them, bow on bow; she tucks them in her petticoats. "I's keep them for thee while thou learns."

It is raining fiercely now, the hall unhousing into mud and thicket, the branch lost in branches, glassy with sleet. The cauldron sunk in mud. The witch bends and smoors the fire. Ashes now. Half light: a cold and clashy dawn. "There now. We's half-moon late." And answering no spoken word. "For t'Nine. They keep back stairs." She flings a sack on her shoulders, sets a basket on her hip.

"Coming?"

Margaret follows.


Small rain. Margaret waked from stalking dreams, toward dawn. So brief these summer nights: the house would be astir by four. Still dusk within, though, in her westward room. Even held aslant above her head, to catch the tide of light, her pages blurred. Even to her night-tuned eyes. She rose and lit her stub of candle at her tinderbox. Ah, that was brighter. Kneeling up, she slipped her hand between the wainscot and the wall, drew out an old tin candle box with all her hoard in it. A pack of cards, some lost; a tarnished ring; a pair of broken spectacles, the glazes fallen from their twisted frame.

She wondered at that last; remembered nothing but a fragment of a dream: a glint and flittering of light, expectancy. A journey. But she'd found them in her pocket, tied about her waist, that morning of her Cloudfall. Hers? But how? A puzzle in perplexity. She sat on her counterpane and turned the bits of glass like mooncoins in her hand, unspent. She held one to her eye, and saw her candle swerve and loom. Further and further out, until the flame dispersed. Mere fog. The other glass? Dwindled it: a spark. Would two at once be clear? A chord of glass? She made owleyes of thumb and finger, with a glass in each. Hand before hand, as if she sighted at a needle's eye. Not that way. This? She moved them in and out, as if she slid a sackbut, peering at the candle.

It leapt at her. A furl of flame. Astonished, she flinched. But the candle was still there on the sill, unmoved. Her hand unburnt. 'Twas but its seeming came to her. A fetch. She laughed in wonderment. *O my.*

Again. "Come, fire." And it flew at her bidding, like a hawk to her hand. A tassel. She held it, warped and haloed, in the glass. Let go.

Again.

Of its own, it guttered and went out.

Stalking and wheeling about her little room, she scried things. Her book, like a great moth to a candle. Her jug, like the moon.

She turned her gaze beyond her window, at the green fields of the sky below. *Come, fold.* It lighted. Here, to hand. And when she loosed it, far away. No stone within its puzzle lost. And not a blade of grass left bent. *Come, fell.* Who'd seen a hillside curtsey like a wave? It moved, removed. *Come, thorn.* Who'd seen a tree in leaf unroot and fly? Alight, without a ruffled leaf? Who'd seen a walking wood? And if a thorn, why not the Thorn? Why not the Sun and Moon?

Long since he'd dreamed of Annot; yet Noll saw her, stitching at a cloth he knew was heaven. Black on white, for it's the back side of the sky. She's taught him that, to read the the grammar of the stars. Strange constellations, yet he knows them all and their ascensions—see, the Owlet and the Urchin, garbed with fruit, the Bear with its bright honeycomb. They two have made them all, the stories of the sky on earth. They've made Unleaving. Now she unfolds another breadth of heaven, saying, *Here's room to fill. What wilt thou?*

*A mermaid with a glass. A tyger.*

Her bright needle flies. Yet all the while he fears the hinderside of heaven, where the ravens are. The Wood is white on black; white leaves that fall from soulwhite branches. Ah, they've stayed too late—*Annot?*

Grevil woke, half smiling, half in tears: for Annot, for the child she left. For the child she was. And puzzled: when did she wear spectacles?

Later Margaret sat with Grevil at his book. Rain as ever, and the soft scratch of their quills. Dip and scribble, pounce and tap. Her thought was elsewhere. She'd need a sort of conduit for light, a pipe. A roll of parchment? No. Heavier. Stiffer. She would need to fix the glasses: so. And so. Covertly, she looked about the room. A flute-case, a map-case. But he'd find them gone.

Outside the window, the gardener weeded and sang. "Hey, we to the other world, boys ..."

In the widow's loft by her closet, there were older woodwinds: a reedless bombard, a shawm. An hautboy in a leathern case. 'Twould do.

"Sir?"

"Eh?" Deep in time. Down the long pleached alley of his pear trees—long

since winter-felled—his father walked, abstracted. White bloom falling on
his bent head, his black doublet. A green thought in a green shade. . . . But the
lass was speaking.

"In your lady's bower, might I handle the instruments?"

"That old virginals? 'Tis lumber. What, to play upon?"

". . . there, the Man i' th' Moon drinks claret . . ." sang the gardener.

"To study."

"As you will."

And the glasses fixed with sealing-wax?

*Thou creeping mouse,* she thought. *Thou wainscot. Nibble at thy master's substance?*
*Lumber. Trash.* Curled within her nutshell mind, she smiled. *Translation.*


Broadlapped, Barbary sat shelling peas; they rattled in her bowl. The door
stood open to the green and rain. She sang:

> *How can I come down,*
> *in the dead of the night,*
> *When there's no candle burning*
> *nor fire to give light?*

A pod of green sisters, a push with her thumb. Another shale. Out in the
wet grass, under the apple trees, Doll chased the sidling ducks, crying, "Dilly,
dilly, come and be killed."

> *There's smocks in your coffer*
> *as white as a swan;*
> *Light down the stair, lady,*
> *by the shining of one . . .*


From her bed, Margaret drew the moon down through her glass, as round as
a drum-head. Tabor to her pipe.


A toy. Her glass was nothing here, thought Margaret: a swift horse hobbled
that would run, a falcon seeled and mewed. Through her casement she could

see but the skirts of heaven, draggled through the hills. And all above, unseen, the mystery and the wheel of heaven. Time's mill turning in the river of the Road. She must get out to it, beneath the naked sky. Must see.

But how? Not through the hall, past the slumbrous dogs, that at a step would rouse and hackle, rising stiff-necked from their bones. But go she must. Bent meekly to her master's book, or working under Barbary's eye, she brooded on her ways and means: with her stripped quill wrote ciphers of her flight; wound wool and longings in a single clew; weighed salt and stars equivocally. She made her wavering stitches with a double thread, of linen and desire, a piercing and a pull the knot did stay.

Window? Here the mullions were too closely barred; and there, the sills too high; from that other casement, she might drop, but never scrabble up again. She needs must come and go; and not be missed. No tower here to climb. Why had they no towers, when they had such skies? But at the foot of her winding stair, beside it in the wainscot, was a narrow door, a sort of stillroom cupboard, and at back of that, a doorway, giving on the orchard. Locked of course. Her key from my lady's tower would not fit; she looked with covetise on Barbary's ring. She missed a clear night; and another, anguishing.

Then on a grey wet afternoon, no hope of going out, by day or night—cloud muffled her chagrin—she set aside her hopeless needlework to climb her winding stair. No comfort in her narrow lodge, nor in the high chamber. Cold hearth, stripped bed, a dwindling store of withered apples: all familiar now. She blew upon the quarried glass; traced patterns in her fading breath. Pinched lavender and balm and borage for the scents. Turned back then with a winter pearmain in her hand.

Now atop the great cupboard, pushed under the eaves, she saw a small chest, like a workbox. Climbing on the chair, she hauled it forward, got it down. Then kneeling in among the lumber in the apple loft, she wiped the dust from it, put back the lid. Folded linen. Nothing strange in that. A needle still in it, half bright, still tethered to its trail of jetty silk: unfinished work. She shook it out, and turned it over in her lap. A smock. So nearly done: it wanted but a sleeve. It was broidered all with rainbows, arched from cloud to weeping cloud, as she had seen them now; but all in black on white. *A sort of book*, she thought. *A spell?* She puzzled at it. *After tempest, see, I come and go.* That much she could read. Snails, butterflies. *I carry my house with me;* and, *I light where I will.* Flowers, but she knew not what they meant. Urchins. *Shan't.* And in the empty room, she smiled. A ship—the Ship—for it was masted with a branching tree, and leafed with stars. *Unleaving.*

For a space she sat and wondered, with the journey in her lap. Then lifted out the inlay with its skeins of silk, its thimble, silver-gilt, and its pillow of pins. Under that, another inlay with some pretty toys of horn and ivory, silver and delf—charms from a yearcake, had she known. A wad of paper, which unfolded was a ballad sheet: a woodcut of a ranting girl in cap and feather, sword a-swash. No more. Yet something shifted, rattled. With her nail, she lifted out a panel, shrunk with time. A key.

And Barbary called up to her, to bring her wardens from the loft.


Ghosted to the shoulder in a fog of flour, Barbary thumped and flicked her rolling pin; she pinched her coffins round. She glanced up at Margaret, wavering on the sill. "All this while for pears? Thou's walked til Babylon and back." Beckoning, the mistress turned them in the frail and pinched. "Sleepy. But will serve." Margaret, turning, tethered to her key and glass, was on nettles to be gone, but Barbary stayed her. "Wait on, and I'll look thy stitches ower. I's just hearing Suke her tally." She turned to the child at the window, knitting.

"Twelve winds, eleven trees, ten sleepers. Say me what nine is."

Sukey puzzled at her wool. "Please you. This heel's all amux."

Ellender, trip-trapping to the dairy, said "It's cloven."

And Cat, "Is't for goats?"

"Monkeys. Same as in thy glass," said Barbary. "Let be." And to Sukey, "Thou's counting, sitha. Look. And let thy fingers mind." Down fell the parings, and she pricked and pranked the pies. Leaves, lattices, a running wheel of hares. "And nine?"

"Nine's for't nine Sisters in a kist o sky."

"Aye, and eight?"

"I could say you three."

"No doubt."

Her needles in a dreadful knot. "Eight ... eight's Brock's keys and locks. Seven's for t'rainbow? No, seven's th' Ship."

"Thou minds what they sing at Elding?"

"Oh, I mind me. An it's songs, I remember." And she sang in her small voice, like dew on a cobweb, clearer than her clouded self: "The sail's o th' siller, the mast's o th' tree ..."

"I's get thee a fiddle to thy school, and thou shall dance thy gramarye. And six?"

"Six for a Swordknot," called Wick Billy from his corner. "And down falls t'Sun."

"Good," said Barbary. "Say me what five is."

He rubbed his nose, all smutched with silver tarnish. "Pies?"

"Nay," said Sukey, pink with assertion. "Five's for't Wanderers. Within and out, and roundabout, and cross t'River twice. And four's—no, twelve were t'winds—four's for't Gallantry where Summer is hanged. And three's for his Fiddlestrings, and t'stars in his Bow."

"Good. Margaret?"

Startled, she could make no tale but, "Madam, I was not so taught."

"No?" said Barbary. "They's strange ways i' Babylon." She unstopped the oven, raked the embers out. "So then. Twa's for't Ravens that bear our souls away."

A chain of stones that broke in running, whirled and scattered on the steps. Elsewhere. A hail of souls.

"And twa's for't Witches that came hither from hence, and bound my lady Moon to't wheel. Set winter turning."

*Bound?* Was that in Grevil's books? And *hence* and *hither*, *never* was and *now*, changed places in her head. Turned inward outward like a glove. It giddied her.

Lifting up her peel of tarts, all gilded with egg, Barbary slid it into glowering dark. "And twa's Leapfire and Lightfast, that's ever at odds, t'ane and t'other, for't mastery o't year. Winter get Summer, and Sun against Sun." She sealed the oven door. "But light and dark is one Moon. And her daughter's Ashes."


"Five for the wandering stars," said Grevil. "So I heard it from my nurse." He thought a moment, smiled, and spoke.

> At eve, the keeper of the day,
> Bright Perseis, at morn;
> At noon, the leaper in the hay,
> Great Hulver with his throng;
> By moon, the reaper in the corn

*To sheave us all, Old Slae;*
*Too soon, the gleaner in his swath,*
*Will reave, Red Morag in her wrath;*
*And sleighting Brock who picks all locks,*
*And thieves them clean away.*

"Well enough," said Margaret. "But they come not in a row, like Jack-a-clocks; but foot it in and out, like country dancers. Cross and cross." Still gazing inward at her sky, that would be outward—O but soon, but even by the morrow. If the door unlocked. There was a glory in her, toward an end: an arrowing. The key hung next her body like the Swan down-diving on the Lyke Road. And the dance was in her, all ablaze. All the conjugations of the planets swift as language, swift as song: a carolling. Now rising, now retiring, at morn, at eve; swift, still; dim, dazzling; before, behind, and turnabout. Now here and nowhere. Tumbling in the sky. She laughed within, as if the key unlocked her. But bending to her page, she spoke most soberly. "They do vanish from the sky at whiles—at random, it doth seem; but never from the dance."

"Do they so?" He tried his pen. "I know them but by chance regard. *O look, 'tis Hulver. See, he rises back of Arket's byre.* And, *Sets,* another saith." He looked not at the room but elsewhere, at a sunlit garden, faraway. "We played a masque of planets at the university, before the lord of Perran Uthnoe and all his kin. 'Twas for his wedding there to Lune, his eldest daughter."

"Were you Hulver?"

Grevil laughed. "Nay. Hulver had a leg; and much ado to get his lines. Our master striped him well for it. Yet he did leap—ah, thou hast never seen it bravelier. And sang like all the stars at morning." On the lawn, the shadows fell. "He was Cloudish, of great family. There was hope of him; but on his going hence to keep his term—as I did not—his ship was lost." He scratched a pattern in his margin, like a knot of hedges.

Margaret knew not what to say. "Is't written? I would read that play."

"'Tis in the elder tongue—but there now, thou art learned." Now he looked at her, all at once shy and challenging. A mischief in his face. "I made the verses." Scratching, scratching. "In a sort, the play did garner praise: 'twas thought satyrical by those who slept through it." He'd drawn a little cloud of asterisks. "I enacted Talith, of the Nine: for whom I'd writ a colloquy." And now a creature in the maze, goat-footed. "Then to rouse the sleeping fellows from their after dinner, comes an antimasque, a dance of woodwos; and so enters Perseis, pursued by Slae: as in the tales."

"Are there tales? Of planets? Of the Nine?"

"Many." Grevil gestured at the heaps of paper, spattering ink. "Hast thou not seen them? In this very book?" He looked about at the disorder. "So. In time, thou wilt, if we untangle. Of the boy who took Journeyman's boat to go a-fishing in, and caught his father's soul. Of Perseis, of course, that was the youngest of the Nine, earthfallen ..."

"Is she not?" said Margaret. "Still a star?"


All in gold and violet, his starry cloak flung back, bright Hulver waits his cue. Stands tiptoe, all the stars a-tremble in his crown. On wires, so they nod his deity. His staff is tipped with light. On stage, the great astronomer, the greybeard, owl-eyed, has piped his invocation to the planets. *See now the Players' Lamp, Ox-Turning Journeyman who mocks the nighted traveller...* Noll Talith holds the book unopened, mouthing word for word. His own and meaningless. How strange that his delight in scribbling should have lit so many candles, branch on branch. The bursar has unlocked his hoard: the ends to go to poor deserving scholars. In the hall, it is dizzying: a blaze and roar, a fire fed on words. In this brilliant artificial night, the astronomer lies down, composing his woolgathered beard, to dream. But here in the withdrawing room, their Law, the real are half shadows: a confusion of stars and satyrs. On the table lie the shepherd's weeds the god will borrow of Tom o Cloud, his broad hat and his budget full of stars. A comet's tail of hair adorns the statue of a long-dead scholar. Wigless Perseis, her train of silver-gold tucked up to flaunt her kidskin thighs, her suit of nakedness, is dicing with the satyrs; Slae, a shy lad, paces, muttering his entrance; Morag, sticky-fingered with nimmed sweet-meats, has ado to tie her beak. Three of the Nine are playing mumble-de-peg; one reads, oblivious; four cuff and bicker like a huske of hares. And Master Wilton goes among them, finicking, exhorting, pinning up. *Seemly, seemly, you goddesses.* And, *Mark the caesura, Master Slae.* But to Hulver, he says only: *Thy dance is deity. O'erleap the night.*

The viols and the hautboys ravel out their braided music. Hulver coils himself to leap. And at the threshold of the stage, a star falls, chiming, from his crown. Noll runs to pick it up, to pluck his sleeve. Too late. The sackbuts call him. He ascends.

Far in the night, Margaret crept down the winding stair, and tried her key in the orchard door. It fit; and with attending to the lock—an owl feather oiled, from her bundle of pens—it turned.

She dared not, yet she must. The glass was in her skirts.

Softly now, she slipped the latch, stepped out among the inky trees. She stood a breath, dissolving in the sound of the river and the scent of green; slipped into it, as water into water, night in night. And ring on broadening ring, she felt the pupils of her soul enlarge. Still stood, attuning to the wider dark. No cell, but shadow to the far horizon. From beyond, there blew a little wind that set the wood astir, that shook the watery leaves. They spattered down on her, small drops of rain. Waked circles to the shore of night. Greywhite on grey, she saw the rabbit on the lawn that stilled and shivered, twitched and stilled; she saw the trembling of the grass. The boles of trees were paler than their leafage, ghosted by the waning moon. A wraithlike blue, limned in lichens, and the burden of the mossblack leaves. An owl belated spoke. So bounteous a dark. When she was brimmed with it, so that a drop would overspill her silence, she looked up.

A star.

One only in the rifted cloud, adrift before the moon; and blotted ere she raised her glass. But there, a dappling of stars, swift-clouded by the shifting heavens. Round she turned. And there and there, a glint of sky, like glimpses of a body in a ragged smock, a shoulder fire-moled, a blue-dark breast. Like islands in the rush of tide, still drowning in the rack. Silently, she called on them, *O stay*. And heedless ran after, through the gate with its stone boys, round the drowsy manor to the upward road. No thought, no longing but to see the open sky, away from the hulk of chimneys and the crowding trees.

Irresistibly, she was drawn to the hilltop and the ring of stones. There the sky would come round again, she half-believed. Envisioned: as a lantern that doth make a world about it, or a silver glass that she had seen in Law that drew a ship from a swirl of colors, as a wick draws fire out of puddled oil. It was the focus. Round it all the riddled heavens would be drawn together in their perfectness, still turning in their wheel of fire.

So she ran, but only to the turning in the hedge, the stile; and there she halted, and she sleeved her face. Looked down at her plashed petticoats, her bare legs striped with grass. Looked up again. No use. The hill was steeper than her onset, and the dark too fleeting for her ardor. Already there were voices in the leaves, a charm and bickering, an endless even plaint. The night was in half mourning, turning back the veil of cypress from its brow. No tint of morning yet—unless in shadows were a ghost of green?

But *see-saw, see-saw* in the hedgerow, like the hinges of the rusty sun—dull vaunt of day—a cuckoo sang its mock.

They were all at breakfast in a flood of sunlight. From the doorway, she was dazzled. "Thou's late abed," said Mistress Barbary.

"Cry you mercy," said Margaret, curtseying. "I slept ill."

"Aye, 'twas a feather in her bed," said Cat. A smirk and elbowing, all round the board. Wick Billy sucked his spoon and goggled.

"Didsta now?" A long considering look.

"Indeed but scantly." Not at all. She'd slipped through the wainscot door as the house was stirring; made frantic rough amendments to her draggled clothes. She dared not drop her eyes; but Barbary's, she thought, missed nothing in the searching light: the stiff-dried petticoat, the damp shoes, rudely scraped.

"Happen thou wants physicking. Thou's have a dish o mugworts to thy supper."

The maids wried their faces. Margaret dipped her submission.

"Come, break thy fast. Quick now. Here's all to do."

Barbary turned to the others. They rose to her nod, in a flurry of napkins. "Day."

Margaret sat, and cooled her cheeks with a long draught of buttermilk. Her porridge was stiff in the bowl.

Barbary was already up and clattering; called over her shoulder. "T'master's rid out til Summerlaw; but thou's weary o thy book, I's warrant."

Seeing Margaret's dismay, the maids overcrowed her.

"Here's out o thy book," said Cat.

"Nay, there's moonshine i't almanac," said Doll.

"At turn o't moon will be our shearing," said Nan, lordly. "And Hob Hurchin's to pipe."

Ellender smiled. "And Tam Sledger's to dance wi' Is Oddin. All night."

Nan tossed her head. "He may please himsel. And what he's brewed, may drink."

"Clip ale," cried Doll. "'Twere brewed this Hallows past. And cakes."

"And delicates," said cat-sleek Ellender. "Dowsets. Curds and cream."

"Thy tongue's to turn it," said glowering Nan. "Thy face would posset milk."

Doll galloped on. "Twelve hundred's to be sheared, says Tom. Then fall to dance."

"Last year I's etten nine cheesecakes," said Wick Billy, unstopping his spoon.

"And were sick on thy long-coats," said Cat. "Thou pollywog."

Sukey, clearing dishes, looked up at Barbary. "An't please you, mistress, will Marget be t'lady at feast?"

"What, yon gowk's egg? " said Cat, "Is *she* to queen it?"

"What's *she*?" said Barbary. "Kit Crowd's mother?"

"Madam Mim there. Margery Daw."

"And why not?" said Barbary. "'Tis not a part that begs discernment." Secure in her ministry, though a cloud of May-fly ladyships should fleet away, she unlocked the spice cupboard. Nutmeg and ginger, saffron, pepper and cloves. A spar of sugar.

"Who is't then? Tell us." A nest of gaping beaks about her. "Have ye choosed?"

"Nan's eldest," said Barbary. A toss of the head. "But Cat Clapperdish is boldest." A caper and a clap. "Doll's bonniest, and likest to a gimmer-lamb." A squeak. "Nell's nimblest—aye, she'd keep her shoes fair in a sheep-dub, an she trod upon another's loaf. And Suke—"

"Nay, I couldn't." Twisting her apron.

"Suke's our piper's daughter and may call his tune."

And she set them all to work.

Margaret, stoning raisins for a century of tarts, heard them singing, to and fro in the long low kitchen, rolling out paste for the cheesecakes—thin as tiffany—and raising coffins for the warden pies. Sad tales of the deaths of maidens to a set of tunes would make a widow skip; and mirth in a doleful key, modal and minor and elegaic:

> *Here's the pink and the lily, and the daffadowndilly*
> *To adorn and perfume those sweet meadows in June.*
> *If it weren't for the plough the fat ox would grow slow,*
> *And the lad and the bonny lasses to the sheepshearing go.*

Ah, but it had a dying fall, as if the petals were a thought embrowned, even in the blooming.

> *Our clean milking pails, they are fouled with good ale*
> *At the table there's plenty of cheer to be found*
> *We'll pipe and we'll sing, love, and we'll dance in a ring . . .*

Margaret had faded from the room. Thought only of the silent dance, the dancers all in cloth of air, of darkness but for scarves of light, faint silver, and the flashing of their crescent feet. They wore the seven planets for their diadems, bright fire at their hilts. Unmasking, they did put aside their brief eclipse. The sun, moon, stars cast off their mantles of the cloud; took hands about the pole. *I was but out of measure with the night*, she thought. *Ill-timed. But if I go before full dark, wait midnight at the stones?*

The Fiddler raised his bow.

Toward midnight. From her window, Margaret saw the stars of summer westering: great Hulver in Ashes and the Scythe sunk deep in grass. Past moonset of a cloudless night.

Time.

With her starglass hidden in her petticoats, she crept down the winding stair, unbarred the wicket in the door, and slipped like shadow into shadow. Breathless with expectancy, she trysted with the Nine. At the sill of heaven, on their Law. She walked as soft as if the moon were owling her, as if the Raven at her back could spy. Death's daughter's child, she feared nought else, no ghost nor witch nor traveller. How brief this summer's night: an island in the rising tide. Even now, it glowed with intimations of the dawn, not stark midnight but owlgrey. Scarce dark enough to see the Lyke Road, faint as foam above her head. She met no stranger but a started hare.

On Law, the greycloaked sisters huddled, sparser than in memory. Her master and Barbary did say they walked. And here, here only was a flawless prospect of the east; as if the circle of the stones were built as frame to it: night's lantern that the east would kindle. Through it, she looked eastward to the harbingers: the Fool, the Knot of Swords. Toward Ninerise. Soon. She wiped her starglass, fogged with gazing. In and out, she walked the maze of shadows, turning Nineward always in her restless hey. Barbary's song was braided through her mind. A summoning:

> *You have three silver mantles*
> *as bright as the sun,*
> *Light down the stair, lady,*
> *by the shining of one . . .*

A star? Still naked-eyed, she gazed until it dazzled. Yes. A knot of stars. She waited as they rose; she bowed and raised her glass. *Come, Nine.* They swirled to her, a skein of swallows—O a crowd, a dazzlement. At once her world was cracked, fell shining. What new stars were these? Dark sisters dazzling. As if her seeing were a breath that kindled, blew the ashes of the sky to embers.

Now Margaret dreamed no more of journeying. Against her night-closed eyes, she saw as through her glass: a coin of sky that trembled, fogging even with her careful breath. A vision circumscribed and yet enlarged: bewildering, glorious, aswarm with stars. She walked starblind, like a traveller in a snowstorm, in the whirl and sting of revelations.

Lying in the dark, on Law, she told the Nine, with pebbles, great and little, on a stone. A henge within a greater henge; a mirror of the smallest, highest of all. A spiral she could cover with her nail. Eighteen. Nineteen. A gemel? Twenty-one. At dawn, she swept them up like jackstones.

It was all to learn again. Not chains and carcanets of stars, but a scattering of stones, unset. She sifted for them, as for diamonds, in a drift of silver sand. There, the Owl's Eye, unblinking; there, the Tabor at the Fool's knee; the Clasp in the Necklace like a clew of light, woolgathered, wound about a spindle of thorn. Torn fragments of a text she'd read in full, an alphabet ungrammared. Notes of music played by one and one that made no harmony.

But there were stranger things to see in heaven.

She'd begun to write them down on scraps of paper: a mouse's nest of them behind the wainscot, with her sketches and her notes.

"Hulver in my Lady's house. He hath a train of Boyes about him, lilly-white: small Starres within his Orbe that dance attendance."

•  •  ○ •              •         ✳    ○ ✳ ✳ ✳        ✳ ✳ ✳ ○   ✳

Remembering, she smiled; then bent the closer to her page.

"The Moon in my Glasse is old." She stopped there. Light enough to blow the candle out, to play at sleep before they waked her. Light enough to write by, and a stub of blacklead: she went on. "Happely she doth go disfigur'd, in the guising of a crone, as Ladies walk abroad in Maskes. If it be not for the sake of Modestie (for all may gaze on her), then perhaps 'tis Vanitie: though she fear not being Sunne burnt, yet she may be Winter chapt. Or else there is a Cloudiness within my glass, a sorte of Cattaract or web. Or else with looking nearly on her radiance mine Eyes be witcht. But she is flawed of Face, like one unpolisht with the Smallpox, who doth white herself to Seeme the fairer ..." Looking up, she saw the moon itself, of lucid gold, of honey, melting on the tongues of morning, in the blue of air. Her light transmuted into song. "... yet she wanes."

Grevil walked out beside his meadows, lifted dazzling from their douse. They glittered in the wind, white aureate. A water green, wave green beneath. Blue undershadow, and the sweetness of the mingled flowers. *Fine hay, but if ...* (No hailstorm, blackrot: he had paid the charm.) Still green but golder, eastward to the rigg, his stripling barley stood, as yet unbearded. At a rippling in the grass like a running hare, he turned. A skylark shrilled its swiftlinked spiring music; but no bird rose. He followed.

"The Road," she wrote, "is made of Travellers." Her book was stitched of gathered leaves, no bigger than her pack of cards: the left hand to its right. She wrote as in a mirror, backward: not in Cloudish nor the old tongue, which her master somewhat knew, but in her cradle tongue, in Norni's language— and in Scarrish runes. No words for half what she would say, so she'd made them up: *starglass. Slantstill.* Notes, conjectures, observations. Reckonings and sketches. Margaret dipped her pen. "... faint Starres and numberless. The Nine ..." Eyes shut, she saw a swarm of stars. "... if they bee Sisters, they are many as an Hive of Bees. What Honey they do make of Ayr and darknesse, I know not. If they be not Nine, I know no Tale of them; and if the Heavens be untold—"

No more. The stars were fading as she gazed, the brief night bleeding into dawn. So brief a night that none had risen, nor had set, but waded to the knee in half-light, dreaming, deep as mowers in a field of grass. All the bright, unlearned stars of summer.

Margaret looked down from the heavens' Law and saw the figure of it standing on the earth. The heavens' rune of stars was mirrored, backward, in the ring of stones. But even that had changed. Like stars in her glass that crowded, riddle beyond rede, the stones had thronged with fainter stones. New monoliths. *The glass has vexed my eyes*, she thought, and rubbed them. Half-light still. But now she saw the new stones were a knot of men and boys, bareheaded, silent. Waiting.

In the bush where she lay, a bird woke, chirred sleepily. None answered.

But the hele-stone walked. It strode from northward, from the wind's eye, with a naked blade: a tall pale moonwitch in a stormcloud of hair. *My lady?* No. Margaret drew a sharp-edged breath. No witch: her image in a bleared glass. A knife-blade eidolon. *Thou mole. 'Tis but a bugbear witch, a shadow on a wall.* No woman even, but a guiser, all in stone-grey, ashes on his head. A man-witch played the part. He wore a hawk-nosed, faintly smiling mask, small atop his lean long body, smaller still amid his storm of hair; he bore a scythe.

The others hailed him, louting low. Crooked knees to him, bowed shaggy heads. Crouching, Margaret shrank, and stared him out of part. No witch. A ropy, ravelled fleece; a mask of bone. A man. What's that but shank and tallow? But a wick for an unseely fire. Whet! Stone on steel rang. Thrice and thrice, the guiser edged his blade. Slow tinder to that spark, he changed. The witch was in him, sightless as a fire by day: a shaking of the air. He shrank, annealed and vitrified by power. His reek of hair rose billowing. Cold fire. Margaret shivered in its blast. *There are witches still on Law*, said memory. The bloodstones in my lady's chain. Her crows. *Lie still. They hunt what flees them.*

Now his daemon roused herself, she mantled in his body. Stalking long-toed in the grass, she turned, now this way and now that. The men stood still as poppyheads; she trod a maze among them, fox and geese. And yet whatever way she turned, her blind mask bent on each of them, it rode unmoving in the rack of time. She danced: the old moon, with the new moon in her arm.

Then all at once, she swung her scythe. And open-armed, the man she struck at leapt the blade. Blazed up, as if he were invulnerable as flame. A challenge. At his cry, his fellows wakened from her spell. In and out amid her trance, they slipped and shadowed, at her very heels: like birds that brave a taloned hawk. Like hares amid the standing corn. Again the witch struck, higher; and another dancer leapt. Bare legs, a bladeswidth from the naked steel. They danced with death. No music but their measure and the wind of her knife. No spell but their serpentine. Always, at the back of it, the rune of blood, unspilled.

The hay's the dance.

By turns, they leapt the scythe. Now high, now low. Stiff men and wary; lightfoot and limber. Stag leaps, goatish capers. A lop and tumble, like a hare. A wallow, like a weltered porpoise; a bogged heave like a sheep. Mute cock-crow. All in silence, quickening toward dawn.

With every swing the light rose and the shadows lay in swaths, as if the moonhag sheared the dark.

By one and one, the men fell back, dropped out. Now three still danced with her; now two. A crowblack fellow and a ragged boy, whiteheaded as a weed. And on this swing, the scythe flashed for the first time, glinting like a gull's wing. The dark man sprang and cleared it. *Blood?* Petals from a crown of poppies, lighting after him. As if her blade had rent the sky. He grimaced.

The boy's turn. Barely made. He staggered as he lighted.

Now the man's. He waited, coiled as a crossbow. Sprang. It was splendid. For the first time, they cried out. *A sun! A sun!*

Swift now, the scythe flashed all about the witch, re-echoing about her like a pyre of lightning, like a bonfire kindled of the moon. It blazed amid the whirl and fury of her hair. Too bright for leaping. Yet the boy jumped, his white head flaring in the risen sun.

He fell like thistledown, to silence. Dazed, unhurt. No man called to him, nor clapped his shoulder. He got up, dusting his torn jacket. Shrugged.

The witch let fall her blade. Her hair drooped mournfully like smoke in rain; her robe clung, dark with sweat, against her body; clung and parted to disclose the naked man. Uncharred and unconsumed. Still passionless, the bone mask smiled. She beckoned to the sullen boy. He came to her; the moonface bent. A kiss. An accolade. And it was ended.

They were scattering to their labors, silent as they came.

Margaret hid.

He passed by her, the witch, long after all the rest. Burrowed in the underwood, she saw him, weary and dismasked, unwitched by daylight, with his bundle of guising. He stank of sweat and sorcery, green rank and acrid as a fox amid the thorns.

## Leapfire

The brat lay like windfall in the grass beneath the ragtree, bruised with birth. He puzzled at the light, the leaves, the dappling of their shadows, doubling as they fell. When Brock came by, the boy was sleeping, nearly covered up in leaves. No fox, no crow, no witch had found him, cradled in the old moon's lap. His blood was not to spill. Not yet. And yet the earth would have him. Crouching by the thorn, she lifted him. He scented of his mother, blood and milk. The down about his head was white as barley. Naked as he came. Piss-wet. She sained him, eyes, mouth, heart; she happed him naked in her coat. Soul in earth in air in fire. He woke and wailed. "Here's a bagpipe that plays of itself," she said, and danced him. "Here's a thirst." Will Starvecraw, she named him. And off she strode with him to be the Sun.

Grevil's study was all shade, a box of drowned green light. Beyond the open window stood the orchard, deep in grass, downsloping to the water-meadows that lay white and shorn. The air was sweet with hay.

Grevil laid aside his flute. As if in Arcady, he'd loosed his bands, laid bare his wrists and throat. A sultry morning. Not a bird. As he studied, he ate cherries pensively, with ink-stained hands. The bowl was wreathed with dragons, blue and white. A rarity, but clouded now, a little crazed. Beside it lay a pair of ivory compasses, a bundle of blunt quills. Drawings of the stones at Askrigg and at Imber Lap.

Margaret at his side was elsewhere, by a river overhung with trees. Ash Beck. *The wood above,* said dreaming. *Here's the Lyke Way in thy glass.* She stood bare-foot in the pebbled shoals, and watched the endless seine and shiver of green fire. *What the Nine are weaving.* Light in leaves. It flickered down and down the river, dazzling and a-dance. A riddle in the rune of light. *If stars . . .* She waded out into the shallows, in the glint and dapple of the stream. It sang. A slow leaf fell to touch its shadow, rising from the air. Rimed. Drifted, eddying; was whirled away. She stooped and flicked a pebble up the stream. It skipped and started, skipped and sank. And at each leap—O wonderful, beyond all hooping—worlds began. As in her glass, enhaloing and interlaced. A skein of stories.

She was happy; and in shadow.

And yet more worlds, unbidden, came. There. And there. Outspreading. How—? Ah, rain. She heard the pattering on leaves. The river dimpled with the dint of rain. Rings wakened. Crossed and fretted and recrossed, until all the beck was one grey breadth of cockling silk. She lifted up her face. Unweaving rainbows—

The red squirrel called her back with scolding.

All gone but the travelling, fading at the limb of thought. *Map falling stars . . . ?* she thought. *Sleave skein?* All writ in water. Gone.

Whisk, her master's squirrel, flounced from table to book-press, book-press to sill, chittering. The birds in the ivy racketed and slanged. She tipped the sanded page. "Your pardon, sir. Go on."

But her master was gazing out the window, a bob of black cherries on his hand like rings. Margaret followed his glance, puzzled. A cat in the currant bushes. Cheesecloths, sweetening in the sun. A mower, scything in the orchard grass.


*O I am slain,* thought Grevil. *I am grass.*

Burnt brown as a warden pear, his shirt laid open to the waist. At every stroke, he strides, he wades through downfall. O brave, the tyranny of youth.

Hard as a green pear, hid among leaves.

Soft as a sleepy pear, brown-sweet and bruising. Butter to the knife. Rough skin, the russeting. The bite of blue-veined cheese.

Brown warden of the trees. That mocks and vanishes.

At dawn. The brush of branches, wet against the face. Further. White as bloom.


Coming down by halflight over Nine Law, dazed with stars, Margaret never saw the boy till he called out. She started, casting wildly for a way to run. Sheer rock fall: not up there. Slough and hag behind her. No. Swift stony water: a long leap. She wavered. And the boy before her in the heather, watching.

"See'd a hind leap yon water. Not i' petticoats," he said.

Margaret faced him warily. He was crouched in a cave of bracken, paunching a hare with a streak of knife. After a moment, she knew him: the white-headed boy, the leaper of scythes. The moon's thrall.

"I saw you jump," she said.

Setting had dwindled him: no leapfire, but a starveling boy. As black in grain as a goblin, imp-ragged, stunted as a scrog of thorn. Half naked, but for sharded rags. His hawkweed hair, that sunstruck was a burr of light, was clagged and sallowy, a ravel of rope-ends. He stank, beneath the reek of blood. He looked at her with cool eyes, green as hailstones.

"I see'd thee skulking. If my lady heared on it, he'd lesson thee."

His lady: the man-witch in robes. Not Annis. "He knows naught of me."

"He could. Thou's awd Noll's fey."

"Master Grevil? Do you know him?"

He stripped the fell from the flesh. "Knaw him? Aye, toyed him for a jacket but two days since."

Puzzlement.

"Jigged him. Danced his dawcock." Blue bone-end, luminous. Raw meat. He looked sidelong at her, mocking. "Thou sloe, thou greenery. Dost knaw what I mean?"

Coldstruck, suddenly she did. "You cheaped yourself."

Now he bent, straking his worn blade in the grass. "'Twas he 'at spilled, not I." He tied the hare, leg through leg. "Cried out. I driven him."

With a cold qualm, she remembered Morag's hands on her: contemptuous, efficient. "Let me go." She gathered up her skirts to get past him.

"Odd on." As if he'd caught her by a trailing leash, she turned. "I see'd thee, owling after stars." There was something in his blood-creased, black-nailed hand. He held it out: a snail shell, whorled and brinded. Tenantless. A coal of fire, it seemed: as if he could blow and it would brighten on his stithy. Night and firelight. A house. A heavens. "Bonny, in't?"

With her hands behind her back, she stared. Said nothing; stayed.

"Called Nine's Bower. Same as stars."

A hand before a candleflame; wreathed hair. A dream? A candle in a cloud of stars.

He closed his hand on it. "Yon hall." He quirked his chin. "Thou's in and out like t'cat. Hunting t'moon."

"So?"

"Eggs." He tossed the shell to her. It lay in the heather at her feet. "Milk. Meal. They's a kist full and ower. Thou could leave 'em by Owlstone, nights."

"They'd be missed."

Impish suddenly, he grinned at her. "Thou say it's for hob."

No stars. No going out: rain beat down sullenly, ran swirling down the muddy cobbles of the yard. No candles left to read by. Restless, Margaret paced the attic by her room, beneath the bare planks, apple-stained. Gaunt comfort in that. The wind seethed in the heavy branches, bowing, blotching out the sky. At last, she sidled down her stair, and crept across the smoke-damp hall. There'd be rushlights in the kist; she'd nim a handful of them, tell her cards. In the passage by the buttery door, she halted, listening. A voice rose and fell in the kitchen, in the cadence of a tale.

"... so, on a winter's night, the moon's spindle near full ..."

Margaret crept nearer, peered round the door. A covey of the maids sat by the fire, all at work; it was Barbary who spoke.

"... a lad come reeling ower hill, a fiddler frae a dance ..."

Caught.

A maid glanced at another, smirking. Needles prinked.

Barbary knit on. "Pricked thysel, Ellender?"

"O no," said the fair girl. "But that Meg Magpie is skulking i't cup-board."

"Stealing cream."

"Turning it, more like."

"None less for thee." Barbary called to Margaret, "Come ben, if thou's a mind to hear."

Still Margaret havered on the sill. The brindled creature by the hearthstone yawned at her. Great elfstone eyes, sleek ash-and-ember flanks. Cruel teeth.

Doll's voice sharpened with disdain. "Not flayed of a kitlin, ista? Pretty puss."

"She hunts," said Margaret.

"So she is made," said Barbary, "as Tib to prattle and Tom to lie abed." Heads bent demurely. "And mice i't buttery I'll not abide." She beckoned

Margaret with her chin. "Blue skein wants winding. Ont dresser."

But as Margaret edged in, there came a stamping in the hallan-end, a wind in the door. "There now," said Barbary, setting by her wool, and rising. "There's Hob." And bundle in apron, she slipped through the screens. They heard the mutter of a man's voice and the clang of pattens. Gone out. Through the door came such a fresh wild scent of earth and water, such a rush and a tumult of water and air, that Margaret nearly turned and ran out to it. Could not, before their eyes.

By the smoky fire, the maids unbent their tongues.

"That'll be fox amid geese," said Nan wisely.

"Tinkers i't barn."

"Filching eggs."

"Firing hay."

Doll said lusciously, "That craw lad's been about. Skulking."

"What's he?" said Margaret. "A spirit?"

Nudge and smirk. "Aye, one o Noll's feys," said Ellender.

And Cat, "If thou gang to't Hallinwood, he'll gi' thee a green gown."

"Get mooncalves on thee."

"Goblins." Whispering. "He disn't have a soul."

"Nor a shadow."

"He'll creep in at window, Suke, and steal thine."

"There now. That he won't," said kindly Nan. "Not without thou call him in by name. And he hasn't none." And to Margaret, "He's nowt. Nobbut beggarly. He were an Ashes brat."

"He should ha' been dead."

"Bled back to't earth—"

"But she hidden him away, his mam."

"So he's nowt."

"Nameless."

"And she's Ashes ever."

Low-voiced: "Any man's."

Sukey Bet uncorked her thumb. "Our mam says he's Mall's basket."

They hooted.

"So he is. Hallyborn. So we's not to clod muck at him. For Ashes sake. And she's gi'en him our Dad's awd shirt when he's begged, and bread." Twisting her apron, pink with unwonted emphasis, she said, "And so Mistress Barbary has. So there."

"Ned's awd stockins," said Wick Billy from down amidst the muddy shoes. He lay there on his belly, dreamily, pushing them about like boats in water, like wagons afield. "I knaw where t'Mistress has ganged."

"Thou disn't."

"I do. Cuddy's getten bellywark. Green imbers, he's etten. And she's ganged wi' a drench." And he bent with his wisp of straw to Nick's great haywains, Margaret's stout cobles, down at heel with clambering.

Clack! went Barbary's pattens on the sillstone. In she came and snecked the door. Shook out her spattered apron; settled her cap. "Here's a clattering of tongues. Do thou make up t'fire, Nan; and Doll, thou scrape sugar. We'll a posset ere we go." Bidding Margaret to her knee, she slipped the blue skein on her hands; and winding up her ball of yarn, began her tale where she had left:

"... a fiddler frae a dance. He heard no bridle ring; but in his road and cross his way there stood a horseman, all i' black ..."


It was clouding to the eastward even as the Nine would rise. The stars were winking out, dissolving in the moon's spilt whey like salt. No glimpse of Journeyman; but Perseis and Hulver lay conjoined. No more this night, thought Margaret. She would in, and write her notes, and rise the earlier. And yet she lay in the cradling heather, gazing at the earth asleep. Asleep.

*The curtains of her journey billow out, raingrey, and wrought with stars. Her bed's a book, a ship. Is time. The leaves lift, turning backward in the tale. Unwintering. The clawed rings of the curtains ...*

Were a nightjar in the heather, churring, changing to a cuckoo's mock. She started up. No bird. That white-polled boy.

"Catched any?"

"I'll away," said Margaret, rising, with her glass behind her.

"Dark yet," the crow lad said. "If thou's bent on play."

"'Tis my work and I have done."

"What, is thou moon's shepherd? Is all thy stars in lamb?"

"I wonder that," said Margaret. "So I wake."

"Thou madge-owl," he said, but absently. Turning gazing at the sky, he was silent a space. "Moon's driven them to fold." He bent to her, all prickliness turned thistledown. "Ayont this knowe. Will I show thee?"

"I must away. They'll be stirring."

"Sun's abed. They'll not afore it, being swinked."

"The mowing ..." But she wavered.

"Hay's in," he said. "Yon field's t'last. But see thou." Softly at her ear. "Come. A pretty flock o stars, and all a-maze i't grass." Coaxing still he drew her on, still turning backward toward the cloud-lapped east.

"There now."

"Oh!"

A cloud of stars. Of wandering stars, Perseides astray. Aglint and giddying. Now there, now elsewhere, in and out, like candles in a maze. A dance. Down-drifting like a scarf of light, silk gauze and silver, spangling, that wafted to the grass and tumbling slowly rose, unravelling. Rebraiding, cross and cross. A net and what eluded it. Ah, there, the cloth of heavens of her dream, but wrought on nothing, on the air itself.

And airy as a conjuror, as grave as any mage, he swept his arm at them.

"Here's t'Sheepcrook; here's t'Black Dog, at Fiddler's heel. Yon's Riddle. Yon's Lantern at t'Ship's mast. And t'Ladle and t'Vixen Dancing." His hand like a pale moth. "Yon twa bright stars is Witches. Sheath and Knife. There's Smith at her stithy. That's t'Owl, waking wi' her one eye open, and Brooch in her claw. That's Sickle and that's Straw, but some call it Thread-Needle or As-Many-As-Will. That's Ewe and that's Shears. There's Fold."

"Fiddler?"

"Aye, to play for t'guising. Didsta fall i' last rain?"

Margaret considered. "Perhaps I did."

His naming made no sense: 'twas spring and winter all at random. A juggerly.

"Does they like thee, yon hey o stars?"

"Not stars," she said. "Slow comets. Planetary. See, they err."

"Owlet." He stooped and combed the grass; and turned to her. Moonspill through his fingers. She could see his sharp face shadowed by it and the will o wisp of his hair. He showed a little flinching creature in the cave of his hands. Against cracked nails and callus, earth-ingrained, she saw its scrawling shadow and its moonleaf greeny glow, that seemed no part of it. That scarce indwelt.

Spill and shadow. She bent, scarce breathing, to observe the thing. A chimaera: a grubbish creature and a lamp of soul.

"What is it?"

"Lateworm." Triumphant. Nonchalant. He opened out his hands and whiffed. Away. "Thou goslin. They foretell."

"Can you read them?"

"Aye." That scornful glee. "That grass will fall."


*So I've drowned*, thought Grevil, turning upward to an endless green. A roaring in his blood. No breath. And far far above him, wavering, an eye of light. *I've fallen through the Sun's eye, fallen burning from the mast.*

He looked to where the crow lad waded, naked as the Fiddler, in the shallows of the beck. Against the stream. *O let me keep this moment ever, ever at the sunstill—only but to gaze. Unleaving.* How he bent, like wind in barley; how he stood. Burnt brown as Tom o Cloud, oak brown to where the leaf turned flower, to the softness and the stirring. And his white head burning in the sunlight, in a flare of silver. Like a comet, perilous and beautiful. *What Till hath writ on Comets. What Antoninus saith.* Ah, now the pyets in his head began, the rumour in his ears. *See now, t'King o Lune is dead.*

"Lad?"

"Aye. Again?" But he came and crouched by Grevil, naked still, and plucked his tousled shirt. Unscarred, unbeaten since his boyhood—Madam's cruelties were of the spirit—Grevil would not strip beside that flawlessness, that damage. He himself was marred, but only with the keeping, like a wanfine vintage, musty with his age and ink. He traced the downless cheek, the collarbone.

"Not over and again, but ever."

Grevil's hand went to his coatskirts, to his pocket, to his purse; spilled out a something glittering on his palm. Sun's face looked up at sun.

"Eh," breathed the crow lad, and bent to it.

A mask, no broader than his thumbnail, bearded with the corn.

"Is't coin? Or what?"

"An ashing."

"Whose?"

"Thy forebears." Grevil turned it in his hand. The face, not kingly but a stripling youth, scarce bearded, seemed to smile. "A digger found it in yon hill by Imberthwaite they call Unleaving; not in my time but my father's father's, and 'twas ancient then. As old as Mally's shoon, my nurse would say." He touched the bright hair. "Thine."

Grevil saw the light go out of him. "They'd hang me for it."

"Why? 'Tis no one's but the earth's, as thou art."

"You knaws me, what I is. I's Ashes' brat, I's nowt." He pulled his rags of shirt on, and his breeches. "When I's dead, I's craws' meat. And there's none sall tell me."

Grevil put the bright thing in his pocket; stood and took him by the shoulder. "Thy tale is written in my book: how Ashes is thy mother and thy soul is Cloud's."

"Burn it." Now he kindled: not with love but dread and fury. "That's not for yer grammary. Yer fool. If he—"

But *If* was swallowed. Almost he had struck his elder, clawed him by the ears: the Master Grevil who could have him hanged. He'd had him by the cock and stones a quarter of an hour since; had jigged him. That was business; this was insolence.

Gently Grevil took the work-rough hands between his own, unclenched the fists. He thought he knew the cause. "No craft in spelling: I do swear it by the Road. I am not the first to write of Ashes and her son. Thou art in a crowd of such."

Still sullen. "Crow lad's what I is. There's nobbut t'ane."

"No, lad. No. For all men die: yet that is not the only tale. Thou art thy own self, and thy tale is thine." Soft, soft now as a snail's horn, stalk and eye: the apprehension of his soul. Not lust but tenderness. Once more his hand delved in his pocket; once more the golden face smiled upward at the sun. He closed it in the crow lad's unresisting hand; he kissed his mouth. And softly, even as the boy had turned, the elder spoke. "Know that I do love you. Will."

As if it burned, the crow lad flung the gold from him. As swift as starshot, tumbling in the sun, it flew, fell sparkling in the water: where it lay.


Grey and sultry. All the trees a lead-roofed louring green; the becks like scratched and sanded pewter. Even in the shaded house, Margaret heard the endless sithe and rustle of the barley. It was bending earthward, light and heavy with its end. Beyond the river, slanting to the sky, she saw it: hoary-headed, all a-dither and a-dazzle. There was thunder in the air, said flurried Barbary: the butter wouldn't turn, the milk was dour, the hens a-swither in the rafters, and the chimney vexed. 'Twould lay the standing corn, she doubted. Grevil had gone out to view his fields with Gill Arket: to bestill the tempest if he might.

That imp of elf-bolt in the air had witched her pen. However carefully she wrote, her page was finger-daubed, all blotched and cockled with her sliding sweat. Blind Os: her quill at fault. Her plait-ends ermined with the ink. She tipped the sand, that clung and glittered on the dampened sheet; took up another page, crosswritten.

*"Of Charmes. For engendring a childe of Stone:*

*"There is a kind of edg'd Chrystal, calld by oure Countrywomen Haile; that beeing taken in a Witches wombe (an she be flawlesse of a Man), with certaine other rites, will breed of her a Misselchild. Of which they say, Shee is Ashes, lateward come. These Flints or rather flawes of Ayr, they say, did fall of Annis in her shattering ..."*

Thunderstruck. Had shattered? Could my lady fall?

*"... the which (though it be reckond Ages past) yet they do call this endris Night; and they do swear it that this child of Hailstone (mirour to herself) shall be no striding Hagge nor Guiser, such as Childern fear, but Annis in her Perfectnesse."*

No more than that. Had fallen, ages past: could fall. But in that wrack her knowing of the heavens overturned. Blind Law had stood eternally, she'd thought: a field of souls. Death's garnering. My lady's dark of moon had reaped them, green and bearded, bled of light. Their ghosts like windlestraws, threshed dry. She saw it now—O now—undone, death's harvest springing up as light.

A rumbling in the heavens, back of Owlriggs. Now a glance and lifting in the leaves. Green dark at forenoon, almost for a candle. Bending by the spattered window, Margaret dipped her pen.

*"Against thunder ..."*


In the north, it rains. There Ashes is called Earthfast, for she never rises; in their brief pale nights, she wades in darkness to the thigh, like one cast up. Her ocean is of earth, of time. She topples in the wave of dawn.

Past midnight. Hail and wind. It lashes at the window, hung with arras and unglazed; it rattles down the chimney, hissing in the fire. At a blow, the shutter claps, and Madam lifts her head and listens. Nothing. Only for a space, the wind has fallen, and the candle curls about itself its winding sheet of wax. She reads again what she written in her letter to her kinsman. "... durst vilifie thine House to meddle with a namelesse Girl ..."

At that she lays aside her pen, and rising, she unlocks her kist. Within, the casket is of iron, hard as dragonscale, inlaid with horn and porphyry and roundels of a glassy stone, nightblack, in which a fire sleeps, half-waking: dragons' eyes. She bespells them. With her charms and with her bunch of keys—not all of matter—she undoes the nine witch locks, turns back the heavy lid. At once, a roke is in the air, of rime. A somewhat glitters in its depths.

She does not touch. She is no virgin; it would kill. And yet she gazes on the stone, desirous. A shard of Annis. Fracted and refracted in its crystal are the starry heavens, flawless of the sun. A frost is on the iron: endlessly the stone within it turns its matrix to itself. It seeks an other to subsume, to cast a likeness of its lyke. Yet cannot hold: without a limbeck of the flesh, it sublimates. And falls, a snow of stars.

A girl. And in her wardship, fatherless: to be reborn. Ah, she herself could envy that annihilation. To the stone she names the vessel: Annot.

Low in the heavens now, the Reaper bends, as if he gathered shadow in his hook, a harvest of the dead. He crouches like a fishing cat. Below him, deeper still in Law, there swims a tawny star.

That sky is in the scryer's cup, the cup within his hall; his hall—ah that no Ashes born may tell you. East of elsewhere. And the sky's his cup; he drinks of it, drinks down the moon. The scythers' witch, who will be Lightfast— though he goes by many names—keeps wake. He watches. In the nightwine is a speck of gold, a spark, slow-tumbling upward; now a flake of fire, now a drowned face, all of gold and wreathed about its head with gold, and every hair a sheave. A souling. Grevil's Will.

He drinks.

"Now?" said Margaret, swathed in apron.

"Back. It spatters." Pink with bending to the fire, Barbary stirred the pan. A slush of beaten sugar in it went to molten snow. "Thou see it didn't gang to rime." Round she stirred. "Else it's all to do ower."

*O strange*, thought Margaret. *Burning snow. A frost of fire.*

On the table lay rounds of paper, written over like the moon's face: Grevil's book turned thriftily to use. She'd copied out those leaves; had cut them—so—for Barbary's pots and pies. The door was open to the day, where Suke and Doll stoned cherries in the garth. The kitchen boy whistled at his scouring. Nan in the buttery clattered and sang.

> *O came there a stranger here last night*
> *To drink till th' day was a-dawning . . . ?*

"'Tis a way of keeping light i' winter. Shares o't sun." Barbary kept stirring. "So: we's have us imbers at Lightfast, as is proper; oranges if there's a ship; a quiddany for Kindling; and at harvest we s'll put up damsons, white and black, for Ashes' ale." She looked at Margaret. "Is there not imbers in thy country?"

*Oranges. They keep in Law.*

"Is there not hallow days?" A spark of sugar leapt and fastened, burning, to her wrist. She sucked it. "Do yer not remember Ashes, there i' Babylon?"

On brittle ground. "We keep not feasts."

"Here's Cloud i' this household." Stirring. "Did thy folk never tell thee of Ashes? Of Annis and t'world beyond?"

*Behind. I left it.* For a moment, caught as in a glass, she knew not coming from her going. Margaret in the deep reached out to Margaret. To pull her in, to drown her. Or to fish her up. She knew not which. Carefully, she said, "I am schooled in goddesses. But I have done them no observance."

"None? Did sun not rise there?"

> *They sought him up, they sought him down*
> *They spared not th' featherbeds a-raking . . .*

Just then, the sugar turned to glass, a perfect crystalline.

"Now," said Barbary. She put the fruit to the sugar. The imbers sank, enjewelling in their essence. Each star embedded in its sphere, becoming it, outspiralling until the heavens were one red. An alchemy.

And O, thought Margaret. *I remember. Was there was not a ring? I was cradled in the moon's lap, and she gave me—Took?* "I had an ashing. That I know. But it is lost."

In and out went the maids at the far end; in bounced Nan, still singing:

> *O I's had many and many's th' maid*
> *But th' likes of yer I's never had baking!*

Barbary pointed with her great spoon. "Stone pots. Did I not tell thee?"

"There now. Be forgetting my petticoats next." Off went Nan. *". . . th'
crockery and platters breaking . . ."*

Turning back to Margaret, the mistress said, "If it ever were, then it's in
Ashes' bag. So come to it, thou will be tellt."


Unclouded and a setting moon. It would be perfect dark. Margaret slid from
shadow into shadow on the way to Law. Her heart beat like a nest of swans,
uprising in a flare and clattering of wings, a wind of prophecy. Time's falconer, she bid it to her hand.

At the crossing of ways stood the Owlstone with its long wake of shadow. Margaret felt within the hollow of the stone. The eggs and the barleycake she'd left were gone. *Crows,* she thought. *Foxes.* But there was something
else in the litter, sharp-edged to her searching fingertips. Knapped stone.
She scrabbled it out: a leafshaped blade, an arrowhead, faintly glittering by
moonset. *Daws' nest?*

A shadow at her back.

The wind that impelled her whirled her round to face—no huntsman,
but the lounging crow lad. "Barley," he said, palms outward in truce. Ale on
him. He reeled a little where he stood.

Foreseeing made her tense and lucid as a waterdrop, ingathered. "Go
away."

"My road as well as thine," he said, and shrugged at heaven, where the
Lyke Road shone like spilled silver. "Broad enough for a fiddler and as many
as will." She saw the flash of his teeth. "Thou's late abroad, Mag Moonwise.
Ganging til a dance?"

"A silent one." Woundless as water, she'd come round again, as if no dart
had pierced. She turned her knowing like a stone of crystal in her mind: the
skyroad within it like a twire of silver, herself like a flaw of air. "Let me
by."

But still he strutted in her way, importunate. "I's gamed wi' Grevil's
sword," he said. "Awd Noll's. I weared it for him, belt and all. Nowt else." He
laughed, leaned closer still. "I garred him kneel for it." A whiff of somewhat
alien, of smoke and civet. "But's there's one I's see'd this night will horse me.
Wouldst thou up behind?"

"Afoot," she said. "Thou wants the manage on't."

"Thou nettlebed." But now he looked at her. "Thou's Ashes born, I'd swear: if ever vixen had a prick and stones."

She looked back at the crow lad, face to face. By the lees of moonlight, he was pale again, as if his dayself were his shadow. He'd cropped his hair, lopped off the dirty clags. Had doused it, seemingly. So lightened, it had lifted. It spiked about his head like thistledown.

She held out the sharded blade. "Yours?"

"Elfshot." He mimed a bow. "My lady hunts."

"Where souls are. Not with arrows."

"Aye, and thou's rid out wi' her."

"I walk."

"Thou jinny-howlet." He bent close to her, breathed ale and awe. "There's bones i'th heather. See'd 'em. Wind blaws through and through him, and there's none has tellt his death." And lower still. "*Her* craws had his eyes."

"They take not souls, I think."

He looked oddly at her. "Thou hailstone. Didsta fall frae t'moon?"

"Walked," said Margaret. The starglass bumped at her knee; the stars fizzed like cider in her blood. She looked to the heavens. "No word. And I'll show thee something."

"Up thy petticoats? Catched me a cunny?"

"In the Fool's cap," she said. *Now*, said her tryst. Not looking back, she turned, and climbed the path.

"Black or white?" he called after. "Thy cunny. Black or white?" No answer. "Squirrel, by thy head." No turning. Far behind, she heard his vaunting echo. "I's a star ... *star* ... thou's not spied." Gone? But he lagged her, shrugged and dallied to the bare hill, crowned with stones. The round earth's nave.

"Here's nowt," he said. "Thou babby. Bare as thy lap."

"No tongue! All eyes!" She pointed heavenward. Bare nightscape. Silence. The crow lad sulked and fretted. Yet he stayed.

The great moon, gold, imperfect—half a token—set.

A star fell, flintstruck: a glint and gone.

"Ah," said Margaret, breathing out.

He muttered softly—a charm?

"Soft," she said. "'Twill come."

Another? Or imagined? There! Elsewhere, at the edge of sight. Faint, fleeting. For a space, no more. And then a nonpareil, a beauty. And its lightsake, hind and doe.

"There," said Margaret.

Rolling back on the grass, the crow lad laughed. "Thou fond! Didsta comb them frae thy hair?"

"No." Six—seven, flick and fall. Like lacemakers' shuttles, this way and that. Nine. Trailing sleavesilk. "I foretold."

"So any goatboy could. Yon's nobbut Hailseed. Falls i't summer fields. I's found it oftentimes. Not catched one. Clarty stuff." A sly look sideways. "Come harvest, Jack Daw dreams o riding, and he spills."

"That's thy lady's talk," she said disdainfully. "More of thy jig."

"Not wi' him, I never—" He sat up, tearing at the grass, his back to her. "Thou urchin. Thou hollybush. Misdoubt thou scattered them thysel."

A memory: oil of orange in a candle flame, swift sparks. "I've never seen them till now." And thought: nor any stars of summer. Nor the sky itself, but through a slit.

"Bred up in a kist, wast 'a?"

"Yes."

He said nothing; but she felt a shift in him, a sliding, like the slump of snow in thaw. Could fall heavy on her. Could resolve as mist.

They lay apart in the summer grass, looking up at one sky. By one and one, the stars fell. Flakes of cold fire. A riddle of embers.

The crow lad shifted in the dark. She saw a tawny star between his fingers like a ring. "Some says they's my lady's lops—Hey!—'Cause they's wick as fleas. And moon's her nail she cracks 'em with." Fleas in a black ewe's fell. "But up east, they says Daw's threshing out yon Sheaf. And Death's his flail."

*A field of corn, all rooted in a sleeping man, a sheaf whose binding is a belt of stars.* She looked for the Hanged Man behind the hill. "He's cut down."

"Aye, toppled. He's til t'fields at dawn." He gazed. "Awd wench I knawed—"

"Ah!" cried Margaret. Scattering bright.

"Said when a star falls, t'Nine is weaving."

Now she glanced to him from heaven.

"Said they's strands of Ashes' hair. Burnt up."

A cold wind at her nape. She watched the bright shears slash and slash the web. The Skein is fate: the stories of the wood above, all braided toward an end. But these lightfallen stars were chancy; they undid. Untold. They sleaved the Skein. "And what thinkst thou?"

He laughed. "Yon sparks," he said, "they's chimneysweepers. Weeds." He puffed his cheeks and blew, outspread his empty hands. "Like that. They come to dust."

"I don't—Oh!"

Like sparks whirled from a burning brand. She leapt up, as if to greet a messenger, with arms outflung. A harbinger, that ran before—what coming? Not the dawn. Her face uplifted to the thronging stars, as if they'd cover her like snow.

The lightstorm struck. A windless rain of light, a swift-scrawled palimpsest, a tranquil fury. Margaret turned and turned to it, light-lashed and whirling in an ecstasy, a-dazzle and a-dance with stars. The heavens' whipping top.

But the crow lad crouched and swore, like one beat down by hailstones. "Get by, thou fool!" As if the sky had shivered like a glass, still crazing; as if the shards were arrows of the Hunt. He caught her by the sleeve and cried, "Get down!" But she whirled away from him. The sky had overturned. Below her stood the stones of heaven, and above, the bladed earth, a-dazzle, like the wind in barley and the scythes that struck: light reaping light. And then no *as above* and no *below*, no *likeness* but light's self; no dark, no otherwere, no *this* and *this*, but *now*: a wave of light that stood and shivered. Stood.


A flickering at the shutter's edge. Not wind. His candle burned unwavering. A summer lightning, then? Grevil rubbed his eyes, that dazzled with his overwaking. And he bent again to study. Not for Margaret's eyes, this Lunish book. Yes, here, as he recalled; he wrote now in the margin, *Star Shott.* "Nostoch understandeth the nocturnall Pollution of some plethoricall and wanton Star ..." *Quaere: if not Slae?* "... or rather excrement blown from the nostrills of some rheumatick planet ..." *Here's catching of colds,* thought Grevil; but he noted, *Hee is Melancholie, rather.* "... in consistence like a gelly, and so trembling if touched." *Our barren wives do gather it; and wantons that would dream on Paramours. They saye a mayd was got with Childe by a falling star; Shee knew no other gallant; and was brought to bed. Of what, I cannot read. Yet being of its temper, cold and moyst—or else by lawe of Adversaries,* vid.: *What does, undoes—they call it* Unmanfall. *The marrish Witches mell with it a sort of grease, that smutted on the bravest Verge will shrivel it. What mooncalves may be got of it, I know not; nor what dreams may come.*

Before her lay a field by moonlight. Not silvery with it, though: as red as leaves in hallows. Light in grain. Earthfire, indwelling, even as the cold quick silver of the moon: slow fire that a breath would blaze. Reaped fire and rustling, bound in sheaves. The sun was harvest.

*For the old moon's bread.*

She knew that.

And a scarecrow—no, a traveller stood, he walked among the sheaves, the embers of the sun in shock. Long-coated like a shepherd, with a broad hat and a staff. His budget at his belted side. His black dog at his heel.

Astray. And wandering as he willed.

*He dreams of this,* she thought. *Of the Unleaving. I am walking in his sleep. The Road*—

The moon's hand waked her.

Barbary set down her water jug. "Past four, and still abed? Thou snail." Grey morning, but foretasting gold. "They's lang afield. They'll be crying t'kirn at Out Riggs, and there's all to do."


Grevil stood dismounted at the headland, looking out upon his field. The last to reap. A good year: it would fill his barns. His sicklemen, of August weary, bent to work amid the standing corn. His bandsters sheaved and stacked. He watched the rope and slide of sinews in a shoulder, in a back; the clinging of a sweated shirt, the gold glint of an arm. They wore broad hats of sunburnt straw, with here and there a wreath of poppies: for they cried the neck today. *A kiss, a clip!* Their Leapfire black and sinewy this year, not fire but its coals. Gib Hawk. White dogteeth in his workburnt face. His mouth—*think not of it*—his mouth would taste of hurts. The bluest eyes.

Noll saw no hawkweed boy among the harvesters, still whiter than the shocks of barley. For the Ashes lad must not come nigh the harvest fields. 'Twas lying with his dam. A blasphemy. *(And if one lay with him? As length to naked length entwined, one sweat? One ecstasy. Or thought of it, between the furrows, then ... ?)* His blood the earth had hungered for, unspilt, was now anathema. His print, his shadow even: they would taint the corn. And yet he was himself the harvest.

In and inward in their spiral, sunwise, crept the reapers with their knives. Noll had a snake-stone, split and polished, in his cabinet. Like this, a spiral, coiled and chambered on itself: but stone. It gendered naught.

A sheaf. Another sheaf. No eddy now: its eye. A patch no broader than his closet standing; then his table; then a man. They ringed it in a running wheel.

Their master now uncovered to his mistress Ashes, she that wed the corn; and stooping for his sickle blade, he joined them in the sacrifice. They waked the corn.


Naked in among the stones of Law, the crow lad who was Leapfire knelt. They'd bound him in a rope of straw. The mask was at his shoulder, bristling, woven of the corn. A crown of it: his power and his overthrow. He knew that passionless and smiling face: Noll's token that would not lie hid. He'd wear it at the last, when he had risen; and unseen, would see.

All round him and below, the fields lay bare. The neck was cried, the stooks were carried, Grevil's ploughland shorn and carted like a drab.

Before him lay his grave. They'd brought him hooded to this place at dark, and laid him in his long trance, in my lady's cleft. At whiles he waited; whiles he muttered to himself old ends of rimes: what he must say. Before the cock-crow they would bid him answer. Soon, it must be soon. How slowly, slowly ran this night; but it was paling: now he saw a little through the meshes of his blindfold. Nobbut sack. All round his burial, the earth was trodden in a maze, a spiralling. Not all the feet that hollowed it were dead. He saw them: shade on shadow in the dawn mist, walking, now this way and now that, and through and through. They mingled when they met, like fire. Ah, but cold.

They walked the Lady into being.

When she lighted she was three. From east and north and south, she rose. Three faces, each and all the moon, his end: her sickle shearing and her mill-stone trundling round, her old black cauldron gaping for his bones.

*A neck! A neck!* the grey cock crew. And from behind him, suddenly, a rope was round his throat and twisted: held until a knife was in each eye, a bloo-dred sun; until a blackness cracked him like a snail on stone. Let go. And naked, blind and burning, hard and helpless, he was turned about thrice moonwise. He was crowned with straw. With sun. A silence but the clack of flails.

My lady spoke then from the north. "Who graved thee?"

He could whisper. "Thy servants sworn to thee. My lady, i' thy lap."

And from the east, "Who got thee?"

"On thyself, myself."

And lastly from the south: "And who will bear thee?"

"Thyself alone."

Three staves struck the earth as one. "Get him up."


The Fiddler, wrapped in Cloud, still slept upon the hills. Outworn with harvesting. *No gazing now,* thought Margaret. She'd go no further on. Turning back from the hillside, coming down, she halted by the Owlstone. She'd cakes for the crow lad in her pocket, from the harvest ale. But there was something left already in the hollow of the stone: a roundness, and the ghost of scent. She knew before she drew it out. A withered orange. Light with age, a shadow of itself. She cradled it and sniffed. *But where——?* They grew not in the wood. What conjury was this? And under it, and stained with it, a playing card. Not hers—her heart had clenched—but cruder. Tallowy with handling, and it reeked of bacca. But the one: old Slae, the coldest of the wandering stars. He sat with his unwilling bride, bright Perseis: the banket spread before her all untasted, and her cup undrunk.

Full naked moonlight now. And at her own chill back, a shadow and a scent of wine. Uncloudish. And another, ranker stench beneath, of man. Of Morag's games. She turned.

So pale—a revenant? An inbreath, caught. And then she sorted what she saw: the crow lad in a fine white shirt, laid open to the waist. As white as deathcap, rising from his rags, gill-pleated to the bands. A lordly shirt. He laughed. "Made thee leap." There were twigs of ivy in his white crow's hair. "S'll make thee tumble next." He held a sprig of grapes up high—*now jump for it*—and higher still, a taunt. He smiled like summer lightning, at a flash, and elsewhere. He was drunk. Not sprawling now but taut with it: a bowstring, and his quiver full of pride and mockery. "I's a star thou's not spied. Riddle me that."

"If it's not in heaven, then 'twill rise in time; if not, thou may'st look for it in Law."

"I'd go," he said. Lordly. "I'd dazzle thee."

"How cam'st thou by that shirt?"

"With tickling trout." New bruises on his wrist, his neck, the color of the grapes. "There's nine," he said. "Then eight." Sleek fruit, unwithered, with a bloom like galaxy. And each a starless night. "I serve a mistress greater than

```
          ALAMEDA FREE LIBRARY
              Main Library
           Alameda, CA 94501
              510-747-7777

   Register #: 01    Branch ID: ML
   ==================================
   07/31/2010  10:06   Invoice # 17819
   Salesperson: CB
   ==================================
   1002
     1            @ each 1.60      1.60
   1002  33341005083984 1364414-0 (fine Inhere
   1002
     1            @ each 1.60      1.60
   1002  33341005052518 1364415-0 (fine Trick
   1002
     1            @ each 1.60      1.60
   1002  33341005084297 1364416-0 (fine Sweet
   1002
     1            @ each 1.60      1.60
   1002  33341007509606 1364417-0 (fine Desert
   1002
     1            @ each 1.60      1.60
   1002  33341007486342 1364421-0 (fine Firefl
                  ===================
                  Sub-Total:   8.00
                  Tax:         0.00
                  ===================
                  Total:       8.00
                  Paid Cash
                  Amount:     10.00
   ==================================
      T H A N K    Paid:       10.00
       Y O U !     Change:      2.00
```

thine own." He bit; he sucked ecstatically, and spat. "Her dark s'll eat thy light."

Mist rose from the river in the dawning. There was light now, even in the wood. Green, green as summer still, the foliage, but in a sadder key, incurling on itself. Bronze green: the summer cast and past. The gressops now had changed their tune. Grevil walked beside the river, up and down, as he had walked and waited since the pale of night. No more. He dared not: he was wanted at the high barn, great with barley. A good year for the corn: the sun had held. He looked at the rain-starved river, bonier, but saw no glint of gold. *Happen he came back for it.* But that was folly: it had washed to sea, or else lay deep within a dub or cranny, lost until a chance discovered it, untarnished and unfaced. The river kept its counsel. Here and elsewhere, a circle started, spread; another and another one cross-faded. *At the ninth,* he thought, *I'll go.*

"Fishing?" said a reedy voice. Turning, Grevil saw the scythesmen's Lady, with his bone mask on his shoulder and his staff, but elseways as a gentleman. "There are rare trout in this stream, I've heard. What luck?"

Grevil chose his words. His neighbor had a jackdaw's eye for trouble, and a restless and malicious tongue. And he had spies. "Good morrow to you, sir. Ill fortune. 'Twas here but yesterday I caught three fingerlings and lost a luck-piece from my pocket. Through a hole. If you see it—" He measured air between his thumb and finger. "'Twas a sort of antick charm, no bigger than my thumbnail. Gold."

"I mind it well," said the witchmaster. "Tom Grevil thy grandsire took it from its grave, where I had laid it with my son. Thy family was the first to break the earth with spades of iron. It is old; it likes not cabinets."

*He's mad,* thought Grevil. *Doting mad.*

Yet still the fellow smiled. "I liked not thy fathers. They did break the Law." He turned away to go, how lightly for his years. At his back, the mask still mocked at summer's fall, unseeing.

"Stay," said Grevil. "A word with you."

He turned, as if he were a card: that face all mystery and malice; this, the lord of high estate, all arrogance. Master-Mistress. "If brief. I have business elsewhere."

"That boy they call the crow lad: he is sorely bruised, beyond all measure of chastisement."

"What care is it of thine?"

"That care I take of any creature on my land, that it be not abused. He—"

"What *he?* It is an Ashes brat. There's game in it, no more."

Grevil drew a breath, but his voice shook. He was losing. "For shame. The boy is kinless; but is of your kind."

"For all I know, he's of my getting." The witchmaster shrugged. "Leave thy fence, Noll Grevil; I know thy care in this. Thou coyst him and he cozens thee; but he is mine." A flicker of the card. "Of earth and of my mystery, and at my will. As thy vixen is thine."

"What vixen is that?" Lost utterly.

"That nameless maudlin thou hast taken to thy bed—Aye, hand to hilt, thou'll not kill earth with iron—"

*Mad. But as a dog is, killing with his mouth.*

Sheer, smiling enmity. "Aye, she. Noll's fey. Now there's a liking I'd not guessed in thee. Whence came this tooth for cunny? Or dost thou use her as a boy?"

"Crows eat thee," said Grevil. "And thy lying tongue. And all thy slanders. These are tales of naught."

"Tales? Are they not thy mastery? Here's law before thy books were made: what's masterless is held in common. Haws in every hedge. But I tell thee: I will give thee thy crow lad for a turn if thou wilt barter. Boy for girl."

To Grevil's shame, his impulse was to flail at him—scratch out that smiling face. A womanish, a weeping fury. Futile. As good score adamant, outstare the sun. When he had mastery of his hands and voice, he said, "Go, play thy vilest fantasies: but on thyself. The girl is innocent; the boy is neither mine nor thine, but hath his will. I do not take." He looked now at the mask of flesh, the face of ivory. Was there a crack? Was there a difference? Nothing in the eyes. "And even nameless, they have souls."

"Do they?" Suddenly the witch's face was mischievous. "Does thy crow lad? I do wonder where he keeps it hid." And whistling up his dark hounds, tall as thunderheads, he strode away.

Getting crawcrooks on the moor for Barbary, Margaret heard a low-breathed whistling in the heather, changing to a stormcock's angry rattle, rising, and the white-haired boy fell in with her. Said little, circling back and back to her, and to and fro, like one of Hulver's moons. But he showed her where the owl had built, the feathers and the bones; and where the imbers grew, blood-ripe, miraculous: at once whole and hollow. Pierced. She set them on each finger's end. He dug where he had left a merlin buried in an ant-heap, skull and body in their perfectness, want-polished, white as elfshot. Each his own garner.

By and by, they came among grey trees, an orchard run to wild. Thrawn trees, flawed apples, windfall in the tangled grass. Thick as stars. *The wood below.* Margaret knelt to scry it, sorting through the heaps. Sitting back on her heels, she cradled—heft and sweetness—sniffed, and bit. Sharp-sour, leaping in the mouth. The crow lad, stooping for his share, said, "Here's bonny."

Leaves in her lap. All round, the bare green hills, cloud-mantled; water, wind. Behind her in the orchard, scarved in mist, knee-deep in tangle, lay a low-browed cottage. Asleep. No eyes in it. "Whose ... ?"

"Awd lass." He knelt in the deep grass, tearing hanks of it. "Gi'ed me bread, times."

"Is she dead?"

He shrugged.

The house empty. "None came here?"

"Witch."

An apple fell; birds cried. He was weaving grass between his hands. A bauble turned and rounded, bristling. Too green: it flagged. "Tellt me stars. What she called t'wood above."

"Stars like mine?"

"Thou stocking bur. Aye, stars like thine, that light mooncalves to mischief." He tossed the bauble to the wind. "Thou's another such teasel as yon twitch-rake. Scritch scratch like a pair of wool-combs. Thou braids of her, awd Jin."

A glint on gossamer. Up and upward into air. She traced it with a craw-crooked finger, dreamily. Blue hands. Far off, a sheep bell clanked.

"Witch?"

Hands flung heavenward, he toppled backward in the knobbly grass. "Aye, witch." He lay looking upward through the leaves. Through his backturned hand, as if the faint sun dazzled him. "She were Ashes."

Kneeling up, he felt amid his rags and tatters for a twisted rag of pouch; undid the string. Raddle and ashes. He smudged a fingertip, and on a stone he dabbed a swift scant pattern: a glyph of stars she knew. The Witches.

"What she tellt me."

He sat back on his heels, the stone between his hands.

"Once afore t'moon were round, there were sisters, Craws Annis and Mall Moonwise. And they span t'moon atween 'em, turn and turn on ae spindle, light and dark. Ae thread. And ilka clew they span a month; and ilka twelve and one, a year."

"What did they spin?" said Margaret.

"For Nine to weave, thou windegg. Yarn."

"But of what?"

An inchworm silence, blunting at air.

"Shorn lateworms?" she said.

"Snick up, I's telling thee." But his mouth quirked; then statelier, he said:

"But Annis, she were high and proud. Thowt ower much on her white hands: so she span no more. And that were Year at far end. She thowt much on her glass. Fair as frost, she thowt hersel. So she's rived her shadow frae hersel, and bound it in an iron brooch, and hid it, lock and key, i' kist. And that were Night fast. And she thowt as Sun would get new shadow on her, so she's cut him down wi' her sickle, sleeping. And she's ground him in her quernstones and she's boiled him in her pot. Tongue and teeth it has, atween her legs. And that were Day drunk up. And she band her sister in a bush o Thorn. And that were Moon lost. And t'Stars she fastened in her glass."

"Not now," said Margaret.

Another silence, needle sharp.

"Lang syne," he said. "So it were Lightfast evermore, for ay and O."

"And then?"

"Twa witches come out o't Otherwhere, fire and frost"—he touched the stone, two fingers to the brighter stars—"and swore that Annis should be bound."

Chin on knees, she was gazing at him. "And?"

He tossed the stone away. "They did."

"Did the sky crack?"

"Aye. Riddled down like rain. Like hailstones. It were stars til t'eaves."

"And the year turned?"

"Like a whirligig."

"And—" She could not say it. *Annis?*

Greendark beneath the branches now. The crow lad sees another dusk beyond it, dawning, and the shadow of the crows. A cornfield. Now he shakes with cold and clacks his rattle, and the cold mist eats his cry. He is hoarse with shouting, but he must. *Craws!* Annis crouches in the hedgerow, waiting; if a crow lights, she will pounce and tear him with her iron nails, and hang his tatters from the thorn.

He leaned to Margaret, whispering, "Eats children."

White morning, like a new leaf, all unwritten. Silver on the lawn by sunrise. Gossamers. An edge of gilding on the trees.

*Autumnal,* Margaret thought.

They'd taken up their scattered work: a heap of Grevil's notes, unthreshed, on flyleaves, foolscap, scrawled in margins, lay before her, interleaved. Her quire of pages, squared and sorted, weighted with a pebble, to her hand. She tried her pen and mended it.

Across the table from her, Grevil stood and read a folded sheet, cross-written, with a haws-red broken seal. Not work. He wore his coat, but no bands; he'd been seeing to the threshers in the great barn, in and out. *Let them glean who want,* he'd said: *'tis garnered. I'll not stint.* All beyond the trees and rising to the stones of the fellsides, the clouds' edge of the sky, there lay shorn fields, unmantled of their summer dignity. He looked out on them. Pale straw a-prickle through the bare brown earth. *White-headed. Back and shoulder for the stroking. Like a cropped lad's neck,* he thought, and stirred. *The nape a-shiver to the hand.*

Margaret drew a little Ship. *Autumnal.* And a new word, *Hallows.* She could taste the curve and edge of it, the quickening: the great stars rising and the whirl of leaves. A larger night laid bare. *Unleaving.* She forefelt it even in her spirit's marrow, great with dark.

A stir and shaking in the orchard leaves, but no bird's voice: Doll asway in the treetops called down to Nan below her, with her apron full of pears.

"Half ripe," called Nan. "There's better higher up."

Bending to her paper, Margaret wrote:

*At Lightfast is the Sun in Ashes; for the which oure Learned Wives do say that she is great with Time. But the lewder Sorte will haue it, that Hee dyes in her, and rises in her Lappe.*

"Do thou tent thee and I's toss." The shaking of the boughs and scrabbling, the plump of fruit.

"O a wasp!" cried Nan.

"But the one, I hope," said Grevil, leaning outward. "I have had them smoked, but the windfalls draw them. How they dote."

Another margin.

*They will let the Sunne no stay in Law, though in sooth it lies a Twelve-Night in that House: they say the Guisers call not at that doore. I have heard oure countrey Fellows tell that Law is Ashes' Bagge, wherein the Soules of all the Dead are gather'd, Coyne untold. Some others name it not; or else, the Riddles that are endlesse Falling or her Cauldron that is fulle of Bones; or in the Lunish tongue (a Traveller at Stallbrigg once), her Virgin crants or Garlande; by the impious, her thing of Naught.*

*The Scythe . . .*

Turning from the open window, Grevil said, "Of what age are you?"

"Sir?"

Looking up, she saw a swirl and settling of birds, like ashes, on the bristling field. A shovelful of cinder-crows. Three gleaners moved aslant the furrows. Slowly, stooping as they scried and harvested. A straw, another straw, to swell the meagre bundle in the hand.

"I know not. Not fourteen, I think."

"Thou gravity." He folded up the letter in his hand. "And of what name? What birth? Will you not swear that you were such a one—Joan's Jin of Askrigg, that was stolen from her cradle while her mother keeled the pot, or daughter of the king of Lune?"

"I am Margaret still. As still I rose. And of no house but this, and at your will: I sojourn here." She saw, as though between her hands, my lady's toy, her spheres: the sun of amber sliding round and round the felly of the year; the moonstone twiring backward through the turn and topple of the stars; the planets in and out, threadneedle, through the starry hey. *Time is where.*

"I see. You are planetary."

All the branches now bore girls. He glanced again, as if distracted, at the green. "My father had those trees engrafted. Luning on an older stock, and all the sweeter for the imping out." Distracted still. He picked up, set down the pebble on a heap of papers. "As thou knowest, I am childless. Makeless. And mine aunt—" Stone, paper, knife. "Well, there are lands. There is a name. And she—I tell this ill." Knife, paper. "This world is unkindly. My name and privilege do ward me from the worst of cruelties, but thou art bare. Beyond these walls, beyond my tutelage, thou wouldst be shelterless from harm." Paper, stone. "I would not see thee slighted at my death. Cast out." Now he looked at her. "So then, Margaret of Nowhere, Margaret Perseis, I would name you as a foster-daughter, as my ward. As Grevil."

As if she'd fallen from the Ship: no up nor down, no earth, no anywhere. No breath. The rush of fires in the dark. "Sir, I—"

"Margaret?"

No answer. What she saw was wing on wing of nightmare stooping on the house: her mother's mother and her bloodnailed servant. They would snatch her from its ruins.

Softly now. "But I have spoken all too suddenly. I see I have amazed thee."

"But ... your aunt?"

His mouth wried. "I have told to her my will. She likes not the alliance." Paper, knife. "But liking must be servant to the law. I can draw such papers that she may not break. Aye, and seal them." He twisted round his massy ring. "This is Grevil's will." Now—only now—he touched her, lifting up her chin. "The land is given: that I cannot change. But I would leave to thee my books."

No words.

"And you? What is your will?"

"I dare not dream of such felicity. If—"

"And if?"

A silence and the stir of branches. "Nothing. Only I would go on working."

"Enough now. The page is dry. We will parley." He sighed. "Get you to the kitchen, hence. They'll want you garnering when Doll hath broke her crown."

Owlset. The Ladle sunken to the rim in stars, like a tin scoop thrust in grain. The Scythe sunk deeper still, but barely embers in the grass. Nine rising. Starring out like thorn.

"Fiddler?" said Margaret. "Fool?"

A shifting in the dark beside her. "Mmm?" His mouth full of stubble goose.

"Thy guising on the Road. What stars?"

He sprawled back in the heather. "See, they's hunting yon Wren." With gnawed wing in hand he traced the sprawl of them across the sky. "There's poor awd Hobby Horse 'at's welted ower on his back. There's Room where they rime."

The great square of the Threshing Floor.

"And Wren's Cage, sitha, brave wi' ribands, and t'Awd Wren hanged."

That whorl of light unspun: she knew it in my lady's Chain. The Clasp.

"Yon's Fool wi' his Knot o Swords. Tabor at his knee. He's one o't heroes. And there's a kemping atween 'em, Leapfire and Lightfast. Sun and his son. Stark battle wi' bright swords. Thwick thwack! And t'Awd Year tumbles down." He flourished with the bone. "And Fiddler's lagged. He's lantered, see, i't Thornbush. They go tumbling round and roundt sky, drunk as owls. And they never catch Wren, and he's catched long since."

"Wren?"

"Aye, well, he's setting there. Aback o Noll's barn."

Margaret called to mind the airy card. A bird in a thornbush. "Why do they hunt?"

"So year is."

For a space they were silent, gazing up at the sky. Giddying. At last the crow lad said, "What d'ye call Fiddler then?"

"The Hanged Man," said Margaret.

Wind in the heather.

He sat up. "Thy folk'll be lating thee."

"Not here."

"Oh aye. Thou's waiting on thy rade to fetch thee under. Bridles and all."

"And back of him, about the Gallows Tree—? Not Witches. Crows," she said. "To pick his bones. They quarrel for his eyes. And there—" Westering. "There's another, swooping down with his soul."

"Fiddler," he said, and hurled his goosewing in the heather. "Thou blindworm. Up there's t'Crowd o Bone that he's lost at a wager. And he's seeking it ont Lyke Road. They stringed it wi' her hair." His voice shook: whether out of fear or triumph, in the dark she could not tell.

She'd not ask. But, "Ashes?"

"Aye, they clipped her for a whore." Rolling to his knees, he pointed. "Yonder on her back, aspraddle. Allt Road atween her legs."

"No," said Margaret.

"Seed full and sack open. Threshed."

"No."

"Aye, and her belly roaring full o flesh. Big wi' Sun's brat. Or any."

"No." She looked where Ashes lay, light-stranded at the verge of Law, the Lyke Road streaming backward like a braid of hair unbound. Her Ring, unseen, beneath her. That way the Hallows tide had borne her, to that darkward shore. Time's shipwrack. Going naked into dark. "No, they took her. Under Law. My lady's … her servants. The Light Horseman. And her Brach."

"There's none such stars."

"Beyond that hill," she said uncertainly. "They would have set. The Hunstman and Hound?"

"Flittin round thy head, more like. Hawk and Handsaw."

"The Swift?"

"Oh aye. And t'Whirlygig. Doll's Dawcock." Here and there, at airy random. "All that nest o maggots i' thy mawky brain, thou windegg."

She sat brooding her knees. "And the Hare?"

"Atween thy legs. Thou fond."

"It would be rising," she said. "I've seen it rising. And the Tower." They were in her pack. She'd dealt them out a thousand times. And in that Tower, in its maze, within its hedge of iron thorn. Beyond that sea. The strangeness of their absence shook her: not her knowing but her sense. As if ascending on a stair she felt a falling. All of these were cards my lady took from her, and all were void: their patterns faded out of memory, their tales burnt out. As if they'd never been. And yet the cancelled stars could still be reckoned in her glass, be counted yet untold. "I could show thee. I'd tell."

He laughed. "There's nonesoever i' this earth has see'd yon stars; but thou has. Digged for them, thou sky-mole. Under Law."

"'Tis where they go; and some do rise again." Her finger traced the fell. "There's Ashes' Ring beneath yon hill. Her soul. They took it of her at the gate—"

"Thou witch." A whisper: but it touched her secrecies. "Uncanny's what thou is."

Colder now, a small wind shivering the heath. "As they will—"

Silence. Even as she spoke, she saw his riddle, rhymed him with a lost card of her pack. "... a star thou's not spied." And she'd given it to burn. A harvest field, a hailstorm threatening; a reaper bending to a Sheaf that was a boy of barleycorn, white-headed like himself. And in his outflung hand, a star. Called Leapfire. She knew it for the seedcorn of the sun renewed. Against the stormdark sky, white crows were rising. Seven. And the brashest carried off a something shining in its beak. *Seven for a secret never to be told.*

The card was burning in my lady's hand; the ashes fluttered to the floor. *Thy choosing, Madam. It will make a game.* Margaret got up. "You can have the cake, I don't want it."

The flower between the leaves was faded, pale as the moon by day. The imprint of it lay across the page, faint shadow on the faded ink: *". . . as Childgrove, which is death to fell . . ."*

"Her book?" said Margaret. A play of Perseis, outworn with reading. In a margin in a brave small hand, much flourished: *Annot Fell.*

"For epigraph." The fled girl's nephew sighed and smiled, remembering. "It was the first I read that set me thinking on the metaphysics, on the stories of the sky on earth." (The shepherd Damasin arose and drew her bodkin, crying out, *Avaunt ye! Hags of night!* And Noll in his black petticoats, a hatchling crow, assailed her fiercely, shrieking out declensions in the old tongue, till she turned him upside down. They tumbled on the floor.) "Above all else 'twas marvellous: there was a star danced in a wood, Unleaving, that did take a shepherd for her love." He pulled his heap of notes toward her. "From here," said Grevil. "Where 'tis marked."

With a blade of barley, awned but empty of its seed, a husk. Margaret turned the book a little toward the fading light, and wrote.

*"The earth may bee divided as the Heavens, into fields. As these, in our demesne of Cloud, call'd Bare Bones, Dearbought, Come by Chance; Cold Hallows, Hanging Crows; Sheer Ash; or Babylon. So likewise do we map the heavens Sphaere, take fallowes of the Element and garths of Law, as these: the Bonny Hind, the Hey (wherein the Nine are bower'd); the Fiddler and his Bitch at heel; the Riddle and the Shears; the Ship.*

"Now *Perseis*," said Grevil, turning to the leaf-shadowed lines. "Where first he speaks."

*"O rare Cosmographie—"*

What voice? She saw another's shadow on the book, the leaves blown backward. Nothing. A wind in the ivy, a small bird's plaint.

*"That wee may cry (as doth the Shepheard in the play, that lookt upon the fallen Perseis, amaz'd), O rare Cosmographie, that shar'st the commons of the Night in steads of fyre, stints of Ayr. Of these (for the greater part) their History is a tale of Nothing, mere Obscurity, but for the Cadence of a starre, chance Fyre; yet some be hallows of the Sunne and Moon. That the Heavens are indwelt in Woods, springs, standing Groves was credo to Antiquitie, who raised them Monuments in upright stones: which carols are the starres' Epitome; the standing houses of the Moone her progresse; Stations of the Sunne.*

*"Yet needs the scion of the Light (scilicet) Barleycorn no vaulted Monument. On going to his naked bed, bare ground, his Seed doth hallow it. His Acte is all. Of his Solemnitie is made our winter's Mirth, that Maske wherein hee's headed and doth rise to dance: the Earth his Tyring-house, the Threshing-floor his Inne wherein his tragedie and Jigg is play'd. The Guisers*

*cry him Room. They bear him in the Sheaf, in* Effigies; *the Old Moon sweeps the way before, and Ashes in her suit of mourning stalks behind. At every Door, they drink his Wassall, of his Bowle, drink down the Sunne . . ."*

She bent to dip her quill; Grevil, mending his, stared silent at the rain, his knife in hand. A thought, like water into water: troubling, mingling with her soul. *Time runs here; he will die of time. And I . . .*

The ripples faded out. She wrote.

*". . . drink down the Sunne that will them wake: in his remembrance is Oblivion.*

*"Wee go not the Sunne's way into shadow, endlesse round to rise; but walk our longways on that paly Road, from earth to Ashes, fallows to the Scythe. We are but Clouds of Earth, instarr'd. The Heavens are indwelt in us: the Sunne that is our marrow, and the scything Moon; the Ship and every wandering Starre. In every Soule is Ashes. In our Nativity is sealed our Death; in every Child his waxe, the Impress of the Sky inlayed: his Lyke Road and his rising, and the journey of his mortall Starre."*

So early dusk. Already now the even of the year, its equipoise: the light ensilvering, the gold ingathered to the barns. And Margaret was late.

There was harvest on the high moor, hurts and crawcrooks. She'd leave to pick with Doll; but Doll had spied a shepherd lad, and slipped away. A moment, she had said; but when the bush was bare, she'd still not come and Margaret, wearying of idleness, had strayed on to the next. But only this spray and that beauty, barely out of reach; this handful, just to even out the frail. They led her down the far side of the fell. And still with her night-quick eyes she saw new garner in the hedgerows, hips and haws and rowans, sloes and brambles, clustered thick as stars. Hers for the picking, for Barbary's winter gallipots.

Now she hurried with her laden basket, shifting it from crook of arm to wrist to shoulder, side to side; she culled it to her bluestained breast. Her garner. Her excuse for dawdling, and her offered recompense for ravelled sleeves, bedraggled petticoats, spoilt shoes. But in her haste, she jounced the berries, and they scattered in the trodden way. Were burst. So she went: halting and hurrying; flurried and dallying; belated and beguiled. Astray.

A moment since, the light lay dazzling aslant a field, pale bright with straw, and climbing to a slate blue sky. They'd counterchanged: the sky was silver pale now and the broad earth shadowed. This was nowhere that she knew: a coign in a crowd of stony fields. She stood.

Long shadow at her feet. Behind her, on the shoulder of the fell, it still was day, still glowing with the embered sun, white ash; but all the sunken path before her lay in shadow, turning always from her way. She felt the glow of her success and flurry fading in her cheek. Cold now with doubt.

Field and fallow now to either side. Rooks quarrelling to their blotchy beds. And in the air, a waft of something sweet and melancholy that she had no word for, that was autumn. Overcrowed then by a shrewder whiff of smoke. She turned about. Upwind of her, a whited field. Like rime. But it was white with ashes: they were burning stubble. Scarecrow figures bent with torches to the straw. Before them ran a rake of fire, a swift scrawl, meteoric: a night, a century of nights of starfall at a blaze. In its wake, great plumes of smoke, white grey as heronry; then dying, darkening in braiding rows, like manes. And the horsemen leaping fire, driving it, all grey with ash.

But the fire only deepened dusk: and there, beyond the fields, was Nine Law, wrongside round. Its haunchbone: in its lap would be Grevil's steading and his hall. They'd not chastised her yet. But then she'd never yet been missed away; was ever snug abed when she was waked. Whipping she could bear, though not before the maids' disdain; but dread of their displeasure— of Barbary's just reproof and Grevil's fret—still daunted her. Best get it over with. No path. But if she cut across the fields, aslant... Yes, that was gainest; and here was a stile.

Lowering her basket to the far side first, she clambered over. She kilted up her petticoats, pinned up a flagging braid; then plunged across the plough-lands, startling a hare. The wraiths of straw that looked so frail, that dithered in the barely wind, bit deep. Sharp stubble and uncertain footing, powdery and plodgy. She'd not gone a furlong, not a quarter of a half, before her shoes were clagged, great formless whelps of clay. As if she grew earthfast, like a standing stone. Or waded to the knee like Ashes, in the dark upwelling from the nightsprings of the earth; as if the fallowed earth bled Law.

A field, it might be, where an Ashes child was spilled; where he might rise, unsowing from the ground, to dance amid the furrows, with his white hair like a wisp of fire. Nameless—but she'd read his litany in Grevil's book: call'd Bare Bones, Dearbought, Come by Chance... Like fire, she saw him leaping, stalk to withered stalk, from now to never was to will. So brief a span: green-bladed, bearded in a summer's space ... Cold Hallows, Hanging Crows ... and hoary-headed, doddering, with the sickling of another moon ... Sheer Ash ... His cradle is a scythe, the frost his ashes ... Babylon.

So brooding unaware, she stumbled on a cairn of stones, half-hidden in the weeds; cried out in falling as her basket spilled. Vexed half to tears, she crouched to gather what she could. Went as still as any hare.

Cold at her hausebone, a shadow and a reek. A something loured at her back, it rounded her: a stench and sentience that walked. A bonebrown woman, all in rags. She bent among the stubble, scrabbling at the clodded earth, as if she'd lost a ring, a knife among the weeds. A gleaner? But of nothing: there was nothing in her seeking hands. A garnering of dark. Still Margaret crouched and willed her on, away, like sleet or sickness or a dream of Law. But the gleaner turned to her and squatted in the furrows, lifting up her ragged skirts as if she pissed. O nothing. Naught: held open like an old sack in a barn.

Margaret turned her face; but only to the chaffwhite face, as in a glass, as if the glass had caught her in its stone. The trance in it was hers: the glint in shadow of the eyes, the mouth agape. The hag of hair, earthbrown, ashwhite, as if the fire had overswept her. There were clags in it like mice, like wasps.

"Moon's put wormwood til her dug," said Ashes. "And she's barred us out her belly. But I knaw a way. Away." Her voice had once been beautiful; was ruined, like a knife corroded in its sheath, a clouded mirror cracked. Like grave goods. "For he's to gang and she mun gape for him. I's ride him cock-horse til my mother's tower, and his cock sall knock her door." She leaned still closer, whispering. The black had swallowed up her eyes. "They's hanged him halter-sack i't stars, yon Gallowsclapper, but I's cut him down. And snaw's his shroud." Her hand, outstretched and beckoning, held crawcrooks. "I sall tell him for his pretty eyes."

"I must go. They wait me."

But Ashes caught her with clawed hands, held fast: a look of cunning sharpening her face. "My lady's made thee all o glass. I see'd thee scrying o't seven stars up Lawside—aye, and at Lad rising. Gazing on thy back." A hawking laugh. "There's a pretty worm he gi'ed thee. There's a hook for it to fish. My lady sees."

No answer.

"He'll have ta'en a ring. My lady sees to it, she's sworn. He'll dance Daw's jig for me, up horse and hattock! And I's ride him tilt moon."

"Let me go." No voice. Her tongue was dry.

But the hag held fast. She groped with Morag's prying hands. Margaret cringed. The memory of them still was fastened in her flesh like ghostly talons. Blacknailed, blood-ingrained. Her iron rings. "Here's a ring for his lickpot. I' thy soulbag." She whispered. "Did it frisk when she kittled thee? Thy granny's craw?"

Bonechill and black sway. Margaret crouched silent. The hands still were busy. They pulled the child's hand to her own foul body, to her nothingness. "Here's teeth and tongue. They slit it, for to gar it speak." It touched. "Will I tell thee?"

*No.* Margaret wrenched away, fell sprawling backward.

Straddling, Ashes haled her up and held her face—O blackness, would she kiss her? suck her breath?—between her own cracked hands, as if she drew her from the dark, from drowning in her glass. *How cam'st thou by my face?*

The hag unsheathed that ruined voice: true metal if corrupt. It pierced and rang. "Rid Ashes, did thy goslin. For a game. Spurred and spilled. Eight held her down for nine to jig. Turn and turn. T'bright wheel's burning i't air, all swords, and down and down they fall." Her breath was earthy strong. "But Ashes cursed 'em, aye, she cursed 'em all. I did. There's one will dance Daw's jig for thee. And t'fiddler gangs afore. Here's siller for his bow. They's stringed it wi' his yellow hair. That's one. So pretty, but it come to dust. I's laid him at my breast. No more."

And still Margaret shrank from her; and still the Ashes held her fast.

And then the men with fire overswept them, shouting. Rakes and torches in their hands. They caught up Margaret, lifted her away, all unresisting as a sack of corn. They clodded stones and fieldmuck at the Ashes. But she ran not like a pelted beast, but stood and mocked. "I's knowed thee, Hoy Bawdrick, aye, I's knowed yer all. I's stood yer. Cock and eyes." Flinging back her fell of hair, she ranted like a queen. "It's what I is, is Ashes. Same as earth is earth. An if I tellt yer, I could dwine yer cocks and blind yer eyes. Set cankers in yer marrybones. I knows yer deaths, and all yer crowd o kindred, and yer spawn. And what I tell, it is."

"Come away," said a man to Margaret. "Here's not for t'like of yer."


At the door stood Mistress Barbary, scouring a knife in her apron. Behind her on the dresser lay a limp grey goose. Sukey's nemesis. "Thou's been missed," she said. Her cool eyes glanced at Margaret's spattered gown, her stained basket. "Fell?"

Margaret kept her gaze level; yet the world jumped and twitched, as in her glass. "I saw a vixen. I was started."

"Aye." Barbary still held her gaze. "Doll's fault, and she's been lessoned; but the next is thine. Fell's not thy study. Thou think on that."

"I will."

"Get thee washed. Thy master waits on thee for supper."

Margaret curtseyed and went.

On the narrow stair she stopped, unseeing, letting maids with a kist of apples bump and sidle past her, downward. Doll went up with bright red cheeks, a wicker basket at her hip. In the broad bare loft, they were making up the bed, lifting and lofting the sheets. Blind with misery, Margaret slumped into her sideslip room and snecked the door.

No use. Her walls were breached, wind-haunted. All about, the air was filled with motes and whispers. *Ganging til a dance?* The crow lad fell like thistle-down, he spilled. *Pinch-ripe*, said Morag, groping as my lady watched. *Whore's blood like her dam.* A stark bare woman writhed and cursed beneath a crowd of men, a spill of bloody froth across her belly. *. . . til a dance?* Again, and over and again, he fell and twisted in a storm of crows. Wryneck and agape. Black tongue. *. . . a dance?* His slow feet turned, to northnorthwest, northwest. *Pike out his eyen*, cried her corbies. Now my lady held a card: the Vixen, burning like a leaf. She cast it down in embers on the floor, and bending, smutched the ash on Margaret, *there*. Grey ash, white belly, tuft of red . . . *Thy secrets*, said a dead voice, whispering. Thea? Ah, but changed: insinuating, coarse. *A hanged lad's thine only cockhorse.* In among the fallows, Ashes fleered and beckoned, lifting up her skirts.

*Sisters?*

And they called to her, *Come down.* But one was Barbary.

"Anon."

Behind her dazed eyes, glimmering, she saw a sea of stars; she longed to plunge in it, to wash away the prying hands, the voices. *Water? Jug.* She spilled it, pouring out. She scrubbed herself: but could not wash the Ashes from her soul.


Still uncertain in his new guise—cropped head, stiff breeches, swordlet—Noll watched the new maid Barbary weigh out her leaves of violet, a white stone worth. A book lay open on the table beside her, though she couldn't read. He'd asked. An old important book with latches, fat and floppy as a toad. He liked its croaking invocations. *Rx drachm ix.* That would be a king of dragons, curled about his gold. Barbary was old as Annot—a chit, so his nurse said, but Imp Jinny's kindred; she'd studied arts. Could draw bee stings; spell coins where teeth were laid; could lick sharp specks from under eyelids with her cool and clever tongue.

"What is't?"

"A cordial." Just so. "For thy father."

Of rose leaves, borage, bugloss, each a double fist; a flake of gold; a coin's weight each of ambergris and hart's horn. Frowning now, she tipped a little more. The scales swung, steadied.

It was Madam who had buckled him. His father saw him not through tears. But she said only, "Mind now: thou art man enough to birch." It was daughters that she wanted.

"Barbary?"

"Aye?"

"Did my mammy die because my sister was a boy?"

"No." Even. "Her tale was ended, is all; she's in Unleaving. Ashes tellt her there."

And Annot? Why did she not wait for him, until he had his sword? He could have gone with her. Barbary unstopped a phial, measured out a knife's point of powder that was mortal. Viper's heart. *How far is Babylon?* And could he follow? Did he dare?

"Could I walk there, Unleaving?"

"Thou'd want company." Brisk now, with the mortar and pestle. "T'world's an ill place, out o doors." Slowing, as she thought. "And inward too. There's woods in beds." Noll saw his mother, lying empty. "'Tis all thicketry. But that's why Ashes. See, her tales is clews. They lead us out."

A silence. "Did—did Madam burn Annot's ashings?"

Now she turned. "Who tellt thee that?"

"Mab. And Ailie." As if a sting were in his heart that swelled it, clenching on its pain; but if she drew it, he would bleed to death. Her cool hand on his shoulder. He clutched it. "They said—said that she was whored. And he that was to marry her, he raged and ranted, and he changed her to a vixen fox and hunted her—" No voice. "They said her bones are in the wood."

"Choughs." So hard, the balance swung and jittered. "Rattleboxes. Thou never mind their viperish tongues, their heads is empty."

"But is't true?"

"Ashes knows." She stood against the light, cool north, but yellowed with the fall; the stillroom filled with it like wine. "Imp Jinny says we's Ashes all, we tell each other's lives. And some nobbut botches at it. Snips and cheats."

With the corner of her apron—clean this morning, so it smelt of wind—she wiped his eyes. "Thy tale of Annot is thine own."

He nodded. *So she's gotten a fine sword and a cap and feather, and she's wandering in the light o leaves. What way? But Tom o Cloud comes to her, and he shows her the moon's road . . .*

"Now then. Take yon book and read me what's to do."


The table was bare of work. Grevil walked his compass up and down it, broodingly. On sentry in a no man's land. "So, Mistress?"

Margaret laid her glass before him, curtseyed and drew back. She had no will in her to flout him or dissemble; Ashes thrilled like venom in her blood.

"Is this thy device?"

She dared not trust her voice. A nod. An eyebrow? "Sir, it is."

"And thy key?"

She laid it down.

"Is't all?"

"It is."

Grevil twisted it about from end to end; peered wrongways down it at his far-withdrawing window. "How—? Ah. 'Tis passing curious. I would at leisure talk with thee upon the working of it and its artifice." He set it down most carefully. "But there is graver matter toward. Thou hast been seen—" She stared him down. "Myself has seen thee walk abroad of nights, agaze with this—this instrument? this optic?"

"Starglass." It felt like a betrayal but to name it.

"Every night?"

"When it is clear."

"Has any met with thee?"

"No one," Margaret could say truthfully. The lad was none.

An outbreath of relief. "Thanks be. I had feared—" And he was terrified: she saw it in his dark-drowned eyes. He stilled his hands. "There are wolfish men abroad, a gang of witches. Huntsmen of the late abroad. There have been—tales."

"I know. You write of them," said Margaret. "Of bones."

"It is my work."

"And this"—she touched the glass—"is mine."

"They would spare not for thy philosophy." He sighed. "I cannot keep a retinue about thee, waking at thy whim—aye, two at least," he said. "A maid for thine honour's sake, a man to guard you both. I am no lording with a train of followers. My servants work. And so must sleep."

"And may they not, if I would wake?"

"Margaret, thou canst not—" Too shrewd: he changed his key. "Thou couldst be injured, soul and body, by a villain. Couldst be—forgive me—whored. In law, there is no reparation, no redress, for outrage on a girl night-wandering, unattended: she is waif and stray. Or even gossip of such thing could undo thee. And being lost, thy name's as weighty as thine honour."

Not pertly, but in sober fact: "I have no name."

"Thou hast thy virtue, which is all thy dowry."

"I do not purpose, sir, to marry."

"No. No. Understand this: thou wouldst be as an Ashes child, as naught."

*I ever was. A hole to fill.* There was a kind of bees' nest in her blood since Ashes handled her, a loathing longing. If she stung not, she would weep. "And Annot? Is she naught?"

A silence. Carefully, he closed the compass, leg to leg. "Is vanished." Cheek in hand, half turned from her. A shining in his eyes, unshed. "In a history, doubtless, she has ended badly. In my tale, she's on the Lyke Road ever. In Unleaving. Let me have my tale." He rose and paced caterways: his old accustomed figure, chair to press to window. "When the great stars rise in autumn, I would go with thee to gaze, to learn thy new philosophy of stars." Another turn. "Happen we could raise a lantern-room of sorts, upon the leads. A stair about the chimneystack."

Hope against all reason rose in her. He'd give her leave to take her glass, to go.

"But thou art shivering, poor mouse. So thou wert frighted by a maudlin?"

*How cam'st thou by my face?* "Not hurt, sir."

"I am glad of that; but there is worse abroad than poor mad Ashes."

And she could not say: *I know. Yet confinement is worse.*

"I would not hobble thee, but less—far less—would see thee harmed." Turn and pace. "Thy fault was heedlessness, and not a wilful disobedience;

and yet the consequence is grave. Unknowing of the law is no excuse." He stood behind his chair, a hand on either lion's head. "Thy glass is forfeit for a month."

"It is my *work*." Her cry astounded her, as if like Ashes in the furrow she had bared her privities to him, her fury and her naked anguish. Raw. She wept as if she bled, unstanched.

He began to spread their papers out, the sorted heaps of books. "So scholarship in Lune was mine: and yet 'twas not my fortune to go on with it. There I had—companions. Masters. There now." He unfolded his handkerchief for her. "When my father died—I being still in wardship, scarcely older than thyself—I needs must leave my wood of nightingales, my books, and study muck and wool. I serve this patch of land. It masters me, it is my office. Noll of Anywhere might have his will; but *Grevil of Low Askwith* is my Ashes coat: I cannot doff my name."

The daemon in her spoke. "So *Margaret* is my office, *Margaret* my coat of skin: I cannot doff my sex."

He looked at her perplexed. "O Margaret, we are not at liberty."

But in a small choked voice, she said, "Yet I would walk that other Road."

"And will in time: but not abroad alone. On this, I am absolute. Thou must swear it, ere thou hast thy starglass back: nevermore to walk by night with it."

Hands between his hands, she knelt then. "On the Nine: I swear."


Will dreams of clapping crows. He has no voice to cry them. Cannot run: his feet are cloyed with earth. The ravens stoop and scythe at him. They're harpies, beaked and taloned, naked to their gashes. That blood rains down on him, and bloody flux. But when they tumble in the air, turn back to front, they're men with glutted cocks. They couple in the air like swifts. But clusters of them, clots of three four seven, writhing and tearing in their joyless frenzy. At the ecstasy, they shriek.

Dry-sobbing, with his crooked arm covering his eyes—they'd pike his eyes—Will struggles on. But a raven stoops and slashes him from throat to fork. His entrails slither out, they loop about his legs and cumber him. *Just finish it. Kill.* But they do game him, gloating. He must run.

And there is Ashes in the green corn smiling, holding out his soul. Her brief bright hair like needfire on the summer hills; her face like dawn. But when he touches her, she's turned to stone, unshapen, cleft. He fumbles in her dry hole for his self, and there is nowt.

He woke. He was lying naked in an icy puddle, in a reeling stench: shit, blood, seed, and stale. A roof above him, and a sill without—forbidden ground. A floor of stone beneath, a gutter running muck. He lay upon a littering of iron: chains, bits, hobbles, flails and rusted scythes. The witchlord and her prize were gone.

And still, as if he'd looked upon the sun, he saw my lady burning on the air, black violet. She wore the bone mask at her shoulder and her witch robe. Naked else. It stood. She held his star as if she'd plucked it from the sky, had blinded night. White gold. *Here's a toy thou'st kept from me. Thy fool has named it. Will,* she said. And at the name the boy cried out as if it barbed him, and the fisher played the line. *Come, Will, I know thy secrets as thou know'st my will. Wouldst game for it?*

His soul.

And he had lost.

He spat the gag out. Tried his limbs, no longer bound. After a time, he could raise himself, and saw the dead light seeping through the slates. And twisting slowly from the roofbeam, now this way and now that, he saw my lady's white shirt hanging like a ghost, the crown of straw.


Morning. Still in his bedchamber, still in his gown, Grevil sat at his papers, hands raked through his hair on either side. By glazes, who'd rear daughters? And with none but himself to blame for her misgovernment, none to chide with, What *thy* daughter did. Mall take the lass, and what's to become of her?

Yon glass, now in his cabinet—'twas curious in her to frame it. If—

No time. He'd business toward—in that vexatious matter of his aunt— and but a stolen hour for his study. He pushed the spoilt page from him, took another, dipped his pen.

A tap at the door. His water can.

Wearily he called, "Aye?"

In came Barbary with a paper in her hand.

He sighed. "Still Madam?"

"Law."

And at her voice, he turned. Her face—still with anger—silenced him. She laid a warrant on his table, with my lady's seal on it: her mask in little, smiling like the scything moon. Unbroken: but he knew at heart the cause, the witch's enmity. O gods, had Will gone mad? "Assault?"

"Thievery."

He broke the wax and read. *O Will*. He stood as at an open grave, stood snowblind. *Burn it*, said his heart. *And beat the ashes.*

"Fled," said Barbary. "Happen he'll win away to Lune." She'd brought a cup for him, burnt wine.

Mastering himself, he stilled his shaking hands, he drank; but saw the servant's face change to an apprehending sorrow. Ah, she knew, they all knew what he felt. "O Barbary, am I made of glass?"

"I's knowed yer a while. Y'll not break." She bent to blow the fire up; he found he was shivering, had lost his voice.

"If I … ?"

"There's nowt as Noll Grevil yer can do but fret or quarrel—and yon witch keeps swords about him. But yer t'Master here—ye wear that power, same as Ashes—and yer part's to see justice done."


The great white featherbed came softly down between the maids' hands.

"… a ring," said Ellender. "And all gold but t'stone."

Cat laughed. "Would look brave on my hand."

"Worth forty plough," said Nan. The brisking of her broom. "Says Nick."

The bump and clatter of Doll's tub. *"Ken ye th' rhyme for grasshopper?"* she sang.

"He'll ride out wi' my lady's court for that."

*"… a hempen rein, a horse o tree …"*

And Barbary called up the stairs.

"Here's that marred girl in a pet," said Nan. "And t'Master waiting his supper for her all this while. It's keeled." She rapped on Margaret's door. "Thou's wanted."


Dusk-drawn, as if the hooked moon caught her through the heart, Margaret slipped from shadow to shadow through the trees under Hallinside. Not her old-accustomed way, familiar now as sleep, but slantwise to it, striking north by west. Leaf, shadow. Outcrop, and the rattle of a started sheep. Whin, thorn. She kept the letter of her oath. No glass with her. At the outwall she paused, intent; gazed up and down the pale road from Ask to Owlerdale. No stirring in the dusk. No sound. Soft as if the moon were owling her, she crossed and stole along the edges of the hanging wood to the Whingate. *Only to the gate, to see the stars.*

But she was wary now, as if she moved within my lady's walls; unwary, for the quarrel in her blood. *Only just to see the stars. No glass.* No matter now: but only that she walk at liberty. If dread of night-things bound her—Ashes had awakened terror—she was still my lady's captive, under Law. The night was stained for her. And then her self was lost.

*Only*—But she saw no stars. Though dark was rising all around her, though it bled and bled unstanched from earth, so that she waded to the knee, the heart, in shadow, still the sky was sickly pale.

Only to the gate.

A stone rattled.

As she turned, she was stifled with a burning hand. A wave of rank scent bore her backward into spring, it whelmed her in a ghostly foam of flowers. Overborne and struggling, she was dragged into the shadow of trees, in a brash and tangle of underwood. "Sneck," said her captor, a hoarse hot shadow at her ear. "Just sneck and I'll not mar thee."

The crow lad.

Wary, he unclapped her mouth; she was silent. His onset had shaken the stars from her like dew from off the thorn. She stood scattered and unhallowed, burned bare in his fire. Surely he was sick, was taken with a fever: racked and glittering and rank with fear. Still he griped her with clawed hands. A white crow, white as harvest: burning like July. Like green hay smouldering. That fox-rank flowering his angry sweat. He shivered; but he held her fast. Spoke lightly, though his swagger shook. "Thou's late abroad, Mag Moonwise. Gettin eldins?"

Cold fury gave her voice. "The wood above's mine own," she said. "I want no leave of thee."

"I's takin leave, thy will or none. I's flittin."

"Then be gone," she said.

He laughed. "Thou's rue that hour. All on yer's to grieve." His voice rose, triumphant, terrified. "Leapfire's what I is. An I leave Noll's land, it fails."

"Go then. And I'll have the sky."

"Go, starve thee. Eat thy moon for bread. Think thy bones will gaze?"

That set her back a step.

"Happen I'll gang for a soldier. Get cap and feather." Still flaunting. "Or take ship. Out Luneward. Hear t'mermaids sing."

Unbidden, she saw a fleet of eggshells tossing in a tub. By one and one they sank. "Not thou," she said. "Thou'rt not for drowning."

That stilled him a space. Then shifting ground, the boy leaned closer still, spoke darkly as he could. "Think on. Thou's not see'd me."

"Nor will I."

"Thou's getten thy master's keys."

Silence.

"He's kists o gold and silver."

"Neither mine nor thine."

"Only but to leave here." Wheedling now. "A handful o silver. Nowt else. And never see me more." He spoke to stone.

"Not an eggshell."

"Marget?" A voice she'd not heard. "They's lating me. To hang." He drew a ragged breath. "For nowt. A ring. A tawdry ring. He—"

"So taking of my master's silver, thou wouldst have me hang beside?"

"They'd never." But he stood appalled. "Not thee. I'd say I forced thee."

"Wouldst lie?"

"My lady lies. If I'd a ring, I'd not beg owt o thee. I never taken owt."

Bare feet in the bracken. "Do you swear this?"

Small and hoarse: as if he spoke against a stricture. "No." As if the halter even now were round his neck. "T'ring's mine. What I is: and he ta'en it. That I swear."

Margaret turned her face. He lied. He lied. "Go hang."

He spat. "Thou marred bitch. Thou maggot. What does thou know o starving, thou in thy goosefeather bed? Thou's slept soft and etten fleshmeat all thy days."

A cold key turned in her, undid her tongue. "What do you know of me?"

"What thou does for thy keep, thou toy." He had her by the braid and twisted. "Lickdish. Thou's to sell, thou babbywhore. To breed. Awd Noll's a reckoning to pay."

Nothing. He knew nothing of her secrets. "Whore thyself."

"What, with Noll Petticoats? I gamed him."

"No. Thy lady's whore. His game. Thou bent thine arse. He mastered thee."

A flash, as of talons. For an eyeblink, she thought the moon had stooped at her: then felt the edge. He'd laid a knife against her throat. "Here's mastery. What it wants, it gets. Here's law." Through a blood-haze in her eyes, she saw the dead hare, skinless but the head; she saw the drawn lip and the glassy stare. "I want what I's owed." He ran a rough finger along the curve of her jaw, from ear to knifeblade. A caress. That chilled her more than any threat. "Thou greenery. Thou glass," he said. Half mocking; musing. Almost gently, he touched the hollow of her occluded throat; traced one small stiffened breast. She flinched; outfaced him. His knife pressed harder. "Silver. And a horse."

Her blood beat against the knifeblade. Still spinning out, the thread.

"Thou? Canst thou ride, crow boy?"

"Aye, cunny. And can pace thee, whip and bridle."

In the wood, an owl cried. She lifted her chin to him. "Thy horse is but the gallantry. Go jig on air."

A fury felled her.

A thrash and tussle in the underwood. She fought. But he held the knife. It won.

Hard-breathing, the crow lad knelt on her, the blade against her throat. It stilled her. She stared up at his blurred white face; heard his harsh breath rale. "Thou see if I can ride." He thrust a knee between her legs, rucked up her petticoat and smock. Chill wind on her naked belly; his grimy, burning hand. Under it, she arced and twisted like a salmon to the gaff. Again the knife stilled her; the hand undid. It skulked and ferreted; withdrew, and fumbled with the rags at his fork. "Vixen." He tweaked her tuft. "Thou vixen." Then he slicked his hand with spit and pried her. *There.*

Lightning.

And with the shock, appalling godhead: a tumult of death. She was made my lady's burning glass, annihilated with her blaze. A voice cried out. Her own?

Dark.

Reeling, dazed with power, she stood. Thrashed down her skirts. He was kneeling in the brashwood, cradling his hand. He whispered.

"Witch. Burn thee."

"My lady eat thee."

She turned and walked down the hill, not blind with rage but lucid, crazed with Law. The air in shards still falling. She did not look backward at the stars.


Ablaze with fury, white as crystal fiery from the blast, Margaret strode down Hallinside. Rage enveloped her, unsouled her. She was turned my lady's vessel: void within and crazing as she cooled. White, straw-white, sullen red: she slaked through fury, shame, despair. Grey ashes. Slag.

Too late she saw that there were torches in the yard. The household was astir. And she was lated: hailed and hunted in a clatter of pattens. Even as she called her rage to arrow her, she knew it spent: a burnt stick whelmed and whirling in an icy river. There was no more heart in her to run. Faces flared out of shadow. Hands caught at her: pinned, plaited, tift and tucked. They did off her draggled apron, scolding; scrubbed her face with their apron corners; smoothed her elf-locked, leafy hair. The crowd bore Margaret away. No running now: the women thronged her, and on either side, a hind held fast. Their dolly, green and fading, like a thing of plaited straw.

A chained dog barked. Another, deeper, hurtling at his rope. Now all: a burden to the shrill of servants.

Looking up, she cracked like cat-ice to a booted heel.

Down from the road from Ask to Owlerdale came a knot of darkness and a scattering of sparks: a rade of travellers in black. Slow destiny. A footboy ran before, a laden packhorse lagged behind, her fate rode on: a horseman and a mantled woman, cloaked and hooded all in black. *I summoned her,* she thought. *My fury called her down.* They brought a stifling dark with them: a scarving, starless night. No air, no flying now. How the torches caught the blink and spiral of the falling leaves. The riders dipped below the turning; rose; impended. They were at the gate. Here, now: the horses stamped and whickered in the courtyard.

"Madam."

Grevil gave his hand to one alighting, a woman in a velvet mask and mantled like the dead of moon. He bared his head, he bent his knee to her.

"Where is the girl?" she said. An old voice: cracked, imperious.

Rough eager hands pushed Margaret forward. Dazed with horror, she sank to her knees. A crooked finger lifted her chin. Light lapped her face: a torch brought close, compelling sight. She needs must look upon her death. And saw—not my lady, but a stranger dismasked: a small face, crazed with age as china is, abrim with power. A witch. No Annis: yet the dark eyes held her gaze. They saw, not through her, but her flaw: where she might crack. "You are long returning," said the Cloud witch. "Daughter Annot."

## Journeyman

*"... goes down at Eventide, her long way under Law; red* Morag *rising now exulteth in her* Kist & Keys ..."

Whin at the world's edge looks to where the stars are setting: at the Road that is a river, at the sea that bears no ship on it—or none of tree—the farther shore that is the impery of death. Her journey: she has sworn.

And from that journey only sun and stars return; and Ashes, who arose from dark, my lady's daughter and her runaway. The Witches walk that Road; the Ravens travel it, who bear away the souls of men, as treasure for my lady's crown. The Huntsman rides and reaves. But no one—willing soul in body— ever made this venture. She cannot. Or not by sea: unless her winding sheet's her sail. Her boat of Cloudish wood is wracked. She's left the bones of it to bleach on no man's sky, to puzzle all the passing dead. A riddle too for the astrologers, a stillborn falling star. Like Journeyman, she haunts the strand of night. This shore her biding place, betwixt.

It was here she met the Outlune fiddler whom the sea cast up. He drowned himself for death of love, and death, dismissive, cast him back. That journey was not his to take. Not yet. And it was here that she and Kit were parted when she told his Thea's death, death's daughter: Ashes, who did choose a mortal love. There, beyond the sea, their daughter is, if any live in that dread country. Under Law. And as Whin's sworn by black and white to seek his daughter, so he's pledged to find her son. Her Ashes brat the old Sun got on her, the boy she'd not give over to the furrow and the knife. No harvest of her blood. So cheating earth, she is forever bound to it: death's journeyman and Ashes ever, teller of the dead.

She turns the lost child's ashing in her hand, the ring of stones. A knot of blood.

No telling.

She has tried. And over and again, she's found herself unbodied in an empty room, has seen a cradle overturned, a burning doll. She's seen a bed, its curtains billowing. Its clawed rings inch and jangle in a moveless wind. Scattered on the floor are painted cards, in twos and threes and gatherings. But as she takes a step, but only one, the floor is sky, the stars are whirling thick about her face, like embers from a brand. And she is falling.

Now is otherwise. Now even as she looks, the pebbles at her feet are dabbled, bright with blood. Her own? The hand is bloodstarred but unhurt.

The ring is drops of blood, is gone.

Not hers.

As mourners do, she marks her face, as her master mistress Brock once did to her: with blood for ashes. Brow and eyelids, cheek and chin. Then mouth. She tastes it.

And the voices wake.

Whin, kneeling at the water's edge, fills up her hands with light. Pale fire: like that shining on the sea that limns the oar's edge, mingles in the wake. It overspills her cup of hands. That light is souls.

The Road that is a River is of souls: not one but many lives in time, a baffling and a braid of streams. The sea is stories. And a wave of them breaks over her: the salt and sting, exhilarating, and the glassy weight. It pulls. The water on her lips is bittersweet.

Whin walks into the sea.


It is another air of water and an earth of light. She walks on puzzled ground, like moorland, in a snow of stars. Not dead herself, she thinks—she hopes— her breath still clouds, her blood beads up and clots, her piss falls scalding on the rime—*there's rain for yer below*. And she desires: she would wap with Kit, left long ago. Not then and never will. She thirsts for it, sweet meddling in the blood. Alive; and yet she does not sleep nor hunger, but for others of her kind.

She drinks snow.

Some times the travellers she spies afar are standing stones; and times—but seldom now—the stones are naked travellers, by one and one, bent onward. Bairns and elders, lads and girls. The dead. But they are blind to her as stones: as silent. Only as they pass her by, she hears an echo of a telling: she is Ashes still.

An old hag with her white hair wild and loose about her, spinning snow. Her distaff is a branch of thorn.

*... my father sold me for a plough of land ...*

A horseman, shod with snow.

Two lovers, clear as glass new-blown, still burning redly where the pipes were broken off: her vixen and his wyrm.

*... at midnight and myself by dawn ...*

Once she came upon a space untrodden, with bloody swords flung down, with gouts and spatterings of blood across the snow. A wreath of gold. Nought else. And now she spies a gallows, raven-haunted, with the corbies made of snow.

*... my songs unsung ...*

Rough-coated as a bear, Whin shambles on. *Ship's thyself*, she thinks. And telling as she goes, she lays a keel of bone.

## Under Law

Keys. Shadows. Eyes.

In her room that now was Madam's closet, Margaret bent her neck to the crow-clawed waiting women, Grieve and Rue. They tugged her laces, twisted up her hair from off her shivering nape and shoulders, pinched her slight pale buds in mockery of ripeness. The gown they'd put her in was rich and strange, of cloud-changed shifting silk: steelblue, stormblue, dizzying with musk and wormwood, old and yet unworn. Her jacket and her petticoat, her stout nailed shoes, were locked away. They turned her round in this garb, as they would buy her on a stall. "Here's all to do," said one, and tweaked a sleeve. Too long for walking in, too low for modesty; chill, billowing and cruelly stayed. "'Twill do," the other said. In silence, Margaret rose and followed down the winding stair.

Tribunal waited in the wainscot parlor, swept bare of work: Madam in a great chair, with unmastered Grevil standing at her side; a knot of whispering servants at the sill beyond. As she passed, he could not meet her gaze; Barbary lifted her chin.

"Come, girl," said Madam Covener, and beckoned Margaret to her chair. There were small things in her lap, like lenses—*No.* But my lady's child did not cry out, nor falter; she was schooled in dread. And it was not her glass dissected. No, the lady held, coin-small and bright, an image to her face: a portrait from her nephew's cabinet. Unlocked, his secrets naked to the eye. And, *Ah,* the craning household said. *Not hers,* thought Margaret. *Not I.* And yet she saw the gown, the lace, the tiring of the pale red hair limned perfectly, as in a dwindling glass, as in the pupil of my lady's eye, diminished.

Turning to her kinsman, Madam spoke.

"It was my brother's maggot, as thou knowst, to wed with an Outlune woman, dowerless and lawless. She did bear him daughters; yet being sickly, of a stillborn son she died. And ere she'd gone a small pace on that road, my brother hurried after, footboy to his folly, as if to light her the way. His bones are laid in Lunish earth. And there he left two girls amongst her barbarous kindred, blood of my blood. As my duty was, I fostered them—" Her glance bade Margaret curtsey. "—myself took ship to bring them unto Cloud, myself unlearned them of their Lunish errors, sained them, schooled and dowered them, and found them Cloudish husbands. Damaris, thy mother—"

Master Grevil bowed his head, hand outward: enough.

"Whelped but a whitely brood: all dead but her cade-lamb. And he unlike to get heirs."

"Madam, I—"

"Her sister Annot—"

All turned toward Margaret.

"—being of an age, was handfast to a gentleman of thirty plough, a lord of great pastures in the north. But on a May morning—"

Grevil broke in eagerly. "She rose before the dawn, and maid amongst maidens, went gathering green. So my nurse did tell it, who did braid her hair that very morn. And laid a cup for her returning, never tasted. Being heedless of our Cloudish custom, she did break a branch of my lady's thorn. And was stolen away under hill."

"And has returned."

Silence. Rain rattled the window glass.

Lifting his palm to her, he swore. "Madam, by this hand, this is no earthly may, but a changeling, nor of Cloud nor Lune."

"That folk are made of air. If they be cut, they wither like a swathe of grass." Again, she looked at Margaret. "If you prick her, she will bleed."

Pensive, Grevil pleached his cuff; then countered. "If mortal, then a stranger to this realm. And by her manner, not of Lune. I—" Now turning of his ring. "I hear no echo of my mother's nor of Annot's voice in hers, and I have spoken with her many months."

"And I have searched her straitly. There are marks about her body that I ken. She is Annot found."

Still doubting. "Well I know that one who ventures in the sunless lands, the sky below, will turn again no minute older than the day she left, were she gone five hundred years—but was mine aunt then a child?"

"No; but thou wast then in petticoats and prattled of thy nurse's tales. Thou'rt dazed with balladry. Thine elders mind her well."

"As I do. Your pardon, aunt: but Annot stood to me as elder sister and as governess, nay, half my mother, and my dearest playfellow."

"Thou her lapdog rather, or a toy to prink. Her fancy marred thee. She did stuff thy wits with nonsense as a monkey's cheek with grapes."

Her mock, it seemed, met air. Grevil's gaze was elsewhere, inward. At last, he turned from memory, as from another room, a gallery. "Yet I know what I do know: that Annot sang."

Madam Covener looked at him, long-lidded. "And this girl does not?"

"Madam, I have heard her not."

"And you?" She turned to the knot of servants. "Does she sing at her needle?"

"Like a cuckoo i't nest," a servant muttered.

And another: "Like an owl."

"Like any crow," said Barbary. "Keeps measure but no music."

A dry disdain in Madam's face. "Think you she took cold beyond?" Then turning to the room: "You see. Their teind is what is dearest to their thralls: wits, eyes, tongues.

*And souls?* thought Margaret.

No murmur now. "They have returned her, but her songs they keep."

The rain fell. In the gathered stillness, Barbary took the image up and studied it. "T'gown's like."

"And the girl?"

"I ne'er laid eyes on her. Awd Mistress Quarrenden, she set me on that summer after. There was t'linen to keep." She set the image down. "And t'lad."

"Then I call one who did." Madam beckoned to a servant at the threshold. "Mab Kelder."

Blind Mab hobbled to the silent girl, and felt her cheek and chin. "Aye, 'tis her, 'tis Mistress Annot, right enough. Did I not tell ye? And didn't I knit her same stockins?"

A murmur.

"'Twas good yarn as ever Jinny span, but she's dead and ashes—poor soul! And she'll never cry holly and ivy no more."

"That will do. Tom Arket."

"Happen she could be," said the shepherd. "I's heared folk gan there and back, and no more changed than delf in a dunghill."

Madam Covener said, "Is this the girl?"

Crook Tom squinnied solemnly at Margaret. "Mistress Annot were another such as yon vixen, aye, bonewhite and blaze. Like as kits of ae kindle."

"And if she is," said blunt Barbary. "What on't? She's away wi' t'fairies yet."

"Such freaks may be physicked." Madam Covener drank deep. "And she is handfast yet. Her lord lives on, thrice-widowed; and has garnered gold on gold, and rare learning. He is great among my lady's servants."

Barbary said, "Would such as he take a nameless girl, a hedgebird?"

"Her name I warrant. And her maidenhead." Grieve glanced at Rue. "She is virgin."

Margaret drew herself still further in. No door, no sky.

"There's one you've not asked." Mistress Barbary turned to Margaret, looked long at her and level. "By t'moon: are you this Annot that were lost?"

A small voice, disused, despairing. "By the moon and dark of moon and all the wood above, I know her not."

"Then tell your name, or wear another's garland to her bed."

Smaller still. "I cannot say."

Madam now disclosed her hand. There lay on it a ring of silver, black with age. "Where got'st thou this? For it was Annot's."

Silence.

"It was hidden in thy chamber. It is found." Flawless Ellender smoothed down her apron. Turning to the whitefaced Grevil, Madam said, "Do you vouch for it?"

He took it, turned it his hand. "It is like her ring. But if it were, the room was also Annot's room; belike she left it there, for she took nothing."

"This she would not leave: it was an ashing of her mother's kindred." Madam bent her gaze on Margaret. "By her face, the girl's a liar. She is Annot."

"Or—"

"Or thou'st taken in a thief and whore. Wouldst see her whipped before the town? Turned out upon the road to serve Daw's pack?" He was silenced. "Now girl, by Annis and her night, I conjure thee: where got'st thou Annot's ring?"

In darkness. Room on room of shadows, and the glint of things that spilled from broken coffers: all the ashings of the dead untold. She would not speak, would never speak: but that her lady's name compelled her. "From one that's dead," said Margaret. Under Law.


Annot stood, scratched and breathless, on a hillside, at the edges of a leafing wood. Wavering, as in a dance half-learned, the music fallen still—*Now which? Now which?* The exaltation that had carried her to this fell back, the wave of it withdrawing from the printless reaches of her heart. Nothing but a shining on the sand laid bare. A momentary gleam. It sank away.

*Ashes? Thou didst call the dance. What road?*

The stars, too, sunken into grey. All vanished now, the Road that she had followed, white as wave-edge, the Fiddler and the Thorn. The Shepherd's Fold. Before her in the paling east, the Nine had faded into air, triumphant. It was May that marked their rising out of Law. *As I hope to rise.* The morning star, bright Perseis, still shone beside a fainter star, she knew not which. *O Perseis. Thy story mine.*

A rustling in the wood behind her. Turning, she looked back. She saw a young man, all in gold and violet: amazement in his face, and dangling from his hand, a garland of the thorn, both white and black. She knew this dance, the soundless music of it moved them both. Now he would speak.


"I find no flaw in it." said Grevil. He looked wearily to Margaret, turning the parchment for her to the waning light.

She looked at a winter hedge of words, at the lash and eddering of quickset strokes. A cage of law, close-woven. Here a crow-blotch of sealing wax; there, a gout of it like blood new-spilt on snow. A hand—long dead and laid in earth—had set her seal on it: a ship like a clinched moon, riding on its keel; a mast of tree, that flowered into stars; and all about it, falling, leaves or stars.

*Lief wode I fall, an light wode spring.*

The riddle in her ring. No stone in it, and yet a skein: a knot of blood.

"It is not my hand."

He sighed. "It is my mother's mothers' ring. Her kindred's, that I wear. And Master Corbet his stamp—" A fiddle and a flaunting crow, blunt-struck, blurred with vehemence. "—both signed and countersigned. Did they chaffer for an eggshell, for a bride of straw, that seal is proof."

She could cipher. "You would sell me."

"No," he said, dismayed. "'Twas none of my doing, by the air and Ashes. I would lief undo." He turned to her. "Think you I would sell a child?"

The crow lad had given her a blade of elfshot, bitter cold and true. She flung it. "You have bought."

Too carefully, as if he bore a cup unspilled, he said, "I do not take." Glasscold and quarrelled. She could see where he had cracked, long since; how still he bore himself in shards. "Go marry."

Madam Covener did up the clasp; she held the mirror to her ward's unseeing face. "Thou wilt mind thee of this chain I gave thee, at thy trothing. I have kept it well." She touched the girl's bright head, close-braided, quenched; sought trembling in the body, still as tree.

The north light, passionless, played evenly on all: the heap of jewels on the table; the woman, soberly and richly clad, still handsome, with the silvered glass; the servant by the window, hands folded in her apron; the girl, pale as frost in autumn, in a stillness of despair.

The woman bent to her casket. "Does she bleed?"

"Madam?" said Barbary.

"Thou hast change of her linen. Will she breed?"

"Scarce yet." The servant made her courtesy contempt.

Madam Covener slipped a ring on a roll of parchment. "Bedding will ripen her."

Sharp-eyed Barbary took up her tray. "He's a taste for green fruit, yon gallant."

"'Tis not his belly will ache for't." The witch half smiled. "Go. I will bid thee."

As she turned, Madam Covener held stones to Margaret's cheeks, half made to hook them in her ears; was checked. No piercings, not a scar. She called to the kist where her own maid knelt, turning out long-folded linens. "Grieve, my needlecase." Her black-browed waiting woman brought needle and thread. "Hold her."

Margaret dared not flinch; she felt the shock of power still, that laid her naked to my lady's thought. This meddling bruised her flesh and spirit; but that rush of godhead was annihilation: it laid waste her soul. Her mind sought shelter elsewhere, amid the stars and numbers in her head: but the air was no liberty, the heavens were no roof. She stumbled in a labyrinth of dread.

Slow lightning, sawing at each lobe. The point was burred with salt. No cry: but Margaret's eyes went wide, her irises half drowned in dark. Pain made itself a door of seeing; made of light a rape. Unwilling tears, yet two or three slid down her captor's hand. "Ah, the stones become thee." She tilted Margaret's chin and gazed. "Thou braid'st of thy grandame that wore them. Blood will tell."

The boy is running, bloodfoot on the moor. He's made his way by holt and hollow, ditch and slough: mud-slubbered, thicket-torn. Lain shuddering and burning in the pale of day. Slept scarce at all, with listening for the brash of hounds. Slogs on now. He is far beyond the fields he knows; knows nothing, but the sea's his only hope. Knows not if it lies east or west. And he might die, if he's not taken. There's a green fire burning in his lights, rust-ropy when he hacks it up; a fire in his blood. And when he drinks to quench it, then a black frost in his gut. As if he's swallowed attercaps. He cannot last.

So at nightfall he breaks covert. And he's running on a moorland, white as if with frost. So light, he's never run so light: as if he's starved away the clag of mortalness. He swivels in the moon for joy. And yet the wind outrides him. *Tig last!* he cries to it. And laughs: Will Shadowslip. Now the air is thick with flying leaves, black leaves before the moon: though not a tree stands by him. Laying back his ears, he runs.

All round him, there's a scent, blood-cousin, that he knows for sea.

Then he hears the cry of hounds. Can feel it in his prick and marrow. In his stones. Can feel the scorching of their breath—No. No, that clamoring is fear. Those flying leaves are ashes, eyed with sparks. He swings about. There's fire on the hills. Not daybreak. North, east, west. As frantically he seeks a trance in it, it closes on him in a ring of gold.

And like the stone of it, he sees the huntsman, all his harness traced in fire, and his mantle of the burning gold upflung. His mount's a roil of smoke and agony. His red-eyed hounds are scattering like a shovelful of sparks; their master falls apart in flakes of fire—a spur, an eye, the flinders of a mouth—still curling inward on himself.

The crow lad drowns in fire, wakes with shrieking.

See, a card is burning in the witch's hand. The last: the Hare, cast down in embers on the ashes of the pack, the Huntsman and the Hound.

In the tale, the Moon-Hare's rising out of Law is liberty; he lopes amid a rime of stars. *See there,* the old wife says. *That star? And that? He's running, and they's never catch him. Nobbut Brock will, for her bag.*

That tale is lost.

Scant light for sewing. Close within the kitchen window, Barbary bent to her needle, frowning, turning Margaret's ruined tawdry in her clever hands. She'd given threads to Margaret to unpick, to save the gold inwoven; but the girl was elsewhere, gazing past the rain-lashed window at the fell. The work lay idle in her lap. While she was caged these endless weeks, the year had turned toward winter, shedding leaves with her blood. The trees laid bare the sky: for naught. Beyond the whirl and slant of wind-torn leaves, her crown of stars moved on unvisited, unseen.

Light mirrored made a second prison of the world beyond, cast all behind before: the fell was white with swags of linen, winter-hedged. Reflections. High in the air, Doll and Nan tripped neatly to and fro about their work: glazed linen slid beneath their skating irons, flakes of lace fell lightly from their goffers, making frost of fire. As she worked, Nan Shanklin sang, abstracted, mournful. *". . . of his needle, he made a spear, Benjamin Bowmaneer . . ."*

Her breath had dimmed the glass; she wiped it.

And in sad antiphony, Doll sang, *"My father was a gentleman, a gentleman was he . . ."* A shirt, a collar. Thump and glide.

A smock. *". . . and th' proud tailor rode prancing away . . ."*

*". . . but he's wed me til an awd man o three score years and three . . ."*

Herself was time's mirror: a glass ghost-misted. Spirits' breath that will not stir a feather yet may stain a soul with longing, with regret. They clouded her, her ghosts. The leaf on stone, the leap of fire that was Thea's voice. Ash of driftwood that was Norni's tang; her salt wind singing to the cradle rocking, empty on the stones: Imbry's cradle, who was dead for Margaret's sake. The lost girl shivered, skyblack on the moor. Her hand was in the frost. And now, beyond that skeining work, Margaret saw Lyke Moor, with its lost souls wandering. *". . . of his thimble, he made a bell . . ."* She saw the crow lad, black as starless night, starve-naked, with his hair like cold fire blown about him, unconsuming. Saw him still behind her eyes.

*". . . to ring that flea's funeral knell . . ."*

A golder fire in the air sprang up. He burned in it. Another. And another. In the room behind her, they were lighting candles, whispering.

"... he's gone intil a hare and hunted, Mab says ..."

"... slipped ..."

"... come full o't moon, they's take ..."

Margaret turned from the ghostly hillside; spoke to blot the voices. "Will you go?"

Pursed lips, drawn brow. Counting stitches. "Sayst?"

*"Hie, Jeannie, hie ..."*

"Will you seek Ashes? At the stones?"

Barbary bit her thread. "That's done wi'." Then sleaving new silk, she said less tartly, "I's beyont moon now. Ashes mun bear."

*"... and sing low, Jeannie, low ..."*

"Oh," said Margaret. "I see."

"Is thy needle a bill-hook? Thou's not lifted it twice this hour."

*"Ye can never mak' a singin bird out o a hoodie craw."*

Margaret took up her handwork, bristling with pins, and drew them; stuck them in a clot of cushion like a heart. Barbary shook out her ravaged breadth. "Here's cats' knittery. 'Twill do for a stomacher." She called to the serving maids, "Y'd best bring candles up. They'll be darkling."

Fain to be flitting, they clipped out.

Dusk in the kitchen, unghosted of its smocks. Rain spat in the chimney, rattled at the pane.

Barbary chose her strand of silk. "I were never Ashes." Another thread, a knot. Swift stitches. "I wanted." Even in her own despair, Margaret heard the longing in the other's voice.

"Why?"

"Not for mastery, but for—" The needle poised. "—draught of light. I wanted Ashes, same as tree wants light. Rain and rooted earth, aye, fairly; but 'tis light in grain. I would knaw that law, that dance; and now I never s'll."

There was a shutter still undone. Only for a glimpse, Margaret looked out on leaves, on endless leaves, wind-paling; at the starless sky, cloud-curded, and the rounding moon. Rain-curtained now the Coffer and the Keys, the ember of the Raven's Eye. Then the servingwoman pulled it to, and latched it. "Go now. Madam waits."

Cold haily night. All folk indoors. Cowering and curing in their chimneynooks like so much bacon. Withered apples in a heap of musty straw. And wanting only fire and fleet: the caudle on the hob; the hangings drawn against the October storm, against the rattle and the sting of sleet. The glory shuttered out. Above them in the smoke, ungazed at, lay the vault of heaven, underdrawn with cloud: the stars in their lightless rafters, hooked. Like so much kitchenry.

*Still there,* thought Margaret, kneeling at the sill. And set them in the sky in order, like a child with her babyhouse. Toys and shadows. Here a cradle of a nutshell; there a thimbling jug of delf. A saltspoon for a ladle: horn. Sad pretty trinkets from a yearcake, a child's wealth long ago: a spindle whorl of bone or ivory, like an ear-bob, wound with tow; a tawdry ring, a cheat of brass and glass for gold; a riddle and a shears of lead.

In the high chamber, Annot's kists lay open, spilling rich and thrifty odors mingled—orris root, ambergris, wormwood and camphire—and outmoded finery. They were remaking her in Annot's image. All her clothing, though excellent, was quaint; and after her long wandering—Madam said—ill fit her.

Madam Covener herself, with Rue her waiting-woman, had the fangling of a bodice. Grieve stitched at linens: fine whitework, as for a bridal or a shroud. Beside her, Ellender, entrusted with a nightcap-in-ordinary, bent demurely to her work. Her bright new thimble glinted. Nan came to mend the fire and clear away, remembering—but only just—to bob.

Then she bent over Margaret's shoulder, frankly gazing at the toys. "Eh now. Isn't they bonny?" She poked the cradle gently with a roughened finger. It rocked. "All this while shut up i't dark. They must been young Annot's— Aye well, thy—" Grieve coughed. "*Yer* eldins," said Nan. Hands ostentatiously behind her back.

"Are they trinkets? Or what?" said Margaret. Her voice seemed small and cracked to her.

"Disn't thou knaw eldins? Thou *has* been away in faerie."

"Mistress Annot well remembers," said Grieve. "As thou, girl, dost forget thyself."

"No harm in maids prattling, an they work," said Barbary, coming up with Madam's burnt wine. "Here's not a lyke-wake, Mall be thanked." She glanced at Margaret's dish, uneaten. "And I's not be having one. T'lass is dowly. She could do with a merry-making, lass amid lasses."

Madam snipped her thread. "I see my nephew keeps unruly servants. Annot's governance is mine."

Unspoken in the air hung Barbary's retort: *Aye, and she fled yer.* "And by yer leave, Madam, servants here is mine. They swears to me. And I answers to't Master." As she spoke, she tidied all the snippets of silk and velvet. "Nan, see thou to't candles while thy tongue is clacking. Ellender, yon thimble's not a diadem. Thou needn't preen."

"Sleeve," said Rue, bristling up with a cockling of conceited velvet and a wristful of pins. "Thine aunt would see the fashion on it."

Margaret stood, and unresisting let the bower-woman turn her this way and that. Breathed ambergris—and now and here were lost. Tip and tilt in memory, the cradle rocked and Norni sang, to speed the voyager to shore. Nan took a knifepoint to the candle-ends.

"Elding now, we kept afore yer come. At seedtime. But o course yer knows that, Not Marget. That's when t'Nine is under Law, locked up i't Lady's kist, and Eldins—she's lallest o't Nine, and shyest, and not to be spied—she seeks 'em through bushes and briars, and right down under earth. She braves Law, does Eldins. And she's getten a sun fra' Mally's kist to light her down, and all Brock's keys."

In and further in, the fire wending in the dark. The scent of stone, of myrrh. The cold mist and the crying out of souls. As if she stood upon her prison's threshold, come to raise herself from dark. *See, Marit.* And she is that child again, my lady's captive, curled in Norni's lap. No warmth, no weight in memory, but O the scent of her, of smoke and ambergris. Her shadow on the hearth, gold-dappled through her drops of amber. With a fingertip, she draws the stars for Margaret to name. A sigil of swift dabs in ashes; then as swift, a rubbing out.

*The Whale, he sounds.*

*And this?*

*The Bear. She comes not under Law. Like Imbry.*

*Aye, she'll win away. For she's wrapped in her eldmother's skin.*

*And her kist's of the Cloudwood.*

*This?*

*The Selkie.*

*Aye, a southern star. He keeps the shoals of Law, cove-haunting. Ay and O my lady's ta'en him as her thrall and ay he slips away. Swims up into the night sea.*

*Up from here?*

*Aye, he'll have found where his fell is hid. And this?*
*The Nine.*
*See, a kindle of kitlins, and the Vixen comes and goes . . .*

Rue's pinches called her back to Cloud, to Annot's bodies. But a moment had passed. Nan dug at the wax, still prattling. "So then o course she finds her sisters and she sets 'em free—that's when they rises, May morning. And then they all sails off i't Ship. There's a guising on't."

"For clownish folk," said Ellender. "And babbies."

"Thou mimsy. Thou's romped it thyself not six moons since." Nan took new candles from her apron. "Aye, it's merry times we has. T'bairns all gets eldins. Tops and tawses. Hoops. Painted whirligigs." She smiled, as at a memory. "Our Doll and me, we was kempions at ninestones. Had dibs in real delf one year, till we hadn't. Cracked."

Still no answer. For the first time, Nan looked at Margaret in her one sleeve. "Will I learn yer to play?"


They walk on, the cold rain turning to a white whirl and a skirmish of snow. The owl-witch Malykorne has kitted Margaret in the tatters of a tinker's coat, the patchwork from her hovel sleeved and skirted; she huddles in it, like a hedgehog in a heap of leaves. Rag coat and slipshod boots, ill-mated, odd and odd. The witch walks quickly. Margaret hurries after, skid and slither, hop and stumble on the clodded coat-skirts. She holds her end up of the creaking wicker basket. It thwacks her shins, persistent as a peevish child; the handle bites like an attercap. With her other elbow crooked against the swarming, stinging snow, she turns her face from the wind. Over her shoulder, sharp and swift, she sees a whisk of fire and a flurry of ice: a creature dancing. Four charry legs, a plume of flame. Jot and flourish. The wind effaces its writing.

"Vixen," says the witch, and tugs onward.

They halt nowhere. Whirl and white.

The witch bites off her mittens. "Reel's running out," she says. Walking she has changed. She looks absurdly young and fierce, like an owlet in an ivy bush. Like a slip of waning moon. "I'll set thee to a place. Thy road's from here."

"Away," says Margaret carefully. *Naked to my lady's crows?*

"Til t'Nine. I's not there." The witch rubs her spectacles. "Nor's she. And after, til Cloud. Where she's not when she isn't."

"Here's like my lady's garden," says Margaret. "Cold."

"Untidier," the witch says dryly. "No walls."

Margaret considers. "It's all one way. Turn and turn, like a maze."

"There's doors, if thou's canny. What's in thy pocket?"

"Snow," says Margaret, divining. "And sticks."

"Toss it up," says the witch.

With bare blue hands Margaret claps and moulds it: a sleety urchin of a ball. The witch's wry mouth forbids questioning. Clumsily, she tosses it skyward: with a whirr and flacker it unfolds wings, rises, white in whiteness, with a cry. Gone.

Still gazing up, she feels her sleeve tugged. "Will it rain cakes, then?" The witch crouches, rolls another ball, in widening, winding circles in the snow; lays bare a maze of earth. The sky turns backward. Margaret follows. Round and rounder grows the ball, as moonwise turns the path: hand-high, knee-high, knocking on a wall of stone. The snowball shatters.

"Back door," says the witch, and shakes her skirts. "Too low for my lady." The basket is there on the doorstep, white with snow. Then she rattles the sneck.

Madam's crows were ever at her back, the one and the other one: like gate-stones, like a threshold that she might not cross. They perched at her hause-bane, and quarrelled for her eyes. Margaret turned her prickling neck to them, and pressed her brow against the windowglass. Beyond the quarrelled panes, she saw slabbed courtyard and a whirl of leaves. Swirl and skitter, rise; unravel, slack and fall. And stir again and scrabble in a hectic gyre, unavailing. No way out. Beyond the cold chimneys and the huddle of slates, she saw bare trees, burnt moorland, the false green gone that had bespelled her to this Cloud: it was winter coming, and the world that she had known. No comfort, but in knowing where she stood: on iron ground. Yet living air.

"Come, Madam. They wait on thee."

At the door of the wainscot parlor, Grieve drew her laces tighter still, half-bared her childish breasts; Rue slapped her pale cheeks, pinched her nipples: so she went a mockery of rose-lipped breathless budding.

Even as she crossed the sill, she caught the stench of sorcery, a tang of iron in the blood. And she knew the stranger even as he turned: the witch, the guisers' lady at the stones. As he knew her—O blindness, he had spied her out. He had doffed the bone mask, bland and pitiless, but his smiling still was mask, his swift regard his scything; and herself the grass that bowed. As he swung round, so must she curtsey, as the lads did leap. That was the dance.

They sat at table, at the wine, all three: wan Grevil and his whitely aunt; her suitor. He was old. Old and harsh, like salt-scarred iron, like a sword sheathed in ruined velvet; old and dangerous. Slaked ash, yet glowering: he still would blaze. No age at all, she saw. Whiteheaded but unwithered. All in black. Hunched as a hoodie crow, but sleek, as if he preened with marrow, plumped on eyes: if winter, then a glut-green January, charnel-crammed. He fed on carrion, but daintily: cracked marrow with ringed hands.

"Master Corbet," said the Mistress. "Here is Annot that was lost; and found."

Round went his knife blade, flecking peel from an orange. Dispersedly before him, lay his broken meats: an eel pie like a castle fallen, battlements in ruin; dregs of wine, sucked marrowbones, disjointed birds. He looked with Morag's eyes at her: contempt, avidity, and cold appraisal. Held her gaze as he would a twisting leveret, ere he knapped its neck. He chose and split a fig with blacknailed thumbs. Still green. Imbibed it.

When he spoke, his voice was wasp honey. "Here's a delicate," he said. "By my neb, the fairies keep a pretty larder. I have heard they feed on mince pies made of children; but never that they candy maidenhead."

"Intact," said Madam Covener. "I warrant you."

"I doubt you not," he said dryly. "But here's a new way to keep cherries ripe. It is a dish that likes me, this preserved virginity, this marmalade. I've had three such green wives stale, ere I laid them in coffer."

Not Death, but Death's pander.

"Sir," said wretched Grevil. "She is young. Could not you give her time?"

"If young, then she will bend," said Madam Covener; and with a shrewd glance at her nephew, "As well thou knowst. Wouldst have it known?"

Down went his eyes. He would not meet her gaze, nor Margaret's; but drew patterns in the salt. "There can be no covenant against her will ..."

"She is sold," said Master Corbet, in that oakgalled voice. "And thou hast reaped, shorn, spun her dowry this three-and-thirty years. Signed and sealed." He tossed a coin on the table. No, an amulet, a little golden face wreathed round with corn. It smiled at her, at anyone. "On this," he said; and turning to his stricken host, "A rarity, is't not? A charm, most ancient in my family, of finding and of binding."

"Come, girl." Grieve and Rue impelled her to his side. He tore a crust of bread, a pinch of salt, and held it to her lips. "Come, Madam. 'Tis thy part to open."

In her ear, she heard Barbary: *Feign; or they will bind thee.*

*My oath? Will that not bind me?*

Unwilling, she must taste his fingers: blood and marrow, and a something charred. Soot-bitter. And with that tang, she tasted knowledge. He would lie upon her like a weight of snow, her grave; mouth, eyes, and every cleft intruded, as roots of yew will break a coffin, and the worms usurp.

*No true knot, if the cord be false.*

Now she to him; and must endure his tongue and teeth. He bent to whisper in her ear. "For a bridegift. Thou shalt see thy cully hang." And his salt tongue flicked her bloody ear lobe. Then turning to the company, he cried, "A handfast. I will hap her well."

A voice spoke. Her own, cold and small. "But halse thee I will never."


Grevil in his study brooded. He had worked whatever sleights and strategems he could devise; prayed fortune for a wind. He could no more. The witch was subtle, and her servants all were spies. Subtle, aye; and cruel as Law. He grieved for Margaret. But she was mewed. He saw her not since that wretched handfast, but in Madam's company. Could not send Barbary to her. Nor slip a note of comfort in a book, for fear of rifling; nor send the book itself but Madam turned it back. "Thou mar'st the girl—as she did thee—with toys of idleness. Her tutelage of late has been neglected; I do school her in her duties."

"Madam?"

"To be nothing. To be filled."

He thought of sly Corbet at the handfast. "This leaping by signatory likes me well. 'Tis marvellous lawful: if I bid then she must bend."

What he gloated on was her unwilling.

How it stifled, though he heard a wind in leaves, a seething in the milkblind heavens. How the candle glared. Grevil, rubbing at his eyes, is elsewhere: Lune in summer, and that crooked room beneath the eaves. Their term is ended; they do keep one gaudy night. He sees Hulver and Perseis, his chamber-fellows, in a haze of wine, still trailing their celestial attire; and the whore sprawled back on Hulver's bed. That godling drinks. A haze of gold on him; a weal where he is whitest. All his gaze on her, her gaping and her sweltering thighs. "Come, chuck," says Ned Perseis to Noll. "'Tis paid for. And the sweetest cunny." Wilting from her clench, he thrashes down his tinsel petticoats. He brings the candle close. And kneeling up, she pulls Noll down on her, to drown in her, as in a quicksand. Her hands at work on his bewilderment. Her reeky mouth. "Come, Noll," says Hulver fondly. "'Tis thine entrance."

He would not.

*Go, let Master Mistress Wilton coy thy cheek, and praise thine asteismus, scrat.*

*Poor sweeting, let him come alone to me. You gentlemen do shy him.*

*So he nill.*

So Perseis had jeered, the whore had kissed and dandled like his nurse; and Hulver shrugged and smiled: and in the dawn, eyes shut and crying out on Peg, had let Noll toy him. And that evening he had taken ship. So Madam in her turn had raged and ranted when he would not marry Hulver's sister-twin, now widowed e'er she wed. That chimaera: his gold in her turned silver, and his grace to gravity; that thing beneath her skirts.

So he would not. Yet had refusal: as Margaret did not.

Grevil stood and swung the window open to the rattle of the rain. Scant still. He let it fill his hands. He laved his burning face.

Abhorred bedding.

Yet he would have drowned for Hulver's sake: gone freely to a greener bed.

It rained now in good earnest, teeming down. And leaning out into the night, he prayed for Will: that he might reach the Haven and take ship.


A moonless dawn. Hoar frost.

Grieve's candle woke Barbary. Silent, throwing on her gown, she followed through the shadowed rooms to Margaret's closet. "Get her washed." So they might summon her to shroud a corpse.

The girl was kneeling in the rushes in her smock. Her face was downcast; her hands hung empty before the welter of blood in her lap. Suppliant. As if she begged her pardon for a thing she'd broken. Her childhood shivered like an egg.

*Here's mischief,* thought Barbary. *She's ower pale for ae night's waking.* A blanched thing in a heap of stones. Like that flower called Star-Naked or Ashes-Bare-Annis, that shivers in the fields of autumn, leafless and forlorn. They'd forced her flowering, she thought. By leechcraft or by worse. They'd ways. And they'd fasted her. And waked. And drugged. The girl was waning with the moon; aye, and moonbent, inward on herself, with flinching. Smudged eyes in a peaked and haggard face.

A whisper. "I am Margaret still."

For a flicker of the candle, Barbary saw another, long-remembered face, and long-denied: a weeping boy, half naked, in a Bedlam coat. *My lass. She needs a woman by her.*

Gone.

His eyes. Yet not his eyes. They had known relenting; they were yet bewildered by the loss of hope. The child's sought nothing.

Barbary set the candle by the bedside; knelt, face to face with Margaret; touched eyes, mouth, heart. "So yer come to Ashes."

There was no caress in her kindness: it was impersonal as rain on earth. She set about her work, stripped off the bloody smock. No woman's body there, poor waft. Scant as a skirret. Bruised, not with beating, but restraint. Barbary wrung out her cloth: all her anger in that wrenching. "Come up." The child endured washing and dressing. No kindness sought, nor justice: she endured. *Reared at a witch's tit.*

Grey dawning. No coal nor candle in the outer room. Yon madams were abroad. Barbary bent toward Margaret, undid her hair, loose-braided down her back and frayed with wear. A knot. Another and another, fine as fernseed. "So. Now yer moonwise, y'll be lating Ashes. Out ont fell." The face was turned from her; yet she felt a stirring in the child, a shift of breath. Barbary took up the comb. She kempt the long hair, cannily; undid each knot, redid it otherwise. "Yer mun gang wi' all t'women, will they or nill. 'Tis Cloudlaw." And lower voiced, "'Twill be Hallows. Happen you may find what door you came by."


A girl in a blue gown opens, with a hand curved round her candle. Light spills through her fingers, stills her face: long-lidded, lustrous as a pearl against the cheek of night. Her gown seems made of sky. For all her ornament she wears bright shears. Her hair is twisted in a cloth, a wentletrap of linen, with a streak of leaf-red hair wound round it, like the bandings on a shell.

"Hallows with you," says the girl and blows her candle out. "Is this the lass?"

"Aye, feathery bonnet and all," says the witch.

"Well met," says the girl. "And long in coming."

Margaret curtsies low.

With a beck, the blue girl raises her. "For thy sojourn, thy house."

Margaret turns at the sill to bid the witch farewell, but she has gone. And the landscape. And the door. The blue girl puts her candlestick amid a throng of others. "I am eldest this time. Siony."

She brings her to a bare room, a bower full of girls at work. So many strangers. All in blue: dusk blue, or deeper, or the liminal bluegreen of twilight. Some wear turbans like the eldest, snailed and turreted like shells; and others, garlands of their own wreathed plaits. A girl in a blue smock bends to her needle, peering at the rents and ravels of a scarf, a gauzy thing. It haloes round her hand like iris. Rainbright in rain, her needle pricks and pulls an unseen thread. Her sleeve is stuck with pins. Another girl, sootblack and silver, crooks a tarnished platter in her elbow; breathes on it and rubs. She glances at Margaret, pushes back her hair with a smutchy hand; then bends to her work. A third stands sleaving out silk tassels, catkins of light. Bareheaded, that one, brief as thistledown. Her dress as pale as if she'd waded in the moon.

Through a doorway, in a farther room, Margaret sees a great bare sort of bedstead, and two girls stringing it with yarn. A gallows harp. A loom. Siony calls to them, "Talith, come. Tiphan! Here's weft."

Two others come, with bare arms streaked with dying, vivid to the shoulder.

They three unlid the basket. "Ah," says Siony. Not clots and tangles of raw wool, as Margaret thought there must be, but skeins, smooth as a child's hair from her nurse's hands; and faintly bright. Like cobwebs. Talith—or is it Tiphan?—kneels, and tells them over, heaping up her sister's apron.

"Corn enough," says Talith.

"But slain apples," says Tiphan.

"Never such a year for lambs."

"Small rain."

"Long summer."

"Late snow."

"Lambswool," calls a girl by the fire. "Will you sup?" A sonsy lass, with clustering curls. There is a faint rose at her hem, that comes and goes. Like dawning sky. Like dreaming. Margaret comes. By her knee, the girl sets out a dish of apples, withered and rosy, and a jug of cream. Sweet froth. The silver spoon bites deeply, to the seeded heart. A year. As in a dream, it dwindles. The blue girl dabs a finger at her iron—hot!—and goes on pleaching buds of silk, of bronze and palest green.

Margaret looks about the room. Clews everywhere, on shelves, in baskets. Skeins. Shuttles and bobbins. A swift of yarn, half-wound. Rush chairs, broad and low, still green; a great long standing board, scrubbed bare, and overheaped with work. Coffers and kists. An inlaid cabinet, a puzzlebox of wood in wood, and hidden drawer in drawer. Most curiously made. She longs to delve in it. The cabinet is crowned with tall blue and white jars, tear-shaped, shining like an April morning.

And the skein of girls.

All about her are the leaf-girls in their long blue smocks, weaving, sleaving, and unpicking, patching and polishing the winter-ravelled earth: not sticks and stars but green.

The dark girl beckons. As she turns, her dress clouds, changing indigo and stormy grey; a star glances in her skirts. Before her on the table is poised a scales full of hailstones, hammered bright; a chamois, and a goldsmith's elfin tools. She holds up her moonbright plate, a mirror. Round and scarry. "Look," she says; so Margaret does, and sees the witch. Her owl face fills it, overbrims. She blinks, and sees herself; but still the witch's cap warped round her, like the old moon's arms.

Behind her, viewless in the glass, the dark girl says, "Your ring. Will I burnish it?" She holds out her palm. Margaret fumbles for the ring. It is black and bent; but it comes up bright to the leaf-girl's chamois. She turns it round and round in her clever fingers, puzzling out the half-worn letters in their endless tale. "*Wode spring leave wode? I fall an light.*" Round again. "*Wode I fall?*" And round. "*Lief wode I fall, an light wode spring.*" It's poised between finger and thumb. "Which this time?"

"I cannot tell," says Margaret. "'Tis endless, like the Skein, the year." She considers. "Unless some stone were in it, like the Sun."

The dark girl gives the ring to her.

Beyond her, the weavers, Talith and Tiphan, wind off a skein: dip and murmur. Long since, Margaret's done for Norni. She remembers with a pang.

"A game," says the blue girl. "One that you began long since." She takes the thread and weaves it, in and out, between her hands; holds out a braid of stars. Time's cradle. "Take it. They'll not fall." Still gingerly, Margaret takes the strands and plays: recrosses, undergoes. The bright stars dance, conjoin.

"As above," says the pale girl, dipping in. "So below."

*Oh, I see,* thinks Margaret. *We keep measure.* A red star, like a drop of blood, falls backward through the web. A pale moon sidles, spiralling. The stars turn tendril in the pattern. Her turn: she weaves.

"Ah." The blue girl takes the web within her hands. It changes.

They play on. Now one, and now another of the sisters takes her turn. Weaving, Margaret forgets all else; until the night within her hands turns dusk, grey fading into farther grey. Her eyes are weary; shutting them, it seems she holds a swarm of sparks. She nods.

"Margaret?" Her hands lie empty in her lap, and heavy, filled with sleep. Rousing, she sees the room is shadowy. The fire is embers.

"Come, see thy web." The sisters at their weaving—Talith and Tiphan, tall Siony—beckon. Margaret comes.

Their web is winding from the loom, a spill of story. It is winter in the warp. But see, a green thread runs through it, recursive. All in green, a green verge in her hand, a child arises from the weft of snow, and where she walks spring flowers. *Ashes?* Now a girl, starfallen, stands amazed. *Ah, Perseis.* Her body is of sky and all the stars: bright Ashes in her privities, the Fiddler in her heart; but inward of her memory, her sisters rise. Her going is a Milky Way. Behind her—she will turn—there stands a woodwo, all in leaves of tatters, red and pale. *O rare Cosmography.*

Now she is running from him, green in green. The leaves are scattered of her gown; or else the leaves create her, she is woven of their element. Her path turns ever to the heart of things, a blackthorn woven in a white, and at their roots a spring. She kneels to look in it, as in a mirror; she is caught. He weaves for her a crown of white and black; he lays her down. When they have done, he strings his fiddle with her hair; and when he plays, she dances.

When she rises from him, he is tree.

Now wood is water, river now in river, rippling and changing. It is sea. A white wave rises from the green; a cradle on it dips and swirls, is carried from her sight. The tree's a ship, still rooted, branching into stars. The moon is in its shrouds; a star falls burning from the mast, a man with sunbright hair. A great wave whelms the ship. Yet overturned its roots are branches.

Now the sea's a field of corn. Round-bellied, Ashes reaps what she has sown; her sickle is the moon. She strings it with her hair; she plays. Her lover dances in the corn, now here, now anywhere. But now three witches stand as harvesters. Inward and inward spiralling, they ring him round. They cut him off at knee. They bind him.

Heavy heavy now, the mourning Ashes rocks the empty cradle that the sea cast up. Her lover's sleeping in a sheaf of corn.

Leaves fall drifting from the tree.

The witches drink of him. They share him out as bread.

There is a child, half-naked, in a field of poppies. Black and bare now, seedheads, rattling in the wind. The child stoops, searching. There is something she has lost: a knife among the weeds, a stone from off her ring. Buried in the black earth, openeyed, there lies a girl scarce older, gashed and naked. Her mirror. Where she has lain, it blooms: the petals her beseeching wounds, her blood her cry. It runs all through the web, that thread of crimson, to the verge—But there the tale breaks off. Warpstrings, like the endless wind.

"Time," says Siony behind her.

Still Margaret gazes. "Is that now?"

"Or will or may be. Or it would have been, long since."

"And ever and again."

"It looks like somewhat from my cards," said Margaret.

"Thy pack is tatters of it," said the eldest, Siony. "They but foretell; we tell what must have been that it might be: the stories of the sky in earth."

"Go," said Talith. "Ask thy sister for thy tale. In there. At her book."

Through a narrow door.

A whirlwind. A babble and a blaze of tongues, all silent but a wind. Leaves rise and scatter, whorling, and are ash. The room is like a lantern pierced with windows; like a cresset heaped with flames. And at the heart of them, a girl's bent writing with a thorn: a word, a vein of words, on each. A book of leaves, unbound.

Unleaving.

"They are burnt," says Margaret.

"But the tree stands," says the leaf-girl.

What she prophesies is scattered even as she tells. The wind has fallen; but the words fly on.

Through the high window, an owl flies in, a clew in its beak like a mouse. She drops it into Margaret's lap.

"Thy tale's for thy telling," says the leaf-girl. "Come. It's all to do." She rises and Margaret follows her. At their feet, the bright web lies like autumn, fleeting even as she looks. The workroom is swept bare.

"Time," says Siony. "You have a key." Margaret gives it her. It fits, and opens on a winding stair. Farther in. The Nine are gathered at the door now, taking up grey hoods and lanterns, turning to ascend the stair.

"Coming?"

Wan and shaken, propped in Madam's chair, false Annot heard a clatter and a jangle coming. The maids beside her glanced and nudged, and bent to their stitchery. In came Barbary with a broad silver bowl, and the dairymaids behind her. Nan in a red cap bore a spindle, and Doll in a necklace of white pebbles held a riddle and shears; half terrified and half ecstatic, crow-clad Sukey shook Barbary's great bunch of keys.

"What is it, girl?" said Madam. "We are much engaged."

"A saining," said Barbary. "To bring Mistress Annot intil t'company o women. Now she's bled." She brought the bowl to Margaret. It brimmed with water. One red leaf floated, slowly spun. "Fetched from Mall's spring at daybreak this were. By a hale maiden, barefoot. What d'ye see?"

Margaret bent to it. "My own self."

"So thou's to be."

Sukey's face fell. "Yer meant to spy Ashes."

Nan tossed her head. "Nay, yer meant to see what's meant."

"Kate Imberthwaite see'd a sheep's head on her. Ever more," said Doll.

"Hush," said Barbary. "Here's rites." And to Margaret, "Touch t'water."

It wavered. For a moment she saw witch enfolding witch, a furl of moonlight and the dark of moon. A rose of sky. Then the ripples faded out, the water stilled. "It comes round."

"So it does. Each moon. Now lave thy face and so it will be."

So cool the water was, and scented of the earth and leaves. A wakening. As if it cleared the fume of magic from her senses Over and again, Margaret bathed her eyes.

Setting down the basin, Barbary held out a towel to her blindly dripping hands. "There now, yer lawful. Ye can late afore ye wed."

Ostentatiously alert and gracious, Madam softly clapped her hands. "'Twas prettily played, you wenches. Barbary, thou hast taken pains with them. Enough. To work."

Barbary curtsied. "We is forehand, I thank ye. Wedding and all." And pinning up Margaret's braid, "'Tis fortunate she's bled this year, or y'd be bound to wait another Hallows for her bedding. All yon baking spoiled."

"Fortunate indeed. The girl is eager for her lord's embrace."

Not a grimace. "What jacket will I air then, Madam? Her sable is warmest, I think. 'Twill be sharpish on t'fell."

"Mistress Annot is too frail to walk out. She will do her observances here."

"O Madam, t'would not be lawful." Shock on all the servants' faces. "By yer leave, Madam, not round here. As Mistress Corbet, she's to have estates and towers; and his sworn folk won't reckon her wed truly, nor her bairns true born, but she's lated Ashes. And that's t'rite on it."

A murmur of assent went round. "So 'tis."

And as Madam gathered herself to reply, the servant clapped once. "By ladle, I's forgotten what come." Barbary took a little parcel from her pocket. "Now then, Mistress Annot. Here's a candling from yer ashmother—awd Madam Selby, ower Luneways. Yer mun write yer thanks and duty to her."

Margaret broke the seal, unwound the lambswool. "Oh," breathed all the maids. A perfect little lantern, silver and moonstone, with a flame in it of topaz. Doors of crystal that swung. "There's a letter," she said.

"Read it out," said Madam.

"'Daughter Annot—'" How strange to read another's letters, wear another's life. In her new-washed clarity, she saw the other girl as real, as lost. She nearly balked; but Barbary nodded her assurance. "'From thy loving Gossip. Wear this Trinkett for my sake at hallowstyde, on thy first lating Ashes. May thy Candle burn bright and longest. May Ashes light on thee, Law take thee not, Brock bed thee.' And sealed with a heron."

"Elinor Selby wrote this? When?" Madam snatched the paper.

"When Annot first bled," said Barbary.

"But that—"

"Were last week, aye."

Madam studied. "I had not thought—"

"She'd be wick enough to bid to't wedding? Nay, an her servingmen carried her, she'd have come, were it back o't moon. And will for Annot's bairn's ashing. Fair fond on young Annot, she is. Would have matched her with her daughter's son."

"A younger son. Died penniless," said Madam. "Master Corbet is a lord of men. She bears me no ill will, I hope."

"'Tis not my place to tell yer, Madam."

"I bid thee."

"An yer will. This marrying in huggermugger likes her not. Wick as she ever were, is Madam Selby. A great lady. She were Ashes twice."

Madam folded the letter in her needlecase.

"And sent nine pound o candles for us lanterns. All virgin wax."

Beckoning Sukey for the keys, Barbary unlocked a kist, took out the stout surrendered shoes. "I s'll just take and dubbin these. Way's mucky, and it's a shame to spoil yon cork-heeled pantoufles."

Bent beggarstaff, a crookback moon trudged slowly down the sky, clad fustily in rags of cloud. Annot walked by its halflight, over moss and moor; half ran, and stumbling, fell. This country was unknown to her, a borderland; her only road, *away*. Toward moonset there came a sharp cold spattering of rain. Shivering in her stolen silk, her city gallant's doublet and hose, she cast about her for a refuge. Just beyond a little beck stood a hill barn. She'd shelter. Sleep in straw.

At the sill, she halted. A rustling within. Rats? Peering, she saw only moonspill in the dust. A shaft of bleak light caught a sickle bound in straw. Sacks. Flails. A grindlestone. A tipsy cauldron, spilling dark.

A laugh.

She swung about. Crouched in among the barleystraw, three hooded women drank. They passed one cup from hand to hand.

"Lost thy knife?" said one.

"I'd not run, boy," said another, as Annot wheeled about. "Dog hunts." A lurcher girned and loured at her feet, all fang and sinew.

And the third: "How it shivers, poor startlin hare." She drank. "Knap it neck."

Kin to Madam's Grieve who gamed with cruelty: she knew it in her marrow, which was turned to bloodred ice. She'd taken her false lover's sword when she ran from him; knew not its manage. Two held her, flung it clanging to the ground. No guise. The first to speak drew back the slide of their lantern. Flare and shadow.

Whores. Annot knew that now. She saw red shoes, a bruised pale breast, a broad hat with a draggled feather. The glint of a knifeblade. "Let me go. I have nothing for you." Shrill bravado. How ill she boyed it.

A black mort, with a blue and scornful eye, leaned forward. Haw as death. "But we's summat for thee."

"Word," said a sluttish drab. Hacked yellow hair. Pissed petticoats and trodden shoes. A limp goose lying at her feet. Spoil. "Thy kindred ..."

A breath indrawn. The boy that was Annot could not mask her sudden hope.

"Nowt for nowt," said a roaring doxy, a tall wench in a soldier's cap and feather. "What's in thy breeches?"

The Black Mort groped her. "Cunny."

"Eggs," said Pissabed, rummaging and seizing all her store. Yolk running down her chin: she slobbered as she sucked.

"Cockseed," said the doxy; then to their captive, "Cut his purse next time. He's filled thine oft enough."

"Cut his throat," said the Black Mort. "Take his cully for thy pimp."

The doxy fleered. "Aye, teach yer grandam to grope ducks."

But the Black Mort held Annot's eye. "Here's word. Thy kindred casts thee off as whore. They's banned thy name and burnt thine ashings. Thou's to die untold."

Black silence.

"Or thou will, but if ..."

No breath to speak. "If ...?" said Annot at long last.

"If thou can show us where thy cully's laid."

"He's craws' meat," said the striding doxy. "Will be hanged i' Law."

"He'll have stolen summat. Say, a chain o gold."

"Or chance a bracelet will be found on him."

"He'll have ta'en a ring. My lady sees to it."

So Madam saw to things. A cheat. Annot said, "He took nothing."

They laughed. "But thou given it."

Annot looked sidelong out of downcast eyes. The knifeblade glinted shrewdly; the rough beast crouched and snarled. No rift. No running. "I know not what you mean."

"Thou liest, vixen's whelp. Thou's trysted wi' a fool."

"If I travelled for a space in company, I saw no ring."

"Think that's why he's to hang?" said Cap-and-Feather. "For a tawdry?"

"For his blue eyes," sang Pissabed.

The Black Mort leaned closer still. "He's to hang for what he took o thee: a ring for his blind finger. That toy were Master Corbet's." Bared teeth: she saw the elfshot strike. "Ah, that bites thee."

Black Mort gazed hard at her. "Not clouded; yet she's cracked."

"There's rare game o that sort wi' us. If it like thee."

"A pretty play." The pale drab swayed and whirled. "Will you have *Aprons all untied*? I'll show thee. Or *Cross my river to Babylon*."

Caressed with nettles. Their words stung like scorpions, like honeyed maggots heaved and coiled. If she spoke she would spew.

Cap-and-Feather leered and licked her fingers with a sharp red tongue. "Thou's a vixen twixt thy legs, same as we has."

"'Twill dance," said the Black Mort. "An it's called and fiddled." She caught Annot's face between clawed hands, and whispered with her charnel breath. "Did it frisk when he kittled thee?"

Fury whelmed fear. Annot wrenched at her captor's hands, but the Black Mort held her fast. She pinched the slight breast scornfully. "There's coin for that. If thou wilt play."

Silence.

Now they closed on her, all three. Red, black, and white.

"Thou's cast away what t'quality would haggle o'er, t'breaking of thy glass."

"Thy fortune."

"But thou's yet unpoxed. Thou's turn a pretty penny still."

"We's a bawd will school thee in gallantry."

"In coining wi' thy purse."

"Thou's slept soft i' featherbeds ere now. Supped sugared wine. Wouldst again?"

But it was comforts of the mind that Annot rued. Sleavesilk and her needlework, undone: she saw her needle in a half-made rainbow, like a slash of rain. Her virginals, the song unlearned; her book, the page turned down. Oh, she was longing for her narrow bed, a book and candle by. For Damaris to lie beside her, silly sisters as they were. For Noll, and winter's tales of ghosts and witches, by a hearth. "I would live honestly, my lone."

They laughed like a rookery. "Whore's what thou is. Thy choice is hedgework or haggling."

"Go, keep thyself. Suck ploughmen and be paid in bruises."

"Fleshmeat thou's have in plenty now. Undressed."

"Raw cream and strokings of a herd o stirks. 'Twill curdle i' thy belly soon enough."

"A ditch for thy bower. Nettles for thy goosedown. Hap-harlot for thy sheets."

"Any man's thy rug."

"And whip's thy breakfast," crowed Cap-and-Feather.

And the Black Mort twisted a great handful of her captive's hair. "Thy choosing. Common whoredom and infamy. Or give thy cully to be hanged, for silence, and thy lot is with our Master Daw."

"Wouldst have thy kindred see thee carted, cry thee whore?"

Still silent, though she clenched her fists until her nails bit. Annot saw not Madam's face but Damaris her sister, pale and sorrowful, arisen from the grave: she held her small son gazing in her lap with great round eyes, as at a masque. *O Noll.*

"Venge thysel. Thou wouldst, for thy ruin."

*Would I?*

Cap-and-Feather preened her knife; lunged suddenly at air. "An thou wilt, he gangs to't gallantry ..."

"But tell us where he lies."

"... wi' a fiddler afore him, Hallows morn."

"He'll dance Daw's Jig."

"Eyes til t'craws."

"Bones til t'heather."

"Soul til my lady's crown."

"And we's to have his flesh," said the Black Mort. "So my lady bids. But say."

And Cap-and-Feather crowed. "A green stick for a witch to ride."

Eyes closed and rocking, swaying, Pissabed crooned. "Ride a cock-horse ..."

"No," said Annot, dry-voiced. "Death gives nothing back to me."

"Not hempseed for thy cockerel? Is thy palate daintier? Then chose what end thou wilt for him."

"There's one teared by dogs."

"That's one. And which is thine?

"One drownded i't ice. Run after sun, he would."

"Is't thine?"

"There's one falls burning frae a mast."

"That likes me. Is't thine?"

They were chanting, ecstatic. Annot struggled in vain. They'd wound and bound a spell about her, a caterpillars' clot of nest.

Now the pale wench set her eggshells in a tub, she tipped it this way and that. She stirred it with a fork. "Here's a cockboat. And another. For my lady to fleet."

The Black Mort picked a witchknot from her crawling hair. "That's one. And here's a wind." It raged in little on her hand. She huffed and sent her tempest onward. In the wooden O, the eggshells rocked.

Another knot. "Will I undo?"

"Thou do. Undo."

A storm swirled in the tub, a whirlpool. Lightnings. Laboring, the eggshells spun. By one and one, they heeled and sank. Now eight, now five, now three, now two ...

Down in the farmyard, the grey cock crowed. Their dog sprang up, a-bristle, barking. The Black Mort swore and seized his collar, flailing at him, but her spell had snapped. Annot leapt for the cockloft, and pulled the ladder up behind. Lay shuddering.

"Fire straw," said Cap-and-Feather below.

No breath.

"My lady cracks no charred bones," said the Black Mort. "Shift."

As the trulls took to their heels, a gabble of hounds took up the basso. Hue and cry. Men called. "Hoy, Bandogg! Ho, Beldam!" Annot peered through a windeye, warily. A rout. Below, the dogs howled and snapped, the shepherds hallooed. "Out on ye! Thieves! Out, whores!"

Too late. Harsh and rancorous, a far voice mocked them. Halfway up Law, Cap-and-Feather turned and flashed her sullied arse, she waggled the gooseneck at her naked fork.

Long after, broad morning, when the clamour had faded, Annot climbed down. The drabs had faded like an ill dream, leaving nothing but a stench and scuffling in the chaff. A scattering of eggshells. But the sword was gone. Out on the high moor, out of sight, she waded in a beck. Shaking, she scrubbed and scrubbed where the trulls had pawed at her, a taint ingrained as ink.


Margaret was earth, she could not wake. Unsinewed, powerless, she could not will herself to rise, to beat with bloodless hands against the rubble and the rock that held her. Could not speak: her tongue was a twisted stump, dry rootstock, in a gorge of stones. No voice; no breath; no sight. Though she lay openeyed, no light would enter and ensoul her grave. The stars forever lost. She lay beneath a fell of dark, and roke and fire rose from her, unwreathing

in a coil of cloud that blotted out her sky. As if she burned, but coldly, unconsumed. Slow tumult in the windless air, a blood-brown dusk. A black frost
on her naked breast, her shoulder. At her fork was moss and marish, bleeding,
bleeding in a bitter spring, a syke. And inmost, burrowed in her secrets, burring out, there grew a clinch of crystal. She was under Law.

... *blood* ... said the raven, perching on her brow.

... *of stone* ... said its marrow, lighted on her flank.

The crows at her cradle. In the windless storm their voices came in
scraps.

... *another Annot is* ...

... *not Annis* ...

A smear of light. *A star*, she thought. *The first of them to fall*—

A scald of fire on her breast.

She woke in the pale bed, in the nightless tower. Under Law. And could
not breathe for Morag, hulked upon her body, mantling with her ashy wings.
Her talons griping in her belly. They bound her with a braid of fire. And
my lady held the glass. But she would not look in it, although the cards fell
burning on her body. Ashes of her stars. *And which next shall I take? Thine eyes? Thy
choosing. It will make a game.* My lady—

And she woke in this world, drenched and shuddering, unselved. And lay,
her blood resounding on the stithy of her heart. There was a drowsing evil
in her blood, an overpowering; they'd drugged her, when she would not taste
their wine, with a fume of poppies, with a cold infusion in a drenching-horn.
It took her will, her understanding; left only naked terror and her shame.
They'd rifled her. And all her power lay in holding back a greater power: as
if they'd brought their candles deep within her, where the powder slept. That
fury wakened could annihilate herself, beside her enemies, and all this house.
The earth, as once the sky.

Now slowly, she remade a world about her, time and space. Her narrow
bed. Her wall. Herself: but recollected slowly, wound about her nakedness. A
sheet of soul; a counterpane of stars. A blanket, as she shook with cold. A
pillow huddled to her chest, to rock herself awake. Between her fingertips and
thumb she pirled and pirled the drop of candle wax, the fallen star.


"She will do," said Grieve; and lowering the candle, snecked the door.

"Aye, another's blood were best," said Rue by the fire. "But our mistress here doth venture much, since none may twice. All others that conceived by Law have slipped ere they had quickened. None were brought to bed."

"If all miscarried, they were false," said Grieve. "There's but one true hailstone left, and hers." She set the candle by the coffer. "It is the last. All eight others hath she sought and studied; it is sure."

"So she would spend it? On that posset-faced puling chit?" said Rue, and handed up a glass. "As good play duck and drake with diamonds in a sump."

"So it be swilled, the earthenware's as good a vessel as the gold: a hole to fill." Grieve took the dram of her and drank. "And there is witchblood in the chit, I warrant you. And none to meddle for her sake. Our mistress dotes on her commodity, despites her, flesh and soul. The smockfaced nephew—"

Rue laughed scornfully. "Is no warden of her honor. Fatherless and friendless, aye. But will be husbanded. Corbet—"

"A beard for her breeding. He will serve us well enough."

"He is no fool, that scythesman. Will he not suspect?"

"A lover? Of that mooncalf? He will find her virgin. And conceit will father it." Grieve unpinned her apron. "'Tis well. Our mistress has her heritage; and the master his game."

"And coney is a pretty dish, they say. That I'm to dress." Rue drank. "I go with her to Corbet: as a gift."

Grieve set the pins straight in her cuff; spoke quietly. "To dress, but not to mar. The governance is mine."

"Is ours—"

A footfall on the winding stair, a shadow and a scent of wax. The servants rose and curtsied. "Is't done?" said Madam Covener.

"Aye, madam, slab and sharp," said Rue, and stirred the pipkin on the hearth.

"The girl?"

"Asleep," said Grieve. "And ripening."

A jangle of keys at Madam's waist, as she unlocked the coffer.

Two witches huddle by a fire of thorn. The cup goes to and fro.

"Here's meddling," says Brock. "Will she bear?"

"Aye, happen." Mally drinks. "Herself; or yon hailstone."

"Could be harrowed out."

"Oh, aye." The small witch holds a garland on her knee, of grey and withered leaves, or none. "Just here's a bitter little herb her mam has plucked for her, when she would rid her belly of yon brat. I's kept it whiles."

"A draught?"

"In time. And if." The witch pours out her cup; the fire flares and dies. "Her grandam wants her glass to fill. Come hallows will she hunt."

"Scent's cold," says Brock. "My journeyman confounds her. For a time."

"Has sailed?"

"At hallows. And herself?"

"Will find herself. Her belly full."

A click of talismans, a flick of smile. Brock's silent else.

"Where one is, two cannot," says Mally. From her cauldron rises up a fog, a frost-hag: they are rimed with it. Below, beyond—there is no word for it—Whin's boat is swallowed up. Blind, open-eyed, she journeys, and the storm begins to rise.

Margaret wakes drenched.

And white in white, the witches fade, black moorland and the winter tree, all but the embers of the fire. Their voices whisper in the sticks.

"... and in her glass ..."

"... is not ..."

Alone in her high chamber, Madam laughed. So it was done: the girl invitrified, and to be wed Ash-morrow. She herself had studied since the last fled Annot; had refined the art. All other witches had miscarried of their stones; had quickened, aye, but then the god-in-embryo had eaten up her vessel from within. Some few had lived a space in agony, half-glass, half-grub: the larvae of transcendence. Some had bled away, some mortified. Some preyed on children and were slain. And all were dead, their souls annihilate. No Ashes of this earth could tell them. Madam closed her empty coffer, lock on lock. But her creature, unborn Annis, would be nourished on the sun, on Corbet's seed. His lust would feed her lust for power, her insatiable dark; until voracious, she had used him up. Drunk down the sun. Then Madam would discard the shrivelled skin of him, sucked dry through his great cock, and reign with widow Annis in his tower. She had staked my lady's soul on it.

*Will hang,* said a still voice to Margaret.

She was on a skyless hill, bent onward, neither west nor east, but wading to the knee in shadow. There was something that she'd lost: a knife among the weeds, a stone from off her ring. Her name. No stubble here, nor grass, but swiddened moorland, and the sift of ash long cold. It fell like shadow into shadow, sparse. Around her lay a sprawl of stones, half fallen in a maze of thresholds, perilous to cross. Whatever way she turned was inward.

She had never gone so far.

Beyond her fled a white hare like a furl of fire leaping from a brand, but paler than the waning moon. Like fire it flared and wavered; and went out.

*That card was burnt,* she thought.

Then she came to the Gallows Tree and saw the crow lad hanged.

He dangled, naked and atwist, agape. She saw his bound hands, writhen struggling against the knotted hemp; she saw his stonebruised feet, now restless, dance on air. She saw his pricket like an angry thorn. His silver hair flared out about the bloodblue face, as if his death eclipsed him. There was something in his tongueless mouth. A stone? And then he twisted and it fell. An egg. *S'll harry thee a howlet's nest,* he'd told her once. *I knaws ae tree.* Stooping she picked it up: unbroken, strangely heavy in her hand. It was cloudblack and scrawled with white, with crossings intercrossing. Runes of stars. What tree? For as she gazed, she saw it fathomless, awhirl with light; she saw unfolding galaxies, feathering like frost. She saw the leaves unscattered of the book of heaven.

*They were burnt.*

*To Ashes.*


Barbed and hooded, masked as for a play, my lady's women brought Margaret down the winding stair. The dream still tranced her, sliding in her blood like sublimate: a bright envenomed clarity, a swaling heaviness. It was the eve of Hallows Eve. So dark a morning still, at noontide, that they bore a branch of candles. Beeswax, as befitted Madam Covener.

"Rare play we had of it," said Grieve to Rue. To Margaret, "The hunt was up, thy lord and all his pack."

"Afoot and riding."

"Earth and air."

"When thou'rt his lady, thou shalt ride with him."

The girl spoke not, but Grieve answered. "Aye, we took."

"A white hare, and alive."

They crossed the empty parlour, shadows and the ghost of flowers, to the high dim crowded hall. It smelled of winter, with a tang that caught her throat, of smoke and damp and mortal dread. Like Morag's kitchen, with its larder of souls. They had dressed her bravely, as befitted Corbet's property; she felt the silver mantle as a tarnish, like a shadow that would slide and leave her naked as the moon. Hard faces turned and stared and mocked.

She knew them; they had leapt the scythe.

Then she crossed a cold threshold, and she knew the place. They stood in Law. About them, silent, there were grey-cloaked women, in the places of the stones, the stars.

Before them stood the crow lad with his hands bound, ringed with scythesmen. Still alive; but the dream had foreshadowed him. Her sullied moon would slide before him; he would flare and die. He seemed now but an afterimage of himself, a scar on sight. Had this poor wretch bestrid her with a knife? Undone the ranting goblin at his fork? Not burning now but quenched. Corbet's men had beaten him; she knew too well that flinch of body, and that bruised despair. Mere pelt and bone and stinking rags, like something that an owl had cast.

He would not look at her.

But Corbet sat asprawl, at vantage, like a gallant at a play. No: like the play itself, a masque of old Slae, he that ate the newborn Sun; and Perseis his bride. He beckoned her; she needs must go. They set her by his knee before the company, brought cakes and wine. Flaunting her, he toyed her bare neck with his civet hand. He whispered with his cold breath, musk and charnel.

"Noll wavers," said Corbet. "See. But he will find for me."

Grevil sat on the dais, with a silver chain about his shoulders, and a scythe against his chair. Before him on the table lay a ring with a great tawny stone. Law's child, she knew it for a soul. As he did not. That puzzled her. She saw it clearly: insubstantial and more real than bread or stone or fire. Real as Law. He turned it in his hand, as if it were a rotten orange at a banket: meat he had no stomach for. And by it, like a crumpled napkin, lay a shirt: a little slashed, once fine, but stained with earth and ashes, and a darker stuff. With blood. And beneath that, bright and scattering—her heart clenched—lay several of a woodcut pack of cards. Not hers, but like.

"Thou nameless known as Crow-lad, masterless. Of no age. Else called

Rattlebag; else Clapcraws, Cloudborn, Ashes-got. These things were ta'en on thee," said Grevil to the lad. "Dost thou deny them?"

The boy said nothing. His warder cuffed him. "No." Sullen, defiant. Another buffet. "No. Master."

"Let him speak or be silent," Grevil said. "Now, boy, Madlin Flint has sworn by lief and law that she made this shirt for Master Corbet; and Nan Fell that she washed and mended it not three days before thy flight, and laid it in his chamber, in a press."

The crow lad's voice was small and harsh. "He gi'ed me yon sark."

"What he?"

"Yon dawcock." He jerked his chin at Corbet. "Him smiling." Margaret saw again the witch's carven mask, the summer lightning of his striding blade. *He* knew. And if he knew her birth? The scythesmen stirred.

"Gave thee?"

"For a jig." He raised his face to Grevil. "My awd jacket were outworn."

"Take care, boy," said Grevil. "Lest thy tongue betray thee." He slid the cards on the table, brooding. "Of what color were his hangings?"

"I were never in his bed. He'd not clart his sheets wi' me." He tried to wipe his snotted face on his shoulder. "Said he'd threshing, at Cock Moor. So I went."

"As whore?"

"Not what I is, it's what I's done. For bread. I'd be elsewhere."

"*For bread*, thou sayest. But a holland shirt? A ring?"

A waggish knave called out, "A lord might tryst wi' a pisspot, at need, but he'd not pay gold to quaff it."

"That man," said Grevil. "Take him out." He composed himself. "Whore is no excuse for thief, if proved upon thee. For the stealing of a shirt, thou shouldst be whipped; for breaking of a chamber, branded; for bearing tales, thy tongue be slit." He paused; and turned the great ring in his hand. "But here is graver matter."

"Ring's mine own," said the crow lad hopelessly. "By Hallows and t'Nine, I swear it."

"Thou? Nameless, masterless?"

"It's what I is."

Margaret watching saw curiosity, doubt, compunction flicker on Grevil's face. He leaned forward. "Has any seen this thing upon thee? In thy keeping? Hast thou spoken of it?"

*I's a star thou's not spied.*

Still he would not look at Margaret. "No."

And if she spoke? But Corbet whispered and caressed her. Filthy things. His cold breath stirred his earrings at her cheeks. It tarnished even gold; it woke them, scorpions to sting. He owned her. He would kill them both.

"Wouldst not have sold it? For that bread thou lack'st?"

"And wha'd believe it mine?"

"None yet," said Grevil. "Thou must prove. How cam'st thou by this ring?"

"I's never had it. Always."

Gibes and catcalls. Grevil stilled them with a hand. "Go on."

"It were given me." Struggling as if the bonds he tried were Grevil's. "See it's not a ring, but when it is. And then yer see it like a ring. Or owt. An orange."

"It is gold," said Grevil. "Valued, and of such-and-such a weight. The stone is adamant." He squared his papers. "It would buy a plough of land, and all its harvests."

Corbet's waiting-man, a sly fellow, called out, "Here's a bold ratlin. I have seen yon ring on Master Corbet's hand before this ditchborn dog was whelped, or ere his mother or her mother whored."

Two scythesmen caught the crow lad as he twisted and spat.

But Grevil looked coolly at the servant. "What hand?"

"Why, his left, sir. By his heart."

"Wouldst thou swear it?"

He would. And a respectable dame, Corbet's linen-woman, swore that he had it of his first wife, at her death. An heirloom of her family, said a third. His old nurse. But of late it grew small for him, and so he kept it in his closet, in a coffer, locked.

Grevil beckoned to his clerk. "Here's a paper of his steward's hand, and sealed." He broke it with his thumbnail. "On his oath, he swears the ember ring was ever on his master's swordhand."

A rustling, as of wind in barley.

Corbet rose drawing with his left hand, swiftly as he'd scythed; then turned his dagger hiltward to the judge, and bowed. "My masters trained me well," he said. "I fence equivocally, with either hand."

He sat, and in the rumour, leaned toward Margaret. "Thou shalt wear it for our play," he said. "And nothing else."

Unwilling Grevil rose. "So. Redesmen and riddlewomen: you have heard ..."

But the crow lad said, "There's cards." A half silence. "I ta'en that pack o them. For gaming wi' a vixen whore. And what I rue me of, is not your charge; and what you'll hang me for is what I is."

In the long withdrawing, Margaret stared at the cards, left scattered on the board. The Hanged Lad. The Horseman. No turning them. They'd not painted Slae like her own: not the Old Year in amongst the guisers with his ivy wreath, but with a billhook, by a leafless hedge. He lopped and plaited it about the winter wren, the Sun. Behind him on the wintry skyline stood a pole with a dangling thing on it, a scarecrow or a hanged man. Crowsmeat. They were all about him, rising in the air. And scattered on the fallow field were drops of silver. Coins. Or seed.

A slow drum beat return. They rose, and sat.

Grevil stood bareheaded, bowed before the Riddlestones. "We will hear your will and weird. What rede ye?"

"Law." One by one, the cloaked and hooded stones came forward, casting tokens in his rattling bowl. Eight black pebbles and a ninth of clouded grey. He shut his eyes, a moment only, soulstruck: like a tree about to fall, unfallen. Then he swept the tally up and showed them to the moot. "Eight and one."

He turned to the crow lad. "Thou wilt hear thy doom."

Dazed silence.

"Cloud will hang thee. Go by that road that thou cam'st, not walking but astride of wind." There were ashes in the bowl; Grevil sained him. "Eyes to the ravens; breath to the blind worm; ashes to air." He took the lykepale face between his hands. "Thy soul, for evermore untold, to Annis, at her will. So be it under Law." And formally, judicially, he kissed him, mouth to mouth.

"If I wrong thee, I will take thy road."

And none but Margaret saw his hand rest, trembling, on the hempwhite hair; nor heard him whisper, "... sorry ..."

But Master Corbet rose and gathered up the shirt. "Well, I'll not ride thee pillion. Here." He bunched and tossed it at the stonestruck boy. "Thou mayst hang in it. I'll a dance at my wedding."

He set on the ring.

## In Brock's Bag

*"There is a darknesse in the* Road, *a rift that runneth to the* Scythe; *but springing in the* Raven *it is call'd her Crawe: wherein my Glasse discovereth no starres. Yet here may bee a deeper Water, and a Catch of Souls.* Brock's Bagge, *our countryfolk do name it. In her secrets is the Soul possess'd . . ."*

Mist all round him. White and still. No road. No sun nor moon. Nowhere.

Bonecold and blinded with the fog, the boy kneels by a standing stone. Half naked, in a slashed stained shirt. Bare neck and legs. No jacket—has he drunk that away? No shoes. And frayed rope knotted round each wrist.

Nothing, he remembers nothing.

*Drunk?* he thinks; and tries to stand.

Reeling, he bows down again, flailed down by a storm of inwit, white black white, like crows that tear, like hailing starfall, like the lashing of a woman's hair, her cursing, as he—black red, the rending of her nails at—*No. Leave off.*

The touch of stone steadies him. Starving cold he is, his wits dunted. Should clap. Get on. Late fire. He rises on whitecold feet and turns. Burnt moorland, rime, that endless mist. What way?

A small jangle and clack, in all that stillness. Like harness; but no horse. He turns, too dazed to ward himself but with an arm before his face, palm outward, and he sees a shadow walk. It shrinks into a traveller: a woman breeched and booted, in a leathern cap, as grey as any brock. There are runes of iron braided in her hair, that swing and jangle; blood and ashes on her coat.

"Where's here?" he tries to say.

"Thy road. And thy lodging."

"Let by. I's nowt."

"There's thy lawing to pay. For thy room here. Fire and fleet." She holds out her scarred brown palm. "Gi's thy ring."

252

"Gone," he says. No voice.

"And i' thy keeping. It's thysel."

And dazingly, he has it, hung about his neck on a cord. He takes it in his hand, and turns it, glowering through his fingers like a wintry sun through ice. That wakes a dread in him. Its fire will dwindle him away, like snow from thorn; lay bare his bones. And if ...? He stamps and feels no buzz of blood returning. Sees no cloud of breath.

A bare whisper. "Will you tell a death?"

The stranger takes and tumbles it from fingertip to finger, burning like an ember; then she quenches it in her bag. "Snaw's to be thy sark," she says. "And wind's thy horse."

He stands earthfast, soulstruck. Cold out, his heart. In Ashes.

What road has he come? He shivers, pathless, in a dazzle of deaths. Again falls blazing from the masthead, burning drowned. Dances naked on the gallantry. Feeds foxes. Crows. Blind worms.

Brock takes his face between her hands, and kisses and kindles him. Blades pierce. Not blood but grief and memory returning, poignant in his flesh. All afire with cold. He shakes. She haps him in her old coat, black as earth; she lays him to her breast, and strokes him, cheek and chin, clagged hair, clemmed belly, and his sullen dart. He rises not; yet he dies in her. She takes him in her lap, and he is nothing, a worm in a hazelnut, a rattlebag.

He is crying; yet no tears will come. "Marget. I never told ..."

"She's not for thy undoing," says Brock, lifting his chin. "And thou's not yet done." She sains him, eyes, mouth, heart. "Thou's nobbut guising for a man; yet thou brings t'sun. Will Ashes."

## Hallows

The lanterns stood unlatched on the sandwhite scoured table. They had hung in the rafters yearlong, from each hallows to the next, unheeded as the moon by day, or like the stars at a child's birth, that work their ministry beneath the sill of night. At Barbary's hest, the maids had hooked them down, and scoured them with sand and rushes. They were old and curious: of horn and silver, ironwork and tin and copper, wrought and pierced with images of moon and stars.

She had unlocked the catmallison for cakes and spicery; laid out a score of good wax candles, even to a scruple.

On the dresser stood the Ashes-supper: soulcakes and sheercake, warden tarts and sharp white cheese, goose pie, gilt parkin, hazelnuts, jugged hare, quince quiddany, a knoll of apple butter and a motte of damson cheese. Now Barbary with her sleeves pinned back bent briskly to the hearthfire, ladling up lambswool in a great turned bowl; and Wick Billy, sticky-mouthed and solemnly resplendent in a turned coat and Nick Hawk's breeches, handed round a plate of gingerbread.

The master, ill at ease, had sained them with a word and gone.

Now Madam condescended to the feast. Behind her, bracketed with crows, came Annot. Silence fell. The great witch played the loving mother's part, bid innocence farewell. In ceremony, kissed her daughter; even sained her candle, prettily. *How glum these hobnails are,* a lady said. For Barbary (in Grevil's name) had bid two or three grave gentlewomen of his kindred—even a Selby—to dress the bridal bed. A quiet wedding, as befit a widower of age: no less in dignity. Will or nill, then, Madam and her waiting women must attend that company, withdrawing to the nobler banket laid for them.

At their going, there was pandemonium, a racket of girls reeling stories, a charm and chitter like a grove of birds: as if October were the kist of May unlocked, with all its green distilled. Gallipots of gossip. *Jug. Jug.* And little wit. Blackbirds and thrushes.

And on the rooftree, the crows. They would follow Annot to the fellside, spying, lest their thrall be fled.

Margaret half-listened, hidden in the chimney corner. An orange cradled in her lap, half-peeled: she had no heart for merrymaking. In this hall but yesterday, the crow lad was condemned; and here tomorrow would she wed his death, her own: their wedding-journey to his gallows.

Just now the maids were teasing Nan.

"Thou's lang and light heeled," said Doll her sister. "What if thou falls Ashes?"

"Happen I may."

"Wouldst thou bid Is Oddin's Tam frae her? Tam Sledger at forge?"

"Happen he'd come," said Nan. And turned about, singing, "... which makes his bright hammer to rise and to fall ..."

"So thou'lt be laid of a brat, come Barley."

"Happen I'd not be," said Nan; but doubtfully.

"How? An if thou dost it head-a-tail, like herrings?"

"Whist," said Nan. "I's have no salt fish. Oyster pies."

Ellender prinked her ribands, smiling. "What I'd take, I'd not give back."

"What, toss him?"

"Toy thysel?"

But heckle as they would, she'd not be drawn. Her silence grew around their teasing like a pearl.

Doll said, "I'd have a flock o geese and keep feathers."

"*Keep nowt*," cried all.

"Feathers isn't geese. Not like eggs."

"Is bloom apples?" said Ellender.

"If happen thou couldst bid a storm, thou might keep snaw."

"Hailstones."

"Wind."

"Keep feathers, and I'd ha' a bed," said Doll. "But I'd not sleep, being Ashes, for t'weight o dark. But lie and shiver, thinking on."

Nan bent forward in the fireshadow, lowering her voice. "There were a lass were Ashes. And a stranger come asking, would she a tell a death? And he'd a mirror."

They were quiet then, the embers siffling as they fell.

Bestirring, Doll cried, "Ey! I knaws what Cat's after." And she sang, as the maids did reeling off yarn:

> *shoemakker leather cracker*
> *balls o wax and stinkin watter*
> *three rows o rotten leather*
> *who would have a shoemakker?*

But Cat Alys gathered up her skirts disdainfully, and said, "If I were Ashes I'd not take me some clownish swain. I'd walk abroad in siller shoon—"

"Rare and mucky they'd be wi' guising."

"—a gown o't green silk and coats o't cramoisy—"

"Aye, that'll wear bravely wi' Ashes' coat. And thy feathery bonnet and all."

"—and a ring til every finger."

"And a fiddler afore thee?"

"Aye, and trumpets and a drum," said Cat. "And ye'd all on ye lout low when I's passing."

Round-eyed, Wick Billy said, "But I were a lass and fell Ashes—"

Howls of derision. "Thou'd wear a smock and petticoats."

"—I'd not. I'd eat sugared syllabubs my fill."

"And give them back? Puke or purge?"

Alys flourished at his breeches with her shears. "S'll ha' to snip thee."

"Won't!" he roared, raising up his dish as buckler. "I's Awd Moon." And he chanted, "*In comes I wi' broom afore, to sweep yon hussifs frae th' door.* And clash 'em, and thrash 'em, and down falls Sun."

"Never mind, Will Constant," said kind Doll. "Thou and Sukey can eat allt tharfcakes, whilst we poor lasses trudge through mire."

Sukey had been biting moons of her gingerbread. "Why can't we gang?"

"'Cause he's a lad and thou's a babby."

"Lasses gang. I's not got a tallywag atween my legs."

"Thou's not yet wanted one."

"Thou's not yet bled."

"Thou'd nobbut ask for a babbyhouse."

But Sukey said, "I'd want nowt. Just to be lating i't dark, and see t'stones walking, and t'stars awhirl."

Margaret looked swiftly up at her. Quite silent: but the light disclosed her.

Nan said, "Eh, then, there's Not Marget moping. What's thy will, if thou's Ashes? Thou's not said."

"Clag Sally," said Doll. A tittering.

And Ellender, "My lady Grevil."

Cat Alys tossed her head. "She's getten awd Daddy Corbet til her bed. And there's her purse full."

"Here's a match," said Ellender. "February Fill-Dyke's to wed t'First of April."

Doll shook her head. "'Tis a blackthorn wedding, January frost in May. 'Twill untimely wither."

"*He'll* untimely wither. I'll lay that he's lost his whirly-whorl."

"Think ye he'll get mooncalves on her?"

"Think ye she'll horn him?"

"Yon fernseed? Couldn't horn a snail."

"And wha'd take her?" The old wheel with a sharp new spindle.

"Will Beggarstaff, Tom Rattlebag ..."

"Tinkers and thieves."

Nan skipped and sang, *"Corbet had her first to wed / But Clapcraws had her first to bed."*

"Clapcraws?"

"He that's to hang, Ash-morrow."

"Wi' a fiddler afore him." Awe and malice in Cat's voice. "'Tis like a ballad."

But now grave Barbary advanced with the mazer bowl, abrim with ale and apples. Lambswool. They fell silent, still with awe or damped and fidgeting. Turn and turn to each of the serving-girls she spoke a line; and each rimed to her, and drank.

*"We know by the moon."*

*"That we are not too soon."*

*"We know by the sky."*

*"That we are not too high."*

*"We know by the stars."*

*"That we are not too far."*

In turn Margaret rose and took the wassail bowl. "Thy word is, *By th'ground,*" said Barbary in her ear. "When there's Ashes cried, i't hallowing, there's one will come for thee. Thou follow." False Annot bent to drink. It tasted bittersweet, of dark: the blood of barleycorn. A froth of apples kittled at her nose.

All but silently she said to Barbary, "You cast the white stone."

No answer to that. But the servant said, "It's mizzling out. Thou'lt take cold i'that frippery." She put a furred jacket, strangely heavy at the seams, round Margaret's shoulders.

Ashes is waked on a dark shore, with the Ring half-buried by her hand.

The year is at its ebb, at Hallowstide. She lies asprawl between wave and shallows, sleep and waking, at the brim of Law. Time-drowned, light-stranded, she is lapped in glimmer, drifted in the shallows of the Way. Its outfall, where the dead lie silted, souls outworn by time. Her telling and untold. They had voices once, and memory; they are ground. They are shoaled about her: numberless and nameless, sand and shingle; with here and there a broken shell. Cloudstreaks cracked and faded, blunted pinnacles, the windings of a heart laid bare.

The Raven stoops to bear away her soul.

Dark-dazzled at the threshold, fire-blind, Margaret turned within a wider air, unbound, and sought the sky.

No stars.

So fierce a pang. It pierced her, pinned her like an angler's worm. She had imagined them so long in her captivity, ablaze in heaven. All her work undone: a harvest still ungathered, that a winter's hail would lodge. But it was cloud above as it was clagged below, mirk dark and mizzling. There would be no otherworld in gaze.

Nevermore.

She stood unmoving on the doorstone of the slurried yard: a cold mist on her brow and eyelids, cheek and chin. Her lamp—unlighted yet—already sweated with the fog; her clothes grey-silvered, hoary. All in Cloud.

And so broad a sky, laid bare by autumn, leafless, even to the skirts of heaven. And a moondark night. She could have seen—

But now at her threshold were not stars but shadows: scythesmen lurking at the edge of sight. Dog stars. Of Corbet's pack. No running.

If she fell not Ashes—ah, then would Corbet's naked will possess her utterly. Blood knowing: she had tasted in his kiss her endless death. His craw would be her universe; the earthing of her grave, her sky. His fell of dark. She would wake to his wolf pelt on her, to the bloodreek of his body, clagged with ravening, acrawl with warlock souls. His vermin. His fleshworm—cold sick loathing in her throat. And colder still, a dread: that he would know in her my lady's part, that crystalline of soul. Would rend her own for what it carried, like a toad its jewel. Annihilate. Leave not a shard of self.

Her hands were at her mouth, to bite—A brightness in the air. She tasted light. Inscape of ennead. Orange in her nails. *The Nine.* The world recurved, refolding round her: the chambers of its cloven heart rejoining, cleave on cleave within its tracery of septs; the ravellings of peel rewinding, scarless but the stem. Pith and bittersweet and curving. She cradled it.

The chasm at the threshold closed: a crack. Time's great rift in her a heartbeat.

She drew a breath of cold clean air, another: lifting up her heart.

*Still there,* she told herself. *Old mole. The wood's above. Thou need'st but shoulder heaven, but a heft and hope of glory.*

Even now not last of all the household, Margaret followed Grevil's servants, through the steading and the intake to the green road over Law. All silent, with their lanterns dark, and the clanging of their pattens cloofed in mud.

A whisper: "Eh, but it's rare and mucky."

"Whisht." Shocked solemnity.

A stumble and a hop.

A giggle.

"... flayed o clarting her shoon."

They were going to the Ninestones, walking back the way she came. The old way new. Slipshod in hallows as she was in May, in her outlandish finery. A maiden still, but barely. All else changed. The shape of air, the weight of darkness, and the taste and tuning of the wind. For solitude, a thrang of company. For stolen liberty, a leash. Her chance had altered: from a web spread wide as gossamer, aglint with possibilities, recrossing and recrossing, to this rope of law, this knot.

Madam's work. Accomplished hussif that she was. With Barbary's lifting of the spell on her came knowing of it: Prick-Madam and her 'pothecary arts, her witches and their malefice had turned her like a new green cheese: a curding and a whey of blood, a working and a press. 'Twas Morag's sort of spell, but ladylike: submission to their gaze and handling; a dulled and dunted acquiesce to her fate. They'd dressed her like a doll of wax. But bleeding, carnal in their lawn and laces: they'd changed her. She could not unspill.

But for this hour, she was free. The further from the house the lighter, striding.

At the crook in the green road, at the gap in the wall, she looked backward at the frame of Cloud, an earthstead stripped to cord and cratch that winter's down would pillow. *Here's still a room*, she thought. *This earth. Within a room of sky. Still closing in. But if the heavens are a painted cloth? and parted?*

Hallowstide. The nap of summer grass, outworn at knee and elbow like a beggar's velvet gown. Slick leaves that scented of decay. Damp air that felted sound. No birds. The chirring of the summer voices fallen silent, with the hushing of the wind in leaves. Here now she heard the brawling of the water in the winter becks, crawse, clapper-tongued; the creak of boughs. The year was old and raw and riotous, a malkin squatting in a ditch to piss. Rag naked in the wind and rain.

Almost her blood rejoiced in it—the trees unbraided to the wind, the nightlong riding and the rant. All undoing and to do. Ah, she'd glory in it, by herself alone. But for the cronying with witches. But for crows.

At dawn, they would gather at the hallows tree, and break their fast— *No. I cannot bear that.* Still the white head flared before her, falling. Jerked and dangled. For her chains of handfast he'd get twisted rope. And darker even than her marriage-bed, the belly of the crow.

A crossroads. She was turned about. Gone thwartwise: and her covey out of sight. No Ashes: she was not of Cloud, was never in the game. *Now. Run,* she thought; and "Oh," she cried. Half sob and half derisive laugh. *In ruined shoes. At Hallows.* She could hear Corbet's pack of bandoggs brashing in the wood. *They hunt.* She nearly cast herself down by the dyke-wall, in a crisping slough, and wailed.

But there was something coming. Quiet as the moon.

At her back, half seen, she felt a gathering of girls. They came by one and two from every windrent farm and loaning, from Lightbeck and from Littledale, from Askwith and Imberthwaite, from Owlriggs and Aikenmoor and Nine Thorn How. Like winter becks, but silent: river into river braiding, running backward to their springs. They lifted her, as water takes a ship; her sail, desponding, filled. They bore her on.

The Old Moon with her lantern, and her eldins on her back.

Looking up at Nine Law in its hackle and its hood of mist, she thought she saw a windthrawn straggled hedge where there was none—bare grass and stone—and in its fold, a tree, a thorn, unleaving in a flame of fire. All a flickering in a mist. She sleeved her eyes. None such. There was a knot of cummers crouching at a fire, occulting it, like kneestones to the standing circle. Their blaze was at sunstill—not a leaping, but a low.

As Margaret browed the hill where the women sat, they rose, turned outward to the lanternbearers with a ring of brands. One, taller than the rest, a stone-cloaked silent woman, raised her hands, palm outward, for a deeper silence; then the others spoke in turn.

"Embers til Ashes."

"Ashes til earth."

"And out o dark, kindling."

"Will ye dance among them all?"

A murmur and a nod, like wind in grass. Margaret dipped and rose.

One beckoned for the lantern in her hands; she touched it with a spill. It flowered. In the flare of light, she caught a glint of spectacles, moonwhite with misting, and a leaf-red cap. Gnarled hands. The latewitch huffed the horn and glazing of her owl eyes; she wiped them in her ragged petticoats, and perched them on her owlish nose. Snecked Margaret's latch.

*Thou see now. All's to do.*

Margaret took her light and bobbed; then turning was entranced. A sort of errant stars had fallen, like a dew of fire: all about, below, beyond her, lanterns flowered on the fells. The embers of the dying year. Its kindling. They were flakes of fire like the swirls and eddyings of leaves, adrift, uplifted on a wind of time. *So many.* Leaf on shadow lighting, leaves on leaves of souls. All wick and wandering. All those who living once had lated here, since Ashes first was earth. All time as one. A wood of girls.

*Unleaving.*

All of them had gone, would go, with Ashes into earth. And she alone would rise in flesh, returning out of dark. Alone would bear the old year's crown, the everturning of her death and life. Yet this ae night her sisters wakened to a silent music, clothing with the tune. A crowd—ah, not of bone, but spirit, all of spirit, strung with souls.

They bid her to the dance.

And still a space the lantern-bearer stood and turned: as if she waited out a figure in a dance. Kept measure. Then it played for her.

It took her elsewhere: to the nonce-wood. In among the stones. Dark, clear within: a rain just fallen, glittering on bare twigs. In and out, and ever in she travelled, willing in a maze of fire, a labyrinth of thorn. Astray. And ever just beyond, she saw another lantern, of a colder fire, making worlds. At every step, the candle called a web, a withying of light about it; and at every further step, 'twas *here*: the light unweaving and rewoven, flawlessly, and not a spark of water spilt. A whirlwind of tranquillity: the world unmoved by moving, as a tree before the haloed moon. *Where I am, is hallows.*

And there came to her an image of the heavens as a burr of light. No outwall and no adamant infixed with stars: no sphere. The crystalline not shattered but dissolved in air. Aethereal. The stars like bright and hanging water swirled about her head. They giddied her.

*So I can do. Still heaven.*

And turning in her stride, she called the creel of stars about her: that wickerwork of light she knew, her cradle that had rocked her sleep. Her ship of dreams. She saw the old bright interlace of patterns. *I am candle and it curves to me.* A lilting in her step; then slower. *Where I stand is why. And if*—Stone still.

She dared not; yet she took a step beyond: and in an ecstasy of fear, she saw the pattern of the moveless stars unwreathe, resolve in strange new shapes. A Bear, a Serpent. There, a Hive of Bees. And still more stars, beyond the stars she knew: a swarm, a storm of them, as many as the snow. But still. It was her mind that travelled. The warp is set; the shuttle flies. How far?

*Can I get there by candlelight?*

Her candle crouched and spired. *Not yet.* Ah, but a little further, but another step to see—

Cold out.

Left darkling on a hillside, downward from the dance. Mazed and mired. All unstrung, the cadence of the silent music fading with the twire of smoke. The dancers fading like a frost, the earth indrawing them. Unriming. Somewhere was a hurlyburly and the whirl of fire. And in the windrent sky were stars. Gazing up, she saw the Fiddler standing, naked in his rags of cloud.


Sand-heavy, stunned and breathless, Whin lay trampled in the roaring dark. A wave clapped hard on her, stonecold and shattering. Not water, though it drowned. Cold fire, quick adamant, edged air. She drowned in Annis, in her endless night, in shards of sky. A wave. Another, clout and harrow. She was dragged to seaward; should crawl. To what ground? Beyond this *now* lay only chaos and a querning sea. Time's millstones, grinding bones for bread. No sun, no moon, no rune of stars. Nowhere.

She scrabbled in the drift for ground.

A colder shadow fell on her, a thrill of malice and a reek of blood.

Harestill beneath a hawk. No flight: and then a wave downtrod her, heavy as a lion's paw.

A clawed hand caught her shoulder, turned her upward to no sky; bent back her naked throat. A hag with a flintstruck knife crouched over her.

No voice.

Whin fended, her bloody hand outward.

This blood above all blood: the hawkwife scented it. She roused, unmantling her wings, outspread her stifling dark. A glint of stone-white body, flintstruck like her knife—she was her knife, all fell intent. A gape of triumph. But a flicker; then she furled. Was a blackclad, barelegged crone, her coats and apron kilted to the hip.

Curtly, she jerked Whin's head backward, thrust a flask between her lips. Half-drowned again, with fire. A drench like molten copper slugged her belly, seared her throat; it scoured like a chimneysweeper's brush. Whin twisted, choked, and spat. A bitter taste, corpse-money in her mouth. Yet it revived her. Burning wire in her sinews, barbs and needles in her blood; but she could stagger to her feet. Must follow.

"By my lady, thou art bid," said Morag.


Had the stars called out to her? A voice, a crowd of them cried out around her, hallowing her name. The hills re-echoed with it, in a whorl of fire.

Ashes that was Margaret looked up. Not eastward where the Nine were rising, like a chalk of silver; nor the west, where Ashes now had set. Gone downward under Law. All round her head, she saw the Guisers at full gallop, in and out of cloud. They'd torn the sky in tatters with their onset: stars and myth and guisers, myth and stars, all whirling in on her.

On earth.

A throng with torches. Waifs of fire scattered upward from the brands: unfurling, fled. A hurlyburly and tohubohu of voices, cry on cry, like a clamoring of winter geese: *Ashes! We's Ashes!* Fire and gabbleratchet, a clangor of wood on iron, the belling of ramshorns, and a drum.

They ringed her like a running wheel.

Men?

No: women by their voices. But in men's coats inward out. Slouched hats
and draggled petticoats. An owl mask, beaked and feathered; tattercoats; a
hood of hareskins, black and white; a pannier worn snailwise; a company of
besoms, all a-bristle at the cobwebbed moon, to sweep the rafters of the sky;
the moon herself, with a great white dish of pewter at her breast, her thornbush at her back; a vixen's brush worn jouncing at a fork; and in among them
all, a greatboned striding woman in a crackpot helm, her grizzled hair unbound and flying out behind her: a skillet for a buckler and a naked sword.

The clangor of the ladles ceased.

All, all of them, the laters and the kindlers and the striding crones: all
louted low to her, with hand and knee, like men. Like ploughboys, all unpracticed in that grace. The great virago, kneeling, turned her hilts to her. And the
stiffest, gravest of them, in the moon's guise, cauled with cloud, made a stiff
leg and a stick, and said, "Hallows with ye, Ashes. And well-met."

Hands to mouth.

"Yer candle's out," said Owl beside her. Barbary. "Cold coming i't frost."
She raised her torch at the Lyke Road.

"A lang way by yer lane," another said.

"Coat's where yer left it," said a fourth.

There was an eddy in the thrang: some swirled toward Grevil's, sunwise;
some north and east, to Corbet's hall. Some, wavering, stood.

"Y'll mind ye," said a fifth, uncertainly. "At home."

And strangely, she did know: she could feel it like a chink left open to a
winter gale, a wind eye in the dark. "Not far," she said.

She led them on. Uphill.

They followed her in silence, but in measure; one behind her played a
reedy little tune on her pipe, over and again: a haunting little hirpling tune, a
jaunty melancholy music, like a bird on a briar. They walked to that wistful
measure, and the *ting* of silver struck. And at the skirts of the rabble, with
a slow whorl and a clack of antlers: for their husbands' horns were in their
keeping.

There were fires leaping up all round them on the hills.

"Here," said Margaret, among the stones. "I live here."

A deeper silence, of unease. The piping bird had flown.

The coat was in the Owlstone, curled up like a coalfox in its den. On the
sleeping flank of it, there lay an owlegg in a garland of haws, like a halo round
the scrawled and clouded moon. Its dream.

Ah, but the scent of it: like a live thing. Wild. Not as a beast is wild, unreasoned ravening; but mindful in its passions: only folk use fire, make patterns of a spattering of stars. She snuffed at it. Of blood and honey like a bear; of earth and ashes like an empty grave, new-opened in the frost. Of time. Kneeling, she touched it, brushed it with a timid finger. It was warm as if a soul had slept in it, but lately risen; and it burned with cold: like frost on fire, snow on swiddened moorland. Smouldering with power.

It would eat her. It was earth.

And being graved in it, she would conceive the sky.

Fearful, desirous, she took it in her arms; she made to put it on: enlarge herself.

"Not yet, lass," said Owl Barbary. "Yer must be waked."

Behind her was a swift low argument: now what?

"Here's nowther maid nor wife," said one. "It's all gan othergates."

"Nor mortal neither, if her bed is Law."

"And when did Ashes take husband or master? As her cradle is otherwhere, I'll stand Ashwife," said Owl Barbary. "But we'll need a hearth."

"Low Imberthwaite's gainest," said Moon.

"Hawtreys," said Owl. "They's a lass will have lated. They'll have an Ash-ale spread."

"Good ale, Deb Hawtrey brews," said Hareskin. "If she's a cup to drink it in."

"That's us," said Vixen, pushing up her mask. "But I'd best run tell our mam y'r coming, or she'll think I's Ashes. And she'd kindle cats." And she took to her heels.

"Doesn't she want more clouts to wash?" called someone after. But the girl was halfway down the far side of the hill.

Margaret looked for her latewitch in the thrang, but they bore her on, jostling. As she was pulled away, she turned, looked backward at the Nine, the stones, until the green road sank between two walls, and they were shouldered out of sight.

They came through a bewilderment of pea-sticks to a cottage, tousled and a-blink, as if they'd waked it.

All at once shy and solemn, the guisers swept the doorstone for her, in slow circles. *Soul! A soul!*

The door was opened by a flustered woman, bobbing, with her apron full of toys. A nearly white smock: but no maid. Roundbellied as a foxglove bud, that children pop. Thin-stemmed. Her wispy fairish hair astray, like owl's down from a ravelled nest. Like withywind. She tried to tuck it in her smutchy cap, but had a saucepan in that hand. Full of old shoes and a mousetrap. "Just tidying a bit. Come in if yer can." Then quailing before the Owl's regard: "That's to say, *Well-met-Ashes-may-you-hallow-all-within.* I's flayed we's all at six and seven here." And over her shoulder, she said, "Here's Ashes to eat yer. Mek yer curtsies."

Behind her, round-eyed, open-mouthed, there was a tussy-mussy of children, as many as daisies, with their faces all upturned. They clutched fistfuls of apron and bobbed; or rather, squatted, bare-arsed boy and all.

"That's not Ashes, it's a lady," said one.

"Husht," said her mother.

"I bring Ashes," said Owl Barbary; and over her shoulder, "Thou, Alys Coteler, and Goslin Crackernut, thou. Stand Ashwives with me. All on yer else, stay without."

The gravest of them, Owl and Moon and Hareskin, came within. They took Margaret's lantern and the Ashes coat, with reverence; then her sooty jacket and her hood, and led her by the fire.

"Ale in plenty. Malbeit new," said Dame Hawtrey, wending through the swags of laundry. "Tib! Thou serve our guests." In the one room, sat the Vixen with her beaver up, nimbling her pick of cakes before the company's descent. Her apron full. "Mam?"

"Here's ashes enough for allt world and their daughters," said Owl, and set the lantern on the hob. A sluff of white ashes, spilling out from the hearth. She knelt by the fire to take Margaret's ruined slippers. "It's a fire o juniper," said Dame Hawtrey. "That's luck. And eldins o Ninewood." She hung out Margaret's stockings on the kettle hook; they dripped on the pudding bag. "And our Sukey Bet? Is she likely?"

"Willing," said Owl Barbary.

Margaret stood shivering in her fine clothes, boned and broidered. Moon and Hareskin eyed her askance, like cats at a crab. *There's fish in that.*

Hareskin stuck her boots, well-tallowed, in the coals. The cat, offended, stalked away. "Eh well. There's bride-cake for't geese i't morning."

Moon drank. "All but t'gander. He'd hatchet for his breakfast. Supped apples and onions."

"Shame," said Hareskin regretfully. "Six pies they were to have, and pluck to't poor. Waste of a haunch o beef. Forby all them raisins i't cake."

A clash of kitchenry. Moon was hunting. "They could have it for Ash-ale."

"Mester Corbet'll be in a tantarum. Thwarted of his dainty."

"He may rant himsel stamping through floor into cellar, but his goblin'll go bare to bed. Here's nutmeg. Does she keep a fork?"

"Not that clout. Cat's pissed on it."

Owl stood unpinning Margaret's limp kerchief, with the pins stuck neatly in her own sleeve, one by one.

There was a scrabbling at the shutters, voices in the eaves. Boys squabbling at a spyhole, like swallows going in a barn. *What d'ye see? Can tha see her?* And triumphantly: *I see'd her arse.* Their catcalls overcrowed by furies: then a clash and a tumbling, thump and crash, as of a ladder fallen down; and on its heels, a lashing and a thwacking. Wounded yelps. A rout.

"Lads," said Moon with complacent scorn. "But we's besoms."

"Eh," said Hareskin. "Mind that Tom o Cloud that were spying at us? Year that Will's Beck were Ashes—Poor lass. Green i't earth."

"Wed at Kindling and buried at Hallows," said Moon darkly. Replete.

"Yer mind him? T'awd luning in a flaycraw's jacket?"

Sleeves.

"Poor fellow," said Owl Barbary. "Mad."

"And they'd a fiddler and all. We'd've had a rare dance."

"Now he's sent for, he can play for t'hanging," said Moon. "Thrift."

Stomacher.

"Thou's til thy bed," said Dame Hawtrey to her tadpole boy. "Or Ashes and her mam will eat thee! In a pie! Wi' *mustard!*" And in a high cracked caw, half gentry and half ogress: "Another slice, my lady? Aye." She crouched and caught him, rolling and squealing, and tickled his belly. "And then we'll *pick* on t'bones, *pick* on t'bones ..." She bore him off behind a flagged curtain.

Now her gown: shaken out with care. Now swift unlacing, aglets flying: Owl unhusked her of her bodice.

"Poor Beck were another such. Russety," said Hareskin. "Head and fork. We's not had a raddle Ashes since."

"Tib's Tabby," said the Moon.

Petticoat.

"Now then," said Owl to Margaret, "Y'll remember what's to do. Same as ever were. Coat's what you are."

Another Margaret, elsewhere and otherwise, had read those words of Ashes: in a drowned book, in a tower, under Law. "Cross all, keep nought ..."

Owl unpinned her hair, unbraided it, the bone pins bristling in her mouth.

"Good. And?"

"Eh, but that's bonny hair," said Dame Hawtrey, coming ben. She smoothed it. "Light through leaves."

"... but silence," Margaret said.

"Aye. Hawd tongue," said Moon. "Thou's mute, but if yer tell a death."

Owl said, "Yer may have what yer will, but not ask it."

"Man or maid, or owt anywise," said Hareskin eagerly.

"Or nowt," said Owl Barbary.

A clattering kept small, as Dame Hawtrey moved from shelf to table, fire to flake. At work.

And Moon breathed barley in her ear: "They's to come at yer bidding, will or nill. But if yer ride a gallop on another's hobby, think on: 'twill fall out afterward."

Owl Barbary said, "So be it. And if any take his will of yer, unwilled—"

"If he as much as meddles wi' yer shadow—"

"If he nobbut pisses upwind of yer—"

"Then by Law, will my lady blast and wither him, her ravens take his soul untold."

"—he's craws' meat."

*I know*, thought Margaret, shaken. *They do clothe me as my lady's Ashes, but I am the thing itself, her creature that did guise as Margaret. Her runaway. There is a cleft in me to hell; and through me, she could burn this world to ash.*

"From Hallows until Kindling, ye may walk by night and take," said Owl. "Whatever's in yer keeping then, is forfeit."

"They unravelled all my knitting that I'd done," said Hareskin.

"Will or no," said Moon.

Owl Barbary: "Yer vixen's yer own."

"But if ye kindle in Ashes, that bairn's blood is Cloud's."

Then they lifted up her smock; they took with it her name, her tongue. Soul naked.

All was changed. Candle; bread; air; bowl of eggs: all commonplace transfigured, numinous: as if her heavens were dissolving in it, light in light. The woman with a jug of milk seemed holy, pouring stillness into stillness from an endless spring of grace. As if the milk were Ashes, Ashes were the cup. As if her soul-in-body brimmed with soul, and still and still the light was filling her, indwelling, and would not be spilled.

The Ashes child was bare as February. Bending like a snowdrop, Ashes' flower, with the burden of the winter. Piercing it. The soul is earthclad that the green may pierce. She is the coming out of darkness: light from the tallow, snowdrops from the earth, Ashes from the winter hillside; and from Law, the child returned.

She is Ashes and holy.

Now the Ashwives knelt to her and murmured "Lady" and "My lady Ashes." Owl, arising, sained her, touching eyes, mouth, heart with rain. "Be of earth. For all of us." She happed the naked soul in Ashes' coat.

Still silently, the newborn wept. Not grief: but only that she felt so light, so strange and light.

"Lift up yer heart," said Owl. And drinking to her, "Hallows on ye." Others knelt in turn and made small offerings: a caudle of milk in a mazer, swirled out a little on the hearthstone first; a something stilled, sweet fire in an eggshell that she was to break; a riddlecake, a little charred, with honey, shared in nine.

"Lie there," said Owl Barbary, folding up the smock. "Moon blanch thee."

With ashes on her fingertip, Owl marked the girl's face: brow and eyelids, cheek and chin. Salt runnels on her cheeks. Then with a handful of grey ash and cinders, flinders of burnt stick, she rubbed her: throat and body, hands and feet. Her hair shone firestreaked through soot.

Moon threw salt on the fire, so it sparkled. Quick now.

Three at once they bent, rebraiding up her hair with runes of iron, charms of silver and of lead. Witchknots. Ashes' sign. A wheel of running hares. Over and again, the moon. She jangled as she turned. They slipped the soulcoat from her shoulders, only to her waist; they clad her in a harden shirt. White-brown as fallow fields in winter; coarser than an old sack on a threshing-floor, but soft with years. Grey skin breeches next. And last, they hung the soulbag at her throat; she bowed her head beneath the cord.

Undone.

She reeled a little where she stood, in snuff. The awe had dwindled into bone-deep weariness. Could not be held. She tasted ashes on her lips; she felt the strange forked hampering of the breeches, skin between her legs. What on earth she most desired, she could not ask in words. Her starglass most of all.

Her book. Her precious pack of cards. All nameless. All forfeit if she took.

"Is't done?" said a small voice from the bed.

"And all to do."

"Will there be oranges?"

"Thy lapful. But thou husht. Here's Ashes."

Awed children, peering round the grimy hangings of the bed.

Oranges. Again, she saw the tawny ring, aglow on Corbet's hand. Again, the crow lad, like an eggshell, crushed. To die without a soul; to hang—But now as Ashes she could take his ring. And not to keep: to give. Could claim his living body. Aye, and silver and a horse. So would he were away.

She would; and could not lift her tongue to speak. As if a stone were in her mouth. Imploringly, she turned from face to face.

"Coat knaws what y'd ask," said Owl.

Delving in the sooty pockets of the coat, she found a great bunch of iron keys in one; a something squared and sliding in the other, wrapped in a cloth. *O my cards.* But altered in her hand: larger, and of lighter paper, rough. Steeped in smoke. Undoing them she saw another set of cards, in woodcut. Jack Daw's pack.

They were for a man's palm: she would need both hands. She cut them clumsily: The Tower. *Ah*, the Ashwives said; and stirred and murmured. Prickling with chagrin and wonderment, at far end of her wits, she thought: *That card was burnt.*


A jangling in the heavens. Mally's in her winter house, whose rafters are the wood above, whose walls are night. You can't get in but she lets you; but Brock's anywhere. In at all doors and through crannies. She's keys to all locks. She lopes in, coatless, and she hunkers by the fire.

In Cloud, a cold wind blows. The feathers of her mattress fall.

Capless, in her crazy petticoats, old Mally stirs the pot. "Is't sure?'

"Aye, braided in her hair." A chink and clatter as Brock turns. "If she's kindled of a stone, she'll carry."

"Good then," says Mally, ladling out for Brock. "Her glass is full."

Taking of the cup, the other drinks. "And if she cast it not? What rough beast then?"

"Carry, I did say; not quicken." Mally drinks of her crooked cup. "Nowt's what my sister is, and nowt will Ashes keep."

"Can thou hold her so? Unquickening?"

"Twa changes o't moon. No more. That long did Thea travail by my sister's malison, afore she lightened o yon bairn. And moon for moon, I's match her. Hallows til Lightfast."

"And if young Marget meet her under Law, and fail?"

"Then nowt s'll eat her up, in outward."

"If Marget win?"

Stars, clouds of stars are canted in her spectacles; then fire, flaring as she turns. "Then we's undone. I't world she's great with, we is nowt." And taking up her broom, she says, "Here's all to do."

Brock thrusts her hand into the fire, and lifts it up; it dances on her palm. "I's off then." At the sill of *now* and *here*, she turns.

> *Nonce would his fancy get,*
> *But Nancy she nill;*
> *Tib shall have Tom o Cloud,*
> *And Ashes have her will.*

The island was bare. Whin, captive, twisted round to look. No castle, as the stories told of Law; no blade of grass, no tree; but a fell of burnt moorland, scald as a fireship, and crowned with stones. All round it raged a wolfblack sea, a wind that ravened on the shore. Above it stood unlifting sky. No sun nor moon, nor slant of light, but mirk and shadowless. No stars. Or rather that they walked among them, or the lykes of stars, in the Unrising.

They moved in silence for a time, still bent against the wind. "Here," said Morag.

They halted at a standing stone. It seemed a rough-carved image of a naked witch, squat-bellied, spindle-shanked, and girning, crouching with her legs agape. Whin saw it was a thrall, enduring, blind as dark. It kenned them and it hated. "Bawbee Mag," said Morag, calling it by name. She took her iron keys and chose one, with a muttered spell; she turned it in the witch's lock.

Earth opened like a grave. Bonecold it was, astounding breath and blood.

*The child?* Again Whin saw the blotch of birds that tore and quarrelled at the dying girl; she saw the bloodwet child upheld. Kit's lass. His daughter, that she'd sworn to find, and bring her, even from the depths of Law.

"Down here," said Morag and Whin followed, down and down a spiral stair, and in and out the turnings of a labyrinth. *They's left me a thread, and I walk and I wind.* She tried their tally on her knucklebones; could make no sense. A thread would tangle on itself, a trail of stones would scatter like a cloud of chaff. They were under Law.

Witstarved, falling in a daze of dream, Whin stumbled on.

She was roused by a reeling stench, a rustling mewling watchfulness. A squalid rancor. They were halted at a cave, howked out of glistening rock. The hag thrust in her torch between the iron bars. "Bred to the stone," said Morag. "They were of thy kind." A cageful of fledgling ravens, blind as worms, and writhing naked in the litter. Wenches to the fork, but winged and taloned. Ravenous beneath. Their mews was strewn with tirings of manflesh, raw bloody bones. Whin stood by the bars: not close. A raven stirred and mantled, gaping at both maws. She was naked, quilling out; she spread the wings that were her hands once, webbed. She was ringed through her privities, that gaped. Her will, her mortal tongue, her soul were gone. Her eyes still knew her fall. And hated.

A monstrous regiment, a blood-dark Pleiades. And of her kind.

A fury waked in her, not whirling but a whetstone. *I see,* thought Whin; and brushed her finger through a smoky torch: that bound her oath. *I will.*

And now they spiralled up and upward; but they came not into light. Bare passages, where hung a few flagged tapestries, all blear with dust. *Her* webs. And nothing else, but here and there, great chests broke open, spilling wrack. Salt-ruined webs of velvet, bletted books. A virginals. Gnawed candles. Cups and oranges, all blue with rot. A sword. And there, the whirligig she'd cried for, that she'd broken, long years since. The knife she'd lost, that cut his cord. Her Ashes brat's. The stubble on her cold neck rose and pricked. That blade had severed her from kind. For what? For nothing but her will. She knew not even if the boy had lived an hour past her leaving him, birth-bloody, on the starven ground. She'd vowed to cut his throat with it, she'd sworn it to the gods: give back to Law what law decreed—his blood. But she had not. Starved earth to suckle him but once: and so she thirsted. She went on.

And in the arras on the wall there stirred a dawnless wind. *What's there?* A glint of mirror. Shadows in the smoke. Were they wafts of her memory? Woven of her dreams? *There,* in the shadow, in the crouch and quaver of the torches—guisers? Faintly as the stars they played, slow-tumbling in an autumn mist, they glimmered in her eyes and faded. Look there, a knot of swords? A cage? And turning, she saw nothing there, a slashed web stirring in a draught. But there, the torches caught a splatch of weld, as ragged as a weed. White hair, as white as chimneysweepers gone to dust. The Sun.

He turned to her from shadow.

All in black. Unmasked. And smiling like a rennie fox.

"Mistress Ashes."

Tumult, as the roaring girls swept onward. "Ashes' will!" they cried. They tanged their ladles on their pans, and blew their mournful threning horns. At every crossroads, and from every stile and stead and scattered cote, almost from every bush, they gathered up guised women as a river in a spate takes sticks. Ashes that was Margaret, dazing in the whelm and uproar of them, stumbled on through the endless night, haled on and hallowed.

"... will. Her will!"

Down and down they thundered, madded like sheep: sploshing hugely over moorland and moss, over leapstones and across a swift loud beck, down a green lane, down a sunken trod, walled and higher walled, the narrower the swifter: down a street. "Who is't?" cried voices. "Clapcraws that's to hang." Their pattens clanged on stone; their voices rang, re-echoing from walls. "Will hang." They spilled into a broader place, pent in. Lapping and cross-lapping, fanning out, like swift water in shallows. Dark: but for their lanterning.

Three suns were dancing in the market square. Down leapfire, up light-fast, and round again the year to come, outleaping both; and like a candle flaring in its fall, as new and new again uprose.

Still jostled onward, Ashes saw the guiser juggling cages of fire, the flames upleaping as their cages fell, the brighter for their downfall. A smith, by her leathern cap. She caught and quenched them, one two three: all but an ember that she pouched. A hail of coppers and a blare of horns. She turned to face the rout. "Here's a clatter," said the smith. "Lang Meg and her daughters, come down frae't hills." A woman by her voice: but breeched, like Ashes. Jangling as she glanced. But coatless: in a patched and singed and sooty jerkin, of as many greys as storm in February. Grey as any brock.

A guiser called out, "I see yer a sleightful wench."

"And if I is."

"We's after a smith. Are ye learned of that mystery?"

"Black and white."

"A master?"

"Aye, and mistress of journeymen."

"Can yer break locks and bars?" said the striding woman with a sword. "There's a bird we'd spring."

"Oh, I's keys til all locks." She beckoned Ashes to her side. "Come, lass. Thou show me where he's laid."

Uncharted here below. Ashes looked all round for the dark tower. None: a dark space, an off-square, set askew; a few bleared candles in the eaves of low houses. All abed? No. Watchful. At the far end where it narrowed ran a river with a stone bridge.

*There.*

By the bridge-end. A round cell in the marketplace, with a cap like a candle-snuffer. Like her lantern: but dark. Absurdly small and like its card, as if she saw it through her glass held backward: but not for laughter, no. Dank-walled and windowless: she knew that dark. That blindness of despair.

From a coign behind it on the packbridge, Corbet and his henchmen rose with swords. All else was nothing.

He was unmasked, half in guising: in a long robe of black sheepskins, with his vizard at his shoulder like a white crow, his familiar moon. Its hair like smoke and ashes. No scythe this meeting, but a naked sword.

He bowed: as if they partnered in a dance.

"Mistress Ashes."

His rout was coming from the trances of the town. At her back she felt the swirl and counterswirl of guisers, men and women at odds.

"Come, a dance at hallowfast," he bade her. Gall and honey in his voice. "Will you have *Cross my river to Babylon?*"

Ashes felt a pull at his bidding: as if his will like a raptor's talons tugged her soulstrings from her heart. But the juggler's sooty palm was on her shoulder. "Bide," said Ashes' champion; and faced him. "Off to thy mummery?"

"At midnight: not without some certain dainties that this rabble would filch. And thou, smutch-bellows? Art thou her champion?"

"I's come for't wedding. Heared there's a fiddler and all."

"Mine? Is put off, they say."

"Thy son and his mother's cockpiece, his daughter and her son. How many's that?"

"I play not at riddles." Hand on hilts.

The guiser stood. "Twa then: Ashes and her will."

"What, that crowsmeat? His bride-bed is a rope."

"Criss-cross, and rope's a bed."

"And a fell for a featherbed on him."

"Sleeps light. 'Twill cast it off as cloud."

"Crows at his cradling."

"And will swing his rattlebag, and flight them. Flaycraw's his trade."

"Yet will hang, for his reckoning. His teind's to pay."

"That ring was not thy gift but his. Witchmaster."

"So the vixen laws it for the lamb." The moonface at his shoulder smiled on Ashes, blind, unchanging in its pyre of hair. "The brat's for the gallows, and that greensick girl is mine."

"Not for thy needfire: Ashes of herself."

"Will this rout of hobnails have a Lunish stranger for their idol?"

"Ashes lights on who she will."

"What need? They could bear about a lolling puppet; and yet drink themselves sottish in her name."

"They's ears."

A dark low muttering behind her; a clenching in the crowd. And still she stood.

His hand grew tighter on his sword; and yet he darted in his glance. His voice rose, reedy as a rackett. "Shall I not have law?"

"Aye. And Law have thee."

"I'll not change words with a juggler."

He turned, disdainful, to the rabble, calling out in his shawm's voice: "Will you loose this dunghill rat to spoil your corn? Breed ratlings of your wives and daughters?" Silence. "Will you teach my covenanted wife to play the whore? To prank at midnight in a tinker's breeks?" Thunderous silence. "I will have whipped who hinders or defies me. She is mine to chastise for her impudence; he is mine to hang: I will take what is mine own."

A woman in the crowd called out, "Which d'ye want, Maister? Lass or arse?"

A storm of jeers and catcalls.

"Breeches is hers by right: Ashes rides rantipole."

"Go singe yer petticoats wi' leaping fires: y'll not leap her."

"First to bed's first wed, awd Craw, and Horn take hindmost."

Still the witch gang held the bridge: a dozen men, well-armed. Uneasy in their arrogance. All drawn. No weapons in the crowd but clods and sickles.

"Fire straw," said Corbet's man, aside to him; but Ashes heard. He thrust his torch at a vent in the prison.

Corbet stayed him with a hand. "My lady cracks no charred bones."

He turned back to Ashes. "If thou comest not now by law, still later thou wilt come; and serve me, will or nill." She stared back in mute fury. "Not a word? Thy tongue will learn its usage, soon enough. And if this night breed maggots in thee, still thou wilt serve. In stews or in kennel: tainted meat I give my pack."

There were horses waiting in the shadows; they mounted, and away.


"My lady's huntsman," said Morag.

"I do hawk for her," he said. "But here's a black wench that I know, though she deny me." He bowed ironically to Whin. "I knapped thy maidenhead. Thou spawned a brat."

"Any mort's same as t'other i't dark," said Whin. "So be it that she's cleft. If she'd a prick yer might remember her."

"I mind thee perfectly. Thy glass a little breathed with country handling; but uncracked."

"There's a marvel, an yer mended it."

"Thou wert Ashes, and bade me."

"There's many been."

"In Crawcrag, a reeky sort of goat-shagged slough."

"They's souls."

"Their Fool had a blue eye and a brown. And thou didst take me for thy will. Thy Sun. White hair, like chimneysweepers—ah, I see thou mind'st. *What's a' clock*, thou saidst, and whift mine ear." He laughed. "Ah, thou gaped for it. Thy milk sprang to my fiddle."

"Y'd have met himself ont road," said Whin. "I doubt men blab."

"They do. Thy cries are commonplace as ballads, and thy knacks on every swagman's tongue; but I did cheap thee first of all. How thou didst game it! Ride-a-cock rantipole, a-gallop, being green. And touse it and mouse it, and tumble and mumble it. *Come in, says cunny to the fox.*" Her voice, in mockery. "And thought it was thy choosing."

He turned to Morag. "What would my lady with this haggard?"

"Happen a lock," said Morag.

"No more than she's used to: stand and take," he said. "But idle work. Thy ravens want a ninth. Let her be seeled and gentled."

"That's as my lady bids," said Morag.

"Has she sport?"

"Aye, when her chit's returned—young Mistress Manseed—then we'll hunt her father's soul, and feast her, and my chucks will have his stones."

"Cold meat," said the huntsman, with a glance with at Whin. "Her crop wants sweeter junketing." Mock tenderly, he coyed her cheek. "There's word aloft that thy fondling's to the gallows. There's a pretty dish of eyes."

He caught Whin's hand before it struck, and bent it backward, so she dropped her knife. "I do not mar," he said. "Carve me or curse me, I am what I am."

"Thou's no man, but a guiser: a thing that walks in men's bodies."

"Worms must feed," said the huntsman. "And nakedness be clothed. I do but change my coat of skin to please me, like burd Ashes. Has my lady Runagate not eaten thee?"

"Aye. And so my bairn did in my belly, inward out. And I's here." Whin sleeved her face, wearily. "Thou'd have got no child on me. Being ghostly."

"Thy brat is father to himself, his mother's cockpiece. Of thy flesh."

"His flesh is promised," Morag said. "It is the ravens' fee."

"Thy regiment was ever coarse." He turned to Whin. But I am curious of meat. Not eyes, but what they've seen, asleep or waking, are my delicates. Yon kite in petticoats but spits 'em out. Crack bones and craunch marrow."

The old crow preened her apron. "Come, girl. My lady waits."


Whooping triumphantly, the rabble stormed the gaol. "Down t'wall!" But with turning round the smith swept clear a crescent in the uproar, as a besom sweeps a hearth.

Even with the keys, the door stuck, swollen; then exhaled a reeling stench. Death cold and close at once: the river's breath updrawn through years of drunken spew and piss, the loose unshovelled muck of terror. From within came a cracked despairing wail. "No. Cock's not crawed. Not yet." And a frenzied clink and rattling of chains, as if shackled he had tried to fight. "Be still thou," said the smith. "And comfort thee. Thou's not for hanging yet." She haled the crow lad out, half-carried him; she stood him on his staggered legs, stripped off his fetid rags and flung them in the river.

Wretched past shame, he moved not to hide himself, no more than would a hunted hare. A poor thing, like an ill-made rush-dip. Naked as a worm.

The guisers howled.

Dazed and shuddering with larger air, he looked about: saw Ashes seeing him. Awe and horror on his stricken face, and now and only now he hid it in his arms.

"Thy death's not yet to tell," said Brock. "Thou's got a hand yet in thy tale."

And turning to the girl, "Here's Ashes' part. Thou keeps t'gate both ways: lap dead and hap living at their hour o birth. Thy mystery is souls."

Ashes looked in stony silence at the boy. What did she know of him, his soul? His fingers prying her, all slick with snot; the lateworm shining in his cave of hands.

"Soul's naked," said the smith. "Thou swathe it."

Ashes looked up and upward at her impery of stars: at the Hanged Man swung above the fell. Tom o Cloud, they called him, Jack Orion: names like any naked man. What swaddling could he give Will Ashes? Not his coat of sparks. The heavens' cloth of gold too fine for such tagrag.

All round the blur of avid faces: not a rag for charity.

And downward? Wet stones underfoot dissolved in lantern light, in glare and gilding, rucked and trampled leaves of gold; in puddled fire; dubs and runnels of the elements. A muddle like mankind. Like figures of a casting half-effaced. She could not read, but saw: a scrawl of glory on a slough.

She flung that mantle over him; spoke silently. *Be thou of mud and fire, Ashes' Will.* And sained him, eyes, mouth, heart, with earth.

As if a spell on him were broken and he waked, the boy shook back his claggy hair. Himself: but all his swagger broken. When he tried to speak, his voice was faded to a raling whisper, a rattle of dead leaves, as if the rope to come had strangled it. "Leapfire's what I is. Slipgallows."

"Thy family is great," said Brock.

The crowd was stirring from their trance. "But here's hunting of wrens," she said. "Out o't whinnymoor intil hollybush, and out o't prickle-holly intil haws."

Two great-armed women, streaked with dyes to the shoulder, seized on him, and ducked him in the sheeptrough, through a lacewing of ice. A great splosh and a gasp as he rose flailing; and then a dousing and a sousing, as if they two were drubbing sheets. They fished him up and wrenched him out, and toused him in a sack to dry: if not as white as milk then sallow as a withy wand, but mottled as the dyers' hands with bruise on bruise.

One gave a mouthful of spirits to revive him.

Another two or three shook out a bundle of fine clothes, now sadly be-draggled: Annot's petticoats that Ashes had doffed. They dressed him up in women's weeds and turned him round in the square, admiring.

He bore it sullenly.

"Here's a pretty ingling for a gentlemen's knee."

"Nay, a maid, so her mammy swears. Ne'er did it but standing."

"Afore if not behind."

"And here's an Outlune gentleman, come up from underhill, to wed thee with a ring." A dozen more pushed Ashes forward. "Walk in, Master Mag-pie."

"Wi' a ring in his neb."

"Aye, steals for his mistress. He's t'Queen o Elfin's bailiff."

"Black as any raven."

"As a chimneysweeper's snot."

"Aye, but cods full o gold."

A new uproar at the outmost edge. Raucous cheers. "Here comes awd Bird i't Bush. Way for Hodge Hedge!" A fubsy little man in his nightcap came panting up from the inn, with two frowzy-headed potboys to elbow him through. They were bearing jugs of huffcap and a noggin of burnt wine. "This'll kittle up yer courage." Her groomsmen held it to Ashes' lips; they made her drink, and drank.

"Here's to thy dawcock."

At which the remnants of her glory slid, awash in mustiness, and overgun-nelled, sank.

The bride tossed back an endless gulp of the ale, with as much bravado as her dress allowed: a mistake perhaps.

A blustering bagpipe and a scrawny fiddle tuned, played snatches off key: *The Magpie's Bagpipe, Aprons All Untied.*

"What's for their supper, then?"

"Old ling and oysters."

"Collops and eggs."

"And where s'll they be lodged?"

"At t'sign o't Moon, in Mall's featherbed," said Brock. "In hallows." And she set the wren's crown as a garland on the crow lad's head, and led them on. The wedding followed: Ashes in her coat the man; the crow lad, crowned with haws, the bride. A stalking, stealing tune began, a maze of turnings in a mist of air. Behind them, there came men and women dancing, longways now, by two and two. Sad mirth and solemn mischief now: all riot combed and carded by the winding music to a skein. They danced with great renown, to small pipes and the soultap of a heartpaced goatskin drum, the plaining of a crowd of bone. It played *Nine Weaving*, the beginning of the world.

"My lady," said her servant.

Scarce Whin could look on her: so black she dazzled, even as the sun inverse. Lightblinded, she must see her still, her image stamped, restamped in burning silver deep within each eye. Her gaze engendered self on self. Outfaced by deity, Whin stood; but flinched her eyes.

And slowly then the god occulted, clouding with a moonwhite face: a woman's. She was old beyond imagining. And silver-new: the moon's last bow re-virgining its birth. As old as the moon is: *Thirteen at hallows,* as the riddle said. Uncounted aeons. *And not bled.* Yet there were lyke roads in her nightlong hair, unjourneyed streaks and sleavings of faint silver, wreaths of light. Unbound in mourning: widowed of herself, self-slain. Unchilded. She was all in velvet rags of night. Her virgin's body, slender as a thorn, was icebound, moveless in a cold despair. Self-broken in her self-raised storm. And wreathed about her rimewhite neck and heaped and braided in her hair, like shatterings of hail, were soulstones, vivider than any Whin had told. She felt the sting and fury of their sentience. But my lady was beyond her reach: no godwitch but a guising, an eidolon. And that wraith itself unstaid. Her semblance flowed from her like mist from ice, subliming in a silver fume, renewed. And still and endlessly renewed, from her abyss.

But at her wrist, Whin saw the braid like living fire. That alone was true: it burned her and it chained.

My lady roused from her brooding; bent her gaze on the captive. She acknowledged.

"Ashes."

"What I is."

"Thou ow'st me blood."

Whin held up her ringless hand, palm outward. "Cannot be held."

"No?" My lady raised her white hand, clotted with its rings, its gouts of soulstones. Beckoning to Morag, she took a cup of bone of her, blacksilver at the lip. "My daughter hath betrayed me; thou art Ashes in her room."

She held out her shallow cup to Whin. "Come, girl, by my knee. A pledge."

Whin shook her head. "Cry you mercy."

"Ah, thou art wise in tales. *Take nothing in the lykeworld: neither flesh nor wine.* But thy gossips have misled thee. Here thou art eaten. Thy heart like a pomegranate, slowly, seed by seed." She tipped the bowl so that Whin saw an eyeblink of the draft. Blue milk. "Thy dam—" She raised it to her lip, and drank. "Thy dam, I think, scarce suckled thee. But cast thee naked to the sea as waif. A witch of the Unleaving—"

"Lish as an otter, aye, and fierce to bite," said the huntsman. "Fish below the fork."

"But served." Again my lady held the cup to Whin. "Now wouldst drink rebirth?"

Whin took the cup, old bone and brown as winter earth; she poured a little in her palm, swirled blood and milk and ashes. "To yer bonny hind," she said, and spilled it on the earth as offering.

"And to the hunt," my lady said; and turning to her servants, "Search her."

The huntsman caught Whin's arms and held her fast, with hands her blood remembered. *Gloves,* she told herself. "Turn and turn," he said. "This time I bid thee. And I ride." Morag set to work with her knife. She slashed Whin's jacket from her back, her shirt and breeches all to ribands; stripped her of her will and all. Turned out the Ashes bag disdainfully. No rings. A barren purse.

"Stop at flesh," said my lady. "For now."

"I'll but redd her for the glass." But Morag's comb undid, it ravelled will and memory and soul. Her nails cracked psyche as she would a flea. *A knot,* the witch's voice said, wasped within her ear. *Will I undo it?*

Blood and milk. Her son lay naked on her breast, newborn, like bruised fruit trodden in the grass. White bloom on him, like sloes. Soft down. Her windfall.

*Will I shear that?*

"No." A low cry, torn from her.

"Time enough for that," said my lady.

"Will I set her to the glass?" said Morag.

"Anon," said my lady. Beckoning, she bid Whin stand before her, naked in her rags. "Here's folly. Thou hast braved the wolfish sea, breached Law. Walked naked to thy weird. Didst thou think to put thyself into a song?"

"I's not so green as that," said Whin. "Tale's eaten me, as is."

"What then? Prig stars to pounce the oversky? Befool me with a bairn of wax? Mine eyes are not yet glass." Her voice darkened. "Or cam'st thou for my daughter's braid?" Stark now, of metal heavier than gold, than lead: bluefaced in her coil of cloud. All slag and cinders but her chain of fire. "To string a fiddle for her bawd thy cockpiece?"

"No."

"What then?"

Whin's tongue was heavy as a stone. Her mind a millstone cracked. Sea-drubbed and clapperclawed, amazed, she swayed a little as she stood. There was no earth, no sky, no otherwise, no in and out, no elsewhere—only Annis, castled in her mind. Herself in self involving, wick in winding sheet. Riddle in rune. And nought in all this wrack of others' memory her own. But silence: and her six wits scuttling like rats in a ruin.

*What's within but mirk and mist?* Long ago, Whin lay on fishnets in a wicker basket, while the guisers stalked and roared. *But I's a sun frae Mally's kist.*

"I could tell a death."


The guiser in grey went before them with the wren's crown on a pole, pale ribbons floating out. When Ashes looked behind, the dance was shadows in a slow hey, endlessly enweaving to a faded music. Longways for as many as will; or that would be or that ever were. *Faint Starres and numberless.* And then had gone.

They were elsewhere, in a wood now, all unleaved but oak. A windthrawn straggled wood, aslant a hillside. On Law. Cloudrooted, it was kindred to the standing stones, but older far: had branched and drifted over them a thousand thousand times. Indwelt.

And wood within that wood, of gold, another wood unleaving. Still and still they drifted, leaf on shadow lighting, leaves on leaves: an endless fall of gold that silent spoke in leaves of prophecy; was fleeting still. *O Hallows.* By the Owlstone, drifted deep in leaves, there sat two sisters, close as moon and dark of moon, that wove one garland on their knees, of light.

*O,* said Ashes silently. No tongue, no breath. All eyes.

Nowhere. And yet—

*A soul. A soul,* called the guiser, knocking with her staff. *For it's cold by th' door.*

*Lift latch,* said the latewitch crossly. *I's get me hands full.*

The leaves whirled up around them; fell. And there was no one but the witch within. No light, no leaves, no hallows. Nothing but an out-at-elbow shabby wood. Setting by a clumsy wreath, the latewitch rose and bustled. Fierce and raggish in her tattered petticoats and leaf-red cap, her hair like a ravelled owl's nest: sticks, mutes, feathers, broken shells, and all.

*Shut door; thou's letting wind out.*

*Leap fire, last fire, fire we sing,* the guiser chanted.

*If it's guising, I's nowt brewed for yer. Nobbut small.* A shrewd glance at the crow lad in his silver mantle, walking in his sleep. *Sun's far astray. Should be wound on t'Spindle, all a maze.*

*Clipsed,* said the guiser, leaning her staff in a notional corner. Then sliding back into ritual, she chanted, *Owl's down and Fiddler born. Year's in Ashes. Will I kindle Thorn?*

*Kindling's wet,* said the latewitch. *Thou could try.*

The guiser crouched and scuffled in the leaftrash, uncovering the ashes of a fire, cold out. She took a handful of black sticks and ashes, and she blew on them. A ravelling of smoke; a little twiring flame, a-dance within her hands. A hearthfire. She set it down and cosseted with sticks until it crackled. Rustling about, she found a crackpot, tipsy on its one leg, canted over. It was full of white rot and spiders.

*Wassail,* said the witch.

*Cold hail,* said the guiser, shaking out the pot. *Cold hail and sneck posset. Thou's ever been a clashy hussif. Crowdling wi' thee's like ingling an urchin.*

*There's owlnuts and arains all up on t'shelf. If thou wants any more thou can sing it thysel.*

*Gi's thy cap, awd lass, and I'll scour pot.*

Still Ashes gazed and grieved.

*All amort?* The witch picked up the dwindled wreath; it dangled idly on her finger. *Lang making. Every year and all, for nowt.* She cast the O of branches on the fire. Even as Ashes cried out in silent grief, it blazed up in green leaves and fleeting flowers, brief as snow; then was russeted and rich with fruit; then firestruck, its every tendril cast in gold, consuming. It was ashes of snow.

*But why . . . ?*

*What thou is, braided i' thy blood. It were twined for thee.*

*And the . . . other. Where . . . ?*

*My sister daughter? Ashes. Wind.*

She looked shrewdly at the girl's face through her owl-glazed eyes. Not avid and abhorring, like my lady's eyes; nor yet disdainful, gloating like her crow's: not kind but true. *Thou braids of her, thy mother. She were Ashes, eld of all.*

All grief entwisted in that poignant grief: that leafblade, firenew, to pierce her heart. *You knew her? Saw her face?*

*Thou knaws her inmost of all. She tellt thee.*

Lost forever now: that ghostly voice, heart-heard.

*Tellt her own death and thy souling in one skein, thy swaddling her shroud; as thou will tell my end.*

A long moment of dismay. *Mistress, I would not.*

*And will. And will know why.* The witch bent for the Ashes garland on the hearthstone. Wreathed in snow: she tabored it. *Thy will is in thy glass.* Bare sticks and withered leaves. She held it up: as if it were a glass between them, each mirror to the other's face. *Not O but arrow. Journey's what thou is. Unhallowing.* Silently, she bade and Ashes bent to her. She set the wilted garland on her brow: sharp thorns, too sharp to wear. She touched her smutchy face. Salt ashes. *Colder, by and by.*

*Here's spring.* A knarl of water in a puzzling of ice. The witch cracked it with her heel, and crouched and filled her gnarly hands. *Thou's dry,* she said. *Will weep thy fill.* And Ashes took the witch's hands within her hands, and drank of them. She tasted hallows and her death. A bitter twang. And then the Cloud ale pierced her from within, it cracked her, as a white thread cracks a hazelnut, unfolding green. *Dost like of it?* She nodded, mute. *Tales,* said the witch. *They go on.*

The trees had bent and gathered now as rafters; were infilling with her kitchenry of stars. *Broom,* she said, and took the guiser's staff. She stooped and gathered up her apron full of leaves, a wicker basket on her hip.

*Back door,* she called; unsnecked the air. She beckoned Ashes and the sleeping Sun. He moved as in a waking dream. A step and they were elsewhere, walking out on skyfell, on a black moor rimed with stars. There was a tumbled sheepfold out back of beyond. The witch tipped out her basket in a blizzard of down, that filled the sheepfold to the corners of the eaves; she shook her apron out, and it was filled with tatters of a coat of leaves. She lifted, lofting out a patchwork of the years of earth to make their bed. Then she took the wren's pole and upended it, unweaving as it overturned: a besom when it touched the earth. She swept slow hallows round the fold.

*Come, lad. Thou sleep.* She took the moonclad Sun by the shoulders, shook him out, as if he were a featherbed of ragged light laid softly on the earth. *Leap fire. Light wood.*

And to Ashes, weeping in her crown, she gave a small thing, as round as a hazelnut, shining as a moon: she held it in her palm. *Keep hallows til thou wake. Thou's all to do.*

And turning at the not-a-door, through which light spilled, she nodded. *I's bid yer goodnight.*


They were bedded, as the crow lad saw it, in an empty house: swept bare, but long since given over to the ministry of spiders and the mapwork of officious damp. As cold as any barn. He knew it though: Imp Jinny's that were dead. Her bare loom and the ghosts of apples. Faint comfort in that. The soulers feared her as a witch. *Ashesfast,* they called her, and they sained themselves: *wore coat turned inward out.* They'd left their swagger at the threshold. Changed their key: the bagpipes shrivelled like a trodden toad; the fiddle shrunken to a quivering of catgut and a windlestraw. The boldfaced drum gone slack. Clipped mirth and cold bawdry now: a whispering haste. They touched as little as they could of Jin's. The bedstead, that was stripped to cord and cratch, heaped up with musty straw and heather and a faded patchwork. A fire in the cold hearth laid, a swift blaze that would die. It cast a creel of shadows on the walls. A cage to close them in like wrens.

Touched Ashes not at all. Kissed him but gingerly. No heart for ribaldry, to toy and kittle with the bride.

*Get Ashes brat,* the boldest of the guisers called; and snecked the door behind.

To bed, but not to bed with her. He cannot; and she nill.

She sat in the fell coat and breeches on the bed, chin resting on her knees drawn up and brooded in her arms: a knot too hard to ravel out. Fierce as an eyas leashed, forbidding as a standing stone. Far elsewhere.

All in the long loud nightmare of their coming hither, she'd paced aside of him, grim and glowering with chastity. For all their raillery, she would not clip him. And they'd dared not shove and grapple her, sained Ashes. In her coat and all. There was elfshot in the air about her, lightning in her collied face, banked fire even in her jangling braids, and hail in her regard.

Colder now; and still more terrible. As black as starcoal, burning cold as

Law. A black thought in a blacker shade. The very shadow of her coat annulled.

*She is Ashes and holy.*

Still shivering with awe and dread, he shrank from her, as if the coat would burn him. He'd been burnt. Could smell the blood on it, as if it were a shepherd's coat at lambing. But the blood was his. They gave the Ashes child to her; they slit and spilled him in her furrows. *Run.* But he couldn't run, naked in this tawdry. They had ringed the house like cats a mousehole; they would take and hang him, shriller in their mockery for his hampered flight. This bed was all his hallows in the wide world. Crows' meat or Ashes' will his choice. Cold sanctuary.

*. . . is Ashes and . . .*

He bent, flailed down by memory. The lash on endless lash of lives.

*Get it into her.* Snail tracks on her body, snotted in her sootblack hair. Stripped naked she is Ashes still: black fleece and bloodclot at her fork. Agape like a nest of crows. Eight hold her down: but still she twists and curses in the filthy straw. *Craws eat thee, cock and eyes.* The bone mask smiling, touchless as the moon; but naked all below. Flayed ganderneck. Crinked hair and tallow and the wrinkled cods. *Thy knees, boy. On thy knees.* He holds the felly of the cartwheel, sick and shaken, in the reeling stench. A scalded strangled red, a glutted red, like something gibbetted: and standing like a forearm and a fist. *Witch. Burn thee.* On his knees in dead wet leaves. A bloodthread at his knife's edge: not to spill, to silence her. He fears her and it mads him. Sets him on. Cold Ashes to his hand: a small tuft, like a leveret's scut; a snail's horn, glistening. He pries. Is withered in her blast. *My lady eat thee.* And again the mask. *Thy knees.*

Ah, he'd swallowed dragonseed. It thrawed in him, and twisted, scale and talon serpentined within his gut. He could not spew it up. So it had spawned. Bred dragons on him. Of his soul. They writhed within him so he could not sleep.

Crow-haunted, all his dark. Asleep or waking.

He had dreams.

A great house like his master's, dark. A silver glass. He looked in it, and saw a mask like his mistress's, that smiled. *Bone of my bone,* it said. *How cam'st thou by my face?*

And waked with shouting,

*Cheat them. Kill thysel.* And even in despair, he laughed. *What, hang?* They'd cut him down to ride. Whatever death he took a mockery to them. A use. If he knew a bane, a poison though? Could taint his carrion. Envenoming.

Crow-haunted in the dark. And still he sat brooding, his garland awry and crumpled petticoats, dandling a straw.

About the dead hour of the night, he heard no latch nor footfall, but a small still jangling; and there came and stood a shadow at their bedfeet.

That greyclad guiser, she that turned the keys. Ashes still.

Lost. No will to fight. He half raised his face, gone stark with weariness and grief endured. A mask like his mistress's, past tears.

Fellcoat and her braided runes: the death of him.

"And how does thou like thy bedmaking?"

At Brock's bidding he must turn and look behind. And there lay Margaret, sleeping in the Ashes coat, as in a den of bears, with her hand curled childishly beside her ghostgrey cheek. Not eaten yet. Still Marget. Marget that had madded him and Marget that he'd teased. Marget he was fond on. There he stood a breath, bewildered: as if a door had opened on a house grown great and strange. A breath, then: Marget that he'd pried and smutched. *My lady eat thee.* And for that shame she'd saved him from the gallows tree. Had see'd him naked as a worm. His soul and all.

A small harsh voice. "... she nill."

"And why should she?" said Brock.

Far and far away he heard the cock crow. Twice, thrice, whitegold, it speared and awned, like barley from the black of earth. He wept.

After a time, still racked and shuddering, he tried to tell her. Hopeless to unravel all. He tried. "Jin's dead. She were kind to me."

"She were greater than that," said Brock; and touched his snotted cheek. Not death but wakening. "Thou knaws what they call this house."

Puzzled. "Fold Hall."

"Same as i't sky," said Brock. "And on that Road." White awe. He felt the cold hair hackling on his nape and all his misery a frost of fear. "Kept house for travellers. Tellt Ashes all her days." And looking at the stark loom where the tales were strung. "See, all yer kind is weftways, hither and yon; but she lived crossways to this world: set warp for t'Nine to weave. Their journeywoman."

She rose and lifted, tucked the sleeping girl beneath the patchwork. "Here's one o Jin's patterns, is Marget. An she'd clicket thee, she'd cheat thy lady Corbet and her lady, that is greater far. And so round again: another Ashes til t'earth. But she nill. And there's an end on't."

Turning from the bed, she made up the fire; found, set on a pot. "Thou sleep."

Still smaller, his voice. "I'd not. I's dreams."

Turning back, she plucked the garland from his brow, and threw it in the fire. In the blaze of it, he lifted up. "Thou lookst like a gimmer ghost in yon nightrail," she said. Stooping, riffling through her pack, she tossed the lad a shirt and breeches: "Get thee doffed."

Then she went and tended to her pot while he strove with the broidered billows, half drowned in petticoats; over her shoulder, she handed him her knife to cut the laces with. Appareled as a man, he brisked himself a bit. Sat up and sleeved his face.

She brought a cup to the bedstock.

"A soul," said Brock, and gave him to drink: a caudle of ale and eggs and barley bread, a-swirl with spices. Strong. It quelled the dragon in his belly. Heartened him. The guiser perched at ease beside him on the bed. They drank together, turn and turn about. She'd meat for him as well: hare pasty with a whet of rowan. Ewe-cheese. Oatcake. He was ravenous, he found.

"So thou's been Noll's ingle."

The boy shrugged.

"Of thy will?"

Cast linen but clean. Fine broken meats. A respite from hard labor and short straw. A coin. A clip. The kindling of his better's needfire; the outplay of his frenzy and remorse. The mastery.

"Ne'er laid stick to me. I liked gadding him." He turned the cup, considering. Half smiled. "But he's mazed like. Maggots in his wits. Talked hobhouchin out o books at me. Did stars dance at Leapfire? Was there elfins at Calderstanes?"

Brock drank. "And thy witchmaster? Mistress Scaldcraw?"

No more in the cup. "I thowt she ... that he'd ... art to gi' me, power and place; but he ta'en." Looking at the stained and shadowed wall. Bare rafters. "Noll's nobbut fond on boys. He's sackless. But wi' my lady ... with him it were ..."

"Will it bruise? Cry out? " She pricked the air with her knife. Quick first, then caressingly. "At this? Will it weep for me?"

A flinch. A shudder. Then an upward nod. That cold sheer smiling enmity: that will to break. So not to weep again, he raged. "And that lickarse Noll, he selled him Marget. He'd ..." There he stopped, with thinking on his rusty knife. The tuft. No better than his puppetmaster. He wried himself, rocking. All unmanned.

"That's all cat's play with him, to dress his meat the daintier. Likes a pretty morsel." And with a sideglance at the boy. "Or green, at any rate. Not ower nice in his following. But thy body's godbait for a greater catch. There's a witchery she has he wants. And so thou had." He stilled; looked back at her. "Thy ring."

Like being lifted up, pierced through. *Thy ring.* And gone. Hope and desolation in his voice. "Yer believe me it were mine?"

"Still is," said Brock. "It's what thou is. Thy soul." She touched his half-bright hair. "And forfeit."

Rousing up at that. "But he—"

"Thieved it. Aye. And others like. He's a lawing to pay for that; but not to thee." And then she smiled, small and sharp as the new moon. "So thou see'd her, Kit's lass. Thea. And she sained thee with a ring. Thou's blessed."

*I's a star thou's not spied.*

Bright shadows in his face now: he remembered and was lifted up. "All i' tatters i' my corn," he said. "And clarted to't knee. Hair like fires that our May lads leap, a-whirl i't wind. Asked would I serve her, and I said, *Owt I can.* And she fasted wi' me, clap and done. And then—" He touched a finger of his grimy hand. "Off her finger, like any queen o Lune, and tossed it i't air to me." Up and upward with his face, as if he saw the spark of it still falling. Not caught: so not yet lost. "I kept that. Ring and word." Aglow.

And overshadowed. "She were Ashes, thou knaws." Brock touched the sleeping child. "And all these other, shadows of her."

Door on door of rooms, beyond the world he knew. "What come of her?"

"She had a daughter," said the god. "And died."

The ember of it fading. "Gone."

"Thy ring? In my keeping. I' my bag."

"How?"

"Thou gi'ed me for thy telling."

Soulstruck, he remembered all: the white road and the dazzle of his deaths; the black earth of her coat, her queynt, his grave.

"Thy will's thine own in me," she said. "To give or take it at thy will; and mine to keep." She took his face between her hands, annealing him: his sharded soul uncrazed. She sained him, named him Sun in Ashes; slipped the

mantle of his stripling body, mud and fire, from his soul. "Now thou can lay
me down and love me. An thou will." He willed it; and she kissed his mouth.


Too bright for leaping. Yet he jumped, his white head flaring in the risen sun.
And there, and there he hung, still dazzling. A-dance on light.

# Ashes

"A death?" said my lady. "One? What game in that, amid so many?"

As she turned the soulstones mocked and glinted in her hair. The hall had vanished. She was nowhere, everywhere: the dark Whin stood upon, the air, the strand, the fury of the sea. She was the reef, the wrack, the harpagon; the dark of moon, her tides; an iron crow struck deep within the rock, the rock itself, imprisoning a crowd of stars. The woundless element, its flaw. And in the coil and midnight of her presence raged a storm, a stinging hail of souls. Dashed ice and driven sleet: but knowing. Sheltering her face, Whin saw the witch uprising in the whirlwind like a spindle to the wheel of night, like a wick of shadow and a whorl of flame. Stark white: a stance of lightning. In the cup of her white hand, the witch outheld a little heap of silvery darkness, hail and sand.

"Choose then. Which?"

No voice. My lady's air was talons at her throat, it clawed her blood and breath. But: "This." Whin made a whiteness, a whorl of cloud round a grain of sand. "Of many, one."


The girl with the red hair woke in Ashes on a cold bright morning, nowhere that she knew. She lay a moment gazing at a dazzle-edged door; until the clink of braided runes recalled her. She was Ashes and alone; and in the witch's narrow bed. Shivering, she sat and pulled the frowsty covers round her shoulders. Cold not with fear nor exaltation, but a still content. A centering. She had known the impery of stars; would know the sword's dominion and the heart's: but this bare solitude ensouled her, selving.

Cold and bare. She rose and looked about her, padding here and there in her worsted stockings, moving in a cloud of breath. All hers alone: a

house. Two rooms, but and ben; a loft by a twisted stair. Adazzle. Dim. The
tumbled bed, a cannikin beneath for use. A stripped loom by a shuttered
window. A besom leaning by the wall. The clothes that had been stitched
for Annot's wedding, scattered on the floor. She gathered them, rejoicing,
bundled them away.

Now for morning. She undid the three-light window by the loom. It
looked out on a garth and orchard, leafless now, but in limned in winter-
silvery light. Where she had sat and listened to a tale of witches: inward out.
Light pooled within her hold and patched it, rippling on the walls. And by
that light, above the panelled bed, a timeworn carving showed: the winged
face of a woman with a pair of shears, but what she sheared was gone. There
were ash pegs driven in the crucks, worn smooth; and cross and cross between
them still a tale of yarn: nine turns of nine. In her trance of understanding
she could read: *sleep safely here, dream well. Wake new.* They sained her; they were
left for her: she let them be.

But how high the sun was. It was very late: near noon, she thought. By
now, she was fiercely hungry; chattering with cold. *Then do,* she told herself.
*Thou goslin. What, eat light? Not stark thyself with cold, at least. Now shift.* She went to
make the fire up.

There was a drawing in charred timber on the hearthstone: a few swift
strokes, a smudging thumb. The Hare. Alive. Ashes studied it: the glint of
quartz the gazing of its wary eye, the swell of stone its flank. The stars in
their just places. Ah, he knew his sky—what other roof had he?—and drew
it well. As on that stone that lay now in the grass without: its perfect daub
of Witches washed away, their tale remembered. As he'd heard it—*O thou
mouldwarp*—from another Ashes, at her weaving. On this very loom. *Tellt me
stars.* She'd read him inward out. His truth lay not in what he told her, but
his tales.

*And the Hare?*

*Atween thy legs. Thou fond.*

*I've seen it rise.*

*And I,* he'd said, but silently. He'd known her vanished stars; had let her
know he'd known: a sort of peace. A pang. For she would ask him for a tale
of Jin's. Could never now. *I would he were away,* she'd thought: and he was gone.
Off with the greyclad guiser, like as not: fierce company, but one who had
the art and wit to keep him from the vengeful pack; if not at ease, alive. *He's
for Brock's bag, caught kicking.*

They'd left tokens though. His garland hanging by a nail from the chimney-breast. On the hearth, a kit full of water and a threadbare cloth; on the sill of the fire-window, a bowl of milk, a napkin full of oatcake and salt butter, and a withered apple, sound and sweet. Nothing in the chimney cupboard, but another carving on the door: an owl.

It would all taste of Ashes.

Could she wash herself? She thought what Barbary would say. *Coat's what thou is. Same as earth is earth.* They'd not leave water and a towel, if not. She hung the Ashes coat beside the ash pegs, with respect. Attire for her calling: not for workadays.

Then she set to work and scrubbed herself by the fire—cold water and no soap—until the towel was black, and her hands and feet were streaked with fainter grey on mottled red and blue. What her face was like she dared not think. No comb.

Then she ate, and felt revived.

Just now she cared nothing for the pother and the choke of ashes, their ill tang in her mouth; the frazzling of her hair; the bite and bruise of fangy metal that she'd slept on, printed in her cheek and scalp; nor yet the curiously fishy bedding. One of Barbary's needle songs was running through her head: *"... thou's a fool without and I's a maid within."*

Taking up the broom, she swept away a confusion of muddy footprints, trampled, overtrampled, to the sill and out the door; and stood admiring her cold clean view.

But not for long: she stood a-shiver in her shirtsleeves now. Rebarring the door, she took the fine furred jacket up, to put it on. All that needlework in vain. She hesitated; shrugged. It could scarce be grimier. But it was strangely heavy, as she now remembered it had been. Pinching, she felt the pebbling in it: well-stitched so not to shift and chink. With the sharp little knife from the Ashes gear, she stood by the unglazed window to unpick the seams. And there was gold in the jacket, like an old tale, sliding out and chiming on her hand: five coins of gold, struck with the Unleaving Ship. She'd no idea what they were worth: a horse? a house? a loaf of bread? *A life,* she thought, for a dazzled blink, envisioning herself, her books; and then, remembering her trade: *A death to tell? But whose?* Cold awe and curiosity.

Bewildered, deeper in, her fingers met a hard-soft packet, and another, nearly slender as the coins. Her breath stopped. Most carefully she drew them out; she broke the seal of one, unwrapped stiff paper and fine lambswool

from her lens. And then the other: hinder and skyward. Within the sheet was
writing, in a hand she knew:

> *Thou needst must travel Light; so I may send thee only (dear as Eyes) what thou*
> *wouldst have. Take of my regard so much as may not burden thee.*
> *The men that bear thee to thy Ship are trew Friends of thy life and Honour.*
> *Go with a fair Wind. Hallows ever on thy Soule.*
> *Think not on my Frailty; but remember mee thy Fellowe clerk.*
>
> *Bartolemy Grevil*

Puzzlement and fierce possesion.

*O my glass.*

*Thy ship?*

*But this is for Margaret, elsewhere. I should give it her.*

And round again: *my glass.* But not her cards, her book. Why not? Were
they still secret, slid behind the wainscot? Seized by Madam and her witches?
Found and burnt as so much trash? Not forfeit, as her glass would be if
Ashes kept it back.

*Why gold though? And what ship? Oh!* And there she stood, agape. *Oh, I see.* The
bandoggs in the wood were Grevil's men. They'd meant to spirit her away.
And in her new rough guise, she nearly stamped. Was she a child that they'd
not told her? Did they think she'd blab? But her old and wary self thought,
but *how* could they have told her? Madam and her crows had kept so fierce a
watch on her that none could speak; though Barbary had stitched and hinted.
*Feign; or they will bind thee.* And, *Thy word is, By th'moon.* Barbary would have lit her
candle, whispering counsel, at the stones. There would have been an uproar
round another Ashes, and a swift encircling of Grevil's men, with swords. A
fine plot, but for chance.

No chance: not in Cloud. The latewitch and the guiser saw to that. Alas
for Grevil's stratagem. They two had made cat's cradles of his tangled web: a
pinch, a pluck, and all was overturned. Spell and counterspell. How much of
all that long strange roaring night had been their work? The crossroads in the
dark? The whelming tide of girls? Her stubborn candle-wick? Oh yes and yes.
The tower and the keys. The bed.

Would no one let her be? She was forever someone else's means: was this
one's dish and that one's candlestick, a sheath for that other one's knife. His
copyist, *his* hobbyhorse, her sealed commodity, his toy, her empty glass: the

engine of their stratagems, device of their desires. A nought to multiply themselves. A hole to fill. Fear and fury mingled with a pang of envy and of loss: for that other self who was Margaret, having taken ship for Lune. She stood unhindered at the bows, with the wind behind her, and the stars about her, wheeling round her mast of tree. Away.

And then she laughed: for all this country dance had given her no sideslip, but her will. That other girl would find a new captivity in Lune: a prison with a vault of stars. Still tethered, though she slipped away. In heart she would have journeyed with her. But in soul now she was Ashes, colder: who could scatter things of childhood to the wind. Unleaving she would journey farthest.

*I would have gone,* she thought. *But I have work to do.*

And looking at the black hare on the hearth, she felt a prickling down her spine. *That card was burnt. That's two.*


As custom was, Barbary brought up an ashing-caudle to congratulate the new-made Ashes' dame.

Master Grevil had ridden out to speak with his conspirators, now thwarted of their charge. To Tiphan of the Nine; to little Etterby the woodwo; Calder that was Slae. A cold returning they would have of it by sea, and all to do again.

But here was work enough within. She tapped at the bower-door where lay the matrons and their maids; was bidden in.

"Ashes is waked."

"And Annot sleeps." The younger Selby took a cup. "This looks not like a nuptial."

Mistress Graves in her nightcap, dizzy with scandal, drank. "*Grief in the kitchen, mirth in the hall,* they say. Or is it t'other way round? Here's all topsy-turvy."

"How does Madam Covener?" said Barbary, up-nodding at the stairs.

"Splenetic," said the Selby.

"I say, let them rage," said Mistress Graves. "Unwedded Ashes." Leaning eagerly. "Didst thou see her will?"

"Named Ashes," said the Selby. "Yet her coat lay not on Annot's bed." She set the cup down. "Thou mad'st her, my girl. Where lay the coat?"

"On Nine Law," said Barbary, "whence she came." She went up to Madam's room.

She'd heard the cry at midnight, coming back: a great despairing shriek. A silence. Aye, she'd lief as not go in. As soon go harrying in Morag's nest of crows. *Best see what they's about,* she thought, and did not knock.

"Ashes is waked. Rejoice yer."

Green as any glass, her face, sea-green as celadon. Flawless in its fury. Bloody hands, though, as if she'd been riving. When she spoke, her voice was mad in measure, like a player queen's.

"See what thou hast done."

"Madam?"

"Thou hast broke my great vessel and the cordial spilt."

"'Tis pity, Madam. Yer mun start again."

A long silence. Then: "So I must," said Madam. "At her kindling." She took the proffered cup and drank. "To Ashes' waking."

"To her wake," said Barbary. She saw the change in Madam's face, could not unriddle it. Exultant dread? *Here's all her stratagems in shards, and—'Tis like she's brock a looking-glass and saved her face.* "'Tis a shame about t'wedding, Madam."

"I am told that Master Corbet did himself repudiate her. Wert thou not of that distempered rabble?"

"Nay, but wi' a graver sort o gossips, matrons and spinsters, at her making."

"A sort of smutched aprons. These country Joans did ill-befit her station. I myself will name her at her kindling, take her coat and crown. Unmake her."

"By yer leave, Madam, 'tis their ladyships, yon sisters, that unmake and make. We nobbut stand gossips in their room."

Contempt and wonderment. "Thou withered impudence. Thou virgin."

"Aye," said Barbary. "Yer crows'd not have me so. I's dry." She gathered up her tray. "I'd lay this Ashes' will's for quiet. Given as she come frae Babylon a maid."

"Her vixen's not been hunted. When it's up, 'twill start."

The servant bobbed. *There's witchery to come, I misdoubt. Still can spin, can Madam Attercap. And bite.* "There's delicates will spoil if they's not etten. I's send our lasses up wi' fleshmeat, cakes and wine." At the door she turned. "And linen. Those hands'll want binding."

A soft knock at Ashes' door: "My lady?" Putting letter, lenses, gold and all in her pocket, she opened on a patched man: almost a boy, she thought at first.

All dusky, with his moledark hair. But then with Ashes' eyes she saw how his lightsome body had been knotted with long work. Still boyish in the turn and carriage of his head, his smile; but hunched of shoulder, weather-worn. Untimely wizened. He doffed and made a leg to her, with hand on heart. "Hallows on yer house." Then he offered what he held: a holly bob. "Beg yer leave, but my dame thowt I s'd first foot yer, being sooty-pated and all. *Black's luck,* they say." And in his other hand he showed a hunch of barley bread, a farthing, and a pinch of salt in paper. "Inasmuch as I can. Siller's hard come by."

Ashes made to speak; recalled herself, and bade him in with a bow.

He gazed about. "Eh, but it's cawd and bare wi'out Jinny. Knit us mittens as a lad. Like poke-bags they were. Fair nettlesome. My mam said she span yarn out o teasels." His turn to recall himself. "Hob Hawtrey's who I is. Balthasar, that is, for me father's sake. But Hurchin's what I is i't guising, so they call me Hob. Y'd knaw our Suke?" *She has a father?* Ashes nodded. "Happen y've not see'd me at t'maister's, as I works outwith; but my Deb she Ashed ye, and thowt 'twere a pity y'd got none o't Ash-ale. Being rushed about like."

She could do nothing but nod and bow, like a poppyhead. How d'ye do and how d'ye do.

He grinned. "They cry awd Jin a witch; and thou another: but yer about as flaysome as our Suke."

How d'ye do again.

No board: so he unladed his budget on the windowsill. Ale in a leather bottle. Ember tart. Lopsided little pies. No soap. A comb. A bundle of rush dips. "Deb were Ashes when we—well, anyways, she said lying i't dark thinking were t'worst on it." He stuck his hedger's gloves and billhook in his belt. "Now yer fettled. Browt firing earlier, but y'd not waked, so I stacked it. Mistress Barbary, she'd have me ears for abricocks if yer fire went out. I's drawed yer water. There's a good clear well i't garth, for all it's upways here."

Another stiff bow. Her grammar limited.

"There's a basket follows up for yer, frae t'Hall. Master Grevil, he's to wait on yer, but he sends word. He says—" Hob squinched his eyes. "He says, *Thou tell her, Hallows on her will.*" Then bending close, he said softly. "There's some i' Master Corbet's purse, and some 'at bays for blood, whateverwise; but some on us thinks yer a brave wench to front him. 'Twere a shame and a spite to hang poor lad. For a tawdry. For nowt. He ..."

No more. A brisk peremptory knock: she needs must open to an eager dame. (Hareskin?) High-nosed as a sheep, but puddocky about the waist, with a shrewd and a roving eye. Awe and avidity mingled in her face. "Yer late abed, Mistress Ashes. Slept well at last, I trust." Clearly she missed nought: the empty bed, very much tumbled in; the man with the bottle; the fine bedraggled jacket. "Hard clambering up here." He took the hint and poured for her. She swirled it, eyed it, drank it off. "But then there's none to overlook yer here. Descry who's in and out."

"None if she takes none. She's a bairn," said Hob.

"Of an age," said the crone. Then turning to Ashes, "Y'll mind then, what's to do."

She dared not shake her head. Would not, for those gloating eyes.

"'Tis Hallowstide," said Hob, seeing her bewilderment. "Yer to soul at every house, be it hovel or hall, where folk has died this year, and tell them." Ashes nodded. "And in likewise yer to wake Sun at Lightfast. Or there's never spring." He was speaking now at both of them: a sort of catechism. "Ashes walks her lane, by moon or dark, and none's to harm nor hinder, but to give her what she will: for Ashes' sake. She bears light out o darkness. Ye mun let her in."

"Aye, teach your granny," said the crone. "I tellt thy dad." She eyed her cup regretfully "So get yersel clad, Mistress. I come to bid yer to a telling."


Ashes that was Whin stands silent in a strange room, in a great house. None that ever she has known; yet knows: as if she's told it into being, told herself into the story; or would tell. She's at the childbed of a girl scarce older than herself: outworn at twenty. They've left the windows open for the soul to fleet; let in a seeking wind, a sift of snow, that stirs the broidered hangings of the bed, that makes the daylit candles dip and flare. Fine candles, breathing honey at the faint cold stench within: corruption, and the overbearing musk and myrrh.

The body wears fine plaited linen, thin as silk; bone lace; black ribands, pearls that in their lustre recapitulate and mock her youth anulled: epitomes of light. And on her, white on white, there lies a finer needlework of snow. At Ashes' touch it sullies, puddles. All in vain, the keeper of the linen dragons it; she scowls at Ashes with her smutchy fingers and her claggy boots. In vain. Her finery's to spoil. That other smock they've burned: the blood was unassailable. This change the last of them. The earth will alter it.

By Ashes' side a slight girl, all in black, bends swiftly to the bed, steps back. A glance of light-through-leaf-red hair. She wakens something. Time runs.

In the cold blue hands, nailbitten like a child's, she's put a knot of Ashes buds, half green, but opening to wither. White and frail. As if the bride has gathered them that morn to bring the year within. As if she were a maiden still, not brought to bed. A lass that's been a-kindling, still a-shiver with the rising in the wintry dark, the whispering company, the carolling: the mischief of holiness. As if she's just now risen from the black earth, pierced the snow. Returned: like Ashes, putting off her coat of earth.

All seemly, all serenity, and beautifully composed: but for her bruised mouth from the gag.

But for her death.

There's been knifework here, the child howked out of her: what lies there is a husk of girl, as empty as a gutted fish.

No breath within.

And Ashes feels her own foreboding worm within her. Since she lay with the lighthaired guiser, with the Sun at Lightfast, she's not bled. Late and morning, privily, desperately, she's drenched and drenched herself; has stolen physick of her grandam, but the winter herbs—grey dust—have lost their virtue, and the knot of blood in her is fast. Will not be twined of her. She teems with it, is rounding with the child she will have left to crows and foxes; with child with loss. *Keep nowt.* She's dreamed of miscarrying; has seen the issue like an imp of fire, like an imber of blood. It danced within her eyes. Now sleepless, sick with purging, she sees slow cinders float before her eyes; she hears the old crows gloating on her fall. Ah, she would flyte with them, give mock for mock. But Ashes has her tongue. At daybreak is her vigil ended: they will strip her of her coat, her crown, her silence; will ransack her, soul and body. Scrub her vixen, scour out her secrets. Claim her bastard for the earth to drink.

But now they bid her by her calling. "Ashes."

There stands the young master, astounded with grief. Not weeping yet, the wound of her severing still white. He is all in sable, unshaven; his handkerchief woven in his gold-ringed fingers, ringbruised with wrenching, wadded at his mouth. He is sick at what he's lain with, what his stones have made of it, no longer *she*: his alchemy.

There lies what he has bred of her: a mewling manchild, squall and stink in swaddling clouts, his small face crumpled like a poppy bud, and gaping with his thwarted mouth.

There stand the bride's young Lunish kindred. All in black, the witch's fosterlings: the dead girl's sickly elder child, a boy in petticoats; her leaf-red sister pinched with grief and rage. Her hands are twisted in her apron, blacknailed with digging, bruised with ice. A green girl and betrothed, for all her whey face and her ginger hair. Her naunt would wed her to a brutish husband, bed her with her death, for pride of alchemy: breed gold. For a tower and a name and forty plough, she fain would bury her, a scant year's bride.

And by the bedfoot stands the foster-mother: she that held the knife, that paunched her daughter like a hare, alive: a widow, dowried of broad lands, a matriarch, triumphant with descent. A witch. Her eyes see through the coat to Ashes' bellyful and smile with scorn. *Thy childbed is a ditch,* they say, *thy mourners crows; thy nameless brat will dung the furrows for my lineage, their bread.* So her shrewd eyes; but before the company her face and bearing say *my lady Ashes:* just so, her deference and condescension as she holds the cup to her: "Drink ye of my daughter's life."

"And to't sun returning," says Ashes in her rusty voice, and beckons to the nurse. She lifts up the child above his vessel of the ravaged earth.

All eyes on him, the cynosure; but Ashes' glance is elsewhere. The leaf-red girl has turned to her. She beckons. *After. Come to me.*

But the telling takes Ashes, as a wind unleaves a tree. She tells an empty cradle, rocking on a sea of gold; she tells a bright leaf whirling from a hand that snatched; she tells a crowd of bone.

Only when she's wakened, risen gasping from the sky she's shattered, from the whelming dark, does Ashes look to see what token in her hand: and sees a grain of sand within a winding sheet, a shroud of light. A pearl.


"So she died," my lady said. "So all you mortals end. What tale in that?"

"A beginning," said Whin. "Will I tell ye another?"

"There is but one. I got her in my glass."

"And then?"

"There is only now."

But Whin thought, *So got herself her precious self, all fettled and unflawed: but never spilled hersel out in her. Kept her for a toy. Why's that? But for a tale o sorts. For then and then.*

Aloud, she said, "A tale's a braid. It goes on."

⌒

Ashes that was Margaret walked behind a shepherd on the Lyke Way: not of stars, but the green road over Soulingmoor to the place of bones. A bright frost in the morning as they set him on his last long way had turned to white mist as they mounted: so that they walked from stone to stone. He lay o'er the green branches of his bier, the sheaf of him, white-bearded, with his sheepcrook and his bag. His broad sons bore him up, his black dogs at heel. Behind him went a guiser with a knot of swords upraised; his old wife followed weeping in the east wind, with her sickle, stone, and cup; and before them all, his daughter's eldest daughter with the lantern of their house to late his way. Last of all before the lesser company of mourners, Ashes followed in her smutched and tangled guise, as black as holly-blotch. She was thinking on the deferent of Journeyman, and mingled with its silver coil, the arc and fall of fire in the juggler's hands: the travelling of light.

Elsewhere and otherwise, she scarcely heard the consort of headcolds, serpent and sackbut, at her back; much less the whispering of gossips.

"... bed were all a-tumble ..."

"Did he spill?"

"Aye, t'sheets was clagged wi' it." And bending to her gossip's ear. "But never a drop of her blood ..."

"... crept out o nights, I heared. All night ..."

"... rare gazing on her back ..."

A bombard blast. "... never thowt to have our nuncle tellt by a Lunish hussy ..."

"... brazen ..." A shawm.

"... be turning out *her* bag come Kindle night ..."

"For shame," said tall Barbary, striding from behind. "And yer kinsman not green i't earth." But she looked grieved at Ashes.

Unseen of all, the raven with the old man's soul flew down and downward on the sheer bright river of mourning, under Law.

At the ring of stones called the Fold, they halted at the sill. The girl with the lantern, bright-cheeked and rough-handed, hoarse with cold, spoke first: "We knaw by t'moon ..." And round the circle of the rhyme, by the sky and stars, until they knew by the ground, and thumped it thrice. A breath, and once again: "A soul. A soul. A mortal soul." And crying out in grief at last: "Lief mother, let us in." Down they set the cold corse on a stone within. Then the solemn guiser, in a gruff shy unaccustomed voice, said, "I were headed and I rise to dance." And last, the old wife turned to the waif in tattercoats outwith, and bid her in: "Ashes. Will ye tell a death?"

Behind Whin in the shadows of the great house, a whisper. *Ashes?*

Even at the threshold, on the hinge between the snow light and the shadows, Ashes turns. Still Ashes, on the edge of infamy, of Whin's disgrace. And it's the leaf-red girl who calls. Her silks, new-starlinged, shiver in the risen draft. Her face is bleak and burning all at once, with fury and despair. *My lady Ashes?*

A child. No elder than herself that was, and greener than herself newborn. The chit would show some pretty trinket that she'd feign to lose, an earring or an amulet, and ask—What is't she'd ask? A hobbyhorse to ride upon? An heir? To brim with death, as did that gutted creature on the bed? To rid herself, howk out some blind mole in her cellarage? Or is it honey with her draught of wedlock that she craves?

*Tell me a ship*, she says. *I would away.*

Ashes' tongue is loosed, true telling. Even now. *Y'd go living?*

The lass nods.

Crouching on the doorstone, Ashes fills her hands with snow. A sea is in them, and a sworl of mist. She sees a marriage bed, at anchor in a sea of blood. Lass 'd go the lighter, then. A pinnace, laden with contraband. She sees its sail conceiving, light of love; she sees the mast of tree. *Alone,* she says. *T'keel's o thy laying. Thine apron's thy sail. Wouldst round?*

*I'd bear it.*

*Infamy?*

The girl in mourning turns her silver ring. Looks inward. Fleetingly her face unshadows. *Lief would I fall, an light would spring.*

Ashes beckons to her, spreads her lap. *Gi's here.*

And the bruised hand opens on a sheath and knife.

White in white: Ashes that had framed the starglass travelled in her outbreath like a comet. Alone and away, after weary company; returning to her hearth, her hold, her solitude. Cakes in her sack. She looked out on her sky below, her landskip all to wander in; and all the wood above. She smiled. No glass: she'd sworn to that. No book. But time and silence, and the winter stars. *And if—*

And if these patterns in the sky are not immutable, not fixed like nailheads in a roof? In mind, she lay beneath a canopy of silver apples, traced in them the changeless patterns of the night. Then Ashes rose, unwreathing like the momentary whorls of leaves that dance, and break away to dance. Unconstellating. Bodiless she rose through apples, and beyond the tree into a moveless fall of leaves, of light. Unleaving. And beyond that in an endless snow of stars. They fell not, but she rose. She tumbled in the air of Ashes, in the stars that broke away to dance. She laughed. *My glass is journeying.*

A moon had rounded and had waned, another moon was new, since she had bled in Annot's place: and still her sheets were stainless as the fallen snow. A sorcery of time. As if a shivered egg had risen, rounding from its fall; as if a rarity of glass, once shattered, had renewed itself, a bubble had unburst. Herself. A secret that she held in wariness, in rising joy. A gift. She had not asked, but it was guessed and given. Ashes' privilege. Her will.

Biting off her black sheepskin mittens, she blew her nails; then in the hoarfrost on a stone, she drew the sign for *sky*: two curves that crossed. The Lyke Road and the Skein: the rune of memory and the run of time.

Mirror to the wider sky, epitome: she left it, for the Sun to take.

Now, thought Whin, *afore she's wearied o me.* She looked into the dazzle and fury of the souls. *Brave now 'd take her fancy.* And she plunged, down-diving through a shattering of adamant to black abyss, a sea-rift where the souls were caved: a den of dragons, sleepless guardians, each brooding on its hoard. Its hoard was self. They reared up at her like snakesheads, rattling their wings. They struck. Their hate was like a stench; their hurlyburly was a cataract, astounding. All about her, in her, venoming her thoughts: a seething, whispering, wailing of disbodied voices, cursing and caressing in a thousand tongues; a clamoring, despairing rant of souls.

*A tale's a braid, is't? Here's clags want combing.*

For they told no tales but riddles. Rants, plaints, wordless lamentation, grievances, mad rages, pangs of memory indrawn about a festering thorn.

*And who undid the nine witchknots? ... I've lost a sheath and knife I'll never ... Lady, will you weep for me? ... Cover her face, mine eyes ... Craws eat thee, cock and eyes ... O bonny babes, if you were mine ... some violets, but they wither'd all ... of stone, cold stone ... and never shall for you ... lest I come search for thee, dress me up grandly ... so much blood in him? ... a thing arm'd with a rake ... woe to my sister, false ... and all alone the grave I made ... How could you lay me down ... by, by lully lullay ... by the greenwood side ... and love me, now? .... two eyes of tree, of tree ... I saw the new moon late ... Come down*

*the stair . . . mine eyes dazzle . . . come down and rock him . . . with the old moon in her arm
. . . that thief and whore is at my door, let no one rise . . . Lief mother, let me in . . .*

Whin drew a long breath. *No wonder t'awd lass is mad, wi' yon chunnering worms
to chide her. Blinded by t'uproar.*

They were all of them untold: that teind of Cloudish souls who had no
friends to bid for them, no ashings. They had died alone, forsaken or too
proud to beg or bend: the witches and the whores; the hanged, drowned, slain
on battlefields; the murdered and the murdering; the mad; the Ashesfast. The
ditchborn brat, his strangling mother, dead of him in turn; the father of them
both. All, all of them—the wolf's heads and the hapless innocents—were
Annis's alike. Crowsmeat. Sleepless stones.

This endless brief while, Whin was listening, listening in the outcry for
her son—not here? O goddesses, not here. But she felt a shifting in my lady.
She would lose her and be lost. No time.

"This," she said, emerging into silence. Stunned with it. The stone she held
was like moonblood. She knew not its tongue.

My lady's blind gaze was fixed on elsewhere. "Bodva of Idho? The whore
is dead of me. Long since."

"Herself?" said Whin in practiced awe. She'd not heard of her, so many
thousand years undone; but an Ashes must be swift to improvise. "I's never
tellt so great a soul. There's nonesuch now i' Cloud."

"Carrion," said Annis.

"So dragons may eat dragons. Did she not—?"

"—dare front me?"

"And so has paid. And will pay, evermore." As she herself would thole, if
Annis wearied of her tale. She thought of it, that endless sleepless ecstasy of
rage, self-companied, self-loathing. Of the tumult and the stench.

"Did I not say thou wert my daughter's vicary? As thy state is higher, so thy
death is worse." Annis plucked at the braid of fire on her wrist, as if it galled
her. "I would hear this witch's end. But so: thou shalt find me, if thou canst,
among my congeries all eight who stole the shards of me, to breed a mockery
of tainted flesh. If thou failst, thou art Morag's and her pander's, for their game
eternally. If thou art perfect, for thy recompense—" My lady raised her face;
reflections of her soulstones rocked and wavered in the cavernous dark, as if the
air were heavier than air, as if light drowned. "I shall tell thee. For a ninth."

A horseman coming. Ashes rose, uncertain and alone: but it was Grevil's voice at her door; and Grevil alone that she opened to, bowing as he had that May morning: but all had changed. "Is it your will that I enter?"

She nodded.

He looked about the bare room, gloves in hand. Smoke-blackened thatch. Bare walls, rain-islanded. Chalked floor, stars fading into dust of stars. "'Tis cold for long study." Constraint; formality; a kind of sorrow. They stood strangely at odds, disproportioned: as if she looked backward through her glass. "If there is aught—I will send such bare necessities as you may want; and such comforts as your state allows." Nothing could she ask in law, but turned her hand palm outward: Ashes' sign. "'Twill come, a basket, if you will or no," he said. "So Mistress Barbary hath ordained." A shadow of a smile. "You need not fear more copying beneath the bread; my horn is dry."

*What should a ghost with bread? with fire? My table is of souls, in Law; my mother bade me eat.*

Still his gaze was sidelong, glancing from her at the sigils, riddle and rede, on the hearthstone. Chalk and raddle and charred wood. Moon and stars. "You read a darker book than I can give you, you that write with fire on the hills." He spoke as from a text: *"That mastery is of womankind: to journey pathless in the dark."*

Still silent.

He picked up a trencher on the table; set it down. "They are afraid of you, the men. Of Ashes." *Of Ashes that they call Death's whore:* but that he could not say. "If you had kindred here, to laugh and say, *My sister guising* or *My brother's lass in breeks*—If I had sway—"

No answer.

"I had hoped—" Again he looked sidelong at the scuffle of signs. "The boy is fled; I am glad of that. He is—but thou knowest, Ashes, all my heart—the boy is dear to me. I thank you for my Will." And to her unvoiced question: "No. If Corbet had taken him, his vengeance would be public. No secret murder but great show. Hanged and gibbeted: as one nails vermin to a tree as warning to all upstart crows."

He wheeled about.

"I would you were beyond the sea; beyond his malice. I would you might be safer under my roof; but mine aunt bears no great love toward you. Yet covets: as she would a string of stones. For this neck or for that: but under lock and key."

She knew that. Still she stood.

Now he turned from the hearthroom to the glazen window, leaning on the sill, and gazing at the deepset pane, that in the gathering wintry dusk gave back his face. As if he haunted Jinny's orchard, looking in, moon pale amid the trees.

*They gather in her trees, the dead. Untold, unleaving, they arise and flutter, swirl and fall. They clamor, silent as the snow in snow, they beat themselves, unbodied, at the windows of her memory, at the doors of sleep. They quarrel for the crumbs of her, her apronful of dreams. They starve.*

"Thou gravity." A low voice. "I could believe that you are Ashes indeed."

*Am I not?*

He stooped and took a brand, and lit her stump of tallow on its dish. So early dark. He stood, the candle shaded by his hand. "They do say, our wise-wives, that each who bears the part is very Ashes, aye, that giddy girl, and this; yet some that wear the coat become it. Mistress Jin ..." Still gazing. Light licked shadow: lapping, lapping at the eaves, and yet the dark still overspilled. "As a boy I would not cross this threshold, no not the shadow of her smoke, for awe. My nurse did say that heedless boys who stole her witch's apples died of cramp; I craved a colder fruit of her, an older root, still green; and would not take, for dread." He set the candle on the table; watched it steadying. "She told my mother's death."

*That cloth is done*, said inwit. *And the loom is bare*

"My father—" A wind in the keyhole, that set the candle cowering in its dish. He broke the furl of wax; it flared. "I am fit for naught," he said. "Old wives."

A longdrawn silence.

"Will you tell a death?" He took the gold ring from his hand. His father's seal, the Ship. His white face overstamped with it: the wax of him all ship and masted ship heeled over, fallen stars. "No kindred. One I—knew." She took it: cold and heavy, canted, sleek: a whirlpool in her hand, the sea his grief. It whelmed her. Salt and wave. The ship of him at breaking ... *Drowned*, she thought. But saw no spirit striving in the wrack but Grevil's, overfraught with grief and love. Clawing in her hair to draw her down. "Not your mourning," said her unaccustomed voice. "His soul." His face in shadow, fire in her hand. From within his coat, his shirt, he took a thing of tinsel, silver-black, and laid it in her hand: a star.

All gold, what she saw then: a huntsman in a harvest field, a restless careless

ranting boy, a-dazzle like the wind in barley. Not to sheave. Cloud towered
at the back of him: it brooded thunder, burnished brighter yet the gold of
harvest. There was hail to come. He held a moorcock in his hand, bloodwet:
still plump with August, ruffled and agape. *I'll the pluck of it,* he mocking said,
*and thou the quill.*

He spoke through Ashes, in her voice. She saw the grief and wonderment
in Grevil's face, as if his soul were sky in which these planets moved. It dizzied
her. *It is a glass,* she thought, *this telling; I can see what is, that never yet was seen.*

She told night-lording Hulver and his starry train.


Cracked, cracked with voyaging, her hands, voice, spirit cankered with the salt
of witches: Whin told on, though wave on wave astounded her. Her ship was
will. No stars to reckon by. No north but in the tending of her blood; no
blood but in the body left astounded in the hall: that slept, and yet took hurt
of travelling. A witchfire played about her mast, now, nowhere, madding her
with visions. There were voices in the shrouds.

My lady was another sky, a sea of air; the souls in it that swam not stars
but cold and burning planets, brilliantly malign: the monsters of her deep.
Whin told them all, the great stones and the islands scattering between; and
telling each, was twinned with her as if they lay within one belly, braiding
blood with blood of hers, and soul with soul.

She'd gone too far for turning, so went farther on.

She told how Bodva of Idho got herself with child of Annis; but miscarried of the stone. A mole, a moonegg of the Witch, and likest to a raven,
so they say—she thought of Morag's thralls, abhorring them—but with a
woman's dugs, a harpy's lust, insatiable. She fed on flesh, quick or carrion,
drank moonblood and manseed; but her prey was souls. Her bane was Askell's
lady, waking by the hallows tree, whereon he hung. That same Asenath slew
her, stooping on his corse.

"And fools made tales of it," said Morag.

Whin dared much; but she dared not drink the cup of bone that Morag
set beside her, black wine and milk; nor eat the strips of withered flesh.

"Go on," my lady said.

"And Hrakki o Scar would use no blood, but argued, *stone o stone.* So she
did match her soul wi' it."

"What end?"

"Her witch is stone and sleeps. I sailed a nine weeks north and see'd it."
But Whin is there now, in its overshadowing. Her small boat shudders on the
waves. The witch is huger than a hillside, black and lucid as the starless night;
but faulted. Flawed through. She's swallowed up the moon and stars, drunk
down the bowl of night; but in her the sky is buckled, like a sheet of silver
leaf, infolding on itself. Cloud coils from her, her hair is boreal, and all that
windward coast a wrack of ships. The stone is cold to crack the marrow, craze
the blood. And deep within lies Hrakki's knife, a sickle like the waning moon,
but nowhere, caught a thousand times in seeming. It is broken. Her sister
Hrima set upon the stone with it, to break a shard, or pry the soul away; and
shattered, as her flesh were ice: her soul was long subsumed.


Ashes that was Thea's daughter dreamed. There was a bowl of pomegranates
set before my lady at her meat. And every lobe of each a clustering of blood,
and every seed a soul. My lady chose; then looked to Ashes, beckoning, as she
did draw her ravens down to feast. *Come, Madam. Here is banqueting.*

She loathed; and yet she hungered for it. Not a word: yet Annis knew.

*For thy bellyful? What wouldst thou give?*

*To eat of it, my lady?*

*To be eaten.* She had split the orb of it; and inward of its lips lay glistening
galaxies, packed world on world.

*My secrets.*

*Thou art glass to me. What other?*

Surfeit and desire and sickening: a rage was in her blood. *All that is,* said
Ashes; and she gave the sky.

It rattled like a dice-box in my lady's hand, a black orb like a blasted
pomegranate; then it split, spilled stars that dimmed with falling. They were
on some lightless shore; the sand was all of stars, extinct. Their ashes. Out
beyond, the tideless sea was stale with tumbling, like a rucked and sweated
bed. *Come,* my lady said, *Thy secrets.* And she raught with bloodnailed hands to
split her, fork to eyes.

She woke. She knew not who she was, nor in what bed; but dry-mouthed,
drenched with fear, she lay upon the anvil of her dream, heart hammering, until the chink of metal, amulet on amulet, recalled her. Ashes. Groping for her
coat, she wrapped it round her, skin to skin, her fingers buried in its matted
fleece; yet slept no more. A daemon in her wept and raged with longing for a

thing she knew not and abhorred; until at first light of a bitter day she rose, and pricked a finger for an ashing. Yet she made no trance; no vision came, no words. As Ashes, she was blinded to herself. She could not tell her blood.


Brief light and whitely fallen snow. Ashes that was Margaret sat wrapped in the old quilt, with Jack Daw's stolen pack spread out before her on the floor, in knots and wheels and magpie cronyings. The cards were old and terrible; the coat had given them. Assigned them: they were something she must need. Warily, she turned and puzzled at them, at the underside of light. Not baneful in themselves, she thought, no more than fire was, or night: but rank with their master's witchcraft, steeped in black sorcery. They scented of him, of his sex; of smoke as from a fire of flesh and bone; of earth as grave. They were tallowy with handling. Yet the bite and dazzle of his blade was in them, and his rancor: the very paper of them buzzing like a wasps' nest. And they felt in some way implicated, tied. As if by turning them, he'd tugged at something: at a leash of hounds, at jesses or a bridle bit; a barbed hook in a bloody mouth. As if he spurred destiny or hawked with fate. Caught fish.

The cards were not her pack she knew, but shadows of them, disconcertingly unlike and like. Strange mirrors of the old devices. Strange guises of the sun and moon; new emblems for the stars. By the constellation, this she held would be the Nine: not drawn as sisters in their tower, bending to their starry web; but as stones of crystal in a coffer, iron bound: as fragments of the shattered heavens, with the stars still captive in their shards. Eight of them: one lost.

Here, in a cater of cards, were half the burnt stars all at once: an ill trick. The Huntsman and the Tower; the Hound and the Swift, still reeling off the lives of mortals. It was painted as a child with a whirligig, running heedlessly, enchanted with his toy. Before his dazzled eyes there lay abyss: a race of water and the great wheel of the mill of bones.

Cinque and sice. The Poppyheads, the Hare. That crone in the stubble field, who crouched and scrabbled at the clodded earth. Were they all of them her tale?

Here, the Ship: but furled of sail and battered, heeling over in a tempest on a woodcut raging sea. A tiny figure, wreathed in picted flame, fell burning from the masthead. Far and leeward lay a louring shore, all wolfish rocks: toward which the Ship was driven. It would break. And on that island stood the Tower in epitome, as in the pupil of an eye.

And here, the Hanged Man, and the avid crows: but each with Morag's face, with women's bodies naked to the fork. White bellies and black—

That she turned as if it burnt her fingers; turned it back, to look on Morag's cold envenomed eyes, her talons and her beak. Her body, as a dreadful mirror of her own: what she might be. What Ashes in the stubble field had urged on her. She could not bear to look; she had to know. The next and then the next. The Scythe. Old Slae, from the trial. She flinched. And turned again, and shut her eyes and scrabbled up the pack. No more. But the image burned within her eyes, black, white, ablaze, as if she'd gazed on lightning: Ashes lying with her secrets agape to the kneeling Sun. Not the worst, not yet. What she dreaded was the Crowd of Bone: to see her mother's endless death.

Abyss and origin.

Shuddering, she dipped her sullied hands in water, wiped them on the Ashes coat. She knelt back on her heels, remembering how in darkness she'd imagined *sky*: a garland of the light, wreathed round with sun and moon, a netted caul of stars. A world no wider than her brow.

And this—blasphemy of stars. This crown of hellebore and nightshade.

It was all too much for her, too much. The wayless heavens and the weltering earth. Vertiginous. Her cosmos cracked and shivered like an egg; her child's true body changing fearfully: untrustable, estranged. She wept now for the dark, the prison of her childhood, for her nutshell full of ghosts. Her realm. Furled and shivering, she mourned the old bright stars of innocence: the wood above, unleaving. Bright cards in a darker place.

*Margaret, do you see the leaves?*

She looked up in sudden wrenching hope. *Thea?* No one there: the shadow of a memory of a voice. She bowed beneath a piercing desolation. *Gone.* Her mother's whispering voice: the guide, the Ship-star of her nighted sky. Far gone, the paradise of Norni's lap. Not hers by right. She thought of Imbry and her namesake. Of her shadow sister who was dead, whose milk she had stolen, whose cradle-place she had usurped. Of her doll that Morag burnt to ashes: as a Scarrish witchery, she said. But lied. All of them gone: her mothers and her sister and her cradle of stars. And she had no tongue to cry.

*I am Ashes of myself.* No answer.

White uninflected light. The fire sinking.

*No,* she thought: *I am braided of them, of their voices telling. I am what they made. They made me to go on.*

And she remembered a small thing lying in the palm of her hand, as round as a hazelnut, shining as a moon: their lives within her life.

With a fingertip in soot, she traced the crossed curves of the sky, of Ashes's rune, on the hearthstone. As she bent, her charms jangled: it was braided in her hair, with others, over and again. Time and memory. They crossed in Ashes.

She could not speak; but she could tell.

She called her cards to mind. On the floor of hardpacked, limewashed earth, she laid them out in memory, Lykewise: the Ship, the Swans, the Nine. The Crowd of Bone, transcending death: unsilenced. She upheld, outspread her hands, as if she took the string of silk from Norni's fingers, overturn and undergo. Almost she felt the ghostly hands that mirrored hers, upholding: give and take. She began.

*Thea. I am telling this in Stars.*

"This one," said Norni, holding out the string of silk. And in and out, her fingers flicked, enweaving web. She spoke the riddle as she wove.

> *No fell, but full of bones:*
> *Fleets featherless,*
> *Walks never, wakes summer,*
> *Winterlong is blind.*
> *A flock of eyes have flown.*

"A tree," said Margaret watching. They had played this game.

"So in Cloud they call it," said her nurse. "They are few in Scar. I had seen none, but their bones cast up in storm." She tugged and it vanished. "I had a comb of tree."

"But you'd seen it in the stars, the Tree?"

"Nightlong in winter, and the worm at its roots." She was threading Margaret's hands. "Ringman there. And under. So."

"Imbry's made of tree." The doll lay in Margaret's skirts, handworn and faceless. "I think she walks there, in the Wood Above."

"And over. See, it grows."

A web between her hands, between their faces. Another riddle. "Is it stars?"

The comb was tangled in the nightlong hair: no planet but a rune of stars. It sang amidst the ranting of the witches: *lully lullay.* Whin knew it for a Scarrish soul, a witch of the Unleaving. It was bone. Not carved but caught in it, as one anatomy of soul, one sentience. It shivered at her thought, all spine. Still telling of the seventh witch, Whin raised that story like a wind, magnificent, to drown her secrecy. Her stormcock's cry was lost in what it prophesied: what it called was tempest. It unskied the hall and vaulted it with lightnings, heaped hailstones to the knee. Unheeded in my lady's trance of ecstasy, Whin touched the windcomb with her spirit.

And she's in an empty room. She sees a cradle overset; she sees a tangle of bright silks. In the roar and crackling of thorns, she sees a burning doll, its blind face like a poppyhead, the petals like a cry. Still swayed by a turmoil in the air, a tumult barely past, the loomstones swing and clack. And further, running further in the pathless dark, a child is crying out.

Kit's lass's bairn; my lady's daughter's child.

*A nurse, she would have had a nurse,* thought Whin. Her mother slain, they must have set her to a stranger's breast: her comfort, her unleaving. Aye, a witch, to fat the bairn on power. Milk of sorcery. Which suckled dry, was then a hindrance to my lady's governing: so quenched. So nothing, to my lady's mind and Morag's. After the unruly grief, the discipline of grief, their pupil should have thought no more on her, than on her last year's leavings. But that nurseling was a mortal child; her nurse a witch of Scarristack: they'd memory and will. Their art was not of Annis' kind, nor any she could sense. It held no power, save what lay between them, child and tender. Not of law but love.

There are snags in the riverrune of story, that unravelled let it run.

Softly, softly, Whin undid the comb, and millennia of night slid free, unbraiding of its knots. One strand, but only one: the souls in it ran down like stars of water stilling from a thorn; like blood. A thaw in the winter, a silence in the storm.

And of itself the comb begins to tell, the song to sleek the endless nightfall of my lady's hair. There is a far voice answering, as if they work from hand to hand; as if a skein of yarn is winding in a clew. The cradle-tide of story rocks between them, nurse and child: Ashes to Ashes, then and now and then.

They tell the Annis witch asleep.

The ravens came at barley, flying from the east. They broke the mist and saw the black cliffs sheer beneath them, flint-flaked with a yell of birds; they saw the steep green rising, and the maze of stones, man-set, a moorweb. They saw sheep, and knew the blackfaced ewe was dying; saw the dead lamb at its fork. They saw a woman by a stone house, grinding at a quern. They stooped. One sat on the rigpole, the other on the wall, crying hoarsely to its make. They'd spied her out. She banned them; they flapped and rose, derisory, and called. A third came wheeling from the law, unmoonwise. Something fell into her lap, a small thing, like a grain of corn: a milkwhite stone. A sort.

Siorvar rose heavily, for she bided her nine moons; she went in, stooping at her low skin door. Her work was doing and undone, and all to do. She would ask her weaving what the stone forespelled; though her blood knew. By the hearth stood her loom of whalebone, warped and weighted down with stones, all sea-thirled: cracked or cloudy, black and white and red. This, green as hailstorm but undying, Tharri Thrasi's dam had found, between the water and the land; that, nightblack with the stars' long swirl on it, had caught between the sea and sky: Pirr, climbing with a strayed lamb on her back, had found it, brought it landward in her mouth. Look, the moon's egg, she had said: that winter brooded it, breastthigh in snow. That round blue rock had drawn a call of whales behind it, flinching on the shore. The stone called sunwise was the eldest, drowned at hallows, found at lightfast burning on the waves.

Slowly, she began to weave. She'd warped the moorit and the shaela threads, in the pattern called the shoal of seals. But as she wove, she saw a strange thing growing in her web. *Tree*, she said, and named it in the Cloudish tongue. Her own had none. She's seen its bones, like an old man's wracked with winters, lying on the shore. The bones of Cloud, they called it, Mallywrack. She knew the rime. She spoke it as she wove: "No fell, but full of bones ..."

*She will sleep this while,* the witchcomb said of Annis. *Go.* Whin took to owl-wise; she rose in spirit, circling to the north, to Scarristack of the unleaving stars. *Bring me my arts. I hid them ere I left.*

At hallows eve, the windwife saw the owl and greeted her: swift, softer than a fall of snow, and sharp as frost to kill. It came from the north, from the eye of the witch, at dusk as the fires leapt. She felt a pang, as if the beak and

claws had torn her, and she knew her time. By moonset, hallows day, beside
the bare loom in the straw, she bore her daughter. Imbry, she named her,
whispering; and saw the cloudblue on her sealdark eyes, her father's eyes, like
sky on rockrent water.


Towards lightfast, Siorvar dreamed of fire. A woman, wreathed in fire, riven
like a stone. Waking, she saw the moon through the wind-eye, waning; heard
the breathing of her bairn, happed soft in eiders, lying at her breast. She
touched the dark head, sleeping. New and wise, she thought: the old moon
in the new moon's arms, that bore it and was born of it, the lighter of its
dreams.

She rose, and going to the kist of tree, took out her eldmother's comb.
It was carved of sealbone, spiny like a hake's back, toothed on either side,
called rime and rune. She unbound her hair. It fell about her, long as win-
ternight, unstarred; and with the runeside of the comb, she combed it, and
began to rime. Far north, she woke the stonewitch, sleeping in a coil of
cloud and wind. She combed the cloud and skeined it, rimed a ring about
the owling moon: a burr of frost, a broch of ice, a storm against the fire-
bringing ship.

But softly as she sang, the wind rose in the roof, the loomstones clacked.
At that, the baby woke and cried; the milk came starting to her breasts.
"Hush, ba," she said, and took her up. "Ah, hush thee, by thy father's fell."
She nursed. The cloud spell slid away, it spilled and spilled away in mist.


Whin saw the pale ship, rudderless, unmasted, make its landfall on the witch's
isle. She saw a fire in the mist, the lantern at the soulship's prow: it shrank
as it came onward, seemed a man. The huntsman, with his straw-white hair,
the color of a bladesmith's forge at full, and he the knife. He bore a round
thing in his hand: a wren's cage, but of iron, hung with strips of mortal skin.
Still bloody, some of them, and others ghostly dry. All knowing, whispering.
Lightfast and alone, he stood before the witch's sill. He stamped.


*Now,* said her heart's tide, running seaward. It ravelled on the Teeth, it broke:
a perturbation and a cloud of sand. Siorvar woke aghast. Still Imbry slept

within her skincoat, brooded by her heart. The stone of milk within each breast thawed, wept. The bead of fire in the nightlamp welled. She drew the windeye's fell aside. Grey shadowless. The dream had been otherwise, ablaze. She saw it still within her eyelids: a skin boat, dip and dazzle on the sun's road, winking into dawn. But it was Lightfast: there would be no day. A paling in the dark, no more, the shoulder of a sleeper waked and turning in his earthy bed. The sun lay long in Ashes, in his winter grave. *The Lyke Road is his dream*, she said, remembering old Pirri's telling, with a pang. She held the babe so fiercely that she woke and squalled. For the last time, she suckled her and cleansed her and bound her to her breast. Then rising, the windwife roped her burden to her back.

She made her way by rake and foothold to the windward shore; set down the kist of tree. It was an heirloom of her lineage: of Cloudwood, waifcast on her treeless island shore. Cloud of the branches, Cloud of the slanted stars: she willed it to its home. Imbry stirred and mewed. Her mother kissed and sained her, touching eyes, mouth, heart with snow; she laid her naked in a furl of skins. No thread to find her, bind her to her mother's fate. Then wading thighdeep in the bonecold restless sea, she set the ark adrift.

*Go*, she willed her. *At the moon's will. Live.*

A wave. Withdrawing on the rake of it, the small ship faltered, but her spell still bore it upright and the tide was strong: it rode. Another and another wave. It slipped and journeyed, rocking on its eldmother's icy lap. She stood and watched the sea long after it had vanished in the mist.

Ashes that was Siorvar's nursling knelt beside an empty cradle, by a hearth, in a stranger's house. A bare room, stoned and sanded. Cold, for all the high-made fire. It was earth ingrained: a taint of mould in it that would not scrub away. The old man's telling had been ceremonious: a form of words, a feat of memory, a mask. This was otherwise.

A stonefaced woman; a bewildered man. The woman held a silver ring out in a workworn hand. It trembled. "Will you tell a death?"

"Tild," said the man. "Her name were Tild. My lady."

Silence.

"She were—she would ha' been nine, come barley." There was something in his great scarred fist. "I thowt as ... well, you'd not 'a knowed her ... it would help."

A wooden doll.

She could not. Not speak, not move, not breathe. Not bear it. If she had her will, she would have torn away the coat and run: anywhere, away. She could feel the shock of beck-brown water as she plunged: she'd wash away her godhead, send the soulbag tumbling to the sea. Throw off this earthish weight of grief, of gold, of deference: their terrible belief.

But at her back she felt the tiding of magpies: those canting gloating gossiping old crones with their hoard of tears. *Here's a pretty thing.* They were waiting to speak for her, interpret. Overcrow. *Sheepnose and puddocky,* she thought. *Magpiety old dames.*

Lifting her chin at them, she took the doll and laid it in the cradle; took the ashing in her hand. A tawdry little silver ring, rubbed bright for her. She turned it on her fingertip.

Could she say, *I am of that place you would send her? Where is neither sun nor moon. And there is no way back of Law.*

In memory, she knelt on stone, her head in Morag's lap. The comb the old hag wielded was of Norni, bone and spirit, made to part them; made to search her charge's head for dreams and secrecies, that vermin of her mortal kind: pick out those maggots of communion. It is tales that make us human. Tales that live.

What story could she tell of death?

*My mother fed me to her crows—*

*No.*

Swayed beneath that storm of wings, with its talons in her heart, she bent and held the cradle's clumsy edge. Unsteady, it upheld her. Creak and thump.

She thought of both the Imbrys. Of her doll in ashes. Of her sister, not in blood but milk. That was Norni's telling by the fire: of that child who would not cross the sill of death, but slipped it, sailed the Lyke Road in her keel of stars. Her child: not cast away but set at large. Unleaving.

Kneeling by the cradle, rocking, Ashes told the Ship.


Whin lighted on the snow. The witch's house and all around it for a stone's cast—garth and fold—was burnt to black glass. But in the rafters of the sky for all to see, safe-hidden, hung the windwife's Comb, her Bearskin, and her Shears: her daughter's heirlooms from her mother's mothers, to the sill of time. Far eastward on the fracted sea, as black as fireglass but moving still, Whin scried a spark. No sunrise in the deep of winter but a ship.

Bent beneath a heavy creel, a woman walked the shore. It was storm-changed, like a man's face back from war: scoured of old thought and restless, while behind his empty eyes death raged. A raw new beach, an old sea. Eyes to the bonewhite shingle, heedless of the crash and sting, she gathered sticks of rimy driftwood, clots of weed. Fire. Enough to char a fish, to seethe a pot. To dry the rags she'd sodden getting fire. Stooping she found a broken wooden comb, half-buried in the sand, and prised it out with cracked blue nails. A shrunk and swollen carving, of a sow? a mermaid? Could be.

Standing up to ease her back, she saw a black thing riding on the waves. A seal? A cormorant? A kist. And riding toward the Teeth. Loosing her creel, she stripped herself, and naked upward to the waist, she waded in: shin-deep, thigh-deep, stunned with cold. A wave drenched her. She caught the kist and lost it, lunged and held it, though it battered, bruised her. Stayed her, as the next wave took her feet. She hauled it on the shingle, with a pant of triumph like a hawk. Waif and stray. Her plunder, wrested from the sea. With bloodless hands and shuddering, she caught up a stone, to smash the lock, to crack the prize.

No prize.

The woman stared in awe and fury at her bitter gift. There lying on a heap of pelts was a naked child. Unswaddled. And alive. A smudge of black hair on its round brown head, a cleft between its kicking legs. A girl. She opened eyes still blue as milk on slate, still gazing on the Lyke Road, on her journey: like a foam of water drawing from a sunk black rock.

Ashes dreamed. On the hearth beside her, Norni held a tangle of bright silks between her hands; she wove it in an endless knot. A game. Her face was like itself, like earth, rain bright amid her dusky hair. *Like this*, she said, and held out the sun.

## Lightfast

Crouched in the ashes in the shadow of the kist, the crow lad waits. It is Lightfast, long ago: they've let him crowdle by the fire, up at Craw Trees. They must. He is the Ashes child. Still young enough to coy, a cub with all his milk teeth yet. The maids have crammed him, cuffed and whispered and caressed. His head swings with huffcap; he shivers with tales. *She'll come for thee. Thou windfall, thou's her whelp. Her vixen will eat thee, pillicock and all.* The black dog's hackles rise. The wind wauls; yet he hears the slow drum and the wheedling pipe, in tatters like the waifs of leaves; then the stamping and the cry. The guisers. They are at the door. You must let them in. At the master's beck, Mall slips the lock and they stagger in with their light burden. The wind of their coming makes the fire crouch, it stirs the smoke; their shadows loom and swale. They are black and ragged in the flare of torches; they are bright with gauds. They bring the sun.

Before them stalks t'Awd Moon, sweeping with her besom of thorn. Her face, grey as hoarfrost, is bearded; she is breeched beneath her petticoats. And lagman, still as shadow, walks a figure in a coat of skin.

She is Ashes and holy.


In the great barn at Grevil's, in the flare and shadow of the torches, Ashes that was Margaret bid the guisers in. The Moon, slow-sweeping, danced before them; and the bustling Fool, a-bristle with his cap of barleystraw, cried out to make them room. He wore his coat of tatters, bore his pipe of bone and goatskin tabor at his knee. Jauncing on a staff, he bore a cage of thorn and withies, twisted in a ball; at every cross were knotted ribands, red and green, and draggled white, black rags and ravellings of gold and silver thread. Mere trumpery: but with her wakened eyes she saw the heavens and the earth in little. Green the holly in the winter wood; the white snow falling on the thorn; the drops of reddest blood. This world: a cage, a crown, a travelling. She saw the rags of heaven floating out behind, the waifs of gold and silver, sun and moon, as if the poor stark wren within were shining. Like a comet in its curve returning. Light foretold.

When the guiser shook the staff, it dazzled—lightning!—and he stamped it thrice to shake the ground. At the threshold he paused; then at Ashes' nod, he crossed it with the circling Moon. All round about the twelve winds, east, north, west, and south, he sained the threshing-floor, she swept, made room to rhyme.

"Walk in," he said.

She knew them all by part. That broad-faced shepherd with the crown of horn. The small man with the bundled swords, the stripling with his pipe and drum. Those ranting lads. The Fool. The Awd Moon, with his petticoats and broom. Herself, with the box of coins, the bag of ashes. And the lad with bright unravelled hair.

Not Ashes' Will. Another boy, hawknosed and sinewy, lithe and light, a-gawk at her. His hair not scattering silver like a bygone weed, but yellow as the broom.

Leapfire.

She would lull him dying in her lap; and he would rise.

Aside and smiling, then she saw the white-haired fiddler, in his broad hat with the draggled feathers, and his moonwhite mask. Old Lightfast who would slay his son. And her heart turned over in its cage; but the white was barley-flour, and the kit a poor cock-headed scrawny thing. He raised his vizard on a snub-nosed puzzled face.

And after him by two and three, some awed, some swaggering, with all their torches burning bright, the guisers gathered on the threshing-floor of Grevil's barn. By one and one, they louted low to Ashes, bending with the knee. She sat upon the sacks of barley in the flare and shadow of their brands, breathed in their scent of smoke and ale and eager sweat.

"Now then," said Hob Hawtrey. "Is all our company here? Mag Moon-wise?"

Ashes startled at that name; slipped into self.

But, "Aye," called the bearded man in petticoats, great-shouldered like a smith. Red cap and rags on tatters, like a slattern cabbage; a besom of thorn. He made his voice small and shrewd.

"Up with your petticoat, have at your plum-tree," cried one of yon ranting lads, and flourished with his sword of lath.

Mag peered reprovingly through empty spectacles, and set them crooked with a charry hand. "Here's prigging of orchards. An thou bites't at me codlins, thou's find a great worm."

"Plays well," said Hob, considering. "We s'll play it so t'night." Squinting at his plat, he pricked it. "Kin Kempery, aye. Nick Knapperty?"

"I's here." The other ranting lad. "And bold as a cockentrice."

"To't wenches," said his mate. "He'll up to them and flisk it, as crank as a cock sparrow. On and off."

"Fil Fadget? And mind thou—see our swords be sharp."

"All fettled," said the small man. "Trim and tackle."

"Wick Billy?"

"What, I? Is't my part?"

"Thou slow worm. I's call thee when 'tis. Kit Catgut?"

"So I is," said the fiddler.

"Crowd on, crowd on." Hob frowned at his paper: which she could see now was a maze of marks. All sigils. Not a word. "So then. Leapfire?"

The yellow boy jumped up. "Take *that*, thou villainy!"

Easily, the old man knocked the lath from him. "Lightfast here, and I's been him since thy father were t'Fool, Hob Houchin."

"Which I is. And that's our tale." He folded up his paper. "Now Grevil's folk is first night as they ever was; then Lightbeck, and t'Rendels up at Nine Thorn How. Second night, we's bound out Aikenmoor, for t'Woodfalls, and langways back through Littledale. And third night, round by Askwith to Owlriggs, and we finish off at Imberthwaite, where Deb has brewed."

A cheer.

He turned to Ashes, bowing for her blessing. "Soft now, my lady. Steal it so—" He showed her, creeping like a cat on ashes. "—when yer stalking bairns. And smutch 'em, an they will or no, and leave none out for Ashes sake. And when we's danced—well, then ye'll do as you's ever done. You knaws yer part."

And then to the guisers: "Lastways: yon Madam up at t'Hall has getten in a pack o gallantry to play to Grevils. Outlune arrygants as dance for gold. Crawsetten conjury they does, to seem t'braver. But they's warlocks all, and swaggerers. And they's cried us for a herd o hinds. Let's show 'em Cloudish honor. Dance 'em down."

A tempest and a hammering.

"Cheerly, my stormcocks, cheerly. Once through and away."

Old Grevil's hall is elsewhere now. It guises all in green, in Woodwo's coat of ivy and his holly crown, his beard of wintry boughs. A green age, hale and hoar with ice. For now is Winter's reign. They burn the Summer-Lyke, a great oak felled; they've stripped and dragged it, all in chains of iron, to the hearth. It guises too, in ashes, with its bright hair blazing from its blackened stump. It sings, devouring; it dances, all the long years of its tale of sovereignty unleaving from the log. For it is knitted up of light, all compact of the Sun. Lord Leapfire. And it would eat the holly, if it could: devour hearth and house and all. Its fire glints and glances in the shining leaves.

*Hush*, says Annot, softly in Noll's ear. *Now comes the masque of witches.* She can feel the stillness in him, and the shiver. *Soft now. They'll not spy thee, thou'rt cowered safe. See, Hobbinoll, I've iron.* And she snips her scissors at the air.

*Do I now?* he asks.

*Not yet. I'll tell thee when.*

Once twice thrice the master of the revels stamps. It is a stranger company; the play's unworn. The rumour dies.

*No tongue! All eyes!*

The play is of the elder mysteries: for Madam Covener is pious, and she keeps old Law. She's taught them. Know you this: ere ever there was Ashes, there was endless night. This world is embers of another world, of wood unleaving.

Here's the haunting hirpling of the little pipe, and now the heeling of the drum.

In comes Tom o Cloud, awd Flaycraw, in his leaves of tatters, leaning on his staff. He turns like a wind whorl in a drift of leaves, and what he's compassed is Cloudwood.

*Once afore t'moon were round, and on a winter night . . .*

"Here's all to do," cried Hob. And roundabout he flustered, like a cat in pattens. Wried his Fool's cap, that looked like a guttered candle. Wrung his hands. "Wae's me."

"Why, what's to do?" said a guiser.

"Here's my lady keeps lightfeast, and she's bid of me a great dish of a wren."

They staggered back, appalled.

"What, beard him in's den?"

"He's rended twenty score o kempions. All bones about his lair."

"He'll reckon thee."

"Crack bones and craunch marrow."

"And wha's to gather up thine atomy?"

Mag Moonwise called out briskly, "Ashes! Here's a telling. Hob Houchin's to die, and he's willed me his bagpipe."

Weeping, the elder shepherd clipped him round the neck. "I ever loved thee"—they clung and blubbered—"and thou ow'st me three farthings and that bacca as thou burnt last Kindle Wake. Here's a bag for't smoke."

"O what's to become o me wife and babbies?" cried the Fool. Down he fell, and took Lightfast by the knees. "Would thou keep them?"

"As me own," said Lightfast. "As they are."

"But for mine and a passing tinker's," Leapfire said. "Her kettle had a hole."

Fil Fadget went about him with a string, taking measures for a coffin.

"By dawcock, what's a wren?" cried a ranting lad. "I's slay yer nine on them—have at yer! Aye, t'awd cock and his whelps. Fit 'em blindfold and bare arse. Wi' a windlestraw, one hand." He slashed at shadows with his lath. "Hah!"

"Good," said Hob aside to him, "but so"—he mimed a stroke, which Leapfire jumped—"and so." It doubled back and smacked his arse. "Plays better."

"Not much pick on a wren," said Fadget doubtfully. A string of babbies swung and rattled on his back.

"Owt else she'd fancy?' said Wick Billy. "I could do her an egg."

"Craw pie."

"Cock pudden."

"Rhubarb and oysters."

"Odd on." Mag Moonwise rummaged up her petticoats, smacked her own hand. "Cheek!" And she howked out a sausage.

The Fool considered it, between finger and thumb. Lofted it. "Flies ill," he said. He stuck a feather of his cap in it. It tilted. A second feather. Now it spiralled and stalled. A third, at a jaunty cock. "So now." He closed on it. A great shrill tirade seemed to pour from his fingers. He smiled; then clouded.

"Aye, but she'd have it in a hare's wame. And they's ill to catch. And t'plucking on 'em—!"

"Black or white?" said a ranting lad—the other one, not he that practiced thwacking at his tail.

"Then all roundt room, up aprons, lating it," said Hob aside to them. "Not Ned Arket's Bet. He'd kill us."

"Nor not Mistress Barbary," said a doleful voice.

"Thou never!"

"No. But I prigged her cherries once. Has a tongue 'd grate nutmegs."

Hob *h'rm'd.* "Now busk it."

And they fell to slap and tickle, snatching at offended air.

Fool again, the Fool bewailed himself.

"And that stuffed in a vixen's belly, in a babby—and they's woe to snatch, worse than honey, O I dare not for its mammy's tongue—"

"I could get yer one for next year," said the ranter. "But y'd 'a to clean it yersel."

"—in a hind's paunch in a bear's maw—"

Here Mag raised her petticoats and smirked. They fell back, appalled.

"—wi' an urchin in its mouth." He drew a breath. "Wi' mustard."

The old shepherd sang out.

> *Night's for her cauldron, her trencher's yon moon*
> *An ye sup wi' my lady y'll want a lang spoon.*

"I could spare yer a babby," said the plaintive fellow with the dolls. "Or me wife, now, she'd pickle rarely."

"And yer tig's a flaysome beast," cried the Fool. "Plays magpie's bagpipes all about yer ears like a hail o wapses til he's run yer mad. He'd play yer nine wits mazy."

"Twins?" said the married man.

"And then t'seething o my lady's pot! There's not breath enough in me to blaw her fire, nor sticks enough to kindle, for she'd have it raw."

> *In comes Mag Moonwise, wi' stock and wi' stick*
> *An ye lig wi' my lady y'll want a lang—"*

The Fool cried out, "O where sall I get a kempion to slay this tig?" And roundabout he turned, and called, "My cockerel for a kempion!"


... there come twa witches out o Lune ...

In come the witches—Rianty and Silvry—in their mantles of the sky, nightblue and starry. Scarves of silvery gauze are at their shoulders, wafting as they turn.

*O brave,* says Annot in his ear. *They've come by the Lyke Road, and they trail it.*

*Are they women?*

*Goddesses.*

Noll puzzles. They are maidenlike; yet wear bright swords and bucklers. Witchery, he thinks: for naked they are boys. Or so his nurse hath said. Their coats bespell them.

*They've lanterns,* he says.

*They're lating Ashes, who is yet to come. Hush now, they speak their argument.*

The world is winterfast, and they will turn it. Annot's told that play to him; has acted it, all voices, in her room. He will remember when he reads the verses, later, later. He will weep. Now what he hears of it is music, fitfully, in gusts: a wind full of whirling leaves, a wild confusion. Some words he leaps at, snatches from the air; most others oversail him.

Now they've gone aside.

Here's Tom o Cloud shivering in the snow. He stamps and blows his nail. He's bristled like an urchin's back beneath a load of eldins. *Kin kindling,* he calls it. He is wood; his words are strange. The witches enter and amaze him; he amuses them. *His dreams do prick him and he flowers.* Annot's laughing at poor Tom, so Noll laughs too, uncertainly. As if their breath would blow him out. He's like a candleflame that burns the brighter for the wind that threatens. He might snuff.

They three will break the winter: they have sworn.

So now they journey in imagined snow. A man you're not to note sweeps back the rushes, laying bare the flags. The ground's chalked out as riddle-stones, as islands in abyss. The ground's bewitched: for what is drawn is chasm. Where they've walked a moment since is fathomless. A cold wind wuthers up from it. Earth gapes for them, and they must cross. Beyond is Law.

An hollow music plays, as if the earth's voice spoke.

They dance the Riddles. Leaping cross and cross them, in a crouch of terror: stone to stone. Noll watches in an ecstasy of fear. A stumble, and they'd fall forever. He can see them, even open-eyed: the black ice of the bodies and the cold white fire streaming upward like a comet's tail. They cannot win the brink. And then another music interweaves: a net of fiddle under over fiddle. It sustains. Now Tom o Cloud uncurls like bracken; now the witches dance the wilder, and the outswing of their lanterns traces fire in the air. They leap his staff, they tumble backward. He dances leaf light and askew: should fall. He never does. The wind that scatters raises him; the wind is story.

Horsed upon huffcap, he is lord of all, of earth, air, fire. He is mounted on the wind, bright shod with barleycorn and summer-spurred, the blood of barley in his veins.

He is Leapfire, lord of summer.

*What I is,* the crow lad thinks. A god in grain. Threshed out. And that other ranting on the floor is but his shadow; and the boy that crouches by the ingle but his chaff. This sword's his own; this bravery of blue and gold. His feats. He's foughten all, and slayed 'em all. They lie about his feet like havoc in a hayfield.

Up and down his golden shadow strides the floor and rants. He brags it, to and fro.

> *Five heroes have I slain at one*
> *And six s'll thole my blade.*
> *Stand forth, awd winter, fell and black*
> *And fight, or thou is flayed.*

And the Fool flings wide the door on winter dark, on frost and famine, and the starving wind. He calls to it. *Walk in, awd Lightfast.*

A cold blast quells the fire.

Here is Law; and everywhere is Annis. Now, nowhere, anywhere: she plays like lightning on the fells. Her black hair fills the room like wind, like night; the candles crouch and flare.

Noll is trembling. Annot whispers, *Will I take thee out?*

*I want to see.*

She colls him; she is glad of his small warmth.

Now comes the slender music of the Cloudwood, like a pattering of rain, and then the twining of the Sisters' viols. Enter three champions. Annot gazes on the brown girl, the witch boy, half in love. In moving, she is perfectness, that still is sullen and farouche. A tarnished Silvry.

*Here is Law,* says Tom o Cloud. *I would be elsewhere, were it on a sinking ship, atwixt a bear and honey.*

*Is the sorceress not here?*

*And happen at her book. I would not for the moon disturb her.*

*We are come to her undoing.*

Turn and turn, the sisters call her down:

> *By the elding of the moon*
> *By the weird of night and noon*
> *That foul or fair befall*
> *By the heavens' rime and rune*
> *I conjure you. I call.*

Down from the fellside in a shock of winter strides Black Annis. She may take what shape she wills; goes now in a witch's like: not dwindled but distilled. The little sun is leashed before her, crouching, like a fire slaked with ash. His mistress wears a crown of souls, like hailstorm, and her very bones are moon.

*Ah,* breathes Annot. This is marvellous. No bloodnailed hag disfigured on a ballad sheet; nor yet an old wives' tale, a bugbear to affright the children. No grisly ghost, that stamping on the floor cries out, *more meat!* This witch is beautiful as frost is, fair and fell. Sheer deity.

Unmasked.

They say a man-witch dances Annis; but no man's throat was ever white as blackthorn, nor his wrist and hand so fine. They say that it's a woman bred to it in dark, that knows no living tongue. That in her secrets, she is neither. Of no mortal kind: a spirit summoned or a waft. The same witch always, anywhere, at once. Herself: for in devouring the mask becomes her.

*Who calls me to the dance?*

*Three journeymen.*

*And I the mistress. Will you gage?*

*For the turning of the sun, we will.*

*This lateworm? What, this lowling? This catchfire gendered on a heap of punk? This Ashes-lap?* He crouches at my lady's feet, his glory dimmed. A golden lad that was, and come to this: a chimneysweeper. She could huff and he would scatter. *Tinsel. But your wager is souls.* She touches him, as if she sains him. *Eyes, mouth, heart: be stone.* Then she turns to the challenge. *I will dance the ay and O.*

Tom o Cloud stands forth. *I will dance the light of leaves.*

But he has not danced but a single dance, once round, when he is done. He whirls his staff at her, and through and through her like a mist. As good kill water with a knife: she slips him still, still-closing, woundless as a white hag rising from the moor. It whelms him. At a breath, he stands astounded, rooted in the earth. His arms, outflung as if to strike at her, outbranch; his leaves of tatters fall. His black staff flowers into frost and breaks. As frost will fell a tree, she fells him; he is winterslain.

Noll is stricken. Annot rocks him in her lap.

*Hush, love. He will rise. I promise. As the sun will rise.* With a dabbled napkin, she amends his face. *'Tis but a winter's tale. Look now, the sisters come to dance for him.*

So fleeting childish grief is: he is rainbow through his tears, he's rapt.

Two on one, they draw on her, at fence. They stand triskelion, a wheel of witches. Then the swords fall clanging to the earth.

*His death was not the wager settled. Still I dance the ay and O.*

The dark witch—Silvry, with her tarnished hair—stands forth. *I will dance the dayspring.*

Sunwise, thrice and thrice around she heels it, leap and landing, lightfoot to the drub of drum. At every turn she raises up her shield a little higher in its arc until—O heavens—she uplifts the Sun. It brightens, burning through the cataract of cloud: an ember at her heel, a shoulderknot of fire, a glory. How it blazes in her vault! It glitters in my lady's crown, like daybreak in a shattering of hail.

And Annis in a rage cries out: *Who slipped my sister that was bound? Who broached her?* Whirling, ranting, how she storms. Her great black sleeves fly out like raven's wings. *Who turned the glass that night may run? Who let her rune of blood to run? How came she lighter of a Sun?* Riddles, riddles. How she stamps it! How she ramps and rages, spurning with her heel.

Annot shivers. In the witch's fury she's recalled her grim aunt stalking from her sister's childbed, bare arms bloody to the shoulder. Three days crying out upon the moon, that would not lighten her. And then the still child in the bearing-cloth, as blue as lead. A girl. And yet again her sister breeds, will kindle ere the greening Ashes rises from the dark. *O my sister. She will rise from this. She must.*

The second witch stands forth.

*I will dance the darklong, and the changes of the moon.*

And moonwise, thrice and thrice around she heels it and uplifts the Moon. At every turn it changes, childing of itself. The riddle read: it is the gendering Moon that does, undoes the knot of blood in woman, and the Moon that lightens her; the Moon that goes with child of mutability. It rounds: is bright edged at the first, a bow new bent; and at the full, sheer silver to the brim. Night's glass.

My lady gazes. She is lost in admiration, in the mazes of the moon. She holds it as a mirror. And it seems another Annis gazes out at her. The one is all of night and silver; and the other bloodfast, hag and whore: her shadow self, outrooted and despised. They draw each other in the glass. They meddle; they are gone. The glass lies empty on the ground.

The witches lift it up, exulting. In it is the sky in little, flawless: sun, moon, stars, and all. A swirl of silver for the Road. All incrystalled in the glass, and still as frostwork on a pane. Down they cast the mirrorworld. It shatters, scattering across the floor like hailstones.

Gleefully, the household scrambles for the shards of Annis; but their garner melts away. 'Twas painted on a round of ice.

And the Sun, the burning boy, uprises. Doffs his coat for cloth of tinsel. But the tree—poor Tom—is leafless still, lies earthfast.

*Get him up,* cries Noll in agony. *She's dead now.*

As if she's heard, the light witch beckons to the Sun. *Wake him: for his dream is done. We played it.* And he sings the morning.

So Tom o Cloud rises up in green, unfolds: like an imp from an acorn, like a catkin from a hazel twig. Shakes out his rags that lie about him like a drift of last year's leaves. He catches up the bright Sun laughing, tosses him, high high up in the air. As high as the rooftree that is green with winter leaves. And there he seems to hang forever, ever falling, shining as the light reborn.

Ashes laughs. *The Road is made of travellers,* she thinks, *and so we are. And so I spy us in my glass: we dazzle me.* All here: Mag Moonwise with her broom of Thorn who sweeps the Way before; the Fool with his Lantern and the Fiddler with his Bow; the Wren they harry from its nest; bold Leapfire; Ashes with her bag of souls. Herself. *The ritual's the Road: we do it, so it is. We dance the sky.*

It swings about her, giddying. Not drunk, she has not drunk with them:

but Ashes dances her. If once she stopped, the stars would rattle down like rain. Like coins for their beggary. Small silver in the bowl of night.

All about her in the night and firelight and snow, the guisers stamp and shout. They've drunk John Barleycorn his health in him, and round and round on setting forth; but they are drunk on heroes, dizzy with renown. As they come they whirl the torches upward, shouting out. They rant for sheer joy of it; they stamp the cat ice on the rutted road. The sky below. And Ashes heels it for the crack; she kicks and scatters flinders like the sparks of autumn leaves. The torches glitter in the star-cracked fragments. Every shard a Sun.

Master Corbet, sweeping up a handful of the scattered heavens, turns and bows to Madam Covener. He opens out his dripping hand. There is a piece still fading on it, fainter than the daylit moon. "Your lady's coin, I think?"

She takes, and it is nothing: water. Glances at his great rings, red as coals. "'Twill serve to turn a mill of yours. Or drown a forge." Or break a ship of his on Law. She's bought him for her paltry niece, with his broad lands, and he will bed the creature, hard—the chit wants manage—but she'll bring an imp-child for a dowry, a daughter in her womb. And yet be virgin, seemingly, by Madam's own well-studied art. There's coin for him, to be her Lady's cuckold and to wear hind's horns. So much for his great rings.

There's tumult in the hall, a caterwauling of a crowd and drum. Her other niece, with her great bellyful, is leaning forward, all agog. The servants call and stamp. The fools are gawking at some jugglery, a tumbler in a tinsel coat. The Sun. Like a woodcut from a tawdry pack of cards. Hedge sortilege. All trumpery, this pack of journeymen; although their mistress has some inkling of the arts of Law. Has six or seven cantrips, but unstudied. Hedgewitch.

Madam smiles. Air and fire, earth and water, and that other element: all one, and in her mastery. She has a stone.

At the door-sill, Annot sets the garland on Noll's head. White buds like drops of milk. Of candlewax and ends of silk, he knows, just snippets; but she's wreathed the snow in it, she's made it real. A secret for his mammy. She parts the arras just a little on a glare and clamour. It is time now. He cannot. A wistful winding music plays. He will.

*Now*, she whispers. *Softly, softly.*

All in green, a green verge in her hand, the winter child arises from her mother's dark, walks barefoot through her shattered crown. But where she walks spring flowers.

He is Ashes and she keeps the year alive.

There's a hushing in the room, a susurration. Like a wind through branches, like a sea: the summertide. The winter leaves with her; she brings the green within, and *in* is not. No hall, no company, no fireside. A hill. At every step a green blade springs.

He carries Ashes in himself: he is a bowl for her, brim full of holiness. So he goes softly, lest she spill. And yet she overspills, and where the drops fall there are flowers. They are white, and rooted in the darkness. Ashes buds. He walks in wonderment.

But in the players' space, amid the dazing candles and the roar, she stumbles and he halts. Looks round and backward. All unwooded now. All faces. Annot?

And the witches who are not look shrewdly on him: would he fall?

He casts about him wildly. Annot?

There. She nods at him, encouraging: begin. But in her face the mischief and the pride have slipped a little, like his wreath. She's fretted for him now. *Don't turn round*, she's told him. *Keep on.* He's done it wrong.

And the dark witch calls, *Pray silence for my lady's imp.*

Confusion: what his legs know is a bow. The crowd of faces laugh, some not unkindly. And the Sun blears out his tongue. Crisis.

But Tom o Cloud lays a warm hand on his shoulder. Steady now. Then stepping back, he quirks a curtsey: half in homage and half prompt.

Later, ever after, he'll remember vividly: the whiff of eager sweat on sweat; how the brown of Tom o Cloud's face is crooked, paint askew on winter pallor; his smile. He'll dream of that: he will be standing at the verges of a greendark wood, afraid, afraid, and he will see it further in, run after. There and gone. Like flick of fire, a falling star. A wish.

But he is *she*, is Ashes now. Tom sets the garland straight.                    .

*Speak, lady. 'Tis your cue.*

No part of his, unpracticed now: the words her own. She speaks her mother tongue, still milky with her draught of heaven.

> *My mother got me in her glass.*
> *Still as snow on snow I pass;*

*But green in greener world I wake*
*And lighter of the dark I make.*
*In my coming I do leave;*
*Death of dying I bereave*

It's silent when she's done.

On the hillside is a door; beyond the door, a fire. On the sill there stands a girl in green to welcome Ashes in. She bids her.

Overcome with godhead suddenly, Noll turns and runs, he buries his head in his mother's not-now-lap, against her mystery. In that drumly hill is laid his sister yet unborn, who will be Ashes.

Tom o Cloud and my Lady sit, playing at the cards for hazelnuts. It's three-and-twenty worlds she's won of him so far; his pockets rattle in her pouch. Unmantled now, unmasked, there's none would mark her: he or she might be a scrivener or a stocking-mender, a hussif or a glover's clerk. Old, young; breeches, petticoats; the dark of moon or light: he plays all parts indifferently, indelibly, and keeps the company's purse. Like Ashes, they are liminal; they live among a cloud of voices, out of door of time. Bar them out and they'll be in at windows. Thieves, some call them, and dissemblers: picklocks of the eye and ear, and coiners of conceit. Brock's journeymen, that walk the moon's road of a history, slip souls like jackets. Tell. They loiter by the screens, as yet unpaid.

The fiddler's filled Tom's mazer cup with Lunish wine, and drinks. The Second Witch eats oranges. Six are too many to juggle. As are five and four. And the First Witch, flown with battle, strays amid the gentry, seeking delicates and praise.

"A pretty Ashes, that," says Pipe-and-Tabor, drinking bacca. "Will we steal her?"

"Yon moth?" says my Lady. "'A plays a maiden rarely, but he's pricked out for another part. His father's master here."

"Milk still on his mother tongue," says the Second Witch. "But mark you, he'll be mumchance when we come the next year. Breeched and cropped."

"Shame," says Pipe-and-Tabor. "Fitted for the quality. Speaks well."

My Lady casts her bones. "His naunt—yon farthing candle—put him up to it. Made his verses."

They look at the girl in green. A stiff provincial finery. An artful hand had laced that stomacher, not hers: she wears it like a prentice, ill-at-ease. Indifferent fair; a fall of reddish hair, like bracken, down her back. A chit. They note her gaze still following the witch boy—sword and petticoats—admiring the sinewed hand so lightly hovering at his hilts, the blackwinged brows. The clear blood in his red lip comes and goes.

"There now, she dotes on Master Leg."

"Who's rapt with his glass."

"That breaks for him."

"Why then, he'll get himself upon a knifeblade."

"A horsetrough."

"A quarrel."

"A spoon."

The witch boy sinks his merlin face into a pot of syllabub.

The girl in green turns round.

And O, the fiddler cries, as if like Tom o Cloud he looked upon the fallen Perseis, amazed: "O rare Cosmography."

"Out of thy compass," says Pipe-and-Tabor.

"Ah, what heavens to be lost in her."

"Thou'rt fickle as the sun, that lies a turn in every house in heaven. Just so many inns to thee. Here's good ale at the Nine and Shuttle, and a brave wench at the Bow."

"See, she comes," says the Second Witch. "Guise thyself." He catches up a mask and plumps it in the fiddler's lap.

And Tom o Cloud sings at him the old tune from the masque, the wood-wo's brag:

> Orion wears a coat of sparks
> And starry galligaskins
> But men may see what man I be
> Without my first dismasking ...

Caught in his confusion, the fiddler's late to rise; the others make their courtesies with hat and leg. The girl with red hair dips and rises like a green wave of the sea. And he is drowned.

"Which of you is Master?"

"I," my Lady says. "And Mistress."

"I am sent to bid you to our supper; so my brother Grevil says."

"And welcome: for we take our road the morn."

"Go you at venture?"

"Mistress, even unto Lune," says Tom o Cloud. "Where 'tis said that hares hold court at midnight, and the moon's their dancing master."

"I would see that." A sigh. "It was bravely done, the masque." The girl in green recalls her errand. "For your pains."

The players' Mistress takes the clinking purse of silver, weighs it in his palm. No stint. Spills silver. Not a moon of it but at its full. He fishes in his pouch. "Here's for your little eyas." Three half-bright Lunish farthings. Owls. "And for his poetry." Another coin.

She turns it over in her hand. There's morning in her face, and mischief. "What, and leave yourselves no Ship?"

The fellow dandling the vizard speaks. "This fiddle is our ship that carries us; our wit our sails. Our wind is your good will."

"Am I an Outlune witch to bind and barter wind?"

"A witch," he says. "No crone."

"Then sit I in the east. Will you not founder?"

"Mistress, in your cold dispraise is wrack; and drowning in your eyes."

"Then I will weep not at your tragedies."

"Nor clap our comedies?"

"Why no, lest with my plaudits I should overset your pinnace. For I see 'tis overigged."

"Thou mermaid—" And he halts, dismayed.

A sword dance of words: they weave, lock, draw. Then silence and a fall.

My Lady speaks: and all that is abrupt, unpolished in the girl in her is grace and maidenhead. She speaks; and what she spells is true:

> But thou art mazed, sweet fool. The wood is dark,
> And I th' moon's daughter in these rags of cloud
> Shall bear thee light.

Tom o Cloud now takes the shepherd's part, his face alight with awe:

> The lady goes with me.
> For that her star is wandering, I name
> Her Perseis . . .

A shrill voice shoulders through the crowd. "Annot? Thou's wanted."

Pipe-and-Tabor shrugs. "Now pat there comes a nurse: and our catastrophe."

As waking from a trance, the green girl stirs and sighs; she gathers up her skirts. "Anon," she calls. "I come." And off through the rout of rustics like a swallow.

Flown.

The fiddler beats his fist against his palm in fury. *Craws eat me.*

They look where a wintry dame, stark upright, beckons from a great chair by the hearth. The green girl curtsies to a man in black, white-headed. Old as Slae. His great rings glowering like a stithy, like a handful of coals. On the table-carpet at his side, there lies a viol uncased. His reedy voice o'ercrows the company. They hear the triumph, not the words.

The Second Witch scowls. "I doubt they've chained her to yon death's head. They'll cry a handfast now."

The fiddler breaks a sword of lath.

And at the door, as if old January's fist were gloved in snow, there comes a muffled knocking and a cry.

The players' Lady turns. "Here's winter come a-begging fire. Shall we hear these country clods their interlude?"


There's a green bough hanging on the door of Grevil's hall. Three times the Fool brings down his wrenstaff—crack!—upon the stone, so that the ribands dance, the bird flits wildly in his cage of thorn. Hob Hawtrey's men cry out, *Sun's in Ashes! Let us in.*

And they call for the maid in the lilywhite smock, who trips to the door and pulls back the lock. Ashes that was Margaret schools her face in due solemnity. It's Sukey's turn, the youngest, in the pride of her silver pin. The keeper of the sill. She plays to her.

But it's a stranger at the door. A qualm: is Suke ill then? in disgrace?

But Hob's her father and the Fool sees nought amiss. *Ye mun let us in. We bring t'Sun.*

And the maid, a young madam—she's a look of Nan about her—eyes them up and down. As an afterthought, she bunches up her skirt and bobs. *Yer all to wipe yer boots, mind.*

*Aye, Road's mucky. All them stars.*

*And shut door.*

In sweeps Mag Moonwise to a solemn music and she clears them room. Oddly, it crunches underfoot. Shards of ice? The Fool slips backward, in extravagant dismay. He dances on the air; recovers.

In comes the gang of heroes, some trampling and scuffling clownishly, but the most of them curvetting, coltish in their pride.

They sing their calling on, and it is glorious: great-rooted, evergreen. It raises roofbeams.

Ashes enters, last of all.

So this is coming home. Half strange already, re-estranged. How small it is, and bright, ablaze with candles. Green with holly. And so great a company within, so many faces. The master of this hall must keep his Lightfast handsomely. She looks about the hall for Grevil and for Barbary.

And sees herself, as in a glass—that pale red hair, that cruel dress—at Corbet's side. He holds a cup to Margaret's mirror, to his bride; and she must drink.

Star-crack and shattering: a heel to the heart. Then deepless cold beneath. It takes her breath away. And rising, scrabbling at the edges of the here and now, she thinks: *But I am Ashes.*

And slowly then, a dawning: *Annot?*

It is Grevil's hall: she knows that. Here is here; but when is now? For the meddling aunt is here—again or still?—unwithered now. Unwintered. But the bridegroom is as old as ever. Old as January. Lord of winter and my lady's huntsman, with his shot and snare of dearth, death, cruelty, and sickness. There is always a bride for him, a new green girl, as there is Ashes, over and again. They reign in hell.

Even in her thrill of fear, she thinks: *but Annot got away.* And then: *Will I?*

Old Corbet turns to her—to Ashes?—beckoning. Holds out his cup. A conjuration? *It is ritual*—she'd have it so—*to greet the Sun.* But in her blood and bones, she knows it as a spell, to bind his once and future thrall. Unwilling, shivering, she is drawn to him: a step, another step. Within his orb, as in her glass, sees a ghostly retinue: his train of brides and boys. All had drunk to him, and all were eaten; they must dance. A step, and he will swirl her in.

But at her back, she hears the loud bewailing of the Fool: the play goes on. Recalls her. When she turns to look, he signs frantically at her: *stalk, stalk.* It is her office.

Slipped in among strangers: an alien, a ghost, a spy. A cheat. Would the

company cry out on her? Demand their own invested Ashes? Think she'd
stifled her, that phantom other? They don't see her: they see Ashes with her
soulbag. She's her coat. Made bold by anonymity, she prowls among them,
stalking children to their dens. In cupboards, under chairs, behind an apron or
the linen-press, or halfway up the stairs. Some flirting with her shadow; others
cowering; some struggling in their mothers' arms.

But stalking, she is stalked. Now in and out amid the revellers, old Corbet
edges up to her. At every turn, she turns from him. At every twist, he tails. *I am
Ashes: we do not conjoin,* she thinks. *You are not in my ephemeris.* A knot of company is
now athwart him, rallying. They clap his shoulder, calling out their lewd con-
gratulations. His bride is young. He is fortunate. And she—! To sheathe him
to the hilt, to take the measure of his puissance. Bear his sons. At every halt,
they drink to him, and he must take his rouse. They none of them see Ashes.

*Are they ghosts then? Am I?* No question, Corbet's real: like Annis, he is
absolute. She tries it in her mind. A place—the sky, a ring of stones, this
hall—though fortune level it, is still the same; time changes. Or else *where*—
space—travels, like a ring on a strand of silk. She runs it back and forth. She
loops the string.

*Where I stand is why.*

*And souls?*

If she's a ghost, she is corporeal, embodied: she can touch the children,
cheek and chin, her fingers slithering in their snotty tears, or gritted on a
brickred rage. A bellowing. She sains them with her thumb, she smutches
them, much as a shepherd raddles lambs. This child is one of Ashes' flock.
Death, pass by.

*. . . in a vixen's belly, in a babby—and they's woe to snatch, worse than honey . . .*

The nonsense is the same. There's comfort.

Now some raffish lads—that pack o gallantry that Hob cried down?—
come sauntering round to watch. Sleek idling fellows, more or less, half in
and out of women's tire. Goddesses dishevelled, slumming it. Constellations
offstage. Capon-crammed, wine-drunken, in their stitchery of silk, they watch
the husbandmen at work.

*. . . wi' an urchin in its mouth!*

*What, no mustard?* says the first of them loudly.

The Fool looks sharp at him. *None, for your mam eats sausages wi'out.*

*Fool's not bad,* the second says.

A scrape and clatter. Madam rises from her chair in anger, and the gabble's stilled. The guising falters for a beat; then at her nod goes on. Her servant slips to Corbet's side, she whispers urgently. A glance at Ashes: *Later*. He is retrograde.

And yet another child peers out at Ashes from behind the tablecloth. There is a giggling, clapped short, and then a humping wriggling in the rushes, like a mole at work. She cannot stay.

But ever as she hunts, she turns: and at the inward of the labyrinth is still the great conjunction of the myth. So many planets in one house—the sky at what ill-fortuned birth? First, the lord of the ascendant, old baleful Slae and his Perseis, his bride: scarce April when he bears her off. Bright Perseis, the errant star, is mutinous: storm clouds her face. Behind them sits the whited moon: the bawd, the panderer. And at her knee, a wan young woman, near her time—as full of child as the plum is of the stone—who pleads her sister's youth, in tears. She coys a child in petticoats, who twists away in loathing of the man in black. Who treads a garland at their feet, let fall. And then like some attendant moon, a young man who is elsewhere, or he would be: in his garden, say, engrafting his new apricocks or down a long pleached alley at the farthest end from all this potherment. A green thought in their shade. No seed of his, this crew of quarrelers, he seems to think, but in-laws merely. Slips.

But then a sweet-sharp sort of body, like an apple-john—an old retainer—says, *Master, 'tis t'wrenboys come to halse us all. Will you not attend?*

Reluctantly, he rouses, turns to the brangle at his board. *Come, shall we hear their catastrophe?*

The crowd is closer now, attending eagerly. The players too: but they dissemble. *In comes I, awd baggy breeks,* says one. *Then mingle-mangle with their yardsticks, and the shaking of the sheets.*

And another, *'Tis their mystery now. Snick up*

Stately, Hob commands the very eye of Cloud. He raps his staff, and bids the champions, *Walk in.*

> *In comes I, bold Knapperty*
> *That were born of high renown*
> *'Twas I that slew t' Scarry knight . . .*

*And brought his breeches down,* says the slighting player.

*'Twas I who fought Rinosserot*
*And brought him to't slaughter*
*By that I made his buttons fly*
*And won my lady's daughter*

*Who's great with child by him already,* says that player. *And will spawn a Sun. See, he brags in her belly.*

*If that be he of noble blood,*
*I'll make it flow like Ranty's flood*

Clish! clash! and down the braggart tumbles. Now only Leapfire stands. In comes old Lightfast who will slay his son.

The nurse tugs Ashes' sleeve. *Mistress?* In her voice is the oddest mix of deference, affront, and worry. *Will you come? You've not sained t'Master's heir.*

Last of all the bairns, she finds the child in petticoats. He's in the wainscot parlor, kneeling with an open book before him on the floor. She knows him.

*We're Ashes both of us,* says Noll. *You're black. And I'm green.* He looks at her. *Does the coat come off?*

And Margaret that is Ashes thinks, *I chose you. Long ago and now. I will.*

Elsewhere, the lath swords clash; the hero falls.

She cannot speak; but she foretells him. At her beckoning, he lifts his face to her. With her thumb she smutches him, on lip and brow. She draws the sign for *sky.* She cannot change his lot, but only prophesy. He is what he was born to be. Though he will die, and leave no kindred of his body, yet his book will live. She marks him out for solitude, for study and regret. *Live and long.*

The fiddle tune begins. *Will you see them dance?* he says. *They are most brave and curious.*

By two and two, and in and out, the guisers dance. They heel it to the small pipe and fiddle, and the thrubbing drum: three tunes. An eerie music, edgewise and ecstatic. They dance with longswords, weaving and wheeling, doing and undoing thresholds, henges, doorways, and at last a knot of swords.

"Ah," said old Pipe-and-Tabor, "but thou shouldst have seen our Mistress Master Morland leap my lady's part. Five-and-thirty year agone, that would ha' been, and Master Grevil there in petticoats. There's none such now."

The fiddler said nothing.

"There's few enough that keep old Law." He knocked the water from his reedpipe. Few to play, and fewer still to set them on. This job would be their last this season. Then wakes and weddings to the hobnail rout, for pence and barleystraw and broken meats. Then nought.

No companies now; or none of quality, his mistress' journeymen. None sworn. Chance men, all of them, rogues and gallowsclappers. Here's my Lady branded for a quarrel, and his cully dead. Here's their Second Witch whipped naked at the cart's tail, he that got a squinch-eyed goblin on a punk. Here's that fiddler that they'd picked up on the road last Hallowsweek. Stark shoulder and a melancholy in his wits. They griped him, and he played a-scrawl. Ah well, their last was hanged.

He sighed and thought of all the witchboys—witty striplings—that he'd taught to play. Their clever tongues.

"Pack up," he said.

And still the fiddler gazed. At nothing. At the guisers' play. Eight or nine clumping lackwits and a red-haired Ashes. Her? Would the fool sweep her chimney?

"What art thou agaze at?"

*The bright hair burning through the ashes. Bracken in the rain. Too far. She's run too far before him; turning back, she bids him on.*

"A ghost."

"Well, I see a quart pot. And the road."

I see a ditch and crows.


Leapfire lay dead in straw.

When Ashes that was Margaret turned there was no child in green. No gallantry, no grief, no huntsman. Nor no great conjunction of the planets. Time had changed the sky. But here was here, and there was Grevil, looking dazed and faintly worried: like himself. His face was smirched with ink or ashes; he was taking notes. And there was Barbary in state attire, like a great frost. *Now* was now. Still Lightfast: for the guisers held the floor, Hob's men. Their mystery was at its crisis. In a moment, it would be her entrance.

"O my son!" cried the Fool. "My only son and heir is slain. Call for a midwife!"

The Sun was trying not to laugh. Perhaps his wig tickled him.

And from the circle in the smoke, t'Awd Moon crowed, "Aye, get thee up, lad, and I's gape for thee." Smirking in her beard, she hoisted her petticoats. "Here's an undertaking."

"Here's a covert," said a ranting lad who peered up her skirts. "Wi' a vixen in't. And eight nine ten young cubs would have a gooseneck for to grease their beards."

"Nay, 'tis an imp-tree of apricocks."

"Up with your petticoat, have at your plum-tree!" Back to their long-practiced lines.

Mag Moonwise set her spectacles askew. "Here's prigging of orchards. An thou bites't at me codlins, thou's find a great worm."

"'Twill make me a rare apple pie."

"Not wi' out mustard," called the Fool.

Here too was gallantry, though down at heel: three witchboys, black, white, red, in fripperies. And there was Madam. At her nod, they swaggered through the crowd; they elbowed. There was one in cap and feathers, sauntering, hand at hilts: a termagant. Her buckler was a dish. Ashes gazed, uneasy, at the second witch, a whitely wanton in a haze of huffcap, and an antick gown of green. There were twigs inwoven in the torn brocade, so many pulled and ravelled threads that it looked like green bearskin or an unmown lawn. With sheepmuck. But she knew that gown. She'd seen it but a moment since, and thirty years ago on Annot. And she knew that bloodnailed hag, the third unseely sister. Knew what deity she mocked, who could annihilate her with a breath: a mawkin Annis. Strolling up disdainfully, from east and north, they broke the guisers' circle. Walked unbidden in their room: the threshing floor where lay the bones of Barleycorn. They perched.

The guisers gave them black looks. Nudged and kicked them. But to stop the guising were to ruin all, hay and harvest: so the play went on.

Beyond the circle, Barbary quirked her chin. The hinds and shepherds nodded and moved in.

Cap-and-Feather squatted by the corpse.

"Here's a knocking i't cellar. Here's a bird flies up."

And Bearskin chanted, growling out, *"The wren, the wren, the king of all birds ..."*

*"Although he is little, his family is great ..."* sang Bloodnails in her glassy voice.

"Shog off," said Pipe-and-Tabor to his fellows. "Clear away. Let's have their mystery clean through."

"Who pays thee?" said the player witch. Half-drew her dagger. "They're clart-arse hinds. We're masters."

"And we once were journeymen," old Pipe-and-Tabor said. "And servants to a greater mistress. Keep thy pence." He stalked off. The shepherds let him pass.

Hob's men were stirring up like bees.

"Put up thy steel, for shame," said Grevil. "Here is holy ground."

The player sheathed; but kept a ribboned chopine in the ring: so Ashes might not enter, so Leapfire might not rise. "We do but game." A dazzling complicit smile. "I hear that your mastership dotes on the quality. Would you see us play an antimasque? Of Slae and Morag? Hulver in his cups?"

"Come away, man. You're drunk." A second of the players' men, the stiff-armed fiddler, took her elbow. The witch in her wavered, slid away. A man in tinsel glared and staggered, swaying in her heels. Fell back a step. The ring renewed itself. "Cloud ale's what you want," the fiddler said. "Away and drench." Then he turned to the guisers. "Go on. We're naught to you, all bravery. We jig for coppers and oblivion. You bring the Sun."

Three kings out of Lune and three of Law hold up their knot of swords—O how the wheel becomes it! See, a marvel in its making. Witchcraft. Now they tumble it from hand to hand. Bold Leapfire that outfaced them all—braved Lightfast and his gallantry—he's spellfast by it and he stands amazed. They coll him with their knives. Still dancing, though the fiddle's silent, and the pipes; the drubbing of their feet their drum. They've ringed him in a running wheel. And all at once they draw and down he topples in the rushes. Dead.

Crouched behind the kist, the Ashes child bites back his cry. The bright ale's burnt away in him, all but the headsway. And the dread of edge: the tale is fathomless and he will fall.

Has fallen with the murdered Sun. His slayers stand, aglow like stithies, soot and ashes sliding down their sweated cheeks. Bright crowns. Their black rags settling, stirring in the draught: the door stands open to the year. My lady's crows. He should clap them from the corse, cry out and clap them; but he dare not for the wintry Sun: old Lightfast with his boneface smiling and his burning hair, his great arms bloody to the shoulder. He bestrides the corse. *O where shall we our breakfast take?*

The crow lad rocks and mourns.

Now the black-browed Ashes steals beside her dead Sun, kneeling; now she takes him in her lap.

Awakening, the bagpipe brangles. Cockcrow.

*Wae's me*, cries the Fool. *Cat's kitted and me eldest father's son is dead. His daughter lies in straw and like to die of toothache. And wha's to milk t'ducks?* The company howl and mock. The crow lad scowls at their impiety. *O willow day, and where's to find a gossip for her lying in?* And he runs about: he looks up the chimney, under the cat. He tugs the maids' aprons and they turn away. They're laughing.

In comes Mag Moonwise, brisking with her besom. The Fool follows wailing and wringing of his hands. *O Mistress, you must come til Ashes! For she's got hersel wi' child by Winter and she cannot lighter be.* He tears his hair away in handfuls, scatters straw. She sweeps it up.

*Aye, bedstraw's what comes o green gowns.*

Walking on his knees. *O Mistress, she will die of her bellyful.*

*And what wilta give?*

*My belt wi' three bright stars.*

*Dead leaves,* says she.

*My cockhorse then, that's siller-shod.*

*I's a besom for to ride away.*

*Me fiddle and me bow.*

*For a ship? But I's eggshells for to fleet.*

*Then I's nowt nobbut mesel.*

She peers sidelong through her glazes. *What's i' thy peascod?* And she ferrets as he frisks and dances—*Oh! Ah! Ooh!*—pulls out a pouch and bacca pipe, still burning, and she sticks it in her mouth.

*And which is it?*

Turning on the wriggling giggling maids, she pokes and kittles with her broomstick. *Aye, it likes thee, does a bit o wood. What's brooded up thy petticoats?*

And she rummages up Betty's skirts, pulls out a rotten apple. *Here's a brave babby, by his red nose, aye, he braids of his mam.* Bet smirks and blushes. *And a squinny, same's his daddy, aye, a brave lad wi' a spade*—they elbow and jeer—*aye, here's catching o moles.* She cowdles it and dandles it and chucks it by the chin; then bites it through. The women shriek. Cheekful and mumping, she hurls away the core.

Now up Gill's smock. A string of black puddings.

A mousetrap from the missus' fork. That makes the crow lad laugh, unwilling and amazed. The men stamp and whistle, crying out, *Snap! its head off then.*

*What do she bait it wi'? Bacon rind?*

*Cut cheese,* says Awd Moon. She ferrets in her bodice for a tit—a turnip, earthy from the ground—and munches. Tosses it to the Fool. *Here, carve thysel a head.*

And turning on her heel, she's elsewise, like the moon that hags. She crouches, casting shade on shadow on the walls. And now she takes the wren's cage in her hand, the ribands stirring in the wind of January like a witch's hair unbound. Its shadow is her other self, her sister. Now she goes to Leapfire's birth. She'll sup him with her ladle and he'll rise. But she halts; and stooping, prods behind the meal-kist with her staff.

*Here's a rat.*

*'Tis Ashes' brat,* the maids cry out. *She hidden him.*

*He's ditchborn.*

*Winter-got.*

*Himself's his father.*

*Why then earth owes him, for he's of her blood.*

The old Moon hales him out, upholds him stricken in the smoke and shadow, in the lickerous light. For all to see: his white hair and his nothingness. Unsouled: an emptiness enfleshed. There are no words now: one roaring in his ears. Ashes opens for him like a bearmouth, bloody; like his grave. They give him to the earth her lap.

*Now,* says Ashes, and she kisses him with open mouth, and takes his breath away. She strokes his cursed head and clips him to her body. Rocking, rocking. *Now. Lay me now.* But Ashes cannot speak. She tells.

So he is dead.

The stench of her: earth, blood, ashes. Wench. He's pissed himself; it mingles, scalding, with her pelt. Her wolfish coat's undone; she bares her tit to him. Slackwhite and the starting nipple, bloodbrown as a flea. He gapes at it, the godthing. Quick he turns his face, wries round; but with her ashy hand, she pries his mouth, she puts him to her dug. He would spurn it out of awe and loathing; but it hards him. Kindles will. He burrows in; he suckles in an ecstasy of need and rage. He bites it in his blissful fury.

And the blue milk spurts, though she's a maid. He fills his fathomless with her, he wins, he wins, he wins.

But she's Ashes, and she's stronger.

Kneeling up, she twists and clenches: with a cry she looses him, asprawl on the rushes in a gush of blood.

Stunned, he sees the sky turned over and the striding stars: the Fool, the Fiddler, and the Swords. And Lightfast with the knife that cut him from his birthright and his ecstasy. The winter Sun his midwife and his death. The old god hales him by the heels, upholds him, over and again, forever.

*Done*, the old Moon says. *Undone.*

*And all to do.*

*Let's finish,* says the Sun. It whispers in his ear, *Crows eat thee, cock and eyes.* Then turning in his splendor, lordly to the crowd, he calls out.

*What have we?*

And the voices cry, as in the harvest field, *A neck! A neck! A neck!*


Her part is silence.

Ashes—any Ashes—takes the dead Sun in her lap and cradles him, soul-naked, for a moment still. And sains him—eyes, mouth, heart—with ashes. But it runs like water on his wan and bloodied face. Is milk.

He blinks in wonderment; he lifts a hand before his eyes, as if she dazzles him. As if she were the Sun. He wakes.

"I were headed and I rise to dance," cries Leapfire, springing up.

And as many as will take hands for the Wakesun, serpentining through the great hall in a mad maze of carollers, and out into the fallen snow. The Fiddler plays for them, astride the starry sky. They shout his wake.


A cold awakening, the fell beneath him stiff with rime, the scent of burning in his blood. Cold out, the ashes of his needfire, drifted on the wind, un-whited by the whirl of snow. Will Ashes lay with winter, naked in her lap. Had died in her, his mouth upon her hoarwhite breast, his fingers twining in the sootblack heather at her plash. Gnarled roots and deepless water. Wellspring. In the blackest ice, whitecracked, worldstarry, he could see the glint of metal, frozen fathomless. Tellings. There were men's souls drowned in her, beyond his reach: a blade, the rowel of a spur. His ring, still falling, like an ember, like a wintry sun. His soul.

And there were voices in the air.

*. . . white bones . . .*

A cronying of crows. They'd pick him clean as stars.

*. . . when they are bare . . . the wind sall blaw . . .*

Far far away he heard the stamp and jangle of his slayers, and the small clack of their swords. His death they tumbled slowly hand to hand, aloft: the knot of swords. His blood was beaded on their music, on the threading of the pipe, the drum that halted with his heart. They took the white road upward.

Frost on fire, ashes on the snow.

It tasted of her body, salt.

A cry went up, like reapers in the corn, the last sheaf won: *In ashes! Sun in ashes!*

Light rent him, and he woke.

No lap. No lover. Gone.

He knelt up. Shadowless about him, white on white, was Law. He knew the road that he must take, his journey. Not the sun's road, Lightfast to Leap-fire through the wheeling year; but the soul's way that spanned it, whiter than the haloed moon. *Yon road's what Ashes walks,* awd Jinny'd said. She'd told him all the stars that run from dayspring to the verge of night, the Gallows to the Scythe. He knew the steadings on the way, the fields intaken from the nightfells, from the starry commons: Mall i't Wood's, inby of morning; Jinny's Fold, outwith; and yonderly, the Lantern and the stony keep of Law. The stations of the soul.

He knew his part; had kempt for it at leaping of the scythes. Not this ae night, but evermore, for ay and O: the dance. And there began the wheedling of a little pipe, a small drum's thud. He followed.

It was all to do.

## Lyke Road

A white stone. Whin sworled it in her palm. Beyond her in the shadow lay no hall, no witch enthroned—that semblance gone—but a waiting silence. But a dark. It drank of Whin. Drank soul and memory from her shallow cup of skull. Cracked marrow for her tales. All else of Annis but that lust for otherness, for story, was unstrung and scattered. Gone: but for the braid of fire that strung, restrung her endlessly, that fed her will. *Nobbut game,* thought Whin. *A pair o lasses sat ont ground to play at cockal bones. Turn and turn: here's toss.* A stone like a seedling moon, moonwhite against her earthblack, bloodcracked hand. *Blood's thy road.* She closed upon it. In the silence, she began. "Once afore t'moon were round, and on a night in Cloud, there were twa sisters . . ."

In Ashes' dream, the Moon brayed bones in her mortar, for to paint her face. The whiter still she daubed it, the bloodier she grew. The hungrier: so hunted for the bones to to crack, to grind, to daub her haggard face. She followed through the sky.

A pounding. Margaret that was Ashes waked, lay still and shuddering, unknowing where she lay. Her bed. Her bed in Jinny's house. The pounding in her heart. Still dark. It could be midnight, morning. They had fetched the sun, but he was slow in coming from his cellarage. No daylight yet to leach the terror from her blood.

Again the dreadful pounding: from without. A stranger at her door. A death. It had to be. She pulled the clothes about her ears.

Again.

And hooly, hooly, she rose up, put on her office with her coat. No more. Then with a candle, barefoot in her shirt, she slipped the lock.

There stood Hob Hawtrey in the sleet and wind, bareheaded, with his black hair and his jacket white-dashed like the bark of blackthorn, and his lantern cold out. *Ah no.* He tried, but he couldn't speak: as if they both were Ashes. But he shook with urgency, as if he ran to fetch a midwife or a surgeon, not a layer-out. He would not look at her, averting with his out-turned hand. Her face. She'd washed it. Even in extremity, he was abashed to look on her, on Ashes in her naked face.

Kneeling at the hearth she sained herself; then swiftly dressed: she gathered breeches, undercoat and stockings, boots and cap. No comb nor mirror now, not if she told. But a coal from the embers, a candle from the ark. Her lantern.

By the moon, they'd parted not an hour since.

They ran.

Sukey opened to them, barefoot in the slushy hallan, and in caught-up clothes. She hurled herself at Ashes, flailing with her fists. "Witch! Annywitch!" she cried, and clawed her face. "Yer didn't sain him." Ashes caught her wrists. *We were coming here tonight,* she couldn't say. *Hob had it all laid it out.* Sukey wrenched herself away, sobbing.

"Hush, love," said Hob. "Thy mam's poorly."

And others of the Hawtrey daughters bent to Ashes, whispering, "She nobbut turned to blaw t'fire—"

"Dad were guising."

"Like that—and he'd slipped her."

"Skirring on t'ice. See'd us do it and he wanted. It brock."

Ashes closed her eyes. As if she fell with him, she saw the black ice whiten as it tipped. She saw the witchboys thwart the guising floor. They broke the sky. Yet Ashes then had worked her mystery in play, had cradled and the Sun had waked. Not here.

Candles in the room.

Deb Hawtrey sat in the rushes with her white-headed boy, quite still, and sprawling on her knees. No lap: she was as great with child as she might go. Her cap askew, her hair half down her back in cat's tails.

She was singing him to sleep.

> *Of his needle, he made a spear,*
> *Benjamin Bowmaneer . . .*

"Love? Here's Ashes."

But she held a finger to her lips, and lulled him.

> *Of his needle, he made a spear,*
> *To prick that flea through the ear.*
> *And the proud tailor rode prancing away.*

> *Of his thimble, he made a bell . . .*

Hob knelt beside them, touched his son's cold cheek, the curve of it. He kissed his lips. No breath. He bowed as if his heart were crushed within him; but he did not weep. "My heart is in the ground." He stood. He had an ashing in his hand, a coin. The smallest of its metal: but of gold. "His name's Arkenbold."

She told the Sun.


Between sleep and waking, elsewhere on that Lightfast morn, the crow lad saw himself: a bright ring in the ashes. Night's journeyman, the winter Sun who walks the road beyond the world's end, over and again. Dayteller. In his setting were the moon and stars.

The god that he'd lain with was vanished.

He rose and went on.


Coming down by Askrigg, bleak and early, Kit—of late, a fiddler with the journeymen, no more—saw a skirmish by the bridge. A young boy set upon by boys and fleeing, pelted with a hail of stones and ice. He skidded on the scree and was down among them, flailing.

"Hey!" In a stride, Kit had two brats by the jackets. Three scattered. "Mob crows. Five on one."

Wick as an eel, one spat and twisted free and ran. From the bridge, he called, "Players! Set dogs on yer."

"Tell our dad!" snuffled the other, writhing under Kit's arm.

Kit said, "Is yon thy brother?" Silence. "Off wi' thee."

He turned back to the stranger boy, crouched warily, shielding his face. Snow ghosted him. For a eyeblink, Kit saw Whin at the sea's edge. *Thou ask at my son.* He sleeved his eyes. Not her son, of course. Long years too young. But like Whin, black as thorn. Another scatterling, a starveling brat. As common as brambles here in Cloud. Ice in his dusky hair, and a trickle of blood. New bruises on old. Rags. Running from his master, thought Kit. Happen from a bad place to a worse.

"Where art thou bound, lad?"

"Away." A norland accent, back of beyond. Eyes blue as mussel shells. A fisher boy.

"Hast bread?"

"I can get it."

"As well now as later." Kit undid his budget.

"I's not begging," said the lad, and stood. "I can work."

Green as April. Kit looked about the bare fells. "Scant fishing here."

"I can run. And carry. Scrape trenchers." He looked away east. "Is there work?"

*Whoring. Thieving.* "For crows. There's lambs dead yonder. And witches hanged."

"Oh."

West, then, or south. Kit thought of travellers who might want a boy. Nick Stiddy's lad was blinded, falling in his forge—or was pushed. A sullen and a smouldering drunk, old Stiddy. Not with him. Cull Marrybone's last moll was bearding, he'd be after a downy. No. And little Tom Stormcock was hanged for a lamb. As good drown.

"Canst thou do aught else? Weave? Thack?"

"I can play yon dub and whittle," he said, pointing at Kit's pack. Pipe and tabor.

"Canst thou?" Kit beckoned him under the lee of the bridge. "Play's a tune, then."

Blue hands. He breathed on them. Then flat and fingers, he thrubbed a beat, three and two; then played *Cats Kindling*, twice through, at a whisper. Not perfectly in voice: a thready sound, shrill and plaintive, like a marshbird. Sandpiping. But with changes. And in time. He looked at Kit.

Who looked at Thea, like the afterimage of a flame. *Do you steal children?* she'd asked. And long ago he'd answered, *Some run away with me.* None since.

"But this day's bread, I've nought to give thee. No roof."

At best. Scant work behind him, with his melancholy like a black dog at his heels. Small work ahead. The journeymen's master had packed him off penniless. No company would take him now: they'd banned him with old Tabor for

a lurching turncoat and a malapert. So that was it. A hireling at wakes, if that.
A sturdy vagabond, for all his bad shoulder. Gallowsmeat. And anywhere he'd
ask for daytell work, they'd know him for the players' fiddler, and a killsun gallantry. They'd broken the guising, and a bairn was dead. He'd best move on.

"Flayed 'em off." The boy looked where the gang had fled.

"Boys. Were they men, they'd've drubbed us both." Or worse. He'd been
whipped at the cart's tail, from dalesend to dyke.

*No hope then,* said the boy's face.

Kit shrugged. "Come up. I know a shieling." He held out a moon's penny.
"Here's for thine earnest. Clap hands." And so done.

"Hall'ee, Master."

"Kit Crowd. Hast thou a name?"

No answer.

"Come up, then, Master Drum."


At the crossroads, Grevil swore. Coming from the Hawtreys in a sleeting
rain, he'd fallen. Frost-nailed though she was, Rianty'd stumbled; though he'd
righted her, she'd had him off. And was away, affrighted in her kittle wits.
At nought. Some marish phantasy, some hobbyhorse. As if a ghostly sort of
guisering had met her in the lane and mopped at her. Shook ribbons of the
snow. As if the way from Imber were the Road.

He fished his hat up from the ditch and looked about. Near dark. The sleet
was fulling out to snow. Nought broken, but he'd had a flailing in his fall. Had
landed on some fickle ice that broke. His clothes were half soaked through;
his hat was quenched. That was bad. A long walk home, round Nine Law.
Gainest over it, but like to come to grief: stray, starve, or tumble down. Back to
Imber, he thought. Tom Shanklin's wife kept Lightfast well, and brewed good
wakesun ale. He could dry himself by their fire. Send Tom for the grey.

Not Hawtrey, who was dazed with grief. A good man. Weeping for his
pretty goslin, up and down, and fretting for the Sun. For who'd bring it? For
there came a man to rake the ashes and the year would die. And who'd wake
it? Though his fellows—Mag Rendal the farrier and little Arkady—assured
him, over and again, that they would dance. Still ashes in their hair, as if in
mourning. Solemn now. But still he fretted, crying out, his son, the Sun. Alas,
poor pretty child, poor rushlight: he was drowned. That fickle ice. And all
about the bier was greenery and candles of sheer wax. The scent of death was

honeyed fire. Small comfort in their master's calling, Grevil thought. He'd done his best: brought spice and candles for the arval, ashing silver for the tale. Left Barbary to wake with them.

As he turned back toward the little hamlet, afoot, he heard a jangle, as of harness. Not his mare: this came from yonderly, up Nine Law. A horseman? If it were, his horse was air. For he heard no clattering of hooves. And who would ride that hill of glass sheer downward? Grevil turned and squinted through the dazzling gloom.

A shadow in the snow. A stone? This side of Imber? Were they walking from the hill? And even in his shuddering, he faintly smiled. His nurse had said the Ninestones danced at Lightfast, when they heard the fiddler.

*Will I see them dance?*

*Aye, and a hare will carry thee, there and back, and thy spurs of silver and its bridle all of gold. When stones hear crowd.*

He called, "Who's there?"

His question always: but the voice was not the antiquary's, curious, amused. It shook.

"Who's there?"

A fire in the sleet bloomed suddenly. No sound of striking flint. A lantern. By its sway and shivering of light he saw a breeched and booted figure striding lightly from the hill. It jangled as it came. A rough coat like a shepherd's, and a lapwise cap. Not one of his own men. Not of man?

A silver light about its head, a hag.

There was Imberbeck between them. Running water. But even as he clung to nursery tales, as to old Tibby's apron strings, he heard the silence of the river. Stayed with ice.

Lightly still, the waft leapt over it. She bid him in a rough small voice.

"I knaws thee, Noll Grevil. Thou's been Ashes."

Dusk. Ashes made haste to the trey stone. At her elbow, gabbling at her silence—there were some took mute for mad—the second ranting lad led on. Kin Kempery with his lath and tatters. "Guising's to gang on. Y'll see. 'Tis all new-vamped." No answer and no pause, as if he jumbled both their parts. "Moon's to play t'Fool, yer see. For Hob's sake. We's been 'hearsing it up Fiddler's house—nay, not Owlriggs, it were changed. I's take yer there. Not far." The way from Ask to Owlerdale.

She hurried after.

Through the daggling of sleet, she saw the torches now, the knot of men. She saw the blot of ivy on their pole, a glimmering of whited hair, outwhited by the snow. The Fiddler. She was in among them when he turned to her, all silent in his mask of bone.

Behind her, all around, she heard a stirring and the clink of metal.

He raised his vizard on a mocking face. Old Corbet, smiling like a rennie fox.

"Mistress Ashes."


Under the lintel of the low door, boardless to the wind and snow, was fire. Mainly smoke, but Grevil, nearly starved with cold, cared not for that. Nor vermin. Crouched over its faint glower, jealously, like dragons with a hoard, were two dark bodies: beggars sheltering from the storm.

"Halse ye," said his new companion, stamping at the threshold. "Here's a drowned man and a ferrier would borrow fire." The beggars shrugged them in. She set the lantern down.

Grevil saw a man about his own age, neither fair nor brown, in middling clothes—no tawdry, but the offcasts of an artisan—who might be light and quick but for a stiffness in his shoulder. At his side, a sloedark ragged lad. Chance met, by need of fire? His boy? The man rose not to Grevil's entering, but stared in horror at the goatshod ferrier, as if he'd seen his walking death. His eyes were drowned in dark.

Grevil knew that face. To swage the awkwardness, he said, "Wert thou not that fiddler but a night ago? That stood champion for the sun?"

Astounded. Not a word.

"And got no penny by it, by this lodging. 'Twas honorably upheld. I looked for thee, to recompense, but thou hadst gone." And Grevil fumbled for his purse.

But the boatman said, "'Twere fairest if thou paid in kind."

"Please you?"

"I has work for yer. A guising." She was busied making up the fire to blaze, and setting on a can of ale. She tossed a budget to the lad. Bread and cheese. He fell on it. "We's drink to Leapfire, and I's set yer on."

Still the fiddler was stone; but Grevil said, "My thanks for your offer"— somehow he could not *thou* her—"but I take no hireling's wages. I am master in this hall—"

"And where's this hall?" said Brock. The shadows wavered on the walls. "Thou's master o nowt. A nutshell. If a worm can lord it where he gnaws. And thy lands are t'length o thee, thy grave."

Grevil said, "I know as you have told me. A soul goes only in a borrowed coat: we are landless all, but only Tom: his coat is Cloud."

"Thou's studied, Noll." An approbation in her eyebrow. "But then thou's been my journeyman, and sworn."

"I made no vow," said Grevil, but uncertainly.

"Nay, thou sealed wi' me lang since. When thou were Ashes. Since then thou's lated all thy life for her, and for a player's coat o Cloud. Now they—" She shrugged at the other two. "They's runned frae't. And three makes up my tale o men. Kit Crowd, Noll Nuttycrack, and Imbry Ask." She nodded at the three in turn. "Thou's lain wi' me, thou's slain for me, and thou I brought to shore."

Grevil said, "Slain? I've harmed none that I know."

"Thou's hanged a lad but two months since. For nowt. His yellow hair."

"Did he not flee?" said wretched Grevil. "I pray he was not ta'en."

But she turned his own words back at him, his sentencing: "*If I wrong thee, I will take thy road.*"

"'Tis a form of words. A ritual. For some." He raised his face. "But I spoke it not in play."

"So thou's to play it out."

At last the fiddler spoke. There was a quaver in his voice: but as a blade still quivers in its mark. Whether grief, hate, fury, horror, Grevil could not tell: a white intensity.

"I'll not be a knife in your hand," he said. "My lass is dead. Our child is forfeit. And I am slain each moment since."

Brock tasted of her brew. "There's men wi' knives that go about to slay t'Sun: and so he rises. And would not if they did not."

He acknowledged. "It is so. But she is dead."

"And Ashes," said the traveller. "So of her ashes will an Ashes rise."

*Riddles?* Grevil thought.

"'Tis a play," the fiddler said. "A cheat. A jugglery of knaves. I've crowded for them."

Diffidently, Grevil said, "I've seen it true. I was Ashes."

And the fiddler bowed his head and laughed: not shrewdly but amazed. "What, you? Were you a player then? Did they run off with you?"

"A boy," said Grevil. "And mine aunt did make an interlude, to please the company. I sang." He looked a long way off, remembering. "But in our hall there was a masque of players. And truly they did wake the sun and moon."

"Ah, but there are none such now," the fiddler said. "All bravery."

Brock said, "All but my journeymen." She ladled out the ale; she held her cup to him. "Would thou raise thy green girl's daughter out o Law?"

"With all my soul." Which lighted all his face—how young he was—and clouded then. "Is't possible?"

"No journey but to travel."

"Then am I your knife."

"It's a fiddler that's wanting. But t'dance is hers."

They drank all round, and swore it by the Road.

"But we've no Ashes," Grevil said. "I am disbarred."

"Ask t'lass," said the traveller, pointing with her chin.

"Not," said the boy, and scowled at them. The men gaped foolishly.

"Thou is and all," said Brock. "A wave child. Cast up on Selbrow in a storm."

Grudgingly, the child admitted, "Aye, Marrit found me. Ca'd me Kist."

"And then—?"

"She sellt me to Slawk Betty, and she bound me til an Ashesfast. Blind, so I led her."

"Begged?" said Grevil.

She looked scorn at him. "Tellt men's fortunes wi' her plash. Wives, when they willed to breed. Wenches, when they'd not, to rid 'em. Boys for practice. Had a mind to whore me, so I run away."

Grevil, horrified and curious, was noting this. An *Ashesfast.* So she that erstwhile had her will of all must give her will to anyone. Selbrow, did she say? A bad old custom.

"So thou's not been Ashes?"

"I's not bled." She braved it for a glance, all honesty; but at a gaze, her courage sank. Her brown cheek paled and burned.

Brock took her by the chin and held her gaze. "Thou was to ha' been Ashes, and there's souls in Law for thee, untold. Black shame on thee."

"There's always Ashes," said the sullen girl.

"Or else there's never spring. A cold year i' Selbrow it's to be."

"Then Ash me."

"At Lightfast? Nay, that's done and done," said Brock, and smiled her little knife-flick of a smile. She turned the girl about as if she were a pot to mend; she rang her metal. "But I'll prentice thee, young Imbry Ask. I's make thy gown o green."

"So, am I for Tom o Cloud? Or he?" said the fiddler, all journeyman now. "If we're to be Sisters, then we must have wigs."

"Which is Lightfast?" said Grevil at the same time. "What of Leapfire?"

And "What play?" said both.

Brock set down the empty cup; she stamped the fire out and banked it. "There's nobbut one. Both halves of it."

"What, with three of us?" the fiddler said.

"There's players ont road this night. All journeymen: and they must come."

They went, all three, with Brock before them. Grevil lagged, half weary, half enchanted, all at sea. For the snow, he could not tell their path: but uphill all the way. Then *somewhere*: pales of shadow in the snow. He looked about him. They were at the Nine Stones, where the earth had opened, and the green child come.

Brock stamped three times at hollowness, as if there were a door. And Leapfire in his crown of barley let them in. They walked between two stones, and were—not *else* but anywhere: a sort of stage. A blank on which the story's stamped: a crowd, a ship, the sun. True coin of history, though the metal be sheer gold or leaden. Room to rime.

There stood his lovely boy, his merlin. That he'd given to the gallows tree.

Who took no heed of him, but rounded on the fiddler. "Thou's not to be Leapfire," said the lad. Updrawn like a candleflame. "He's mine by right o't ring. I kempt for him, I kempt 'em all. I beat."

"I'd not dream of it," the fiddler said.

The crow lad looked about the circle. "But here's no Ashes."

"There's to be," said Brock. "She comes by another road."

He turned that over. "So if she's laggard, then I never rise."

"So it looks," said Brock.

"I's hazard it. I want a thwack at Daddy Lightfast."

They do say, *When the door is opened to the wind, up leaps the candleflame.*

Now at last he looked at Grevil. Not his face, but at his sword. "I's need that." And he took and put it on.

The fiddler turned to ask their master mistress Brock the way.

There the lantern stood; but she was gone.

No word: but all at once they drew. And all about her, at her throat, there flashed a knot of swords. Of steel. Ashes saw the torches glinting in their blades, as if the fire licked them and it bled. Across and cross her, eddering: a hedge of steel.

And she felt nothing, nothing but a bluewhite fury: *I have work to do. They will not end it. They will not.*

The mistress of the witches now had doffed his guisering. Put off his mawkin Annis with her ropy fleece of hair. Unmasked of Corbet. Stood himself alone: Jack Daw, that some do call my lady's huntsman. But his hunt is only for himself. He smiled.

"Here's the moon come down to me," said Daw. "Herself in her white smock. Is that not brave? But her darkness likes me better: in her wane and on her back."

He turned to his antimasque. "Tonight we play the Moon in Ashes and will foot it at her wake. I call the dance: longways, for as many as will."

They belled like stags at that, they sounded and they stamped.

Still none would lay a hand on her; but fenced about, she needs must go. Borne off in howling triumph. If she stumbled, then they drew the halter of their knives still closer round her neck.

All about were torches twisting, flakes of fire whirling up like leaves. She saw his rantsmen only in torn snatches, in and out of light. They all of them went masked, in red or yellow, or in black, in fells and feathers, and their stench was bestial: hags, stagheads, boars and bulls. All wreathed in ivy, or in misselcrowns like spills of seed, with staves and antlers ivy-garlanded. Some few had birdskulls braided in their hair. And one went all in tattercoats. Of yellow leaves? Not leaves, she saw in horror, but the hands of children: flayed, beseeching. For a tail, a snakeskin of a cock and balls. She knew the player witches by their tawdry: Bearskin, Bloodnails, Cap-and-Feather. And she knew a ranting lad, a boy that had these two nights guised with her: Kin Kempery. Who would not look at her, who could not look away.

When they hear his fiddle, they must dance: the dead of soul.

They led her to a threshing floor. They'd left the great doors open to the wind, for Lightfast. And the snow blew in, in wraiths arising like the chaff of summer, like the ghostly murder of the sun.

Still the rantsmen would not touch her. She was still death's heir and vicary, her voice on earth: and she was holy.

"What, flayed of Ashes?" Daw cried out. "Like mewling children hid behind the door?" They shook their heads; but none stood forward.

"None of you have cocks? Then I'll unsain her." Lightly, Daw struck down the ring of swords, and stepped within their circle. Knife at throat, he stripped her of her coat of skin, upheld it. Brandished.

Still they waited on her voice to ban them all, cry out, bring down a fiery whirlwind on their heads. But she was mute.

She had another adversary. In her mind she saw black flakes of ashes of a burning card—the Tower—drifting down. But almost at the ground, they wheeled and winged, arising as a pack of crows. They hunted.

"Hah!" He shook her godhead, as a terrier a rat, and tossed to it to his men. How they gnarred at it and worried it, like dogs about a wounded bear; but could not rend it.

Bolder now, he slashed her other garb—her jacket, breeches, shirt—to ribands on her back.

Still mute. For this was not the nakedness she dreaded most. Now even open-eyed, she saw the ravens seeking for a way, a windeye, into here and now. They must not spy her out. She feared him, soul and body; but she feared her grandam more.

"I see my lady paints," he said. "Yet Ashes will to ashes go, for all thy pranking in thy glass. It ill beseems thy bridal bed. Come, Madam. I will have thee naked." And stooping he took up a handful of the sharp-edged sleet that puddled at their boots and scoured her, face and body, to the fork. Between. Cold filth ran trickling down her naked breasts, that stiffened with the chill and loathing of his touch.

Still mute.

Arms wried behind her back, he turned her to his men. "Look. Look. She swelts for it."

Lust, awe, horror, and contempt. A goblin glee. And yet—

"T'other bitch were blind," called out a man.

"We'll come to that," said Daw, still smiling. And her soul was cracked. *O my stars.* "But first I'd have her see our play. And last of all."

He cut the soulbag from her neck. Undrew the string and rummaged in it, brisk as a midwife in a brothel. Even his gang were silent, appalled by the blasphemy. That hoard of souls might be their kindred, lovers, friends. Their fathers and their mothers, bent with laboring; a brother in a far-off war; a green girl, much beloved, who had died unwed; a child newborn whose only tale was Ashes'. Hinds and shepherds, maids and tinkers, artisans and lords. He spilled them on his palm. All dust, the golden lads and girls. The tawny ring? Not there. He picked among the trinkets, toyed with them; he tried a child's ring on his fingers, longman, lickpot and his horny thumb: far too small for him. But here's a pretty coin of gold. He licked his fingertip to pick it up, no bigger than an elm seed: Arkenbold's. The Sun's. He glanced at Ashes, mocking openly. "I rolled the orange on the rotten ice. Thy Fool was in the way."

At that she tried to curse him, break her vow: and she could not. What she could utter was a speechless shapeless noise, a tongue-slit twittering. *Tu-whit. Tereu.* And at her gibberish a great fear lifted, and they mocked.

"She'll not tell tales of us."

"Aye, there's better uses for her tongue."

"Think you my lady will have gloves of her?"

"He'll take her arsy-varsy then. Your kidskin's dressed with dung."

Bloodnails laughed for admiration. "Here's a fiddle fit to play our mystery on her bones. An she be set in tune, the crowd he makes of her will wake the dead."

Daw let them triumph for a space; then stilled them, held her open like a sack.

And she was powerless. Her struggle was with Annis. She was holding back the storm of her, as if she held a nightmare by its mane of lightning, in the ramp and plunging of its madness, thundershod. She choked the bear deer vixen burning child within her that would out, the black hare and the crow's outcropping. In the cold flesh of her body she could feel the raven quilling out: a monster, barbed and taloned, brutal. It would own a raven's apprehension, knowing only flesh and gaudery; but a woman's body, cold and perfect to the nethermouth, the bloody and abhorred fork.

He spoke now as a priest, a hierophant of hell.

"Earth gapes for you." Black silence. "See ye not this narrow road in her, so thick beset with thorns and briars? That way did you come of Law, and that way will descend, no more returning, to the underworld. That road is death."

His rantsmen groaned like branches in a storm.

"But this ae night, this Lightfast at the dark of moon, when Slae doth lie in Ashes, joying in her lap, the lord ascendant: on this very night, the way lies open, and the passage back from death. Who takes that narrow road with me this night, will live immortal."

She was holding back the earthquake now: a wood of lightning, thunderstroke on stroke, that all at once would outburst through the very stones—through her—and shatter them.

The rantsmen stamped and chanted now: one word, one word, one word.

Daw undid his cock. For all his cold and finical contempt, his mincing malice, he was stirred: his rage was at his fork. It stood to blunt and batter at her privities.

But first he'd pry her soul.

He seized her by the hair to pull her down, and howled. She felt the runes in it uprising in a whelm of power, like the white-hot embers from a forge. Unwilled. The hammer falls, the sparks fly up.

He fell back in a fury, cradling his hand.

Everything had stopped: light, time, space. Here. Now.

Then Bloodnails spoke. "Unwitch her."

Annis dreams. Her knowing is untellable; but in her sleep—unmoving, open-eyed—is fire. Whin feels it, braiding upward endlessly. It seeks her vengeance for her daughter's treachery; it seeks a vent. The earth will crack of her, cal-cine; the sea like molten glass will slump and shatter, falling endlessly within and in her void. Not ocean but a snow of salt. She would consume it all, to swallow up her faithless child. Her sleep is fathomless: the grave, unbirth, abyss. Her waking will annihilate.

It was braided in her hair, the witchery. It crackled like a fire of thorn, it spat and rang. It must be cut.

There was a sickle on a nail. Turning back for it, Daw spied a glitter, like a bit of ice, amid the rag and ruin of her Ashes coat. Unthawed? He picked it up: another witchery, of glass. No power in it he could feel but in her pain. So he held it up to her, and mocked her through its O of ice. Then cast it down. He cracked it underfoot. Again that wordless cry. It joyed him almost to the frenzy. Down he thrust her, naked, in the slather and the shards of glass. He set his knee upon her, pulling back a great bunch of her hair, as if he would cut her throat. But no: he sheared her godhead. Hacked it off like straw. He rived it in great handfuls, roughly, with his sickled knife, and cast it to the winds.

And at a whirl each handful that he strewed was fire, scattering bright, uprising on the air; each strand of it unbraiding into light, and fiercer light, as if the wind were bellows: red to golder red to sun at noon. And brighter still, bluewhite. Ablaze. A storm of light, like starfall but arising. Fire flaughts. The rafters of the great barn were a sudden sky, a fret of fire.

And down upon his witches fell a riddling rain of fire, a hail of elfshot. Cinders of the runes. The men shrieked and cowered, cursed and howled. Some stayed to beat the smouldering harvest out with snow, and kick it cold; most fled at once: not now his standing gang of heroes, but a rout of running men.

Shadows in the barn. *Plock. Plick.* The last few clinkers of the magic fell and scarred the earth.

And there was nothing in his hand.

Undone.


Ashes leaps up laughing, in a flare of ecstasy. She catches up her coat. Daw's done it. Thinking to unwitch her, he's unbound her with his sickle, set her free of Law. *Undone. And all to do.*

She calls upon her sisters, *Ashes! Ashes!* And they all rise up.


The wood was overgrown, thought Grevil, since his father's time. By day he could have walked it endlong in a dozen verses; but the new-called journey-men had staggered round and round it for a candle's length, hallowing and brashing to affright the urchins. Puck-led and perplexed. There was a good path up Owlriggs: but no. They must gang by Unleaving, so Brock had said. By candlelight.

*When yer come to't door, y'll have found it.*

*What door?*

*There's nobbut one. Thou ask at Mag Moonwise.*

He bore the lantern. And perhaps his eyes were dazzled: for beyond its burr of light, he thought he saw a drift of leaves, the shadow of an endless fall. He thought the snow was moonlight. When he lowered his candle, he saw a slushy little copsewood, ending but a stone's throw from his hand. Perhaps the lantern made the wood.

Kit Crowd came scuffling up to him. "But thou art mazed, sweet fool ..." he quoted; and then ruefully: "This wood *is* dark."

"*And I th' moon's daughter in these rags of cloud shall bear thee light.*" Grevil finished it. "Why a lantern, then, if not to see?"

"If we be stars, we bear it to be seen: so lantered men may gaze on us and say, *By t'witches, I's drunk.*"

"Go we blind, then? Do we company their rouse?"

"Being stars, we stray not, for the Road is broad." Kit looked about. "Have we tried yon marish path?"

"Twice or thrice. It ends here."

Kit rimed, reminiscently:

> *My tower's where thou'lt never find.*
> *They's left me a thread, and I walk and I wind.*

"If stars," said Grevil casting back, "then the Silly Sisters: fools by heavenly compulsion. And the girl, by her despised petticoats, twice Ashes." He looked about for her: a scowling silent little impet, black as thorn. There, in among the scrogs.

"And the lad must be Leapfire, so he says—yon sword's a great argument— and being light of heels, then Tom o Cloud. I hope that he be quick of study."

They looked where crow lad practiced with the sword, in his private ecstasy. "The rogue will have the edge off that," said Grevil; but his heart leapt with the lad. A painful joy. *Alive.* That he unwillingly had sentenced: yet had done. So was lost to him. "And I the Fool."

"And by this kit of catlings, I the Fiddler. So our play is fitted. Like the tinker's ass, three legs and one eye blind. For it halts with no villainy to whip it on."

The crow lad swashed.

> *Stand forth, awd winter, fell and black*
> *And fight, or thou is flayed.*

He danced beyond the candle's limen, in among the wafting leaves.

"How does he that, that tumble?" said Kit marvelling. "In a wood, no less." With an updragged branch he tried the swing askew of it—*I will dance the light of leaves*—and tripped himself up. "But how would he know the play? It is the gallantry's sworn mystery."

"And in books," said Grevil. "I have read three or four of it; from Lune even." He looked at the crow lad. "I wager he has not."

They called the stripling and the girl to them. "D'ye know the masque of the Silly Sisters?" *What gentry stuff is this?* said their stares. "The Witches?"

"Cracked t'sky," Will said warily. "Them?"

"Know'st thou the guising of it?"

Now he was shocked. "There's nobbut one guising, time out o mind and evermore. It's t'*guising.*"

They asked silent Imbry.

"They stown away her Comb and taken Ship wi't."

"Ashes?" Imbry shrugged. "Her Comb?"

"Stars." She pointed up at cloud through branches. None the wiser. So she took a twig and scratched the pattern in the snow. The Crowd of Bone. "Called storms wi' it. For soulwrack for her shore. But I's not heard on a guising of it." She scuffed it out. "There's carols for't Ship."

*"The sail's o th' siller, the mast's o th' tree,"* sang Kit to her startlement. And aside to Grevil, he said: "Elding play from Arrish. That won't be in books."

"It could be," said Grevil. "There's that fallen oak again."

"Comes round like a burden." Kit pondered. "So: will it do in halves, this play? Or must we put it back together? 'Tis like an egg in flinders: it will hatch no cockerel to crow the sun."

"Patch it?"

On they travelled, in a hey of plays

*I will dance the light of leaves.*

*Stand forth, awd winter, fell and black . . .*

*. . . The lady goes with me. For that her star is wandering, I name her . . .*

*. . . Leapfire bold. Walk in.*

*But thou art mazed, sweet fool. The wood is dark . . .*

*. . . in a vixen's belly . . .*

*His dreams do prick him . . .*

*. . . and they's woe to snatch, worse than honey.*

*Let him in . . . .*

*. . . in a bear's maw . . .*

*. . . and he flowers.*

*By that I made his buttons fly.*

*O rare Cosmography.*

*. . . wi' an urchin in its mouth!*

*I will dance the dayspring.*

*What, no mustard?*

*Still I dance the ay and O.*

"Enough," said Kit. "'Tis not a play but a gallimaufry. It wants a frame." He thought a pace. "Tom's the hinge—no, Tom's the heart of it; Ashes is the hinge, it turns on her. Like so—" With steepled fingers and his thumbs he made a three-cornered figure. "Here's Witch and Witch and Ashes at the point—"

Grevil did likewise. "—and Ashes and Fiddler and Fool." Point to point they met and twisted over, gimmaling like guisers that would make a lock of swords, a star. It encircled an imagined sacrifice. They drew.

"And so he tumbles down," said Kit, "and rises up. Both of him."

"Yes," said Grevil. "Yes. Could we do that?"

"Not as we are. Still only three of us." Kit looked at the lantern. "That candle's near out. Have we another?"

"No."

"Our play is like to be brief, then. With a bergamask of bones." Kit hunched for cold and jigged a little, dolefully.

But on a sudden, Grevil stamped. He would have struck his hands together, but for the lantern. "But look you: down he tumbles, Tom o Cloud, and off with his coat then, and rises up Leapfire. Guising underneath."

"*Yes,*" said Kit. "'Twould play in dumbshow rarely well." Then he clapped and kicked the leaves up. "And when he lies in Ashes' lap, she doffs *her* coat, and rises up in green. She springs."

For a moment Noll looked inward. "And happen green Ashes and the Sun may wed?"

"'Tis then a comedy," said Kit. "And so a jig and done."

"So may it fall."

The lantern snuffed. But they were standing in a kitchen garth, within a hedge of thorn. Imbry was putting snow down the crow lad's jacket. And a moon was setting.

"By trod," said Kit, "how came we here?"

"From elsewhere," Grevil said. Noll spoke with Tom's remembered voice. "*Here is Law. I would be elsewhere, were it on a sinking ship, atwixt a bear and honey.*"

"*Is the sorceress not here?*"

"*And happen at her book. I would not for the moon disturb her.*"

And she is running through a cloud of Ashes. Before her, white in white, they rise, as if she's breathed them on the air: a hey of girls, whitesilver as a wood in April, frost and flowering. A blackthorn winter. She is woven in their dance. Like thorn amid their blossoming, her ashen black and bloodstreaked self enwreathes itself in whiteness, in the mingling of the may. A garland, all of Ashes.

Turning back, she sees the steep of heaven, like a hill of air, of crystalline: sheer nightfell. It's the way she's come. She sees the endless snow of stars beneath her, giddying. Far far below her in the fathomless, she sees—O marvellous—a toy, a plaything from a mage's baby house, a bluegreen bauble like a seeing-stone. Or like her own eye looking up at her, an iris. Cloud in cloud inlapped. She laughs for wonder.

*Where I stand is why.*

She's on the Lyke Road, in among Nine Weaving. In her glass. What she has seen with it, now is: a myriad of Nine. As if her seeing of it made this *where*, this *now*. A wood upwelling through a map. *O rare Cosmography.*

And still inchoate. From an Ashes, all invisible as air but in her edges, silvery black, there rises up another Ashes; from *her* nakedness, another still, unbraiding from her body in a silver frost, subliming. Sky of sky. In each of them, in knee or shoulderblade, in brow or cleft, there is another silvery wood at dance, another flowering of light. In their becoming is their perfectness, their everlasting in their birth. Here is time's nursery.

*Will be its ashes?* But she puts that thought aside.

For now and ever now, she dances with her sisters to a silent music, to the Crowd of Bone. Itself and all alone it sings, at Lightfast: when the Ninestones hear, they carol. In their myriad is grace, enwheeling her: a power not of regiment but commonality.

Turning in the dance, she sees one who is otherwise, who dances like a flame of fire in the mist. But she is elsewhere always, here and gone. Or she is any of them, lighting as she will on any, as she does in Cloud. As ever, she's the last still burning, who was Ashes first of all. Their ember. Last of all of them, her daughter sees the crescent of her, turning always from her sight; she sees the quenchless fire of her hair.

She runs after.


Black-thacked and skew of timber, this cot has a louring look. The journeymen stamp and trample to a halt in the up-churned yard. *"Cold by the door and my candle burns low . . ."* says Grevil, trailing off. Bold Leapfire hawks and swaggers; green Ashes sleeves her nose.

"Seemly, seemly, Master Drum," says the fiddler; then something changes in his face, a light and shadow. Softly, ruefully, he says, "If thou's a lad, thou doff thy hat, see."

"What now?" says Grevil.

"'Tis the Fool his office to knock; and the Second Witch to conjure."

"Am I that?"

"Turn and turn. We'll cast for it."

"Talk then. Yer t'grammary," says the crow lad. Not fondly: but he speaks. Grevil looks backward at the scuffled snow, that is crossed and overcrossed with footmarks, like the writing on a page. What's said can never be unsaid. Unsentenced. He begins, *"By the elding of the moon ..."*

The door opens, and a fierce small person in the Awd Moon's petticoats peers round it, like an owl in an ivy bush. Leaves of tatters and a leaf-red cap. Owl's beak and elfshot eyes, redoubled in her glazy spectacles. One glass is cracked. It gives a scornful and a mocking twist to that eyebrow.

"If it's guising, yer a bit few."

They look to the Fool. He bows to her, with backswept hat and hand at heart, louting low as to a goddess: to the Moon.

"We bring the Sun. All else is mummery."

No hilt to finish up his flourish at.

Kit bows. The crow lad, capless, jerks and hinges, and the sword pokes sideways. Imbry, with her cap in fist, ducks.

She looks them up and down. The strangers to the world, bewildered in it, yet the ones who made the game; the child the ship brought over; and the flaycraw. Landfallen, lightborn, lost. It happens over and again

"Yer late."

Grevil rises. There's a mischief in him now. "Mistress, we were much amazed. Your wood is riddling; and no maiden came to light us hence."

"Get in with yer."

They duck after through the low door, into heaped and crowded otherwhere, a looming dusk. Her workroom. In the dim and glimmer, slowly, Grevil makes things out. Or up. A fire, with a canting cauldron. Swags of washing or of cobwebs, maybe? Chaos and old nighties. All her mending and remaking, endless. Are they baskets of hailstones? Creels of cloud? Her carding combs are snarled in it; her spindle faintly gleams. Leaves, feathers, eggshells. Lanterns in the rafters, and a sickle hanging: and low as her roof is, Grevil knows he cannot reach them down. Here is earthsky. The Unleaving.

The lad is still casting about for a guiser, for some horny-handed smith in petticoats. "Is Master Moonwise in?"

"Moon's what I is. Would thou beard me?"

In the flash of her regard, he winces; but he stands his ground. "So yer Ashes like, Mistress? It gangs round yer?"

"Aye."

"Will yer dance?"

Grevil gapes horrified. And yet it tickles him, the thought of froward godhead frolicking in garlands. *Here's an undertaking.*

"I'd not set foot i' Law, else there's a thunderclap, and nowt hereafter. She's where I's not." She sets her besom in a corner. It roots and branches. "But I's swept t'Road afore yer." There's ale on the fire; she ladles it out. "Now drink, and I's fettle yer, and set yer on."

Grevil watches as the cup goes round. Imbry's avid and unwilling, scowling at the taste: as if it were the thing of naught that changes everything, desired and despised. The crow lad, Kit are tranced, twice-tasting of each drop, as if the draught has wakened echoes in them, memory or dreams: *I know this; I remember now.*

When it comes to him, he raises it to Malykorne. There stands her cross-patch avatar, her mask of irony; here lies her true reflection in the cup, brimful of her: sheer light. *"O light, and genitresse of Light, that walks Night-mantled, taking Heaven for a maske ..."* He drinks. It tastes of hallows and his death. Would make him poet, take his voice: and all at once. A whip and halter to the soul. He will wake for it, weeping, all his life.

The eyebrow in the cracked lens quirks at him.

No words now but a childish rime. His nurse's. "I see the moon, and the moon sees me ..." He's forgotten. "Hally us all."

"So now," says the Moon. "Off away, when yer kitted out. Here's properties."

"What, have you stuff for a guising?" says the fiddler. "For a masque?"

"Whatever's i't sky. What yer ask at. Not else."

"By your leave, a moment." The Fiddler and the Fool consult in hurried whispers.

"Busk, busk!" she cries, and thwacks her ladle on the pot.

"A coat of sparks," says Kit.

"A cap of tatters," Grevil says.

She beats the fire so the sparks ·fly up; they swarm in the rafters, in the

swags of washing. She pulls down a woadblue jacket, smouldering. "Here."
She thrusts it in Kit's hands; he takes it, warily. But it is cool as lateworms to
the touch, then cold as frost; the embers breathe and brighten, at his shoulders, at his belt with three bright stars. Astonished, he can only duck his head
in thanks.

In a corner is a bunch of withies, red and white; and on a shelf, a bundle
of rushlights in a wisp of hay: the Fool's coat and his cap of tatters. In her
hands they glow a little, faintly: a wistful flittering light. Will dances in the
wisp. Donning them, dithering back and forth, the Fool tries out a line or two.
"O my son!" he cries. "My only son and heir is slain. Call for a midwife!" But
his mourning's for the crow lad's love.

"Witches next," says Kit aside to Grevil. "What d'ye think?"

Boldly, the Fool calls for "mantles of the sky and mirrors of the Sun and
Moon."

She takes great swathes of dusty arainweb, that in her hands are bright
with dewfall, shining as the Road, and pins them round the Witches with her
thorns: petticoats and scarves. From kist and cupboard, hook and nail, she
scrabbles out a clanging armoury: kettlecaps; stomachers of cullenders; grat-
ers for greaves. Here's a rusty great frying pan for one, a ladle for his sword.
Here's a sickle for the other, and a sieve and shears.

Bemused, Kit studies his unreflection in his pan. "They are beardless boys
who play this."

Grevil gazes in his riddle; turns it to his fellow. "We are old now, and un-
fair." Men dressed as women dressed as men. Each in the mirror of his other
sees a mawkin: not fair witchery but striding termagants.

What else? *They're lating Ashes, who is yet to come.* "We've a lantern," says Grevil.
"But no light."

Kit upraises a withered apple-john. *"What's within but mirk and mist? But I's a
sun frae Mally's kist."*

"Here's apples in store," says the witch, and fills their pockets, lest the russets run out and leave them darkling.

At the witch's beckoning, Kit bends to her. She pins his mantle with a
clumsy iron brooch, a ring and a raven's head, inimical. The ring runs grating
through its single eye; the beak's the pin. Old, old: and perilous. But tangled
in it is a snarl of stuff from a workbox: threads and needles. A dangling spider
takes his measure. "I'd not game wi' that," the witch says. "It's worked another
time, but ill."

She turns to the crow lad, who glowers haughtily. "I's Leapfire, lord o't dance. And I's a sword will make awd Winter skip. Nowt else."

"Crawing, crawing," jeers Imbry. "Thou dies in a bush. Takes Ashes to get thee up."

"Thou scrog o thorn. Thou lop. Thou limpet."

"So thou's to dance soulnaked i' thy sark?" The old Moon's knuckle lifting up the crow lad's chin.

Hand at hilts. "Sun's what I is."

"I's beard thee." The Moon takes a winnow fan of barley, tosses it; so when he jumps, he's all a flare of gold. The air about him dazzles blue. He splinters sky.

When Grevil can speak, he says. "And he's Tom o Cloud as well. His coat?"

Bending to the floor, the Moon picks up, shakes out a heap of leaves: an urchin tumbles out, offended. Stalks snuffling away. It's a coat of sorts, a wood with sleeves.

"A cup and a staff—" says Grevil.

The staff is leaning in a corner—no, it's rooted there, and branching. It unleaves; and yet is never bare. He's caught a leaf of it, dry, curling. Beech. Hazel now. Now oak, now ash and thorn. Down fall the pale and yellow leaves, and light; their fellows rise to meet them, they are mirrored in the air … He drops the leaf. He's in a hovel, in the smoke. The tree's a staff. When Mally gives it to the lad, he leaps it, swinging round. And still it's rooted, though it travel.

Here's a footed little mazer cup. Wormeaten, with a ring of blackened silver round it. Ah, he knows that cup. They drank of it. Not all the dreams were ale.

"—and a hat with a feather," says Kit.

Drenched and battered, with its broken plume, Grevil's now is fitted for the part. He looks to the Moon; she nods; he gives it to the crow lad with his blessing, lays it lightly on his head.

Now for the silent girl.

"I'd play yon bear," says Imbry, "and I'd harry 'em off."

They stare at her.

"Bear?" says Grevil.

"What bear?" says Kit.

"Thou poppyhead," the crow lad says.

"'Tis not in our book," says Grevil kindly.

"Craws eat thy book. I'd want some Northern stars. Unleaving." She points up in the rafters. "So I'll have yon Bear. And t'Comb, and t'Ship. And if we's not got dancers, then we's best take t'Knot o Swords."

"Aye, that's witty," says Kit, admiring.

"Ship's thysel," says the Moon. "Mind that." And she gives the girl an old horn comb, agrin with half its teeth, and a pair of rusted scissors; then she clambers on a basket on a kist to reach the rooftree, hauling down a great black fell of fleece. There's ice on it, still glittering.

"'Twill be brave as Ashes' coat," says Imbry. "Will I study my part?"

Kit says, "Black Ashes has no lines. You may do it extempore. When Tom is slain, you grieve his falling, in among the leaves." He makes a dumbshow of weeping.

"Colder, by and by," says Grevil sighing. "A gown for green Ashes."

"What's that to be? Awd hay?" says the crow lad scornfully.

And Kit can't help murmuring, *"Aye, bedstraw's what comes o green gowns."*

But Mally takes a nutshell in her hand and huffs on it. It sprouts, unfolding little plaited leaves, green leaves. A gown, as crimped and shining as a new leaf is, and sticky from the bud. Then she takes an eggshell full of milk and drops the shale in it. Plock! A coronet of drops splash up, and fall a garland of white buds.

Rough as she is, Imbry skips; she dons them. Turns. On her, they are a wave, as green as any glass, and crinkling white.

"Let's see thee lady it in that," says Noll, jealous of his part. A girl disguising as a boy disguising as a girl. "Softly now. To music."

Kit takes the fiddle from his pack: a poor crank instrument, and scrannel-voiced. He's nursed it as he could. Bending, he begins to tune. Looks up, as if he's heard a voice. And Grevil sees him see the crowd of bone that's hanging in the roof, unstrung. He looks and longs. And yet he sees in it a greater shadow than mere death. Would he dare speak for it? Or leave it hanging there and live, to marvel and to mourn?

"I'll have yon crowd," he says.

"Unstrung?" says Malykorne.

He nods.

"'Twill cost thee."

"I have paid."

"And will."

He says, "Its playing is beyond my art. Its silence outdoes me."

"Thy silence for its voice?"

Without a word, he hands his fiddle and his art to her.

He knows what road we're going, Grevil thinks. So do they all. As I have known but as a proposition on a page, mathematically; but he with his soul. If A then O.

"Imbry," says Kit, "I'll beg that pipe of thee a little while." He plays green Ashes' dance, "The Nightgrove, or, The Embers Ashes," steadily enough. Imbry paces gravely to its measure.

Noll behind the curtain sees the darkness parted on a glare and clamour. It is time now. He cannot. He will.

"Well measured," says the dancing master.

Imbry nods, all business. "And my part?"

"I'll tell it thee." Light and shadow on his face. He kneels to face her.

> *My mother got me in her glass.*
> *Still as snow on snow I pass;*

She rehearses as he speaks; but overlapping her, as wave on ebbing wave, Noll Grevil takes it up, goes on:

> *But green in greener world I wake*
> *And light—And light—*

He stumbles. Forgetfulness? Or feeling? Kit goes on:

> *And lighter of the dark I make.*

Turn and turn; then as one:

> *In my coming I do leave;*
> *Death of dying I bereave*

"Where got you those lines?" both say.

"Of mine aunt," says Grevil, "that was lost."

"Of my mother who is dead. She made them."

"Her name?" His voice shakes.

"Annot Lightwood."

"Not Covener? Not Fell?"

"She would not say. She took her mother's mother's name for dread of her great kindred." He turns his face a little from the fire, shamefast. "I am lightborn. She knew not my father's name."

Grevil's gazing back in mingled joy and grief and perturbation. Found and fallen at a breath: and dead.

"She had an antick ring of her, which too is lost, of silver, with a posy: *Lief wode I fall, an light wode spring.*"

"That Annot was my mother's sister; thou her son, my cousin that is found."

They embrace. No words, no words.

Then drawing back a little, but to look on him, on Annot in his face, Noll says, "Thou art like."

On a sudden, Kit laughs. "But thou art *Noll*, then. Noll that was Ashes, Noll that took his physic like a soldier—"

"Tales."

"—Noll Hobbinoll that told her histories of the sky." Then looking at his fool's coat and his ladle sword, "So now we're in one. On the Road to Law."

Noll says, "And I am with you to the end. But why?" And in that word is all the road before them and the grave, whence none return.

"My daughter is there."


*Go and catch a falling star,* thinks Ashes.

Gone.

And giddy with the turning, damp and breathless with the chase, she pauses: and at that the light falls silent and the dance is shadows in the mist, is stone. So now and ever now it falls, still so; and yet has long since fallen, and is yet to fall. Time echoes, echoes.

Now is here.

Half naked, but for slashings of her office, Ashes stands amid the Ninestones, at the sill of heaven. She's come where she is most herself: where she can see. She knocks at air.

A girl in a blue gown opens, with a hand curved round her candle. Light spills through her fingers, stills her face: long-lidded, lustrous as a pearl against the cheek of night. Her gown seems made of sky. For all her ornament she wears bright shears. Her hair is twisted in a cloth, a wentletrap of linen, with a streak of dusky hair wound round it, like the bandings on a shell.

*Hallows with you,* says the girl. Not Siony this time. Another holds the candle, and another ever: eldest shifts from star to star.

*And with you, and all of you,* says Ashes. Is it Talith? Or Tiphan?

Turning to the light within, she calls her sisters from the weaving. *Come. Here's our youngest sister from the clouds below. Here is Eldins.*

They gather. All in blue: dusk blue, or deeper, or the liminal bluegreen of twilight. None with fiery hair. They speak in wreaths of words, one twining with the next.

*Ah, you braid of her, your mother—*

*Thea, that is music—*

*Embers of her Ashes, bone of bone—*

*A tale of her telling.*

They have a smock for her like theirs, ungirded, of the greenest sky.

*I am smutched,* says Ashes. *I will sully it.*

She thinks of Corbet's hands. But looking down she sees her body—if it is her body—scoured as with spindrift, all her cuts clean as paper, stinging. They are salt, the Ashes, like an ocean of girls. Not water. When she touches, gingerly, the shorn spikes of her hair, her hand is silvery with ashes. Fire-singed. Burnt Eldins.

But the coat's unchanged: still black as earth untainted, hallowing what's laid in it. Bones and the bright gold circling them, or fallen from the ears, like seed from barley. It is Ashes' lap, who lightward travels, greening. A generation of light.

They dress her with their deft hands. Though the gown is of air, she cannot see herself through it: yet if she walked before the moon, its light would shine through her, the gown and all. She eclipses nothing. Is she bodiless? One brings a bowl of milk, and one a riddle cake, unshared. And thankfully she finds that she is clemmed with hunger, dry as straw; can eat and drink. She sups. They bid her to their workroom.

*It is nearly done. Will you see?*

And walking in, she stands—*O heavens*—lightstruck. For their web is marvellous, beyond her telling. See, the Lyke Road's on their loom, the green world and that other woven with a mingled skein. Unleaving and the lowering stars that rise and set, the sun and moon, and all the storied sky. The scattered leaves bound up.

*It still is weaving,* says a leafgirl. *Still to do.*

*Ashes tells the warp.*
*A cloud of Ashes, and a Crowd of Bone—*
*Herself and all alone, she sings, her one plaint always: of her death—*
*With her, rough maids on whom the godhead falls—*
*And that great Ashes under Law who sings the stones from Annis' crown—*
*And the warp's of all their heartsblood.*
*Soulstrings.*
*Lives.*

It shifts as Ashes looks at it, the Bear's a Ladle.

All the constellations change like wind on water, wavespell: but the sky's the sea, eternal. For the Nine have woven in it all the stories of the world at once. There's guising in it; there are cards from Jack Daw's pack, high rimes of ancientry, and tinkers' rumors, to and fro, like weeds beneath the waves. There are runes and riddles sunken deep within it, like the wrack of ships: she's read them only in drowned books. From Cloud and Lune, and east and west; and north as far as Scarristack beneath unsetting stars, they come: the ritual and unremembered, silly and unseely, courtly mummery and country matters, light and dark. As if her cards, and all the packs of cards now scattered through the world were gathered back, unwintering, like dry leaves to a tree, now green. As if the pages of her Master Grevil's book—how he would marvel if he saw—were glass, and story after story overlaid.

Here's the Fiddler in his variations, but himself's the tune. He's picted in his tattered guising, in his glory that bestrides the sky: the Hanged Lad and the Hallows Tree, the Flaycraw, and the Sheaf.

Here Ashes walks the sea's edge, to the knee in shadow. To her, from her, endlessly the pale of water shifts. The tide's eternity. Her lantern swings and halts. And at her feet she finds a ring half-buried in the sand. She tells it. Ashes rises from the dark, and at her feet spring flowers: so the Road is white with her journeying. And Ashes sprawls in darkness, great with light, no lighter of her child. The Ravens fall on her.

For the constellations of the underworld are here, and the mourning of the stars that journey in the sky below. She sees the Coffer in the Ewe in Lamb, the Reaper's Attercap. And yes: she sees the Nine in their imprisoning, in Annis' tower under Law, as well as in their exaltation, weaving in their web; and earthwise, as a ring of stones.

Here are bloodnailed Witches from the crow lad's tale; and Sisters from the masque, with their epitome of painted ice; and ballads from the book left open on her bed in Law: "... one king's daughter said to another ..."

And here and everywhere are Norni's tales of the Unleaving, from her island in the farthest north. See, here's the windwife's Comb, that's toothed on both sides: so she brings the storm and binds it, rime and rune. The Road's her Hair. But cludderfolk do call her Crowdybone. Here's the Selkie that can daff her coat of skin—*that's Ashes*, Ashes thinks. Here's the Bear our elder-mother, she that quarrels with the Sea to have our bones, and thunder is their strife. The Warpstones in her Loom are Nine. They've woven Norni's stars who lost them, and her tales, who died untold. She never saw the sky again when she was taken. Nor the sea her strength and lover, and the eldest of her blood. Nor yet the one child of her body, Imbry Ask. She put her from her breast, and set her in a boat adrift: that Annis might not eat her soul.

The Ship's a cradle on a sea of dark. Her milk's the Road.

And here is Law: a girl sits reading in a story, in a garden made of stone. *What is it lives within a maze, within a wall, within a hedge of thorn? And on an island, not a winter's day in riding round. Yet she's never seen the sea.*

But she looks up at it: the earthsky and the sea of fires. On it sails that Ship whose mast is rooted in the dark, and branching into heaven. See, its leaves forever fall as stars, light never on the earth below.

The sky's her self and story. It is all the mother that she has.

And at her back, a voice says, *Margaret, do you see the leaves?*

*Thea?*

She is glass between an emptiness and night, a window for the frost to etch that presence. And it cracks her. She cannot see for tears.

*Are you grieving for the fall of light? Unleaving?*

*Colder, by and by.*

*Yet you will weep.*

*And know why.*

Cold in her pocket, safe within the Ashes coat, she has the other lens. Her starglass. As she holds it out, it fills with candlelight, is gold as morning. *I would know why*, says Margaret. *It's what I am.* Bright Perseis who brings the dawning and the dissolution of the lovely night. Burnt Eldins with her toy of fire. She knows it: she would make a thing as beautiful, complex as theirs, a One-of-All; but in her mind. A tale of numbers that would end their sky.

She's not spoken, but they answer her in thought. *So you will, if you but live.*

And so she would: but now she weeps for Ashes, for the world that will have been.

*Keep your glass now.*
*What you will do with it, will us undo: your mother and us all.*
Still wet with tears, she lifts her face to them. *Then why do you let me in?*
*You're Ashes still, until your kindling—*
*Ashes, and you bring the Sun.*
*The guisers call you on.*
*The weaving waits on you.*
*It wants but a tale.*

The way's through the witch's featherbed. She tumbles them in, and they're otherwheres, anywhere you like. The silly men pace on together, clattering of plays, of Is and Not; but Imbry laughs. She is Ashes, and she has her Will.

*I would thou were away*, she says.

*I care not what thou will, thou whin.* The crow lad struts his sword.

He's made her gown of flowers, so she makes his shirt of snow, his jacket of the sleet. He turns and touses her; they tumble on the moor. The sword's an awkwardness. *Thou hurt. Thou juniper.* He kisses where he's burned with snow. *Thou bramble.*

*Aye, thou chimneysweep. I catch.*

*I's hurtle thee.*

*Thou flaycraw. How?*

Pushing up her smock, he fills her lap with nettles and with violets.

*Now will I, thou ragbush? Will I now?* He kisses. *Now?*

*Aye, now,* says Imbry. *An thou will.*

She makes his horse of January, mounts him on the wintry wind. He spurs.

A daze and dazzlement of cold: the sun in snow. It covers her, it fills her eyes, mouth, heart. She pierces it, she flowers.

The Fiddler and the Fool, the Sun and Ashes, are on the road somewhere. From Ask to Owlerdale, thinks Noll; Kit thinks Hare Law, the way from Kempy Mag's great barn. But somehow in the witch's cupboard that is full of Cloud: she's popped them all in—lad, lass, and new-found cousins—like a bundle of washing. They've talked all this while, the cousins. Not of folly in love, of the tangle of unwisdoms in their family's amorous history—Noll's lad, Kit's lass, Annot's lover—nor as yet of foundlings and of children lost. Not here.

For it still is nowhere, though their lantern makes them room. The Road's no place for winter's tales. Their talk is not of where they're going but of whence they came: the sisters, Damaris and Annot. Their mothers. They remember variants of Annot: maid and mother, dowered and dishonored, Cloud and Lune. But her stories were the same.

"... Tom o Cloud," says Noll.

"Ah," says Kit. "Did she tell thee of Brock's bagpipe?"

"That plays of itself? An I cried, she would call me that."

"Aye, and tuck me under her arm and down-dangle, up and down bravely till I laughed."

"Then was I Tom o Cloud," says Noll. "Locked up in Law, in the witch's glass castle. And off she strides with me, to be the Sun."

*"Ah, but he's for Mally's lap, she haps him all in snow. It's winter and her loom is bare. Wood's her cupboard, and her walls are thorn; her bower's all unswept. Thou can't get in but she lets thee. And she's Tom o Cloud's nurse. But Brock—ah, well now, Brock's death's gossip and she's keys to all locks. Will I tell ye how Brock stole him?"* says Kit, in an old wife's voice. Imp Jinny.

Noll looks back, the way they'd come. Bare moorland. Has it not been wood all this while? And a moon but a moment since? At full? No stars above: they walk on them. And if their lantern fails ... ? Bewilderment. "I fear me I am wood, but cousin ..." He waves at back beyond, where a door might be. "Was that—? Were they—?"

"Our mistresses? Aye." Kit paces on. "They've dealt with me before."

Now Grevil remembers. *Thou's lain wi' me.* Cold awe at that. Himself had craved so poignantly, so long, for but a glimmering of otherness, a foolish fire; but meddle with a goddess? Is he cousined with a myth?

The myth speaks ruefully. "I am something overparted in this play."

Still Grevil says nothing, but Kit answers his unspoken words.

"I cannot. Yet I go on. Like a gossamer, from thorn to briar." Dark all round them and the lantern travelling: a parenthesis of light, a walking interlude. "I would sooner go a shadow. It catches not."

A hill aside of them, and in and out of wood, they hear scuffling and taunts. The others' lantern sways wildly. Then it stills, but their shadows leap.

"Ottering," says Kit.

Grevil sighs. "Is it wise? Here?"

"I think it makes earth of air. As one that's to hang makes air of ocean: for he may not drown." Then turning back, Kit says, "Did she sing thee the riddles?"

"What, kitrum katrum?" Still elsewhere.

"Aye, that. Mindst thou the air?"

Distractedly at first, Noll sings, "I have nine sisters beyond the sea, And these are the gifts they sent to me ..." It's riddles, and a pattering of nonsense, to a tune that catches like a thicket of thorn. It snags him.

*When the Ship's in the acorn, there is no keel ...*

Under and over it, Kit begins another song. Noll tangles, trips up.

"No, keep on: 'tis in parts."

And with a clash of keys like Brock's bag jangling, they start again, and break down laughing. Third time's the charm: they right their reel. Noll sings his pit-pattering. But underneath and counterwise, like the slow part of a round, Kit sings an older patterning: "I have two sisters beyond the sea, And these are the gifts they sent to me ..." His burden's all of trees: a wood for the wanton fire, a world arising through the nothingness of Law, and Noll's dark ship a-sail in it. A spring upwelling through the riddles.

At first, heeding time and interval, they scarce note what they sing; then hearing, they stumble.

"... *embers of a crowd of bone* ..."

The Ship founders. The wood is gone.

"Where got you that?" says Noll.

"Of my mother." Astonishment: as if he's raught in a bird's nest for a egg and found a owl. As if a toy has bitten him. "She got it in her travelling, she said. Of a Norlander."

"Or made it herself?"

Kit upturns his hands. "I learned to prattle it, parrotwise; I had forgotten till now."

"Again, I pray thee. I would learn this part."

Song and countersong, they interweave: a net of riddle under over riddle. It sustains. The world is thin here, cat ice, and the void is fathomless. The Riddles bear them up, all four.

*One is a root in a flaw of stone*
*Two is embers of a crowd of bone*
*Three is kindling in an ashen bowl*
*Four is a shadow with an only soul*
*Five is a trance in a hey of stone*
*Six is a swarm in an ivory comb*
*Seven is a seeing in a silver pin*
*Eight is a souling in a coat of skin*
*Nine is a cauldron of a sickle blade*
*Nought to these is all that's made*

They walk in silence for a space. The wood behind them falls to nothing
like the ashes of a log.

Musing, Kit says, "Here's matter, but confusedly."

"Yet may be rede in it, as in a runish text," says learned Grevil. "Art thou
a journeyman? Of Cloud, that is."

"Not sworn," says Kit. "Nor like to be."

"I have read of a Hallows mystery that was played by them long since, of
Death's Gossips. They bring nine ashings at—that other mistress—her birth.
Might this not be remnant of that mystery?"

Kits casts backward into memory. Her candle low, his mother bending to
the fine fine needlework for other backs to wear; the copies of music for others, idler than herself, to play. Ink on her fingers. Pins in her sleeve. Prick song.
"She did call it the Bear Song."

"Bear," says Grevil. "Bear?" And he calls out, "Imbry?"

Underfoot is no earth. Ashes walks on light, on memory of light, sootblack
and silver like the ashes of the moon. But for telling she would fall.

*I am in my glass; I travel light.* She tells herself her journey, step by step, as if
she's writing in her book. Here is that rift in the Lyke Road, called the Belly
of the Crow, the Crop, the Rattlebag, the Riddlestones. Brock's Bag.

In the shifting sliding of the tarnish is a glint of gold. A souling? If it is,
she hears no whisper of a tale. See there, another, drifted over with the dark-
dust of the Road. And there and there—faint myriads of suns that prick the
nightmoor, dimly glittering. Time's embers. Though a fire settling would sing:
these mortal suns, long cold, are silent.

Looking up, she sees my lady's Ravens wheeling overhead. They know their gain. They follow the seedsman; they follow the sword. So here about her is a field of souls, unfurrowed nightfell, sown with deaths. Unharvested, unsprung.

Stooping—for she would know why—she burrows in the dark. It tingles like a bank of snow, so light that it is merely cold; but the silvery blackness slides away from her. It cannot be held. Shadowing, it edges her with silver, shining like the moon in swift eclipse. It lights her briefly; leaves no stain.

But the coin of gold is real: has form and gravity. Is worn, as if with years of handling. There's a woman's face on it, not quite in profile: turning back as if to call another on. Her metal bears no coin stamp of authority: she looks not lordly but exultant and afraid. As if she ran in ecstasy to meet her death. But why? No telling. She will keep her secret; but she dares you follow.

Another step, another coin. On this, a boy, despairing. His mouth is open in one voiceless howl. And a third, a nullity, a newborn child. They clink a little in her hand. She cannot carry them; they weigh her down. She leaves them in a drift of dark.

And here a potsherd, written over with a fraction of its tale. She puzzles but she cannot read its emblems. Why a red horse? (Broken.) Why a wheel of running hares?

Here, a flint of elfshot, like a knife; and there, a shard of bone. She flinches: she has seen too many in her childhood, under Law. But this bone seems not charnel, but a frame of soul. If it were strung, it could have been a crowd of bone, to sing the spirit's death and journeying. It's daubed with char and ruddle in an ancient glyph: the Nine. And here's a long bone with the Fiddler's belt, the Three: but thirled in it, to make a flute. Unplayed. A cup of skull, from which the teller would have drunk her inspiration. Yet unfilled.

And here, an earring for a sorceress, a sibyl: in a ring of gold, an owl-eyed woman, winged; and yet a striking owl, with hands. Of all of the ashings, this still has a distant voice, still fainter than a dry leaf on the wind. It cries the same words over and again. *Of stone, of stone, of stone.* Like a bird's cry: but its plaint is knowing. It despairs. Ashes, hearing, understands all tongues; but this is strange to her. A flinder of a foreign tale. A leaf, of many, one. The tree long fallen in another world, its leaves dispersed and scattering. That tree was myth. Untold.

Then deep within the sky she hears—has heard unknowing all this while—another voice, half chanting, hoarse, demotic. Ah, she knows that rhythm with her blood. An Ashes tells. The dead souls string their scattered bones with her, they sing their tales through her. And singing, are set free. It's her breath fills the sail, that they might journey.

The traveller stands wondering. Askant, she sees a flickering of light. She turns. Too swiftly gone. But *there.* A spirit rises from the dark, a spiralling of soul like fire. The flower of that field. Another and another rises, briefer than the grass, a braid of fire, soul on soul—and see, the barren field's a meadow, summering the dark.

She is nowhere. She would fall; but Ashes sings the Road, sustains her.


The journeymen walk on. They're out on skyfell, on the soundless dark: a black frost faintly rimed with stars. Far far below them in Soulingdale, the river runs.

The crow lad sees a desolation of moorland, heath burnt over; he sees the cracked stumps of the waystones fallen, girning at him in the mist. He sees the midnight gallows, and the thing on the pole. But Marget's lateworms light him on. And he's steel at his side: that's sun and moon to him.

Kit sees neither sun nor moon; but sees the bright hair burning through the snow, the small face turning back at him, to bid him on. His lass.

Noll sees a greendark wood. He is afraid; but further, ever further in, he sees a flicker like a fall of leaves. Tom o Cloud.

But Imbry looking back sees the Horseman following. Nightshod, his riding makes no clatter on the Road. His mantle, like a smoke of silver, rises, rises from his burning cold: he is made of it, remade. Half turning back, she takes the Comb of stars, and with it, rime and rune, three times she combs her sloeblack hair: and of it, all about him, springs a thicket of its thorn, its leaves of fire.

## The Sun In Ashes

Cold by the door: which is notional. A heel might drag it in the sand. Yet cross that sill and there is no returning: not by any road. A tower of stone may fall; these shadows never.

Kit looks at Grevil, Imbry at Ashes' son. No pipe nor fiddle plays, but the blood's still beating fast between those two, like the tumbling of drums.

Irrevocable.

*I will,* says the Fiddler. *Thou didst last. Turn and turn.*

*Two may ride on one horse,* says the Fool. *Do thou knock and I'll call.*

*Both at one,* the Fiddler says.

The staff seems to branch for them, a ride of thicket of one root; it woods them in a little O, a fetch of fall. Cloud walking. It is rooted, though it moves with them like lantern light, it dips and sways. The leaves forever fall.


My lady calls Morag.

*Madam?*

*My glass.*

For the eighth witch is telling: spin it finely as she can, Whin's thread is near done. She will play it out; but they will find her jugglery, her sleight. For naught.

The old surveilling crow unlocks the casket. Long since they've had sport.

A thunderclap.

All pause: as if the turning of the key has drawn it, or the tale has conjured.

Twice, before the echoes of the first have died.

Three times the herald beats his staff. Three times three times it echoes in the timeless dark and wakes the shadows. *Sun's in Ashes! Let us in.*

In the abyss and labyrinth of Annis' dreams, Whin lifts her head and laughs. *Guisers! By stithy, is they mad?*

And all the souls screak and gibber, like a treeful of birds at a hawk.

*Morag? Go. Harry this impudence.*

She nills it, avid for the glass, the game. But at the hammering and cry, a something catches at her throat, it hooks her like a silver pin and pulls her thrashing to the door: no daemon now nor fury, but a monstrous little fish, blind, spiny, benthic; a fingerling of needle teeth, crushed small by self abyss. That pin is law: it hales her.

*If they come as guisers, you must let them in.*

*Was there not a sea?* thinks Ashes. *Round my tower?* She remembers rummaging through chest on broken chest of sea-wrack, heaped and spilling; she remembers mourning for a congeries of books, sea-ruined. In her childhood was the sound and tale of storms. *I was islanded. I know that.* Here is dry. She's standing in a wilderness of air, unsouled. The voice has gone.

And there is nothingness beneath her feet. She reels.

*Thou flittermouse, thou worm. 'Tis nowhere here. Get on.*

She feels the roundel of glass in her pocket, makeless now. It recollects her in its O. *I do it, so it is. I walk the sky.* She cannot sing her road, but she can riddle. *So: a sea but not of water? What, of time? Of tales?* She claps her hands once, softly; stamps. *Of travellers, of course.* As atomies of spirit, apprehension, will: thought travels where it will, through earth, air, fire, or imagined seas. It arrows on.

The warp is set; the shuttle flies, light swift, beyond the web.

They cross no threshold, but the dark is altered: not vertiginous but prisoning, the cellars of the sky. Out beyond on the nightfell, on the steep of heaven, blackness awes. This inner dark intimidates, it crushes: yet is but an anteroom, a lobby to annihilating dark, the womb of night within.

The crow lad sees a great stone hall where Corbet sits in judgment. At his side, as pale as ashes, crowned with bone, sits Marget, naked as a needle. Flaunting her, he coys her breast, he paddles in her plash with soulringed hands: his winter bride, his thrall.

Kit sees a crossroads on a darkling moor; he sees the gallows tree, sees Jack Daw swaggering with his gang of whores. There's one—O gods—there's one with shorn red hair. A clawed fist seizes on his heart; it drags it through his ribs. She turns, the witch-child in her tawdry finery, the fireship; she kills him at a glance, contemptuous. It mocks the pain it gives. Not Thea, no: her child and his. Their daughter.

Grevil sees his mother in her grave. He looks down on her, her bruised face and the flowers withering. She's empty, open like a coat for Ashes to put on.

But Imbry sees work to do. Her prentice piece. She slips away, as Brock has told her. *Steal it so.*


Imbry eels her way through the maze of passages, all interwreathing, spur and spiral, like a cage of thorns. A net. She slips it, minnowing: that seine was spread for greater souls, for gods and heroes and high witches.

*Keep ae hand ay to't wall,* said Brock: but Imbry knows where the godhead is, same as like fire, only cold. The awe is like a loathing, like an ecstasy: the wound and its cautery, the venom and its trance, as if unwillingly her soul is frenzied at a rape.

*Nobbut Ashes,* she tells herself: *awd coat's what she is.* She's led blind Ashes. Washed her when she's pissed herself; dilled her when she's waked with ranting, rocking of herself and crying out, *There's one falls burning frae a mast. And which is thine?*

*No.* She mun keep her wits about her, like a needle, eye and end, and all follows. Mind her way: *in's ae thing, but out away's another.* Her blood sings in her heart to drown the terror, in a wordless lalling. No cradle song: but in the drub and driving of the tune, it's for the waulkers at the wool, the threshers in the barn. It sings the tumbling of the drums. Mouth music.

The way turns inward to the eye of Law. She feels the seawind of my lady's melancholy, and a few small drops—ah, not of rain. A sliding shiver and a knowingness. A spatter of souls. And she's in a mist of them, a firefog, a throng of ghosts that mingle through and through her, beading in her started hair, and sliding down her spine. Black spirits and white, red spirits and grey. Her milk-eyed mistress. Thrimni who was drowned; his sons. The windwife who had sold the charm. Life-starved, they mouth at her, athirst for what they cannot feel, that cannot warm them. They are thronging at her eyes, mouth, sex, to drink the tumbling of the blood. Cannot.

Crazy with fear, she flails the air and shouts, *Shog off, yer malleyshags. Ash black yer, will yer leave me go?*

Desperately she fumbles for the comb to scatter them like lice; but feels it

sleeking through her heartstrings, sleaving out her fear. It lulls her, lulls her,
though the hand is bodiless, as no hand ever has or will.

*Mam?*

Illusory.

The child, the bride, the mother: shadows all, all air and malice.

Crying out, Kit catches at his nameless child to sain her, and she changes
to a slithering snake, unfleshed. *Hold fast,* he thinks, bewildered: but it's gone
in a shrug of silver, writhing burning through the rock like molten silver in a
snowbank, lightning through a cloud. Quicksilver in its moving; in its venom,
sublimate. His hand's unburnt. Daw and his drabs are punkfire, scattering like
a kicked clump of puckfists, in a smoke of spores.

*Thou's dead, thou crawsmeat. Draw.* The crow lad grips his sword and glowers.
But the daemon and his thrall are mist: not of water but a fume that catches
at the throat, that stops the breath. A bitterness.

The earth has closed about its hoard of bones. *Still dead,* thinks Grevil. *And
will be and be forever. That is no illusion.*

Gone.

All but the maker of the interludes: she slipped the lock; now bars the
way. A daemon, bloody to the shoulder, soberclad: white apron and black
cap. A crow-faced malignancy. Morag: Kit remembers her. But sees her now
unswaddled of illusion; sees her nakedly. She is atrocity. Had love so muddled
him, that fool he was, so mittened up his wits, that he could see this harpy as
a servingwoman, this hell as a castle? He drinks lye to look on her. He sees
again her kitchen, heaped with game; sees her squatting with a hare to gut, that
never was a hare. The clawed hands forage in the blue meagre flesh.

*. . . in a vixen's belly, in a babby—and they's woe to snatch, worse than honey . . .*

Here is Law.

Noll touches Kit's sleeve, questioning.

"Her servant. She that held the knife," says Kit; then looking round, appalled, "Imbry?"

"Stalkin brats," says the lad and hunches doubtfully. "She'd not be held."

Grevil gapes. *Children? Here? In this—?* Then he sees Kit's face. His child. He
takes his cousin's shaking arm, and it is wrenched from him.

The old crow says, "Your suit?"

The Fiddler bows. That mask at least can move and speak: though in it,

Kit is curled and howling. "Tell your mistress that we bring the Sun." The guising looks at her. "And take what belongs to it. The living are not hers."

"Thy whore is dead," says Morag. "Eaten and shat."

All his soul and body rises to a shriek; but his will wears the mask: "I know. I would have my daughter."

"As she is?" The pebble eyes evade him.

The crow lad has half drawn; Grevil's hand restrains him.

"Even as she is."

"As you have bidden, so you must play it out. So Law is kept."

"And your mistress?"

"Will attend no gallantry; but after she will see you paid." Hands folded in her apron. "You will wish for that easy death you slipped: merely to be eaten, soul and flesh."

By now the hall is full of spirits, crowding in, still crowding: lap on overlap like water, fall on fall. If leaves then ill-intended, scrabbling at their faces, avid of their senses, hating them. If water then a blood-dimmed tide.

The Fiddler turns to his fellows. "Now, my brave boys. Once through and away." He takes the staff and it sinews him: he's furled of sunlight, rooted in unsullied earth; he's lapped with bright water, leaving into air. A breath. Another. "Now."

Overturning the staff for a besom, now the Fiddler's the Moon. Light from her imagined lenses glances all about, it dances in death's rafters like a cloud of fireflies. Like Cloud. And she dances too, slow-sweeping round her fellows, driving back the drift of souls, the shadows. Where she sweeps is hallows. Where her sister's not, she is.

The Fool bustles on, like a scarecrow to the stake. But in the players' space, Noll halts. He's overwhelmed. His terror shakes him, even to sickness, and his tongue is dry. Like a shamed child, he's pissed himself. Confusion: what his legs know is a bow. So much: and nothing more. Not his name, his sex, his kind. If he speaks, he will whimper.

The Old Moon brisks round him officiously, brushing at his legs as if she would sweep him up and out. And at the touch of twigs, he feels Tom o Cloud like sunlight on his face, like leaves and light through leaves. And every leaf a word, a page, a story of the world: no tongue he cannot read. *Speak, lady. 'Tis your cue.*

The play begins.

Whin's braided the eighth tale into a ninth, of a witch's daughter. All this endless while she's held my lady in her glass, with gazing on her glittering self; she's stilled her with the comb. It lulls, it lulls her, sleeking out the nightlong hair, soul starred and scattering. Brightness falls from her. They sit in glittering drifts of hailstones, in the blood of souls.

The one is left: my lady's daughter that were Ashes. Kit's lass, that went with child afore she'd bled, and could not bear it for her mother's spell. Old story, that is, but turns out mostly otherwise. If they still lived, the guisers out beyond—poor gaudy fools, cold hail they'd get from Morag and her huntsman—would be telling it. *O Mistress, she will die of her bellyful.* In the guising, the Old Moon saw to that. Undid, and let her lighten of her bairn. A Sun, and every year a Sun in Cloud: but under Law, a lass. And she'll not rise again to dance. Fordone and no undoing her. And yet, thinks Whin, her death's still fiercely brooded, like a living thing. But why?

*Or cam'st thou for my daughter's braid?* My lady's told her what she fears, forbidding her, and fear's both lock and key: as Brock's own journeyman Whin knows. So the braid's what binds her to herself, the virgin to the rock? There are laws to the godgame. *Stone breaks scissors, scissors cut braid* ... No knife. They took that first of all: as if mere smithy craft could scathe their woundless immortality. She did wonder at that. Small chance of thievery without a blade.

Unbraid it? She's tried. This will not sleave with singing. Even but a thought of it runs fire through her nerves; a touch would burn her hand to bone and cinders. Wake the dragon: who would blast, annihilating.

And yet while Annis slept, Whin's wound a coil of hair about my lady's wrist, herself in self involving. Night and fire mingled, bone and blood.

Can't tell her daughter from herself.

Time's past. And having glutted on the guisers, Morag will return, and there's an end on it. While then, Whin tells. Her voice is giving out, a husk and gravelling; her thread is done. Nothing for it but go on.

*What is your nine O? Green goes the Ashes O ...*

She plays as the guisers do, for the sun returning: for time.


He is Leapfire, lord of summer.

Up and down his golden shadow strides the field and rants.

The place is anywhere. The mind, avoiding nullity, will have it *here*: a field, an empty ring of stones, scant snow. It will have illusion; or it mads. All here is emptiness; all but the scythe blade rusting in the fallows, rootbound: that is real. The Road's end. Otherwise is blackness bleeding through imagined frost, a cat ice on abyss. They walk on rime.

But Leapfire—ah, he's glorious, the Fool thinks: like a fire, where he is, is center, and he curves a world about him. As he strides, bright flaws of fire seem to break from him, stream upward like a comet's hair. He flames amazement.

The Sun cries out his challenge in the Fiddler's silence:

> *Stand forth, awd winter, fell and black*
> *And fight, or thou is flayed.*

And the Fool flings wide—no door. There is no outwardness, no hearth, no hallows in this world. Though even nought is bounded, this is limenless. Winter's where they stand, their everywhere: nought else.

Yet he summons it. *Walk in, awd Lightfast.*

Nothing comes. The Fool twists his cap of straw; the Fiddler sighs; Leapfire quivers like a bow.

*Walk in.*

But he precipitates; falls out of air. Sharp-sided, many-faced: he is the scythesmen's witch; the guisers' Lightfast; Master Corbet, glittering with rings; Old Slae that carries off the weeping Perseis; Jack Daw, whiteheaded, all in black, greenblack and broken swagger, like a swung cock at a fair. A pack of selves, and all one self: the Old Sun, hoary with expired light. Old crow of all.

They know him well, though each a face of him. That cold sheer smiling enmity: that will to break. He speaks not to Leapfire, lord to lord, but to the upstart crow lad, feathered out with guising.

> *Onward comes the rope-ripe boy:*
> *My seed, mine enemy, my toy.*
> *Falling, he will gar me rise;*
> *My crows will eat him, cock and eyes.*

Summer deigns no answer, draws; then letting fall his belt, ungirding godhead, he stands forth.

*'Tis Leapfire calls thee into't ring;*
*Lief would I fall, an light would spring.*

Smiling, Winter draws his sword: old steel, sheathed in ruined velvet, scarred with use; bright only at its edge, death-polished.

Leapfire attacks. Youth and rage will carry him through seconds of his onset: enough to startle Daw, almost to daunt him. He falls back a step; but artfully. He lets the boy wear himself out with slashing, futile in his fury; parries him at will. A chance scratch seems to bloody Daw's arm; it frenzies his adversary. Then leaning forward, as if inquiring, Daw disarms him. The sword spins over and half over, clangs on the ground. Daw sets his foot on it.

The Sun, eclipsed, looks back at him with dark-drowned eyes. His face is almost blank with horror.

"Yield?"

*Live,* thinks Grevil; though the Fool must watch.

Leapfire cannot speak. He shakes his head.

Stooping for the sword, old Lightfast tosses him his own.

Once more the boy assails him, slashing in a frenzy at the smiling face, stabbing at air; once more the old god thrusts.

And Grevil stands as if the sword has pierced him, slain with shock. He sees the boy transfixed and twitching; sees the old god, face to face with him, caress him, kiss his mouth, blood-welling. "Whore. And whore's brat." Then the god withdraws, he shakes his sword free from the toppling body.

The ground shakes, unmooring.

The crow lad falls, blood runs; the world begins.


Even through the tumult of souls, Whin feels the shadow at the door: that will be Morag and the glass. Her end. She lifts her face to meet it square, defying it—and startled, nearly laughs. She's looking in another sort of mirror, at another self.

There's a thief in the shadows, crouching. Cap and fellcoat: with a gang, then, of guisers. They'd have sent their Ashes as they played. Who stares at her and shivers. Mirror's not the other way. Whin sees the girl see no great witch, no hero, but a journeywoman in a sark of blood. Old blood, inglorious. An elding body. Grey black and gory, like a badger in a trap.

Fordone. She can feel the drumming of the Ashes' heart from here. Mad scared and—Whin laughs silently—reverberant with sex. What, here? With ghosts? And how can Annis not feel the roar of blood, like sea-break in a cave?

Feels nothing, only self. Does naught, only brood on absence. That's why there's Morag: for her talons, for her eyes. And she has just now been diverted. Stepped outby.

Still telling, rising to a roil of story, Whin beckons to the brat: *Soft now. Blind, not deaf. But quick.*

The brat—O marvellous!—upholds a glint of metal. Tosses it. Whin catches, clumsy with her long travail; she cuts herself on scissors. But she knows their metal in the marrow of her spine: that knife with which she cut the cord. Her son's blood tempered it.

Softly, softly now, she closes on the braid.

As the blades meet, round about her neck she feels the guisers' knot of swords, their wheeling to the measure of her heartbeat, fast and faster in her terror, giddying—and all at once they draw.

Her blood's the braid. It leaps from her, unbraiding from her body in a rush of red. It whirls away in fire. Felled.

Darkness.


Ashes comes to my lady's tower, to the threshold: where is nothing still, but absolute. Its gravity annuls her. In her veins is lead, envenoming; her soul is in a slow eclipse. On groping for her lens, she sees it milkblind, blank as any stone. Her gown the Nine have given her, of twilight, now is leached as white as ashes, livid. She is home.

Three times she stamps the groundless air. Dry-voiced, she calls to death, "Lief mother, let me in."


Sea-heavy, torn like water, towering: the night sky breaks in fury on their heads. The goddess rises up in tempest. She is called.

Imbry cowering in the wrack waits death. Confusedly, amid the lancing of the lightnings, the contusion of the thunderclaps, she sees the stars, wave-warped, as if the sky were ocean; sees the tatterings of light. Then the nightwave overwhelms her, and she's drowned.

Long afterward, her stopped heart beats again; she draws a saw-edged
breath.

*My lady?*

Gone.

Sea-hammered, thunderstoned, she raises up her head. She sees the other
Ashes lying trodden like a shipwrecked sailor.

Dead?

Creeping warily along the ground, Imbry touches her. Still breathing.
Turns her. Cold as stone though. Swounded. Where the ravelling of the braid
has touched her are a thousand wales, fine whips of fire. Blood on blood. The
sark of older blood not hers, may be: she's weltered like a midwife. But she's
ill enough, in truth, and stinks of kenneling. Rag-naked, rope-cut, chapped
and cracked and starved.

Imbry haps her in the bear coat; then for want of else, she combs her dirt-
rough hair. That's all the comfort she knows. But it works: the Ashes wakes.
And not mad: her gaze is curious, self-mocking, shrewd. "I's old for saining."
A leaf-scratch of a whisper.

"Thowt yer were drownded," says Imbry. "Thowt I were."

"No chance, brat. Thou's to hang." Grimacing, as if her bones ache, the
Ashes sits, runs fingers through her hackled hair, as if to free them with the
fading spells, to limber. She considers young Ashes. Black imp like herself
were. Like a hollybush dragged through a chimney. Aye, she'd scratch Sun's
face. "Thou keep yon comb then. Keep it well."

"I is." Then remembering, Imbry fetches out a leather bottle from her
budget. "Our master mistress Brock, she sended yer this."

"Here's rain in April. Halse ye." Whin drinks long and long before she
lowers it and sighs. "Ah. That'd set stones to dance." And seeing Imbry's look,
she passes it over. "There's a snuff yet i't bottle. Cloud ale."

It's water.

"Pull's up, lass, and I's lag thee after." Stiffly she rises, raxing. "If it's guising, thou's work to do."

At that, Imbry startles. "Craws! I mun gang now. They's be lating me to
lap Sun."

"So thou's done," says old Ashes, smiling. "Had thy will. And will."

Imbry pinks: not with modesty.

"Wick sword, has he? He's been thumping yer awd Lightfast then?"

"We's brought no Winter," says Imbry. "T'witch said bid him and he'd
come."

Whin knows what Lightfast loiters here. She pales. "Run, lass. Thou's wanted. Run."

No Ashes.

Grevil takes her part in silence. Holds the dead Sun in his lap and cradles him. No words, he has no words. He gathers up the sheaf of him; he rocks, he rocks him at his breast, the bright youth: Cloud in Ashes. Closes the astonished eyes. He strokes the rough bright hair, the cheek forever beardless now. He sains him—eyes, mouth, heart—with hand alone. No tears. He cannot weep as yet. He bends to kiss the cold mouth, bright with blood. Still warm—O goddesses—and clotted with his death. As warm as embers. Yet no breath will kindle now. The play does not go on: the sun rise dancing and the summer wake. No spring will come.

Gently, Grevil lays the body down.

The Fool picks up the Winter's sword and turns to Lightfast.

Slowly, slowly, Whin that was Ashes strives against my lady's tide of rage. It runs athwart itself and baffles in its riddling rocks. She wades in it, waist-deep and oversoul: a turbulence of witches in a nightmare sea. Like weed they wind about her, red and brown and virid black; they importune. She's combed them, so they cling to her. She tangles in their greenwhite hair.

Bone weary: she would lie with them and drown. A solace. But her work's to do. She follows Annis in her fury, bright as moonblaze on the water. Clear path if she could ford a way.

Far far ahead of her, the Ashes that was Imbry dodges, dances in a blind-man's hey. Well she may chance with lightning, being sea-born, so a hero by her birth. She's hunting Annis hunting blind amid a cloud of witches, in a labyrinth of self-made ghosts: the ruins of her mind. The goddess cannot see for voices.

Yet she runs and rages, streaming fire like a falling star. What's called her down, dishevelled, from her brooding?

Not the guisers. They're trumpery for Morag to dispose. No, she's bent on something else, a soul beyond all others in her avarice, a lust more jealous even than her daughter's braid.

A glass. Whin sees in Annis' mind a child of crystal, firenew, still glowing from the blast; the reddest where she's broken off in shards. A vessel. Empty and unsouled. And all her lust is but to pour herself as mist into that void, possess it utterly. Whin sees the canting of the heavens in that narrow space, the swirl and settling of stars; and then the seal of godhead and the absolute of night. The child will crack of her.

Kit's lass's bairn. Whin's sworn to him; so she must stand for her, come what will.

Far off, she hears the lamentation of the guisers, mourning for the Sun. That's Ashes' journey. Send she's not too late. But Whin sees, as she is cursed to see, forever and again, his death. She knows by heart his loveless birth; has waked with dreaming on his life. A chance brat, scatter-sown. A windclock whirled away. Her son.

The Fool picks up the Winter's sword and turns to Lightfast. Fronts him. *He will die*, thinks Kit. *I cannot bear it, death on death.* But Grevil throws it down at Daw's feet. It falls clattering. It's wood—a painted prop.

The old god laughs. "'Twas a rare jest that the boy should bring his death with him. Expedient. And I unarmed." He opens out his hands in mock transparency. Grevil says nothing. "Not the first thing of yours he's been spitted on; though much the hardest." Nothing. A sly look, and that buzzing, balming voice. "Whores will talk. They carry tales like pox: no doubt he gave you mine." Still mute. The god looks round. "What, no mystery? He will not rise? Your bush is belated."

*"His death was not the wager settled. Still I dance the ay and O."*

*Is he mad?* thinks Kit. But it is spoken well, good voice and good discretion. Noll touches his shoulder, sketches with his knee a hint of curtsey. Still he speaks in that clear well-measured player's voice.

*"He will rise. I promise. As the sun will rise. Look now, the sisters come to dance for him."*

*I see*, thinks Kit. *He runs it backward: it is all to come. Another Ashes and another Sun.* They've hinged over to the masque now, to the witches' mystery. Tom's the heart of it; the hinge, the double-jointed paradox, is Ashes. *In my coming I do leave; Death of dying I bereave.* It's the play itself has power, not themselves. Like Ashes: in herself the girl who takes her on may be a fool, a rantipole, a scold, a slut; she may be giddy, greedy, vixenish; but in her hands are life and afterlife and death. The mystery works itself each time, it hallows nonsense, turning silly into seely sisters.

So: Brock's journeymen will play, *ad hoc*, apocalypse. A poor forlorn hope to storm so dragonish a citadel, but two are all they are. Kit holds himself in witch's wise, and takes his sister up; he curtsies to a ghostly gentle audience. *"Be not affrighted, ladies, he will rise; 'tis writ in the catastrophe. 'Tis but a winter's tale: a dream of ghosts."* And saying, he would make it so: would write the script anew. *We do it, so it is.*

They go on with the masque of witches: playing sisters playing greater sisters, shadows of the light.

*"His dreams do prick him and he flowers."*

There is power stirring, they can feel it: as a blind man in a wood can feel the spring. And so can Daw: for circling like the stalking gallantry, he seeks to break the charm. A false knight at the crossroads, in his cockblack broken swagger, down at heel. At every turning, he is there: he holds a mirror to their inward littleness, to Noll and Kit.

"Here's players: swordless and unstrung."

Not wordless though. They shrug.

"So he would rise for a wench: not for thee." The scythe swings at Noll.

The dancer leaps. "But I am Ashes; he will rise for me."

"A pretty love, to bed him on a gallows tree and hard him with a rope. He died despising thee."

A stagger, but a leap: it clears.

A swing at Kit. "Thou know'st I delivered up thy vixen to my lady's table, and my cully here did carve."

A leap in silence.

"But I gamed her first: we had good sport."

Kit sees his Thea as he saw her last, in labor: whitefaced, warping like a swelted candle, wrenched with pain. Dismissing him to save him. But the Witch says, *"How came she lighter of a Sun?"*

Closer, coldly at his ear: "Thy daughter's like her dam: fire at the fork."

Hands clenched, but still he plays.

"I had her in her mother's belly. And but an hour since. In company."

At that Kit's tempted to his useless knife, to stop that damned voice, and slash its smiling, cancel it; but as the Witch dissolves, he feels a flaught of fire at his back, a swirl and spiralling. The strings are flying to the fiddle: Thea's and another's, trebling her alto, making of his burden harmony, the three as one. *Ah, she braids of her mother.* It is strung in time, in tune. Will sing, itself and all alone: the one tale always. Truth in riddles. And it sings: *He lies.*

Yet Daw sees nothing; nothing hears.

Kit laughs.

Dismayed Jack Daw falls back a step: as if his scythe hit rock. Then he opens out his hands, aglow with rings, and in his honeyed voice, he coaxes. "Come, I'll trade with thee: which of these for thy broken kit?"

When an armed man bargains with a traveller, there is something that he fears. Kit shakes his head. "Too gaudy for the road: I would be set upon."

The old god turns to Grevil, wheedling, holding out a great ring with a tawny stone. "See, thine ingle's soul: and thine, to hang about thy neck and dandle; but for thy marrow's wilfulness. He would deny thee. Cheat thee of thy consolation and thy power. And for what? A toy."

*Coal and jugglery*, says the witch's glance. *What he? Here is Silvry and Rianty.*

They go on with the play

*"Is the sorceress not here?"*

The old god glances sidelong; barely, but they see him twitching. *Ah*, thinks Kit: *so that's the way of it. He fears the cat. We mice do call her in.*

*"And happen at her book. I would not for the moon disturb her."*

Brisk now, officious, the old god chivvies them. "Enough. Here's silver and thy door." He stamps and the circle's broken.

"You must let us in," says Grevil, setting by his part. He wries his signet on his finger; but he lifts his face: speaks truly. "It is law; and under Law most binding: your dominion as our realm of day is founded on it, dark and light. Forbid us and your night is forfeit: death will be no more."

*We are come to her undoing.*

Kit gapes in admiration. Daw parries easily.

"As guisers: but you masque. As journeymen you must be bid. Or hang as gallantry."

Grevil's caught off balance; but Kit stands. He remembers a hillside long ago in Lune, a moonish boy, half drunk: a fiddler coming from a dance. "Did not my lady's servingman come bid me play? And give me handfast of a silver coin? And seal it with his kiss? That holds."

And Grevil, lawyerly: "But played you to this household?"

"Not a note. For my gear was taken."

"So by the rule of riddlery, 'twas binding, yet is unfulfilled. He must pay his reckoning and hear you out."

They speak assuredly, but quail: a slender chance.

It holds.

"I bid thee—"

"Here's his word," says Grevil.

"—to no Lightfeast."

"Aye," says Kit. "A wedding, you did say—"

"But I hear the bride is fled," says Grevil.

"—and an ashing of the bairn."

"Then take your gold and be gone," says Daw.

"An if please you, that is not his suit: there was a play contracted, and as yet unplayed. By the huntsman's summoning, that bond is still between you. Signed and sealed."

"Then let you play to the kitchen; you are not for the hall."

*The wasp likes not my lady's web,* thinks Kit. *Nor yet does Madam Flyblow.*

And the fiddle sings: *My lady will have him, for the smutching of her glass.*

Grevil still is dry. "As my lady's seneschal, you spoke for her: let her sleep or wake, her audience is bid. And if the play displease her, yet the choice of it was yours."

*Here is Law. I would be elsewhere, were it on a sinking ship, atwixt a bear and honey.*

"And if I should refuse?"

"To wake the sun, having bidden it? The law is exact: you owe a sacrifice. A black cock's blood."

There are rings now on Daw's hand: a high king's ransom, were they not of snow. "Then give your piece: a masque or what you will, so not this farrago. It is unfitting for this court."

"Why, then a comedy," says Grevil, bowing, white as paper and inexorable "If a wedding you want, then a wedding you shall get."

"And an ashing," says Kit. "For here's a bonny sun a-borning, and a midwife to hand."

"What think you? *Slae and Perseis?*" And Grevil turns to Daw. "'Tis an old play, very choice in rhetoric, in old high Cloudish verse: it tells how Slae did carry off green Ashes for his bride in darkness; but the harper had her first to bed. He sang her out of Law."

But Kit is watching Morag watch the body. The stone-eyed servant's word-sick, circling the carrion and looking for an opening to stoop. Her argument is talons. For the huntsman's promised her her fee. Cock and eyes.

"And afterward," says Kit, "an antimasque, a most lamentable comedy of the wedding of Jack Daw and Widow Maggot Pie. They sing it all about the norlands—it was made a ballad to the tune of 'Babylon.' No doubt you've sold the sheet?" He's babbling; but he wards the body from her scavenging.

"*He put his hand all in his coat, and he pulled out a gay gold ring ...*" sings the Kit witch, and unpins old Mally's raven brooch. He holds it outward, beak between his knuckles; but he need not strike. She gazes, this way, that, admiring, adoring. The ring is Morag's mirror, and it holds her; as the witch holds onto it, but barely in his hand, for it wakes to her: outquilling, living, leashed. He holds it like a falconer: a raven, goddess-eyed; a great-winged woman, cold and perfect to the fork. She changes to its mirror, ravenwise; and wing to wing with it wheels round. Twa corbies. How she courts herself! Each gazes at another Morag, all of night and silver.

"Ah, see how she preens herself, the pretty lass," he cries to Grevil. "How she flirts, the bonny bird."

"Alas, but she is handfast to a lord of land. All graves are his demesne, all dead his retinue. His train is numberless; they dance the Lyke Road, longways, to his tune: a crowd of bone."

"She will be married this night: to one who loves her least." Kit turns to Daw. "And we promise you: you will not like your sheets."

"Now," says Grevil.

And the First and Second Witch stand forth. Turn and turn, the witches speak:

"*By the elding of the moon ...*"

"*By the weird of night and noon ...*"

They conjure Annis: call her to the dance.

*Lief, lief,* a shadow calls, re-echoing. *Lief mother, let me in.* The air is full of voices, leaves before a coming storm: fled prophecies. And pale and yellow mingling, dark and red, they fly, unleaving under Law. *By rime and rune, I conjure you.* The colder blows the wind. Wood rises: not as timber but a web of cracks. *I call. I call.* It flaws eternity.

At the heart of it, a bonfire dies.

The wind beats down the leaves, it quells the fire. It is death.

The witches are no more, nor men: but mere astonishment, the circles where a stone has fallen in a pool of dusk, outspreading, o and wider O. The waves will touch her edges; they will be no more.

The raven and her glass fly up into the branches.

Jack Daw stands. He has no power but his voice, to turn the self against itself, despairing. And a cord is at his throat, of tales: the hemp is memory, is fire.

Imbry hurls herself against the air, which now is stone.

Whin gazes at the boy, as bloody now as at his birth. But crying then and flailing, drowning in the air his enemy. Not now. A bonny boy. As she did then she learns him now again by heart: forever now.

The wave astonies them.

The blood in them is silver, running perilously bright and heavy in their veins. Imperative. All memory and all that's mortal vanishes: a smoke, an emptiness. Lost wax. Death casts them and will crack.

*Who calls me to the dance?*

The ripples die like echoes to the sill. An Ashes there, who speaks.

*A journeyman.*

Annis and her daughter's daughter, child and death. They come at once, they call each other into being, glass to glass.

Time stills. The air is tranced. Dark-dazzled, like a world enstoned in crystal: dark within, but lightedged, and refracting light. Green Ashes travels slowly, slowly in the timefrost, in the trance of light. A mote in Annis' gaze. They see her as a crescent, heavy, like a raindrop streaming; but of fire. Ablaze but coldly now: a silver negative. She labors in eclipse.

*Too late,* thinks Ashes. *I will be too late.* Her atomies are all but still. The heart, breath, soul in her will cease to tell her threefold story: descant, burden, drone. Already Ashes that was Margaret is effaced, is palimpsest. What Annis sees, she is: a hole to fill. A tuft of red hair flickering about a cleft. A limbeck spilling smoke, a ruined alchemy, a phial of swarted glass: she sees it, canted over in the ashes of a smithy, crackling with the crow god's fire, infumed.

And in that glass, another glass inclosed: my lady's vessel is with stone.

*Who let her rune of blood to run?*

That howl is felt with other senses: as a shattering of blood, a boneshake. And the ghostly wood is felled, as if a scythe had struck.

My lady turns on the usurping huntsman in a bluewhite firestorm, annihilating with a word, a hand. But in her glassy dark, his doom creeps onward at a stone's pace, crack on crack of fire flaring out: a wickerwork of knives. Her lightnings inch, slow-scissoring. Anathema itself congeals. As slowly as it comes, he cannot flee his death. He watches it, agape, a shriek slow-tarnishing his face.

The greater fury now will fall upon her child's abhorred brat: the hole with legs, the whore, the anarch. Crow's meat, excrement begotten of a ruttish fool. His cockspawn. Her flawless glass made carrion. The goddess scrabbles at her wrist. She will unbind the fiery braid of hair, her daughter's whoredom, as a whip to flay this upstart Ashes, flesh from bone: each stroke eternity.

Not there. Not Thea's but another coil enwreathes her, this of night: wyrm-wound about her, endlessly engulfing self, as if the Road turned serpent. Frenzied now, she claws at it, as if she could unburn its blackness. It will not undo. The dragon eats herself.

The god cries out. Of that great howl of rage and loss, in Cloud a mountain cracks, an isle in Scarristack is drowned. Her cry eclipses light; it is an O that swallows up the sun. Eats Ashes.

Out of Ashes, in that utterness of dark, there shines a coronal of light. An ashing: silver like her father's mother's ring. Ashes tells herself.

"I am Ashes that was Thea's daughter. She is dead of me. I tell the stars."

And she upholds her lens, the last, and gathers up the sky in it. Draws Annis, night and Law, and all the heavens in one glass. A world incrystalled. She has thought to shatter it: a sacrifice, as dear to her as eyes. The breaking of the sky would serve. That last apocalypse of witches held, from shattering to now, nine thousand years. It set the world a-turning, moonwise; but it scarred. She puzzles. *Ah, but if*—And Ashes lifts her face, as to a snow of stars. *I do it, so it is. Unbound the sky.* Delighting now but solemnly, she holds the sky in little on her hand; she breathes on it, the pattern of the moveless stars dissolving like a frost, unfolding endlessly. She makes Law infinite, uncoils the serpent; she unstrings the stars.


Crows light upon the gallows tree, the Old Sun dances on the air.

Kit sees a playing card, a woodcut in a woman's hand, alight. The fire glitters in her rings, reglows. She wears the Hanged Man's gold on every finger, and his tawny stones. His card consumes. She casts it down in embers, and the scraps of ash fly up: as ravens, coal-eyed, calling in their cynic voices. They are bodied like women, naked to the catch: white-bellied, welling blood. They're avid.

Imbry sees a straw man burning on the moor. The witches dance through him, and through and through. They rant and whirl and caper to the goat-bagged pipe; they kick him, scattering sparks. Their shawm's of his legbone, their drum's of his fell. She leaps the fire and laughs.

Still gazing at the world between her hands, green Ashes heeds no play. She sees the light still travelling: a winnowing of worlds, their stories all untold. She sees the pattern of the Guisers whirled and scattered in the endless heavens like a broken chain of stones. She sees the Fiddler's belt unstrung. His sword is buried in a barrow-mound of night.

Noll Grevil sees a knot of swords of lightning at the monstrous throat. O strange and terrible: for he himself is dancing with the silent men, the weavers of the wyrd. They slash. The body topples, headless. Then it rises like a roke, if mist could bleed. The little music threads. They dance it, over and again.

Whin sees the Old Sun burning burning on a masthead: many-winged, black, manifold. His mane is glorious. His gallows is the Ship. He falls, still burning from the mast, will fall and burn forever, quenchless in the sea of night.

All stand in awe, in exultation, dread.

Then a great sea whelms them, not of water but of time.


Guisers and journeymen lie tumbled on a darkling shore, amid the wrack of stars. No castle, not a stone nor shallow where it might have stood. No witch, no gallows, and no crow. By one and one they rise and stare about them at the timbers of the Ship, and at the wreckage of their world's mythology: a sickle, buried to the haft in sand; a sieve; a shuttle wound with bloodred yarn; a bunch of keys, rust gouted; ruined hay, a dazed goat browsing it; the rootstock of a thorn, salt-bare. The tideline is a zodiac. They wake and wonder.

All but Leapfire lying slain: the Sun's in Ashes, and the Scythe in flinders at his feet. He's threefold dead: pierced through and drowned and broken on the rocks of Law. There's an orange lying by his hand: his tawny ring. His soul.

Whin crouches by his body; touches with her work-rough hand his cold entangled hair. The coin she's paid for crossing is of gold, and of her make: her winter's son.

Kit holds the frantic Imbry, crackling like a cat. "Let them be," he whispers. "That's his mam."

*Her son,* he thinks. *O goddesses, she's found my daughter. I have failed her son.* Too much, it's all too much, between his joy, apology for joy, his guilt and grief. He scarce dares look at Thea's daughter, nor away. He is in awe of her: a sorceress. In love. Distressed at her ill use: the hacked hair and the bruises. And pierced, in the very finding, with his loss. So much like Thea—ah, that line of cheek and chin, those eyes. Her brow, her lips are like his mother's. Annot's. Like his own. But she's a child no more. Past fathering. Past wanting him. He fears she'll vanish like a trick of light. A lending.

Ashes that is Thea's daughter, that was Margaret in another world, in Cloud: she gazes at the boy, astounded, grieved. *How came he with the guising, here?* And the crow's voice in her says, *Thy curse. That rope will not undo.*

Grevil stands. *No right, no right at all to mourn. No kind of his. No lover.* Yet it's he who stoops to take the ring up, sandy on his palm, sea-clouded; and he turns to the Ashes at the crow lad's side, the elder of the three. "Will you tell a death?"

Whin takes it in her hand. No more Brock's journeyman, but mistress Ashes. Only with a look, she stills them all: the shivering of the Fool, who's not yet wept, who when he does will break down utterly, heeled through; the Fiddler's sad bewilderment, his sorrow at his joy; Imbry's fury; green Ashes' disbelief.

*What I is, is Ashes. Same as earth is earth. Her coat that she put on.*

The play's not ended yet.

Ashes takes the crow lad in her lap, she cradles him. But for Imbry's coat, she's naked, wearing naught but blood, as if she'd just then given birth. Her nakedness is office. And her part is silence. She slips the ring on his cold finger, where it gleams a moment like a raindrop, like the sun through sliding water: gold and gone. She sains him: brow and wound and gender; eyes, mouth, heart.

He stirs.

All others now are still: as if unbreathing they can give him breath. Out beyond, the sea breaks, birdless, on the shore.

"Will," says Ashes. "Wake thee."

And he takes a shuddering breath. Another.

*Done.*

The blood runs shining from his side. The gash, gut-spilling, knits itself: an angry seam, a scar. She traces it. Death's nave.

*Undone.*

He wakes.

*And all to do.*

Will lifts a hand before his eyes, as if she dazzles. "Ashes?"

"Get thee up, lad. Thou's to dance another where." She sits back on her heels. "It's all to do ower. All down t'Road."

·  ⟳

Yet they linger a space, but to drink Unleaving. Whin's been kitted in the coat of sparks, laid by her Ashes coat for now; she's kindled fire of the thorn. The night is clarified by fire: the mirk turned deeper grey, but starless yet. Unblue. As restless as the flame, Will paces; the others hunch and brood. Here's nothing: but a space between sleep and waking, now and nowhere, sea and strand.

Whin's been mulling ale in Rianty's saucepan helm; she calls him. "Here's drink. Thou's a cup i' thy tatters."

So he finds, having rummaged through the Cloudwood coat: a little wooden cup, wormeaten, so the lip is oakleaf edged. As thin. She fills it from Brock's bottle, nearly: she has that much left. Cloud ale.

Rising, Whin gives the cup to Kit. "Halse ye."

"And hallows ye." He drinks of it, and all his life without is shadow. Here is light, the heart of it: pale fire, and the endless fall. Unleaving. He wakes wood. Still falling, leaf on leaf, he's earthfast, root and crown. Eternal, he is time. Through a tranquil storm, he turns to Ashes that was Thea's daughter. Light through leaves. His vision fades before her, cloud before the moon. He sees her mother's face in her, the old moon in the new.

Long long ago, a dazed boy took a cup and drank to eyes like these. *Is this the moon?* he said. A goddess: and he knew her as a lover, breath and body; yet he knew her not. But in the folly of their play they got this miracle. *Thy mother was my dearest love, my heart; and thou*—No words, no words.

But Grevil takes her by the arms. "Margaret," he says, appalled. *Margaret,* thinks Kit: their mothers' mother's name. "What scathe is this? How cam'st thou here in hell?"

"Here was I born. And thought to die here in myself; yet live, unkindly. I was Annis' glass."

Kit then to Grevil in astonishment: he asks the least of it. "You know her?"

Grevil shakes his head. "Not as this—epiphany: but barely, if this dream be true. As Margaret, she is of my household; has been for this half year and more. I took her in, a waif. But you?"

"I never saw her face, nor thought to see it; yet her mother was to me still dearer than my soul. We were captives here; and fled."

Thunderbolt on bolt. Astounded, Grevil looks at them, from face to face, with doubt, with wonderment, with kindling joy. "By the ladle. Hand is not more like this hand. Ah, Margaret, here's thy father that has sought thee to the end of Law."

Still Margaret stands, as if amazed. "You were Thea's Kit? Who took the braid?"

Kit dies. "That he."

The stern young face—still childish—gazes through and through him. "Ill-done: for you did twist a halter with that hair. Her death and my captivity." She gentles then. "Yet she did love you. In the end."

He cannot speak.

Bricks and timbers of the house still fall on Grevil's head. "O but then— thy father's Annot's *son*. Thyself's thy father's dame. Here's law confounded."

Gravely she looks on them, the newfound cousins, as she would a pair of gloves. "Then we are kindred. You are like." She curtseys. Even swayed with weariness and battle, even marred—bruised face, cracked lip, the hacked hair like a carted whore's—she bears herself as Thea's daughter.

Kit takes her small hand, roughened by her journey; raises her. "You are like her. Like yourself: no other."

Then she takes the cup of him, and drinks.

She sees the old unshattered heavens, come together like the moon in water, all unflawed. An O. She journeys in the Ship, whose mast is rooted, flowering in stars; they fall upon her, white as thorn. She's standing at its very bow, that breaks the black night, voyaging: the Road's her wake. And there are islands … But it fades.

Turning with the cup, she sets it on a rock. She beckons Imbry to the circle: Ashes bids Ashes. Yet she speaks as child to child. "I pray you: let me see your comb." She takes it as a relic, turning it; her face is sorrowful. "They call you Imbry. Were you cast up from the sea?"

"Aye, and if?"

"We two are sisters then. Thy mother was my nurse. Her milk was salt for thee, with grieving for thy loss, her mourning boundless as the sea."

Imbry stands between doubt and blazing. She would scorn—*aye, throwed me to't fishes, and to worse, to dragging up by whores and witches*—but the comb says, *Kept thy soul alive.* She nods warily.

The other bends and whispers softly in her sister's ear: "Her true name in her tongue was Siorvar. She told me as they—told me once, so one might ash her." Norni being dead, they'd given her her milk to drink: a cup of it, with certain blood. That guilt she would not tell. But stepping back, she says, "A windwife, a witch of Scarristack. She taught me somewhat of her art; yet I was young to practise it, and too much overlooked. She sang it as she dressed my hair; but I am shorn of it, of art and nursery. Sister, I would learn of you to braid."

She gives the cup to Imbry Ask, who drinks. At once that black imp's in a whirlwind, white on white, of snow and spindrift. Bending on, she sees a field of snow, and knows it for the sky, as yet unstarred. She sees the tracks of stars across it, godprints; sees the Hare's Trod and the Bear's Tread, and the Vixen's swift three Leaps. Then tumbles down and downward to the hearthfire and the dance. She's naked but a fell of stars. No music have they in the norlands, but the nimbling of the tongue, the struck skin's dub: mouth music and the tumbling of the drums.

And Imbry turns to Will. "Halse ye and halter thee. Thou bragfire raggamuff. Thou hempseed."

"Thou cattle-plash. Thou sough. Would thou gulp me?"

"Aye, skin and soul. But if thou eat of me."

Drink he must: and sees in it the Swords, slow-wheeling, turning ever to his hand.

He would give the cup to Margaret, but the ritual forbids. Self-crossed in love, he stands, and all his acts athwart and thwart him. He would look at her, cannot so much as lift his face. His inwit gnaws him like a bandogg's bone, old meat.

Here's Marget that he's fond on. Marget that he's fought for. Marget that is Ashes, eld of all, and Thea's daughter that he's sworn to serve. And Marget that he's meddled: pried her with his snotty fingers, and a rusty saw-knife at her throat.

So he's fought old Daddy Corbet for her sake, he's died for her; yet he's fallen and she's won.

The cup is burning in his hands; his heart is stomach, is a drabbled rag wrung out. He shrugs and mutters. "Then I's sorry. What I done."

But Margaret says, "I kept that snail's shell. In my box." He lifts his face a little, curious: sees hers, unsmiling but alight. "But the lateworms I do keep in memory. And will."

"You'd not map those."

"I have not the calculus."

A ghost of old bravado. "Thou arain-web. Thou urchin."

"Chimneysweeper." And she opens out her hands.

But Whin's seen Grevil hanging back, and draws him in. "Will. Here's one who's not drunken."

So he must face his judge; his trick; his fellow journeyman. A curt upward
nod. "Noll." All this while, he's fed on fury: on the sentencing, the truckling
of the man to Corbet; on the cruelty for naught, for cowardice. He's glutted
on contempt. *Aye, spur on, yer gentryship, I's jigged thee, naked as a worm, I's heared thee
groan and whimper. Wiped my hands of thee on grass. I driven thee.*

But what he sees within is Noll's hand on a book. He turns it to the boy.
*There now.* And the page is full of images, bright painted creatures, birds and
flies. All spellbound. And they bind the boy, who gazes. *Wouldst thou learn
that art?* And, *Aye,* the boy says. *I could do that fine. That gressop's legs is all awry. Is't
Lunish?* And Grevil: *I could teach thee. Give thee colors.* Lake and madder. Useless
in the muck of byres, in the roofless wind and rain. All paper dreams. He'd
drunk away the lead of silver.

The boy who speaks is half-remembered: young. "Could I keep hat?"
Grevil nods, as if his heart would spill. "—and feather."

Noll drinks: he sees the harvest field, a-dazzle through his tears. He
drowns in gold.

That over with, the lad lopes off to the sea's edge, wading in to wash the
blood away. He strips his shirt.

Grevil gazes. Shaken to the bone with beauty, he forgets his courtesy.
The cup, unnoticed, still is cradled in his hand. Kit takes it gently, hands it
on to Whin, full circle. She drinks her last of Cloud; what Whin sees, no
one knows.

Whin sets the cup aside; looks up at Kit: and all is changed between
them. In that moment is awakening, regret. A knowing of the other, soul
and skin. A love autumnal: like the first bite of the first half-ripened russeting: sharp sweet, springing in the mouth. A harbinger of frost.

And yet they resonate: as if they two were fiddles, on a sudden set in
tune: but will not play. As if the key has shifted and the canon overturned,
as turn it must—and then breaks off. No cadence now. No chance.

Bending to her task, Whin gathers up the scattered properties. They'll
take them all away: the cup, the staff, the knot of swords; the shirt, a little
slashed, once fine, but stained now, bloodied with his death.

"If it's guising," says Kit, "you're a bit few."

"A sword and a bush," says Whin, nodding at Will and Imbry. "So it
ever was."

Down at the sea's edge they're running, leaping overlapping waves. Imbry has the great black coat on now; she splashes Will, he lashes with the

knotted shirt, he dodges. Exit, pursued by a bear.

"Two?" says Kit.

"Three. There's master: which I is."

The sea booms; the fierce young voices cry and challenge. Running back along the sand, they edder Margaret, in and out. She walks along the shoreline slowly, stooping. She is getting shells and pebbles, turning them between her fingers, on her palm. Some she keeps, and others casts away. Beyond her is the ocean, undiscovered.

"No," Whin says, though he's not asked. "Nobbut three." She draws a crossing in the air: chiasmus. "We's skyward, and sworn; and thou and thine is earthfast. See, it's done here. And no more to do."

Nothing left beneath the moon, thinks Kit: he sees the round earth like an orange peel, sucked dry. "But why?"

"It's what thy lass did."

That stabs at him. He bows his shoulders, wries and rocks. "She meant no—"

"What she is. What she were born for. Same as I is Ashes." She looks outward. "Late," says Whin.

"There's never morning here."

"There's morning now: it's changed."

"Dark's all it is."

"Aye, and will be nowhere when 'tis light. Time's turned and coming in. We's best away afore it whelms us." And it's true: the dark is paling now, it thins. Out of nowhere, there's a little wind.

She's scavenged up the skywreck, bundled in a scrap of sail.

"If it's done—" he says.

"Done here. There's elsewhere all to do." Knot on knot, she's tying up her pack: new stars for the otherworlds, all down the Road. "It's all in thy cousin's book, I'd wager. Witch stuff." How she binds it, bowing to her work, half singing to herself. "*We'll riddle and we'll fiddle, and we'll make the sun go round . . .* It's a rare good play, t'guising: Sun dies in Ashes' lap and rises up, himself. All bright i't sky. But nevermore i' Cloud: there's none can raise him there. He's dead. Like I is." Knot on knot, she binds it. "Like thy Thea: but will rise up shining, over and again. For ay and O." And now she looks at him, holds out her hand. "Thy crowd."

Kit flinches; but the ghost of this has walked his heart: *no more.* And it is empty now: a shell with no sea in it, sung out. Unstrung.

He gives it.

And she takes. She looks as he's remembered her, a little greyed. "All over and again. I'd rather once."

A kiss like summer lightning: distant, bodiless, all light.

No more. The journeymen have gathered as she stamps the fire out, and quenches it with sand.

The parting's brief. All this interlude has been a maze of glances, gazes, weaving and withdrawing like the knot of swords. Cross and cross: and when it's made, it's all at once unmade, and brings the heavens toppling down.

But they get up, go on, as people do; they change things, being who they are. Will's angry and aspiring; Noll grieves; Margaret wonders; Kit and Whin regret; but Imbry sees what comes. All are loved in some way, not as they would chose; and all but one desired. Noll is odd man out.

Whin takes his shoulder. "Hallows on yer orchard, Master, to blow well and to bear." She looks for the last time. "You that way, we this way."

The guisers turn—not inland—upward, climbing into air as if the heavens were a hill. They go by the pack road, white with stardust: Imbry running on ahead; Whin loping with her jangling pack; and Will, Will lagging, looking backward at his Margaret.

They come like hoarfrost and are gone. In their packs are dreams, lies, memories: the patterns that the mind makes of the scattered stars, the toys and engines of imagination. At your bidding, they will play for you the histories of the sky: the moon's brief comedy, the downfall and the death of stars. For silver, they will wake your dead; for gold, will sain your marriage beds. Some say they do steal restless wives and children: that is false. For they take nothing but your dreams, though some run after. If they come as guisers, you must let them in: the slouched one with her bag of ashes; the patched one with his broom of thorn. They bring the sun.


So Whin and Will and Imbry fade: not dwindling into space as travellers do; but paling as the morning stars do, overtaken by the light. *We drown*, thinks Margaret: *there isn't dark enough to bear us up.* For even as they watch, the night grows thin. The sun will not bring life and color to the shadowlands: it will efface them, white them out like snow. A cloud of reason, overwhelming myth. Her edges now begin to blur. She thinks, she tries to think if anyone—the Nine?— has told her of a road returning. But the light's dissolving will and memory.

At her back she hears the sea, the booming and the swash. It catches at her throat, the tang. They turn to it, all three.

There's Brock. She's waiting in her sooty cap between salt water and the strand. As black as a stithy, as apt as a knifeblade fitted to its haft. To hand. Her boat's drawn up. "Lowp in," she says to them. But Margaret's clumsy: parts of her too light, too heavy all at once. Unstrung. She staggers in the sand. She falls. So Master Grevil and the other man—her father?—help her on, half carry her; they wrap her in their coats. They launch. The boat is real and splintery and cold. It grits beneath her feet; it rocks and shudders on the waves; it wallops. Giddying, she cannot tell if fire or water, fever or the swell unsettles her; but feels the thinness of the hull that bears her on the cold abyss of sea. *Water*, she would say, but knows no more.

## Conjunction

Look now where the sky is bloody, there beyond the heath. You see those two great stars? And there, a third and brightest? In that twelfth of heaven called the Harvest Field, that bright, those baleful stars conjoin: black Slae who breedeth melancholy, and my lady's crow, old Morag, see, a red star like a raven's eye; and at their feet, bright Perseis, that green girl they would master, who would not be owned. He ravished her from heaven, bore her off to be his bride; the old crow dressed her for his bed, her table. Yet she rises, she eludes them, flawless of their blight. All three are there enskied. They brighten with the falling dark. They hang.

So you may see them in the great dance, crossing and recrossing heaven, siding in the starry hey. Now they arm; now gypsy; now withdraw, and for a time they meet not, east or west. In heaven is a dalliance, disdaining as they pass: *thou harpy* and *thou whoreson kite.* They do but trifle. But in hell, they're wed.

In Law they will be joined forever, and their bride-bed is a rope. Jack Daw will hang, undying. Winged and taloned, she will set upon him on the gallows tree, devour with her beak and bloody mouth. She ravens on the thing she loathes. Each scrap of him is sentient; each gobbet venom in her gorge, her gash. Each day he is renewed: his flesh, her stomach for his flesh. The crow will eat him, cock and eyes.

# Moonwake

Near light now on a moorland. Anywhere. Black frost; a scant of snow, unsettling, driven on in wreaths before a restless wind. The girl is running, running blindly from the witch gang. They are vanquished, far outstripped, hailed down upon with baneful fire: but they've scathed her, and she cannot shake the terror from her blood. They hunt her down, the half men, guised as wolves, bears, boars; yet smiling with their mannish teeth. No other beasts would gloat.

But she herself is half, is meddled. Stripped of Ashes, she is no one. For her soul is in the elderwomen's keeping: they unselved her when they sained her Ashes. At her Wake, they would have taken back her coat, her silence; given her her name. But she is scoured, shorn, unhallowed: not by rite but violation. Daw has stripped her of her godhead and her will, ransacked the soulbag that was in her trust. That rape is graver than her own. Even but to wear the daggings of the Ashes coat—and she is naked else—seems blasphemy.

The girl runs on.

The first pain is a thunderclap: a shockwave and a flash so fierce it seems to be outside her, greater than herself, an element. An ocean. Like a wave it scoops her out, her inlets and her harborage, withdrawing in a long harsh grinding ache. It staggers her; she bears it. Bent and clenched, she keeps her feet, fights hard for breath, hangs on.

It's faded. She goes on a little way, a little further, toward a fold, a thorn tree.

At the second shock, she's riven, and she burns from roots to crown, her tree of nerves white-fiery. Green and burning: for another half of her has gone by the sky road and the outland sea, another half has won. She cannot piece her selves together.

Looking back, she sees a spattering of blood on snow. She feels blood sidling down her leg, a snailing, then a stream. Leaning on a wall, she lurches for the gap in it, for shelter.

At the third she's felled. She lies with what has come of her, her issue, at her side: a splatch of blood and splinters of a thing of crystal. *O my glass,* she mourns, *my starglass,* thinking she's miscarried of her secrets. But the shards are of an Annis witch: a wizened, knowing thing, a crazed and shattered sentience of glass. A goblin child: as midnight black and lucid, edged as elfshot, and malign. Each shard of it another witch in embryo, an imp. It has my lady's face, cracked through.

Since the master's horse had come back riderless, the house was in an uproar, kitchen and hall. Barbary had sent out all the men, three riding, and the rest in pairs afoot. The first were back straight way with news: that Madam's horses were gone. And Barbary, hastening to her chamber, found the witch and all her servants fled. "We'll hunt her, then?" "No," said Barbary. "You'll fetch Master Grevil. Happen he's been nighted." They went abroad with lanterns, flails and forks, to seek for him. In twos and threes: for there was mischief stirring. Witches. Rantsmen.

Barbary kept the fire up for their returning, got wine and physick and old linen ready for whatever ill befell. Waited. Worked. No good in sitting idle. Stilled the wauling of the maids, who had him spirited by goblins, set upon by thieves. Turned witch and fled with Madam. But her mind was elsewhere. They should have been back by now, if only with tidings. Ill news travelled quickly. If he weren't at Shanklin's—Well, it were a steep road up from Imberthwaite, and ways were icy. Crown, collarbone, ankle? Send it weren't his back.

At nine she sent the maids to bed, wittering and clinging; all but Nan who'd some sense to her, if told sharply. Asleep now in the chimneycorner, with her stocking on her lap. She'd scarce knit an inch.

And if—? No heir. He'd not wed, being as he were, so he'd gotten none. It all would go to some far Outlune cousin and his stranger retinue. And all this household, masterless. Turned out upon the road.

No more to polish. Still no word.

Far in the night, it was. The fire sank and sang. The shadows crept from their corners. Barbary half drowsed: she'd waked the night before with Hawtreys' bairn. Her thimble fell; she heard it on the hearthstone—*ting*—like a little bell. And looking up, she saw young Master Noll. Eight winters then, or seven. He was by the dresser, with his pale red hair, that curled like oak leaves in a frost, and in his suit of mourning, overdyed. She saw where she had mended it, that elbow. He'd be wanting candles, then—a sickly child, and ever at his book. He begged them of her, as another child would cakes. Begged tales. Not coaxing prettily, but as a prentice to his master. Ah, now he would speak—A log fell. He was gone.

Shivering, she bent to make the fire up: no blaze would drive away that cold of doubt. Ill news, to see his shadow walk. Could he yet live? And over and again, like children's tales, she saw what might have been. Stolen by his faerie folk for sporting, under Law? Tumbled in a fell-dyke? Ah, like Hawtreys' lad, poor bairn. His bright hair rayed out in the ice. Moon send no crows to him. Waylaid by Corbet's men? Or Madam's? There was wickedness abroad this night. She knew it in her blood.

Just then, she heard the dogs start up. Beldam and Bullen in the yard: the one and then the other one, then both at once. Then all the housedogs in a frenzy. Grevil's hounds. She heard the stumbling running feet and the hammering at the door; but when she drew the bolt, only Wick Billy tumbled in, white-cold and sobbing. "Ashes—"

Nan woke crying.

He could not get his breath, but panted, "Sun's not—Ashes—"

She took him by the shoulders, steadying. "What is't, lad?"

"Sun's not brought—"

Nan wailed, "O waly and there's winter ever. World's at end."

Barbary slapped her silent. Then she poured a cup of wine for Billy, and he drank.

"There weren't Ashes. Smith Rendal and all, they waited but she never come. And Sun's not brought." He sleeved his face. "They says Awd Slae's abroad wi' his gabblerack. They hunt. He's stown her away for his whoring, and there's never light again."

*Corbet*, thought Barbary. He'd a grudge at this household, master and ward. And he would spoil what he could not possess.

There was no one left to send. "Nan," she said. "Thou keep fire up. Thy master will be cold returning. And let none in but of our house."

"I's flayed, oh, I's flayed."

"Thou's nowt to fear, thou goose. Hearth's been hallowed. Give Billy o't bread and wine. He'll sit with thee."

She was fettling as she spoke: stout shoes; her mantle and another mantle, wrapped about a hot stone from the hearth; burnt wine; a good sharp knife, the same she jointed sheep with. Clambering up on the kist, on tiptoe she unhooked a lantern from amid the rafters, the oldest and the plainest of the hallows twenty. She would need it. She was lating Ashes.


The child is cradled in the old moon's lap, as light there as a garland, light as leaves. The moon with her gnarled hands combs her daughter's sleep, undoes the ravels of the night. Her sleep is long as wind. Her dreams are leaves on it, and leaves. They're drifted deep in time.

A traveller would see none of this: a windbent thorn, with pale rags tied to it; a stone; a spring. Yet here is hallows. He might pause and leave a coin within the hollow of the stone; or tear a strip of scarf to flutter with the fading hopes, the rags of twilight and of dawn. Or she might make a pilgrim's journey to the spring, to drink to fill her womb; or trample cross and cross it with her muddy boots and flock. They'd not get in.

In comes the journeyman, old Brock, and crouches by the spring. She cracks the ice to fill the cup. She drinks to the childing of the moon, a caudle of Cloud ale. *Wassail.*

*Cold hail,* says Malykorne. *She bears it light.*

Brock looks at Ashes in her lap, and Annis. Turning, they are each the other, new of old: the cauldron and the sickle and the cold bright bow. *Hard travailing. She'll live?*

*Outlive this world and all.*

*Thou's gossip?*

*An thou stand wi' me.*

*I'll that. Thine ashing?*

And the old witch takes her spectacles and huffs them, moon and moon; she folds them, bow on bow. *What's thine?*

Brock drops a great bunch of her keys. They jangle falling. *But she's to find locks to them.*

Then Malykorne unhaps the bearing cloth of earth, of cloud, of fire: she upholds the naked sky, unswaddled.


A fold, a thorn. A sweep of snow, but endlessly refigured by the wind: no tracks in it. No where. But even as her candle—all but viewless now by winter dusk—went out, Barbary saw the blood on snow.

*Ashes. We's Ashes.*

It's what she'd always wanted, standing last. The vision. But a few steps farther on, she saw the huddle of the Ashes coat, greyed out with snow, the brush of hair, banked fire: Ashes, lying in her blood. *O sisters two, they's killed her.*

She had seen ill things; had cut away a mortifying breast. But not a goddess raped.

Kneeling, Barbary swiftly touched the lips, the pulse. She lived. But could not live in company, so smutched, defiled. The hacking of the virgin's hair was sheer contempt. It said: *she opened to us of her will. She joyed in it.* It said *whore.*

Capably, reluctantly, she turned the still girl upward, studying the belly and the thighs. No seed. No snailtracks, nor no ruttish scent on her. But blood and blood. Far wrong in that. *With . . . knives?*

Her hackles knew before her eyes did: witchcraft. And she found the outcome of it: at the virgin's side, the monstrous birth. It swayed her stomach like a chasm, fathomless; it blackened in her sight: would take her eyestrings in its talons and would wrench them. But she willed herself to look upon it. Fathom it. There's no undoing in the dark. And yet she gazed on it but warily, behind her out-turned hand, as if she looked upon eclipse, dark-dazzling. Her fingers all were edged with silver, spilling silver; and she saw the chalk of bones. It burned with cold, a cloud of it, a hag. And it gazed back at her, with fractions of a face. All beautiful, all damned. It would possess her—not her belly but her mind—with rage, iceblack and lucid. For she knew all at once what Madam Covener had done, her sorcery. Not merely forced a green child for an old man's bed, but bred of her a blasphemy.

*Keep nowt,* they'd told her at her making. Here was nothing.

Wordlessly, she asked Imp Jinny, who had taught her; and was answered. *Sain it, grave it, as it were a stillbirth. For it has a soul.* She looked about her for an ashing, anything: a pin, a coin. She wore no ring. She took a pin from her cap and blessed it, and she named the hailstone: "Annis Ashes' daughter, mother to thyself: I name thee. Light hap thee, at thy crossing over." And she drew the sill. "Daughter of thy daughter Ashes, sister to thyself: I bid thee, Annis, go in peace. Lyke to the earth's lap, lightly on the Road. Unleaving be thy soul."

And she in she, the goddesses rose up, greysilver, in a cloud of Ashes. For a breath, they lingered, young and sorrowful; then fading into air, were gone.

Now Ashes that was Margaret stirred and murmured in her sleep. Mistress Barbary took her in her lap, as in the guising overturned: a shadow for the sun.

She happed her in the stone-warm mantle, chafed her. A brave lass, a brave lass: she could feel the strong slow heart, the warmth returning to her body, even to her hands, her feet. Could feel the kindling of a fever: she'd want nursing yet. A long way from her bed.

Just at daybreak, Barbary took Ashes' coat, her silence, gave her back her name: "Margaret, wake."

And echoing, she heard a man call, "Margaret?" He was running uphill, breathing hard and raggedly; she heard the rattle of the stones dislodged. If it were Corbet, let him come. Let him look to his ballocks. She'd a knife. But looking up, she knew him for that fiddler with the gallantry who'd spoken for the sun; but long before that as the desperate boy who'd pleaded for his lass. And in her pride of piety, she'd spurned him: for the sake of ritual. For maidenhead. In longing to be Ashes she was Annis in her pride, disdainful of the grieving heart, the errant flesh. No more.

When he saw them, he cried out, crouched eagerly to take his daughter up. She signed to him: *asleep.* He turned and beckoned wildly to a second traveller behind him: Master Noll, much worse for wandering, and hatless. But unscathed. The faerie-hunter, home from the hill.

She could not rise to curtsey; but she nodded. "Morn t'ye, masters. Here's your lass returned from travelling; she'll live to comfort ye. Come up, we'll bring her home."


Waking from that long strange dream of Cloud in Ashes, Margaret's running in the labyrinth, in Law. She wears the heavens as a chain of stones. Her collar and her clew: it leads her down and down the spiral stair. The necklace breaks, the stars unstring. They roll and scatter on the stones; are lost, forever falling. There are cracks in Law, unfathomed. But she cannot stop to pick them up, the moon is hunting her.

And now she's in a boat alone, but for the silent journeyman. Above her is the starry sky, the bloom of galaxy; below—ah strange, the sea is full of stars. The ship is flying now, the sky is water. A single planet, steadfast, clear, shines out: the Boatman. For they call it so in Cloud, she thinks. She must remember now to speak their tongue, for all's translated here. The ship's the moon and shadowed by the moon; it follows, shattered in the water, coming round and round, still closing.

*Cup,* she thinks: she thirsts but cannot drink of it. It brims with light.

The pale ship is the moon, cloud-canvassed, and the moon a bed, its ghostly hangings great with air; the clawed rings inch and jangle on the yards. Crows crony on the masthead. Grave as doctors, they confer, they parcel her. The sea is fretted now with islands; the rocks are thronged with seals: dark, indolent, and sleeky creatures sloping off, incurious. They slide into their element. But some are Norni's people, with her great eyes. How they stare at her, a bare forked thing. Their changeling and their charge. They slip from her her skins of earth, air, fire: fell on fell. Clay-cold, as pale as cloud; then skydark, pricked with light. Her body's moled with stars. They roll them, fine as vellum, for the steersman. Soulskins. Maps.

The sky is paling, streaked with fire; she is made of sky, she burns and shivers. Where she bleeds is morning. Sleepless as the day, she watches as the Crow stars fade. Seven a journey, six for a thief. She has stolen herself. Uncaged, ah, cut away from Law, outlaw, she wreathes, unwreathes the broken chain. Not dreaming, no. It's only that she feels so light, so strange and light.


Will is on black moorland, climbing. It is half light, neither sun nor moon but shadowless. White frost in patches and a mist arising from it, shreds and tatters of a scarf.

No stars. There'd not be Margaret.

But she's standing by the Owlstone, small and cold and straight. A willow wand. A candle, with a flickering of fire about her head. Her hair. Had they bound her to the cart's tail, cried her for a vixen and a whore? Shorn her for a lunatic? She's naked but her smock, as if she's risen from her bed; and barefoot on the whinnymoor. In frost. She'd starve o cold. Dread catches at his throat. *She weren't—?* No. No, he sees her cloud of breath. But wandering in a fever? Mad?

*Thou's late abroad,* he says. *Marget.*

He cannot read her face.

*The wood above's mine own.* She stands on a puzzling of oak leaves and ice that glitters with the moon in it, in shards. No moon, no tree but where she stands. *I come to gaze.* He sees her glass with her, that charms the moon and stars from the sky. And she's tablets of wax to spell them down.

No stars.

She looks him up and down, half smiling. *Here's bravery. Cap and feather and all. The Road has prospered thee.*

There's rings on every finger. Gauds. His hand goes to his hilt: and power. He begins to fear, unknowing how this came. He would unbuckle, belt and all. Ungird. He'd lay them at her feet: his sword, his rings, his mantle of the sun. Cannot: for what he's ta'en.

But she mistakes him. *Put up thy sword. Thou hast what thou didst levy of me: silver and a horse.*

*That's not what*—But he's forfeited. One kiss is all he craves of her: her child's cold mouth, but sweet as water. That he never took, so never tainted. All other memories of her are black with shame. Her sweet small breasts; her low of fire. Her Lunish talk. Her maddening. Herself.

*She's not for thy undoing,* says Brock's echo.

And he says, *I'll take no leave of thee.*

*Not of thy will, but must. We meet but as the night and day, in dreaming, and the river lies between.* She is her cloud of breath, condensed of it, all air; and if he reached for her—*Win up, win up. The wind is bridled, and thy river's yet to cross.* But even as she speaks, she's fading, mist in mist. She seems to hold a cup of frost: that lingers last of all, bloodred, abrim with sun.

He's lying in a lap. Another, darker cloud looms over him. Not mist but firesmoke and fog. Wet ashes. Drops rain down on him, they sidle. *Will you drink?* the ghost says, echoing. He hears a stamp and jingling, of his waiting horse? A whickering dance? But he remembers now, they bring the hobbyhorse. He hears the cockcrow, or the bagpipes mocking it. And O, it breaks his heart with light. It draws him up and up, still struggling, into ritual: a room of smoke and firelight and rumour. Hobbleshow.

Then the drum beats, and he must awake, away. He rises up to dance.


Looking up, tranced Margaret sees a flint of sun, struck glinting from its wheel: another sun. And then, another and another sun, the fellies of its wheel of frost; but still. It is the year's cross, quartered in its turning. Three suns, beside, aside, above the sharp white sun, at hilt and hilt and pommel of a wintry sword. It dazzles in her eyes. The sword is in the starry hill; the witch is sleeping, naked in her bones of frost, blacksided in a coil of cloud. The white sword's pierced her through. And Margaret stretches out her hand to it and sees that it has cut her bonds. The ends unravel from her wrist, a bracelet of bright hair, plaited as the living blood; but cold, as cold as hail, and darkened as iron in an ashy forge. Then she's slipped. She sees herself the bright hawk balanced on the rimy wheel, the wheel about to turn. *I have flown myself,* she thinks. And dazzled, staring at the three, five, shivered suns, she winks. The windgalls vanish in the sky; the hill is stone.

Will is riding on the nightfell, upward from that silent shore. His mantle of the burning gold flares out behind him as he wades the river: bright a moment, dusk and ashes as he mounts the sky. He's clad in sunrise and its setting, and the black of night between them; but his bones are of the earth. New-fallen snow lies next his body, whiter than a weft of linen, finer stitchery of frost; his coat's the mirk black rain. He wears a windgall at his breast, and at his back, a moonbow, arrows of the sleet. Upon his hand, he wears a stone of fire. Hailshod and unbridled, he is horsed upon the wind. His spurs are January.

When it lightens, we do say he rides. There's thunder in his gait.

He rides by the gallows where the sun will hang. All paths lead ever to that crossroads, to his shadow self, his day. That other strode the heavens, bright and ragged, in a belt of stars. But he is silver that was golden once. He scatters brightness. *Ah, like this,* says Ashes, *like a chimneysweeper.* Leaning to her listener, she opens out her hands, she whiffs. *He comes to dust.* Forever he is whirled away, unsilvered, in the windrush of his riding. Still he scatters, he is endless. Slash him: all within is light. The falling stars are called his seed.

On bitter nights, you cannot see him, sky in sky, but for the glinting of an edge of silver, like the turning of a crystal in the moonlight, like the limb of fire on a glass new-blown, still fiery from the blast. Her breath ensouls. And in him, edge on edge refracted, is another sky aslant: the Ship, the Gallows, Ashes at his heart. The Road's within him, and his riding. See, a littler horseman with a ring upon his hand, epitome: and in that stone, another heavens. All the stories of the world are in him, starry in his veins.

Fading from her lips, he clouds a little. Crazes. There is salt of blood in him, his flaw: he cracks with it. His shattering is storm. A white hag rises from him, streaming from his horse of air, subliming. He is silver on the trees.

Look for him riding on the scar of heaven, on a black moor rimed with stars. Night's horseman.

He will take you up behind.

### Unleaving

Cold sunlight, clean linen. Comfort: down and fire, and a fall of snow without. An absence—ah, the soft weight and the winding of her braid along her body, coiling and consoling her. Margaret woke remembering.

A presence. There was a stranger at her bedside reading. Or was reading but a moment since: with a finger in his book he looked at her. An anxious pleasant face, but overwatched: as if she were an apparition in the heavens, long-awaited, clouded over and now clear. He'd Master Grevil's slate-blue jacket on, ill-fitting him; a fairish beard and hair, not sorrel. Like and unlike. Grevil's cousin. Thea's Kit.

He smiled. Swift-chasing light and shadow in his face: an April visage, had she known the month.

"Good morrow, daughter."

She blinked in the light.

"Mistress Barbary would have thee shuttered; but I argued thou wouldst wake to sky."

The chamber was not hers: she was in the great bed, in the loft.

"Madam—?"

"Fled."

Shadow chased light. A silence. She turned, half sat, to see what book he read; he held it up. "*Perseis.* 'Twas my mother's—Annot's—book she left here, long ago. She oft did speak of it, regretting: though she had it all by heart. And played it to me as a child in coats, so I did learn it of her, leafmeal. But in game: and so more surely than I got my grammar." He smiled, reminiscent. "Though chiefly I did beg of her the masque of bears."

Inwardly, she saw the frontispiece, the woodcut: Perseis appearing to the wondering Shepherd in the wood, the wood unleaving. Oddly drawn: the toyish trees scarce higher than the lovers' heads, the leaves in folio. The lady naked but a scarf of rainbow, black on white, a garland of the stars outblazing in her comet's tail of hair. As if she'd fallen from an almanac. And he long-coated, with a broad hat and a crook. His budget at his belted side. His black dog at his heel. From a window in the heavens, in a curling of cloud, the Eight upheld their hands.

She spoke for him. *"O rare Cosmography—"*

He took her up. *"Let fall my lantern. Thou art only light . . ."*

*"But thou art mazed, sweet fool. The wood is dark . . ."*

And turn and turn they played the scene, forgetting here and there, uplifting on the wave of measure, carried by the tale. The lovers meet in greenwood, in the fall of leaf. They spring. The play's a winter's tale: it draws towards darkness, to a storm of grief and partings, even to the deep of hell; and yet will end in reconciliation, lightly, with a dance.

"In another Tale she dyed," wrote Grevil in the autumn after. "For their meeting was by Chance: as when a Starre falls. We doe say, *The Nine are weaving*; but their Weft is gossamour, it drifteth by the Wind. In otherwise, her Shepheard swain had tarried on the hill, or slumbering late had dreamed a lesser Faire than he had lost a-bed: so waking was bereft of her. Or else, new-fallen Perseis had met not Tom o Cloud, that should have hail'd her, but a loitring Man in black, a rabble of his Drabs behind: so she was fallen utterly." He paused, biting his pen. How the light danced, flickering at the edge of sight. He rubbed his weary eyes. "The Warp is sett; our lives, light as Shuttles, fly and fall. I have seen young Countrie lasses play at Ninestones, casting up and catching pebbles, very featly. As they play they chaunt a Rime, as *Talith, Tiphan to the East, &c.*, two Sisters to a wind: there being Eight by their reckoning. The ninth is Chance."

Leaves whirling down, a crossroads. Long ago. Too late the boy saw the journeyman, saw the swirl of his long coat and hurried by, head down. *Past. Don't look. Keep walking.* But a staff swung round before him, tripped him up and barred his way; a strong hand caught his shoulder: not unkindly but inexorable. Hauled him up and turned him round. "Here, boy. How cam'st thou by that jacket?"

"It were given me." Wried shoulder, ducked head.

"By?"

No answer.

"Thy name?"

"Aiken Drum, sir."

"Well then, Master Drum. That's Crowd Catling's good silk doublet and his murrey hose. And as I wager thou'st not killed and eaten him, I take you for a thief. Hast thou not bid him stand? And standing, spill and die?" Head down and turned. A shake. "He gives the offcast of his bravery to none but minions. Yet would not this suit, for he plumes himself on it. And least all would he adorn thy whey-face with his scarlet. It goes ill with thy sorrel pate."

A moment, and the whispering fall of leaves. The journeyman raised the lad's chin, gazing at his face. He whistled softly. "By trod. 'Tis Ashes' governess, the maker of plays." Her blush betrayed her. Gentler now, but no less stern, he loosed her collar. "Were you not at Low Askwith, Lightfast last? And taught that pretty child his interlude?" She remembered that voice: Tom o Cloud's. "Speak, lady. 'Tis your cue."

No answer but a bitten lip.

"So you're Covener's niece? Corbet's handfast?" His arm dropped to his side. "We'll be hanged, boy and all."

"No." That startled her to protest. "No. What I have done is my fault only."

"What, took your own maidenhead? Or rather, Corbet's: for it is his in law."

"I know."

"There are broadsides up at every crossroads, nailed in every inn. Gold offered for your taking, aye, and retribution sworn. Look. Here." He showed a paper like a ballad sheet. A woodcut girl. "If this is laid on us, the quality is damned. For which I thank you, Madam Minx."

She folded up the page, quite small. "If they find me, then my kin will— burn me?"

"They'll not deal kindly with you. No."

"They would wed me to my grave, to January. Is that kindly?"

"No. I would not give a rat to Corbet for his dog to worry; I've heard tales of his cruelty. But what of us? Shall we hang for your heedlessness?"

"And if I sheltered with a silly widow? Or a gang of begging children? Should they hang? Their lives are dear to them as yours to you."

He looked at her. "An argument. Yet such would spare your honour: which is all your worth."

"I must deal somehow with mortals; else I die. I would not kill myself."

"So went you with a common journeyman?"

"Are you not?"

"I offer no enticement. But with this rattlepate, this fiddler?"

"Not for his sake." Annot twined a lock of hair about her finger, bit it; raised her face. "I would away at a venture, for I could not stay to wed. At Maying, for 'twas only then I'd leave to walk abroad: that once. And met him in the wood, as Ashes had foretold me, pat upon his cue: I broke the thorn." A treeful of small birds rose all at once in fret; they flocked another tree, as bare. They leaved it with their plaint. "Like you, your fellow did remember me; he praised my verses—and my outward self, my mouth and eyes, but that I counted less. And yet I plumed myself. He flattered as the fox the crow." Again the birds unsettling. "And being green, I did believe him. Could I go with you to join the gallantry? I said. For I would study how to guise. Would boy myself. And he said he would prentice me." She wrung her feathered hat. "Oh, I am a fool, a fool."

*To leave thy featherbed? But with a wolf in't.* Softer now. "Were you in love that you lay with him?"

"Fifteen," she said, "and had a tryst with story. I would put myself into a song."

*"'Twas they who put the grey hawk's feather in her bed,"* said the journeyman. "All know that we steal wives and daughters. Did you dream on us?"

"I fled a nightmare. There were none would speak for me against that match, but my brother Grevil, who is timorous. My dearest sister, who is dead. *Here is Law,* I thought, *nor am I out of it:* so bid an Ashes tell me of my fate, forspent my prophecy. As they will do, this Ashes spoke in riddles. *Thy ship's i't forest,* she did say. *Its shrouds are fourfold strung.* I saw his fiddle and I thought—"

Her listener did not sing: *Then touch but her smicket and all's your own.* He bit his tongue. "And so he told you pretty tales of love, and sighed and swore? He toyed you and he teased?"

"He asked no leave of me, but took." A silence. "Having once, he said, I must henceforth. To pay my lessoning." Annot thought of the bedding. It was all a dark confusion in her mind of shame and stirrings, awkwardness, sharp pain, rank sheets or mast and nettles, twinges of uncertain bliss. It cloyed curiosity.

Gently: "May it was and now October. So he's left you by the highway? He'd a friend?"

White then red, and white again. "I would not."

Too far. He'd gone too far with her, in anger at his friend. "I do pray your pardon, mistress, for my ill-considered speech. My brother has foredone us all; I hold you faultless of his crime."

He knew his fellow player: fathom-deep and babbling, for a time, of love and goddesses; then up he'd spring, dry-dolphining through other's tears. Still lighting on the next divinity, and then the next. He made ducks and drakes of maidenheads; he feasted on young hearts like cherries. Surfeited. But like an orchard-thief, well-willing, he would share his sweets. His fellows held their drabs in common like their books and their bacca pipes, their stockings and their souls. 'Twas even generous to her, he'd think: a virgin spoilt is but a penniless green girl. She'd be fortunate to have him find a spark for her, a gallant. One a trifle marred perhaps, not outright tainted. At any rate but one, not anyone: she'd not come yet to standing work in alleys and the cart.

"So you ran?"

"Aye, at midnight. I took for my recompense his sword and bravery; and left him sleeping, with my smock and petticoats."

"Would I had seen him wake." Tom o Cloud heeled over laughing. "Petticoats! And provincial petticoats, what's worse."

"Do you players not woman it in coats?"

"Catling will not: so is but a fiddler. Let him frisk it in his Cloudish smock." He lay back on the grass, still green, and looked up into the leaves. "Now then, Master Not Annot. We journeymen go everywhere and all at once, like moonlight. We are made of tales; our livery is broidered all with tongues and eyes: in brief, we are your only rumourers. What say you if we noise abroad that you were stolen by the fays? They took you—hapless child—from the greenwood and under hill to dwell. 'Twill be news in every inn and market, aye, from Scarristack to Lune, and ballads sold of it."

There was mischief in her eyes now. "I would make them, an I may."

"Would you so? To what measure?"

"You may sing it to the tune of 'Babylon.'" She stood and walked a pace; then turned. "How she rose amid her maidens all, and combed her yellow hair—not red, 'tis not poetical—and in the greenwood met—"

"A lord of elfin?"

"No. The queen herself, and all her courtiers, her rade, in crowns of blackthorn that is mother to the slae, and mounted on black hares—"

"'Twould play well, an 'twere staged." He rose and turned on her, all frost and flowering thorn. His look would wither May, downcast the stars. "How durst thou break a branch of mine?'"

"The wood's my own."

"It springs of us. 'Tis rooted in our dark."

"And reaches to the light." She casts her handful of bright leaves to the wind. "And so they take her crown, her maidenhead. Her tongue." Her back was to him. "Think you that would sell? We'll get a man to cry it, street to street."

On a sudden grave again, he said, "You must away from Cloud. For tales or none, your folk will hunt you. I can walk with you to Luning Haven. No further: I am sworn to meet the gallantry—among them your betrayer, he whose windpipe I would gladly throttle, and whose blood I may not spill. We meet by Hallows, for our winter tour."

"Walk with me?"

He held his dagger with its point to him. "By the Moon and Ashes, I do swear: I will touch not a button of you, not a hair, but by your leave."

"I do hold you by that oath." She curtseyed. "But with me? Is that not perilous?"

"They look not for my prentice, Master Drum."

A fleeting smile; then fret. "I have no silver for the crossing; nor honest means to get it. I took nothing when I fled from home."

"Sell his frippery."

"'Tis stolen. I do wear it of necessity, but coin it I will not."

A turn and scuffle through the leaves, then back to her. "Make us a masque: of what mystery you will, so it be shaped for four men and a boy. I have ink and paper for the writing of it, and will pay for it your passage to Lune."

"I could do that." And her February face unclouded. "I would like that."

"Then your quills shall fledge you. Will I see you to the ship?"

What her legs knew was a curtsey. But Tom o Cloud laid a finger to his lips; he sketched a bow: half in homage and half prompt.

She bowed in turn, most courtly in her prentice part: all footpage, all aglow.

"And Master Drum—?"

"Sir?"

"Are you with child?"

As if he'd struck her: but it must be said. He would not now see her left, a stranger, unprovided. Annot shook her head uncertainly, then nodded; shook again. She didn't know. She didn't know how she could know.

"If falls, 'twill fall." He gathered up his bundles. "Come then. We've miles to walk by nightfall, if we'd lie not at the Nine."

As he turned to the crossroads, back toward Fallowing, she saw the fiddle at his back. He looked at her, over his shoulder. He smiled. "Most journeyman can play a crowd. I second."

In her lantern-room toward morning of another Lightfast, turning from her new glass, Margaret wrote: "... clowding to the North: the *Ship*, the *Vixen Dancing* veil'd in snow. The *Crowd of Bone* ..." Her sister woke and cried; was danced. The footsteps came and went below. "... at rise. The old *Moon* joyeth in her Riddle; as the *Sunne* in *Ashes* lap doth labour to his Joye." Drowsy, she leafed backward through her notes and ciphering. No moment when the sky had changed, yet all had. "Perseis hath changes, even as the Moon herself; doth maske—or Seemingly—in all her Figures, now as one and now the Other goddesse: but the lighter, great with Dark." Still backward, to the winter of another year. "The *Witches* wade the nightshore, in the shining of the *Road.* The *Sheath and Knife* cast up like sea-wrack, lost and found; the *Kist* long buried in the Sand. Rash *Hulver* in his falle ..."

"I like not this moon," said Pipe-and-Tabor. "I would die abed."

"In a boy's mouth and a bacca pipe in thine," said the Second Witch.

Covertly, the First Witch was fingering his downy cheek and chin, his lip. Shadowed? "Then he should away: there's nought here but stockfish and oysters."

"Has not thy voice cracked?" said the Second, all mischievous condolence.

"But a cold. This filthy norland fog."

Lightfast of the year they'd parted, drum and fiddle: Annot sailing Luneward to uncertain harborage, her new love turning North with the gallantry. They lay the night at Uthwind, on the dockside. From their jettied window, they could see the Tilda Shoop, as great-hipped as a marketwoman, shift and creak and sidle on the waves. Her master liked not setting forth. An ill wind sang and jangled in her shrouds, a peevish little wind; all day, the gulls upcast themselves at random, settling and unsettling. The small rain turned to sleet.

Crowd Catling their fiddler, turning from the sleeted view, went on: "The Blackthorn is the swifter: she doth bring the lord's daughter of Perran Uthnoe to wed in Lune. The day is named, a fortnight hence: she sails the morn."

"We sail," said my Lady, "at the moon's will." Her painted cards lay spread before her on the table. Northern stars: the Ship, the Swords, the Vixen Dancing. "Lying in her daughter's arms, as now, she doth devour fortune."

Pipe-and-Tabor went on cording up the boxes, counting up the properties against his list. "The moon her silver mantle. For the sun, a periwig. One yellow doublet that was torn. Tom o Cloud his coat of leaves ..."

The boy'd been juggling with an orange, round about his hand, and round, like ivy wreathed: as if it could not fall. A second now. A third. But withered, so it would not balance with the others, blue and slumped. "I would away from here. I weary of this dark."

The First Witch drank. "Uthnoe? Old Ranulph's daughter? I saw her gown that they praised so for the needlework; 'twas nought."

"In itself 'twas fair enough," said the Second. He stretched his tawdry stockings to the fire, where an egg was roasting in the ash, beside his hissing sweltering boots. "'Twas she that ill-became it. A peely-wally puling thing, still hanging on her nurse's pap. He'll not get a heir by her these five years."

"Not he. But thinkst thou Crowd will bed her ere the bridegroom can?"

Still the fiddler wheeled about and paced and argued, like a player: he had caught the trick of them. He used his stage. "They are fools who would not journey hence. Such a wedding comes not twice in ten years. All the gallantry of Cloud and Lune are bid to play at their solemnity; and we—not least of them but bravest—should outdo."

"Five swords, with belts to them ..."

"'Tis not a combat, that I know," my Lady said. "A calling rather: for the sky must fall. We are for Cloud, then, and the masque of witches, when the wind has turned."

"Cloud is but to play before a hobnail rout, for pence and ale. There's gold for us at court."

"There's gallantry for thee," said the Second Witch. "Hast thou not made conquest of the lady's waiting-woman? Not the sheep but the black hare?"

"Ah," said the fiddler, sighing. "She is frost and fire, incomparable."

Tom o Cloud looked up from his letter. "And so like nothing: neither fire nor frost, nor damask rose nor thorn, but only Gill who will. A thing of nought."

"I see 'tis January with thee, Cloud: thy wit is bare."

"And thou art dog days, as thou ever wast, Crowd. Thou wilt loll thy tongue, and rage, and rig it."

Crowd laughed. "Summer liketh me. I do not reap, like sunburnt laboring men, but leap and sing. I am a gressop." He undid his purse. "But look you, journeymen. See what a pretty fairing I would charm her with." A comb and glass of jet and ivory, like blackthorn garlanded around a pool.

My Lady turned, elbow on chairback. "I'd not take those aboard, Master Fiddler, on whatever ship. 'Twould not be wise."

"A gown of green silk, for the new play of Elfin ..."

As if in idleness, but merely for the hand of it, Cloud stroked the folds of silk. A mothwing dangled in a web. No scent of Annot lingering, but salt and wormwood, smoke and ale and players' sweat. "I am for Lune," he said, "having some brief errand there, but—"

But the Witches now had snatched the gown, and danced it, jeering at the fiddler. "By tit, here's Crowdy's coats."

"Did he not look a vision in that mantle, like a nymph descending to the inn-yard?"

"Like to queen it at a May-game, with a bellows-mender for a consort."

"The very pot-boys were amazed."

Hand on hilt now, the fiddler scowled. "Shog off, you open-arses. Let you sail, go wallow in your leaky tub. There's not a cock among you lot can stanch her. I am for the lady's wedding; you may play her lying-in."

"That is thy will, then?" said my Lady.

"Aye, Mistress. With your leave."

"So be it. Tide's at three, if her master will put out. Here's silver for thy crossing." She swept her cards aside to count it out. "A fair wind follow thee."

The fiddler found his dignity, and bowed. "And you, my Lady, and you all."

His bundle and his box were packed, his fiddle in a fleece, fell outward. Round the room he went, bright-faced, in a flame of triumph, clipping and clapping, tugging ears. "Jog on, you Cloudish jades. I go before you as harbinger." He clipped Tom hard and cheerfully. "A wench is *like*," he said. "And simile thine only picklock."

"If thou needst break in. I have a key." A gressop's what it is: in winter it goes. "Fare you well," said Tom o Cloud.

At the threshold, his mistress recalled him. "Oh, and Master Crowd? Remember: there's thy reckoning to pay."

*O look!* A star fell burning from the Ship. The children in the meadow wheeled about, entangling in the summer grass. *There.* Nowhere.

*Ah, that's one,* said Margaret. *The first.*

*Is't fortune?*

Turning all, their faces to the heavens. *In a sort. The Nine weave—O it sunders! Two and three.*

*O brave. Two riders on a horse.*

*'Tis not like counting magpies, One for sorrow—Four—They weave what will have been that it might be.*

*A paradox,* said Kit. *Five, six! Ah, but Noll should see. Has he forgot?*

*Is writing. Weaving in his way.*

Swifter now, as if inspired, the lightstorm scrawled the sky. A moving palimpsest.

Behind his love, his late-found Siony, Kit walked. Small Annot on his shoulder slept. The others waded through the summer grass, they dreamed: bright Phoebe, chirring like a drowsy gressop; wondering Tom; and Will and Whin. His daughter Margaret still would gaze.

In memory, a child was playing on a fiddle, scrawling notes. Beginning it again. Kit knew that tune, green Ashes' entrance to the stage. He was remembering a low room high upstairs in Lune, all eaves; his mother writing by the window, crowded close to spare the candles. He can see her breath. Can see her fingers, pricked and stained. She copies music for the players, or their words on long rolls; she mends their tirings. Sometimes she will hold her head and sigh; count pennies; weep and rage. Or laughing, she will mock the words she copies. Sing. They dance to keep them warm.

It's a cold room or it's stifling; and it slants. If he lets it go, his wooden horse will travel of itself, roll down away. And on the hundredth trip, she'll turn and rant at him, and cuff; but sometimes she'll get up behind. They'll journey. They are in a winter wood, or on the Road to Law. In Cloud in April.

Anywhere. Their cold and crooked room.

Not bare: above them in the rafters hangs a crowd of goddesses and kings. There's Hulver's godcloak, slashed with violet and gold; Slae's stockings, black as ink but shining, and his hempen wig; bright Journeyman's black bag and Morag's beak. A mask for owling in. A robe for to go invisible: they wear it both in turn, and call like echoes, mocking, as the other hunts and blunders. *Here, mam. In the air.* Here's Perseis her rainbow scarf, his mother says. And laughing she puts on the starry gown, and rustling turns to him. She speaks.

No more. The others had gone in; and last of all now, Margaret walked homeward to the hall. Her skirts were heavy with the dew, unsilvering where they swept the grass. To bed now, and to sleep. The stars were fading even as she looked. *But lo, night-braving Perseis embarks, At morrow-tide ascending heaven ...* Ever and again, yet otherwise each night. Her study. At the crook in the green road down from Law, she saw the chimneys of the house; she saw the light in Grevil's window. Still his candle burned: and she would weep. She knew not why. For mortals and their burning brief desires. For herself. One last time turning, Margaret saw the day-star where she lay in Thorn, the branches of it withering with sun; and Brock amid the Witches, etched on ice. And there: great Hulver lay in Ashes, ember into coal. *A flawless night,* she thought: *a fair nativity. Illusion. Where we stand is why.* The wheeling planets do not swerve and wend, now here, now anywhere, like children in a game. There are no striding deities, no figures in the sky: we set them there. For ecstasy and dread, for lanterns as we late. For tales. The sky's unstrung. Yet we make patterns: out of light, of love.

In Cloud, in winter, full a year since the fiddler's ship was lost, the journeyman walked on. He wandered. By his heart was Annot's letter, folded and refolded, grimed with many hands. Much-travelled: but had come to him at last in Uthwind.

> *At the Knot of Swords, by Mris. Aislaby, in Lyke Street, Lune:*
> *To Mr. Thos. Cloud with my Lady's journeymen:*
> *I lodge now with a fiddler's Boye, call'd Kit. Thy play is done.*

And then a line of *Perseis:*

> *". . . he's cradled in the old Moon's lappe . . ."*
> Thy loving prentise,
> Not Lightwood
> ix August

In Lune; and he in Uthwind, then in Cloud.

She could scarce have written more; old Corbet had his spies. And indeed all his company had read it over ere it came to him, the seal of it long broken. They had jeering bid him jump for it; still plagued him mightily about his Lunish ingle.

His boy. Or not: 'twas equivocal. A Kit, a crowd of bone. And Crowd the luthier of flesh—or not, and yet had played on her—was drowned. Ill tidings travel swiftly. Strangely, his rival's death had ghosted him: as if the child's two fathers needs must mirror. He drew himself in breath upon the other's glass.

And yet when first he'd read the letter, he had laughed for joy. As if he'd juggled with the sun, had made it rise. The first of all mornings.

Ah, but how could he sustain them? Would he ever see the boy, if he did braid of him? See Annot? Lying as they did in Lune, over sea and spell.

At dawn he'd left those hobbyhorses in the Bag at Aikenmoor, to snort away their ale and boying in three beds. He'd walk to clear his wits.

A sunless dawn. A silver-frost. It purfled all the brown leaves, edge and vein. How still it was, the endless fall of leaves—He scuffled on a pace or two and halted, looking up. Leaves fell like snow, as if their source was endless: tatters of the sun. It was winter. Elsewhere, anywhere in Cloud, the trees were bare.

*By hallows,* said the player softly, and he laughed for wonderment. Uncovering, he lifted up his face, he turned about. Still falling and would fall. He'd played the mystery an hundred hundred times, had danced the light of leaves as Cloud his master and my lady taught him, as their master-mistresses taught them, and backward to the spring of fall. He was prenticed to it as a child, no older than Not's Noll; the first of his alphabet was birch. By his conjury, his art, he called the wood about him out of air: waked wood, and so it was. Nine years he'd worn the coat of tatters, played the fool, waked wood; and now the wood waked him. Now he was shadow that the light did conjure. It did but play him for a scene; would set him by. It took from him his mortal heart—its bruising and its care—put in two eyes of tree. He walked, admiring.

A little and a little further in, he saw a spring. It welled up through the leaves, lapped ice on ice, the knarl of living silver spilling secretly away. Cloud ale. Tom's wassail cup. He knelt and cracked the ice and filled his hands. So cold, as cold as time; and when he drank of it, he tasted earth and leaves. He tasted memory. He drank to the fiddler's boy; drank down the Sun.


In Cloud. Late summer, lingering. A year since Grevil named a green girl out of Law his ward. Once more, the pears were ripe for plucking, and his endless book undone. Paling with the night, at last his candle spired and went out. Grevil set aside his pen; came slowly from his text, as from another world. It was.

Dusk here. He could see the white leaves on the table, scattered, and the window edged with grey. He rose and raxed his stiffness, rubbing at his inky fingers, yawning like a gulf. There was something he ... Now what was it he was to wake for? Ah. *There will be starfall*, Margaret had said. *Toward morning*. Past then, unremarked. She'd tell him what he'd missed.

To bed now: but his wits were thronged with images, as bright and silent as a snowfall. Other worlds. He'd never sleep. Not if he drank a gallipot of honeyed stuff. He'd take a turn about the orchard, then, to settle him. The night air would be fled.

Down he crept, and softly through the wainscot room—Kit's now—to the orchard door. Unlocked: so Margaret also waked and worked. He stepped out among the trees. Will-haunted still. A year since they had lain together, drowning; since he'd named what he would lose.

Unsilvering now: the moon had set. A ghost of green beginning. Here and there, he saw the glimmering of arain webs, like rafts of silver on the grass. *Tom's clouts*, his nurse had called them. Ah, the sweetness of the apples slept, unwedded to the day, when loving sun would waken fire: the scent was all of green and shadow, earth and air. The laden boughs bent downward to the grass; they brooded shadow. Further on, an apple fell. Another. And a wintering bird awoke.

But he was orchard now, in green dissolving. Green. The leaves rained down their silver on him, rivers of the moon. If he but reached his hand, infallibly, he'd pluck the ripening sun.

A something mewed and rustled in the grass. He startled, in that instant all unspelled. Went still. The cat? Had she, the wicked creature, got a bird? He clapped and cried out, "Scat!" No swift cadenza in the grass. No streak of marmalade.

Then softly, lest he tread on wounded game, he swept about him. *There.*

A naked child, newborn: a windfall in the grass. A starfall. See, its down of silvery hair still danced like fire round its head. Still travelling though it fell. "Thou will o wisp," he breathed. "Thou lateworm. Catched thee." As he bent to take it up, he saw the other: golder, sleepy as a pear, pricked out. By heaven, twins: a manchild and a maid. Willfallen, ah, he had no doubt, and embers of the stars.

How Barbary would scold.

One by one, he raised them to the heavens, laughing. *O you gods!* They woke and starred their little bodies, furious with life. They damsoned and they squalled. Stripping to his shirtsleeves now, he wrapped them in his study gown. He bore them like a garland, branches of the wood above, its fruit and flower, to his doorsill: to his house, to bring it down.

In, summer!

# Kindling

Ashes now, the world my mothers got. All burnt to ashes in my glass.

I, Margaret called Lightwood, leave what may not journey with my soul to Imbry Ask, descendent of that Imbry who was seawrack, and is starry, and of Will, the Sun in Ashes; and of Annot Lightwood, daughter to my father, Kit. Her study is the world I ended: what I knew. She riddles earth, tells ashes. Scries Cloud, its monuments and midden-heaps, as once I delved the air. She raised young Hulver's ship.

I leave to her my glass, wherein Nine Weaving was unravelled. They were sisters once. Didst know? I saw not sisters but a scattering of stars: the knot's within the braiding mind. I told them with my glass. And so resolved, I drew them, scattered, in my book. A swarm. Like bees, like fireflies. Like corn amid a cloud of chaff, still flying from the fan: the seed of worlds. They were, and are now *like*. The sky was storied once, didst know? That galaxy of stars wherein we travel, turning, was a road, a river of my lady's milk. Was cloud and now is law.

*Colder, by and by,* the Nine said. Cold now in Cloud, in January. Even by the hearth. Beyond the sill, the stars that I unstrung. Unhallowed, of my will: I would know *why.* A clear night, dark of moon. Bright Perseis at riding, Luneward, on that endless sea. I wait the tide with her. I dip the pen; I pause. My shadow on the page my company. No owl nor raven such as witches keep, but silence and the quilly frost. Its talons in my bones. My bird is time, that gripes my shoulder, perches on my hand. Old bones. Old scrabbling mole. I keep my burrow, in my shabby jacket. Soft as ash. No tiring for my lady's grandchild.

I will tell this in my hand.

Go on.

I leave to Imbry Ask a fiddle and a ring.

I leave to her my pack of cards, that was my mother's legacy, that was a witch's hoard. All painted with the stars at Cloud's nativity. The wood above. A rarity, but spoilt for game: nine cards are lost. My lady took and burned them; these I kept. I turn them over now: the fortunes of a world that is no more.

The Hanged Lad, this. The Crowd of Bone. They strung it with my mother's hair; it sang her death. Here's Ashes, walking on the white road out of death. The Rattlebag. The Tower and the Ship. All stories once. No more: the sky's unpainted and untuned, the wood unleaved.

No Hare, and never was: my lady burnt it.

I was Ashes.


Their drum's the moon. They come in silence on the white road, rising from the hill. They are as they are painted in the cards: the Vixen Dancing and the Bear; old Ashes and her daughter, kindled of her; or the Windwife and her Comb. They are Persephone who must descend—look there, the pomegranate in her hand—and there, her mother who will seek her, even into hell. Whatever you do know them as, they are. The Sisters. See, the Fiddler goes before them: you will follow in the dance. Or as old Jinny tells it, by the fire when the wind is cold, he is the Horseman. He will take you up behind. And when it thunders, she will say: *he rides.* Or he is Dis in his great chariot, nightwheeled; the World Ash or the Hanged Man, or the Huntsman in his crown of horn. He is as you remember him: Orion, Odin, Oberon, the Erl-king, Icarus. Whatever you have dreamed.

They are night's quality: the moon's own company of players and her starry masque. They are the winter's tales.

Brock's journeymen, they bring the sun; and at its forge, they make or mend the fortunes of the world. They hammer out your dreams; their anvil is the night. They are myth's artificers and the thieves of sleep. They take your wits, your memories, your soul. No threshold that they cannot cross; no heart they cannot break.

And then they play the one true story, of the world's creation or its end. They play the turning of the year, the tempest, and the resurrection. They play the tumbling of the drums.

At dawn, they will vanish.

In the heavens now, wheeling and tumbling, the guisers faded into mist. *Exeunt omnes.* In her tower, Margaret looked up, laid by her crowquill pen. Her candles one by one had guttered; and the last of them burned pale. Near morning. Time now to descend. Not lightly now. In dreams—and over and again of late—she still ran down and downward on a winding stair; her chain of stars whirled outward and away, it broke and scattered. Ah, she flew. As light as starfall. Then she woke still in this body, thrawn with time. Too old to weep now for a dream; but mourning for the self that wept.

There was a story Barbary had told: of a girl who walked to the world's end for a wonder, for a scrying glass in which to read the mysteries of the world: and saw in it herself, grown old. So she had bought with her journeying old age.

So it was.

Coming down through her chambers, tower and bower, Margaret saw them as a stranger would: wheels and shadows of great wheels, epitomes of light in brass and glass and boxwood. Instruments of unheard music. Engines of time. The rooms themselves looked small and shabby now, wormeaten, paperchoked; the hangings that were brave once, threadbare, ravelled almost into cobwebs. And at their center still, herself the artificer and the arain: Mistress Lightwood in her web of night.

She shook her head. These mazes were but fantasy. The rooms were still her own; they fit her as a snail its shell. Beside her, she had kept, most dear to her, the relics of her centuries: the play of *Perseis;* an inlaid box, a half-embroidered smock in it; a book of scraps of paper, gathered leaves, with childish notes on stars; her cousin Grevil's work, *Reliquiae Nebulosae; or, Remains of Cloud.* Leaves pressed in it, and flowers. Here, the music Kit had written for a crowd of other hands to play; here, laid on it, a spindle-whorl: the owl of bone his dark-eyed Siony had brought from Scarristack, her bridegift. There, the toys of long-dead children: Grevil's twins, starfallen; Siony's fierce Til, in mourning for her own, her sea-drowned father; Margaret's brother and her sisters, lateborn, much beloved. Phoebe's whirligig; Whin's babyhouse, Will's drum; and Tom and Annot's ashing cups. Inch-deep in dust. And on a heap of manuscripts, a shell. Age-clouded now, as light and brown and brinded as her hand. *What's all this Mallywrack?* old Barbary would say. *My life.* But there was none such now as Barbary to scold and set to rights. Who now remembered her? Who knew of Malykorne, of Annis, in this other Cloud?

The old astronomer set down the shell.

She had outlived the world of her begetting. When she broke the sky, dissolved it—and herself in it—the gods departed, that were half her kindred. Not at once, but slowly, slowly, as a tree might backward grow, unrooting from this earth. And history, that had gone through endless involutions in their hands, cat's-cradled, braiding, now was linear. Was so much string. No more she'd meet her shadow on the road; no more would Ashes wake the Sun. The world was otherwise.

Cosmography began. Now *here* and *elsewhere* had been fixed, surveyed, the round earth's corners unimagined. Cloud that once had lain *beyond*, or *farther in*, or *north-north-westward of the moon*, was mapped. No will o wisp about it now: no *there and back again*, no *long and light*. Of old the Cloudish coast was spellbound, and its sea the sky. Its ships had journeyed by the art of windwives, calling on the Witches: they who came from elsewhere. Time went all one way now, and the great ships to and fro. They took the wind's chance.

Now the sky itself had slid askew; or rather, Cloud was on a toppling earth. They saw the seasons falling slowly backward under stranger signs: the spring arising in the Reaper's hook, the Ship star out of true of North, Unleaving sliding like an eiderdown, shrugged off in sleep. Unfast, the laggard Sun slipped backward out of Ashes' lap. It waked now in the Scythe.

*What I do undoes.*

With age, the world had cracked, all ills crept in. War, dearth, new plagues and tyrannies. And yet not all was evil that did come of change. Not even law. She had descended once to town, the old mad she-philosopher, the legend and the mock of men, to speak in Sillycourt against judicial hanging. Not that first time nor the fifth or sixth: and yet the law had passed. Daw's wooden horse no more would gallop; and his tree bore no more fruit.

Jack Daw himself was dwindled to a chimney shadow, to a winter's tale: a figure of vague comic menace. They did burn him, hallows night each year, for stealing of the old moon's daughter. He was made a man of straw. The elding lads did bear him door to door in effigy, to beg his firing and ale: black tatters and a mask, slouch hat and broken swagger, with a sausage at his fork. Awd Strawhead. *Penny for the guise!*

A bugbear to affright the children. Ah, but so was she, with her great eye fixed on heaven. They did shun her as a witch: Mag Moonwise. She will lure thee in with gingernuts and *tell* thee.

At the window on the landing, she looked out. How straggling now the

orchard grew, half wilderness, and hoar with mistletoe. A haunted place.
Small wonder they did call her witch.

Not all the bairns had run from her: Is Hawtrey stayed. Ah, long ago: the
last of all the maids that Barbary had sworn. A wispy child, like Sukey that
had been her aunt; but dark like Hob. All cap and eyes, she was, and smoth-
ered in a great rough apron. Clumping boots. She'd come to lay the fires, but
had stayed to learn the glass, observe, record. It was Is who'd first discovered
the great comet; both had written papers on it for the new Society. Herself
alone had seen it twice return; would not again, she thought. They'd named
it Arkenbold, for Hob's lost boy, the pretty child who'd chased the sun out
on the ice.

No, not all she'd done was ill.

She thought of her new starglass that her cousin Noll bespoke for her,
that was a copy of the old remade, with lenses brought from Lune; and then
the newer and the newer still, of Cloudish make, refined and reinvented. Then
the tower and the domes; the letters and the papers and the learned books; at
last the colleges. Noll's joy. Though barred to her by ancient privilege, barred
to Is and Annot and their shining daughters. Still, she could rejoice for him,
the boy called back from paradise to study muck and wool. He'd walked amid
his budding grove—had given it—in hope of nightingales; had sat until the
dawn in conversation with his other selves, his burning boys. Who'd withered
into doddery old men nid-nodding in their gowns—alas, she'd argued with
them at a century or three of tables—rousing only at a pretty dish: old wine,
a syllabub, a pheasant. *I'll the pluck of it, and thou the quill.* But she had time; she
had her gossip Mally's knack for meddling; and at length, she had her school:
her College of the Nine.

Coming down through the music room, she looked about with pleasure.
Here was once the wainscot parlor where old Covener and Corbet sat, like
crows dividing her. Here she was made handfast; here she sained the child
who would be Master Grevil. She had made of it a reinvention of a memory,
of a bright dark closet full of wonders and of dust. A cabinet of curiosities:
of wood and ivory inlaid, of woven silk and wool. Here stood a cabinet compact of boxes; here a gathering of china, blue and white, a congeries of summer mornings. At her table, over tea, had come new poets and mathematics;
chocolate from Ind; the art of fugue. When Noll and Kit discovered coffee,
joy was unconfined. There had been much music here, a changing consort,
played by children of the house, their children and their children's children.

Still it murmured like a shell about her, echoes of the salt immerging deep of family, the sea of generation. Ah, not mute: like instruments untouched, and long unplayed. Like strings the memories would wake. Their voices lingered.

Slowly now, she crossed the old hall: where the guisers and the gallantry had played. Where she was Ashes. Where the crow lad long ago was tried and sentenced. Still as cold in here as ever, with the timbers of the roof not underdrawn. She would not have it ceiled. Up there about the rooftree that is green with winter leaves, the Sun still seems to hang forever, ever falling into Tom o Cloud's arms. No groundlings now but she; though some who watched him then still did, stared out from portraits. Smutched as colliers.

*Oh the chimneys: I regret.* Wheels not of light celestial, but of iron, strap and cog: still turning, ceaseless as the sky, but purposeful, entrapped. The trees that fell, the fires that devoured them. The shuttles multiplying, myriads of nines. The children in the dark. The choking sky. Not Cloud but smoke. All risen from her burning glass, her brave new world. The Scythe's Age, as they called it now. And yet that clattering of looms had raised the towers of her Weavers' College: light and learning, founded on the engines of the night.

*I would know why,* thought Margaret. *It's what I am.*

Much like her mother, Kit did say; yet more like those she mirrored, left hand to their right: cold Annis who did think the stars in darkness, so they were; old Mally who did keep the wood. *I am both hands clasped,* she thought, *the light and dark of moon.* But even that was flawed now, but a wizened orange of an earth.

*Colder, by and by, the Nine did say. And yet I mourn for what has been. I see the leaves; they light about me, gold and dying, and I weep.*

Since the fading of the spellbounds, and the shifting of the balance; since the coming of the Outlune ships, there had been wars. Men had fallen to the scythe in swathes, and beardless boys, unbarleyed yet: no harvest, for no end. *I would know why.* Her nephew, Kit's Tom's restless Will; the boy Is Hawtrey loved, untold by her. The Arkets fatherless; the Shanklins childless, that had three tall sons. All gone: like chimneysweepers, that are gold and come to dust. Yet ever windborn, lighting never on the fertile earth. Unsown. She wondered: had her countryfolk once killed an Ashes child and spilt his blood, in innocence, to feed the earth, to slake its hungering for dead? A sacrifice of one for many? All in vain. They all were crow lads now, all Ashes. Still she raged against the dying.

At the threshold, she swung back the heavy door to let the dawn come in, white mantled. Winter-crowned she came, and walking printless in the snow. Her smock was of the pleated snow. It ruffled at her heels. But where she walked sprang flowers; where her shadow fell was light. They'd spread no rushes for the coming lass to rest, nor brimmed a bowl of milk for her. The maid that slipped the lock did wear no gown of green; she sang no carol to the greenfoot girl. But grey and bending on her blackshod stick, Margaret stood, no slip in flower but a stock of thorn: the last of all her world to keep that rite of innocence. There were none now who remembered.

Winter and summer, you must let the guisers in: they bear the sun. But as for spring, you must call out to her: she rises from the winter dark. You meet as in a glass. She pulls you from the deep of time; you drown in her undying.

Now, here, at her doorsill, in a curving drift of snow, there lay a bunch of frail white flowers. Snowdrops. Yet as far as Margaret could see, the snow lay printless and unmarred. Were they frost in flower? Of a garland for a bride of snow? But bending for them, yes, she saw and felt green stems, the nodding of the buds, a-tremble; even in the cold, they kept their pure green scent of hope, expectancy.

Old Margaret bent her face to them; and softly she spoke:

> *But green in greener world I wake*
> *And lighter of the dark I make.*
> *In my coming I do leave;*
> *Death of dying I bereave.*

Then looking to the dayspring and the dawn, she called to Ashes, Ashes to arise.


All in black she rises, walking from the earth. In winter she is naked branches; she is darkfast, drinking snow. The wood, the winter grove, is all of Ashes. Islanded in mist, ah, see the nightblack girls: in spring they wake and whisper, with their leafless hands unbraiding for the dance. They shake their silver tresses, that were bound. They wait. Alone the green girl rises, breaking from her bark of night. She flowers, starry from the wood, whitenaked. Light of darkness, spring of winter: over and again reborn as Ashes of herself, of Annis. Greenfoot in the snow she passes, white in whiter mist. At every step a green blade springs. Her wake is light.

She follows the uphill winding of the beck, the misty Lyke Road to its spring. It rises on the nightfell, high amid the stones.

By the Owlstone, drifted deep in leaves, the grey thorn crouches, capped with haws. Her lap is full of snow. But see now, see the old witch hiding in the tree? Leaves puzzle into ragged skirts, gnarled branches into hands; rucked snow is ragged apron. There she sits and knits the summer. At her foot, her winterspring wells up, a twirl of silver spilling endlessly away. With every stitch in time, she's younger, water-sleek and ruddy-fingered, wickening; she's braided now with birds. Her petticoats are green. Glancing up with her spectacles, she sets the early sun a-dance.

She lifts her chin to Annis, beckons. *Sister.*

*Sister.*

They embrace, the blackthorn and the white; the sisters mingle, intertwine, as close as moon and dark of moon. They weave one garland of themselves, of green: a hey of light.

## Acknowledgments

Above all, with thanks to my first readers: Deborah Manning, the goddess of fractally evolving fiction; Sonya Taaffe, who enticed me to the underworld; and in the later rounds, Lila Garrott, of the archipelago of index cards.

The Nine, as Margaret found, are many. With thanks to those many others who have worked with me, the co-creators of my Cloudish mythos: to Nick Lowe, Tibs, and Geraldine Harris of Jomsborg, where it all began; to my silly sister Faye Ringel, to whom I first told the stars; to Delia Sherman, Mary Hopkins, Caroline Stevermer, in the early days; to Paula Tatarunis, Sue Thomason, Chris Bell; to Sherwood Smith; to Farah Mendlesohn; to Rachel Elizabeth Dillon; to Elizabeth Willey, for the glorious eleventh-hour gallop; to Gavin J. Grant and Kelly Link of Small Beer Press for asking, and for their bookish attentiveness to everything, from text to typography.

With thanks to my dear twin Barbara Breasted Whitesides; to Sylvia Adamson for the art of reading; to Lucy de Gozzaldi for the leaves and marbles; to Betsy Hanes Perry for Lady Fettiplace's jam; to Annie Lenox for the hats; to Joan Corr; to my community of friends on GEnie and LiveJournal; to the Readercon gang; to Sue Thomason and Rory Newman for taking me to Cloudish landscapes; to Chris Bell for the bluebell wood; and to all those great and generous writers who encouraged me, not least to Diana Wynne Jones, Michael Swanwick, John Crowley.

With thanks to Anon, for all the ballads; to the singers who revived them, green leaves from old roots; to June Tabor and Maddy Prior, to the Watersons and Carthys; above all, to the late miraculous Lal Waterson for "The Scarecrow."

With loving thanks to my mother, who first gave me books.

## About the Author

Greer Gilman (nineweaving.livejournal.com) is the author of the novel *Moonwise* (which won the Crawford Award and was shortlisted for the Tiptree and Mythopoeic Awards), and of the World Fantasy Award-winning novella "A Crowd of Bone."

Her short fiction and poetry have appeared in magazines and anthologies such as *Century, Trampoline, Salon Fantastique, The Year's Best Fantasy & Horror,* and *Women of Other Worlds,* and she has contributed to *Modern Fantasy Literature* (Cambridge University Press) and the *Journal of the Fantastic in the Arts.*

A librarian, she lives in Cambridge, Massachusetts.